What Girls Are Good For

A Novel of Nellie Bly

Copyright © 2018 by David Blixt

Third Edition by Sordelet Ink

Cover by Next Chapter

ISBN-13: 978-1944540463

www.davidblixt.com

Published by Sordelet Ink
www.sordeletink.com

WHAT GIRLS ARE GOOD FOR

A NOVEL OF NELLIE BLY

DAVID BLIXT

EDITED BY ROBERT KAUZLARIC

SORDELET
ink

Books by David Blixt

NELLIE BLY
What Girls Are Good For
Charity Girl
A Very Clever Girl
and coming soon
Stunt Girl

THE STAR-CROSS'D SERIES
The Master Of Verona
Voice Of The Falconer
Fortune's Fool
The Prince's Doom
Varnish'd Faces: Star-Cross'd Short Stories

WILL & KIT
Her Majesty's Will

THE COLOSSUS SERIES
Colossus: Stone & Steel
Colossus: The Four Emperors
and coming soon
Colossus: Wail of the Fallen

Eve of Ides - A Play of Brutus and Caesar

Shakespeare's Secrets: Romeo & Juliet
Tomorrow & Tomorrow: Essays on Macbeth
(with Janice L Blixt)

Visit www.davidblixt.com

FOR TARA

CONTENTS

AUTHOR'S NOTE

From its founding, the city of Pittsburgh did not have a consistent spelling for its name. Named in honor of William Pitt the Elder, it was originally spelled *Pittsbourgh* in a letter written (amusingly enough) by a Scotsman—who no doubt rhymed it with *Edinburgh*—and it sometimes appeared in print as *Pittsburg*.

The American pronunciation of *burgh* as "berg" led to variations in spelling right from the beginning. This ended in 1911, when the city successfully petitioned the federal government for an exemption to a law that knocked the *h* from the end of every city ending in *burgh*. From that time forward, *Pittsburgh* was the only accepted spelling.

There are newspapers and companies in this story that use the *h*-less spelling. While I have used the correct spelling of the city in dialogue and narration, I have kept proper names such as the *Pittsburg Dispatch* as they were in 1885.

For ease of reading, I have corrected typos and infelicities in the excerpts of articles within the novel. Additionally, casual racism against many cultures and ethnicities was commonplace at the time. While removing them entirely would be to pretend such views did not exist, I have edited particularly egregious references so as not to be jarring to modern readers.

"The way she walks, she lifts her foot,
Then she brings it down,
And when it lights there's music
Down in that part of town.
Nelly Bly! Nelly Bly! Never, never sigh,
Never bring the tear drop to the corner of your eye..."

– 'Nelly Bly'
Stephen Foster

I

LONELY
ORPHAN GIRL

WHO IS THIS INSANE GIRL?

SHE IS PRETTY, WELL DRESSED
AND SPEAKS SPANISH

SHE WANDERED INTO MATRON STENARD'S HOME
FOR WOMEN AND ASKED FOR A PISTOL TO PROTECT
HERSELF — IS HER NAME MARINA?

A modest, comely, well-dressed girl of 19, who gave her name as Nellie Brown, was committed by Justice Duffy at Essex Market yesterday for examination as to her sanity. The circumstances surrounding her were such as to indicate that possibly she might be the heroine of an interesting story. She was taken to the court by Matron Irene Stenard of the Temporary Home for Females at 84 Second Avenue. The matron said that Nellie came to the Home alone about noon on Friday, and said she was looking for her trunks. She was dressed in a gray flannel dress trimmed with brown, brown silk gloves, a black straw sailor's hat trimmed with brown, and wore a thin gray illusion veil. The closest questioning failed to elicit any satisfactory account of her. During the night she frightened the minister by insisting that she should have a pistol to protect herself. She said that she had some money in a pocketbook, but somebody took it away from her. Her voice was low and mild, and her manner refined. Her dress was neat fitting. The sleeves were the latest style.

In court Nellie was not even terrified into giving any account of herself when informed that she was charged with insanity. She was perfectly quiet and went willingly with the matron. The burden of her talk in reply to many questions put to her by the matron and Justice Duffy was this: "I have no father. He is dead. I don't know where I came from. I am going to New York. The hat is not mine. I have forgotten how to speak Spanish. Oh, how many questions they ask me, why should they ask me so many questions? I want these men to go away. That man is a reporter. I don't want anything to do with reporters. I came on a railroad. That is the way I always go. I don't see why my private affairs should be made public. I came to try and get work. But I do not know how."

The girl had in her pocket thirty-three cents wrapped in white tissue paper, and a black memorandum book in where there were some rambling and incoherent writings.

—*New York Sun*
Sunday, September 25, 1887

ONE

Unquiet Observer

PITTSBURGH, PA
WEDNESDAY, JANUARY 14 1885

"HE'S AT IT AGAIN!"

Frying an egg on the stove, Mother had her back to me. "What's that?"

I shook the newspaper as if it had rendered me a mortal wrong. "He's at it again!"

Sarah entered the kitchen, my nephew on her hip. "What's happening?"

"What's happening?" I retorted. "I'm going mad, that's what's happening."

Sarah pulled a face. "Why now, Pink?"

I threw down the offending newsprint. "This column in the *Dispatch*. Oh, he's driving me crazy!"

Hurling a sigh in my direction, my sister-in-law sat and began knee-bouncing her baby. "Really, Grant, why does Auntie Pink bother to read if it only gets her riled?"

I didn't like her calling me Pink. I didn't like *anyone* calling me Pink. But since Charlie still used the childish name, his wife felt entitled. Rising to help serve breakfast, I was tempted to be smart with her. *Better to read and be riled than not read and be ridiculous.* However, with Mother at the stove, and Albert and Charlie in the house, and Harry, and the baby, and the lodgers, maybe this wasn't the moment to sharpen my tongue.

Scraping an egg onto a plate, I decided to enlist Sarah in my outrage. "The Quiet Observer has returned to his backward turnings!"

Again addressing her baby, Sarah said in a loud whisper, "I think Auntie Pink is in love with the Quiet Observer."

I spun so fast I nearly took the next egg with me. "What?!?"

Sarah murmured in Grant's tiny ear. "No woman talks about a man that much unless she's in looooove."

I flushed a bright crimson. *What gall!* Fine, yes—I had enjoyed reading the Quiet Observer's pieces in the *Pittsburg Dispatch*. I'd considered his columns to be well written, amusing, and harmlessly avuncular. I'd imagined him as a kindly, old, bespectacled gentleman in a knit cap, with a pipe jutting from the corner of his mouth.

Everything had changed a week earlier, however, when the Quiet Observer had tackled a popular topic of the day: the working woman. In a piece maddeningly titled *What Girls Are Good For*, the Q.O. had espoused the typical line, railing against "those restless dissatisfied females who think they are out of their spheres and go around giving everybody fits for not helping them to find them," claiming they were "on the lookout for gnats" and "constantly swallowing camels." He summed up his revolting thesis by saying that every such woman "should make her home a little paradise, herself playing the part of angel." With her husband as the Lord Almighty, no doubt!

The Quiet Observer had summed up his piece with one utterly damning line: "Her sphere is defined and located by a single word—home."

Instantly, in my imagination the Q.O. transformed into a burly, bullying, moustachioed brute in a bowler hat, with a cheroot sticking out of the middle of his face—a man's man, a bounder, a masher, a monolithic enemy of modernity and maidens everywhere.

The idea that my outrage disguised some sort of girlish admiration was just the kind of nonsense I was decrying. My frustration stemmed from his words, from the repulsive—and repulsively common!—ideas he expressed. *Do I need a hidden motive? Can't a girl even feel what she feels without being told she's wrong?*

Despite Mother's inevitable disapproval, I was on the verge of savaging Sarah when Harry came in, all smiles. Only fifteen years old, my youngest brother was nicer than the rest of us put together. He slipped into his seat, thanking me for giving him breakfast, thanking Mother for making it, and thanking our little nephew "for sharing it."

Charlie came in right behind Harry, bussing his wife on the cheek and patting his son on the head. As I plunked a plate in front of my middle brother, he grimaced. "What flea is in Pink's bonnet today?"

Sarah knew a good weapon when she had it. "She's in looooove."

With heroic effort, I ignored her. Instead, I lifted the newspaper. "Listen to this tripe. Here's a man calling himself 'Anxious Father' who wants advice about his daughters. 'I have five of them on hand, and am at a loss how to get them off, or what use to make of them.'"

"Marry them off," said Charlie simply, digging into his breakfast.

"Not every girl dreams of marriage, Charlie." My voice dripped with disdain.

Charlie shrugged. "Not every man dreams of being a clerk. But here I am." That was my middle brother: plainspoken, dogged, honest. Rarely sweet, but never mean.

Lacking a ready answer, I read the rest of Anxious Father's letter aloud:

The oldest one is 26. She paints some—I mean she paints pictures and crockery. The next is 23. Her taste runs to music, and I must say she isn't bad at the piano or singing. Then comes Anna just turning 21. She is of a moral and religious turn, spending most of her time going to meetings of one kind and another, and collecting money for the poor and the heathen. The next one is a regular clip. She says she is "18 and don't you forget it." She can come as near paralyzing a wash tub or knocking a piano out in one round as any one you ever saw: and I do think she can slap up a meal in about as short order as the next one, and when she takes a turn through the house with a feather brush and a dust rag you would think a blizzard had broken loose or there was an explosion of natural gas. When the rumpus is over, however, you will find things in apple pie order.

The other one isn't of much account no way. When she was little she had fits and didn't thrive well. Some of the doctors said it was worms and others thought it was her nerves. She sits around and reads stories, drinks hot water, pieces crazy quilts and jaws.

Now what am to do with them? I can make out with Nervie. She is the worker, but the others keep me awake of nights thinking about them. Mother says to marry them off. I would do it in a minute if I had a chance, but they don't seem to catch on well.

If you will give me a few pointers you will greatly oblige.

"Poor dears," said Sarah, bouncing Grant on her knee as he groped up at her face. Charlie said nothing, wolfing his egg and drinking down his tea.

"I'm sure they're pretty enough," said Harry, eating over his plate so as not to soil his school clothes.

"If their own father doesn't brag on them, then no," said a nasty voice from the next room.

My stomach clenched, as did my fists. Albert, eavesdropping again. I couldn't wait for my eldest brother to get married and move out. He wasn't Charlie—he wouldn't go on living here after the wedding. I hoped.

As ever, Mother cut to the heart of things. "And what does the Quiet Observer respond?"

"Don't encourage her, Mother!" called Albert with mock despair.

He was too late. I was already heading toward the most incendiary passage. "First, he says that if Anxious Father wants advice, he ought to write to Bessie Bramble. Having absolved himself of the necessity of actually giving a sensible response, he launches into his screed." And I read:

Some people are always in trouble. . . One woman always has sour bread, another is sure to have a headache on the night of her favorite opera, and another never hears the latest gossip until it is old. This is all bad enough, but it drives the iron deeper into their souls to know other women who get all the gossip while it is fresh and fragrant, are always looking their very best when there is an opera ticket around, and who have won fame in breadmaking with the same brands of flour and yeast they use.

"Some people do have all the luck," said Charlie. "No use crying."

"Of course not," I said.

"Then what's the matter?"

I shook the paper. "*These* are the problems he thinks we deal with? He thinks *this* is what keeps women up at night?"

"I know I'm always worrying about what to wear to the opera," remarked Mother, to general laughter. If she had learned one thing in her life, it was how to diffuse tension.

I was unable to take the hint. "Here's the best line."

In China and other of the old countries, they kill girl babies or sell them as slaves, because they can make no good use of them. Who knows but this country may have to resort to this sometime—say a few thousand years hence? Girls say they would sooner die than live to be old maids, and young men claim they cannot afford to marry until they get rich because wives are such expensive luxuries.

I slapped the paper down upon the table. "Luxuries! It's men who are the luxuries women cannot afford!"

My outburst brought predictable reactions. Poor Harry looked down into his runny egg as if he might miraculously find a steak beneath it. Sarah sent a glance heavenwards and sipped her tea—she didn't eat breakfast, so as to regain her pre-baby figure. Mother went still, folding in upon herself.

Chewing, Charlie said, "Be sensible, Pink. How would women live without a man to look after them?"

I positively bristled. "Really, Charlie Cochrane? Tell me now, how would *you* live without a woman to look after *you*? You have three of us to sew on your buttons, and cook your food, and clean your boots, and raise your son. The rent is paid by Mother, while you save your money. She buys the food, as well as the clothes on your back. So tell me, who is the provider here? You're quite as beholden to your mother as little Grant there is to his!"

Slamming his hand down onto the table, Charlie stood. "I have to go to work." He stalked to the door.

Startled by the violent noise, Grant's lower lip started shaking. With deep reproach Sarah snapped, "Elizabeth!" At least she wasn't calling me Pink.

I felt that stab I always got when I tried to make a point and it didn't come out the way I meant it. I'd only intended to make Charlie see that his view of the world was cockeyed. Instead, I'd shamed him and challenged his manhood. But that was the way with me: quick with the comeback, ready with a retort. The first thing out of my mouth was always sharp. Unladylike, they called me. "Too quick for your own good," they said.

Shooting me a glance, Mother held out her arms to the baby. "Give him to me." Sarah passed off Grant and dashed to placate her husband, navigating past Albert, who lingered in the doorway.

"Don't mind Pink, Sarah," drawled Albert over his shoulder. "She's just frustrated because she's not fit for any work, and no man will have her."

"That's not true!" cried Harry, coming to my defense. "Lots of boys admire her."

I appreciated Harry's intention, but his words set my teeth on edge. Was my worth only measured by the interest men had in me?

"None of them want to marry her, though, do they?" Albert maneuvered into Charlie's seat to eat what was left behind. I pulled the plate away and put it in front of Harry. In answer to Albert's glare I said, "He's still growing. You're all you'll ever be."

Albert carefully resumed his smirk. "Don't worry. Once I'm married I'll make it my job to find a husband for you." With that, he disappeared behind my cast-off newspaper.

"Does Lizzie need a husband?" asked a voice from the back stairs amid a thunder of footsteps. A moment later, Tom Smiley burst into the room, broad-shouldered and pugnacious. "Tony's a bachelor, and has good breath."

Tom was followed by our other lodger, Tony Orr, who was handsomely boyish with pink cheeks and strawberry blond hair. "I chew mint, that's the secret."

With Grant still in her arms, Mother started to rise, but Tom waved her away from the skillet. "Don't trouble, Mrs. Cochrane. I can fry an egg."

"Burn one, you mean," said Tony, playfully slapping back and forth with Harry. "And it's two eggs, numbskull."

"Language." Passing little Grant to me, Mother gently interposed her fifty-five-year-old frame between our lodger and the stove. Acquiescing, Tom sat down and poured himself some weak tea.

Turning Grant around in my lap, I let him grasp my fingers with his tiny fists. Tony pointed to my shoulder. "Oooh, sorry, Lizzie. Baby gack." I looked down and his pointing finger flipped up to tap my chin. "Gotcha," he said, and received one of my arsenal of scowls in return.

From the stove Mother said, "Are you boys heading out today?" Their packed bags stood at the foot of the stairs.

"Yes, ma'am," said Tony. "Company's close to completing the changeover from narrow gauge."

"Finally!" said Tom.

"Yes, the Baltimore and Ohio Short Line will soon be ready for use," concluded Tony.

"You'll be in Washington tonight?" asked Mother with some coolness as she served an egg to Tony.

"Yes, ma'am," said Tom. "For a week at least."

Mother was calculating the lost rent. My own depression was more personal. "Wish I could go."

"Go where?" asked Tom, sitting down to eat.

"Anywhere," I replied, bouncing Grant in my lap. "Washington, to start."

"It's Washington, Pennsylvania, not D.C.," observed Tony dryly.

I was undeterred. "I wish there was a job on the railroad for me."

Both men laughed, without saying why. They didn't have to. What job was there for a woman on a train? I had to bite back several utterances. Mother's presence was a great deterrent, and Grant was a beautiful distraction.

Harry's head was down. Tony chucked him under the chin. "What vexes the little man?"

"Nothing," said Harry, determinedly looking down.

Tony puzzled, then groaned. "Oh, Harry! Oh, I'm sorry, I completely forgot."

"What?" I asked.

"I promised him I'd take him to the skating rink tomorrow. Harry, I didn't know we were heading out of town so soon. I'll take you the moment we're back, I promise. Is that all right?"

Harry nodded, brave in the face of disappointment. His expression made me want to smother him in hugs. But he was too big for that, so I said, "I'll take you."

Quick to let go of a hurt, Harry's face broke into a huge smile. "Really?"

"Yes, but you'll have to help me stay upright."

"You're a better skater than I am."

"You're being kind. I'm all akimbo. And," I added acidly, "I'm told I resemble a weasel when I skate, my face is so contorted."

Albert shook the paper. "I only speak the truth," he said, lying.

"I'd pay to see a weasel on skates," remarked Tom cheerfully. "Good money."

"How much?" I asked, my voice becoming a little husky.

"We'll all go," said Mother, cutting off any hint of flirtation. "A family outing. It's been too long."

"Can we afford that?" I asked.

She let her eyes hold mine a moment before answering. "I think we can manage."

Terrific. Mentioning money in front of Tom and Tony was a mortal embarrassment to Mother. First Charlie, now her. I was on a roll.

As bells chimed from Saint Catherine's, Albert tapped Harry on the shoulder. "Time to go. You can walk me as far as the streetcar line."

Harry kissed me on the cheek, then Mother, and then he poked little Grant on the nose. "Be good. Be. Good. And remember, your first word is *Harry*."

"Which is more than his head is," said Albert critically. "Late to come, early to go. Bald as an egg by thirty, mark my words. Bye, all. And Pink, don't worry. I'll pluck you a husband from the streetcar on my way home." He chortled at my horrified expression.

Mother watched my brothers twist and turn out of the narrow kitchen, passing Sarah on her way back in. With a scowl, my sister-in-law whisked the baby from my arms and took him upstairs for his breakfast, ostentatiously ignoring me.

Mother looked at me with a pinched expression I knew too well. "Are you done with the paper? I'm certain Tom and Tony would enjoy it."

That brought me back to what I had been reading. Unlike Harry, I never willingly parted with a grudge. As our boarders divided the paper between them, I said, "You don't think women should only be in the home, do you?"

"Of course not," said Tom.

"No," agreed Tony. "We need some in the dance halls, too."

"Anthony!" chided Mother.

"Sorry, Mrs. Cochrane." Grinning, they ate in chastened silence, reading the paper while I cleaned up. Then our lodgers picked up their bags, donned coats against the wintry air, and bade us farewell. "See you in a week or so!"

The moment they were gone, I plucked up the *Dispatch* to read the article again. Busing their dishes, Mother chided me. "They list the jobs in the classified section, not the agony columns, Elizabeth."

Elizabeth. I hated Elizabeth even more than Pink. And the pet names were worse. Liz, Lizzie, Beth, Betsy—all awful. Though I did appreciate the queen named Elizabeth, who had ruled well and never married.

I should have been proud of my surname: Cochrane. Judge Cochran's girl, that's who I was. Only, no one in Pittsburgh knew who Judge Cochran had been. The name meant nothing here.

During my brief stint at boarding school, I'd added an *e* at the end, wanting distance from my half-brothers and sisters, Father's first family. Charlie and Harry liked the change, and eventually even Mother went along. Far away from Cochran's Mills, we became the Cochranes of Pittsburgh.

Elizabeth Jane Cochrane, familiarly known as Lizzie, Pink, or Pinky. Names that didn't fit.

Just as my life didn't fit.

I helped Mother with the dishes, then we made up the beds. As we unfolded sheets, Mother said, "Remember, Kate is coming with little Beatrice on Friday."

"For how long this time?"

Mother sighed at me. "For as long as she needs."

Straightening a counterpane, I felt a stab of vindication. My little sister had married one of our old boarders, a sleeping car conductor. He wasn't good enough for her, and Kate had never forgiven me for saying so. Or for being right.

The arrival of Kate and her daughter meant that I would have to move into Mother's room. Honestly, I didn't mind, and it would be wonderful to have little Beatrice in the house again. She and Grant and Harry were the bright spots of my little sphere.

A woman's sphere. Again, I fumed over the Quiet Observer, with his Chinese girls and sour bread and operas. Putting snap into the corners of the sheets, I thought of confronting him, and of all the things I'd like to say.

Only it would come out wrong, like everything that spilled out of my mouth. *If only I could choose my words beforehand. . .*

That's when I made the decision.

With the morning chores finished, Mother went to lie down. That's when I crept down the stairs and scrooched myself behind the tiny writing table in the corner of the living room. Pressing a pen nub onto a fresh sheet of paper, the words tumbled out of me as if I had slit my own wrists for ink.

> *To the Quiet Observer,*
>
> *I have read with interest your recent observations and advice for the young women of America, and Pittsburgh in particular. While I have no doubt these are your honest and fair-minded thoughts, there are perhaps some aspects of a woman's life that have been neglected in your studies.*
>
> *You seem to think a woman's life is poor if she is not the receiver of fresh gossip, if she cannot look fine at the opera, and if her bread has gone sour. Perhaps if a woman is wealthy, perhaps if she comes from a*

good home, perhaps if she does not want for clothing or food or shelter, then perhaps what you say is true, and these are her occupations. For such women, employment is a choice, not a necessity.

But let us take a less affluent example. Perhaps she is someone you have observed on the omnibus, or in the street itself, rushing ahead in last year's clothes with her hair a little askew and her hem a little frayed. Perhaps she is someone you have tut-tutted over after touching the brim of your hat as she passed, thinking that if she only took a little more care, she might find a husband.

Could you but look inside the chapters of her life, you might find less to scold and more to admire.

Consider this in your future advice to fathers—girls are fortunate to even have fathers to write on their behalves. My own father died when I was six years old. He was a wealthy man, twice married, with fourteen children spread across his life. A soldier and a judge, a businessman with a town named for him, he died without a will. Almost at once, his eldest children, my stepbrothers, sued for their part of his estate, forcing my mother to sell our fine house and lands and reduce myself and my brothers and sister to a much smaller home.

Mother had been married before, but that husband died young, so she'd married my father. Now twice widowed, she still did not seek work outside the home. Instead, she anticipated your advice and married yet again.

Her third husband was a sinful man full of promises and the easy courage one finds in a bottle, with all the attendant anger and sullenness. That marriage ended as it should have done, in divorce. It might as easily have ended with me orphaned entirely, as he was prone to fits of violence.

At fourteen, I applied and was accepted to a prestigious school in Indiana where I might gain the education required to be a teacher, one of the few occupations my sex is permitted. After a single semester, I discovered I could no longer afford the tuition, for what my stepfather had not squandered on drink and my relations had not stolen at law, my guardian had mismanaged.

I am not yet twenty-one, and have no inheritance left.

My family moved to Pittsburgh to chase work, and for the last several years I have attempted to find respectable and gainful employment. I have tried my hand at tutoring, nannying, and housekeeping, all to no avail. Even kitchen work doesn't last, as other women consider me too small, too slight, and treat me shamefully.

Everywhere, I am considered willful, inquisitive, and outspoken—traits you doubtless deem praiseworthy in a man, but dreadful in a woman. At the same time, my two elder brothers, despite being less educated than myself, have landed suitable office positions. Alas, their wages cannot support them, their budding families, my mother, my little brother, and myself. In fact, it is up to us to support them.

I write not for pity but to correct your errant notion that a woman's sole sphere is in the home. I have more in me than suits my "sphere." If my home were my sphere, it would soon cease to orbit, but rather fall into the sun and be consumed.

I am determined to work at working until I discover my proper "sphere" and become as independent in finance as I am in spirit.

So tell me now, as a girl of a respectable family who, through no fault of her own, has no money, no father, and no prospects, what am I to do? Is selling myself in marriage the only option? How is that different than a life of shame? How is an honest girl to make a living?

In short, what am I good for?

I await your answer.

> Your friend,
> Lonely Orphan Girl

Exhilarated, I read it over. Perhaps there were too many *perhapses*. A couple of better phrases came to mind, and some snappier retorts, but nothing to make my argument stronger.

I considered showing the letter to Mother, but she wouldn't enjoy my frankness about our family situation. So after addressing an envelope— "To the Quiet Observer, *Pittsburg Dispatch*"—I bundled up and walked to the post box on the corner.

It was snowing, but the air smelled of sulphur, which was only fitting in a city labeled "Hell with the lid off." Pittsburgh was a center of industry, which had its drawbacks. I walked into a floating cloud of soot, from which I emerged choking and brushing my coat. The stench was in my nose, and the taste of copper on my tongue, not unlike blood. *Ah, the flavor of home!* During the previous four years, the quality of the air had grown briefly better, thanks to a push from the natural gas men. But coal was too attractive, and the city was back to befouling the skies.

Like most Pittsburghers, I wore my city's blackened reputation with pride. Head held high, letter clutched in my fist, I reached the small metal box at the end of Miller Street. Opening the hatch, I allowed the letter to linger between my fingers for a moment, hovering between idea and action.

Then I opened my fingers and let it drop. The little metal door clanged shut, and the letter was beyond recall.

It was difficult to turn around and go home. I kept waiting for something to happen. But nothing did.

Not yet.

Two

Round and Round

FRIDAY, JANUARY 16 1885

AIR WHISTLING IN MY EARS, I wove between swaying, tottering bodies as wooden wheels propelled me to ever-greater speed. I hurtled across the varnished floor like a runaway train.

"Rinkomania," they called it. Suitors brought sweethearts to hold hands. Mothers carted children there to exhaust them and loosen a few teeth on caramel apples. Invalids came for exercise, which, according to lore, was how Mr. Plimpton had invented the roller skate in the first place. On his doctor's orders, he had ice-skated until the spring melt had prevented him. Refusing to let the weather slow his convalescence, he had added wheels to his shoes. Thus a craze had been born, indoor rinks replacing actual ice-skating, even in January. It was new, and it was everything.

Flushed with excitement, I was completing another circuit of the rink when Harry waved me over. I steered for the gap in the rail.

"I'm as tall as you," he said proudly from the higher step.

It wasn't that impressive, as I was just five feet, five inches in height. Yet I couldn't be mean to Harry. "And you'll be taller still. Taller than Albert."

Harry's grin was shy. "He won't like that."

"Poor him. Here. Hold my hand."

"I don't need help," he protested with the asperity of a young man clutching a woman's arm.

"Maybe I need yours." It wasn't true, but it salved his teenage pride. In moments, he and I were arm in arm, finding our stride as we fell into the ranks of skaters.

After two happy circuits, the band started playing "The Jam On Gerry's Rocks," a signal to the young ladies to vacate the rink so that the lads might have the freedom to race.

I pretended not to notice the exodus of women. I liked racing. As the tempo of the music picked up, I released Harry's arm and started picking up speed in time.

The first pinch caught me by surprise, only because I thought I was moving too fast for such shenanigans. It was harder, too, than most streetcar pinches. I quickly learned which racers to avoid as I sped faster and faster around the rink.

At first merely an amusement, I quickly became an embarrassment to my fellow racers. A girl skating faster than half the men? Intolerable.

I dodged the first elbow, but the second rocked my ribs. I ducked an outflung arm and nearly spilled as my skirts brushed my wheels. Hiking them up, I gritted my teeth and raced faster.

I passed Harry, who had found his sea legs. Charlie was out there, too, gliding happily like a duck on a pond. I waved, and he shook his head, smiling. Then he frowned at something over my shoulder.

Too late, I turned. A man sideswiped me, knocking me into the rail. I grabbed hold as my skates carried on and managed to keep upright. I looked for my attacker, but he was gone, vanished into the mass of men.

Watchers beyond the rail made a fuss over me. I shook them off and started to skate again, but the song was ending, and the race with it. Furious, I did one last circuit, allowing my eyes to unmist and my throat to open again. When I finally approached a break in the rail and stepped off the rink floor into the milling masses, I was able to hold my head high.

Unbuckling my skates, I saw Mother seated at a table with Sarah and Grant. I decided not to join them. Instead, slinging my skates over my shoulder, I added myself to the throng congregating near the refreshment tables. I needed something to drink.

Not that I could buy anything. I had contributed a dime to the evening's entrance fees, all I could reasonably spare. No hot tea for me. But water was free.

As I waited in line, I suddenly wondered if the rink hired women. Why wouldn't they? A woman could take a ticket or serve lemonade just as well as a man. Probably better! The place was certainly profiting from women. It might at least hire a few.

But, no. As I looked around, I saw that everyone working there was male. Which led me to think of all the ways women spent money there: the fee, the rental of skates, the refreshments. But also on pretty new shoes—keeping cobblers in business—and the streetcars they took to get there. Newspapers were making a fortune from advertisements in the women's pages, being paid to entice women to spend their money there of an evening. *Yes, this place owes it to women to hire at least one. . .*

There was a fresh pinch on my elbow. As I raised my fist, I heard Albert say, "Hello, Pinky."

"Hello, Bertie." *Use a name I dislike, I pay in your own coin.* I lowered my hand. "Not skating?"

Albert pretended to stretch his shoulders. "Have to leave something for the other fellas. Don't like to show off."

"Since when?" I asked.

"Since I decided one member of the family making a spectacle is enough. You looked ridiculous out there."

"So ridiculous they had to knock me down to keep me from winning," I retorted.

"No, just for being you, Lizzie. To know you is to want to knock you down."

"It must run in the family, then. I have no idea what Jane sees in you."

This was a lie, alas. He was a handsome devil, my brother Albert, with his neat dark hair parted in the middle and fine moustache waxed at the tips. The only thing that diminished him was his height—he was barely half a head taller than me.

Albert's handsomeness was an insidious gift. That, and his ability to become someone else at a moment's notice. To Mother, he was the ambitious son to whom one gives all in exchange for small thanks. To Harry, he was vaguely abusive in a boys-will-be-boys manner. To his fiancée, a lovely young lady called Jane Hartley, he was the very picture of manners, consideration, and uprightness.

To me, he was a terror.

Now he just grinned. "Jane sees a man who will protect her from an existence like yours. But I'm forgetting—you like your life, don't you?"

"Not particularly," I said. "Some parts are repugnant."

"You don't find men repugnant, though, do you?"

"What does that mean?"

"You prefer the company of men. Even if they treat you a little rough. Best watch out. There's a word for that kind of girl."

"I know," I said. "Independent."

"Unladylike," he answered.

"Intelligent."

"Immoral."

"Capable."

"Loose."

"Strong."

"Slattern."

I would have gasped, except he wanted me to. His cheeks were burning with excitement. It was tempting to use the palm of my hand to make one cheek even redder, but his fiancée Jane chose that moment to return. "My, what a crush! What was that you were saying, Albert?"

At once, Albert was all solicitude. "I was explaining to Pink about the pattern in your lace. She thinks it's too ornate, but I think the intricacy makes it fine."

"You *should* like it," she said, teasing. "You bought it for me."

"So I did! But then, who else can I buy things for? My sister likes plain things. It's her nature."

"I said nothing about her lace—" I began.

"Oh, do stop lying, Pinky," said Albert with real pain in his voice. "You never fool anyone. Oh, listen, Jane—it's the Lovers' Stroll, calling us." And without sparing me a glance, he took Miss Hartley by the elbow and reentered the rink to the strains of "My Wild Irish Rose."

I remained where I was, seething. *Imagine* him *calling* me *a liar!* And here we were, scrimping and saving to keep shelter over our heads, while Albert used his salary to dress himself in fine new clothes and purchase expensive gifts for his betrothed. We were empowering him to live in a style that was beyond his actual means. *So nice of us!*

I glanced at Mother. She had taken little Grant so that Sarah might join Charlie in the Lovers' Stroll. I considered going over and complaining about Albert—his selfishness, his nastiness. But Mother always found excuses for him, or else told me I was exaggerating. Like the time a man had shown up at our doorstep with his daughter to say Albert had gotten the girl in the family way. Mother had played confused, and then, in her most civil and solicitous tone, she'd asked how the girl knew Albert was the father. The implication had caused the girl to cry and the father to storm from the house, dragging his daughter by the arm. The poor fallen girl had called Albert's name over and over, while Albert himself had remained out of sight the whole time. Cad and coward all at once.

But it had taught him a lesson. There was nothing he could do that Mother would not excuse.

Popular fiction in my family said that I was the troublemaker. It wasn't true. I was never a trouble*maker*. That was Albert, who sowed trouble like a farmer sows wheat. No, my sin was that I pointed out trouble when I saw it. I refused to stay silent. Which, to a lot of people, was the same as causing the trouble.

I was talking myself into spending my last nickel on some Necco Wafers when I heard a squeal in my ear. "Lizzie! Lizzie Cochrane!"

I turned in time to be embraced by a woman my age with blonde hair, big dimples, and a too-wide smile. "Ada! It's been so long!"

"Too long," she agreed, hugging me. I'd met Ada at the rink the previous summer, and we'd quickly made a habit to skate together to keep the mashers at bay.

"I know," I said, sighing. "We haven't been here in weeks and weeks."

"Me neither," confided Ada. "Come along. My date is fetching refreshments, so I have a minute, and he can't be jealous of *you* on my arm. Let's be lovers."

Laughing, I swiftly rebuckled my skates, and then together we rolled out onto the polished floor and fell in with the rhythmically rocking couples. "So what's new? Are you still housekeeping?"

Ada pulled a face. "No. The lady of the house said I smiled too much. Funnily enough, just after her husband complimented my smile. No smiling now, I'm afraid. I'm a factory girl."

A fist clutched my heart, but I tried to remain diplomatically neutral. "And how is that?"

"Dull. Exhausting. Demeaning. I work from seven to six every day, with just a half-hour break for lunch, and only earn four dollars a week. Which is why I haven't been coming here. Nickels are dear."

"I'm so sorry." I squeezed her arm. "But you're here tonight!"

"Thanks to Benjamin." A smile flashed across her face, but it was perfunctory, gone as soon as it appeared.

"Benjamin?" I asked.

"A clerk at a bank. I met him on the Shady Avenue streetcar. He asked me where he could take me for a good time. I said here. That way if I fall, I'm in good company." She laughed.

I forced myself to laugh with her, feeling hollow inside. For a woman, *fall* was a word loaded with meaning. I decided to take her literally. "Did you hear about the New York girl?"

"The one who died of a broken head?" said Ada at once.

"Yes," I said, then added pointedly, "from a fall at a roller rink."

Ada lifted her shoulders in a careless way. "Lucky for me that most falls aren't fatal."

I changed the subject to the one that had consumed me for two days. "Speaking of the news, did you see that article in the *Dispatch*? The Quiet Observer's answer to the Anxious Father?"

"Lizzie," Ada chided, bumping my hip. "I can't afford a paper."

"Let me tell you, then." I related the whole piece, and for two circuits of the rink we heaped abuse on the Quiet Observer. When I told her of the letter I'd written, she gasped and clutched my arm tight. "You didn't send it!"

"I did! I swear, I did!"

Her face flushed and her dimples deepened. "Oh, thank God for you, Lizzie!"

We went on to discuss the case of the roller-skating bigamist who had been in the newspapers. A man called Osborn had wooed a rich heiress at the roller rinks of Ohio. Unfortunately, on the day they had wed, his other wife in Pennsylvania had given birth to his son. There was a warrant out for his arrest, and we laughed as we pointed at all the men in the rink who might be him, hunting for a third wife.

"This is just like life," said Ada. "Around and around, looking at men, hoping they aren't scoundrels."

"And trying not to fall," I added warningly.

When the music ended, we returned to the rail to find Ada's young man waiting with a pair of lemonades. "I spiced them," he explained with a wink. "To warm you up."

Accepting the drink from him, Ada introduced me. "This is Lizzie. She's my friend."

Benjamin spent a moment appraising me, his eyes stroking my figure from heel to head. He lingered on my face—beyond doubt, my best feature. Many a man had said they admired my eyes, which they'd alternately described as deep, limpid, soulful, or "containing the sadness of the world." Mother said my eyes were perfectly even. Harry said my eyes were pretty. Albert said they were too large and that I held them too open. "They make me feel exposed," he'd said.

The rest of my face was plain enough. Round, with eyebrows that looked like a painter's afterthought. A solid mouth with a thin upper lip and a full bottom one. I was least fond of my nose, which turned up just a bit. But my ears didn't stick out, and my skin was smooth—a victory of sorts.

Not that any of it made up for my lack of a figure. I never tried to fool anyone into thinking I had a bust, and I was too thin to have curves in other places. Plain Lizzie Cochrane.

"Nice to meet you." Benjamin the bank clerk had apparently decided against throwing over Ada for me. He took her hand and said, "Ada, drink up! I'm sorry, Lizzie, that I don't have one for you."

"That's fine." From the smell of Ada's cup, I was grateful. I could not have coped with so much whiskey in my lemonade.

"Allow me to give you money for one," he said, offering to pay to be rid of me.

His eagerness to have Ada to himself made up my mind. With a pathetic simper in my voice I said, "Oh, Benjamin, I'm *so* sorry, but I have to steal her away. I have a terrible problem and I need Ada's help to solve it." I took the drink from her hand, returned it to him, then pulled Ada into the crowd.

Once we were out of earshot, she said, "You shouldn't have done that, Lizzie!"

The anger in her voice surprised me. "You don't mean you wanted to stay with him!"

"I certainly did," she snapped. "At least until he bought me dinner."

I jolted to a stop. "You don't mean that."

"My stomach means it. I haven't had a proper meal in days." Ada yanked her hand from mine. "I'll see you, Lizzie." With that, she turned and skated back to her beau.

Dumbstruck, I watched her rejoin him and, at his obvious urging, drink some of the doctored beverage. Then, turning their backs on me, they entered the rink together, his hands on her hips.

Well. It was clear what Benjamin thought girls were good for. The awful part was that Ada seemed to agree.

Feeling utterly miserable, I returned to my family's table. Harry was there, nursing a swollen lip and holding his elbow. Mother was waving the rink doctor away. "It's only a bruise."

"Or five," I said, sinking beside him. "What happened?"

"I got into a race!" Harry's triumphant smile clearly hurt. Just as clearly, he didn't care.

"He didn't win," said Albert, drawing near with Jane.

"He made a good show," said Charlie.

"And made sure not to break anything," added Sarah.

"You don't know that unless I examine him," persisted the doctor.

"He says he's fine," snapped Mother. Of course, she desperately wanted the doctor to look Harry over. But we couldn't afford whatever fee the doctor would charge. "We should be getting home, everyone. Harry's done for the evening, Grant is fussing, and Kate's train is getting in soon. Someone should meet her at the station."

"Jane and I will do that, Mother," volunteered Albert. "Then Kate and I will see Jane home and be back before you're in bed."

Mother kissed Albert in thanks and the eight of us departed the roller rink.

I was fuming. *I* wasn't finished skating. No one had even asked my opinion. If I had said anything, I would have been called demanding, or selfish, or headstrong. *That's Pink. Always making trouble.*

So I stayed quiet and fumed.

BREAKFAST WAS BOISTEROUS. MY NIECE Beatrice had evidently discovered her singing voice since I'd last seen her, and she woke to greet the day with her full-throated two-year-old soprano blaring "Oh My Darling, Clementine."

> In a cavern, in a canyon,
> Excavating for a mine,
> Dwelt a miner, forty-niner
> And his daughter, Clementine.

All three of my brothers found it hilarious to hear their tiny niece singing the slightly racy song, a parody of the sad ballads that were going out of fashion. Mother was none too pleased to discover that her granddaughter knew every lick of it. I saw her throw doubtful looks at Kate, but my sister was too bone-weary to notice. Already she looked older than her nineteen years, and she clutched her coffee like a drowning man does a spar.

I might have sung along, but I was busy flipping through the *Dispatch*. I was disappointed. Though I knew they would never publish my letter, I'd hoped it would land on Bessie Bramble's desk and she would use it to take the Quiet Observer to task. But there was nothing from either of them. The only exciting story was one about an attempted jailbreak in New Mexico where a deputy sheriff had held off a band of eighty Texas cowboys. The rest was about the capstone on the Washington Monument and the colonization of Africa.

Beatrice pranced past me, stomping and singing:

> Light she was and like a fairy,
> And her shoes were number nine,
> Herring boxes without topses
> Sandals were for Clementine
>
> Drove she ducklings to the water
> Ev'ry morning just at nine,
> Hit her foot against a splinter,
> Fell into the foaming brine.

Idly turning the paper over to the "Mail Pouch," I froze like a rabbit in the open. At the top of the page dedicated to letters to the editor, in its own square and printed in bold letters, was a message:

LONELY ORPHAN GIRL

If the writer of the communication signed "Lonely Orphan Girl" will send her name and address to this office, merely as a guarantee of good faith, she will confer a favor and receive the information she desires.

My heart hammered. I felt like a naughty child called to the front of the class to have her knuckles rapped. An appeal to identify myself? To reveal my name to the newspaper office? What could they possibly want? Had I broken a law? Had I slandered someone?

I mentally retraced the letter I'd written. No, it had been absolutely proper. Pointed, perhaps. Maybe a little blunter than they were used to. But there was nothing in it that warranted a scolding!

Was it a scolding, though? Surely if the *Dispatch* wished to, they could have published my very personal letter and written a scathing response. Instead, they had printed this queer query. *Guarantee of good faith?* Whose good faith? And what favor could they confer?

My brothers were now singing along:

> How I missed her! How I missed her!
> How I missed my Clementine,
> But I kissed her little sister,
> And forgot my Clementine.
>
> In my dreams she still doth haunt me,
> Robed in garments soaked with brine;
> Then she rises from the water
> And I kiss my Clementine.

Did I dare go? To go was to reveal myself, my true name. No hiding behind a *nom de plume*. No safety in sending letters from home.

Would I meet the Quiet Observer? Could I beard the lion in his den?

Never in my life had a moment of decision announced itself so clearly. Did I dare? Did I?

> Oh my darling, oh my darling,
> Oh my darling Clementine,
> Thou art lost and gone forever,
> Dreadful sorry, Clementine.

Lost and gone forever. . .

It's silly to think that a song made up my mind. But popular music had a grip on my life, one that I wouldn't understand for weeks—even years—to come. In that moment, listening to the male voices of my family laughing at a woman who was lost forever, I made up my mind.

If I'm going to be labeled a troublemaker, I might as well make some trouble.

THREE

DISPATCHED

SUNDAY, JANUARY 18 1885

TALL AND IMPOSING, THE DISPATCH Iron Front Building was, to my mind, pretentiously old-fashioned. The face of the founder, Colonel J. Heron Foster, was there upon the crest of the roof, above a row of five circular windows and just below the American flag. With its arches and high narrow windows, crenellations, fleurs-de-lis, and pediments, it was positively garish.

The windows along the ground floor were plastered with posters that proclaimed the *Dispatch* to be THE LARGEST DAILY PAPER IN THE STATE and to have 8 PAGES DAILY! and CIRCULATION OVER 15,000! Newsboys shouted headlines along the busy street, and I had to navigate between them and several men warming the chilly air with a heated discussion of the Knights of Labor and the possibility of a railroad strike.

I would have enjoyed the excitement and bustle if I hadn't been scared out of my wits.

I'd lied to Mother as I'd bolted from church to streetcar, telling her I had a job interview. We were too much in need of money for her to frown. Instead, she had wished me luck, adding, "And mind your manners."

Pushing through the *Dispatch* doors, I found the interior looked surprisingly new. They had gas laid on, and modern paper on the walls. Yet it was as though, having once updated the building, they couldn't be bothered to clean anything. The wallpaper was uneven in color, and the tarnished gas jets hissed in fits and spurts.

A doorman approached, eyeing me from hat to boot. "If you have an ad to place, you can leave it with me."

I shook my head. "I—I was asked to come to the offices."

"The editorial offices?"

"Yes, please." I had no idea.

"Fourth floor. Ask for Madden." Hiking his thumb toward the stairs, he promptly forgot about me.

As I began my ascent, I heard cranking and thumping from somewhere behind the walls. Were those the presses? Were they powered by electricity? Pittsburgh wasn't using much electricity yet. Charlie kept saying that if he had a brain in his head he would abandon his job at the rubber factory and learn how to wire up streetlamps.

I had no time for the excitement of electricity, having to contend with those hideously steep stairs. Several times I caught my heel on my coat and had to cling to the inset stone railing. *It would be so typical of my life if I stumbled and broke my ankle. Or my neck.*

The placement of the newsroom on the top floor spoke volumes about the value of reporters—if a fire broke out, the men would roast but the presses could be saved. The quality of the noise at the top of the stairs was different than it had been below. Above the clackety-clack of typewriters, I heard male laughter through the transom above the lone door in a long wall. Up and down the hallway there was no other office. No door with MADDEN stenciled upon it. Just a frosted-glass portal to the newsroom: the brain of the paper, and its ego.

Lifting my gloved hand, I tapped on the door so softly that it wouldn't have startled a bird.

Nothing.

Steeling myself, I tapped again, more forcefully.

"Come in!" snapped a voice.

Clutching my bag and my coat, I turned the handle and took the plunge.

Like our city, its newsroom was full of smoke, only these clouds came from cigars, cigarettes, and pipe tobacco. Together, they created a luxuriant musk that made me light-headed.

At each desk sat a man with a Remington typewriter and a stack of disordered papers, along with blotters, inkwells, pens, pencils, cigarettes, matches, tobacco pouches, baseballs, licorice, photographs, and the bric-à-brac of the modern reporter. The sight of it all was more intoxicating than the smoke.

All typing ceased the moment I stepped into the sphere of men. Journalists with their shoes upon tables bolted upright like schoolboys at the arrival of a teacher. Voices trailed away mid-sentence. Those on the far side of the frosted door craned their necks to see what had caused the silence.

An office boy hurried over. He couldn't have been more than fourteen. "Can I help you, Miss?"

In a choked whisper I said, "Mr. Madden?"

The boy inclined his head, bringing his ear closer. "Beg pardon, Miss. What was that?"

Swallowing and hiding my shakes, I said, "I would like to see Mr. Madden."

"There he is," said the boy, pointing. "Mr. Madden! This young lady is here to see you!"

Expecting some venerable bespectacled patriarch, I was startled to see a man with only a hint of gray at his temples. Mr. Madden had a round chin, large ears and nose, and the saddest eyes I had seen outside a basset hound.

In response to the boy's hail, Madden turned from a conversation and crossed the room. "Yes, Miss?" His smile looked tired.

"You asked me to call today."

A wrinkle creased his brow. "Did I? Forgive me, I don't recall."

"You didn't actually specify the date," I corrected myself. "But you advertised that I should come here for the answers I sought."

After puzzling a moment, light dawned. "Oh! The girl who wrote the letter! Yes, please!" He gently took my hand from the doorknob and drew me into the newsroom, closing my escape behind me. "Come into my office and we'll chat. Thank you, Willie," he added to the copy boy. "Why don't you see if there's some tea or coffee to be had. This way, Miss. . . ?"

"Cochrane." Only after answering did I realize I had unthinkingly surrendered my anonymity.

Mr. Madden led me to a corner office with half-glass walls and a door, where he could conduct private meetings and still keep the newsroom under his eye. The frosted-glass door bore the moniker GEORGE MADDEN— EDITOR.

On the way, we passed one particularly tidy rolltop desk, behind which sat a tall man of about forty years with electric eyes and rosy cheeks. He gazed at me with keen interest. As our eyes met, he gave me the slightest nod of encouragement. I managed a weak smile in return before entering Madden's office.

"May I take your coat?" After hanging my coat on a rack, Mr. Madden pulled out a chair, then perched on the edge of his desk. "Well, Miss Cochrane, I'll tell you, that was quite a letter."

After removing my gloves, I folded my hands in my lap to keep them still. "Was it?"

"Yes." His brow knotted. "Might I ask, just for verification, that you relate some of the contents?"

"Oh," I said. "Are there imposters?"

"You never know. It's a queer business, newspapers."

"I don't know if I can quote it exactly. I wrote to challenge your Quiet

Observer's assumption that women care more about bread and opera clothes than their means of survival."

"Right. Again, just for certainty, how old did you say you were when your mother died?"

"My mother is alive," I said at once. "I was six when my father died."

"Right-o," he said, relaxing a little. "Forgive me. As you can imagine, we've had several letters from women in response to the recent Quiet Observations. My desk is buried in them," he added, pointing. "A dozen young ladies, all of them outraged." He plucked up a sheet from the top of a pile. "Here's one, calls herself Becky Briarly. Says Q.O.'s name should be the Queer Observer. She writes, 'In our Eastern cities there are more women than men. What are you going to do with the surplus? Change Horace Greeley's famous advice to young men to suit the case: "Go West, young woman, Go West?" Perhaps you could send us on consignment to a marriage-broker. The cars might be labeled PERISHABLE FREIGHT, WESTERN-BOUND MAIDENS, HURRY UP, KEEP ON ICE.'"

Madden looked up, perhaps expecting me to laugh. I merely raised my brows.

He plucked another paper from off his desk. "Or there's this one. Dubs herself Fatima. Says she's always liked the Quiet Observer, but now he's revealed himself to be as crazy as every other son of Adam." He scanned the page. "Ah-ha. Listen. 'I am old enough to vote, if selfish man would give me a chance, yet not so old but what I may reasonably hope to see the day when women will march to the polls in a solid phalanx and assert their rights.'" Again Madden gave me an appeal. "You see?"

I wanted to be cool, dispassionate, to answer him with poise. But I never behaved as I liked, so I bluntly demanded, "What's the matter with that?"

Madden let the letter fall as if it had soiled his fingers. "It doesn't answer. Won't change a mind, won't persuade a soul. It's argument, and maybe good theatre. Will such letters sell papers? To be sure. Will we publish them? Of course. But they don't advance the *debate*. They don't make a dent in the argument against women." In earnest now, he started to pace. "Any man will read that letter and say—forgive me—that it's just another woman who hates men sounding off, and there ought to be a law against it."

He paused to level two fingers at me. "*Your* letter is different. Your grammar may not be all it should, but there are ideas in there that smack of newness. Because you're right: Wilson entirely neglected orphaned girls in his piece. Girls who have no choice but to work."

"Wilson?"

"The Quiet Observer. That's his real name. Erasmus Wilson."

"Oh," I said, then frowned. "What's the matter with my grammar?"

He ignored me. "Your letter has heart, but it also has an angle no one's talking about. Perspective matters in this business. And no one has your perspective."

"Bessie Bramble—"

"Bessie's terrific, but she comes at the girl problem from the top down. You come at it from the ground floor. To her, women are an idea. To you, they're people."

"Of course we're people!"

Hopping back up to perch on the edge of his desk, Madden wagged a finger at me. "There! Not *they*. We. *We're* people. That's it, exactly." Lowering his hand, he plucked up my letter from his cluttered desk. "Now, you don't want us to publish this. It's personal, and while good reporting always feels personal, it can't be about the reporter himself. Here's what I'd like: if you're game, I want you to write an answer to Wilson that removes your own story, but keeps all the perspective."

"But without my story—"

"I phrased that badly. Don't speak just for yourself. Speak for all the girls like you. Right now, they don't have a voice. For one day, in one column, you can give them one. Does that interest you? I'll pay you, of course," he added. "Three dollars for one article."

My face must have been comical as I waded through surprise, delight, anxiety, and reluctance all at once. I did a lot of blinking. "I don't know."

He nodded. "Naturally, you're hesitant. You've never done this kind of work, and it's daunting."

"It's not that." My forefinger was worrying my lucky thumb ring. "I was on the verge of saying yes when you offered to pay me."

"Ah. And you don't want me to think you're mercenary in your aims."

"Yes."

"But you also need to work."

"Yes," I said, grudgingly.

"I apologize for insulting you. I should have laid it out up front. Miss Cochrane, I asked you here to meet you, speak to you, hear your view, and then, if I liked what I heard, offer you a chance to write for the paper professionally. I think you have something to say. But that's my opinion. I need to know if *you* think you have something to say."

My spine straightened as though a spear had been lashed to it. "I do."

"Good. Fifteen hundred words, day after tomorrow."

Five minutes later, I was on my way out of his office. The handsome older man at the rolltop smiled at me, but I was wound too tight to respond. I wanted to shout, dance, and hide all at once.

I had told Mother I was going to a job interview. *Turns out I didn't lie!*

FOUR

OBSERVATORY

I WAS HARDLY THROUGH THE DOOR before Mother was there, taking my coat and asking how the interview had gone.

"I have an opportunity to prove myself. But I must write out some passages."

"Oh! Is this a teaching position?"

"Instructional," I said evasively. "If I do it well."

I couldn't tell her. Not yet. What if I made a hash of it? I wouldn't be able to endure Albert's mockery, nor Sarah's knowing eye roll, nor even Harry's sweet attempts to comfort me.

Worst of all would be Mother's disappointment. So I kept word of my opportunity to myself.

Happily oblivious, Mother shrugged. "Well, no one's in the sitting room. Just be sparing of the ink." A prescient admonition.

An hour later, all I had were crossed-out words and ink-stained fingertips. It wasn't that I had nothing to say. It was my usual problem of *how* to say it. I was trying to take Madden's words to heart. Because he was right: this was not about me. It was about all those other girls—the ones like me, only worse off. The true lonely orphans of the world.

I loved the notion of being a voice for others. But I had absolutely no idea how to write, except through my own experience. After hours of fruitless scratching, I retired in high dudgeon to my temporary bed in Mother's room.

Her capped head was already on the pillow. "How was your writing?"

"Dreadful. I have no ideas. And apparently my grammar is atrocious."

"I'm sure it's not," she said soothingly.

I lay awake long after she had fallen asleep, my finger passing over and over my lucky thumb ring, my mind roving over the day's events. It was all so exciting. Such an opportunity.

If only I could grasp it.

LOOKING THROUGH NEWSPAPERS FOR INSPIRATION the next morning, I was stymied. There were no fresh Quiet Observations to pounce upon, no new letters to spark a conversation on the plight of working girls.

But as I was flipping pages, an event notice caught my eye. At lunchtime that day, there was to be a rally for women's rights at the Allegheny Observatory. "Mother, how would you like to visit the Observatory today?"

In the end it became a family outing. While Harry went to school and Charlie and Albert went to their jobs, Sarah and Kate bundled up Grant and Beatrice to brave the elements with us. Kate seemed to prefer the idea of remaining home to sleep, but Mother was able to shame her into joining us for Beatrice's sake.

While hunting for a needle to repair a loose coat button, I had to venture into my own room for a moment. When I knocked, little Beatrice said, "Come in!" before Kate could stop her.

My sister was dressing, her blouse not yet entirely buttoned at the arms. I saw the fading mark of bruises. Bruises the size and shape of a man's fingers. Kate glared at me. I explained about the needle and left as soon as I had it.

In the hallway, I leaned against the wall, lips pressed tight, fists bunched. Poor Kate. No wonder she resented me. It's so much easier to forgive someone for being wrong than for being right.

It was January in Pennsylvania, so there was snow on the ground. The previous January had seen record snowfall, over twenty-four inches, and this year looked to keep pace. With Grant's baby carriage covered against snow and soot, we started out for Riverview Avenue.

The Observatory grounds were popular for picnics and gatherings. In the summertime, I liked to sit and read novels borrowed from the Women's Circulating Library. Not by good-for-you novelists like Dickens or Hugo or Dostoyevsky, or even Henry James, whose *Portrait of a Lady* I wanted to love. No, I enjoyed Jules Verne's scientific imagination, Mary Elizabeth Braddon's eerie forebodings, Wilkie Collins's sense of the dramatic, and the sheer gothic romance of Hugh Conway's *Called Back*. In short, I liked the so-called penny dreadfuls and shilling shockers.

One novel I was dying to read was the new Mark Twain, due out the previous December, but recalled due to a printer's error. It was so galling to know that in England the Brits were enjoying *The Adventures of Huckleberry Finn.* But I had already written a lot of it in my head: the further exploits of Tom Sawyer's band told from Huck's point of view. I hoped Twain's next book would be *The Adventures of Becky Thatcher.*

Arriving at the Observatory, I couldn't help wondering what Jules Verne would do with such a telescope, one of the greatest in the world. It had originally been open to the public, but like all things public, it had been taken for granted and fallen into disuse. So it came to be part of the Western University of Pennsylvania.

Two years earlier, all of Allegheny and greater Pittsburgh had been made proud when the Observatory's director—Samuel Pierpont Langley—had transmitted, across the whole country, the wireless signal that marked noon for the new Eastern Standard Time and set up the different time zones for North America. So far, Standard Time was working perfectly, and money came in from across the country to pay Langley for observing noon each day.

If it had been summer, we would have strolled the green. But the air was biting. Pretending surprise, I pointed to a large temporary pavilion. "Why not take shelter in there?"

Kate saw women carrying signs and turned to me, glaring suspiciously. Sarah rolled her eyes. But Mother took my suggestion at face value, and we were soon warming ourselves in the crowded tent. There were far too many bodies to allow the baby carriage to enter, so while Sarah fussed over little Grant, I scooped up Beatrice and affixed her to my hip, where she craned her head at all the ladies in their fine hats and fur coats.

Already, I was regretting my inspiration. These women were of the class to which I had originally been raised, wealthy and refined. But even had our family not fallen on hard times, these were city ladies. They would have looked down on me as provincial even if I had worn their fox ruffs and kidskin gloves.

There was quite a range of ages, at least, so my youth did not mark me as completely out of place. But the women my own age were hardly sisterly. I heard them tut-tutting my clothes and making snide remarks regarding my inelegant hair.

I never liked to fuss about my appearance. I saw hair more as a nuisance than an adornment. For that reason, I kept mine in a braid at the back of my neck. With my thrice-mended worsted coat and my simple hat and scarf, I was perfectly respectable and unassuming. Best of all, my outfit was easy to move around in.

This was in direct contrast to the women about me. Twice as many women could have taken shelter within the pavilion, were it not for the shelf bustles, which extended derrieres by a good foot at least. It was *à la mode* for women to dress as if they intended to ride a horse, so under the furs and stoles there were fancy riding coats, artfully unbuttoned to show the plumes of ruffles beneath. How many layers those women must have worn, just to artfully display those ruffles!

"Oh, you sweet thing," said one woman in mock solicitude. "It is so cunning to show off your child by dressing down so as not to compete with her."

Hearing the titter of the mocker's friends, I smiled back. "I do what I can. But however I dress, I'll never be as pretty as you. Your cheeks are so rosy, your skin so white. Do you have tuberculosis?"

There were gasps all around. Eyes wide, the mocker turned her back on me at once, smacking me with her bustle. No longer giggling, her friends huffed behind their hands.

"Why did she do that, Auntie Pink?" asked Beatrice. "You told her she was pretty!"

"Some girls think it's clever to look like they're sick. They see it as romantic to look like they're forever dying."

"That's silly," said Beatrice.

"Yes, it is very silly," I said loudly. "Especially as we know being sick isn't a mark of beauty, but of being unclean." Not yet out of earshot, my tormentor stiffened. *A hit!*

Another woman saw Beatrice in my arms and smiled with disapproval. "You brought your daughter."

There was no point in saying she was my niece. "It's not too early to fight for fairness."

"Too true," she said, nodding dutifully, then corrected my grammar. "It is never too early. But I think this a bit busy for my little ones just yet. And too cold! No, they are at home with the nanny until they are of a more suitable age."

The implication was obvious. Only an irresponsible mother would not leave her child at home with a proper governess. I wondered if it occurred to her that not all mothers had governesses at home.

Yet there were tiny dependents in that crowd. Many women had brought along their most prized companions, their lap dogs—pugs and terriers, most of them, sometimes in silly bonnets and always with a basket of sweets brought just for them. As I heard snickers directed at me and tut-tuts at the beautiful child on my hip, I was sorely tempted to shout and startle the pugs into relieving themselves on the laps of their "mothers."

The meeting came to order when several women ascended the dais to protest in stately fashion for women's rights. Most of the talk was about various fundraising notions, but several ladies complained about holding an outdoor event in such weather.

"Now, now," said one woman. "If we cannot brave a little chill, how can we prove to mankind that womankind is not, as they tar us, the 'weaker sex'?"

"Not weaker, but certainly more foolish!" called a voice in the crowd. "If we cannot find means to meet where it is warm!"

Fortunately, the gathering was made more purposeful by the next speaker, a woman called Alice, who made an impassioned speech about a woman having the right to her own wages. "It is nearly forty years since Seneca Falls! It was then, just after the passing of our state's Married Women's Property Act, that women gathered to declare our rights as people in this nation! Since then, we have waged a brutal war to defend the rights of oppressed Negroes in the South. But for us—who are half of this country yet have no voice in the running of this country—our rights are stripped from us the moment we marry.

"As Elizabeth Stanton said then, if a woman is married, in the eyes of the law she is civilly dead. True, today we have a right to our own property, and we are not held liable for our husbands' debts. That is true in Pennsylvania, New York, and a majority of states—but not all! Worse, in all but four states, married women still have no right to their own wages. That is true even here, today, now! A woman who works owes her wages to her husband! Is that fair? Is that just? The men in Washington talk of fighting injustice. But who is ever going to fight a war for us? No one! We must fight it ourselves!"

The crowd was in a lather. Noting the odd mixture of spiteful feminine voices and yapping pugs, I found myself thinking, *None of these women have worked a day in their lives.*

Mother touched my arm. "Grant is fussing. We should go."

Expecting me to argue, she was surprised when I started elbowing my way none too gently through the women around me. Outside already, Kate took Beatrice from me the moment we emerged. Doubtless, she thought I had been attempting to indoctrinate her daughter.

I was quiet during the walk back. The wind was less intense, being at our backs, and the sun had emerged to give the illusion of warmth. But it was only an illusion, not the genuine thing, which seemed apt. I had hoped the meeting would spark my imagination. But there had been more light than heat.

Mother fell in step with me. "I thought it was an excellent point about wages."

"It was. It is."

"I'm sorry if you wanted to stay."

"I didn't."

"Then why such a long face?"

"That was as much a social gathering as a call to action!" I blurted.

"None of those butterflies actually care about the plight of women who have to work!"

"That's a bit harsh," said Mother.

"It isn't! To them, working is something that they want the right to do if they choose. They aren't thinking about the women who *must* work."

"And why do you think that is?"

I looked at her blankly.

"Because they don't know them," said Mother. "The women you speak of are too busy working to attend rallies."

What was it Madden had said about Bessie Bramble? *"She comes at the girl problem from the top down."*

Girl problem. That was it, right there. It wasn't the ordinary girls who were the problem. It was ordinary girls who *had* the problem. A problem no one seemed able to solve. Like the Gordian knot, or the riddle of the Sphinx. . .

A puzzle.

The moment we arrived home, I excused myself. Closeted in Mother's room, away from prying eyes, I began to write.

THE GIRL PUZZLE

What shall we do with our girls?

Not our Madame Neilsons; nor our Mary Andersons; not our Bessie Brambles nor Maggie Mitchells; not our beauty or our heiress; not any of these, but those without talent, without beauty, without money.

What shall we do with them?

The anxious father still wants to know what to do with his five daughters. Well indeed may he inquire and wonder. Girls, since the existence of Eve, have been a source of worriment, to themselves as well as to their parents, as to what shall be done with them. They cannot, or will not, as the case may be, all marry. Few, very few, possess the mighty pen of the late Jane Grey Swisshelm, and even writers, lecturers, doctors, preachers and editors must have money as well as ability to fit them to be such. What is to be done with the poor ones?

The schools are overrun with teachers, the stores with clerks, the factories with employees. There are more cooks, chambermaids and washerwomen than can find employment. In fact, all places that are filled by women are overrun, and still there are idle girls, some that have aged parents depending on them. We cannot let them starve. Can they that have full and plenty of this world's goods realize what it is to be a poor working woman, abiding in one or two bare rooms, without

fire enough to keep warm, while her threadbare clothes refuse to protect her from the wind and cold, and denying herself necessary food that her little ones may not go hungry; fearing the landlord's frown and threat to cast her out and sell what little she has, begging for employment of any kind that she may earn enough to pay for the bare rooms she calls home, no one to speak kindly to or encourage her, nothing to make life worth the living? If sin in the form of man comes forward with a sly smile and says, "Fear no more, your debts shall be paid," she can not let her children freeze or starve, and so falls. Well, who shall blame her? Will it be you that have a comfortable home, a loving husband, sturdy, healthy children, fond friends—shall you cast the first stone? It must be so; assuredly it would not be cast by one similarly situated. Not only the widow, but the poor maiden needs employment. Perhaps father is dead and mother helpless, or just the reverse; or maybe both are depending on her exertions, or an orphan entirely, as the case may be.

GIRLS POORLY PAID.

What is she to do? Perhaps she had not the advantage of a good education, consequently cannot teach; or, providing she is capable, the girl that needs it not half as much, but has the influential friends, gets the preference. Let her get a position as clerk. The salary given would not pay for food, without counting rent or clothing. Let her go to the factory; the pay may in some instances be better, but from 7 a.m. until 6 p.m., except for 30 minutes at noon, she is shut up in a noisy, unwholesome place. When duties are over for the day, with tired limbs and aching head, she hastens sadly to a cheerless home. How eagerly she looks forward to pay day, for that little mite means so much at home. Thus day after day, week after week, sick or well, she labors on that she may live. What think you of this, butterflies of fashion, ladies of leisure? This poor girl does not win fame by running off with a coachman; she does not hug or kiss a pug dog nor judge people by their clothes and grammar; and some of them are ladies, perfect ladies, more so than many who have had every advantage.

Some say: "Well, such people are used to such things and do not mind it." Ah, yes, Heaven pity them. They are in most cases used to it. Poor little ones put in factories while yet not in their teens so they can assist a widowed mother, or perhaps father is a drunkard or has run away; well they are used to it, but they mind it. They will very quickly see you draw your dress away that they may not touch it; they will very quickly hear your light remarks and sarcastic laugh about their exquisite taste in dress, and they mind it as much as you would, perhaps more. They soon learn of the vast difference between you and them. They often think of your life and compare it with theirs. They read of what your last pug dog cost and think of what that vast sum would have done for

them—paid father's doctor bill, bought mother a new dress, shoes for the little ones—and imagine how nice it would be, could baby have the beef tea that is made for your favorite pug, or the care and kindness that is bestowed upon it.

But what is to be done with the girls? Mr. Quiet Observations says: "In China they kill girl babies. Who knows but that this country may have to resort to this sometime." Would it not be well, as in some cases it would save a life of misery and sin and many a lost soul?

IF GIRLS WERE BOYS,
quickly it would be said: start them where they will, they can, if ambitious, win a name and fortune. How many wealthy and great men could be pointed out who started in the depths: but where are the many women? Let a youth start as errand boy and he will work his way up until he is one of the firm. Girls are just as smart, a great deal quicker to learn: why, then, can they not do the same? As all occupations for women are filled why not start some new ones. Instead of putting the little girls in factories let them be employed in the capacity of messenger boys or office boys. It would be healthier. They would have a chance to learn: their ideas would become broader and they would make as good, if not better, women in the end. It is asserted by storekeepers that women make the best clerks. Why not send them out as merchant travelers? They can talk as well as men—at least men claim that it is a noted fact that they talk a great deal more and faster. If their ability at home for selling exceeds a man's,

why would it not abroad? Their lives would be brighter, their health better, their pocketbooks fuller, unless their employers would do as now—give them half their wages because they are women.

We have in mind an incident that happened in your city. A girl was engaged to fill a position that had always been occupied by men, who, for the same, received $2.00 a day. Her employer stated that he never had anyone in the same position that was as accurate, speedy and gave the same satisfaction; however, as she was "just a girl" he gave her $5.00 a week. Some call this equality?

The position of conductor on the Pullman Palace car is an easy, clean and good paying business. Why not put girls at that? They do many things that are more difficult and more laborious. In the banks, where so many young men are employed,

GIVE THE GIRLS A CHANCE.

They can do the work as well, and, as a gentleman remarked, "It would have a purifying effect on the conversation." Some people claim it would not do to put woman where she will not be protected. In being a merchant traveler or filling similar positions, a true woman will protect herself anywhere—as easily on the road as behind a counter, as easily as a Pullman conductor as in an office or factory. In such positions, receiving men's wages, she would feel independent; she could support herself. No more pinching and starving, no more hard work for little pay; in short, she would be a woman and would not be half as liable to forget the duty she owed her own true womanhood as one pinched by poverty and without means of support. Here would be a good field for believers in women's rights. Let them forego their lecturing and writing and go to work; more work and less talk. Take some girls that have the ability, procure for them situations, start them on their way, and by so doing accomplish more than by years of talking. Instead of gathering up the "real smart young men" gather up the real smart girls, pull them out of the mire, give them a shove up the ladder of life, and be amply repaid both by their success and unforgetfulness of those that held out the helping hand.

However visionary this may sound, those interested in human kind and wondering what to do with the girls might try it. George M. Pullman has tried and succeeded in bettering this poor class. Some of our purse-filled citizens might try it by way of variety, for, as someone says: "Variety is the spice of life." We all like the "spice of life": we long for it, except when it comes in the form of hash on our boarding-house table. We shall talk of amusements for our girls after we find them employment.

LONELY ORPHAN GIRL

FIVE

RAZZY

TUESDAY, JANUARY 20 1885

FIRST THING THE FOLLOWING MORNING, I went straight to the *Dispatch* offices and placed the pages—and my future—in the editor's hands.

Perched at the hard edge of the oak banker's chair that faced his desk, I watched Madden's face as a parched man stares at water in a glass just out of reach. He read without any expression at all. When he reached the end, he went back to the start. "You went over your word count."

"I—sorry."

"Not sorry," he said absently. "Just don't do it next time, or I'll cut your article down myself. You don't want me doing that."

"No, sir." My heart thrilled. There was going to be a next time!

Finished, Madden crossed to the door and stuck his head out. "Here, Razzy. Read this." He held out the pages to the handsome reporter at the rolltop along the wall outside.

"Please don't call me that," said the man as he accepted the pages.

Madden was already closing the door, grinning. "Going to drive him insane. How old are you?"

"Twenty."

"No, you're seventeen."

I blinked. "And next year?"

Madden shrugged. "Thirty-five, or seventy. Whatever we need you to be."

I couldn't stand it any longer. "So, you like it."

Madden's sad expression softened with his smile. "I do. We need to find places for breaks—readers need to have internal headlines, they're like resting posts, little oases for the eyes."

I frowned. "I should know that. I've seen it a hundred times, but never really noticed."

"No reason you should have. And subheads. Hm." He began making notes. "'Some Suggestions on What to Do With the Daughters of Mother Eve.' 'The Old Fields of Labor Overcrowded.' 'How the Average Employer Discriminates Against Petticoated Workers.' 'The Road as Safe as the Factory.' That last one will draw some eyes."

"So will the mention of petticoats," I added wryly.

Madden was unabashed. "You want men to read? Promise them something. You don't have to deliver."

"There's a name for that."

"Yes. Journalism."

"Doesn't that make me immoral?"

"No, it makes you a writer."

A writer. It was a profession that had never occurred to me. There were female writers I admired. But I didn't have the skill, the know-how, the right kind of mind. Or the education.

"A writer," I repeated, my mind all akimbo.

"Part of me wants to send you to school out there," he said, waving a hand at the newsroom, "for polish. But your unvarnished style has its own charm."

"You're calling me uneducated. I'm not."

"How much school did you have?"

"I had two years at the Indiana State Normal School. I had to leave for health reasons."

Madden's expression was neutral. "In your letter you said you had one semester and left for financial reasons. Which is it?"

I froze. This habitual lie had gotten me through job interviews, explaining my lack of a diploma. I'd forgotten I'd written the truth in my first letter.

I opened my mouth, then looked down. "One semester."

"So, no health issues?"

"No," I assured him.

He stared at me for a moment, then nodded curtly. "Good. And that's an important lesson in newspapers: always remember what you've written."

A rap on Madden's door coincided with its opening. Out from behind his desk, the man called Razzy was even bigger—over six feet tall with broad shoulders, arms like saplings, and hands the size of ham hocks.

One of those hands was holding my article. Madden raised his eyebrows. "Well, Razzy? What do you think?"

The veteran reporter closed the door and leaned against it. "Provocative. A lot of our more vocal readers will write angry letters, which will keep the whole conversation going. It won't hurt sales."

Madden raised his eyebrows. "Yes, Razzy, but what do you *think*?"

The tall man, at least twice my age, directed a kindly smile at me. "I think she doesn't want to hear what I think."

I straightened a little in my chair. "I assure you, I do."

Mouth curling at the corners, he spoke in a patient tone. "I think it's naïve, and a little misguided. Asking a man to give up a job so a woman can take it just means that the man is out of a job."

"Oh, is that all it means?" With his nods and smiles and encouragement, I had thought he was in my corner! "I'm afraid, sir, that I am not the one who is naïve and misguided."

The reporter's moustache covered an infuriatingly polite smile. "Oh?"

"Your assumption is that a woman working takes away the job of a man. This presumes that men have to work and women do not. But for many women, not working means starving. Even married women. So let me ask you this: would you ever conceive of a working man taking away a job from a woman? And if not, is that not a signal of faulty presumptions on your part, and not on the part of working women?"

Madden grinned. The reporter glanced at him, and the editor held his finger like the barrel of a pistol and blew upon it. "She found the flaw in your argument, Razzy, and hit a bull's-eye."

The reporter shook his head. "I don't think it's my presumption. I think it's how things are meant to be. Women have their sphere, men have theirs. I presume you read Bessie Bramble's piece the other day?"

On Sunday, Bessie had finally responded to the Quiet Observer, stating plainly that "All women are no more adapted to keep house than men are fitted to be good tailors or shoemakers." She'd asked if society would have been better served if Harriet Beecher Stowe had kept to cooking three meals a day rather than writing *Uncle Tom's Cabin*. If Florence Nightingale had tended to her sewing rather than the running of hospitals in Crimea. If Clara Barton had tended to her home rather than the soldiers of the Army of the Potomac. If Pittsburgh's own Jane Grey Swisshelm had kept to cleaning her pots rather than writing her polemics against slavery. She'd concluded:

> When a woman who is cut out for an artist, a writer, or a preacher is put into a kitchen instead, she may become resigned to it and make the best of it, and do fairly good work, but never the best of which she is capable, and her draw in the lottery of happiness will prove to have been a blank. A round woman in a square hole is as much out of place as a man in a like position.

"I read it, and I agreed—especially the part about not everyone being suited for their 'spheres,'" I added tartly.

"And I agree. But that does not absolve them from *working* in their spheres. I was a soldier. I'm not naturally inclined to violence, but as a young man my country needed me and I went. I got shot at Perryville, and I was along for the walk on Sherman's March."

"I'm sorry," I said, not entirely certain what I was apologizing for.

Still leaning against the door, he waved that away. "I'm saying, I wasn't cut out for that, but I did it. Because that's a man's lot. That's my sphere. It's what's expected. If we all stop doing what's expected of us, nothing gets done. Only lunatics and zealots will run for office, or fight the battles. And then mankind loses."

Realization dawned. "You're the Quiet Observer."

Startled, he came away from the door to shake my hand. "Where are my manners? I should have introduced myself. Erasmus Wilson."

I just stared at him. With an embarrassed smile, he slowly withdrew his hand. Madden chuckled. "Razzy, this is our Lonely Orphan Girl, Elizabeth Cochrane."

"A pleasure. And please, Madden notwithstanding, everyone uses surnames here. I'm Wilson."

"No, you're the Quiet Observer." He was not at all what I had pictured. He had hardly any gray hair at all, and his moustache was close-cropped and neat. With his large frame, vibrant eyes, boyish face, and gentle manners, it seemed almost unfair. "You're the man who conveniently ignores reality to talk about how things *should* be, not the way things are."

"Really?" asked Wilson, still infuriatingly polite. "Isn't that what you're doing?"

"Me? How on earth—"

"You talk about how women *should be* employed. You have an ideal where there is plenty of work for everyone. Jobs and money for all. But it's not an ideal society we live in. It's the real world, where jobs are scarce and money is tight. In that world, men must work because they're not equipped to do anything else. We're not cut out to clean or nurse."

"Nor are all women!"

"I'm sorry, Miss Cochrane, but women are biologically tied to the homestead. They bear the children, they feed the children. It is purely the nature of things."

My chin lifted in defiance. "That may have been true of pioneers, though I seem to recall a great deal of farming done by women as well as men. But this is 1885. We are no longer a hunting society. We are civilized, with modern machines that do the work for us. Can I lay rail tracks? No. But can I ring a bell, or fill out a ledger, or open a door? Yes, I can."

"Of course you can," he answered. "But *should* you? The answer is clearly no."

"It's less clear to me. We're here arguing something *I* wrote. Me. A woman."

"Yes," he agreed. "A woman responding to something written by a man."

"Meaning, we're actually discussing your ideas, not mine?"

"Well, actually, we're discussing Anxious Father's question of what to do with his daughters."

"I thought your idea to emulate China and murder them was a very good one."

Wilson looked wounded. "I know it's not always clear in print, but I was being ironic."

"I wasn't. Better death than the life some young women are forced to lead."

"Miss Cochrane, I hope you don't mean that."

"I do. How would *you* enjoy being as capable as any man—as smart, as quick, as diligent, as dedicated, as hard-working—and yet have every door shut in your face if you try to move beyond your so-called sphere?"

Wilson shook his head ruefully. "I wouldn't. But men are stronger and more capable than women. I'm sorry, but it's just a fact."

"No," I declared, "it is a *belief*. I would ask you to judge the women of your life, look at their abilities. Who among them has not endured as much hardship as any man, and yet carried on? Can you tell me that the women in your life are truly less capable than the men?"

For the first time, his expression clouded. Looking right at me, he said, "Yes. I can."

I didn't know quite what to say. I seemed to have angered him, but I had no notion of what I'd said to do so. Troublesome me, I refused to buckle or look away.

There was an uncomfortable silence, then Madden cleared his throat. "Razzy thinks your piece will stir controversy, which in turn will sell papers. I agree. It's a fresh voice with a unique viewpoint. Well done." Reaching into his desk, he drew out a checkbook and scribbled on it. "Three dollars to Miss Elizabeth Cochrane."

I should have been elated. Instead, I received the check feeling somewhat queasy. Wilson's sudden dark cloud had blanketed me, and I didn't know why.

Madden tried to remove that cloud with an over-bright smile. "Razzy, I'm going to see if lightning strikes twice. Miss Cochrane, this time I don't want a reply, but something original. No plucking at Razzy here, at least not to start. We'll see if we can get a full-blown feud going. Capulets and Montagues here in our in-house Verona. Then everyone will buy the paper to see the latest volley in our own civil war. So long as it remains a *civil* civil war," he warned.

Shaking off his frown, Wilson perked up. "Oh, I have no doubt that Miss Cochrane will tailor her words to fit decorum. It will be up to me to keep the debate on a suitably elevated plane." He turned to me. "So tell us, Miss Cochrane. What does the Lonely Orphan Girl write about next?"

Thinking of Kate, I found I had my topic ready. I told them, and both men paled.

MY FIRST ARTICLE APPEARED ON page eleven of the *Dispatch*'s Sunday edition on January 25th. I had a whole column to myself, with a little spillage onto the next. Madden had suggested removing the word *Lonely* from my name. "It'll make too many men think you're unable to attract a man." Bristling, I agreed.

I read the column through, then read it again, trying not to quibble over this word, that phrase. Instead, I reveled in the thrill of knowing that, all across the city, women and men were about to settle in to breakfast and read *my* words. Maybe discuss them. Maybe argue over them. They would go to church and discuss them there. Ladies in their luncheon clubs and sewing circles would bring me up. "Did you see what was in the *Dispatch* today? That Orphan Girl talks real sense."

Not everyone would see it as sense, I was sure. Certainly not the fine ladies of Allegheny, whose eyes I had blackened so viciously. "Who does she think she is, telling us how to support women!"

But some would see the sense in it. Men and women both. Madden was proof of that. Not every male would be as stubborn as Wilson.

Wilson. I wasted a good deal of time thinking about the Quiet Observer. He wasn't the relentless curmudgeon I had conjured in my head. In some ways, his good looks and nice manners made things worse. That ready smile, that calm politeness, that twinkle in his eye. He hadn't dismissed me out of hand. He'd heard me out before countering with the tired arguments he couldn't recognize as antiquated relics.

But there had been something very certain in his "Yes. I do," something powerful behind his insistence on the weakness of women and the strength of men. It hadn't felt like blind obedience to the way things have always been. I wondered what it could be. And the more I wondered, the more interested I became in Mr. Erasmus Wilson, the Quiet Observer.

I reread his old columns, as far back as we had kept papers. Slowly, the Q.O. changed from my nemesis to my objective. If I could win him to my way of thinking, I'd win everything.

The place to begin was my next piece. It had to be better than the first one. That meant I had to receive criticism. For that, I needed to register an audience's response. And where would I find a better audience than my family?

I waited until after church, when everyone gathered in the kitchen as Mother cooked supper. Taking up the newspaper, I said, "I'd like to read something."

Albert groaned. "It's not more women's nonsense, is it, Pink?"

"I'd like to hear you call it nonsense when Jane is in the room," I answered tartly. "She seems quite an advocate for women's rights."

"And yet *she's* marrying," retorted Albert, with obvious implications.

"More fool her," I said, but too softly for Mother to hear me.

Albert heard, though. "You know you're only jealous, Pinky. No man will have you."

"That's not true," said Charlie, grinning. "There was that neighbor boy back when she was four. Wrote her letters and everything. Wonder where he is today," he added with a wink at me.

Albert scoffed. "Except he was twelve. What, Pinky, is that the trouble? You like older men? I know a few I could—"

Chopping onions, Mother said, "Why don't you read to us, Elizabeth?"

Albert subsided and I began to read, now and then sneaking a peek over the paper at my family. Mostly, they looked bored.

When I finished, I said, "What do you think?"

"I don't see what's wrong with hash," said Mother. "We're having it tonight." Behind her back, the rest of the family exchanged glances. That line, at least, had resonated with them.

"She's right about one thing," said Charlie. "Poor people being used to it doesn't make it better. I've always minded when my pockets were empty."

"It does make you appreciate the life we have now," said Sarah, squeezing his arm.

Lost somewhere behind her eyes, Kate said nothing. I looked to Harry. "What did you think?"

Harry blinked. "Me? It was fine. Though I don't think a woman would take my job. I want to work the railroads, like Tom."

"Then you're luckier than whatever reporter Pinky just ousted from a job," said Albert.

Everyone looked at him, including me. It was galling. Of all my family, he was the only one to recognize the words as mine.

"What gave me away?"

Albert stretched his legs toward the stove, pretending to warm his toes. "That story about the girl earning half what the men earned. I remember you telling me about it. As I recall, you asked for more, and he fired you. You always have a reach longer than your arm."

"That's right," I said. "And now I have a better job than you. Life is funny sometimes."

He wanted to retort, but the rest of the room was a hubbub of exclamations and praise. I produced the three dollars, cashed earlier in the week. As much as I would have liked to have kept the check as a memento, it was far too valuable an addition to the household funds.

Harry hugged me. Kate asked for the paper so she could read it over more closely. Sarah was impressed in spite of herself, and Charlie was actually laughing. "Wait! You wrote one column of newsprint and earned what I make in a day? Clearly I'm in the wrong business!"

"Well, it's just this once," said Albert. "It's not as though she's a reporter."

"Actually, Albert," I said with real smugness, "they've already asked for another."

Albert pulled a face. "I didn't know the *Dispatch* was that desperate. What more could you possibly have to say?"

"Albert." The tone of Mother's voice said he had reached the limit of what she considered appropriate.

Shrugging, he rose and sauntered from the room. I was relishing his defeat when I was suddenly hugged by Kate, who was on the verge of tears. Beatrice saw her mother wiping her eye and said, "What's wrong, Mommy?"

"Nothing's wrong, my little bee," answered Kate. "Auntie Pink has just made us all really proud. She's a writer. See? She wrote this." My niece looked at the words on the paper as if she could read, then began cheering and dancing.

Sarah set Grant into his basket and pulled her chair closer to mine. "Tell us all about it! How did you do it?"

I told them the story, which they all seemed to think demonstrated much more bravery than I'd felt. By the end, they applauded and asked me to read the piece over again. Glowing with embarrassment and pride, I did.

All the while, I was aware of Mother listening, still working on the meal, her back to me. When I finished my second recitation, Kate, Sarah, and Charlie all fell into a discussion of women's rights, with me at the center.

When I couldn't stand it any longer, I went to stand beside Mother. "Can I help?"

"Mm? Oh, no, dear. It's almost ready."

"I didn't mean to insult hash. It was just an example."

"And a good one. 'The spice of life.'"

"So you liked it?"

She glanced at me. "Oh, it's very good, dear."

And that was all she said about it.

From the table, Kate asked the burning question. "What are you going to write about next?"

I took a breath. "Divorce."

The silence that greeted me was deafening.

So much for being the hero of the evening.

MAD MARRIAGES

THAT BREAK HEARTS COVERED BY CALICO
AS WELL AS BY SEALSKIN SACQUES

LOOSE MARRIAGE AND
DIVORCE LAWS

"Bavaria has just passed a law forbidding the marriage of people who have received public charity within three years, who have not paid their taxes, or who, by means of dissolute habits, laziness or poverty, are likely to make the home wretched." What a blessing such a law would be to our country. What untold misery, unhappiness, and even murder, would be saved. Of late much is written of unhappy homes, brutal husbands, unfaithful wives. Peruse any daily paper; you will read of two, perhaps a half dozen sometimes, petitions for divorce on account of desertion, unfaithfulness, brutality and other similar pleas to have the matrimonial knot cut. Petitions for divorce are as common as marriage notices. Governor Pattison's suggestions in his message regarding divorce laws are, to say the least, commendable, but to get to the root of the evil and save all after regrets, dig up the marriage laws, prune them, bud on good, strong, sensible laws and the fruit will be good. Divorce laws will then not be necessary. In fact the better way is to grant no divorce.

In Pennsylvania a man or woman, either drunk or sober, as long as they are able to stand up and clasp hands, can be married without one question as to his ability in supporting a wife, as to her ability to make a good wife, or to make home comfortable. It is not asked if they are capable to raise children in the right way. They promise to "love, honor, and obey," without one thought of the solemnity of the vow, without one intention of trying to keep it. Poor men without trades, without homes, without one dollar laid by for a rainy day, with cruel tempers, brutal instincts, with a surprising love for the bottle containing spirits that do not tend to ennoble or better them, have the ceremony performed, and many women similarly situated, with hot tempers and shrewd tongues. What can such ill-sorted marriages bring forth? They naturally disagree, have a large family—poor man's luck—that they cannot support, are unable to feed, to clothe, to educate, to instruct as to the right way to live; to what end do they come?—to the almshouse, workhouse, reform school, brothel house, penitentiary, and in a few short years depart this life with a sin-stained soul to fill an unhonored grave. The sins of the parents are indeed visited upon the children.

Not only to the lowly do such mad marriages bring misery, but in the higher walks. Money, the god that does everything, will many times close the world's mouth, if not its eye. The children born of these will have every advantage; nevertheless as many hearts ache under silk and satins as under calico. The bond of matrimony hangs like a millstone around the necks of as many of affluence as of poverty. There are just as many brutal husbands, just as many unfaithful wives, just as many wretched homes among the lordly as among the lowly; but money helps in a great measure to make life bearable.

MARRIAGE A VENTURE

Reformation is necessary, but how is it to be obtained? By simply making the divorce laws stricter? Surely not. Marriage is truly a leap in the dark. The most common excuse is, "How did I know it would end in this way? He or she was my ideal before marriage, but there has been a dreadful change since." Truth enough. Young men while courting are all that can be desired—polite, kind, indulgent, generous to a fault, while at home they may be unkind to their mother, disrespectful to their father, tyrant over younger brothers, may even strike their sisters. Where is the girl that would marry such a man? But they are in the dark and eager for the change. It is the same with the sweethearts. The young man finds them neat and kind, the parlor in trim order. She is a good hand at euchre, sings sentimental songs and plays racquets on the piano. He congratulates himself on finding a treasure, an angel, when lo! and behold, she is a Tartar; goes to breakfast with uncombed hair, without a collar, sleeves torn out of dress, shoes unbuttoned, slaps her sister, scowls at mother, gives father impudence and wages a war of words with her big brother. Where is the young man that would marry her as she is; where is the man that would wish to make her queen of his home, mother to his children; that would willingly say the fatal "I will" that would bind them together until divorce released him? But he also is in the dark. The cup of married life is before them, and with a vain, conceited idea that they know what it contains, they eagerly snatch it while holding it to their lips during their engagement. They dream of the nectar and bliss, they drink, surprise too great for expression awaits them. What looked like the richest of wines turns to the bitterest of gall; the scales drop from their eyes; they behold with disgust each in his true color. Life is not the thing they planned out, and so grows unendurable; finale—a divorce.

A young man drawing a comfortable income has a widowed mother, who has doubtless worked hard to give him a start in life, and helpless sisters. He lets his aged mother work, and allows his sisters to support themselves where and how they will, never has 5 cents or a kind word to give at home, dresses in the height of fashion, has every enjoyment, gives his lady friends costly presents, takes them to places of amusement, tries to keep it a secret that his mother and sisters work. If the fact becomes known, he will assert positively that it is against his most urgent desire. Will he make a good husband, think you? Where is the girl who, knowing this, will give her happiness, her life, into his keeping? But it is not always the case that both parties are deceived.

OLD MAID BUGABOO

Some excellent men get wives who make their life a torment; some splendid women get husbands who are brutes; some people marry for money, some for love, and many marry because they don't want to be old maids, Bessie Bramble to the contrary notwithstanding. To be called an old maid is just as great a "bugbear" as it ever was, except to one that is very smart and intelligent, whose duties would interfere with domestic life. "I am surprised that she married him knowing him to be a confirmed drunkard," said one lady to a friend on the Manchester street car the other day. "Yes, it is strange; but then, you see, she got married." Great consolation. Let this man be what he would, she married him and escaped old maidenhood. However, few women will marry a man knowing that he drinks, but if they do walk into misery with their eyes wide open, make no exit for them in case of fire. If they will embrace unhappiness make them do it knowing it is for life. As a rule women will marry a man believing his promises to do better; but men will seldom take women likewise. Reformation of the marriage laws is necessary. "But for the funeral baked meats that the bridegroom sees in the future, would he so joyfully fall in with the marriage procession?" But they don't look forward to the "funeral" now, but to the divorce, as they fall in with the marriage procession.

It is strange, but true, that as people grow more enlightened marriage produces more misery and becomes a less sacred tie. It is not so many years back since they married for life, not with the understanding that if unsuited, a divorce could be easily procured. Then, if from some desperate cause they were compelled to be divorced, they were shunned by society and no one had courage enough to marry the divorcee. Let the Bavarian law be passed here. It will prevent misery. Let the "leap into the dark" be lighted, so that it may be seen, before you jump, just where and how you will land.

How shall it be done? Can there be a better way than to provide that before marriage a licence might be obtained, with testimonies of the friends of both parties as to their dispositions, so that they may be seen as they are, not as they pretend to be? And if after knowing all of each other's bad qualities they conclude to marry, make the law provide that the tie shall last so long as they both shall live. Then strike out the divorce laws. Have a provision also that it will be a criminal act to swear falsely, or for a minister or any party holding the right to marry without the license and accompanying testimony. Let the young girl know that her intended is cross, surly, uncouth; let the young man know that his affianced is anything that is directly opposite to an angel. Tell all their faults, then if they marry so be it; they cannot say "I did not know," but the world can say "I told you so."

NELLIE BLY

Six

WHAT'S IN A NAME

SUNDAY, FEBRUARY 1 1885

I STORMED INTO MADDEN'S OFFICE AND THREW a crumpled newspaper down on his desk. Vibrating like a lightning bolt trapped between heaven and earth, I demanded, "Who the devil is Nellie Bly?"

My article—the divorce piece I had written so well, so daringly—had appeared that morning. Madden had even used my title: mad marriages. But it hadn't been signed "Orphan Girl." Instead, it had been attributed to "Nellie Bly."

Madden had given that piece, of all pieces, to someone else? Put someone else's name on *my* article?!

The paper clutched in my grip, my salary in my purse, I'd come to hurl both at him before storming out of his office forever. But first I had to know one thing. "Who the devil is Nellie Bly!?!"

Astonished, Madden's face broke into the most boyish grin imaginable. "You are."

I blinked. "What?"

"You are," he repeated. "You're Nellie Bly."

It was not at all the answer I had expected. Still standing, I said, "What do you mean, *I* am Nellie Bly?"

Madden folded his arms defensively. "Well, 'Orphan Girl' outlived her usefulness. She was dandy for your rebuttal to the Q.O., Anxious Father, and Bessie Bramble. But the newspaper can't hire orphan girls as full-time members of the staff."

My jaw must have looked funny, hanging open like that. "What?"

"I'm offering you a job, Elizabeth Cochrane. Or should I say, Nellie Bly."

When faced with good news, I always fought back. "Why Nellie Bly?"

Enjoying himself, Madden was blasé. "You needed a new name, and I didn't have much time. They were screaming for copy. I wanted something catchy, pithy, and I called out there for suggestions. There were lots of answers—you don't want to hear most of them. Benji, one of the copy boys, came in whistling 'Nelly Bly,' and for the next minute we were all singing. You know the song?"

"I know it."

"'Nelly Bly, Nelly Bly, bring da broom along, we'll sweep de kitchen clean, my dear, and have a little song.'"

"I know it," I repeated. "Everybody knows it."

"Ex-*actly*!" Madden waggled two fingers at me. "Which is why it's perfect. Every time they see that name in print they'll smile and start humming without knowing it."

I was unconvinced. "How does a made-up colored girl connect to me?"

"She wasn't made up," protested Madden. "Story goes, Stephen Foster was serenading a party when a serving girl poked her head out. She was scolded, but Foster said she could stay, asked her name, and wrote her a song on the spot. 'Nelly Bly hab a voice like de turtle dove, I hears it in de meadow, and I hears it in de grove.'"

"I said I know it!" Popular as they were, I had never been an enthusiast of minstrel shows, or their music. "What does that have to do with me?"

"Foster was a Pittsburgh boy."

"That's it?"

"The founder of the paper was named Foster, too."

I waited, but he didn't say anything else. "And that's the only reason you have?"

Madden shrugged. "What more do you need? You didn't want me to use your real name, did you?"

"You could have let me pick my own name!"

"You weren't here. We were under a deadline. You can pick a new name for next time. Like I said, I'm putting you on the staff."

"As what, the next Bessie Bramble?"

"No. I already pay a woman to write opinions. Your perspective isn't so unique that I can justify the salary for two."

"Oh? How many men do you have writing opinions?"

Madden held up his hands. "Before you boil over, listen. I'll be able to justify the cost if you're something other than an opinion writer."

"Such as what, a copy boy? Is that why I'm called Nellie Bly? Am I supposed to sweep up after everyone? Am I Viola, dressing in breeches?"

"Dress as you like," said Madden. "I never tell my reporters what to wear."

That brought me up short. "Reporter?"

"That's right, Miss Cochrane." He leaned back and tented his fingers behind his head. "I want Nellie Bly to be a reporter. I'll send you out on stories. It's hardly unusual, that. There are plenty of women covering flower shows and markets. But I want stories from *your* point of view, stories no one else is getting, because they don't even know they exist."

"Written by Nellie Bly," I said mulishly.

"Whatever name you want."

I pointed at the paper. "I want everyone to know *I* was the one who wrote this!"

"You didn't. Nellie Bly did. Sorry you don't like it, but it's too late to do anything but steam on. Like the girl said, 'a rose by any other name.' Does a name matter?"

"Of course it matters!" I exclaimed. "People follow writers they connect with in the paper. 'Mad Marriages' is bound to stir people up. If Nellie Bly never writes again, they'll think they managed to silence her!"

Madden was unconcerned. "It's up to you."

Fuming, I recalled something Mother quoted whenever my stubborn streak was blazing—my father's order of action: "Determine Right. Decide Fast. Apply Energy. Act with Conviction. Fight to the Finish. Accept the Consequences. Move On."

Determine Right. The name didn't matter. The stories did. I sighed. "You spelled it wrong."

"What?"

"The name in the song is Nelly with a *y*, not *ie*."

Madden uncrumpled the newspaper. "Huh. Look at that. Want me to fix it next time?"

"No, don't. If I'm stuck with it, at least it's different from the song. Just don't be so high horse about my punctuation in the future." I offered a slight smile. Slight.

"Fair enough." His battle won, Madden leaned back magnanimously in his chair. "I take it that's a 'yes.' You want to be a newspaper man."

"I do," I found myself saying. "I truly do."

"Good. We'll start you at five dollars a week until we see what kind of reporter you are."

"Do I get a desk?"

"A good reporter doesn't need a desk. They're out reporting."

"Which is why Wilson is always here," I said, unkindly.

"Now, now! Don't be that way. He's a good egg. And a very good writer. In fact, you should get some tips from him."

"Over my dead body."

Madden shrugged. "As you will. Now comes the hard part. Pitch me some story ideas."

He liked my very first idea, which I later discovered was rare. As I prepared to go, Madden called, "Where do you want your checks sent?"

I almost gave him our home address, but instead said, "I'll pick them up."

He shrugged. "Okey-doke. Leave the door open."

I exited his office into the open newsroom, looking around with a sense of ownership. That was why I said I would pick up my pay: I wanted an excuse to come to the newsroom as often as possible.

From the rolltop desk just outside the office came a voice I knew. "Congratulations," said Wilson, rising to tower over me.

"Thank you," I said, fidgeting with my coat buttons. "I suppose you disapprove."

"Not at all. I like it when hard work and gumption are rewarded. Please, have a seat," he said, pulling up a chair from an empty desk for me.

I considered refusing, but I was intrigued enough to oblige. "Isn't that a contradiction?"

Wilson sat back in his chair. "The *Dispatch* has a history of hiring women. Story goes, old man Foster hired a woman to write for him and told any man who protested he could take his hat and walk. Of course, he was under tremendous pressure at home. His wife was vice president of the local suffragette movement."

"Maybe he was a believer," I said.

"Maybe he was henpecked," said Wilson with a grin. "Most husbands are."

"Are you?" I had noted the wedding ring the first time we met.

His "Of course not" was perfunctory. Then he said, "I enjoyed 'Mad Marriages.'"

"Oh? I thought the topic was too racy."

"Divorce is with us, whether we acknowledge it or not. I was just surprised to find your point of view more traditional than mine."

"It's not!" I said indignantly.

"You advocate for a removal of all divorce laws from the books. To force people to stay married for their whole lives, come hell or high water. Begging your pardon," he added with a blush for his curse.

"Yes—after making sure the bride and groom confess all their flaws in front of witnesses before the wedding! The point was that divorce would be unnecessary if people went into their marriages with their eyes open."

"It's pretty to think so. But that doesn't allow for people to change. They do, you know."

"Are you divorced?" I asked.

"Of course not," he said. "But marriage isn't like death or taxes. It's ever -changing. Rather like boarding a ship bound for a trip around the world.

You can prepare, but the weather can still surprise you, and someone can grow sick at sea."

"Or the ship can sink," I said.

"Yes," he agreed. "Which is why we must keep divorce legal, and rare."

"And stigmatized. We shame women who go through it."

"Men, too. And that's a fine way to limit it. Otherwise marriage would be meaningless." His eyes danced, and the lines around his mouth curled. "If you wanted your 'modest proposal' to succeed, you should have lobbied for an abolition of marriage entirely. *That* would have turned heads."

"I—wait. . . what?" It took me a moment to perceive that Wilson was teasing. He had divined that I hadn't been serious in my proposal, and then he'd pretended in order to make me argue.

Seeing my consternation, he chuckled. "Every writer worth his salt wants to be the next Swift. Alas, only Twain has succeeded."

"So far," I said.

"So far," he agreed.

Wilson's grin was like a plague—try as you might to resist it, it was infectious. Fortunately, I managed to keep from smiling until I was out of the newsroom and heading down those treacherously steep steps.

ALBERT WAS WAITING TO POUNCE the moment I got home. I had barely closed the door before he was waving a copy of the *Dispatch* in my face. "What's this, Pinky?"

I pulled off my gloves a finger at a time. "A newspaper. Some people read them."

"You know what I mean. 'Mad Marriages.' Mother says that's you. What's this about young men sponging off their widowed mothers?"

"Just something I've observed."

"You're attacking me?"

"I'm not attacking anybody," I replied sweetly. "I'm merely asking if that kind of man is husband material. If that describes you, that's hardly my fault."

Realizing his mistake, he changed tack. "You know Mother is mortified."

That stopped me. I had been too angry about the name change to ask anyone's opinion about the piece. I'd read the byline, thrown on my coat, and stalked for the streetcar into the city.

And I took the paper with me, so how did they. . .

"She saw how upset you were and sent Harry for another copy. We all read it. Everyone's upset. Kate thinks you're referring to her, Charlie and Sarah think you're talking about them—"

"You think I'm talking about you," I supplied.

"And the whole time, Mother knows you're actually talking about her."
I noticed the empty coat pegs. "Where is everyone?"

"At the park. Harry is taking Bea sledding. I wouldn't follow if I were you," he added, blocking my path to the door. "You're on thin ice as it is."

Rebuttoning my coat, I shouldered him out of my way and returned to the chill outdoors.

It was a ten-minute walk to the park. When I got there, I saw Harry dragging little Beatrice on a sled. There were lots of other children, but only a few adults, all huddled under the roof of a wooden gazebo. In the summer it was open to the air, but during winter it had shutters and a stove.

Kate was at the entrance, watching her daughter howl with delight. The way she said, "Hello, Pink," a little too loudly meant that she was alerting Mother to my presence.

Mother was standing near the warm stove. Brushing snow from my coat, I tentatively approached. "Hello."

Mother looked at me. "You ran off so quickly. Did you get your problem sorted out?"

"I suppose," I said with hesitancy. "I mean, it's fine."

"Good."

We stood for a moment, Mother warming herself, me waiting for the cutting disappointment in her voice. Finally, I couldn't endure the suspense any longer. "Mother, about the article—"

"It's very good. Better than the last one. I only have one question."

I braced myself. "Yes?"

"Who is Nellie Bly?"

I stared. Seeing the hint of a smile on her lips, I sagged with relief. "I guess I am."

SEVEN

"ADA! ADA!"

My friend Ada had been on my mind ever since our meeting at the roller rink, but I didn't know how to find her. Waiting at the rink seemed unproductive. I recalled her mentioning a specific streetcar line, so I took up a position on Shady Avenue first thing in the morning, and began the hunt. I must have been a curious sight, peering under caps and hoods to see the faces of women on their way to work.

My quest bore no fruit that morning, so in the evening I returned to repeat my spectacle-making performance. I was about to give up, when I spied Ada crossing the street. Her blonde hair was visible, which was odd in such cold weather. But I was thankful, because it was her hair that caught my eye.

Dashing across the street, I dodged horses, dogcarts, and people on their way home after ten hours of work. "Ada!"

At the sound of her name, she turned. "Lizzie?" Instantly, her expression went from surprised to wary.

"I'm so glad I found you," I panted as I skidded to a stop beside her. I almost lost my balance, and she had to grab me to keep me from falling. "Thank you. Whoo! Hello. What are you doing? I want to take you to dinner. Unless you have plans?"

"Plans?" Ada loosed a sour laugh. "No, I don't have plans."

"Then what do you say to dinner?"

Ada studied me, likely wondering if I had become a church girl, some kind of reformer out to save souls. "Dinner where?"

"Anywhere you like," I told her, then added, "Within reason. My new job doesn't pay that much."

Her face brightened. "Are we celebrating?"

"Yes! But I need your help."

Intrigued, and now fairly certain I did not mean to judge or upbraid her, Ada took my arm, and together we went to find a restaurant. This was always a difficult chore for women not in the company of men. We could have gone to a hotel restaurant and been served in the Ladies' Ordinary section. But that was costlier than either of us were accustomed to. If it had been earlier in the day, we might have found an ice cream saloon near a dry goods store. But those offered either salad or ice cream on their menus, never a good piece of meat. Women were thought to be either abstemious or indulgent, never just hungry.

The establishment we ended up at was called Abe's Brewery. It offered cheap meals for laborers and also served as a boardinghouse, with box rooms and side rooms. Through the window we could see other women, and not of low character, which encouraged us to enter.

It was packed inside, but we were able to lay claim to a corner table near a drafty window. As we shook the chill from our bones, a young man approached to offer us a choice of coffee, tea, or cocoa.

"Cocoa," said Ada. "We're celebrating. My friend here has a new job."

"Congratulations." As he returned with the cocoa, he was a little too familiar. Introducing himself as Abe's son Daniel, he patted my shoulder. "It's such a shame. You're far too pretty to work, both of you."

"Thank you, Daniel," said Ada, fluttering her lashes. She'd perked up in his presence. Perhaps it was the cocoa.

We ordered food. The menus were fairly standard for working-class fare, divided into five-cent and ten-cent dishes. As it was my treat, we both splurged and ordered from the pricier list. I had veal cutlets while Ada ordered liver and onions. Daniel departed, promising to make her dish himself.

"He's nice," said Ada.

"I think he likes your blonde hair."

Ada laughed. "Why do you think I take it down at the end of the day?" Perhaps recalling my attempt to save her from her date at the rink, she folded her hands before her. "So Lizzie, tell me. What's the new job?"

I told her, and she was unabashedly joyful. "Wait! You wrote 'Mad Marriages'?"

My eyes widened. "Did you read it?"

Ada shook her head. "Sorry, no, but some of the other girls at work were talking about it. The married ones, especially. They said they wished someone had made their husbands confess all their faults before their weddings."

It was wonderful to hear just the reaction I wanted, coming from exactly the people I was writing for. "Well, I need a new story, and I thought of writing about you."

Ada flushed. "Me?"

"Girls like you. Factory girls. Girls who work long hours for little money."

Suspicion crept into her face. "Why?"

"Not to lament your lives or make an example of you," I assured her, my palms held up. "No, I want to shine a light on you. Men like the Quiet Observer don't believe you exist. I want them to see you, the lives you lead, and stop them from calling you lazy or willful or anything like that."

Mollified, Ada pursed her lips. "What do you need?"

"I want to hear about your life. You, and the other girls. Are there any you think would like to talk to me?"

Once again Ada loosed that sour laugh. "If you buy them a meal, they'll tell you their whole life stories. A meal, or a drink," she added.

"Can you ask them to meet with me?"

Ada considered. "I can think of three who would come out, at least."

"Wonderful! Thank you, Ada!" I pressed her hand, then took a sip of my cocoa. "Now, tell me what questions I should be asking. I don't even know what kind of factory you work in."

It turned out to be a cigar factory, where the girls used their small hands to pack and wrap tobacco into tight paper shells, which men consumed in clubs that women were prevented from even entering. The contrast couldn't have been more pronounced.

It didn't take her too long to tell me about the work itself. Eleven hours each day, surrounded by tobacco. "The worst part is that the smell never leaves. It gets into your hair. And if you're not careful, your fingers get stained." She removed her gloves and showed me the patches of discoloration caused by handling tobacco all day. "Everyone thinks I smoke."

"How much do you make in a day?" I asked.

"Depending on how many cigars I get done, I can make as much as a dollar. But an average day is seventy-five cents."

"I see." I had to be careful not to let my outrage show. "How many girls work there?"

"About twenty-five. Sometimes the tobacco runs out and the girls are sent home with no pay."

"So there's no guarantee of work."

She shook her head. "And if you get sick, you'd best find your own replacement, or another girl will take your position. Sick girls pay an extra dime just to be sure the girl in her place doesn't steal the job while she's covering."

"So the girls pay their own replacements not to steal their job?"

"It works, mostly." Looking up from her cocoa, she started at my expression. "Did I say something wrong?"

"What? No."

"You look angry."

"Not at you," I said soothingly. "I'm angry at your job."

"I'm lucky to have it," insisted Ada. Then her face brightened. "Do you think the *Dispatch* is looking for another girl reporter?"

I suddenly felt a kinship with those sick tobacco girls. I didn't want anyone swooping in and stealing my job, either. "I don't think so. But I can ask."

Ada nodded, knowing what that meant. Instantly, I offered to buy her something sweet for dessert. *My* extra dime—only it was to assuage my guilt.

I GOT HOME LATE, SMELLING OF CIGARETTES and beer. Daniel had offered us a small glass of the house brew, and we'd accepted—though I'd insisted on paying for it. All told, I'd spent seventy cents on that dinner, as much as Ada earned on an average day.

Most of the house was asleep, but Kate was sitting up, looking out the window for me. She greeted me as I dropped my coat and darted past her toward the washroom. After four cups of cocoa and a glass of beer, it was all I could do to keep my eyes from floating.

We were lucky to live in a house with flush plumbing, something I'd heard of, but not experienced, as a child. In this one way, life in Pittsburgh was superior to life in Apollo. On such a cold night, the walk to an outhouse would have been murderous, and sitting down would have been uncomfortable when the wind shifted.

As I came back, Kate was laughing at me. "I miss those days."

I headed to the pegs and hung up the coat I'd shed as I'd burst through the door. "What days?"

"The carefree days." Kate's expression was wistfully envious. "So, who was your date with?"

I sat on the stairs to unlace my boots. "My friend Ada. The one at the roller rink. She was telling me about her job."

"Oh." Kate seemed mollified. I hadn't been out living it up with a man. There was no reason to envy me. "Albert is furious with you."

"Then it's a good day." Easing a foot free of its boot, I wiggled my pinched toes.

"That piece about divorce upset him."

"No one made him read it."

"I suppose not. He thinks you were writing about him."

"He's not as stupid as he seems."

I regretted the confirmation the moment it passed my lips.

"So you *were* writing about us," said Kate flatly.

"No," I said, wrestling the other boot free. "I was writing about marriage and divorce."

My sister shook her head. "You want to drag us through it all again."

I felt my back going up, and had to fight to keep my voice level. "No one's dragging anyone through anything. I wrote about a subject I have an opinion about."

"Oh, you're just full of opinions, aren't you?"

I placed both boots on the floor to dry, then stood up. Whenever I was attacked, I liked to meet it on my feet. "And you aren't? You're always telling me to get married, to find myself a man to take care of me."

"Because you should!"

"Why? Because misery loves company?"

Kate stared at me, and the look of disgust on her face was something I hadn't seen since the worst days with Ford. She rose and stomped up the stairs to my room, where she closed the door firmly.

"Well done, Pink," I murmured to myself. "No, you're not a troublemaker. Not at all."

EIGHT

CATCHING A MASH

WEDNESDAY, FEBRUARY 4 1885

THE NEXT EVENING, I MET ADA again. She told me she had lined up three women for certain, perhaps as many as seven.

Though delighted with this news, I went into a mild panic. I had already spent a good portion of that week's pay. When Ada asked if we should all gather at Abe's, I did the math and quickly suggested someplace more private. If worse came to worst, I could invite them home. *But then they'd be subjected to my family. . .*

Fortunately, Ada was all enthusiasm and full of helpful ideas. "I'll ask my landlady if we can use the sitting room! She's an old battle-axe, but for a nickel we can have the room all evening. And maybe some of the other boarders will join us. They're factory girls just like me."

Mindful of Ada's promise that I would feed these ladies, and not knowing how many would attend, the following afternoon I took a streetcar to Penn Avenue and Stanwix Street, where the massive new Joseph Horne Company Department Store building stood.

I hadn't been shopping in almost a year, and as I lingered near the dresses on display, I noticed something new. Whereas a customer once had to ask for the price of an item, there were now little cards with numbers beside every garment or trinket. I'd heard of this happening over at the new department store on Fifth Avenue, Kaufmann's, where they proudly declared their egalitarianism: "The same price for everyone!" Alas, Kaufmann's catered only to men.

With a mental note to return on my next payday, I wrenched myself away from the ladies' wear and headed over to the consumables, where I ordered two supper baskets.

Baskets were the ideal fare for a gathering of ladies. Inspired by the rage for picnics, department stores were creating ready-made baskets containing biscuits, fruit, buns, and milk. I had one basket made up with egg and celery sandwiches, the other with fruit sandwiches—Graham bread with a little whipped cream, fruit jam, and slices of steamed prunes. Then, with a basket on each arm, I plunged back into the streets and set out for my first interview, heading to the address Ada had given me.

It was a drab place of unadorned brick. Ada met me at the door and let me in to a room with wallpaper so faded I almost couldn't see the pattern. But it was clean, with no hint of dust, and quiet, like someone holding a breath.

Waiting for us in the foyer was a woman no taller than myself, but far more imposing. With block shoulders and steely hair pulled into a severe bun, she squinted at me, a lifetime of feeble eyesight pinching her face. This was the landlady. I offered the promised five cents. She tucked the nickel away and started setting down rules. "I don't know you. You're not one of my girls. But you're a friend of Ada's, so I'll say this once. No drinking. No loose talk. No swearing."

"Of course not," I said.

"You'd best not be here to protest your rights or such," she said scoldingly. "I want no sign painting or chanting here."

"Unless it's to promote temperance," murmured Ada.

"What's that?" demanded the older woman.

I interceded. "No signs, no chants."

"I lock the front door at ten o'clock."

I nodded. "We'll be out by then."

She glowered at me. "And no men. Ada here has trouble with that one."

Ada pulled a face behind her landlady's back, making it difficult to answer with a straight face. "The good news is, I don't."

The landlady had exhausted her list of commandments. But she was suspicious of my ready agreement. "What will you be doing in here? I think I have a right to know."

"I'm a reporter, and—"

"A reporter!"

"Yes. With the *Dispatch*."

"A girl reporter," repeated the landlady, as if marveling at a two-headed cow.

"She wrote 'Mad Marriages,'" supplied Ada.

"I don't want any trouble," said the landlady.

"I'm just taking interviews. About living conditions. Ada suggested we meet here, as it's the nicest place any of these girls live." That mollified her, so I decided to add more honey. "What's your name?"

Taken aback, the landlady frowned. "Mary. Mary Keneely."

"Thank you, Mrs. Keneely, for letting us into your lovely home. I can't promise you'll be in the story, but I can promise we won't disturb you."

She insisted upon examining the baskets for bottles of liquor. Disappointed at finding none, she helped herself to an egg sandwich and moved off toward the back of the house.

With Ada's help, I set about unpacking the baskets. We were just pouring tea when there was a knock on the door. Expecting one person, I was surprised to see four women file in. They seemed sheepish, and one of them, Clarice, admitted she'd almost turned away, but the other girls had arrived. Together, they had been emboldened to knock.

Even inside, two of them refused to remove their coats and gloves, so they might escape at a moment's notice. We enticed them into the sitting room, where the food was all laid out. Ada wanted to wait for others, but I had a sense that these were the only girls coming. If the others had even set out, they had probably obeyed Clarice's impulse and fled from the door.

Ada and I seated ourselves in straight-backed chairs, while the rest took seats on the sofa and love seat across the room from my oh-so-fearsome presence. They sipped their tea or milk from small cups Ada had borrowed from the kitchen. Their food went untouched on their laps.

Trying to smile warmly, I looked at them all. "Thank you for coming. Ada explained why I want to speak to you?"

"Yes," said Clarice.

"I want to know why," said another, called Patricia.

"Why what?" I asked.

Patricia folded her arms. "Why you want to write about us. We don't want pity." Two others nodded.

"I'm not here for pity," I explained. "I'm here because the men at the newspaper office don't believe you exist."

I saw their backs stiffen. They had all taken the time to look pretty, yet each bore marks of fatigue identical to the ones etched on Ada's face. I reminded myself that they had already worked a full day.

"Don't exist?" echoed Patricia.

"They think all women who work do it for the sake of making a point. They don't know what it's like for a girl to be hungry, to have to choose between medicine and a meal. They spout all kinds of nonsense about women needing to stay in the home. And they put it in the paper. You've read it, I know you have. Don't you get angry when you read that?"

"Every time," said Patricia.

I fixed her with my gaze. "That's why."

Ada looked around, her eyebrows raised as if to say, *What did I tell you?*

"You wrote that piece about marriage?" asked a girl called Lily.

"Yes."

She squinnied at me. "Have you been divorced?"

"I've never married."

"Smart girl," said Lily, softly. "Saddest day of my life."

Patricia said, "You can't write anything bad about our employers. You'll get us fired." There was a murmur of agreement.

I hadn't thought of that. Or rather, I hadn't thought about the consequences of writing negative things about factory owners. These girls needed the work they had. If they went tattling, they'd be fit only for places that didn't ask for references. That was worth a shudder.

It would be a shoddy thing if I used my new job to help them lose theirs. "I promise. I won't write anything bad about your employers."

Clarice began to eat her sandwich, and Marcy, who had not yet spoken, nibbled the edge of a biscuit.

"So where should we start?" asked Ada, the eager hostess.

If I was not going to ask about their employers, that scratched my first dozen questions. So I did what my mother always did when at a loss—resort to compliments. "You all look very well put together. Do you dress this nicely for work?"

Marcy paused in her nibbling, which made her seem even mousier. Lily shook her head slowly. Patricia snorted, and Clarice said, "No."

That was interesting. I looked to Ada. "The other night you said you let your hair down after work."

Ada nodded. "At the job I keep it in a bun. Don't want to be too pretty."

"Draws the wrong sort of attention," agreed Patricia.

All the girls agreed, even the silent Marcy.

"Do you not want attention at work?" I asked.

"No," said Clarice.

"Why?"

They all exchanged glances, unspoken language passing between them. At last, Patricia said, "We aren't going to say anything bad about—"

I cut across her. "I'm just trying to get a sense of what your life is like, generally. Is it because any attention might lead to wrong ideas?"

Clarice said, "It's not just the men."

"No?" I asked.

"No. If you try to be too pretty, the other girls will think. . ." Her voice trailed off.

Patricia filled in. "They'll think you're not there to work, but for the main chance. And if the other girls turn against you, God help you."

"Amen," said Marcy softly.

"So you don't make yourself pretty for work?"

"We have to look nice, or we'll be fired," said Clarice. "We just can't look *too* nice."

"I don't know what you all mean," said Lily, raising her chin. "I like looking nice for work. I like compliments."

"So you do dress up for work?" I asked.

"I dress nicely," she admitted. "I do my hair."

"And put on makeup," said Patricia, under her breath, but not so quietly that we couldn't hear her.

Lily reddened. There was an unspoken rule about wearing makeup. Only two kinds of women could paint their lips and line their eyes: those at the very top of the social strata, and those at the very bottom.

"Your hair is lovely," I told Lily, trying to deflect Patricia's cattiness. "Do you always wear it down?"

Lily replied a little stiffly. "I like to look nice when I go out. At home, there's only my husband to notice me, and he never does."

"He did once," said Ada.

"Yes, how did you get that husband, Lily?" asked Clarice coyly.

"By catching a mash," said Patricia with real smugness. Again, Lily flushed.

"Catching a mash?" I asked, frowning as I wrote down the phrase. "What's that?"

All five girls looked flustered, as if caught gossiping in front of their mother. They looked at each other. They looked at their food. They studied their shoes. Finally, Ada said with a shrug, "It's what I was doing that night at the roller rink."

"Oh," I said, very matter-of-factly.

Ada rose. "Let me freshen your drinks." From somewhere, she produced a small flask. I don't know what it was, but every girl except Clarice accepted a slug of it in her teacup. Maybe I should have foregone the whole meal and taken them to Abe's instead.

I had my pencil tip hovering over my pad. "Catching a mash. Can you always find company?"

"Oh, yes." Clarice sounded scornful. "There are plenty of men just waiting for a chance."

"How does it work? Do you flirt with your handkerchief to attract them, or will they accost you without encouragement?"

"Handkerchief!" scoffed Patricia. "Very few of us use the handkerchief now."

"So how does it work?" I repeated.

It took some more prodding from me and hemming and hawing from them. Once it became clear I wasn't going to look down on them, they explained all at once, together:

"You bump into a well-dressed young man on the streetcar."

"Or get him to notice you by letting down your hair."

"Some fresh gents will come up without a signal, but most of them wait until you look at them and smile, or they'll make some remark for you to answer. I can go to town if I wish, and no man will look at me. And I can go for the purpose of flirting, and every one of them will be looking and tipping." By which she meant tipping his hat.

"After chatting about how bored you are, he invites you someplace else for a drink, maybe even a meal."

I nodded, writing down their words in my little pad. "And do you go?"

"Not the first time," said Ada. "You start by promenading around, let them gallant you home. Then you make a date. On that date, you let him buy you lemonade, or tea. Then something more."

"'First they abhor, then embrace,'" said Marcy, quoting something to herself.

I said, "Did none of you never know any nice young man who could call on you at home?"

"Oh, yes." Clarice's face twisted. "One called on me sometimes. But I had no decent place to entertain him, and he never asked me anywhere. He called me 'nice,' belonged to church. But I've found that the worst men in the city will treat me better than he did. Neither will they try to persuade me to do wrong as much as he did. I dropped him."

There were nods. This was common.

I was nodding, too, even though I was confused. "But, wait—you're saying the worse sort of men treat you better?"

"Yes," she said simply. "I've had them, after making proposals I rejected, advise me to discontinue my ways. They plead with me to drink no more, and point out where such a course will lead me, however flowery some may paint the way."

Patricia broke in. "There are many that brag what they can do and stop at nothing to get their ends accomplished." There were murmurs of grim agreement. Everyone knew that type, too.

"Then you drink sometimes?" I asked.

"As much as he'll buy, and I can swallow," said Marcy, contributing to the conversation for the first time.

"And what does he want in return?"

"No more than you want." She raised her plate, and with some shock I realized she was comparing me to the mashers.

I didn't like the feeling, but that did not stop me from asking, "So what do they expect in return?"

"Sometimes a promise of another date," said Ada, drinking her doctored tea. "That's what Benjamin got."

"And did he get the date?"

Flushing, Ada nodded.

"Is that all they want?"

"You know what they want," said Patricia harshly.

"I don't, unless you tell me," I answered. "I mean, Lily got a husband out of it. Is that what they're looking for? Marriage?"

"My last one was married already," said Clarice. "I didn't know it then. Only after." She studied her plate.

"After?"

"After I fell for him."

"And by 'fell for him,' you mean. . ."

Clarice said nothing. Patricia looked at me sternly. "It's an expression."

"I know. What does it mean?"

"That's a stupid question."

"I'm sorry. What does it mean?"

"It means fall," said Patricia.

"Let your foot slip," said Ada.

"Take a tumble," said Lily.

"Down to Hell." Mousy little Marcy was surprisingly hard-bitten.

I nodded. "Sin, you mean."

"Sin," snorted Patricia. "What are you, a good little Protestant girl?"

"No," I said. "Just a reporter."

"Reporters don't ask questions like that."

"Why not?"

"Because they don't want to hear the answers."

"Well, this reporter does. So let me ask you this—why risk your reputation in such a way?"

"My reputation!" Patricia's cheeks were rosy. "I don't think I ever had one to risk. I work hard all day, week after week, for a pittance. I go home at night tired and longing for something new, anything, good or bad, to break the boredom. I have no pleasure, no books to read. I can't go to places of amusement—for want of clothes and money—and no one cares what becomes of me."

Ada reached out to squeeze Patricia's hand. "We care, love."

Patricia continued as if compelled to finish her statement. "I used to take a walk to try to forget myself. I would speak to men for fun. Now, I couldn't go back to the same dry, unchanging life."

"What she's saying," added Ada, "is that catching a mash means that for at least one night we have someone who cares about us. Who likes us, thinks we're special. What girl doesn't want that?"

"Even if it's pretend?" I asked.

"Even then," Ada agreed.

Marcy shook her head. "It's more than that. I drink—it's not that I like the taste. It's that I like myself more tipsy than sober." She lifted her teacup for Ada to refill. "I drink to make me happy. I go out, tired and low from a hard day filled with work. I drink, and I'm flooded with warmth. I am renewed, reborn. All my troubles fade, and all the years. I drink, my weary feelings leave me, my cheeks flush, my eyes sparkle, and I am a new being."

By this point, Marcy fascinated me. She couldn't have been older than I was, and she had clearly had a good education. Yet here she was, the hardest of them all. "Do you never tire of such a degrading experience?"

"Sometimes," Marcy admitted. "When I go home from work, I feel sick and disgusted with the world, and with myself, and wish I had some respectable place to go, or something to employ my mind. But I don't, and so I commence to wonder if many of the other girls are out, until the desire to go and see is so strong I can no longer resist." She laughed. "Two hours later, drinking my wine, I wonder at my reluctance to go!"

Just then we were interrupted by Mrs. Keneely checking on us. I was astonished that she remained ignorant of the alcohol. Even if she couldn't smell it, she should have been able to tell by the flushed cheeks, the slight swaying of Marcy, and the overloud speech of Ada and Patricia. Yet, because there were no bottles of anything but milk in plain view, she seemed satisfied and let us alone.

As the evening went on, Marcy was particularly eloquent. I discovered she was the daughter of a teacher, had been raised surrounded by books and learning, and had entered the adult world impoverished and alone.

But she's hardly alone, is she? There were hundreds of girls like her. Thousands. All quiet and mousy on first glance, yet desperate to be noticed.

On my way to the interview, I'd intended to ask these girls about the work they did, their hours, their conditions, and more. We never even broached those subjects. I simply listened to them peel back the rind of their lives. By the time we rose to depart, I was feeling very protective of them.

Lily lamented going home to her husband, and was halfway serious as she tipsily suggested catching a mash "for old times' sake." The others thanked me for their meal. I could see they were each concerned they had said too much. Patricia reminded me of my promise. I assured her I would do nothing to lose them their positions. "You didn't even tell me where you worked," I reminded her.

Marcy was at the door when I caught her arm. "You quoted a poem earlier. . ."

She looked at me, then said, "Pope. Alexander." Then she recited:

> Vice is a monster of so frightful mien
> As to be hated needs but to be seen;
> Yet seen too oft, familiar with her face,
> We first endure, then pity, then embrace.

She pulled up the collar of her coat and departed, swaying a little unsteadily.

Thanking Ada, I left her with the remaining food—as well as twenty cents to cover her helpful lubricant. We kissed each other on the cheek, and then she shut the door on her horrible little boardinghouse.

I experienced a kind of giddy confusion. On the one hand, I had wonderful material. On the other, what a dismal, degrading life they were living. *There but for the grace of God. . .*

That night, as I penned my piece, I felt obligated to warn *Dispatch* readers not to be too quick to cast stones:

It is too true that the poor have no enjoyments. The old adage runs "All work and no play makes Jack a dull boy." Likewise Jane a dull girl. Although it would be infinitely better dull than to lead such a life, yet if no amusement is offered them they will seek it and accept the first presented. No excuse can be offered for girls with pleasant homes and kind friends; no excuse for the men who can seek amusement elsewhere. But the poor working girl, without friends, without money, with the ceaseless monotony of hard work—who shall condemn or who shall defend?

Owing to the girls' restriction about not mentioning their employers, as well as my self-imposed goal of not judging them, the piece ran too short. I decided not to add their self-judgment and sarcasm. Though hard-earned, those qualities would do little to win the public to their side. To fill up space, I instead inserted some clever gossip I had heard during my day of waiting at the streetcar stop for Ada. It was amusing, I thought, to include the prattle of teenage girls who themselves were looking to catch a mash.

Early the next morning, I read it over before sealing the envelope addressed to Madden. I wished I could have used their names. Names made everything personal. Names, and faces.

As the corner mailbox clanged shut like a metal dragon snapping its jaw, it occurred to me that the only name in the article was mine. No, not even mine. Nellie Bly's.

Which made Nellie Bly the voice of every woman without a name.

NINE

THE GIRL TRAP

THE ROWDIES OF THE NEWSROOM were full of lasciviousness on my next visit. Praising my piece, they asked for the names of my subjects. "For follow-up interviews," they said.

I smiled at them, murdering them all with my eyes. "They asked if there were any handsome men working at the *Dispatch*. I lied and said, 'Yes.'"

They jeered, then one fellow called Hal Ranger grasped my hand and bent his knee to me. "If you need to practice catching a mash, Miss Nellie, I'm your masher!"

I pulled my hand away just as Wilson stepped between us. "Mind your manners, Ranger. Or I'll be forced to mention this to your wife at Sunday mass."

Ranger obediently returned to his desk. "At least it would make for a lively sermon." The others laughed.

Wilson escorted me toward Madden's office, muttering, "This place is filled with roaches. Both the insect and the other variety."

"My knight," I said. "The roach slayer."

He frowned at me. "Well, what did you expect, with a story as lurid as that?"

I stopped in my tracks. "Lurid?"

"'Man-Mashers'? That can't be real. Women don't behave that way."

I stared dumbly at him. "You're saying I made it up. Is that what you're saying?"

Blanching, Wilson hastily held up his hands. "No, no. Not what I'm saying at all—"

"Because I didn't. They do that."

"I'm sure you were a good reporter, repeating exactly what your subjects said. Doesn't mean it's true."

I folded my arms. "So I'm not a liar, just vapid and gullible?"

He shook his head, exasperated. "I wasn't saying that at—"

I lifted my chin at him. "What if I said I went with them?"

I don't know what made me say it. But the lie was worth it to wipe Wilson's eye.

A voice came from over my shoulder. "Tell me you're kidding." Madden was standing in his office door.

"About what?" I said.

"That you went out with these young women to catch a mash. The paper could be sued. Or given a bad name." It was clear which was worse.

Part of me wanted to shock him and say that I had. Part of me was appalled that he thought so poorly of me. And part of me was angry at being appalled. *Aren't I trying to make a case that there's nothing wrong with these girls? What kind of hypocrite am I, to look down on them?*

The truth was, I *did* look down on their lives. But not on them. Theirs was not a life they aspired to. Any one of them would trade places with me in a heartbeat. As long as that was true, I could abhor the lives they were forced to endure, but I didn't have a right to look down on those girls.

I wasn't denying it, and Madden was becoming livid when Wilson stepped in. "Don't let her fool you, Madden. Our Nellie's a naughty girl, but she's not wicked. She didn't say she had. She just posed a hypothetical. No reporter cares to be called a fibber. My mistake." He turned to me. "I apologize."

Madden stared at me. I stared back.

Surprisingly, Madden relented. "Sorry. Of course. I just don't want the paper to be accused of contributing to the city's declining morals by having its reporters out man-mashing. Good Lord, what a phrase you've coined!"

"I don't think it's original to me," I said dryly.

"It is now. Congratulations. The churches are all going to be sermonizing on man-mashers come Sunday." He gestured toward his office. "Come on in."

Wilson gave me a pat on the shoulder and then returned to his desk.

In his office, Madden handed me my weekly check, for which I was awfully grateful. "I spent my last one on a meal to get the girls talking," I said.

Madden frowned. "How much?"

I knew the answer to the penny. "Three dollars and forty-one cents."

Madden went back to his desk, removed some cash, and made me sign a receipt. "Don't make a habit of it. I'm already running through a fortune in blue pencils marking up your articles. Now, what's your next story?"

Stung by his casual insult to my writing, I was a little huffy. "I'm not sure. I don't feel like I'm done with this one yet."

Walking me to his office door, Madden laughed softly. "I'm not sure how many more the good people of Pittsburgh can take. Okey-doke. Come back tomorrow with five ideas." A yell from across the newsroom drew him away.

"He really likes you," said Wilson from his desk.

I cocked my head at him.

"Not like that! I mean he sees something in you. In your work."

"Because it's a good story."

Chuckling, Wilson shook his head. "No, it's not."

Blood simultaneously fled and flooded my face. "What?"

Sitting at his desk, Wilson put his feet up and turned his amiable face toward me. "It was sensational, but it wasn't a *story*. It was gossip."

"You spiteful thing! It most certainly was not! It was about how these girls are forced to live."

"Forced by whom? That's what the story is missing. The trouble is, Nellie, you start off with a punch, but the second half is nothing. It has no point. It's just prattle overheard on the streetcar, such as any person in this fine city can hear. Gossip. Which is what your writing has been so far. There are a lot of ideas, but hardly any cohesion. There's no *point*. You're driven by emotion. Which only makes sense. You're a woman. But if you want to succeed, you'll need to do better. You'll need to do real reporting, which involves facts. And no one has ever taught you how."

I placed my hands on my hips. "And who is going to teach me? You?"

Wilson spread his hands. "I don't think you'd want me to."

He said it with such smug affability that I balled up my fists against my sides. "Then tell me who, exactly, should have taught me? Even if there were schools for reporters, they wouldn't accept women, and certainly not working women. When I was twelve I wasn't offered a chance to become an office boy to run errands and learn the trade."

"Because, as you just noted, the term is office *boy*—"

"Of course it is. Because girls aren't allowed to learn a trade. You claim I shouldn't be a reporter because I don't know how. I don't know how because I'm not allowed to. I called it the Girl Puzzle, but it's really more like a Girl Trap!"

"Traps require bait. Maybe if you'd stop trying to—"

My outrage boiled over. "Stop trying to be more than what I should be? Or what *you* think I should be! If you had your way, I'd be out there smelling like tobacco and beer and catching a mash, rather than making a respectable living doing something that I'm clearly good at!"

It was only when I came to a crashing halt that I realized the hum of the newsroom had ceased. Silence hung as thick as the tobacco smoke. All of the men were staring at me in slack-jawed astonishment.

Wilson, however, was still smiling. "If I had my way, you would have no cause to shout at me. Obviously, I am at fault. I apologize for upsetting you."

I saw how it appeared to onlookers: the gentleman calming the hysterical woman. *The Girl Trap, indeed.* I took a deep breath. "If you had insulted a man's work the same way you insulted mine, he would have knocked you down."

"But I would never—"

"Have spoken to a man the way you spoke to me. Thank you for admitting it."

His smile wavered, replaced by an uncertain wrinkle in his brow. It was as much of a triumph as I was likely to achieve.

"Well, this has been a delight," I told him, my voice reeking of sarcasm, "but I must be going." I turned and marched out of the newsroom door, only to come up short against those ridiculously steep steps, ruining my exit.

Behind me, I heard laughter—low at first, then louder as the jokes began to fly. I heard some genial cussing, and was tempted to reenter just to frighten them. Instead, I took hold of the stone railing and, turning sideways, began my descent.

A solicitous hand took my elbow. I turned to offer my thanks. It was Wilson. At once, I jerked my elbow from his grip. "I can manage, thank you."

"I'm certain you can manage anything," he said, descending beside me with his pipe clenched between his teeth. He had thrown his coat on in a hurry, and his hat was in his hand. Finding his help refused, he was free to hold his pipe in the other hand as he matched my headlong pace. "But I wanted to say something."

"Do you require the last word?"

He reddened. "I came to apologize."

"You already did that."

He loosed his damnably boyish grin. "I had the sense it was not accepted."

"How very astute. You should become a reporter."

Wilson shook his head. "Must everything be a fight?"

Reaching the first landing, I halted to gaze at him. "I wonder if that's what the southern slave owners said before the war."

A flash of anger. "I fought in that war."

"Oh? On which side?"

As his jaw clenched, I felt a perverse satisfaction. "On the side of right, of course."

He was significantly taller than me, and I wanted to look him eye to eye, so I took two steps back up the way we had come. "I take it you mean you fought for abolition. But slaveholders believed they were in the right. Demands for equality are always disruptive to those who feel superior."

"Women are not slaves," said Wilson. "There are no bonds from which to free them."

"If you believe that, then you're right—I'm not a very good reporter. Yet." With that parting shot, I marched by him and exited the building.

Rather than go home, I wandered about the city for hours, fuming. *Imagine that middle-aged sack of male platitudes trying to instruct me how to be a reporter!* Worse, he had clearly thought he was being kind. Avuncular. Magnanimous. He wanted to offer advice on how I could be a better reporter? What did *he* report? Not facts! No, he just shared the gobbledegook inside his own head. Not even thoughts—*feelings*. That's what his Quiet Observations amounted to—a collection of feelings about how the world should work. No rational argument, no penetrating chain of reason. Erasmus Wilson was the epitome of the writer who wrote what he felt. He didn't deal in facts, or write from his own experience.

Experience was the key. Facts, not platitudes. Real life, not gossip.

I had to be *better* than Wilson, better than all the other reporters at the *Dispatch*. I had to have facts to back up anything I said. I had to see things with my own eyes. Experience them. Then no one could accuse me of lying, or writing from a place of emotion.

"LIZZIE?" SAID ADA, BLEARY-EYED AS she stared through the gap in the door.

"Mrs. Keneely let me in," I told her. "Sorry for the late hour. I have to ask another favor."

She drew her robe tighter around her. "What do you want now?"

"I want you to get me a job at a factory."

II

MISS PUSH-
AND-GET-THERE

HER MEMORY CLOUDED

THE INSANE GIRL ON BLACKWELL'S ISLAND WHO HAS
NO RECOLLECTION OF HER PAST

It is a sad case. A young lady of eighteen years, nicely attired, showing in her speech and bearing every evidence of having been well educated and tenderly reared amid refined associations, becomes insane, without any identification whatever, and is to-day an inmate of the female asylum on Blackwell's Island.

This is the fate of Nellie Marina, or Nellie Brown, as she indifferently calls herself, who, on Friday last, asked permission to stay over night in the Home for Women at No. 84 Second Avenue.

The matron of the institution thinks she was sane when she came there, and that her lunacy suddenly developed a few hours later.

Dr. Braisted, in charge of the insane pavilion at Bellevue Hospital, who studied the case with much interest after the girl came under his charge, thinks she had a lucid interval when she entered the home. Even after entering the hospital she was apparently sane and logical in conversation the greater part of the time, except when the subject of her chief delusion—a belief that people were seeking to kill her—was brought up, or when any persistent effort was made to learn something of her antecedents.

If she has any friends they have not presented themselves. "The one series of statements to which she is faithful in her various conversations with us," said Dr. Braisted, "is that her father and mother are dead, and that after their deaths she lived with her grandmother and had a maid."

Her grandmother, she told the doctors, died recently, and the girl thinks she remembers having a fine watch, an extensive wardrobe and a large sum of money. She does not know how she came here, and quietly declines to believe she is in New York.

"She never seemed to be restless," said Dr. Braisted. "Her delusions, her dull apathetic condition, the muscular twitching of her hands and arms and her loss of memory all indicate hysteria."

A commission consisting of Drs. Braisted, Field and Fitch yesterday adjudged her insane and she was committed to the asylum on Blackwell's Island.

There is no evidence that she has been treated with any violence nor that she had been involved in any unfortunate love affair, nor that her own conduct has been marked with any moral improprieties. With much tact and delicacy she was closely questioned on these points by one of her own sex without exhibiting the least indication of anything but surprise.

—*New York Herald*
Sunday, September 25, 1887

TEN

THE FACTORY GIRL

TUESDAY, FEBRUARY 10 1885

ADA'S FRIEND LILY WAS EMPLOYED by Oliver Bros. & Phillips, one of the largest manufacturers of iron in the United States. She worked on the floor where nuts and bolts were made. Ada told her I would like to take her place for a day.

At first Lily was hesitant, but I promised I was not interested in taking her job. "In fact, you can have my wages for the day. The newspaper is already paying me." With that understanding, she wrote a note in which she pleaded illness and stated that I was a competent girl who could take her place.

Which meant I had to understand what to do.

"I'm a pointer," she told me. "We cut the raw bolt at the end, so the nut can catch it. Don't wear anything hanging. Cover yourself, but be able to roll up your sleeves, and keep your skirts at your ankles, no lower." Then she explained in very simple terms the work she did, and how to appear knowledgeable.

Leaving home long before my wont the next morning, I shivered and slipped my way to Water Street on the South Side. *I hate the world before dawn*, I thought as I switched from one streetcar to another, grumbling all the way to the Oliver Bros. factory. Nestled neatly between the river on the left hand and railroad tracks on the right, the site consisted of three massive buildings, each with smokestacks that belched horrific blossoms of noxious clouds and dust into the roseate sky.

Uncertainly, I joined a crowd of workers waiting outside. A whistle blew, the gate went back, and what appeared dead and deserted became animated. Wheels groaned and screeched, belts snapped.

I followed some girls to the second building and up the stairs, pausing only long enough to see the massive furnaces and vats of molten iron. Having been told whom to ask for, I found Mr. Lansing in his office. He read Lily's letter, then sized me up. "Not much, are you?"

"She said you don't have to be strong to be a pointer."

"It's true, pointing isn't heavy work. But you can't be weak, either. And it takes concentration. You can focus, I hope? Not chatter away all the day? If you're a talker, I'll put you in with the nutters-on."

"Excuse me?"

His eyes rolled up to the ceiling and back. "Look, if you don't know the terms, you can't—"

"I can do the pointing," I said hastily. "Just point the way."

He ignored my inadvertent pun. "Go put on an apron and tell one of the girls to show you to machine eight. I'll be by in a bit to see how you're doing."

In the dressing room, all the other girls had already removed and stowed their coats and were flying hither and thither, rolling up their sleeves and tying on coffee sack aprons. Taking one, I imitated them, and then asked a freckle-faced girl my own age where the pointing machines were. "Come along," she said. "I'll show you."

While we walked, she made small talk. I mentioned Lily. "I don't want to let her down."

"That's sweet," she said. "What's your name?"

"Lizzie," I told her. "Lizzie Cochrane."

"Ginny." We shook hands. "Oh, your hands are so smooth. Say farewell to that!"

That sounded ominous. I decided it was time to start interviewing. "Do you like your work?"

She shrugged. "Better than a stick in the eye."

"Do you find it hard?"

"Heavens, no. It's easy enough when you once learn how."

"Do you never get tired?"

"Not often. When I get tired of sitting, I stand up, and when I get tired of that, I sit down again. We can stop for a while if we wish, but most of us want to make as much as we can in a day, so we work right along. Here we are. Number eight. All yours."

I was looking at a not-too-large machine that had pedals like a sewing machine. Attached by a belt to the main pulley, it was already in motion.

A broad-shouldered man in coveralls set a bucket beside my machine. He stared at Ginny, who smiled back at him. "Good morning, Christoph."

"*Guten tag*, Ginevra," he said in reply, making the G hard. He examined me, but when I did not speak, he shrugged and walked toward the stairs.

Watching him go, Ginny leaned close. "It's cute that he can't say my name, don't you think?"

"Cute," I agreed, staring at the machine rather than the man.

Seeing my obvious hesitation, Ginny took pity. "Here, I'll do one." Stepping up to my machine, she plucked up a raw bolt from the bucket. With her left hand, she placed the head of the bolt into a socket. Then she stepped on a pedal, causing several steel knives to leap up and kiss the bolt.

I jumped back, and she laughed. "Just make sure your fingers are away before you step on the pedal."

"I will," I promised, watching in fascination as the knives trimmed the end of the bolt into a neat curve.

"Release here, and the bolt drops." She demonstrated, letting the bolt slide into an iron pan. "Then put them in the box, and one of the boys will be by to take it on to the cutters. That's it!"

Thanking her, I took my place before the machine. Reaching down into the bucket, I plucked up a bolt. I was very tender with that one, and it fell out before I could step on the pedals—I soon learned I had to really ram the bolt into the slot before it would stay. Careful that my fingers were nowhere near the blades, I stepped on the pedal, and hey presto, the job was done. I proudly pressed the release, the pointed bolt dropped, and I reached for another.

My sense of accomplishment faded as the morning wore on. My shoulders began to ache. I imitated Ginny by switching between sitting and standing. Alas, nothing could be done for my hands, which became filthy and chafed. I felt very proud when I was given a bucket of bolts of a different size and figured out how to change the settings of my machine on my own.

After a while, I stepped away to ease my shoulders and started questioning the woman at the next machine over. "What do you think about all day?"

"Nothing. Day's too short if you want to make money."

"Aren't you exhausted at night?"

"When I started, I would be kept awake at night by the clatter still sounding in my ears, and my arms felt as if they were still moving. But you become accustomed to anything." Her pace didn't slacken while talking, and I felt her disapproval so strongly that I returned to work.

By midmorning I had learned all I could from pointing. The next time my box was full, I forestalled the wandering boys and carried it myself to the second stage: the cutters.

The cutters were directly across from the pointers, but they worked at much larger machines. There was a sink full of oil that pumped constantly, keeping the bolts lubricated through the cutting process. Unlike a pointer, a cutter regulated her machine with her hands, not her feet. The bolts were placed in the center of the sink, then shoved in hard. While the dies ground the threading onto one bolt, the cutter was already placing a second bolt, as the machine cut two at a time. Thus a cutter was constantly alternating left and right, dropping each completed bolt into a vase on either side. Naturally, with all that oil, the cutters' hands glistened with filth.

Setting down my box beside one, I said, "Here are some more."

"The boys can do that," she answered.

"I needed to stretch my legs." I nodded at her machine. "Your work looks hard."

"Heavy. But no harder than anything else."

"Would you not rather do housework?"

She laughed. "No, indeed! My time off is my own. Besides, I make more money here."

"You don't like housework?"

"I'd like it well enough if I had a house of my own. But all the places I've tried it, the girls are treated lousy by the mistresses. When I'm out of work here, I go to housework, but I'm always glad to come back when they need me."

"Do any girls ever leave here to work in houses?"

"One, not long ago. She'll make less for more work, poor fool. She was a good worker, never got less than twelve dollars a payday."

"When is payday?"

"Every two weeks."

That's more money than I'm making as a reporter. Perhaps I should stay, I thought as I returned to my machine. After pointing a fresh box-load of bolts, I wandered away to another cutter and chatted her up. "I suppose you'll stay here until you get married."

She never looked up from her machine. "Don't know as I will ever get married. I'll work here as long as they'll keep me. You can't always tell how a marriage will turn out. I say it's better to work and be happy than to be married, still have to work, and be miserable."

A woman after my own heart.

After bolts were cut, men known as washers dumped them into perforated zinc buckets and wheeled them on wagons to large tubs filled with boiling soda water. When washed, the bolts were then taken to the "nut-tappers."

"Excuse me?" I said to Ginny upon first hearing this sobriquet.

In answer, Ginny pointed at the largest of all the machines, the tapper, with six pedals and six pulleys. These operated sharp, threaded steel drills that cut holes in the nuts. "That's the worst. You have to sit all day."

Sidling up to a nut-tapper, I watched her quick, skilled hands deal with six nuts at once. "Do you like your work?"

"At first, not so much. But now. . ." She shrugged.

"You do that so speedily!" I said in genuine astonishment. "How long have you been here?"

"Ever since they started hiring us." By which, I assumed she meant girls. "Four years."

Four years, and they had seventy-five women here. "You must have been good to stay so long in one place."

"I came to earn a living. I mind my business and go ahead. That's all that's asked of us."

Even with frequent breaks to chat up my fellow workers, it was one of the most grueling days of my life. The dim light, thick metal smell, and incessant thumping of machines conspired to make me light-headed. Worse, several men eyed me as a fox eyes a hen that strayed to the edge of the coop. One, bolder than the others, came right up to me, so close that I could almost taste the sausage he'd eaten for lunch. I had to slip away between a gap in the machines too narrow for him to pass through.

That aside, the work itself was utterly monotonous. The factory girls were treated like machines, and machines required no relief, no joy. Upstairs on the third floor, where I did not go, girls screwed the nuts onto the bolts and then bundled the finished products into boxes strung with twine. Beside the door to the third floor was a sign: positively no singing.

At the end of the day, I waited while my work was weighed. The supervisor was disappointed by my paltry offering. "Maybe less talking next time?" he suggested.

"What does that number mean?" I asked.

"The timekeeper reduces the weight into thousands, and you're paid by that measurement."

"Lily will give me my share," I answered. "Use her name."

"As you like," he said, crossing out mine.

That night I arrived home weary and aching, but filled with experience and observations. My fingers positively itched to write the story.

But first I took a bath.

MADDEN READ MY STORY WITH HORROR. "You actually worked there?"

"For a day. Let me tell you, Mr. Madden, it was the most exhausting day of my entire life. The place was foul-smelling, the air thick, the heat high, and the work both mind dulling and ceaseless. We were given a water break every two hours, and just fifteen minutes to eat any food we'd brought with us. We started before dawn and ended long after dark. We had no sight of the sun all day, as all the windows were closed."

Madden tapped his cigar ash into a tray. "I don't suppose you're worried about being sued for fraud?"

"Fraud? What fraud? I did the work. Now I'm writing about it."

"I'm not sure I like it."

"That's too bad. Because I'm not finished."

He was halfway through a puff and choked on it. Coughing, he said, "Excuse me?"

"Mr. Madden, this is just one factory out of dozens in the city. Women do all kinds of work. I have a friend who works rolling cigars," I said pointedly. "You should hear the stories she tells."

Madden removed the cigar from his mouth to stare at it. "Never learn how a thing is made. Spoils the enjoyment."

Placing my hands flat on his desk, I leaned in. "Imagine a series of stories about the women who work. Reveal them as sisters and daughters like any other girls. Make the people of Pittsburgh *see* them."

I could almost see him disappear behind his eyes as he considered it. The appeal was obvious. The story was sensational. And a series! Nothing was more appealing to a newspaperman than a series—except, perhaps, a scoop.

"Okey," he said, stubbing out his cigar. "It's not as though you're lacking for material. Or novelty. But you're not going in to work at each factory."

"Why not?" I demanded.

"For one thing, they'll catch on. For another, it's not how it's done. From now on, you'll approach it like a reporter. And you'll start with Oliver Brothers. Go back, say who you are, ask for interviews. Do it properly."

"Fine," I huffed.

"And I'm sending Billy Pelletier with you."

My hackles rose at once. A man? "Why?"

"Easy there, Miss Prickly. Pelletier is an artist. Pictures are the thing to run with a story like this."

It took me several minutes to cool off but, on reflection, I actually liked the idea of having an artist along. I had promised not to malign any of the girls' employers, but one image would speak volumes.

I DID AS MADDEN ASKED, AND SET UP an appointment for interviews. Upon arriving, I was amused to find the factory noticeably cleaner. Even the air was fresher. The women were all clearly primed for my arrival and had nothing but praise for their employers.

I already knew how I would handle this obstacle. I started out by asking perfunctory questions about their current work, about which they could sing paeans of praise. Then I subtly asked if this was their first factory job. When the answer was no, I prompted them to speak about their *previous* employers. I received more truthful answers, and the eavesdropping Oliver brothers could not complain, as they looked positively spiffy in comparison.

Ginny recognized me, of course, but thankfully said nothing, and I did not ask her for an interview. That would have been awkward for us both.

Only when I reached the third floor—unseen on my earlier visit—did my composure fail. This was where the nutters-on threaded nuts onto bolts and then packaged them for shipping.

They were all little girls.

I halted in the door, staring at girls who should have been in school, or running through fields, or playing with dolls, not threading bolts or sweeping metal shavings.

Approaching one, I introduced myself and asked why she wasn't in school. "I'm through with school," she said scornfully. "And father don't make enough money to keep us all."

"How old are you?"

The child shrugged aggressively. "I don't know just how old I am."

"Well, you look to be eight or ten."

Again, the shrug. "I dunno. Maybe I am."

I wanted to feel outrage, but then I thought about what I'd been doing at that age. That had been during the Ford years. I could hardly say that, if given a choice, I myself would not have wanted to be at work instead of home.

The next day, I turned in my revised copy. The moment I entered Madden's office, he produced a blue pencil. My initial annoyance at the implication turned to horror as I saw how often he was forced to use it.

But for once he did not chide me on my grammar. When he finished, he sat for a time, his hangdog face looking particularly heavy. "Okey," he said at last. "Let's run it."

THAT FIRST STORY RAN WITH a magnificent banner:

OUR WORKSHOP GIRLS
WOMEN'S LABOR IN PITTSBURG.

Pelletier's art was terrific. The women looked less tired in ink than in life, which would please both the bosses and the girls. It pleased me, too. The prettier they looked, the more these women would become people in the minds of the *Dispatch*'s readers. The more they became people, the more sympathetic they would be.

In the byline was the name Nellie Bly. My name. I was growing to like it.

I saw Wilson later in the week and asked him what he'd thought of the story.

At least this time he didn't dare to question my veracity. He simply removed his glasses, shaking his head while puffing on his pipe. "It's a real shame. Those little girls."

"That's what they're good for," I said.

Wincing, he pointed the pipe at me. "You're telling me they wouldn't be better off at home?"

"What home? They don't have a real home," I told him. "For them, it's a choice between this and nothing."

He just kept shaking his head. "I can't believe it."

"Then keep reading my stories," I told him.

ELEVEN

EXCHANGING BARBS

M Y NEXT VISIT WAS TO H.B. SCUTT & Co.'s factory on Bingham Street in Southside, where women made barbed wire. "This is the only wire works in the world where female operators are employed," I was proudly told.

The place was at least congenial to the senses, being painted, well lit, and well ventilated. Also, there were obvious fire escapes, and two dozen Babcock fire extinguishers. Evidently, they were careful. As well they might be, with two hundred and fifty girls working machines throughout the building. At that number, they more than doubled the amount of men working there.

I was most impressed by the machines themselves. They were wonderful. Far from dirty, these devices gleamed—I later learned that the workers were forced to clean them every Saturday. And they seemed to function almost independently, needing only to be fed wire.

The wire itself was produced by my old friends at Oliver Bros. and delivered in huge coils. The Scutt women loosened the wire and spooled it onto mammoth bobbins. Then the machines took over, and the women had nothing to do but make sure they kept going.

"I never worked before I came here," one confided in a rush as she managed two machines, "and at first I was very much ashamed to be a factory girl. I was afraid to look at the others because I had always been told that factory girls were the worst girls on earth. But I've found some very nice, sensible ones here. Some are rough and swear, but aside from that I don't believe we have a bad girl employed here. I've learned a girl can be a lady as well in a factory as in a parlor." I adored this quote and made sure to use it.

Moving upstairs, I watched the barbing machines in action. Each girl fed her barbs along the wire, judging the distance by eye alone. She had to keep moving at all times, lest a patch of wire remain barbless. Some girls were using tabulars in place of barbs. Unlike barbs, tabulars were not sharp, so the girls could be less exacting with their fingers.

"You feed very rapidly," I complimented one girl.

"I should. I've been here since they started."

"All the girls appear to be old hands at this."

"Most have been here at least two years."

"I suppose you're exhausted at the end of the day?"

"No. I hardly ever feel tired."

"Oh? So what do you do when you go home in the evenings?"

"I have no home. My father and mother are both dead, so I board. I never go anywhere. I always stay in the house."

Her no-nonsense replies did not seem curt or spiteful, so I pressed on. "I've been thinking of boarding. What do you pay, if you don't mind my asking?"

"Five dollars every two weeks."

"That's very reasonable. Do you board here in Southside?"

"No, over in Pittsburgh."

"Really? What time do you have to be up to get here by seven o'clock?"

"I generally get up at five or five thirty."

"And how much are you paid?"

"Seventy-five cents a day."

"As much as the men?"

"Yes. But if we go over production, there's a cash premium." Hence her unwavering concentration.

"What's that machine over there? It looks new."

"It takes scrap wire and turns it into a kind of nail."

I pointed again. "And that one?"

She had to wait to look, and her glance was lightning swift. "A staple machine."

"And what kind of barb are you using there?"

"The Oliver Twist. It has two points. The four-pointed barbs are called Cactus, or Holdfast, or Scutt—it was invented by the owners." She frowned. "Excuse me. I'm losing my concentration."

I thanked her and moved off. While Pelletier drew my friend at her machine, I paused by one of the supervisors. "How do you like having women working here?"

"Meh," he said, tossing away his cigarette. "I'd rather have men."

"And why's that?" I asked politely.

"These women are cranks."

"What makes them cranks?"

He looked at me as if I, too, were a crank. "They want to work!"

At lunch, the women all found spaces—on the floor, in corners, between machines—to eat. Spying one pretty blue-eyed girl who was not eating, I chatted her up. Her name was Gwendolyn. "My brother brings my lunches," she said. "He'll be here."

But it was a long wait, and when her lunch finally came, it was a little girl who brought it. "My sister," Gwendolyn explained.

The sister ran up, breathless. "Pat had to go to town, so I brought it!"

"You were slow enough about it," said Gwendolyn crossly. "I thought you weren't coming at all."

"I have something for you. I thought I would bring it over so you wouldn't be in a bad humor." And the sister produced a paper box.

"Oh!" cried the blue-eyed worker in sudden excitement. "It's a valentine! Danny told me he'd sent one, but I thought he was only making fun!" With eager fingers, Gwendolyn flung the box open. Inside was a beautiful blue satin valentine.

A crowd formed at once. "Oh! Let me see it! Isn't it lovely? When did you get it? Do you know who sent it?"

Looking at that expression of affection, I was inexplicably melancholy. Not that I wanted a beau. But there was no one in the world who cared to send me kindnesses.

Focusing on my work, I said, "Since you have someone to send you valentines, I suppose you also go out in the evenings?"

Gwendolyn raised her chin at me. "No, I do not. I never go out at night. He comes to the house and I always stay in."

"What do you do in the evenings when he's not there?"

"I make knickknacks and do all kinds of fancy work. I like to do such things. I know some girls who go to balls and such places, but I've never gone."

"Yet!" laughed another girl behind her back.

"You're lucky," said yet another. "My father makes me keep house in the evenings, after working here all day. If I had a minute to spare, I'd be out having fun, not doing fancy embroidery."

A span of experience, right there. Yet nothing like mine. I had no father to make me clean house, nor a suitor for whom to sew and wait for at night. I pined for neither.

Yet as Pelletier and I returned in a carriage from that set of interviews, I felt acutely alone.

THAT LONELINESS EASED SOMEWHAT as the letters began pouring in. After the first story ran on February 15, Madden called me into his office to read them. After the Scutt & Co. story appeared a week later, he assigned me a desk of my own. "You get more mail than I do, and it's burying me alive."

As my desk was not far from Wilson's, I quite enjoyed tweaking the Q.O.'s nose by loudly reading him the joyful missives from women who were reading my articles with avid attention.

Wilson took my ribbing with good grace, and cheerfully teased me in return. "When letters full of praise come in from men, read me those."

The other reporters in the newsroom fell into two camps. There were those who felt daring, having me in among them, and made passes at me. Then there were the others who deemed me an unwelcome intruder. These tended to go to lunch or off to track down a story if I ever sat at my desk for more than ten minutes. If they stayed, they made sure to make rude remarks about passing wind, or dancing girls they had seen, or feminine figures they admired.

Wilson admonished them from time to time—"Leave off, roaches!"—but he also gave me a look that said, *What do you expect? You don't belong here.*

It is natural, I suppose, when given a choice of unwelcome attentions, to gravitate toward the more flattering. I started to socialize with the handful of "roaches" who weren't shunning or insulting me. We would go out to a saloon at the end of the workday—a decent one, well swept and well lit, with large windows facing the street and no tinny piano or room for rent upstairs. Mr. Pelletier joined us, acting as a kind of chaperone, though I made it clear from the first that I had no need of one. "Don't get fresh, any of you, or there'll be an article about masher reporters." That kept them in line.

Once they became used to me, the roaches seemed to like having a woman in their midst. They claimed it elevated their discourse.

For my part, I quite enjoyed talking to men about events around the city. I had long suspected that men gossiped as much as women, but on matters that were more relevant. I enjoyed those debates—the vehemence, the surety, and most of all the bluntness of their talk. It was almost intoxicating.

But in truth, I was hardly at the *Dispatch* often enough to enjoy that feeling. I was out hunting up my next target, identifying the next factory, or crafting new questions for the women I would interview.

I was finding my stride.

NEAR THE END OF THE MONTH, Madden called me into his office. "Nellie, come here."

I obeyed at once, rising from my desk to cross the few feet to his door.

It was entirely lost on me that I had begun to answer to Nellie Bly.

I plopped down in the chair opposite Madden's desk, cheerfully unconcerned. He produced my next piece. I saw blue pencil marks all over it. "We can't keep doing this."

I felt my blood drain. "Doing what, Mr. Madden?"

"I can't keep rewriting your pieces."

A wave of relief overtook me. I wasn't being fired. "I can work on my grammar."

"It's not the grammar. Heaven help me, I can deal with the grammar. No, it's the structure. Structure matters. In this piece here, you bury the best line and lead with nonsense. I don't care as much about how a thing is made as about who makes it. You have a grasp of what goes into a good story, Nellie, but you have no idea how to grab a reader's attention."

When being criticized, instead of admitting fault, I usually resorted to defiance. "I seem to be grabbing some attention, at least of those who write letters."

Madden held up a hand. "Now, now. Every reporter has to learn something. As I said, you have an eye for good stories. You just haven't learned how to tell them yet. You have a point of view. It's what I hired you for. You get these girls talking, which is terrific. It's just that when it goes down on the page, you need guidance." He glanced out his office window.

Following his glance, my back hardened like cement. "Oh, no."

"Oh, yes. I want you to run your pieces by Razzy for the next few weeks. He'll help you craft your reporting into the right shape."

I groped for an objection. "If those men out there see me asking the Q.O. for help—"

Madden waved a hand. "So do it out of the building. I don't care, so long as I don't have to spend hours each week reworking your stories. Use this." He handed me the one he had corrected.

I took it without removing my eyes from his face. "Must it be Wilson?"

"I've already talked to him about it." I opened my mouth, but he cut across me. "That's all, Miss Bly."

Back at my desk, I tremblingly put things into their proper places, donned my coat, hat, and gloves, collected my bag, and headed for the door. If Wilson was watching me, it was out of the corner of his eye. He didn't speak.

It took a long streetcar ride and a longer walk for my burning rage and shame to abate even one degree. I didn't fully cool down until I was locked away in my room, where I studied the corrected article.

I saw how much Madden had been forced to move around. He was not being cruel. He was doing his job.

I didn't like admitting I didn't know something. *I don't suppose anybody does.* It wasn't that I thought I knew everything. No, my problem was that I wanted to be good at whatever I put my hand to. I hadn't been an instant virtuoso on the piano, so I resented practicing, because that implied imperfection.

Having discovered a thing I was naturally good at, and interested in, and eager for, having my deficiencies pointed out was like having ice water thrown over me while I slept—something Albert had once done to me.

I flopped down on the very bed where that had happened, recalling the shock, the fear, the humiliation. What was this, compared to that? What Madden had said was galling, yes. But he hadn't said it to gall me. Looking at the paper with all of its blue marks, I knew he was being honest. This wasn't an assault on my character, or a slight against my being a woman. In fact, by fixing my articles, he had been treating me as he would treat a man. *That* would have been the outrage: *not* being told to fix it.

And his idea of handing me off to Wilson—an older man, married, with whom I was on speaking terms—was a far better solution, in the circumstances, than putting me in close contact with one of the newsroom roaches. With Wilson there would be no possible scandal.

It was only when I thought of Wilson's patronizing smile, his handsomely weathered features, his *aw-shucks* charm, and his endless politeness that I felt sick. *Ask him for help?* Death would have been preferable.

And yet. . .

You want to be a reporter. If that means swallowing some pride, well, you've done it before. Besides, practice had eventually made me proud of my piano playing. So, too, would instruction make me a better writer.

I flopped over on my mattress, feeling the cork shavings shift to make way for my sharp elbows. What I had to do was make such a name for myself that no one could question my skill ever again. And if Wilson was the means to do that, then I would use him to glean as much knowledge as I possibly could.

Nevertheless, there was only one way I was going to be able to stomach it: I would have to educate the Quiet Observer in return.

In bed in my own little room, I began to smile.

T HE NEXT DAY I WALKED right up to Wilson and said, "Mr. Madden has instructed me to have you review my articles for structure. At his insistence, you are to teach me how to best construct a story to keep a reader's attention. I agree, on two conditions. First, that we do not ever speak of it here, or in front of the roaches. Agreed?"

His expression was amused, and a little embarrassed. "Agreed."

"Second, you will not question the content or point of view of my stories. You will help me create the best version of the story I want to tell. Do you agree?"

His damnable dimples were out, ludicrous in a man of his years. "I agree."

"Excellent. Where would you like to meet, and when?"

He considered. "Fort Pitt?"

"Where would we sit down? What about Delmonico's?"

He rubbed his neck. "Are you made of money? I'm not. Drat! I wish I could just take you to my club."

"Yes, it's a shame women aren't allowed in clubs. Maybe I should go with you and write a story about that?"

"How about we wait a little," he suggested sheepishly.

"I thought as much. Monongahela House?"

He looked genuinely taken aback. "A hotel?"

Blushing, I nodded. When he rejected that out of hand, we both bent our brains to the problem. We spent a moment lamenting the city's decision to reject Andrew Carnegie's offer of a quarter-million dollars to build a library, because that would have been the ideal place to meet. But the city elders had considered the upkeep of a library to be outside the bounds of what tax dollars were meant for.

We eventually decided to meet that afternoon at the Observatory, which was unquestionably proper. With that settled, I handed him my latest piece, nearly indecipherable with Madden's corrections. Wilson raised his eyebrows, then hunkered down to read with a promise to have some ideas for later.

I went to collect Pelletier from downstairs and we headed off for our next set of factory interviews. As I walked, I preened a little. I was going to have Wilson help me construct articles that flew in the face of what he believed. My satisfaction came from knowing that this forced partnership would at least be equally disagreeable for us both.

Surprisingly, though, it ended up being rather pleasant. After an exciting day of interviewing another set of factory girls, I arrived at the Observatory to find Wilson full of ideas and pointers. He was completely helpful—at no point did he argue with what I wrote, only the way in which I presented it.

Best of all—or worst, depending on your point of view—the end result was superior to what I had begun with. When my third story drew more mail than the others combined, I settled in to learn everything Wilson could teach me about structure and hooking a reader.

I wondered if he realized I was, at the same time, teaching him that girls could be good for a "sphere" other than just the home.

TWELVE

TONE IT DOWN

ONE NIGHT, I ARRIVED HOME bone-weary from another day of interviews. It was freezing out, only five degrees—a new record low. Hunkered down in my stiff clothes, I didn't notice Tom and Tony's damp things by the door, nor did I see the chairs strung together in the hall until I tumbled over them.

I heard them burst with laughter from their hiding place upstairs. Face down, heels over head, I called out, "Mother!" and Tom and Tony scampered away before their landlady could arrive to chastise them.

Climbing gracelessly to my feet, I pushed the chairs out of my path. I found Albert reading a newspaper in the sitting room, reclining in the window, his feet up on the sill. "You couldn't have warned me?" I said.

"I was *just* about to," replied Albert lazily. "But you have such a quick stride. And so deep! Are you certain you're not a man?"

"Are you certain you are?"

Unfortunately, I said it just as Mother arrived. To quell her frosty glare I waved at the chairs. "Tom and Tony."

"I'll speak to them," she said. "But right now I can use your help in the kitchen." This was Mother code for, *I wish to reprimand you, but in private.*

Albert waved mockingly at me and returned to his newspaper—not the *Dispatch*, I noticed.

Following Mother into the kitchen, I found myself being handed potatoes to skin. "I must say, Elizabeth, that I have noticed a coarsening of your speech since you began visiting that newsroom."

Elizabeth. Terrific. "I wasn't profane, Mother. And besides, it was Albert. We've always been that way. I don't think we can count it against the newsroom."

She relented a little. "Perhaps not. You do have a sharp tongue when you are displeased. But I notice you appear more displeased than before you took on this work."

"I'm not," I protested in complete surprise. "I love what I do."

"Then why insult your brother?"

I flushed with indignation. "Did you hear what he said to me?"

"Yes, and I shall speak to him as well. But it strikes me that you must accustom yourself to such comments. If this is to be your career, you will be sneered at much more caustically than you were by Albert. You know how people are. How they *talk*." There was bite to that last word. "If you cannot take criticism, you will forever be on the defensive. And that is unattractive."

I paused while peeling a potato's eye to roll my own. "Mother. . ."

She placed a pot of water on the stove. "I am not just referring to potential husbands. Spiteful women are not admired. They are called shrill, or bitter, or jealous. They are derided. And to allow yourself to be insulted is to show that others have power over you. You show them their opinion counts for something in your heart. The moment they realize they have power over you, they can exploit it."

I frowned. If somebody made me angry, I wasn't supposed to let them know it? Then what would stop them from doing it again? And if I buried my true feelings, how would that help me?

Mother had never been one to show her true feelings. Back in Apollo, when someone would spy the bruises on her wrists and she'd turn away their queries, I had thought she was just being stoic. Rather, it appeared to be a philosophy of sorts.

"A *man* is allowed to show his anger," I said.

"Yes, he is," Mother agreed. "But if his target is unworthy of him, he is looked down upon."

"As being unchivalrous," I added with mild scorn.

"Yes."

"So, because I am not a man, I should learn to absorb insults and smile?"

"No." She put the potatoes on to boil. "Because you are a woman, you should learn to not let it show that they hurt you."

I frowned at that. "I'm not sure I can tamp down my feelings so much. It's hard just to keep from screaming during these interviews."

Mother raised her brows. "Screaming?"

"Shouting, then. Telling off the managers and the male workers, and the women themselves who tolerate their lives. But I remind myself that Nellie Bly is there to hear their stories. Mother, you should hear their stories! And the letters! Dozens of them, women wanting Nellie Bly to come to their workplace next. Based on just the letters I've received, I could keep doing these pieces for the next three months!"

"Would that be healthy?" Mother seemed skeptical.

"For the women I write about, it would be. Maybe something can be done to improve their conditions, or even their wages."

"Healthy for you, I mean."

That surprised me. "What?"

"As I was saying, you seem angrier. I thought it was just the insults. Now I see it's from watching these commiserable women toiling each day. Hearing their stories. Being helpless to fix things."

I thought about that for a long moment. "I don't think I'm angrier than before. It's just that I have more evidence that my anger is justified." I paused. "And I'm not helpless. In one way, that's worse. I now have the power to change things. So I feel like I have a responsibility to do just that."

Mother was silent as we cooked. But she had a little smile on her face.

THROUGH MARCH I VISITED FIVE more factories, and the corresponding stories ran each Sunday. In every one, I kept to my rules. I reported what I saw and what I heard. Facts. Wilson could offer no complaints.

My goal was different from his, of course. Always in the back of my mind was the fear of hurting these women by causing them to lose their positions. So I said nothing to vilify the workshop owners. In fact, I went out of my way to praise them. Perhaps too far. I copied down their blithe assurances of the health and happiness of their employees, while turning a blind eye to the cockroaches and shuttered windows and bad air. I heaped praise wherever I could, without lying outright. In not calling out the owners, I was thinking back to my one semester at the Normal school, where we'd read a lot of Shakespeare. One phrase in particular had stuck in my head: "Brutus is an honorable man." Praise repeated often enough becomes an insult.

Besides, I didn't really want to write about the factory owners. I was there to write about the women. And write about them I did.

The forelady at Schmertz & Co. was unhappy with my presence until I began to interview her. "I can tell you how to make a shoe, complete from beginning to end," she bragged, chin high. "My father was a shoemaker, and ever since I was a tiny child I have worked at the trade." She had left her father's shop and come to Schmertz. "It takes the patience of a saint and the eye of an eagle to get along here. But the girls we have understand their business, yet they have to learn to do men's work."

She meant that they needed to learn how to make men's shoes. But there was a delicious double meaning there.

Each week, I labored to turn the public's opinion of the factory girl on its head. I told stories of girls who toiled twelve hours to earn a single dollar. I quoted them about their lives, their mode of dress, the type of labor they performed. I turned them into people.

And that, it was soon made clear, was a problem.

I WAS AT MY DESK ONE day when Madden appeared at his door. "Bly. Come in here."

When I entered his office, Madden closed the door and told me to sit down. It didn't bode well. Nor did the fact that he sat in his chair rather than on the edge of his desk.

Brows knit, he looked at me. "Don't you ever smile?"

"When I feel like smiling. Is something wrong? I thought the last article was better."

Madden stroked his moustache. "It was, it was. No, it's something else. There are pickets outside Oliver Brothers."

I felt a tiny glow of excitement, but tried not to show it. "Really? Why?"

"Because of you."

"I didn't write anything negative."

His eyebrows lifted. "You don't consider an eight-year-old girl working there to be negative?"

"She might have been ten."

Madden held up a hand. "Don't, please. You had to know it would stir up trouble."

I stopped playing coy. "Mr. Madden, you wanted me to give these girls a voice. Who needs it more than an eight-year-old girl working in a factory?"

He lit a cigar. "I'm not saying you were wrong. But the Oliver brothers had lunch with O'Neill and Rook, and the subject of their conversation was you."

O'Neill and Rook were the *Dispatch*'s publishers. I knew the names, but had never met them. "I take it they were not impressed with my piece."

"No, they decidedly were not."

"What did they say?"

Madden puffed. "They asked if there were any falsehoods in the piece. They told the Olivers that if they could point to a lie, they could dismiss you."

"And they couldn't," I said.

"Correct. I just wanted you to know the conversation happened."

My fists tightened. "Am I being told what to write?"

"Do you need to be?"

"Mr. Madden," I said slowly, "I know I'm new at this. I'm not as hard-bitten as you fellows. But I can only stomach so much."

He blew an impressive ring of smoke. "Then be subtler about it."

FOR MY NEXT STORY, I tried for subtlety. At the McKinney Manufacturing Company, where women were tasked with making hinges, there were yet more young girls, all aged seven to twelve. This time I didn't even talk to the little girls, but instead conversed with the foreman about them.

"It's not our custom to take 'em," he told me. "Not that young. But their mothers, see, their mothers come with tears in their eyes and they beg—*beg!*—for work for the little ones so they can help out at home. Now, we don't just take the mothers' word for it, either. We send someone to the home. But if we think we can help these miserable little things by giving them work, we do."

I dutifully reported this, cleaning up his language to make him sound less rough. And in the article I added, "This is undoubtedly an act of kindness and charity, and if this rule was lived up to by all employers of child labor in the two cities, many a home would be cheered and to many worthy ones extended a helping hand."

"Subtle enough?" I asked.

"We'll see," Madden said.

THE STORIES RAN ON SUNDAYS. Each Friday I met with Wilson, when he would lament my style in general, and one thing in particular. "Kid, you cannot keep putting yourself into your stories!"

"Whyever not?"

"Because that's not how it's supposed to work!"

It was still bitterly cold out-of-doors, so we were meeting in a saloon on Strawberry Way, just two blocks north of the *Dispatch* offices. It was a common haunt of the roaches, and to Wilson's dismay the bartender recognized me right off and pulled my preferred small beer.

Wilson let that pass, as he was busy protesting a passage in my latest piece, where I quoted myself as saying, "There are some people who think factory workers are horrible," which allowed the woman I was interviewing to answer, "Well, they are as good as the ones that look down on them."

"You cannot quote yourself making such statements!"

"It's what was said!" I countered. "I said the one thing, she said the other. How is that inserting myself into the story?"

"You could tailor the quote so you are not involved. Simply substitute 'factory girls' for her use of 'they.'"

"I should alter what was actually said?" I asked coolly. "How is that good reporting?"

"Then what about this line of yours? 'That the world may always appear as bright and cheerful to you as it does today is the sincere wish of Nellie Bly.' Tell me, you naughty girl, what has that to do with the price of fish?"

"You write platitudes all the time, oh Quiet Observer."

"I am a columnist. I'm paid for platitudes. *You* are supposed to be a reporter."

"I *am* a reporter!"

"A reporter doesn't make himself the story!" insisted Wilson.

"She does if she's me!"

"Please lower your voice," said Wilson, wafting his wide hands downwards.

This absolutely enraged me. "You raised yours, too!"

He shrugged his wide shoulders with that affability I found so infuriating. "I'm a fallible man. In a lady, a raised voice is a tragedy." His brow wrinkled, not in consternation but amusement. "You know, when you get angry you lose your Pittsburgh tone."

"Oh?" I said sharply.

"Yes. You sound almost regal."

That startled me. "What?"

"Well, it's said that in the hills of Western Pennsylvania, the people have an accent that dates back to the time of Queen Elizabeth. That means that when you get mad, you sound just like Shakespeare would have." He chucked me under the chin. "Smile for me, at least, Viola. To show we're friends."

If he meant to flatter me, he had mistaken my mood. I was ready to shatter glass with my voice, or toss my drink in his face. But I smiled. I smiled because I had a secret. Truth was, I had deliberately inserted myself into these stories. Reading the letters that piled up on my desk each day, I noted that the women who wrote were very focused on me as a person. They praised my bravery. They commended my witty banter. They cheered my choice of topics and my dogged determination.

Those were the letters from women. The letters from men were far less praise-filled. They said I should never have been hired. I had no business interfering in the lives of the factory girls, who deserved their lot in life. I should just find a husband and stop warming a seat that belonged to a masculine posterior.

Some of these letters were vitriolic, some merely patronizing. Of the two, I preferred the vitriol. At least those writers were being honest.

Of course, not every woman approved of me, either. Many a housewife lamented my choice of work, choice of topic, or manner of writing. I pictured them pausing in their writing to feed tea to their lap dogs, then thought of them no more.

Being Nellie Bly was becoming a badge of pride. And keeping Nellie Bly at the forefront of the conversation gave her strength. Each Sunday, I thrust her under the nose of every Quiet Observer and forced them not to look away.

But this Quiet Observer was not at all quiet about my shortcomings. "And another thing—why do you often simply repeat what is told to you?"

"I'm a reporter. I ask questions, people tell me things."

"And sometimes they lie. Sometimes they lie to make themselves look better. Sometimes they lie to feel important. Sometimes they say they don't know anything when they do."

"It is not a sin to plead ignorance."

"Tell that to Pontius Pilate."

"Are you accusing me of washing my hands?"

"Not at all." Removing his glasses, he pinched the bridge of his nose. "I'm simply saying that you sometimes come across as credulous in the extreme."

That stung. "So, again, not enough facts for the Quiet Observer."

Wilson drew a breath, then released it. "Kid, listen. Do you know what men think of women reporters?"

"That we should go home and tend to our own little *spheres*."

Acknowledging the hit, he pressed on. "Women do not lack wit, to be certain. They have sympathy by the bushel. They own energy, and often imagination. But it is said that women lack the good judgment required to write a story. That, and they have a lamentable style." I flushed, but he waved this aside. "I've seen much worse in several of my colleagues. But, because you are a woman, it is chalked up to your *being* a woman. Does that make sense?"

"What? But—that's—I—" I sputtered. "That's utterly unfair!"

"I agree. It is also true. Because there are so few women working as reporters, you, kid, represent them all. As far as style goes, it doesn't much matter. That can be fixed—I hope," he added with a wry smile. "What matters is judgment. Your judgment must be superior to a man's. Because where a lapse in good judgment in a man is written off to him being a foolish individual—"

"—in a woman it is because she is a woman." I smiled at him. "You know, you may well become a suffragette."

Wilson was so surprised he dropped his glasses onto the scarred table between us. "What?"

"Mr. Wilson, you are not saying anything that every woman does not already know. I'm just astonished you've learned it in so short a time."

Wilson chuckled ruefully. "It's tempting to say I have learned nothing, and so tee you up for a wicked slice. But I regret to say my opinions have not changed. It's just that I've come to. . . well, kid, I'd rather not see you fail." He grinned, adding, "It would reflect badly on *me*, you understand." His eyes twinkled.

I should have wanted to hit him. Instead, I laughed.

Thirteen

Flower Girl

I HAD BEEN EXPECTING THE FACTORY GIRL series to go on through the spring. I certainly didn't lack for material. So I was quite surprised when I handed in a story in the middle of April and Madden said, "Excellent. This will wrap it up nicely."

"Wrap it up?"

"Yup. For eight weeks we've enlightened the people of Pittsburgh about the plight of the factory girls. Time for something new."

"I don't have any pitches ready," I told him.

"Lucky, then, that I have one for you. I want you to write about Arbor Day."

I blinked. "Arbor Day."

"You know what it is?"

"That Nebraskan idea, where everyone goes out and plants a tree?"

"Last year they planted over a million. Governor Pattison is proposing an Arbor Day here in Pennsylvania. Write about it."

"You don't know what I think about it."

He smiled. "I'll be interested to learn."

I was vaguely dismayed. I still had two factories in mind to visit. But I also had to admit we had probably mined the depths of surprise and outrage on the life of the factory girl. I didn't want her to become boring. Her, or Nellie Bly.

Though less than enamored of the subject, I threw myself into the piece, with a history of the tradition and a quote from the governor himself. It was exciting to go to his office and ask!

Madden was pleased with the piece. "Fine, fine. Let's not derail you. Let's keep you on plants. There's a flower show to benefit the Pittsburg Library Association."

"That's not until next week. What should I write about for this Sunday?"
Madden shrugged. "Something earthy."
My next headline read:

THE POSIES OF OUR GREAT-GRANDMOTHERS
STILL POPULAR AND PRETTY AS EVER
SHRUBS THAT THRIVE IN THIS SEASON
HOW THE IVY GREEN COULD BE UTILIZED
TO BEAUTIFY THE SMOKY CITY
WHEN AND HOW TO USE THE PRUNING KNIFE

The following week I attended the flower show with my family.
Fraught with the potential for tension, the excursion itself ended up being
surprisingly pleasant. With Albert's marriage approaching, we were able to
look at various types of flowers for the ceremony. As I wrote the article, I
attempted to please my mother by listing Albert as one of the "prominent
citizens" Nellie Bly sighted at the show. If he appreciated it, he didn't say.
    Wilson, however, noticed. "Is your brother a prominent citizen?"
    He always surprised me. I had expected to be badgered once again for
placing myself in my story. A florist had asked me if I knew the language
of flowers—I had said I'd never bothered to learn it, and he'd replied that
I must not have ever been in love. I included it deliberately in the piece to
dissuade some of my fellow reporters who had begun hinting at making
love. I thought a dash of cold water would do them well.
    Expecting an assault on that front, I was unprepared for Wilson to bring
up my brother. "He's getting married in a week. I thought. . ."
    "Thought what?"
    "Nothing. He was there. I mentioned that fact."
    "Without mentioning that he was your brother."
    "His name was buried among all the other people."
    "Why?"
    "Why was it buried, or why mention him at all?"
    "I know you buried it," said Wilson, with the infuriating smugness of a
man who thinks he knows what's in a woman's head better than she does
herself. Then he proved himself right. "You were ashamed."
    "Ashamed!"
    "Kid, you put yourself in your stories without batting an eye. I wish you
wouldn't, but I can at least approve of the fact that you usually don't try to
hide it. Whereas here, you included your brother, but hid him at the end. If
you wanted to bring attention to him, you would have interviewed him."
    "How do you know that?" I asked.
    His boyish grin flashed. "The Quiet Observer, remember?"
    "Not so quiet at the moment," I mumbled.
    "Forgive me, kid. I truly don't mean to pry. And for once I'm not telling

you your business."

"You aren't," I repeated with heavy skepticism.

"Absolutely not. I couldn't care less if you mention your brother, your mother, or your whole extended family."

"Then why bring it up?"

He patted my hand on the tabletop. "I want you to recognize why you're doing it."

Wilson was gazing at me in a particularly penetrating manner. I pulled my hand away and focused on my tea. Finally, he said, "Lonely Orphan Girl."

I blinked. "What?"

"The name you chose. Before you were our naughty Nellie Bly, you called yourself an orphan."

"Yes," I said. "Because I am."

"I thought your mother was yet living."

I nodded. "She is."

"And you have brothers?"

"Three. And a sister."

"All older?"

"No, actually. Two above, two below."

"Dab in the middle," observed Wilson.

"Yes."

"Hmm." There was a long, insufferable pause as he considered me. He was not looking at me as men often did: to tease or flirt or mash or belittle. His interest was warm, but distant, as though I were a delightful but wounded puppy, adopted by a friend.

Uncomfortable under his scrutiny, I changed the subject. "Did you see the announcement from Boggs and Buhl? They've installed a telephone and are taking orders for deliveries. Deliveries! They'll deliver their goods directly to a home. There might be a story there. I wonder how they do it. Do people carry the goods, or do they use a horse and carriage. . ."

The Quiet Observer just sipped his coffee while I prattled on. Observing. Quietly. It drove me mad.

ALBERT WAS MARRIED IN A LAVISH ceremony thrown by Jane's family, the Hartleys. We were all guests at their home in Tarentum, a town just outside Pittsburgh. To my fury, Albert paid for clothes for Charlie and Harry, but not for Mother, Kate, or me. It was only due to my wages that we were not shabbily dressed before our new in-laws. Albert had counted on me being unwilling to allow Mother to look poorly, and he'd been right.

Still, the expense was worth it to see Albert leaving our lives. He had already leased a house in a nice, middle-income neighborhood not far from his work. With luck, he would be too lazy to come home, even for Sunday dinners.

To Albert's consternation—and my utter bemusement—a great deal of the reception was focused upon me. Apparently, I had become something of a celebrity. Or rather, Nellie Bly had.

I only realized it when my sister Kate caught me by the elbow and dragged me around to meet one gaggle of people after another. She didn't introduce me as Lizzie, or even Pink. "I'd like you to meet my sister, Nellie Bly."

At first they thought she was joking, but when I confirmed my identity, I was mobbed. Every woman there found a reason to come over and shake my hand or ask me about man-mashers or factory girls. Even in Tarentum, the name Nellie Bly was well known.

It was a head-swelling half hour until Albert came over with a particularly nasty gleam in his eye. "What's this about Pink being a reporter?"

"Albert, shouldn't you be with your wife?" I asked.

He paid me no mind. "She's not a reporter. She's an actress."

"An actress!" For a moment I thought he was going to accuse me of being a fraud before all of his guests. What he did say was far less kind.

"Nellie Bly is a role! She likes the stage, and hiding behind a false name. She longs to become someone else—but never for too long! No, once the show has opened, she writes her own review and then moves on to the next role. But I warned her, if she keeps trying to be everything, she'll never be anything." For the first time, he addressed me. "You think you *helped* those women in the factories? Hardly. You exploited them and then left them. At least the factory owners pay them for their exploitation. Are any of them better off today because of you? Is anyone?"

Kate and a few other women came to my defense. Myself, I was speechless. "Excuse me. I think it's time for my next role—the guest with the headache." I escaped the small chapel yard to take the air down the hill.

I was leaning against a tree, my fancy new hat in my hands, when Mother arrived. "You should return," she said crisply. "You are missed."

"I'll come back in a little bit."

She waited. When I didn't move, she said, "Don't lean against the tree, dear. You don't want bark clinging to your dress."

Dutifully, I slung myself upright. "I don't want to go back."

"Why not, Elizabeth? Or should I say Nellie?"

She thought I was deliberately spoiling my brother's big day. "*I* didn't mention Nellie Bly. I didn't bring her up. And if I'm out here, I'm hardly trying to draw attention."

To my mind, Mother's sigh was a little theatrical. "I suppose it is something we must all accustom ourselves to. We have a famous reporter in the family."

Looking up, I saw she was smiling. She was so changeable, my mother. From scolding to approving, like the fall of a coin.

She held out her arm, and together we returned to the reception.

I HAD BEEN WORKING AT THE *DISPATCH* for almost three months before I met the other female journalist there, the formidable Bessie Bramble. One afternoon I discovered, among the jumble of letters on my desk, a note in beautiful script asking me to tea at her house the following Saturday.

I wrote a reply at once, thanking her and accepting the invitation. I had always liked pieces under the Bramble byline. Two years earlier, the state had been considering reforming the divorce laws because too many women had been petitioning to be free of their husbands. Bessie Bramble had caustically observed, "No happy wife, whose husband treats her as he ought, ever applies for a divorce. Reform men, and the question is solved."

In print, she was prickly. She had started out as a music reviewer, savaging most local performances and praising only a handful of truly talented musicians. But her scope had not remained limited to music for long. She wrote a great deal about school reform, women's wages, social clubs, wicked husbands, and quite often about the priests who used their pulpits to keep women downtrodden. The name Bramble was appropriate: she was never comfortable, and liked to keep pricking the consciences of her readers.

Outside of her writings, I knew nothing at all about her, other than her real surname: Wade. From her address, Swissvale Avenue in Edgewood, I understood that she moved among the highest of Pittsburgh society.

That being the case, I took care to dress well. I wore a new blue dress that reached right up to my throat, closed by a black brooch I quite liked. And I took extra time with my hair, forming it into a neat bun. I had just begun to regularly wear my hair up. Down, it was too often stroked by the worst of the roaches in their not-so-subtle mash attempts. If that kept up, I would simply cut it off and tell people I'd had a fever.

Topping off my ensemble with a hat I had purchased for the wedding, I ventured into the world of high society.

The Wade house was newly built, and clearly only recently occupied— there were still packing crates lining one side, waiting to be sent off or turned into kindling. After passing through the gate, I traversed a brick path, climbed the porch steps, and knocked on an imposing double door.

It was opened by a servant. After my hat and coat were taken away, I was escorted into a lovely breakfast nook full of sunlight. The walls were painted white, and the dark oak of the doorframe and windowsills provided texture and grandeur.

There I met Mrs. Elizabeth Wade.

"So *you* are Nellie Bly!" exclaimed my hostess as she rose to take my hand. Nearly fifty, she wore her whitening hair pulled into a bun on the back of her head, yet she left enough of her fluffy bangs free to soften any severity. She wore oval glasses just the size of her eyes and didn't bother to take them off to make herself prettier, as most women did. Her mouth was nearly lipless, just a straight line beneath her ample nose, but there were laugh lines all about it. Humor was never far from her. Twice my age, she was just my height, but double my girth. Not to say she was fat. Rather, she bore the appearance of a stocky, no-nonsense schoolteacher.

Which, as it turned out, she was. "Principal of the Ralston Industrial School for Boys," she informed me. Born Elizabeth Wilkinson, she was now Mrs. Charles Isaac Wade. As the wife of a prominent banker, she could have lived a life of leisure. "But I've always preferred to work," she said. She had begun her career as a teacher, and then had risen to assistant principal and, finally, principal.

She spoke with the slightest trace of an English accent. Her father had brought the family over from Liverpool four decades earlier. She'd met her husband in the church choir, and they had two children: a daughter of fourteen years and a son just my own age.

When she mentioned her unmarried son, an alarm bell started clamoring in the back of my head. But thankfully Mrs. Wade only invited me to the next meeting of the Woman's Club, of which she was a founding member—along with the pioneer of female journalism in Pittsburgh, Jane Grey Swisshelm.

Then she settled in to question me.

I answered her queries brightly, offering the best side of myself. She was delighted to discover that she and I shared a Christian name, which was also her daughter's. She was sympathetic when she learned I had been unable to finish school due to my health, and was certain I would have finished at the top of my class, as she had. I talked openly about my late, doting father the judge, but skirted discussion of the harder times and Mother's remarriage, calling it simply "a difficult period." She stated that she was more than impressed with my achievements, especially for one so young, and asked exactly how old I was.

"Mr. Madden says I am seventeen," I replied.

That brought a smile to her lips. "Ah. Slightly built as you are, it is certainly plausible. And forgive me the impertinence. We older women should know better than any not to ask for a lady's age. May I assume, though, that you are not younger than seventeen?"

"You may so assume," I agreed gravely.

"Well, well. Miss Cochrane, I am enamored of you. Entirely enamored. To have made a name for yourself so young, in so short a time. And to have utterly flummoxed Ras Wilson as you have."

I brightened. "Have I?"

"Oh, he cannot stop talking of you. I imagine if he and his poor wife had a grown child, he would want her to be just as you are. I assure you, he is immeasurably impressed."

"He hides it well," I said.

"Yes," she said, with a sad smile. "But then, the luckless man is accustomed to hiding his personal likes and dislikes. I think that is why he is such an engaging, if misguided, columnist. He resides upon a cloud of his own making, looking down at humanity from on high, keeping us all at a distance."

That perfectly summed up Wilson. "I hope to puncture one or two of his less realistic notions about women."

"I wish you luck! I am tempted to name him a lost cause, but I do not believe in them. And if ever there was a writer to challenge him, it is you." She picked up a book from the table beside her, and I felt my throat catch as she opened it. It was a natty collection of all of my stories for the *Dispatch*. I had a set of those exact clippings in my bedroom, though mine were less carefully scissored.

She turned gently from one to the next. "I thrilled at your first foray into writing. The whole of Pittsburgh owes you a debt for your series on the women travailing in our factories. Do you know how many factories there are in this city?" Chagrined, I shook my head. "Nearly five hundred. Fully a third of them staffed by women, most of whom are single. In fact, only ten percent of working women are married. Fifteen percent are divorced. The rest are single girls attempting to make a living for themselves."

I flushed. *Why didn't I think of finding these figures?* They made my case for me. It was not women who *wanted* to work who took jobs, but women who *needed* to work—women with circumstances very unlike those of my hostess.

Meekly, I said, "I wish I had talked to you beforehand."

Mrs. Wade set down her cup in alarm. "Oh, no, my dear girl! Your instincts did not betray you. Figures and numbers are cold. You gave these girls faces! That was the genius of your articles. You presented women not easily written off. They were not simple, or homely, or deserving of contempt. Your work has the whole city abuzz with pity, and a movement is afoot among my peers to lobby for better conditions and wages."

"If I may suggest," I said quickly, "the greatest change these girls could receive is a daily wage. The piecemeal pay, for each item completed, varies greatly from summer to winter. In cold weather, in unheated factories, their hands move more slowly, so they complete fewer pieces, and therefore earn less."

Mrs. Wade clapped her stocky hands. "Excellent! Clearly, you will have much to say at my ladies' group. Now, to my reason for asking you here. After your daring piece on divorce, and especially in light of your thrilling ventures into the factories of Pittsburgh, I waited with bated breath to see what your next piece would be." She arched one eyebrow. "Imagine my surprise when it was a series about flowers. Pardon me, and I could easily be mistaken, but you do not look like someone who enjoys the labor of the earth."

I laughed a little. "No."

"Nor I. As you rightly stated, not every woman is suited for every womanly thing. Now, your flower-show pieces were very well done. Though your eye for fashion is a little less discerning than what the readers of the ladies' pages expect, it was certainly a breath of fresh air. But if I may be so bold as to ask, were those stories your ideas?"

"No," I answered frankly. "Mr. Madden suggested them."

"I see." She closed the book on the clippings. "They are womanizing you, my dear."

"Womanizing!"

Seeing my shock, she allowed a smile. "Forgive me. Not womanizing in that sense. You see, my dear, in recent years newspapers have made the astounding discovery that women purchase things. That women, in fact, do most of the household shopping. Hence the Women's Pages, featuring marvels like which sauce goes best with duck, or the surprising medicinal uses of sarsaparilla. Most women reporters are relegated to writing about shopping, or homemaking, or child-rearing. Or," she added, "scrutinizing the latest fashions at flower shows."

The blood drained from my face. "I see."

Bessie Bramble took my hand in hers. "You cannot—*cannot*—allow yourself to be remade into a more comfortable version of the woman you are. Resist the Women's Pages. They will forever try to put you there. You are a reporter, one with an instinctual grasp of stories that normally go unseen. You are a voice for women, for the impoverished, for the dispossessed. You cannot allow that voice to be silenced!"

In a small voice I said, "What do I do?"

She leaned back, raising her chin imperiously. "Make them uncomfortable.

Do not give them reason to fire you, but also offer no reason for them to forget you. Occupy your desk in the newsroom. Take the stories Madden gives you, as a good reporter should. But make them your own. And in the spaces between, find the stories *you* want to write. Find them, and make Nellie Bly a name the powerful should fear."

A fist had formed in my throat. I swallowed hard. "I will. I promise."

FOURTEEN

INFORM AND SELL

THE FOLLOWING MONDAY FOUND ME sitting at my desk, perusing the latest batch of letters addressed to "Nellie Bly." There were fewer of late, and they were much more approving. Women with fine handwriting praised me, and men said they much preferred my new choice of topics.

It was utterly damning. Bessie Bramble was right. I was making people comfortable. As far as society was concerned, I had found my proper "sphere."

I marched right into Madden's office. "I'm done with flowers. I want to write about the Economites."

"Who? Those nuts who live in Warren County?"

"Is it nutty to live frugally?" A piece about thrifty living might lead back to talking about working women, who were so often forced to pinch their pennies.

"It's nutty to bury seventy-five thousand dollars in silver coins for fifty years." The hoard of rare coins had been put up for auction earlier in the year, bringing the Harmony Society, as they called themselves, into the news, where I'd first heard of them. "But go ahead."

It was not a long journey to Economy, Pennsylvania, but as it was an overnight trip, Mother accompanied me. Upon our arrival, I met members of the Harmony Society, who seemed perfectly nice, even if their ways were strange. They held all things in common. Any money they earned went into a general fund. There was only a single store, where things were taken by necessity, at no cost. And every member of the community was required to remain celibate. Even married couples were forced to live separately.

"I don't see them lasting very long," quipped Mother, a remark that had us both laughing behind our hands.

During the train ride home, Mother asked what I desired for my birthday. "You will be twenty-one. And we are in funds, thanks to this new career of yours. You deserve to treat yourself. What would you like? A new hat? Shoes?"

I knew exactly what I wanted. "A lawsuit."

Mother started, then closed her eyes. I bit my lip for a moment, wondering if I was in the wrong. But no. I was not insulting her. I was seeking justice.

When my father had died, I'd been left an inheritance, but the money had run out just six months into my education. For seven long years I had been itching to sue my former guardian, Colonel Samuel Jackson, for frittering away my money. He had been too generous to the children of my father's first marriage—all adults—and had neglected to preserve any of the money due to me, Kate, and Harry.

Whenever I brought it up, Mother would refuse to file suit against him on her children's behalf. "I have had my fill of the courts," she would say.

The moment I turned twenty-one, I would have standing to file the papers against the Colonel myself. And I intended to do just that.

But that didn't mean I needed to involve Mother—at least, not until a date for the hearing was set. Seeing her injured spirit, I sighed. "What about a new traveling bag?"

THE ECONOMITES ARTICLE WASN'T A SENSATION, but I'd thought it would be enough to lead to another piece about either money or chastity. That wasn't the case.

"You're going to interview an opera producer," Madden told me.

"An opera producer," I repeated dully.

"E.H. Ober of the Boston Ideal Opera Company. You'll like her. She's a businesswoman. She's made a fortune on the stage, and now she's retiring."

"That should go to Bessie. She handles the arts."

Madden loosed a wry chuckle. "Miss Ober would never let Bessie through the door. Five years of scathing reviews, with some spiteful personal remarks thrown in for good measure." He felt my skeptical gaze on him and opened his hands. "What, you only want to write about destitute women in business?"

He had me there. Recalling Bessie's advice to take the assignments Madden gave me and make them my own, the piece I turned in was a paean to women who dared to work:

It is shameful to state, yet the fact remains, that in this enlightened age there are many who think all labor, except housework, belittles a woman, and who look with holy horror on one who has courage enough to elevate the regular routine laid down for the fairer sex and enter the manlier domain. Plenty of women will eke out a miserable existence at some so-called "light work," while the world is full of good, comfortable places that require only energy and pluck to assume. Some few women can be named who have bravely struck out according to their own pleasure, and have succeeded. Honor to them. If there were more the world would be better.

Madden was right: I did like Miss Ober. I especially enjoyed some of the quotes she gave me. When talking about her pioneering work as a female opera producer, I asked her, "Were you not afraid of failing?"

"Afraid of failing?" she repeated with a smile. "No, I was not afraid. I knew people who had started out before and failed; and also knew many had started out and succeeded. So I had just the same chance as any man."

"What is your opinion on women entering public life?"

"I think if they are fitted for it, all right. Women are just like men—some may be fitted for a position that another could not fill; but I say, what they can do, let them. If they have energy and pluck to start out and take care of themselves, they should be praised for doing so."

"What treatment do you receive in dealing with the men with whom you are thrown in contact?"

"The best, the very best from managers, landlords and all. I cannot complain of one thing. My sister always travels with me as an assistant."

I received complimentary tickets to that evening's performance and took Mother, who was beginning to enjoy being privy to my excursions. I wondered if it reminded her of when she had been married to the most important man in Apollo.

Next, Madden asked me to interview a chorus girl, and then a young piano prodigy. Gritting my teeth, I did as he asked.

I was nervous about meeting the chorus girl, but the moment I did I was ashamed of myself. "Mention a chorus girl," I later wrote, "and one thinks of a big, loud-voiced, flashily dressed, ill-bred woman who would rather be dressed in pink tights than petticoats—a woman devoid of all principle." My intimation was clear: a woman willing to fall for any man on any night.

However, I was met by a girl my own age, clad in a light blue housedress with a plain white linen collar. Her golden hair was dressed in two simple braids.

The moment we were seated, I blurted out, "Do men ever make love to you?"

Her eyes went wide. "You're a girl. How can you ask such a question? Of course they do! Members of the company are forever making love to one another. Showmances, we call them. Then in every new town the girls are hounded by mashers who wait at the door to take us out to supper. Some of the girls ask the fellows for presents, and they always get them—jewelry, flowers, and candy, those always lead in the gift line. And the love letters! If you saw them you would be mortified. Men get mashed at first sight, and compose long letters declaring their undying love and such rubbish. We girls get lots of proposals."

While I enjoyed her honesty, I was angered at her circumstance. She had a profession she was good at, one that took skill and training and physical perfection. Yet was forced to endure endless unwelcome attention. Many would have said it was attention she was after—she was a performer, after all. But should she dance in private and starve, instead?

My second artistic interview that day was with a Miss Clara Oehmler, who could play the piano perfectly without being able to read a note of music—which, truth be told, made me quite envious. But she was unassuming about her skill, and when I wrote of her, I offered my best definition of a young woman: "innocent, unaffected, and frank."

My next assignment was to investigate a new malady that was being called "hay fever." I did so, and wrote vibrant passages about the lack of fresh and wholesome air in the city, as well as the unhealthy eating and overwork that drove both men and women to die "as the dog dieth."

Thus began a war that would last all spring and summer. Madden would hand me an assignment fit for the Women's Pages, and I would dutifully turn it into a piece that reflected Nellie Bly's worldview.

I covered rude clerks, warning them, "In this age of wonders, one can entertain an angel unawares; they may be poor today, tomorrow they may strike oil or work out a patent. Then they will remember who treated them well."

I covered the Schenley mansion, making much of its thirty rooms being continually uninhabited as the Schenleys preferred to live in England. In lieu of the absent well-to-dos, I interviewed their servants, and struck reporting gold when one of them turned out to have once been undermaid to Queen Victoria herself.

I turned every assignment into a stealthy attack on common wisdom, the wealthy, and those who looked down on women. And I felt a sneaky pride in doing so.

By this time, my weekly meetings with Wilson were less focused on my writing structure—not because it had improved, but because he had thrown up his hands in despair. Instead, our conversations were more often about the newspaper business itself. With twenty years of experience behind him, there were things unknown to me that he took for granted.

Now basking in summer weather, we were no longer confined to ice cream parlors or saloons. With its hills and the river flowing through it,

Pittsburgh was a city made for walking—so long as one could endure the gusts of burning sulphur or the sudden cloud of soot. But even with the polluted air, sunshine occasionally crept in enough to provide a pleasant day. Wilson and I often strolled along the river, or else met near the Observatory for an amble across its grounds.

One day at the Observatory, I lamented my latest assignment. "Does Madden think that I, of all women, have advice about the styling of hair? Honestly, Wilson, look at me. Does it appear to you that I spend time thinking about my appearance? Me, the factory girl?"

It was shabby of me, fishing for compliments. Wilson did not swallow my hook, instead squinting as if in pain. "Miss Bly."

His formality did not bode well. "Mr. Wilson?"

"I must tell you something. I feel it would be wrong not to. But you must promise not to pucker."

I raised my gloved right hand. "I vow not to lose my temper."

He eyed me with suspicion, then in he plunged. "About that factory series. At the end of March, Madden had visits. And letters."

"From grateful women, I'm certain."

"And not-so-grateful men," observed Wilson. "In particular, men who own factories."

My spine straightened. "I never said a word against the factories."

"You didn't have to. Just by describing the lives of those girls in such detail, you made people see them with fresh eyes. And the drawings did the same thing. It's one thing to consider a handful of unseen fallen women toiling away with needles or glue. It's quite another to see those pretty faces juxtaposed against the drudgery of their lives. The factories could be the most airy, pleasant places on earth, and it would still not make up for the lives these women lead."

"So you feel for them?" I asked.

Wilson nodded. "I do. I truly do."

"So you've changed your mind about working women?"

"On the contrary," said Wilson, his good cheer unperforated, "your fine work has only made me feel my point more strongly. Women should not be forced to work. As a man, I abhor the idea of any woman living as you describe."

I shook my head. "Same old Wilson."

For a moment we were both smiling: me at him, him at me and also at himself. He never smiled at me as other men did, all teeth and leering. His lips, pressed together beneath his moustache, were friendly and yet restrained. *And handsome. . .*

Suddenly blushing, I quickly returned to the point. "What about those visits?"

"Ah. Yes." Wilson's smile vanished. "They wanted the factory girl stories to stop, and threatened to pull their advertisements. Imagine the shoe and cigar ads gone from the paper. And not just them. *All* the factory owners threatened to pull out. They were each afraid you would tackle them next." I opened my mouth, and he held up a hand. "You promised!"

"I'm not—!" I took a breath, then with forced calm I said, "I am not puckering."

"Good. And don't blame Madden. Remember, he is in the newspaper business, and that consists of doing just two things: informing the public and selling papers. Always aim for the first, never forget the second."

It was excellent advice. And once I had left him and given into my rage by stomping around the city for a good two hours, I was able to consider it, and absorb it.

Inform, and sell. Nellie Bly would always do both.

FIFTEEN

FAILURE TO THRIVE

NEAR THE END OF THE SUMMER I was pleasantly surprised to find myself the subject of a brief interview for an upcoming book called *The Social Mirror*. I was portrayed in a word portrait: "In person 'Nellie Bly' is slender, quick in her movements, a brunette with a bright, coquettish face."

As much as I rankled at *coquettish*, that was far from the worst part. I had stupidly offered my full name in the interview, and someone—I had a sneaking suspicion who—had then supplied more details, including my nickname. Thus, my entry listed me as *Miss "Pink" Elizabeth Cochrane.* Pink!

The piece ran on, stating, "Animated in conversation and quick in repartee, she is quite a favorite among the gentlemen."

To my dismay, that was certainly becoming the case. No longer did Nellie Bly receive admiring letters only from women. Now men were writing, but not to scold. No, like the dancer's mashers, these men wrote to make love to me! Meanwhile, my newsroom suitors were growing more persistent—even those that were already married. It was outrageous!

I only made things worse by complaining of this at supper one night within the hearing of Tom and Tony. From that point on, they wrote me ludicrous love letters, full of flowery phrases and descriptions of the improbable feats of chivalry by which they meant to win my affection.

I was not amused.

"It's your own fault," Wilson informed me on one of our Friday afternoon rambles. "I warned you. If you keep putting yourself at the center of your stories, your readers will think, not about the story, but about you."

"Tut," I replied. "People see an article with my name on it and know that if I wrote it, it must be worth reading."

Wilson laughed. "Do you know the word *hubris*?"

We were walking by the Block House, the oldest building in Pittsburgh. They had demolished Fort Pitt years before, but the old redoubt—used in both the French and Indian War and the American Revolution—had been turned into a residence. It was owned by the same Schenley family who were absentee landlords to much of Pittsburgh.

"I read the piece about you," said Wilson. "Why 'Pink'?"

My cheeks reddened, betraying me. "The story goes that when I was little, my mother disregarded the grays and blacks little girls wear. She dressed me in white stockings, which brought out my natural color."

"Suits you. Always standing out in a crowd."

I elbowed his arm. "That remark might not be considered complimentary."

Wilson's eyes twinkled as we strolled down the brick sidewalk. "It was intended in no other way."

I sighed. "The odd thing is, I wanted those black stockings. While the other girls admired my clothes, I longed for theirs. I always felt as if I were being singled out for ridicule."

"Then why accept the name Pink? Surely you could have requested your Christian name be used."

We walked several steps without either of us speaking. Growing uneasy, Wilson started to apologize. "If I've offended—"

I held up a hand and he stopped talking. Together, we strolled to the river's edge. I picked up a stone from the grassy plot of land and pitched it across the water.

"Well thrown," he said. "The *Dispatch* should have Nellie Bly infiltrate the Alleghenys as a pitcher." Afraid of giving me ideas, he hastily added, "Not actually."

I kept my eyes fixed on the water. "My father was the first to call me Pink. I like to think it was his compliment, his way of saying I was as good as any son to him."

Wilson nodded. "Pink being a boy's color, like red is a man's."

"I even enrolled in school under the name Pink. But no one likes to be teased at every turn. As I got older, people turned my nickname into an insult. 'Pink cheeks,' they said. What was I so ashamed of all the time? What had I done?"

"Poor kid," said Wilson consolingly. "Children can be cruel."

"And some children never grow up."

Wilson laughed ruefully. "A low blow!"

I had been thinking of Albert. Instantly contrite, I put both my hands upon his arm. "Oh, no! Q.O., I didn't mean you!" I looked up at him, pleading for forgiveness.

Under the brim of his hat he wore a startled expression. Slowly, he withdrew his arm and stepped back. "My mistake. I should know better than to imagine you waste time thinking of me." Before I could reply, he pressed on, brightly. "And of course you are entirely correct. Most men are still boys at heart. How many of us look back on our youths as the best time of our lives, when we were carefree and unburdened by a lifetime of choices. Perhaps that is why so many men behave childishly—they long to return to the simplicity of youth. Hm. There might be a Quiet Observation in there." He bowed to me, only half jokingly. "I am indebted to you."

It was only a few more minutes before he withdrew his pocket watch and stated with shock that he had no notion it had grown so late, and he had an engagement at home. I said I completely understood. "Please give your wife my best regards."

Wilson assured me he would. Then he was gone.

My heart was racing. *Did I do something improper?* I had only touched his arm, as I might have done on any other occasion. I had certainly thrown my tiny fist at his shoulder many times before.

So why did this feel different?

IN AUGUST, I INTERVIEWED a Civil War hero, Colonel William Sirwell. He died just twelve days after my interview, as if he had been waiting to tell his story, and once it had been told, he could relax into his final sleep.

One of the ailing soldier's remarks resonated with me. "Pick your battles wisely. Know your own strength. When you do take ground, you must hold it. Plant your flag and stand."

The following Monday, I marched myself into Madden's office. "I want a column. Not for stories about summer dresses and pug dogs. I want to write what I think. Same as Wilson."

Madden studied me with those perpetually mournful eyes. "Okey. We'll give it a go."

My first column appeared on September 6th, with my name quite small. I made Madden rectify that the following week. The week after that, though my name remained large, my column had shrunk by two-thirds.

It was my own fault. Just as with reporting, writing opinion pieces took some getting used to. My first few attempts were—to be kind—limp. I struggled to make them interesting, with mixed results. After demanding to speak my mind, I made a paltry show of it.

I took dinner table comments, or things overheard on the streetcar or in the office, and attempted to give each one a point. When I wrote about a drunken husband returning home or a backroom dogfight, I was trying to write about the abuse of innocents. In a sly nod to Wilson, I even included an account of the increasing number of women attending baseball games.

If he saw it, he did not say. Our Friday afternoon meetings had mysteriously ended—not outright, but with delays and excuses. It was especially galling as I was proving a feeble columnist and could have used his advice. *I used to have opinions,* I thought. *Where have they gone?*

I found them the fourth week, and from Harry, of all people. He had gone to an event at the Young Men's Christian Association, and talked that night of all the fun he'd had there, playing games and singing in a clean, positive environment.

I posed a simple question in my next column: "Why is there no comparable organization for women?"

In so doing, I inspired dozens of letters and accidentally picked a fight with none other than Bessie Bramble. In her very next column, she chastised me for slighting the Women's Christian Association of Pittsburg. She informed our readers that the members of the association did not have much money, but did much in the way of charity. "That they are so quiet and silent about their good works, that Sister Bly did not know such an association was in existence," she wrote, "shows how well they have been taught the silence and submission theory, so long held and enforced by the church."

In reply, "Sister Bly" politely informed Bessie that in all my talks with the working women of our fine city, I had yet to hear of any benevolent society offering aid to them. What we needed, I said, was "a place where poor girls will find inducements to spend their leisure time, especially evenings—a place that will offer and give assistance." Though I made certain to couch my terms—"While not daring to offer our humble opinion against that of a talented writer and learned lady like B.B."—I also pointed out that saving just one soul through actual *help* would offer "a brighter reward than a lifetime spent in prayer."

The responses poured in, all of them in unanimous praise. I had stumbled upon a topic that was admirable to everyone: providing a safe haven for penniless women to spend their leisure hours. One letter suggested that I set up a reading room, so women would have an alternative to the skating rink.

Wilson finally broke the awkward silence between us as I walked by his desk. "A fine solution for the man-mashers. Well done, Miss Bly."

I stopped in my tracks. "What?"

"I said 'well done.'" He noted my stricken expression. "What's the matter?"

I shook my head. "If the Quiet Observer approves, I have almost certainly lost my way."

He looked genuinely wounded. "Or perhaps I can recognize good sense when I read it."

"Why start now?" I snapped, moving past him. If I was sour, it was because I felt like a failure: "In any event, Madden just axed my column."

"No shame. Just not your beat. You're a reporter. Stick to that."

But my reporting assignments did nothing to improve my mood. Madden sent me to do stories on rubber raincoats and made me turn in two full columns on a local minister with a collection of fifty thousand butterflies. Butterflies!

As a suddenly prominent member of society, I was asked to be part of an entertainment committee for a delegation from the Mexican railway. Though I spoke no Spanish, the men from Mexico were quite flattering to me. I offered to write up the story, but Madden wasn't interested.

More and more, I was detesting my assignments. This culminated in December, when I declined every story he offered me. They were, each one, women's goop. In their stead, I proposed stories about prostitutes, about the poverty-stricken, about the homeless, about the starving.

Madden rejected every single one.

What am I still doing here? I thought as I left his office one day. True, despite my lack of a byline, I was still receiving a paycheck. *But I am a reporter now, with a name!* If I wasn't happy, I wondered why I couldn't move on. *What is holding me to the Dispatch?*

I was still puzzling over this when I received an invitation to attend Wilson's annual Christmas gathering. It being my first holiday season at the paper—and maybe my last—I threw caution to the wind and decided to go. *Why not? It's not as if I have a real career to ruin at the moment.*

Dressed nicely, my hair up, I splurged on a cab, though I could have walked. Wilson's home was in Allegheny, like ours, just closer to the river. Not quite as fancy as Bessie's, it was well-kept and spacious, with real warmth in the paint and molding.

"Nellie!" cried Wilson as I joined a flood of other revelers stamping snow from their boots. "Let me take your coat. I'm delighted you decided to come."

"Hi, Q.O. Nice bonnet." He was wearing a Father Christmas cap that looked ridiculous. Were it not for his moustache and creases, he might have been a boy playing pretend.

To my shock, Wilson blushed. "My wife insisted."

I leaned forward to lightly embrace him. He gave me a brief peck on the cheek, then turned his head and called, "Mrs. Wilson! Here is Nellie Bly!"

"At last!" came a cry from across the cramped vestibule, and I suddenly found myself in a sideways embrace, my arms pinioned and half my face squashed into a breast.

Mrs. Wilson was an oddly proportioned woman: too large above, too skinny below. Her dress did not flatter her, nor did her bun, which pulled her hair back to show an unfortunate amount of scalp between the thin strands. Yet she had a ready laugh—so ready it could be jarring, bursting at the smallest comment to ring about the house.

"So this is Nellie Bly!" she exclaimed, holding me at arm's length before kissing me on each cheek.

Mrs. Wilson ushered me into her home and plied me with punch and cheese and Christmas cookies. She asked if I enjoyed embroidery and promised to embroider me a pillow sleeve with my name done all in flowers. Then, seeing someone else, she vanished, leaving me breathless.

"Something, isn't she?" said a voice in my ear.

I jumped, sloshing a little of the punch from my glass. "Madden!"

"Sorry. You haven't met Sissy before, have you?"

"Sissy?"

"Her childhood name. She's an experience."

"She seems lovely," I hedged. "Effusive."

Madden grunted. "That's one word for it. She's on good behavior. I dreaded the days she came to the office."

"I've never seen her there," I said.

"Because Razzy has forbidden her from entering the newsroom ever again. I think she was in the hospital for a week after that blowup." The expression I turned on him made him blanch. "I don't mean—no, Wilson would never—" He paused, then lowered his voice. "She is like a bandalore." He mimed the toy with his hand, running an imaginary disk up and down on a string. "I think tonight we will see up. It's Wilson who bears the brunt of *down*. I hate to think what it would have been like for their daughter."

"They have a daughter?"

"Had," said Madden sadly. "Died an infant, about six years back. Failure to thrive. I think that's about the time Sissy began. . ." Again, he mimed the bandalore, up and down.

I looked over at Wilson. If I was to be honest with myself, I had girded myself against any ill feeling I might have for his wife. Certainly, meeting her, she was not what I'd expected, and I was unaccountably pleased.

That puzzled me, and I chased my own feelings. It finally occurred to me that I was pleased to learn of her inconstant nature.

It occurred to me that I was pleased that Wilson was unhappy in his marriage.

It occurred to me what that implied.

Meanwhile, they had lost a daughter, a little girl. I wondered what her name had been. I wondered if that was why Wilson called me his "kid" so often. I wondered why it made us closer. He'd lost a daughter. I, a father.

What does that say about our motives for friendship?

Shaken, I threw myself into conversation. Exacting several kinds of penance from myself, I spent a good portion of that uncomfortable evening closeted with Bessie Bramble, allowing her to harangue me about all the good that the Christian women of Pittsburgh did on a daily basis. "Especially at this blessed time of year," she observed.

"I appreciate everything you say," I answered when she paused to draw breath. "And I am sorry if you felt my writing besmirched the good Christian ladies. But, forgive me if I'm mistaken, I thought you were not a great believer in religion."

Her patrician gaze became haughtier. "Do not mistake religion with church. I fully believe in Christ's message to mankind. What I cannot abide are those imposters of the pulpit who choose to interpret Biblical parables as literal truths in order to dominate and diminish our sex. Examine the story of Genesis, and you will note not one but two pernicious myths. First, that knowledge is evil. What better way for the Church to keep us docile than to keep us ill-informed? Second, that woman is the cause of sin. We bear the blame, we are told, for the evils men do. Thus, we have no cause to complain when we are abused or neglected. Even anatomy partakes of this slander. A man bears an Adam's apple. Science tells us that this is what lowers a man's voice. But it is named after Eve's partner who, like her, swallowed the apple. However, we are told, it stuck in his throat, leaving him less sinful than Eve."

"I had no idea," I said, feeling keenly my own lack of education. "Why do you not write that?"

"Because I would never set ink to page again. Every battle comes in its time. Twenty-five years ago, the battle was slavery. Today, it is suffrage. The battle for the heart of the Church has been raging for centuries. Sometimes the reasonable are victorious, sometimes the asinine. No war is ever won. There are merely times when hostilities cease and an armistice is called. One hopes that one has gained enough ground before the cease-fire bugle is blown."

I laughed. "I interviewed a colonel at the end of the summer. He said something similar: 'Plant your flag and stand. Never retreat.'"

Bessie Bramble frowned. "That's absurd. Sometimes one must retreat, or else risk the whole war. Not every piece of ground gained is vital. If Lee had not chosen to stand at Gettysburg, do you think the war would have ended the way it did? The town itself was of no consequence. It was only because he invested it with his whole army that it has import today. A war was lost because a good general refused to give up bad ground. Thank God," she added.

"Thank God," I echoed, then smiled brightly at her. "Mrs. Wade, how did you become so wise?"

She laughed. "I have experienced much kindness. There is privilege in a full stomach and freshly laundered clothes. Oh, and travel! Travel, dear Miss Bly, is the most important teacher one can have. To see other cultures, hear other tongues! My best advice to anyone is to travel to Europe or the Orient and get exhilaratingly lost. There is no better education in the whole world!"

At that moment there was a tinkling of glasses signaling it was time for the host and hostess made a short speech. Or rather, Wilson attempted to make one, only to be repeatedly interrupted by comical asides from his wife. She was unquestionably amusing, and many people laughed good-heartedly. Then she would smile and repeat what she had said, like a parrot.

At one point Wilson was mid-sentence when she opened her mouth and I saw him catch her hand in his. She chose to interpret the rebuke lovingly. I watched their fingers interlock as she pulled herself close to him and bussed his cheek. He was embarrassed, as well he might be. The kiss seemed almost desperate to me. Her eyes were wide and liquid as she looked first at Wilson and then at the room at large. Her cheeks were flushed. I knew the signs of drink, and this was quite different.

Several things happened at once inside my head. Wilson. Eve. Madden. Gettysburg. Divorce. Bessie. Travel. The Women's Pages. The *Dispatch*. Albert. Mother. Father. Ford.

I found Madden laughing in a crowd of reporters and pressmen. Sneaking up behind him, I stood on my toes to place my chin beside his ear. "I quit."

Before he even had a chance to turn around, I spun away and left the party.

I WROTE MADDEN AN OFFICIAL LETTER of resignation the next day, joking that he would not have to invest in so many blue pencils in the future. I made sure to thank him repeatedly for all of his support and guidance, and for making my career possible. "I would be happy to work on a freelance basis in the future," I wrote, "should a story arise that requires the voice of Nellie Bly. Rest assured, so long as I have that name, I will think of your kindness and generosity." Like a coward, I snuck in and left the letter on his desk after he had gone for the day.

My letter to Wilson was equally appreciative, if more honest. "I'm leaving for a good cause, though it might appear shabby. I simply refuse to be relegated to the Women's Pages. One must stand on principle. That, I'm sure, is a position the Quiet Observer shares." I signed it "Your Naughty Nellie" and left it where he would see it.

I cleaned out my desk late in the evening, so as not to draw attention. The last thing I wanted was to depart in the full glare of the newsroom lamps. I put all of my clippings into a portfolio, placed my notebooks in my bag, and tottered down those steep steps for what could possibly be the very last time.

If my reasons were murky, I told myself the decision was sound. I had been so busy making my name that I hadn't noticed I was losing the cause. And who was Nellie Bly if not a writer with a cause? A bicycle upside down, wheels in the air.

Besides, there's nothing to hold me here. Nothing, and no one.

As I departed, I was certain of just one thing: Nellie Bly was not about to write on anyone's terms but her own.

SIXTEEN

RUNNING TOWARD AWAY

LIFE AT HOME WAS MUCH more pleasant since the departure of Albert. It was as though the air had been purged of some noxious cloud. The walls themselves seemed less crowding, the furniture less cramped.

I was sad, though, to realize that little Harry wasn't so little anymore. After turning sixteen, he had taken a job in an office, making more money to start than I had—which I confess caused some resentment in me.

Charlie, Sarah, and baby Grant still lived with us, with Charlie contributing more to the household than Albert ever had. And both Tom and Tony were still kicking around whenever they weren't off jaunting down some railway track or other for their work. So the household wasn't missing my income.

I was, though. Not the monetary value so much as the sense of worth. It was one thing to stand on principles. It was another to be silent after finding your voice.

On New Year's Day, Tom, Tony, Harry, and I were playing cards for matches and discussing our New Year's resolutions.

"I resolve to learn to sew," said Tom. "Two cards."

"Good," I said. "You can start with the button on the dress I wore yesterday."

"Only if you wear it while I sew, so I can stick you."

"You should resolve to smoke less, Tom," said Tony. "Costs too much."

"Bad for you, too," said Harry. "Or so Mother says."

"That's not what the Indians say," replied Tom. "Did you know, they didn't have a word for *smoke*? They used to say they drank tobacco."

Tony laughed. "Where did you hear that?"

"In El Paso last month. What, you don't believe it?"

"No. Because I don't believe everything someone pours in my ear."
Tony turned to me. "What's yours, Pink?"

"Two cards," I said.

He grinned. "Not much of a resolution, but here you go."

"A book," I said. "I want to write a book."

"A book?" asked Harry.

"Why not? Look at *Bootles' Baby*. Half a million copies this year."

"That was written by a man," said Tony. "John Strange Something."

"Winter," I said. "And he's a she. Used to be a newspaperwoman in
London."

Tom looked impressed. "I hadn't heard that. Well, good luck. Make me
a character and I'll read it."

"You are quite the character," I said. "Harry? What's yours?"

Harry reddened. "Never be late to work again. Three cards."

Tom ruffled his hair. "It was one time!"

"Leave him alone," said Tony. "The boy's industrious. We should all
work so hard."

"What about you, Tony?" asked Harry.

"Mexico," said Tony.

"Mexico!" exclaimed Tom. "Damn—I mean, drat. I should have said
that."

Weighing my next bet, I was distracted. "Mexico?"

"Line's finally finished," said Tony. "Dealer takes two. In just three,
maybe four days, you can take a train from here straight to Mexico, sunny
land of the gods."

"Bullfights and señoritas and lazy siestas," agreed Tom. "That's the life."

"Absolutely," said Tony. "Okey-doke, Pink. Your bet. Pink?"

"She's cheating again," said Tom.

"She never cheats!" exclaimed Harry. "Albert just says that to hide his
cheating."

"The game *has* been smoother now that Albert's not here," admitted
Tony.

"She's not denying it, though," teased Tom.

Turning to me, Harry nudged my arm. "Lizzie?"

"What? Oh. I, ah, I fold." I set my cards down and stood.

"See?" said Tom. "Cheating."

"Where are you going?" asked Harry.

"I—I, um. . . I don't know."

Except that I did. I was going to Mexico.

I DIDN'T SLEEP A SINGLE WINK that night, and the next morning I practically ran to the corner to hail a taxi—there was no time for the streetcar! Stomping up the familiar steep steps, I brushed past the copy boy and the reporters startled by my return.

Wilson wasn't there, but Madden was in his office. Face flushed, pulse racing, I marched in and closed the door. "I want to go to Mexico."

Startled, he leaned back in his chair and raised his brows. "Happy New Year to you, too, Miss Cochrane."

"Happy New Year. And it's Miss Bly. Send me to Mexico."

"In a hot air balloon?"

"I had an invitation from that Mexican delegation last fall. I mean to take them up on it. Make me your correspondent in Mexico."

Tempted to laugh, his impulse died when he saw I was in earnest. "Do you even speak Spanish?"

"I can learn."

"Do you know anything about Mexico?"

"Not as much as your readers will, once I'm there."

"Why?"

That was the question I had been pondering all night. "I need to see the world. I need to live outside of Pittsburgh, outside of Pennsylvania—out of America. And there are stories there. The stories I'm good at telling: how other people live."

"And it's exciting," he said.

"Yes!" I agreed with a laugh. "It's exciting. It will sell papers." I watched his eyes narrow and pressed that point home. "If it's exciting for me, it will be doubly exciting for the *Dispatch* readers. Their own Nellie Bly, off on an adventure. It'll be reporting and serial drama all in one. We'll inform the public, and at the same time entertain them."

On my whole way over to the office, as I rubbed my lucky thumb ring under the sooty spray of the taxi, I imagined how difficult he might be. And now I could see his struggle play out on his face: It was an excellent idea. It would sell papers. And he hated it.

"I have to say no."

I wasn't discouraged. I had known he would start with a *no*. "Why?"

"Because it's lunacy."

I straightened. "The word *lunacy* comes from *lunatic*, which means 'swayed by the moon.' Are you saying I'm swayed by the moon, George Madden?"

He blanched, knowing enough about women to know that such a comment could bring no good. "Most Americans think life has been swell for the Mexicans since their emperor was deposed. But I hear things. It's not safe."

"Would you warn a man away?"

"I would, yes."

"Would you let him go?"

Madden considered. "Yes."

"So let me."

"No."

"Why not?" I tried not to yell.

"Because I don't want your death on my conscience."

"Me either. I promise not to die."

"The answer is no."

I grew mulish. "You can't stop me."

"That's not true. The trip is expensive. I can decide not to pay for it."

"You can," I agreed. "All that means is that I travel among the indigent, live in cheap rooms, eat bad food. But I'm going."

"A week of that and you'll turn right around."

Madden knew that argument was a mistake the moment it emerged from his mouth, and he winced as I said, "Oh, I will, will I?"

He sagged a little. "Look, it's a terrific idea. Nellie Bly on the road. Just choose somewhere less dangerous. Go to New York for a week, write stories about life there. I'll pay for that."

I resisted the urge to fold my arms like a child in a tantrum. "You don't want me as your foreign correspondent in Mexico?"

"I won't be responsible for you putting yourself in danger."

I nodded. "Fine. I wonder if the *Gazette* would be interested."

Madden stared at me. I didn't budge. We both knew that another paper wouldn't hesitate to poach my name and send me haring off. And if I died, so much better the story.

I had won. We both knew it. Given that I was certain to go, there was no point in me not going for the *Dispatch*. The only remaining question was whether Madden was willing to cut off his nose to spite his face.

At last, he closed his eyes. "When do you leave?"

I'D IMAGINED THE ENCOUNTER WITH MADDEN to be the second hardest fight. In that, I proved correct. But I'd misjudged which would be the hardest. I had thought it would be gaining Mother's consent. Yet when I told her my plans, she hardly batted an eyelid.

"Good for you," she said. "But you must look after your health. You remember what happened to your great-uncle on his trip around the world."

I'd been raised on stories of great-uncle Thomas and his three-year voyage around the globe. In many ways, he was my model for heroism and adventure. But that trip had utterly wrecked his health. I promised to be careful, and Mother seemed content.

No, the fiercest battle arrived in the form of Wilson.

A knock on the door summoned Mother, and I was startled to hear the Quiet Observer's voice asking to see me. I felt my cheeks flush, and I had only a moment to wonder if I was quite presentable. The dress I had on—if not the one I might have worn had he sent advance word—suited me well enough, with its high buttoned neck and brocaded bodice. I did, however, wish for lace at my collar and cuffs.

But he hadn't sent word, and didn't deserve my best. *Besides, what do I care about what he sees me wearing?*

As Mother showed Wilson into the sitting room, I rose to make introductions. "Mother, this is Mr. Erasmus Wilson, who writes under the name Quiet Observer. Mr. Wilson, this is my mother, Mrs. Mary Jane Cochrane Ford."

Mother's eyes widened a fraction when I added *Ford*. Honestly, I didn't know why I'd said it. It was cruel, and I felt myself flush in shame. I had no idea what Wilson made of that.

As ever, Mother was adept at smoothing over an awkward moment. "So, it is thanks to you that my daughter has transformed into the formidable Nellie Bly."

Hat in hand, snow melting on his shoulders, Wilson parried her smile with his dimples. "Hardly, Mrs. Ford. She came into the *Dispatch* fully formed and entirely formidable. Which must be due to you."

"How kind," said Mother. "And please, it is Mary Jane. Or, if you must, Mrs. Cochrane. I am divorced."

"I—yes, I know. I am so sorry." Less adept at dissembling, Wilson faltered. "Forgive me, but I had to call. I must prevent your daughter from making an enormous mistake."

"Oh, dear," said Mother. "Perhaps I should stay." She looked at me. Though annoyed, I couldn't prevent her, and she turned back to our unexpected guest. "Can we offer you something, Mr. Wilson? Coffee? Tea?"

"Tea would be lovely," said Wilson.

"Then you must promise not to discuss matters before I return," said Mother, rising. "Elizabeth doesn't make tea." She bustled back to the kitchen, leaving the door open to eavesdrop.

Forced to make small talk, Wilson smiled at me. "You don't make tea?"

I shook my head. He waited. So patient, so infuriating. It was a reporter's trick he often urged me to use: leave a lingering silence until things became so uncomfortable that the subject felt compelled to fill the void.

I hated that it worked on me. "When I was a little tot, I decided I wanted some tea. So I poured the entire contents of a five-pound canister into the pot and filled it with water."

Wilson began to laugh. "Oh, dear."

Entirely against my will, I felt a smile brewing. "It was like 'Jack and the Beanstalk.' I burned my hands trying to hold down the lid, and soon it covered the stove and the kitchen floor. I had to be rescued by my mother."

"And you haven't made tea since? That's not the Nellie Bly I know."

"I don't like not being good at a thing."

"No one does." He gestured to the upright piano on the far side of the room. "So that's for show?"

"Not at all," said Mother, returning with Wilson's tea and saucer. "Elizabeth is quite skilled. She can play both the piano and the organ."

"My sister Catharine's better on the organ," I said with perfect fairness. But it was true that I enjoyed playing the piano. Until becoming a reporter, it had been my most constant release.

Mother brought tea for her and me, then seated herself at a small distance, leaving us free to discuss what had drawn Wilson to our modest home. Of course, I knew very well what had brought him. I gave him no time to voice it and attacked first. "I can't fail to notice you didn't come calling when I quit the *Dispatch*."

Wilson smiled ruefully. "I was hoping you had found yourself a nice man and planned to marry, having gotten this reporting bug out of your system."

Mother's expression was hard to read, but I thought she disapproved of his frank statement. I know I did. "Is reporting a disease? It hasn't been fatal to you."

"No, but it might be to you in Mexico. Please tell me you—I was about to say, 'tell me you are not serious.' But of course you are."

"Of course I am," I agreed evenly.

"Then let me say, it will not be what you think. As dangerous as Pittsburgh can be, here at least you have friends, family, a home, a refuge. You also have policemen, courts of law, and a newspaper industry that is free to publish whatever it likes. In Mexico you would have none of those."

"There are no police in Mexico? No courts? No newspapers?"

"Only a semblance of them. And you would be a foreigner. Your rights would not be paramount."

I shook my head like a mule. "Then I will write that story, too."

Wilson nodded in resignation. "That's what I imagined your answer would be. I know how powerless I am to change the mind of Nellie Bly."

"Then why come?"

He leaned forward, his hat dangling in his clasped hands. "To beg you to take someone with you. A chaperone, or at least a companion. Someone to be by your side, so you are not alone on your travels and explorations. A young girl alone in a foreign land is an invitation for disaster."

"What kind of disaster?"

"All kinds. Besides the personal dangers, you are putting the *Dispatch* in danger. What if something should befall you? Our readers will hold the paper responsible. What were we thinking, sending our beloved Nellie Bly to Mexico?"

I laughed. "You make it sound like a journey to Hell. It is only Mexico."

"You say that, having never been."

"Have you?"

"No." At least he had the good grace to admit it.

"Then I think we will both benefit from a trip south, to have a firsthand account of what Mexico is really like."

"I would." His voice carried real urgency. "If I could, I would. My wife. She is—she isn't well. I cannot leave her."

I had not meant my flippant answer as an invitation. Yet somehow he had inferred one. And, more, he had clearly thought about it!

Keenly aware that Mother was watching, I said, "I wouldn't want you to."

I was fairly good at reading people. That, and a sense of dramatic justice, was what made me a good reporter. But Wilson's face went through such a rapid series of emotions that I couldn't capture them all. I saw hurt and relief and surprise and despair, but it was hard to say which won.

When next he spoke, his voice was level. "If not me, then for God's sake take another reporter from the *Dispatch*. Madden will pay for it."

My spine grew steely. "Absolutely not."

"Why?"

"Because then my companion will write all the important stories, while I sit about, writing on Mexican gardening and the fashion of women's shoelaces!"

I expected him to laugh, but he did not. "I see. This is another Nellie Bly crusade. But remember: crusaders often do not return, and if they do, they are never whole."

I laughed. "I don't mean to wage a war!"

"Of course you do," said Mother unexpectedly.

Both Wilson and I looked at her in surprise.

"You are your father's daughter. He was a judge, interested in justice and fairness. Like him, you cannot help but try to right wrongs."

That was possibly the most wonderful thing Mother had ever said about me. Had we been alone, I might have burst into tears. With Wilson there, my chin only wobbled for a moment. Then I lifted it to look Wilson in the eye. "Bessie Bramble told me to choose my battles. This is one."

Wilson's moustache bristled. "A good general does not go into war unprepared, undermanned. Take reinforcements."

I shook my head. "Taking anyone is admitting defeat before the train leaves the station."

"Does that apply to everyone?" asked Mother. "Or only other reporters of the male sex? I think having a companion is sound advice."

I glanced nervously at Wilson, then back to Mother. "Who?"

"Why not a member of the family? Certainly none of us will outshine you."

I frowned. "Harry? He just started work. And Charlie has Sarah and Grant to support. Kate has Beatrice."

"None of them."

"Not Albert!"

"No, not Albert." Mother looked at me expectantly, her hands folded in her lap.

I was later ashamed at how long it took me to parse that look. "Mother— would *you* like to go to Mexico?"

Her lips thinned. "Only if you want me." Before I could answer, she went on. "I could ask Catharine to live here while we are gone, to look after Harry and keep house with Sarah. Beatrice will be better off, and Grant can play with his cousin again. They won't even notice I've gone."

"Of course they will," I responded. But I said it in a placating tone, not a protesting one. It felt cowardly, but I was relieved. For indeed, though I would never have admitted it, I was a little frightened of going on such an adventure alone. My pride was at war with my sense, and up to now pride had been winning.

This, however, was an option I had never even considered. "Mother, if you really mean it, I would be delighted to have your company."

Mother swelled happily in her seat, then turned to our guest. "Well, Mr. Wilson? Does that quell your concerns?"

From his expression, it did not. Two women wandering around Mexico was hardly better than one. But he could not say so. He merely bowed his head. "I am delighted to see there is at least one person on this earth with the power to make our Nellie alter her course, if only a few degrees. I am sure that, with you present, she will avoid any undue risks, and return to us sooner, safer, and full to bursting with stories."

He soon departed, and I stood in the window watching him as he ventured out into the snow. His step was sure. He did not appear to be downcast. And why should he? His visit had not been in vain. In one way, he had won: I would have a companion, a chaperone, for my grand adventure.

Mother and I were heading to Mexico.

III

ONE BUTTON
IS ENOUGH

HER MEMORY STILL GONE

NO ONE CLAIMS THE PRETTY CRAZY GIRL AT BELLEVUE

JUSTICE DUFFY BELIEVES THAT THERE IS A ROMANCE IN HER STORY, BUT WARDEN O'ROUKE DOUBTS IT

The well-dressed girl who wandered into the Home for Women on Second Avenue on Friday, and who said she was Nellie Marina, and again that she was Nellie Brown, is still at Bellevue Hospital. The doctors are not certain that she is insane. She says continually that men are going to kill her, and that she would kill herself if she only knew the name of the poison she wants to take. She has lucid intervals, when she talks sensibly enough about what is going on around her, but she appears to remember nothing of the past. Dr. Braisted, the physician at the insane pavilion, takes no stock in the theory that the girl is suffering from the effects of drugs. His opinion is that she is suffering from hysterical mania, but he is not certain that she is not romancing. He admits that her case is a puzzle that will take several days to solve.

The girl is probably a Cuban, and, as far as can be inferred from what she said on Saturday, it is believed that she lived in New Orleans. She walked into the nurses' room in the pavilion, with a heavy shawl wrapped around her neck and shoulders, to see a SUN reporter yesterday afternoon, and complained of the cold. She said nothing, but stood staring until the reporter spoke.

"Where are your relations?" she was asked.

"They are dead," she answered, sadly.

As the nurse took her back to her apartment the girl said: "I never saw such a lot of crazy men as there are around this place."'

"They are not crazy men," said the nurse. "They are reporters."

"They must be crazy to question me," she answered.

Justice Duffy said last night that he was deeply interested in the girl. She was a Cuban, he thought, and had been waited upon by slaves. She called them in Spanish peons. She probably journeyed here by water, for she expressed a desire to leave by the ocean.

"There is certainly a romance," said the little Judge, "behind her fragmentary story."

Warden O'Rourke of Bellevue said that he considered the girl a humbug.

—*New York Sun*
Monday, September 26, 1887

SEVENTEEN

ADIOS

WEDNESDAY, FEBRUARY 3 1886

WITH MADDENING SLOWNESS, EVERYTHING was put into place. Tom and Tony created our itinerary as far as Mexico City. Madden paid for the tickets. I thanked him by filing a story on women's charity work that would warm Bessie Bramble's prickly heart. It was my only published piece in January.

Meanwhile, the household was in an uproar. Harry was alternately excited and jealous, wishing we had made the trip before he had started work. Charlie was amused, Sarah exasperated. Kate was delighted to leave her husband for a few months and bring Beatrice up to Pittsburgh. Albert was mockful, saying I lacked the gumption to go anywhere without our mother's skirts to cling to.

But nothing could take the gloss from my excitement. I was doing something new, going somewhere unknown, and would soon see things with fresh eyes. This might not be the grand tour of Europe that Bessie had praised, but it was by far the most exciting thing I had ever done. Even disguising myself as a factory girl hadn't given me such a lift!

The only extended travel I had ever done was to the finishing school. I'd been a student then, with very specific instructions of what to bring. For this trip, I packed clothes and necessaries with only my wild imagination to guide me as to what I might require. I was in serious danger of overpacking until Mother pointed out, "It's better to bring too little than too much. We can always buy a hairbrush there. And then you'll have a souvenir."

So it was that on a gray January morning, we went to Station Square to board the Panhandle Express. We'd said most of our goodbyes at home, but

Charlie took the morning off from work to help us with our bags. At the station he passed them off to a Pullman porter and then helped Mother up into the Pullman car.

I was about to follow them when I felt a gentle grip on my elbow. Turning, I half expected to see Wilson. But no, it was Madden. He lifted his hat and handed me an envelope. "Some extra money never went amiss. Wire when you need more. And start writing the moment you leave the station. I want copy as soon as possible."

Tucking the envelope into my coat, I was genuinely touched. "Thank you, Mr. Madden." I glanced behind him. "Is Q.O. with you?"

"Razzy? No. Why?"

I shook my head. "No reason. I just thought he'd try to talk me out of this again."

"Do you want to be talked out of it?"

"No!"

He tapped the brim of his hat. "Then safe travels, Miss Bly."

Charlie called from the top of the train stairs. "Pink! The train will leave without you!"

"Pink?" asked Madden.

Shaking my head, I scampered up the steps into the car and took a seat, vibrating with excitement.

I needn't have hurried. It was ten more minutes before the train actually departed. I saw Madden and Charlie shake hands, introduce themselves, and fall into conversation. At one point they both laughed, which piqued my temper. *Clearly, they're discussing me! Thank God Albert didn't come.*

Charlie and Madden remained by our window and waved goodbye as the engine lurched once, twice, then began rolling. They were soon engulfed in steam as we pulled away, hurtling into a new life of adventure.

I could hardly sit still. I didn't know how to behave on a long-distance train. I felt trapped in my seat. I decided not to rise until someone else did. Once they did, I thought I might go to the dining car, or the observation car. Having more experience and far more patience, Mother decided to nap.

We were traveling in a line of Pullmans. I realized there might be a story in that. Determined to be industrious, I called the porter over to ask about them. He was a handsome black man with his hair worn close, his face clean-shaven, and not a speck of lint on his cap or buttoned coat.

He was more than happy to tell us the provenance of our conveyance. "All the cars on this train, Miss, were built at the new Pullman factory on Lake Calumet, south of Chicago. Each car is seventy feet long, with lacquered walnut finish and inlaid decorative carving."

"All of them are made in Chicago?"

"Lake Calumet, Miss. South of Chicago."

"How much does a worker there get paid?"

If my question surprised him, I was equally surprised by the answer. "Miss, my cousin took a job there last year. He's paid one dollar and thirty cents a day."

"And how many hours a day does he work?"

"Oh, ten or eleven. It's good work, Miss, and there are many things to enjoy in his free hours. Mr. Pullman has created a whole town, with churches, theatres, parks, and a library."

"That's very impressive."

The porter nodded. "Mr. Pullman is very generous. My cousin says one of the other men had his foot—well, he was injured. He's getting half his wages paid for the rest of his life." Someone across the car called, "George!" and the porter begged our pardon as he went to help them with their children.

Looking to Mother, I said, "I wish all employers were as generous."

"I do not," she replied from behind her closed eyelids. "It would lead to malingering. A lifetime of half pay for a foot? Some men would think it a bargain at half the price."

I knew which man was on her mind. Ever since Wilson's call, the name of Ford had hung in the air between us. My fault. It had been an unspoken family agreement to never again mention his name.

Feeling guilty, I rose. "Would you like to visit the dining car?"

Mother agreed and together we moved down the train. Stepping from one bumping, thumping car to the next was fraught with peril. As the ground raced visibly beneath our feet, I held Mother's hand, and she mine, and together we traversed the gap to the car where meals were served.

The combination of the food and the rhythm of the train convinced me to nap that afternoon. Or *siesta*, as I remembered to call it. Knowing only a handful of Spanish words, I had to get the most out of them.

After a siesta, we chatted with our fellow passengers, few of whom were going half so far as we were. Most were headed for Chicago or St. Louis. No one in our car was heading as far as Texas. I felt a shimmer of pride— *Mother and I are pioneers!*

It felt strange, traveling west in order to go south. But Tom had assured me that if we went south first, our trek would take much longer. "More stops, and the rails aren't as sure. Best head over to St. Louis, then on to Texas from there."

That night, our porter made up our beds in the sleeper car. I remained awake in the upper berth, listening to the sounds, feeling the shocks and tumult of the wheels traversing the rails beneath us. I felt a sense of wonder for the achievements of mankind, that such things could exist in the world.

Man could do so much. Surely Woman could achieve more, given the chance.

D URING A STOP IN CINCINNATI the next morning, several new passengers greeted the porter by name. "Good morning, George" and "thank you, George" rippled up and down the car.

When his duties were finished, the luggage was stowed away, the new passengers were comfortably seated, and the train was underway once more, I called our porter over. "How does everyone know your name? Do they ride this route often?"

The porter smiled with polite indulgence. "I wouldn't know, Miss. All porters are called George."

"Oh. Really? Why is that?"

"After George Pullman, our employer."

I was shocked. "But—forgive me, but isn't that what used to be done to slaves? Weren't they all named for their master?"

He nodded. "Yes, Miss. I believe that is so."

"That's appalling! What is your actual name?"

For the first time, he looked flustered. "Matthew, Miss."

"Well, Matthew, here is at least one passenger who will use your proper name!"

"Thank you, Miss. It's very kind. May I get you another drink, Miss?"

"That would be very kind, Matthew. Thank you."

As he retreated from our embarrassing conversation, I fretted. I had admired George Pullman for his decision to employ only Negroes as Pullman porters. It had given employment to hundreds of former slaves. Tom and Tony had said it was a job they would have wished for, and Albert had often joked that they should put shoe polish on their faces to apply.

Now I perceived an uglier side to Pullman's operation. Hiring former slaves ensured an air of subservience in his employees. And some of his customers might feel empowered to behave badly in front of a Negro tasked with serving them.

That night, in the relative privacy of our sleeper, I asked Mother about this, and she offered a different perspective. "Only the rich are waited upon this way. By employing these porters, Mr. Pullman offers people of the middle class an upper-class experience."

"And perpetuates the notion that black people are here to serve," I said through pinched lips.

"And pays them wages to do so," she countered.

That sent my brain whirring. In my "Girl Puzzle" column, I had suggested the employment of women as Pullman porters. After actually riding on a train, I imagined what that would look like in reality: wearing pretty dresses, serving drinks, forcing smiles, and accepting all kinds of boorish behavior. All while reinforcing the notion that women were subservient to men.

On the other hand, it was a job. It was employment. Surely it was better than being a factory girl. Or was it? Was it better for the individual girl, but worse for *all* girls? At what point did the benefit to the individual become a detriment to the whole?

I had no answers, and that troubled me. The debate raged inside my brain until the motion of the car finally rocked me to sleep.

AS TOM HAD PREDICTED, OUR progress slowed once we reached the South. When I asked Matthew about this, he informed me that not every rail line was built for an open throttle. Thus our speed was reduced from the breathtaking fifty miles per hour to around thirty-five.

Though we were no longer racing toward our destination, the slower pace did allow me to take in more of the scenery as we passed from St. Louis to Little Rock. To my amazement, it had suddenly become summer. When Matthew had made up our bunks the previous evening, the world chugging past our window had been slumbering under a blanket of snow. By morning, there were green trees outside, and the warm air in our car made a fool of my shawl.

From that moment onward, I spent all my time in the observation car at the back of the train, which had windows facing behind us. There was even a terrace of sorts out the rear door where one could stand in the open air and view the land as we chugged through it. I wasn't even in Mexico, yet I was already seeing things I never had before: cotton fields and wide empty plains, counterpointed by mountains and rivers and dotted with the occasional homestead.

I was amazed, and not just by the landscape. I saw all kinds of people living lives as foreign as if we had already entered another country. I saw women plowing fields while their lords and masters sat on fences, smoking. I'd never longed for anything so much as I longed to shove those lazy fellows off their perches. As we got further south and west, I was glad to see those fences—along with their unbecoming ornaments—disappear. Of course, then the men just slept under trees.

One afternoon, I saw real, live cowboys riding along the plains. I was seated on a folding chair as the train moved along at a "putting-in-time" pace, when I suddenly spied two horsemen on the open plain to my left.

They wore immense hats—sombreros, I mistakenly thought then—and shiny spurs, and lassos hung from their saddles.

Cowboys! Mine was one of the many imaginations that had been captured by Wyatt Earp and Doc Holliday's fight against the Cochise County Cowboys at the O.K. Corral. I had read somewhere that cowboys wore red sashes, so I raced back to our car and interrupted Mother's reading. "Mother, give me your scarf." It was red. Bemused, she handed it to me.

I dashed back to the rear platform and began waving the scarf at the two men on horseback. Belatedly, I wondered if they might shoot me. But they both lifted their wide-brimmed hats from their heads, just as any man would have done on the streets of Pittsburgh. I laughed, and it must have carried, because, with a sudden burst of their own laughing voices, they urged their horses after us!

Other passengers came to join me, and still more pressed against the windows, waving to the cowboys as they chased the train. The horses' hooves never seemed to actually contact the earth, concealed as they were in the great cloud of dust that bore them along behind us. At last, the horses tired and the train pulled away.

I waved to the cowboys one last time, wondering what might happen if I were brave enough to abandon my mission, and my mother, and leap from the train into their arms. I'd never considered myself a Romantic. Yet those two young, sun-browned men, so cheerful and carefree, would come to haunt my dreams.

THE FOOD ON OUR JOURNEY BEGAN to distress me. I had thought that the West would be a land of plenty: steaks, butter, cheese, cream, and more steaks. I could not have been more mistaken. On those occasions when the train stopped to cool down, all we found available was hard bread and salted meat. Not a creamery in sight. *Thank Heaven for the dining car!*

I was also not sleeping well. My own bed had been a refuge to me for so long that I had been unaware of how it would feel to sleep in sheets I had not washed, in a bed I had not made. By nature, I was not an early riser, and the trouble I had falling asleep only made waking me that much more of a chore—one that Mother accepted, but not without comment.

Wherever the train stopped, the local folk would draw near to see who was inside the painted car with its polished wood and shiny brass knobs. We made genial conversation, and I was amazed at the accents and how politely everyone treated us. I remember one black woman drawing near me as I sat on my chair at the open end of the observation car. "Good mornin', missis."

"Good morning," I replied.

She laughed at me in a truly kind way. "Missis, why are you sittin' out here, when there's such a nice cabin back there?"

In a conspiratorial whisper I answered, "My mother is in there."

She bobbed her head sagely, then carried on her way with a wave.

It was foolish, but ever since I had been saddled with the name Nellie Bly, I felt a kind of kinship with black women. I was always wanting to run up to them and introduce myself. I didn't, of course, because that would have been ridiculous and self-important of me. Yet the kinship existed, if nowhere but in my imagination. It allowed me to see them, whereas to most everyone else they were invisible.

Just as Matthew was invisible, except when needed. He was always there for us passengers: shining shoes, moving luggage, fetching items or drinks. Trying to set an example, I made sure to tip him often. After all, it was the *Dispatch*'s money.

The evening of our sixth day onboard the train, Matthew came to inform us that our beds were turned down. "We arrive at El Paso early in the morning."

"Already?" Part of me wished the ride would never end.

"Yes, Miss. Would you ladies like to be awakened beforehand, so you are not in a hurry to dress?"

Mother answered. "Yes, thank you, Matthew. A half an hour's warning would be splendid." He touched the brim of his cap and moved off to make the same discreet offer to the other passengers in the car.

I had no notion of what the actual time was when he wakened us. It was black as pitch outside the curtains, and I could hardly open my eyes as I struggled into my clothes in the upper berth. *Ah, the glamour of travel!*

"It's so dark," said Mother. "What on earth will we do when we arrive?"

"I'm glad it's dark," I said. "I don't have to bother with my hair or my boot buttons."

I finally got my dress fastened and my nightdress stuffed into my bag just as the train started slowing. My feet had barely found the floor when I was staggered by our lurching halt. As Mother and I emerged from the Pullman car, we were thrown amidst a frenzy I had only witnessed from a distance at other stations. Matthew and the other train staff were racing up and down the platform with lanterns on their arms, seeing the luggage properly bestowed.

We stepped past the chaos, and no one paid any attention to a drowsy pair of women seeking comfort and familiarity. Quite a change from being waited upon hand and foot for almost a week!

"I shall fall into the arms of the first man who mentions marriage to me," I yawned to Mother as we wended our way through freight and baggage. "Then I will have someone to look after me."

"One must look after one's self," she answered tartly.

I wanted to say I was only joking, but again the shadow of Ford loomed. She was right: it was important not to depend upon a husband. *A lesson hard learned.*

There were no cabs, but it hardly mattered, because we were informed that no hotels were open at that hour. Instead, we exhausted travelers were all heaped into a waiting room, where men, women, children, dogs, and baggage were bestowed in one promiscuous mass.

It was a dreary scene. Some slept, some ate, and in one corner of the pile, a cluster of men shared a bottle as they dealt greasy cards by lamplight.

"I can't stay here," I said.

"We could sit outside," Mother suggested.

I took her arm in mine, and we returned to the platform. It was too dark for a view of the landscape. And it was surprisingly chilly. I had imagined Texas to be hot all the time, even at night.

"I hate five a.m. in El Paso," I said mutinously.

We watched the train depart, our hearts longing for our lost berths. Then I spied a man with a lantern who had not departed with it. Apparently this was the station master. I asked him if it was true that there were no hotels open at this hour.

"Too true, I'm sorry to say." Seeing my wilting expression and my mother's age, he took pity on us. "But if you ladies would be satisfied with a second-class house, I can take you to my home. My wife sometimes takes in lodgers from the railway."

I laughed, and Mother had to quickly explain. "As do we, though ours are railway workers." Sleepily, we told him of Tom and Tony as he conducted us to his home.

How foolish we must have seemed, walking off into the night with a man whose name we did not know, to an address we did not know, for what kind of accommodations we did not know. Fortunately, it was only a short walk through the sandy streets. The station manager had spoken the truth, and there was one room unoccupied. He introduced us to his wife, we paid our fee, and then we closed the door on the world. With real gratitude I collapsed onto the bed. I thought I might have felt Mother slipping off my unbuttoned boots, but in truth I was already asleep.

EIGHTEEN

NAKED INTEREST

APPARENTLY, IT HAD BEEN THE TRAIN bed that kept me from sleeping. Or perhaps I was tired enough that it didn't matter where I laid my head. All I knew was that I slept well past sunrise, and it was the warm sun shining across my shuttered eyelids that finally made me groan and roll over.

"Pinky? Are you awake? Do you feel rested enough?"

Face buried in the crook of my arm, I said, "What are you doing up already?"

"I've been up this hour. You slept so well, I didn't want to bother you. But it seems a shame to sleep through our only day in El Paso."

I rolled over again and squinted. Mother was seated beside the open window, and sweet scents I couldn't name came in with the air that ruffled the curtains.

Instantly, the exhaustion of our midnight arrival vanished like a bad dream. Full of energy, I leapt up and set myself to dressing, brushing out my hair and actually buttoning up my boots.

Our host, home from his night shift, was eating his supper, which coincided with our breakfast. From him we learned that the first train we could get for Mexico would be at six o'clock that evening. With nothing else to do, we decided to explore El Paso.

"What does El Paso mean?" asked Mother as we set out.

"It's Spanish for 'the pass,'" I told her.

She made a face. "Not really!"

"Really. Tom told me."

She shook her head. "It's like the broken Spanish a child pretends to speak. El traino, el tracko."

Grinning, I joined in. "El streeto. Phew! El heato."

It was indeed already warming up as we entered the hustle and bustle of a growing junction town. Several railways were centered there, the better to reach all points on the compass. We were fortunate to not require a hotel, as they were thronged with some people stopping over for work and others staying the whole of the winter.

It turned out that El Paso was actually two cities: one American, one Mexican. The Mexican town was called El Paso del Norte, meaning "the pass of the north." The two were separated by the Rio Grande.

"Just like Pittsburgh and Allegheny," observed Mother in wonder.

We hailed a hack and took a ride around the city, with our driver acting as an impromptu guide. His name was Edward Olivar, and while his English was tinged with Spanish, I had no trouble at all understanding him as he pointed out the sights.

Some houses were made of brick, built in the modern style, but there were occasional adobe huts at either end of town. I asked if they were comfortable, and he assured me they were. "I own one myself."

"Isn't there any grass?" I asked, looking at the vast stretches of dirt and dust.

"In private gardens, señorita." It was my first time being offered that title, and I felt absurdly cosmopolitan.

"What about across the river? Can we go?"

"Certainly, señorita." Señor Olivar gently turned his horse and took us across the bridge into El Paso del Norte.

The difference was startling. The American town was a bustle of invention and progress. El Paso del Norte felt as though it were back in the Middle Ages. In some ways, it was more pleasant on the eyes. It had grass and shady trees, and a queer stone church older than the town itself.

As we rode, Señor Olivar extolled the virtues of the grapes grown on the Mexican side of the Rio Grande, though he noted that the marvelous wine made from those grapes had to be smuggled across to the other side. "And the tobacco! Do you smoke?"

"No," we said in unison.

"Good. It is a filthy habit. But many Americans fill their pockets with tobacco from this side to carry back with them."

"Is there a lot of smuggling?" I asked.

"To be sure! And both ways. A bar of soap costs in Mexico three times what it does in El Paso."

"Don't the customs officials object?"

Señor Olivar shrugged. "Why should they? A bottle here, a nice perfume for his wife there, and he does not object. Less expensive than paying the fee."

Mother pointed. "I should like to visit that church." It was clearly the most respectable structure in the city, big and clean and dark.

Señor Olivar clicked his tongue. "I would not advise this. The padre does not like americanos."

I frowned. "Whyever not?"

"He preaches that the old ways are being left behind. That schools for everyone give the people ideas, keep them from enjoying life the way our grandfathers did."

"Of course he doesn't like schools." I suddenly found my inner Bessie Bramble. "Education is evil because the Bible says Eve plucked the fruit of the Tree of Knowledge of Good and Evil. Women are evil, and knowledge is dangerous. The only truth in the story is that the apple stuck halfway down Adam's throat, proving that you cannot educate a man!"

"Perhaps we should avoid the church," said Mother.

"Perhaps so," agreed Señor Olivar, wide-eyed.

We learned a great deal during our ride. Señor Olivar's sister's husband was in the prison, a long, single-story adobe monstrosity. It was a prison without cells, we learned, where the prisoners and the guards all mingled together to while away the progression of the sundial. It all seemed quite civilized, until we learned that the jailers were not at all particular about ensuring that the prisoners were fed. "There is not enough food for a sick *gato*. It is worse for the Americano prisoners, I am sad to say."

"There are American prisoners?"

"Of course. So close to the border, we get many men wanting to steal from the unfortunate Mexicanos and then flee across the river. Sometimes they are caught and jailed, and, if they are too uproarious, they are lined up and shot." In case his meaning was unclear, he mimed with his finger. "Bang, bang, bang."

"Don't the guards get in trouble?"

"For shooting escaping prisoners? Why?" Señor Olivar winked at us. "Do you plan to remain until Sunday?"

My horrified mother said, "Alas, no."

"We catch a train tonight," I added.

Señor Olivar sighed. "A pity. Though a cockfight is not fitting for a lady, the bullfight this Sunday will be uproarious."

"Best hope the bull isn't shot," I said.

"Shot? No-no. The bull is stabbed."

"Or stabs," I added hopefully.

"No chance of that! The horns are sawn off."

"So the wretched bull has no chance of defending himself?" I felt even more outrage than I had for the shooting of the prisoners.

Señor Olivar shrugged. "He is a powerful brute, and it takes art to end his days."

"I'd hardly call it art," I said.

"Shouldn't you be writing this down?" asked Mother.

She was correct, of course. I tamped down my outrage and began making notes of everything Señor Olivar shared with us as we continued through El Paso del Norte. As opposed to the bustle on the other side of the river, here men were idle—having apparently been instructed by their priest to be so—smoking their cigarillos and lounging and wondering why Americans were incapable of enjoying life. Smallpox was rampant in the streets because vaccination, like education, was deemed irreligious.

I could hardly believe that only a river separated this place from America. It was quite a shocking first exposure to Mexican life, and I hoped it was not representative of the whole.

I could soon stand no more of Señor Olivar's "hilarious" anecdotes, and I brought our ride to an end. It cost twice what such an outing would have run us in Pittsburgh, but then I was beginning to notice the inflated cost of nearly everything around me. *Just the kind of information that's of practical value to my readers!*

We had a choice for our return to El Paso. We could wait for a ferry, but that would cost five cents between us, so we chose the streetcar instead, which was a penny less. The driver informed me that this was the only international streetcar line in the world. I jotted that down at once.

Once on the American side for the last time in the foreseeable future, we strolled the avenues of El Paso without a care. People on the street seemed very friendly. By chance, we struck up conversation with a woman named Mary, who was in El Paso on her doctor's orders. She offered to show us a place where we could get some good food. "Thank heavens," I said. "I want a full stomach before we leave tonight."

"You're taking a train this evening?"

"Yes," I said. "To Mexico City."

She took my arm. "Then take my advice and buy a basket of food to bring with you. There are no dining cars on the trip south, and the food once you cross the border. . ." She shuddered.

She also suggested that we exchange our money in El Paso, and so we did, getting a premium of twelve cents on every dollar. We picked up our baskets as advised, and, as shades of night enveloped us, Mother and I collected our luggage and boarded our train.

It was nearly empty, with only two men heading south. One was a handsome Mexican, presumably returning home. The other was a young American with a waxed moustache. I asked him a few questions, and he seemed cheerfully dishonest as he answered them. His name was Donley, and he claimed to have come down from Chicago. Though he wore a pistol, he insisted he was merely traveling for his health. Perhaps it was true, in its way. Chicago had that kind of reputation.

No sooner had the train started but it stopped again on the far side of the river, where our baggage was thoroughly checked over. That troubled Mother, and I teased her. "Are you smuggling something?"

"It's embarrassing to think of strange men pawing one's garments."

For my part, I thought it was thrilling. But then, men were far more a concept than a reality for me. Unlike Mother, who knew the best and worst of men, and love, and marriage.

We whiled away the meantime at a restaurant. Amusingly enough, our first meal in Mexico was Chinese. I found the clingy rice to be edible, but flavorless.

When we were notified that the train was ready to embark again, it was so dark out that we had to cling to each other to find our footing as we stepped into our car. We retired to our berths and let the train rock us to sleep as we hurtled headlong into Mexico.

"THIRTY MINUTES TO DRESS FOR BREAKFAST!" At the call, I yanked up the window shade and gazed out at the landscape, only to meet a vista devoid of any interesting feature save the odd cactus. "Sunny Mexico, land of the gods," I observed wryly.

"Think how people describe Pittsburgh," replied Mother, pulling our shade shut for modesty's sake.

Our new Pullman porter told me to call him George, and cheerfully refused to offer his real name. That upset me, but not nearly as much as the breakfast we ate when we stopped. There was no restaurant, no hotel, not even a house to offer a meal. In their stead, an old freight car had been converted into a makeshift buffet kitchen. All the food was laid out on a table. In the main it was flat bread, beans, and some kind of charred meat. The coffee was tepid and sludgy.

We quickly escaped back to our train car and the basket we had intended for our lunch. The cold chicken made a tolerable breakfast, and we saved some peach preserves and dried figs for later in the day.

What recovered my mood was the weather. Having escaped January in Pittsburgh, I felt genuinely sorry for those luckless souls we had left behind. The air in Mexico was sultry and free, and Mother and I set up folding chairs on the rear of the observation car to watch the land unfold behind us.

The further south we traveled, the more interesting the land became. The sky seemed further away, less oppressive than at home, and even when there were only cacti in view, at least they were tall, with fascinating blossoms.

Apparently the natives found the sky to be warm and inviting as well, because they chose to bare themselves beneath it. I was unaccustomed to the sight of naked men, so at first I averted my eyes. But after the tenth or eleventh man, I adjusted to their habitual nudity and gazed freely.

They stared at us in equal fascination, and Mother surprised me by seeming more concerned for their comfort than our modesty. "Why should they care for our sensibilities? They are as God made them. I only hope they are warm enough at night."

We had to abandon the observation deck whenever we pulled into a station, for the natives would swarm up to the train to beg or try to sell us flowers, eggs, goat milk, or strange purple tubers. Once, while Mother was purchasing flowers through a window, I bought one of the tubers. Turning it over in my hands, I found it to be the oddest thing, and through the window I asked a half-naked man what it was called. He did not understand me, but kissed the coin I had given him and mimed eating the tuber.

"It is called *tuna*," said an accented voice at my shoulder. "Not to be confused with the fish. It is a fruit from the prickly pear."

It was the handsome Mexican passenger. He introduced himself as José Antonio Garcia. I gave him my name—my real name—and then asked, "Prickly pear?"

"Yes. You might see one in a greenhouse in London or New York. Here, they grow to twenty feet, and they grow bristles to protect their delicious fruit. Hence their name. That kind man has already shelled it for you, so there is no fear of thorns. May I?" Taking the fruit from my hands, he produced a knife and split it into quarters for Mother and me to eat.

It was refreshingly juicy, and I said so. "Then you might enjoy the beer they make from it. It's called *pulque*." Whipping my notebook out, I asked him to spell it for me. If there was one thing Pittsburgh readers would want to know about, it was beer.

He described pulque as having the appearance of milk, and told me it had once been considered sacred. Hearing that, I decided to leave it out of my reporting, imagining what would happen if men in Pittsburgh could bring beer to work that looked like milk, and call it holy.

As the train resumed its travel, I waved farewell to the natives. "Do they never wear clothes?"

"As seldom as they can," replied José Antonio, taking a seat across from us. "They cover up in rain, when it comes. If needed, they wear a rug with a hole for their heads that covers their bodies."

"A strange custom," said Mother.

"No stranger than other peoples'," he observed. "For instance, in

London, men and women dress in clothes so restrictive and confining that these natives would think themselves bound."

"London!" I exclaimed. "Is that where you're coming from?"

"Most recently." He then informed us he had been traveling Europe for the last two years, though most of his time had been split between England and Spain.

The charming Señor Garcia became our impromptu guide for the next leg of our journey. The following day, he was in the midst of teaching me a few Spanish phrases when suddenly his gaze became fixed out the window. He pressed himself close to the glass, peering out with a smile of pure bliss. "I have not seen one of those since I left."

Taking positions beside him, Mother and I watched what looked like a wispy tornado moving across the barren land. "It is a sand spout—what you might call a whirlwind."

"It's beautiful," I said.

"Enjoy it now," he advised, "for soon the spell is broken, and the sand falls to the earth again."

"To be trod underfoot," I observed.

More Mexicans had joined us at the last stop. One of them, seeing our interest, broke into our conversation. "I once was caught in one, señorita. It is frightening. But I learned how to break it apart and save myself. I shot my pistol into it, and it collapsed at once, as if murdered."

Señor Garcia wore a dubious expression but did not contradict the tale.

As promised, the sand spout suddenly vanished as if it had never existed. It struck me as poetic—in one instant, the fierce storm reached a thousand feet high, choking and terrible and beautiful and wild, and in the next instant it vanished, its component parts dispersed, left to be ground underfoot by some lonely mule crossing the plain.

As we settled back into our seats, we were regaled with more tales from the other passenger. One was an amusing anecdote: during the construction of the railroad, wheelbarrows had been imported for the native workers. Not knowing what to do with them, they'd carried the wheelbarrows upon their backs. "Even when shown how to use them, these natives did very little work. They are weak of arm, and of head," he said dismissively.

"Not all of them," observed Señor Garcia.

"No," admitted our neighbor, "but they would hardly be where they are if they understood *trabajo*, no? They cling to their beliefs, and cannot understand what is new. You must not judge all Mexicanos by these simple folk, señorita," he continued, addressing me. "Would you believe that many of their homes are simple holes in the ground! The smoke creeps out from the doorway all day, and at night the family sleeps in the ashes. They do not lie down, but sleep sitting up! These people!" He laughed, shaking his head. "So backwards. At first, the trains were regarded as the Devil, and the passengers his workers. Once, a settlement of natives decided to overpower the Devil. They took one of their most sacred and powerful saints and placed it in the center of the track. On their knees, with great faith, they watched the advance of the train, feeling sure the saint would cause it to stop forever. The engineer—who I guess had little reverence for that particular saint—struck it with full force. That saint's reign ended, let me tell you! Since then, his fellows are allowed to remain in their accustomed nooks in the churches. The natives still have the same faith in their powers, but are not anxious to test them again." He laughed heartily.

I noticed Señor Garcia shake his head. I wanted to ask why, but we were interrupted by the conductor. Begging our pardon, he offered to show us a strange and magnificent sight. Naturally, we were interested, so Mother and I followed him to the rear platform of the observation car.

"First, señoras, please do not credit that tale. It is an old one, often told, and of no more truth than old wives tales." When I thanked him, he smiled and pointed. "Now then, here is the strangest mountain you will ever behold."

It was certainly startling. Rising from the barren plains like a nose on one's face, the mountain seemed to be made of brown earth, but it showed not the least sign of vegetation. It looked to be as tall as the Brooklyn Bridge—at least, based on the pictures I had seen—and it was about the same length, in an oblong shape. It was perfectly straight across the top, as if some giant had cut it with a scythe.

"When this railroad was first being built," said the conductor, "I was with a party of engineers sent to survey the land. To get a good view, we decided to climb that mountain. From here, you cannot see the vegetation, but it is covered with a low, brown shrub. Can you imagine our surprise when we got to the top to find it was a mammoth basin?"

"No!" I exclaimed, peering for a better look.

"Yes! That hill holds in it the most beautiful lake I ever saw."

Having just been advised of the falseness of one story, I was hesitant to accept a tale that seemed even less creditable. "That sounds wonderful."

"Oh-ho! It is not more wonderful than thousands of other places in Mexico. In the state of Chihuahua is a *laguna* with water as clear as crystal. When the Americans who were superintending the work on the railway found it, it had been many days since they had seen any more water than would quench their thirst. Accordingly, they decided to have a nice bath, and some dozen or more doffed their clothing and went in. However, their pleasure was short lived. Their bodies began to burn and smart, and they came out looking like scalding pigs!"

Mother's hand went to her mouth. "What happened?"

The conductor shook his head in sad amusement. "The water is strongly alkaline. The fish in the lake are said to be white, even to their eyes. They are, of course, entirely unfit to eat." He inclined his head. "You do not write that story down?"

I dutifully did, though I was unsure if I would include it in my narrative.

"So you are here to write about Mexico?" He clicked his tongue. "I hope you are better than the others."

"Others?"

"The other reporters. I must say, we do not think much of the people who come here to write us up."

My head snapped up. "Whyever not?"

"Because they never tell the truth. One woman came to make herself famous. I could see she had no interest in Mexico except as a fairyland. She pressed me every day for more and more fantastical tales. One day I told her that, out in the country, the natives roasted whole hogs, heads and all, without cleaning, and so served them on the table. She jotted it down as if it were true!" He laughed.

In a polite tone I recognized as critical, Mother said, "If you tell strangers untruths about your own land, can you complain that those same strangers misrepresent it?"

Flushing, the conductor muttered that he had not thought of it in that light before, and then said he had to return to his duties.

As Mother and I settled into our camp chairs, I said, "That's why a good reporter never believes what she is told, but what she sees. What she experiences."

"So those tales are useless?"

"Unless we want to leap from the train and go hiking up that mountain, or find the lagoon that burns. I can certainly include them, but with the disclaimer that I did not see them."

ABOUT AN HOUR LATER, I spied something along the road behind us, a cloud of dust more horizontal than vertical, and certainly different from the sand spout we had seen that morning. Opening the door to the car, I begged Señor Garcia to come join us. "Is that another whirlwind? A dust storm?"

Peering to where I was pointing, his face grew grave. "Those are horses. They come for the train."

"Bandits!" I exclaimed, craning my neck. Mother began gathering up her knitting.

"Not illegal ones," our new friend corrected us gently. "They are from the government. To escort the train into the larger stations, and quell any trouble."

"What kind of trouble?" I asked.

Glancing at his fellow Mexicans on the other side of the door, he kept his answer vague. "There are many troubles in Mexico. It is the toss of a coin if those men are more help or harm."

That was both distressing and very interesting.

At the next station, to our delight, we discovered a trove of tomatoes and strawberries for sale—though we were fooled by the first vendor, who had placed stones at the bottom of our little strawberry basket to add weight. A lesson well learned.

The native vendors wore loose white pantaloons made of muslin. With serapes around their shoulders, sombreros on their heads, and leather sandals on their feet, the men looked positively well-heeled. The women, too, were less as God had made them, with skirts of raw cloth tied about their waists and the customary rebozos wrapped around their heads. So many of them carried babies that they seemed to be standard issue.

The armed men did not approach the train, but they watched us as we came into the station and rode after us until we were well away from it. It was certainly the most enticing part of our adventure so far. For while there would ever be interesting tidbits of cultural differences and peculiarities of the terrain to report on, I sensed a more compelling story lay below the surface. I sensed danger.

It would be months before I found out how real that danger was.

NINETEEN

WELCOME TO MEXICO

ON SATURDAY MORNING, THE FOURTH day after we'd left America, Mother and I disembarked at the call of "Mexico City!" Only there was no city—just a train station and a few desultory buildings.

We looked about in confusion until Señor Garcia took pity on us and explained that there was only one rail track laid into the area and we would have to use other means to reach the city proper. "You see the line of carriages? They are all licensed by the government. The color of the flag denotes the quality. White, first class. Blue, second. Red, third. They are priced accordingly. We are fortunate to arrive in the daytime," he added.

"Why?"

He grinned. "Because at night they remove their flags and double their prices."

"It is a comfort to think cabbies are the same the world over," Mother murmured.

Señor Garcia offered to share a carriage with us. I was initially afraid that with our luggage there might not be room, but I had not reckoned with the practiced skill of the cabbie, who cleverly strapped our bags across the roof. After many protests, I convinced Señor Garcia to split the fare with us, assuring him that the money came from my newspaper.

The ride took almost an hour, during which time he gave us advice about the city. "Choose landmarks to guide you. Do not rely on streets' names. Every block has a new title, and every square a different name. It is not so bad as Venice, where they do not even bother to label their streets. But there, at least, you may hope to find your way. Alas, here it is a forlorn hope. Do you have a hotel?"

"Yes, the Hotel Yturbide." Seeing his smile, I said, "What does that mean?"

"It is the name of our emperor, Agustín de Iturbide, who won independence for Mexico."

"Your George Washington!" I exclaimed.

"If President Washington had declared himself emperor, fought a war against Alexander Hamilton, resigned in disgrace, had his presidency nullified, and ended in exile in England."

I nodded. "So, less George Washington, more Napoleon. I'm surprised there's a hotel named for him, then."

"It is the palace where he lived when in command."

"Our hotel is the royal palace!"

Again, the indulgent smile. "Yes. It is at least a hundred years old. I believe it is designed after a famous palace in Spain. Do you happen to know which floor your room is on?"

I shook my head. "Why?"

"The lowest floor will be the cheapest. On the higher floors, one may escape any possible dampness, and there is more sunlight."

"And a view," I said hopefully.

"And certainly a view," agreed Señor Garcia.

"Dampness?" asked Mother.

"Mexico City is built in a basin of sorts. Once it was a lake called Texcoco. They drained it two hundred years ago, but it is sometimes still subject to flooding."

"Oh, dear," said Mother, looking at the passing streets for signs of rushing water.

Staring out the other window of our carriage, I saw what our companion meant about street names. After traversing the grand Plazuela de Santiago, we turned left on the Calle 15 de Mayo de 67, which became the Calle 21 de Junio de 67 before becoming the Calle de Miguel López. All of these were the same road. After we passed the Plazuela de las Guerras, the road transformed into the Calzada de Santa Maria. Asking the difference, I learned that *calzada* meant *carriageway*, as opposed to a *calle*, a simple *street*.

We passed a theatre with a great deal of bustle before it. I did not see the name of the play, but the painted figure of Christ's crucifixion on the sign remains one of my first impressions of the city.

The street changed names three more times before we turned right onto Calle de San Francisco and stopped at our destination. As our baggage was freed, Señor Garcia pointed back the way we had come. "This is an excellent location from which to explore the city. Back that way is the Alameda, a large park that is both beautiful and peaceful. If you continue east along this street you will find the *catedral*." He slipped into proper Spanish on this final word, and I could sense his delight at being home again after so long abroad.

He offered his address, and asked if Mother and I would like to take the air with him once he had visited his family. I said that would be very agreeable, and we chose the next day to meet, allowing us all to acclimate to our new surroundings.

With our bags on the bricks, the driver climbed aboard his rig and lifted the reins. I called out to pay and found the driver unwilling to take my coin—Señor Garcia had already assured him of the fare. Frustrated by this unwelcome gallantry, especially after we had made a bargain, I shouted after the carriage as it bumped off down the street toward its next destination. "I insist on paying you when we meet tomorrow!" A pretty picture I must have made: the tiny American girl shouting at a retreating carriage. Passersby might have thought we'd been robbed if Mother hadn't been laughing.

"Shall we?" she asked at last.

Hotel Yturbide had certainly been a palace once upon a time. Its façade had faux fortified towers at either end. However, their martial effect was quite undone by the carved female figures holding up the bulbous pediments along the top.

At the front, set between two massive pillars, a thirty-foot rectangular archway was topped with an impressive carving that included two bare-chested men with muskets, surrounded by overly ornate flowers and tasteful geometric shapes. Both men were looking up at a lone face emerging from the carved botanical madness, but for the life of me, I couldn't figure out what the face was meant to represent. Amidst all the carved chaos I spied a random mermaid, which made me laugh.

The hotel itself was based on a style we would come to recognize as common in Mexico. The archway led to a wide, open-air courtyard ringed by hotel rooms on each floor. We were greeted by a clerk who spoke enough English to check us in. He seemed very friendly. Perhaps his affable manner was meant to offset the coming disaster.

Things seemed well enough at first. Our room was on the third floor, far from the feared dampness, if not at the pinnacle of comfort. Upon entering, however, I noticed that the red bricks of the floor were old, worn, and somewhat uneven. The room itself was quite large but utterly airless. The only ventilation to be had was achieved by opening the thin pair of glass doors that lead out to our small external balcony, which faced the building next door, almost close enough to touch. There were only five items of furniture: a table, a washstand, a wardrobe, and two small iron cots set in either corner.

I waited until the door closed behind the porter before giving vent to my feelings. "Well, this is miserable."

"Pinky," said Mother reprovingly.

"It's like a cell."

She ran a finger along the wall. Dust came away on her glove. "It *is* less than opulent."

"I wonder if that's where the word comes from. *Misery. Miser.* Does cheapness bring unhappiness?"

"Do not mistake comfort for happiness," said Mother, setting about unpacking. "If you became an heiress tomorrow, would you be happier? Or simply more comfortable?"

"I imagine I should not be more unhappy," I replied tartly.

Ignoring me, Mother began airing out our clothes and hanging them up in the wardrobe to uncrease. I stepped out onto the balcony, hoping at least for a view to ameliorate our squalid accommodations. *Alas, frustrated here, too!* I could just make out a ridge of mountains off to my right, but only if I leaned out close to the building butted up against us. Hardly poetic.

From that moment, things went from miserable to outright comedic. We could not make ourselves understood at dinner, the food was wretched, and after a single night in those beds we were neither rested nor refreshed.

"We must change rooms," I said.

Down at the desk, the hotel manager was very sorrowful. "My house is yours. You have but to command me." Yet he did not lead us to a house, but rather to another room, one of no better quality. This was my first encounter with the habitual Mexican phrase "It is yours"—a charming pleasantry with no actual meaning.

"We must change hotels," I said.

Mother nodded. "We will ask Señor Garcia."

So, rather than seeing the sights, we spent our first full day in Mexico City finding new accommodations. Fortunately, Señor Garcia was able to ask around, and by our second evening we had transferred to a private home in the same neighborhood. "Hotels are no way to learn Mexican life, in any case," he advised.

I noticed Señor Garcia was showing me particular attention. The last thing on my mind was some wild Mexican romance, so while I thanked him with real gratitude, I declined his offer of another meeting the next day. "I have to go meet my fellow newspapermen."

This had the benefit of being true. I was in Mexico as a reporter, and needed to turn in stories for Madden to keep footing the bill. If it helped me escape potential romance, all the better. The last thing I wanted was to be the typical maiden who fell for a handsome stranger while traveling abroad. I had more important things to do.

THERE WAS NO ACTUAL OFFICE for American reporters. Instead, I was reliably informed, they congregated in a French café on the west side of our park, Plazuela de las Guerras. It was called Café Mijo, named for the proprietor's wife. A cosmopolitan place, it was fairly expensive—one look at the price of a cup of coffee made me wonder what kind of expense accounts these reporters were on. Back in Pittsburgh, the roaches from the *Dispatch* ate and drank as cheaply as possible without contracting food poisoning.

But Café Mijo (with the *j* pronounced, because it was French) happened to house a number of great Mexican and expatriate literary types. As Wilson had once noted, every reporter dreams at heart of becoming the next Mark Twain. Thus, my fellow journalists spent their time slowly sipping their cups while rubbing shoulders with the likes of Manuel Gutiérrez Nájera—a name which meant nothing to me. But everyone else seemed very impressed!

I entered the place without Mother. I doubted any of the fellows had brought their mothers with them, and didn't want to lessen my standing among my peers.

Stepping inside, I was pleased to hear my own language flying about. However, my pleasure immediately dimmed as I noticed two women smoking and writing in notepads. I had thought my notion of being a female reporter in Mexico to have been a wholly original one. I quickly learned there were no fewer than six women there before me, though none so young as I. That made me a kind of pioneer, I supposed.

I spent a good part of the afternoon there, collecting stories and learning the tricks of sending reports home.

"Telegrams are for catastrophic events only," explained Mr. Theodore Gestefeld. He was the editor of the *Two Republics*, an English-language newspaper printed right there in Mexico City. "For the rest, send express letters. Your editor will thank you."

Mr. Gestefeld had been there a good while, having worked for the *Chicago Tribune* before settling into expatriate life and making Mexico his permanent home. To me, he was a gold mine, and not at all stingy with his advice. To hear him, Mexico City was full of promise: a winter resort, a city for men to accumulate fortunes, a paradise for students, a haven for artists, and a rich field for anyone interested in the curious, the beautiful, and the rare.

"You must remember, there were cities here before America was even discovered. Why go to Rome or Cairo for ruins that have been pillaged when you can see ancient temples here that are everything they used to be." He waxed poetic about the neighborhoods and talked lovingly of the literary salons at the nearby Casa de los Azulejos—the House of Tiles.

He invited me to attend one, and I promised I would. "Though I won't understand much."

He frowned. "You don't speak Spanish?"

I shook my head. "No."

"Huh. You said *gracias* just now with such a perfect accent, I simply assumed. . ."

"I'm a good mimic. I have about five words, and *gracias* is three of them."

Gestefeld clicked his tongue. "That's a shame. A real pity."

I felt the urge to make things right, to not be lumped in with the other reporters who fell for stories like the ones the conductor had told. I leaned forward in a manner a little too earnest for a young lady. "Look, Mr. Gestefeld—it's true, I don't speak Spanish. But I want to *experience* Mexico. Not just from our room or at the American watering holes. I want to see the real thing, tell stories that do it justice. I don't want to use the guidebooks and just see the sights. I want to get to know the people. Those are the stories I want to write. If I can't find them, I'll just turn around and go home."

He studied me a long time. "Okey then," he said in his best Chicago way. "Who knows? If you stick around long enough, you may pick up some of the language. But to stay, you have to keep sending in stories that'll make your editor happy. Who's your editor? Madden? Don't know him. But all editors want the same thing, really: stories that keep readers buying papers. What have you written so far?"

I told him about my articles on the journey. "Fine, fine," he said. "But now you'll need a hook. Something tragic, yes? Something to make your readers bawl their eyes out and shake their heads." He was smiling as he said it, but the smile faded. "Here it is. Saddest thing I ever saw. When I was fresh out of Chicago, looking for stories, I saw a policeman here talking to a boy. A crowd of locals had gathered around them. Full of journalistic instinct, I went up to investigate. The boy, I found, belonged to one of the many families who do odd jobs for a little food, and sleep in some dark corner at night. Strung to the boy's back was a dying baby." I gasped, and he nodded. "Right? Its little eyes were half closed. It was nearly dead. The crowd was watching in terrible fascination as the little guy gasped out his last. The boy had no home to go to, and no idea where to find his parents at that hour. So there he stood while the babe died in his serape."

Stricken, I said, "That's terrible! At least in the States they would have a home to go to."

Gestefeld arched an eyebrow at me. "You think that doesn't happen at home? Of course it does. But back home, it isn't news. Just like reporting it here wouldn't be news. Kids die every goddamn day—pardon me."

I waved away his casual cursing. "Then why should I put it in a story of mine?"

"Dios mío!" he cried, sounding perfectly Mexican. "Because when you tell the tale, it's from a colorful locale. They will think the same as you, and say, 'This could never happen here,' which will make them feel good about themselves and their country. And *that* will keep them reading. *Qué lástima.* That means 'what a pity,'" he added.

He went on to give me advice on where to eat, what foods to avoid, where to accept water and where to only take it after boiling. "When in doubt, order coffee. It is cheaper and better than at home, and all the ill effects will have been boiled away."

He was so helpful that, in the end, I took him outside and introduced him to Mother, who was whiling away her time looking at the shops. He charmed her and invited us for dinner later in the week.

I went to bed that night feeling fairly satisfied. With a room in a private home, a local acquaintance who spoke English, and the goodwill of a local American newspaper editor, Nellie Bly was primed to begin exploring Mexico!

TWENTY

LOS SERENOS

SEÑOR GARCIA'S ADVICE TO NAVIGATE by landmarks was entirely sound. We started referring to "the house with the falling plaster" or "the church with the over-tall steeple." The only street in the whole city that made sense to me was the main thoroughfare, called San Francisco—like the city. The first block was designated First San Francisco, the next was Second San Francisco, and so on. When lost, we learned to ask policemen the way to San Francisco to regain our bearings.

There were police on almost every corner, certainly more than at home. They wore blue suits with nickel buttons and were topped by white caps with numbers on them. At dusk, they donned overcoats and hoods, which to even my unromantic eye made them look just like the pictures of veiled knights. I imagined that in the olden days they would have carried a sword in place of a club.

At night they disappeared into doorways to sleep, leaving red lanterns in the street to mark their posts. Mother remarked, "It's good to know police, like cabbies, are the same in every country."

The police had one unfortunate habit that affected us directly. Our window was just above one policeman's post, and every hour he blew his very loud whistle. When I asked Gestefeld about this, he informed me that in small towns, instead of whistling, they called out the time of night. "One o'clock! *Tiempo sereno!* All is serene at this time."

I put a hand to my mouth and imitated yelling. "Three o'clock and all's well!"

"Exactly. The local kids call them Los Serenos. The Serene Ones."

"They seem lighter-skinned than most," Mother observed.

"How observant, Mrs. Cochrane. Yes, the government does not permit the police to employ natives." He noted our surprise. "Oh, that's hardly the only thing the natives are barred from. Most government positions are closed to them, along with anything that smacks of authority. Some reformers tried passing a law to fund literacy for them, but it went down like a skewered bull. Speaking of which, have you been to a bullfight yet?"

"I have not," I said, "and would not care to."

He shook his head. "I understand your hesitation. But if you want to truly understand the Mexican character, you must attend the opera and at least one bullfight." With very little grace, I accepted his invitation to take us the following week.

My agreement stemmed from gratitude. Gestefeld had inadvertently handed me a topic worthy of Nellie Bly: the mistreatment of the natives. It had the oppression angle, as well as the benefit of being so overlooked. I salved the pangs I felt for my opportunism with the thought that no one else was telling their story. *And it's a story that deserves to be told!*

I dove in right away, posing questions of anyone who spoke enough English to answer. But mostly, I observed. I watched the native women with baskets on their heads, the men bearing bundles on their backs: baskets of laundry, eggs, charcoal, or roots, bundles of fruit or game, and cages of live fowl. Men arrived from the mountains every day, coming in droves of twenty-five to fifty, bearing burdens that averaged three hundred pounds. Mules were only used for profitable enterprises, like meat or the alcoholic pulque, which arrived in swollen pig skins.

Once, it was not a bundle on a native man's head, but a tiny coffin. As he passed, rich and poor alike stopped to doff their hats. I was touched. Mother dabbed her eyes.

Death was surprisingly common, and treated with a great deal of religiosity. One day, Mother and I spied a crowd gathered around something on the sidewalk by a construction site for a new hotel. Drawing near, we saw a body—a native laborer had fallen to his death. He was covered in a white sheet that was too short for him. His sandals stuck out comically, and I had to pinch my arm to remind myself that a man had died. All around us were mutters of "The Virgin rest his soul" and "Virgin Mother grant him grace." Then a policeman arrived to command the body be taken away. Some workers rolled him in the sheet and put him in a wheelbarrow.

"Let's follow," I said.

"Don't be ghoulish," snapped Mother.

"I'm going."

Mother sighed, and together we followed the makeshift hearse to a backstreet yard where coffins were constructed. In fact, every establishment on the block made coffins, causing Mother and I to dub it Coffin Street.

The joiner in charge of the yard ignored the dead man, literally leaping over him to doff his hat to us. He then dragged us through his house to view his coffins and described in a torrent of Spanish how fine they were, all while smoothing their linings and wiping their handles with a cloth from his pocket.

I pointed to a coffin. "*Nombre?* What is it called? *Qué es?*"

"*Qué. . . Ah! Es un ataúd.*"

In halting Spanish, I said, *"Tu ataúdo es muy bonito."*

Delighted, he bowed and began repeating a phrase we had heard often. *"Sí, señorita! Es tuyo."*—"It is yours."

It took another ten minutes to convince him we were not in need of a coffin. Finally, Mother dragged me out by the arm, laughing softly. "Serves you right."

"Well, honestly!" I cried, less amused than she. "What would I do with a coffin? Perhaps he looked at me and decided I am not long for this world."

Mother scanned me critically. "You *have* lost weight."

"So have you," I retorted.

"It's the excitement," she protested.

"It's the food," I growled, in counterpoint to my ever-aching stomach. I felt like I was starving.

Yet food was always available. Almost everywhere we went, we saw women making tortillas for sale, spitting in their hands as they worked cornmeal into batter, and cooking on greasy pans blackened by charcoal.

Watching one such operation, Mother declared, "I will never touch a tortilla again so long as I live."

Many days, our wanderings were dictated entirely by our stomachs. Finding a good restaurant became our chief goal. Our palates had not adjusted to the flavorless concoctions we were offered, nor had they come around to the peppers that made our eyes stream just by smelling them. Too little flavor, or too much: that, to us, was Mexico.

Even the bread was troublesome, because they let it harden to the point of cracking one's teeth, and there was an utter lack of butter and a complete absence of jams.

I had thought we were safe with simple meat dishes, but we had the unfortunate experience of learning where our meat came from. Twice a day we'd see a plodding old mule or a horse that had reached its second childhood. Strapped to its back would be a long iron rod with multiple hooks, from which dangled meat that was exposed to all the mud and dirt of the streets, as well as the hair of the animal. Each beast was accompanied by two basket-bearing men with their trouser legs rolled to their knees to keep from being stained by the dripping blood. In their baskets they bore the parts of the dead animals that had fallen by the wayside on their dusty trek.

There were only two street vendors I was willing to patronize: the fruit seller and the aguador, or water carrier. The aguadors were ubiquitous, with their water jars suspended from their heads. Unfortunately, I sometimes saw them refill their jars from the public fountains—fountains that people were also bathing in.

At meals, I was reduced to fresh fruit, rice, fried pumpkin, and boiled cheese. Mother was more of a soldier than I, forcing down food I declared inedible, like the hideous mixture called chili.

Yet, being both proud and frugal, I insisted we avoid the American fare in the expensive hotels. Occasionally we would venture into a French restaurant, or an Italian one. I found myself amazed by the cosmopolitan aspirations of Mexico City.

"It is the president," explained Señor Garcia one afternoon in the park. "He envisions this as a new Paris, which is part of the reason my return has been so successful. After living in Europe so long, I have insights to share with the city council. They hope I can help them lure architects and chefs from Paris and Rome."

"Do you think you'll succeed?" I asked.

He shrugged. "I love Mexico. But there is only one Paris."

"Perhaps I can travel there next," I said lightly.

Señor Garcia took my hand. "I hope you have no desire to escape Mexico. Or Mexicans."

With Mother helpfully watching, I was able to slip my hand out of his and pat his shoulder. "Of course not! I've hardly begun. By the time I'm through, Mexico will want to throw me out."

I SOON FINISHED MY FIRST ARTICLE about Mexico City. I began by framing the city in a warm light, talking about how the best sights in Mexico aren't the cathedrals or fountains, but the people. Then I got down to business and described the native people:

Their lives are as dark as their skins and hair, and are invaded by no hope that through effort their lives may amount to something.

Nine women out of ten in Mexico have babies. When at a very tender age, so young as five days, the babies are completely hidden in the folds of the *rebozo* and strung to the mother's back, in close proximity to the mammoth baskets of vegetables on her head and suspended on either side of the human freight. When the babies get older their heads and feet appear, and soon they give their place to another or share their quarters, as it is no unusual sight to see a woman carry three babies at one time in her *rebozo*. They are always good. Their little coal-black eyes gaze out on what is to be their world, in solemn wonder. No baby smiles or babyish tears are ever seen on their faces. At the earliest date they are old, and appear to view life just as it is to them in all its blackness.

They know no home, they have no school, and before they are able to talk they are taught to carry bundles on their heads or backs, or pack a younger member of the family while the mother carries merchandise, by which she gains a living. Their living is scarcely worth such a title. They merely exist. Thousands of them are born and raised on the streets. They have no home and were never in a bed. Going along the streets of the city late at night, you will find dark groups huddled in the shadows, which, on investigation, will turn out to be whole families gone to bed. They never lie down, but sit with their heads on their knees, and so pass the night.

When they get hungry they seek the warm side of the street and there, hunkering down, devour what they scraped up during the day, consisting of refused meats and offal boiled over a handful of charcoal. A fresh tortilla is the sweetest of sweetbreads. The men appear very kind and are frequently to be seen with the little ones tied up in their *sarape*.

Groups of these at dinner would furnish rare studies for Rodgers. Several men and women will be walking along, when suddenly they will sit down in some sunny spot on the street. The women will bring fish or a lot of stuff out of a basket or poke, which is to constitute their coming meal. Meanwhile the men, who also sit flat on the street, will be looking on and accepting their portion like hungry, but well-bred, dogs.

This type of life, be it understood, is the lowest in Mexico, and connects in no way with the upper classes. The Mexicans are certainly misrepresented, most wrongfully so. They are not lazy, but just the opposite. From early dawn until late at night they can be seen filling their different occupations. The women sell papers and lottery tickets.

"See here, child," said a gray-haired lottery woman in Spanish. "Buy a ticket. A sure chance to get $10,000 for twenty-five cents." Being told that we had no faith in lotteries, she replied: "Buy one; the Blessed Virgin will bring you the money."

The laundry women, who, by the way, wash clothes whiter and iron them smoother even than the Chinese, carry the clothes home unwrapped. That is, they carry their hands high above their head, from which stream white skirts, laces, etc., furnishing a most novel and interesting sight.

Here I inserted Gestefeld's story of the dead child before going on to describe the natural beauty of the native women, and how the men wore their hair long. Bursting with revelations, I related many things I'd observed and more I'd gleaned through sources I trusted—Gestefeld and Señor Garcia, mostly. Then I closed up the matter of the natives:

As a people they do not seem malicious, quarrelsome, unkind or evil-disposed. Drunkenness does not seem to be frequent, and the men, in their uncouth way, are more thoughtful of the women than many who belong to a higher class. The women, like other women, sometimes cry, doubtless for very good cause, and then the men stop to console them, patting them on the head, smoothing back their hair, gently wrapping them tighter in their *rebozo*. Late one night, when the weather was so cold, a young fellow sat on the curbstone and kept his arm around a pretty young girl. He had taken off his ragged *sarape* and folded it around her shoulders, and as the tears ran down her face and she complained of the cold, he tried to comfort her, and that without a complaint of his own condition, being clad only in muslin trousers, which hung in shreds from his body.

Thus we leave the largest part of the population of Mexico. Their condition is most touching. Homeless, poor, uncared for, untaught, they live and they die. . . Their lives are hopeless, and they know it. That they are capable of learning is proven by their work, and by their intelligence in other matters. They have a desire to gain book knowledge, or at least so says a servant who was taken from the streets, who now spends every nickel and every leisure moment in trying to learn wisdom from books.

That servant belonged to Gestefeld. I met him one day when he came running up to Café Mijo to deliver a message. Gestefeld read it and smiled at me. "There is to be a party tonight. Dancing and singing. Would you care to go? And your delightful mother, of course. Your chance to see Mexican social life in action."

I had little interest in Mexican social life, certain that it was exactly the kind of thing the other lady reporters would be covering. But I could hardly refuse. *Besides, I might meet more English speakers with whom I can strike up friendships.* So Mother and I put on our best apparel and walked to the House of Tiles for a soiree.

It was lively and charming. The relationship between music and dance seemed inverse to their counterparts in America. The music often stuttered and hopped from note to note, whereas American music of the day was fluid. Yet the dancing was smooth and liquid, quite different from the jump steps and heel-toeing in the dance halls at home.

For songs that were sung, I made it a game to listen for key words I recognized—*agua, amor, mujer, hombre, caballo*—and then make up a story to go along. That was the night I learned that all Mexican music requires the word *corazón*—the heart—to feature in every song. Either a villain was stabbing the singer through the heart, or else the hero was leaving his heart behind to make a better life for his family. Always, always, the heart.

One similarity to home was the love of the waltz. In America that poet of the piano, Chopin, was still all the rage, whereas in Mexico they seemed to have blended the European waltz with traditional street music in a fascinating way. As it filled my ears, I found myself swaying along with it.

I was still swaying when Gestefeld arrived to introduce an elegant American lady. "May I have the honor of presenting Mrs. Charter. She is here on missionary work. Mrs. Charter, this is Miss Cochrane and her mother, newly arrived in Mexico. Miss Cochrane is a reporter for a major newspaper in Pennsylvania."

"How daring!" The missionary's eyes were slightly derisive. "And how are you finding Mexico so far?"

I answered with a torrent of observations, all of which sounded ridiculous when spoken aloud. I ended by adding, "I hope Mr. Gestefeld will show us sights less common to tourists."

Gestefeld rescued me. "I am thinking of taking them riding to see Chapultepec."

Mrs. Charter applauded that idea. "Marvelous. Of course they must ride, and take joy in the park, see all the fine people."

"I wish we could," I said, panicking a little. "But we have nothing appropriate to wear for horseback. It's not something that comes up much in Pittsburgh."

"Oh, you mustn't let that prevent you! No, you will wear my own riding habit. The coat might be a trifle loose, but your feet are small, like mine. And I am certain I can find gear for your fine mother. Send to my hotel, and I will lend you them gladly."

We then discussed her missionary work, which seemed largely to consist of her reading passages from the Bible, in English, to natives she cornered in the marketplace. She only did it two days a week, she informed me, as she found it exhausting. But she was certain she could see the light of Christ kindling in the "pathetic peasants' eyes," especially when she offered them a meal along with a Bible verse. "They have only the example of Rome, and of course, that is no way to find Christ." I smiled, then turned away, pretending interest in the dancing.

Mother was critical. "If she was offering them food and preaching Islam, I wonder if she wouldn't have seen the light of Mohammad in their eyes." I had been thinking the same. But it was hardly our place to criticize charity, however it was given.

We met another half-dozen people, passing polite comments as the music swelled around us. In a strange way, I was a novelty: the tiny American girl with the eager eyes and the mocking tongue. Suitors were persistent, and twice I accepted offers to dance. Mother, too, was politely courted, but she declined all offers, a wistful smile on her face.

"We used to have parties," she told me. With a quick laugh, she waved a hand. "Not like this, of course. Not so many people, and no guitars. But, oh, the parties we had!"

"When?" I asked, falling into a chair, breathless.

"When you were little. You don't remember?"

Sipping champagne, I shook my head. "I'm sorry, I don't."

"Oh, your father loved them. The Judge was a very sociable man. Though I suspect he held parties in order to argue. He would find a man who felt strongly about a topic, a contentious topic—slavery, suffrage, temperance—and then argue the opposite side purely to see if he could win the debate. The Devil's own advocate. It drove me mad. I never knew where he actually stood on any issue." She glanced at the musicians. "Then the Judge would hold out his hands to me and we'd dance until he lost breath."

I listened, enraptured. Mother never spoke of my father. As if the years of hardship following his death made the memories too bitter. "I wish I remembered him."

"You don't? Not at all?"

"Flashes. Like lightning. A present. Pushing me on a swing behind the house. His step on the stair. But not more."

She stroked my cheek. "You were very young."

"What was he like?"

"He was the best man I have ever known," said Mother simply.

After that pleasing pronouncement, a frown crossed my brow. "A shame that cannot be said of his sons."

Mother looked at me in shock. "Elizabeth!"

"I didn't mean my brothers!" I corrected at once, though I made a mental allowance that I *did* mean Albert. "Not my full brothers. I meant Robert and John and George and, and. . ."

"Thomas and William," supplied Mother, as I had forgotten the names of my other two half-brothers, children of father's first marriage. It was excusable, as they'd been fully grown when I was born.

"Yes. Them! To say nothing of Maryann, Isabel, Angeline, and Juliana. Aren't they all peaches?" I'd omitted my youngest half-sister, Mildred. She was nearest me in age, being eleven years my senior. She had never been unkind, as Mother had helped to raise her after her own mother's death.

"They are not bad people, Elizabeth."

Incredulity was printed on my face. "Of course they are! Mother, they threw us from the house! Made us sell it, so they could get their hands on their blood money!"

"It was their inheritance. Look how angry you are at the loss of yours." She sighed. "They saw me as a gold digger."

"And us? Their brothers and sisters? Were we gold diggers as well?"

"Elizabeth. They had lost their father, too."

"Which makes it excusable? Can you imagine if we'd just been allowed to live in the house until we were grown? We would never have had Ford in our lives. . ." Seeing her face redden, my blood froze. "I'm sorry, I didn't—"

"I understand," she said, clipping her words as if with shears. "Allow me to say, Elizabeth, how terribly grateful I am that you allowed me to be your chaperone on this trip. As I am clearly dreadful at protecting you."

I opened my mouth—to protest, or argue, or apologize, I wasn't sure. But she was already on her feet. "I am tired. It's been a long day. Please don't trouble yourself, I can hail a cab."

Quickly, I gathered my things. The delightful evening was spoiled. By me, and my unending parade of grudges. *Always the troublemaker. Or, at least, always making trouble by pointing out uncomfortable truths.*

We offered our thanks to Gestefeld and his wife, who had thankfully been dancing during our spat. Then we headed out into the street. A blue-flag cab was readily available for the short trip to our lodgings, and we paid the extra fee for second-class travel.

Twice on the way I tried to speak, but lost my nerve. It was only as we were getting ready to extinguish the lamp in our room that I found my tongue. "Mother. I'd like to say something. Two things."

She didn't speak. Neither invitation nor refusal.

"I don't require protecting. And I'm glad of your company."

Still she said nothing, but I could sense her relax a little. I hoped that by morning, all would be, if not forgiven, at least more easily ignored.

TWENTY-ONE

DAY OF REST

SUNDAY, FEBRUARY 14 1886

THE NEXT DAY WAS SUNDAY, and Mother and I rose in strained near-silence. Our monosyllabic interplay was a dance I knew well. I could not appear too buoyant, for then she would think I wasn't taking the quarrel seriously. But if I remained utterly silent, she would accuse me of punishing her for having feelings of her own. A treacherous landscape, filled with pitfalls.

Fortunately, we had a diversion at hand. The previous evening, Gestefeld had arranged a full itinerary for us: a ride in the country, an afternoon at the bullfights, and an evening at the theatre. "A typical Mexican Sunday," he had explained.

"What about your duties at the paper?" I'd asked.

"No duty on Sunday."

"No? Whyever not?"

"Because no papers are published on Monday. In Mexico, no one is expected to work on Sunday. It truly is a day of rest. Quite civilized, actually."

We were to begin our day of rest by attending church. "Though not the Cathedral or the Basílica de Guadalupe," he had advised. "See those later, when you can linger and admire the architecture. No, go to San Jerónimo on the far side of the park, or else to La Profesa. You'll have a better experience."

So before dawn, with only a few shared words of necessity, we obeyed the summons of the bells and crossed the park to Templo de San Felipe Neri, commonly known as La Profesa—"the Professed." Once a Jesuit abode, it had housed a famous conspiracy that had preferred a dictator to the rule of the masses, which lead to the rise of our friend Iturbide as president.

As a church it was definitely ornate, but neither fish nor fowl—it seemed to have a foot in both the seventeenth and eighteenth centuries, with its head in the nineteenth. I overheard a pair of tourists discussing its importance as a transition between early and modern baroque design. Knowing nothing of architecture, I took their word for it.

Personally, I was far more interested in the people. As there were no pews, everyone knelt on the floor to pray. There was a complete lack of hierarchy. A wretched beggar could kneel beside a wealthy dandy without drawing comment. Very different from home, where the janitor at our church was expected to remove any indigents from view so they would not spoil the prayers of the prosperous.

As we entered, Mother and I were hissed at. It was startling, and took me several moments to discover why. "Take off your hat," I whispered to Mother, removing my own. The hisses subsided. I noted that ladies wore lace coverings for their heads and faces. They also wore black, quite in opposition to the colorful Sunday costumes of home. I wondered if we had inadvertently stumbled on a funeral. But no, this appeared to be a regular Sunday service.

I didn't understand much of what was preached that morning, no more than I would have understood a Catholic mass at home. But I learned the Latin responses, and murmured them with everyone else. I did not know if it was proper to take Communion, but I was game and would have risen to take the cup and wafer if Mother had not restrained me.

The service ended and, despite the early hour, we exited to find the street absolutely packed with people. The sun was barely up, but the markets were positively thronged. Bands were playing in the parks, and all the shops were open. The flower merchants were mobbed. Wandering hawkers peddled ice cream, pulque, candies, cake, and a dozen other delicacies.

Sunday was a popular moving day, as well. For months to come, Sundays would show us cavalcades of well-dressed people carrying furniture from one abode to another. Even policemen, their arms polished and gleaming, their horses finely brushed, transported their belongings on Sundays.

I had imagined, in such a religious country, that Sunday would be a true day of rest. But it seemed to be the most vivacious day of the week!

Though tempted to shop, we hurried back to our rooms. The next part of Gestefeld's itinerary was a ride to see the castle of Chapultepec.

Having taken Mrs. Charter at her word, we'd sent to her hotel to borrow riding apparel, and expected to find it waiting at our rooms. Upon our arrival, however, the messenger had only an apology. "The señora had no idea you meant to ride on a Sunday. She expresses her surprise that you would require riding gear on a day meant for prayer."

I was quite frustrated, to say the least. While I fumed, Mother was calm. "Beggars and choosers, my dear. The shops are open."

I shook my head to that. I was not about to spend good money on fancy riding apparel for just one day's ride. "We'll go as we are."

Most of the ladies we had observed rode sidesaddle, which called for a habit that was long on one side and bifurcated beneath so as to conceal the leg while ahorse. I did my best to duplicate this effect by draping my one large shawl around my waist and using Mother's red scarf to cinch it in place. "There!"

Mother imitated my achievement with the shawl, then looked up. "What about our heads?" We had no wide-brimmed hats such as we had seen others wearing. Mother ended up using another scarf around her head, while I, believing one hat to be as good as another, took my tall, rounded bonnet and plopped it on top of my head.

When Gestefeld and his party arrived, they discovered us in our improvised riding gear. Observing their expressions, Mother whispered, "They must think we look like gypsies."

They complimented us, of course, though with wide eyes. One young caballero asked, "Is this common riding attire in America?"

"Oh, yes," I told him nonchalantly.

Gestefeld introduced several gallant men, including a pair of diplomats and a writer for his newspaper. The Mexican members of our party were quite young, and eyed me as a fish eyes a skewered worm. With the distinct feeling I would be courted throughout the whole day, I was once again grateful for my mother's presence.

Which I owed to Wilson.

I was thinking of him when a fellow with a thin moustache came up. He appeared to be our guide, and I had the momentary thought that I much preferred Wilson's fuller moustache to his. "Are you ready, señorita? You appear concerned."

My concern came from Wilson, who was half a continent away. I shook it off. "All ready."

Our guide wagged a finger. "No, no. First, I say, '*Vamos?*' You reply, '*Con mucho gusto.*' This means 'with great pleasure.' Now try. *Vamos?*"

"*Con mucho gusto,*" I said, smiling.

And we set off to see the paradise of Mexico: Chapultepec.

IT WAS A GLORIOUS MORNING RIDE. I was incautious in my saddle, for which I paid in soreness several days thereafter. But I had not ridden since my childhood and had never mastered the reins as I did after watching our guide. I mimicked his clicks and jabs, and the horse beneath me responded to my every whim. With my red sash wrapped around my waist, I felt like quite the proper cowboy.

Mother was perfectly at home in her saddle, and rolled her eyes at my glances in her direction. I recalled her riding out with Father, and wondered if that was when she had mastered the skill. *Or had it been with her first husband, perhaps?* A question worth asking, when we were on more steady ground.

Besides, this was a day for vibrations and vistas. I could have been happy enough just to ride all the day through, even without the sights promised us. But sights were what we were there to behold, so I tried to catalogue them.

My first surprise came when we arrived at a tall set of gates guarded by both mounted and unmounted soldiers. I thought it strange to have to pass through guarded gates to enter a park. But apparently this park was also home to the castle that was the seat of government.

Our journey took us along the Paseo de la Reforma, which cut through part of the massive park on the north side of the hill. The boulevard was so wide we could have raced five teams of horses abreast. It seemed a remarkable achievement. When I asked Gestefeld about it, he said, "It was originally called the Paseo de la Emperatriz, after Maximilian's wife Carlota. He had it built after the style of his home in Austria."

I wondered how long it had taken to build, and I was acutely aware of how spare my knowledge of Mexican history truly was. "He didn't reign long, did he?"

"About three years from arrival to arrest," said Gestefeld. "You know his history?" I shook my head. "He was a royal Habsburg, but a younger brother, so he made his career in the navy. When the French invaded Mexico they asked him to become the emperor. He refused, until some Mexican monarchists convinced him."

"I'm surprised America didn't object."

"We were a little occupied in '63," observed Gestefeld.

"Oh. Of course. Still, I can't imagine the Mexican people were pleased to have an Austrian ruling them."

To my surprise, our Mexican escorts shrugged. One caballero said, "No-no, of course not. Yet he was better than some. He forbade the labor of children."

"He forgave the debts of the poor," added another fairly.

"And *la emperatriz* raised vast sums to house the destitute," remarked a third. "Together, they adopted Iturbide's children, so their heirs would be Mexican."

Gestefeld smiled at me. "Local feelings are complicated, as you see."

Not for me. As un-American as it might seem, I was suddenly in love with the deposed emperor. "He seems quite the humanitarian."

"Perhaps, señorita," said the first speaker. "Perhaps he could have been, had he lived in different times. But his coming dispossessed the great Juárez, hero of the people."

I looked to Gestefeld for explanation. "Benito Juárez," he explained. "Their Abraham Lincoln and King Arthur in one. The once and future emancipator."

Our most loquacious companion nodded. "However fair Maximilian might have been, he was, as you say, not Mexican. And when he tried to strike down Juárez and the rebels, it only hastened his end. All of Mexico rose up."

"It helped that the French withdrew their troops," added Gestefeld. "And our war was over, so we were able to exert a little influence, too. Monroe Doctrine and all that. He was arrested, tried, and executed. Firing squad," he added.

I wondered if he had been shot by the very children he had liberated, then realized that with only three years in his grand office, those children had barely grown at all. "What happened to his wife?"

"Went mad. I understand that she's living in Europe, denying to this day that her husband is actually dead."

"How horrible!" exclaimed my mother. "That unfortunate woman."

To console us with diversions, the caballeros pointed out several fine statues. "There, the explorer Columbus. There, the last Aztec ruler, Cuauhtémoc. And there, on the horse, Charles IV of Spain."

"Really?" I asked, surprised.

Our guide shrugged. "It was made during his lifetime. They talked of melting it down after *la Revolución*, but wiser heads prevailed. It is a thing of beauty, and part of our history. It would be foolish to deny either."

I nodded, though it seemed strange to me, honoring someone who was considered an enemy of the nation.

The boulevard was more a place to be seen than to see. Fashionable people promenaded themselves, showing off their fine clothes, best horses, and new carriages. The conveyances far outshone those in Pittsburgh. We saw tally-ho coaches, elegant dogcarts, English gigs, and handsome coupés, all drawn by the finest hot-blooded studs in the world. Cream-colored horses with silver manes and bobbed tails that would have caused slack-jawed crowds to gather in the north were entirely common in Mexico City.

Among the moneyed set, the fashions were extraordinary. We saw powdered women in high French opera heels, covered in lace, brocade, and fresh flowers, walking alongside men in tile hats and long coats, with knobby canes and heels taller than those of their female companions. I found it remarkable that while the men wore tights to cover their legs, the fashionable women went out with only the stockings of Eve.

Several women stared at my strange riding habit. One even clicked her tongue at me in distaste. It made me laugh, which I was glad to see infuriated her.

"The trees are enormous," observed Mother.

Gestefeld laughed politely. "Oh, believe me, they are dwarfs to the ones further on."

"These trees are the silent witnesses of history," said our guide. "They provided shelter to Montezuma, Cortés, Iturbide. Here is where our Niños Héroes laid down their lives to defend their country. Here is where the last battle with your country was fought forty years ago."

"And now it is to be the home of President Díaz," added Gestefeld, piquing my reporter's interest. He informed me that the palace had been vacated as a residence since the fall of Maximilian, and been made the home of the Astronomical, Meteorological, and Magnetic Observatory. "But three years ago the observatory was moved to the archbishop's home in Tacubaya. Ironically, that was just after President Díaz broke his vow to step aside and instead ran for reelection. He won, of course. Now Chapultepec Castle is going to be his presidential residence."

Just then, we emerged from the trees and I saw the castle itself. Situated at the top of Chapultepec Hill, it was not my notion of a castle, derived from storybooks. It was more a palace, though with a rough stone base. Only two stories tall, it was impossibly wide. A modest tower rose from what looked like the middle—which was undergoing construction—with a number of peasants and craftsmen swarming over it, even on a Sunday. President Díaz meant his home to be both modern and impressive.

"It is the only honest-to-goodness castle in North America to have housed royalty," observed Gestefeld.

Impressed as I should have been, I thought of our own proud observatory in Pittsburgh and imagined some rich politician claiming it for his home. *Shame on President Díaz for taking this palace back from the people!*

We rode around the castle nesting on the hill above us. Once, as we were crossing a stream, I remarked to our guide, "Chapultepec. What does it mean?"

"Grasshopper," replied our guide.

Imagining some dark invocation, like "sacrifice" or "hill of God," his answer made me laugh. "Why? Because it's shaped like a grasshopper?"

"Some say so. But there are many insects in the forest as well. Personally, I think it's named for them."

Around the back of the castle, we reached another gate and encountered a scene worthy of an artist's brush. A small adobe house stood beside an old aqueduct. Its front porch held half-clad Mexicans selling coffee and pulque to passing horsemen.

There was quite a line, with everyone waiting their turn. Our guide assured us we would want something to drink before the next leg of our adventure, so we dutifully took our place in line.

Through the nearby gate came a constant stream of natives with burros bearing burdens destined for market. There must have been two hundred mules between us and the gate, but the beasts were the souls of patience as their masters waited in line for their drink. It was so amusing that I laughed, wondering which ones were the animals lining up to drink and which were the tolerant masters. Then I realized that I was in line with all the rest, which only made me laugh harder.

A song was being sung by those waiting, and also by those who had drunk more than one helping.

> *Sabe que es pulque—*
> *Licor divino?*
> *Lo beben los ángeles*
> *En vez de vino.*

I asked our companions to translate. They took a moment, carefully omitting anything that might be inappropriate for a young lady's ears, but at last emerged with this genteel ditty:

> Know ye not pulque—
> That liquor divine?
> Angels in heaven
> Prefer it to wine.

The pulque and coffee shop was not the only enterprise at hand. Some peóns had decided to compete by boiling water for tea or cooking small strips of meat on flat stones over charcoal fires. The wives of these entrepreneurs sat about knitting, weaving, or cooking their own repasts, which looked far better than the half-cooked strips of mystery meat offered up on sticks to the riders.

Our turn came, and Mother and I accepted our coffee, which was absolutely miserable enough to make me gag. "I should have had the pulque."

"I could not have blamed you," she agreed, surreptitiously dumping the contents of her cup onto the earth.

Remounting, we turned toward the gates and headed out into the sun-dappled wilds beyond the borders of Mexico City. Here the Paseo de la Reforma ended, so we leapt a ditch and galloped off into the open space before us.

It started badly, as we traveled through a cloud of dust for at least a mile, unable to see or breathe. Even the horses were coughing.

"Is it always this way?" I asked through a mouthful of grit.

"This is uncommonly bad," said Gestefeld, barely audible for the hand across his mouth and nose. I could only grunt in response.

Finally, our guide decided we should find shelter until the dust settled. "There is a hacienda nearby where we get a drink and change roads. *Vamos*."

He did not mention who lived at the hacienda, and we did not ask, so I was quite surprised when we came to a village of natives going about their daily business in spite of the sand.

"These are the Huichol," our guide said once we were under cover. He paid them a few small coins, and they rushed past the straw mat that served as a door. In moments we had cool water to slake our thirst and wash the dust from our throats.

Refreshed, I studied the home, which looked to be wholly organic—not adobe or brick, but something else entirely. "What is it made from?"

"The leaves of the maguey plant," explained our guide. "They use it for everything: clothes, construction, rope, even alcohol. For centuries it has been so."

The sand soon began to clear, and I smiled to see naked children running out of doors. Not far off, a herd of horses sheltered in the shade of trees. One native with a bridle in each hand was leading the horses two by two toward a walled pond. He, too, was entirely naked. With a horse on either side of him, he waded into the water, the animals docilely ambling along with him. Together they walked straight through the pond. At one point he entirely disappeared, with only the horses' heads above the water. Then the trio rose together on the far side, glistening and beautiful.

Resuming our journey, we started up a high hill with a monument visible at the top. As we ascended, we passed several plain wooden crosses. The inscriptions asked travelers to pray for the souls of the deceased.

I'd never been one for retaining literature. I tended to remember plot and characters more than poetry. But one line from Byron came forcibly to mind:

> And now I'm in the world alone,
> Upon the wide, wide sea:
> But why should I for others groan,
> When none will sigh for me?

The monument atop the hill turned out to be a marble memorial for the Mexicans killed defending Casa de Mata and Molino del Rey—the House of the Dead and the Mill of the King. It troubled me to think that these memorials were to men killed by Americans.

The mill still functioned properly, with no sign of the old war upon it. Behind it stood Dolores—the City of the Dead. I found the cemetery disquieting in its beauty, with its strange wooden statue of Christ holding the globe in his palm, its many candles and flowers, and its plucked lawns encompassed by apple and peach trees. Eating fruit grown in a graveyard seemed ghoulish.

Fortunately—for us, at least—a funeral was in process, so we could investigate no further. Consequently, we skirted Dolores, which took us through a thicket of resentful pulque plants that pricked the legs of the men and tried to pull my skirt clean off. The horses suffered worst, and were obviously relieved once we were clear of them.

Next, we reached the gorgeous ancient city of Tacubaya. Where once had resided Montezuma's favorite chief, now lived Mexican millionaires. A band was playing in the central square, and the markets were so lively and cheerful we bought two small jugs of cream, overpaying scandalously.

Our guide halted atop another hill, pointing to a weather-beaten frame house and waterwheel. "The name Tacubaya means 'where water is gathered.' Inside is the spring that has offered water for hundreds of years."

Gestefeld began describing how the water made its way to the aqueduct. I was less interested in the mechanics of it than in the woman doing her washing in the trench alongside the waterwheel, and the two boys with buckets hung along poles on their shoulders hauling water back home.

The day became a blur, and I later had to reconstruct so much through talks with Mother and Gestefeld: La Castañeda, the great pleasure gardens. The natives shooting at birds for sport. Mixcoac, with its own gardens and the remains of the American barracks, and the terrible puns on its name. Shaking his head, Gestefeld explained that Mexicans loved bringing Americans here. "Once, some fool referred to the town as Miss Quack's. They will never let us live it down."

One unforgettable moment was our encounter with the shaggy, curly-horned cow that startled us on our shortcut to the paper mill. We had evidently intruded on her private grazing land, for she charged at us as if she were a bull. Laughing, we turned to fly like Mr. Vanderbilt racing Maud S.

"We have eluded our bovine assassin," said our guide once we'd leapt a nearby trench.

"But I've lost my hat!" I replied, hand flapping the air over my head.

That ignited a series of protests from our Mexican companions, who had remained respectful and amused by our trip so far. Seeing an opportunity for gallantry, they vied with each other for the honor of retrieving my lost chapeau. So violent did their oaths become that I was afraid it would come to blows. At last, one overmastered the others by simply leaping the trench and riding back toward my hat, once again entering the domain of the territorial heifer.

"He might be killed," said Mother breathlessly.

"If only we had some *capeadores* to distract her," cried one fellow. "Señorita Bly, you have been to the bullfight?"

"No," I told him. "Not yet."

"She's going this afternoon," said Gestefeld.

"Ah, but you must allow me to be your escort!"

Smiling, I gestured to the brave fellow rescuing my hat. "That honor must go to him, mustn't it?"

The gallant's eyes twinkled. "If he dies, may I take you?"

"What a horrible thing to say!"

"He's close now," said our guide.

We all turned our attention to the cow, who was raising and lowering her head and scratching at the turf. But she allowed him to dismount and pluck up my hat. Back in his saddle, he gave her a brave salute and then raced back to us, leaping the ditch with bravado.

As I replaced my hat, I thanked its savior. Wary of giving too much praise, I added, "Naturally, she let you retrieve it. She is a woman, she understands. Clearly she is proud of her headgear, and would never deny my mine."

It was considered a highly witty comment, though the young men laughed perhaps a little too much. During the whole ride back, they kept exhorting me to smile more, grinning at me and performing ridiculous saddle or rope tricks to make me laugh. It was aggravating.

We reached our rooms a little after one o'clock, having ridden nearly thirty miles. Though my hat had been rescued from the cow, it had not preserved my face. My cheeks were blistered from the sun, while my nether regions were blistered from the saddle. It was time for siesta, and I longed to drop onto my bed without even shaking the dust from my clothes.

But I could not. We had just time enough to change our attire before heading off to our first bullfight, and after that, an evening of theatre.

Sunday—a day for relaxation!

Twenty-Two

Bullish

"THAT WAS DISGUSTING!"

People all around me were hooting and cheering like Romans howling for the blood of Christians. Below, in the center of a dusty ring, a horse was being dragged off by a lasso wrapped around its still-kicking feet while a furious bull stamped and huffed and tried to shake off the barbed spears in its flanks. It was monstrous.

Before that afternoon, my impression of the Mexican people had been wholly positive. While deploring the government's treatment of their natives, I had found the people themselves to be charming, polite to a fault, almost tranquil. I'd considered both the men and women to be models of gentility and manners.

The bullfight shattered that illusion.

The first inkling hit me during the narrow-gage train ride to the arena. We had to travel a fair distance into the countryside, as bullfighting was banned within the city limits—to avoid rioting, I would later discover.

The military was out in force, all silver-buttoned and buckskinned, armed with gun, revolver, sword, dagger, mace, and lasso. They were the best-paid soldiers in Mexico, Gestefeld informed me. "And the fiercest."

"How so?"

He waited until we were past a clutch of them. "They were all bandits, and worse. Then President Díaz hired them for his military. They'd just as soon kill you as look at you, and they never question orders."

I looked back over my shoulder at them. "The perfect soldiers."

"They certainly think so," remarked Gestefeld. "A bunch of daisies."

Flower metaphors being popular at present, to be a daisy meant that one was the very best. Daisies also stood for purity and innocence. I had a sense that Gestefeld's use of the phrase was ironic, in both ways.

Upon leaving the train station, we immediately entered the arena, which was very like a racetrack. As members of the press, we had box seats on the shady side, above the rich spectators, while the penurious sat in the sun. I supposed that our box was more comfortable than the common stands, but packed in on hard backless chairs, I was not disposed to enjoyment. My thighs and adjacent regions were still sore from the horse ride, and I was already dreading sitting for a few more hours.

But I soon discovered that few people sat during the bullfights. They rose and waved and hollered and cajoled, cheering first the animal and then the men. It seemed that all of Mexico was pressed into these stands, young and old, rich and poor, women, men, and children, all in their best attire, all eager for the sight of blood.

In the press box I saw many faces I recognized from Mijo's. There was the reporter for *El Monitor Republicano*. His neighbor wrote for the *Mexican Financier*, a dual-language paper chock full of ads from the States. Further down the row was a writer for *La Patria*. And Daniel Cabrera Rivera from *Ahuizote* was there, dozing beside an artist doing a satirical sketch of the fight before it had even begun!

Yet I supposed he had the correct idea—it was best to get a jump on things. I took out my notebook and started scribbling details to fill the time. The fence enclosing the ring was painted in patriotic colors—red, green, and white—and there were no fewer than three platforms set in the crowd for musicians to play.

I saw a lone man in fine apparel approach a box just below us, followed by a uniformed boy. Their advent gave rise to applause. "Who is that?"

"*El juez*," said Gestefeld. "The judge. He decides who scored the best hits, insists on certain moves, disqualifies contestants, that sort of thing."

I made some notes. "How are judges chosen?"

"Appointed by the city. Though, interestingly, the fighters have a right to refuse a bad judge."

"A bad judge?"

"One who makes them take extraordinary risks. Once they've accepted a judge and are in the ring, the judge's word is law. A fighter can be fined for disobedience, and the crowd can turn against him."

"And who is the boy?"

"His bugler. He toots out the commands to the fighters below."

Someone was approaching to join the judge. "And that?"

"The town mayor. Every fight needs to be held in someone's honor."

"And those sticks they're hanging on the wall?" I was afraid I wouldn't like the answer.

I was proven correct when one of the caballeros, the one who had rescued my hat, took up the answer. "Those, Señorita Cochrane, are the *banderillas*, the barbed spears. The decorations on them take all week to craft, but it is marvelous to see tinsel or the Mexican colors streaming behind a racing *toro*."

His neighbor said, "I so hope today's fight is as exciting as the one two weeks ago."

My caballero agreed. "It was a very good fight."

"What makes a good fight?" I asked him.

"The *toro* was ferocious! Three horses killed by a single bull, one man's arm broken, and Bernardo Javino barely escaped with his life! It was glorious."

Gestefeld leaned close. "At eighty-two, Señor Javino is one of the oldest bullfighters in Mexico, and the most revered."

"He has killed four thousand bulls in his time," said my caballero, before shaking his head sadly. "But he should have retired long ago."

"He lives on his salary," said Gestefeld.

My caballero was disgusted. "His nephew should support him. *He* is the coming man! Were I a woman, and didn't have the perfect specimen of manhood to worship—I mean myself, of course—I would fall in love with Juan Moreno. Much as that pitiable woman!"

"What woman?" I asked.

"That same day, a man was gored, and a woman—not his wife—came shrieking from the stands to murder the *toro* herself. The unlucky mistress succeeded in being hoisted in the air atop his head and carried about the whole arena, only to be cast aside. It was a wonder she survived, but she did—much to the dismay of the man's wife, who had watched the whole thing with a broad smile on her face. In the end, the mistress staggered from the arena, her dress in tatters. But she had her revenge! She paid good money to buy that bull's heart and eat it that night. So I suppose both women achieved their revenge. Ah! Here! Watch!"

Dazed by this casually sordid tale, I watched a kind of parade unfold below us in the ring. First entered El Capitan, the matador, followed by eight *capeadores*, two *picadores*, and then the *lanzadores* on horseback, lassos twirling. I had to admit they were all very handsome in their satin knee breeches and colorful beaded and tasseled coats. Curiously, they wore false hair under their hats, tied back into a pigtail, which Mother called a Chinaman's knot. Then came three mules, two clowns, and an old man with a wheelbarrow. All bowed to the judge and mayor.

The matador, this young Juan Moreno, was six feet tall with broad shoulders and uncommonly fair features. As he swept into a fantastical bow, the whole crowd roared, "El Americano! El Americano!"

I turned to Gestefeld. "He's American?"

He laughed. "No. With his light complexion, they call him that."

The crowd leapt to its feet, making me jump. "El toro! El toro!"

The clowns and the old man retreated with the mules while the fighters formed a semicircle around a tall door, poised to strike. With flourish, Juan Moreno approached the door, flung back the bolt, and leapt aside.

At once the bull burst forth, and I saw that he already had two of the barbed banderillas sticking out of his neck, prompting his eruption from his dark cell. As our driver in El Paso had said, the bull's horns were sawed off. "What kind of sport is it when all the danger is on one side!"

No one heard me. Below, the bull was racing toward the capeadores and their flutters of silk. They put on quite a show, goading and dancing. Most were artful in their escapes, but occasionally the stampeding bull forced them to hide behind the six-foot-wide wooden *burladeros*.

When the crowd grew bored, trumpets blared and a *banderillero* raced out, twirling his decorated stabbing sticks above his head. The beast paused, pawing the ground like a baseball batter at the plate. Then he lowered his head and bellowed.

Despite my reservations, I found myself riveted. And I was certainly not alone in holding my breath—the arena was silent. However, I was probably the only one hoping the bull came off the better of the exchange.

It was not to be. With a pirouette any ballerina would have been proud to make, the man twirled safely past the charging bull, who now had two more banderillas sticking out of his neck. The beast roared again, this time in agony. Some evil genius had devised a way to insert firecrackers into the banderillas so that they ignited when stuck. The spears quivered with every move the bull made, popping and sending up dramatic puffs of smoke.

My caballero turned to me. "Was that not splendid?"

Through clenched teeth I said, "It was very skillful. And utterly barbaric."

He laughed with pity for me. "No doubt you are correct. But in Mexico, only two things stir a man's blood: a love affair, and a bullfight. They are not unlike. The wooing, the little wounds, the dance, the gifts, a kind of, how you say, *seducción*."

"Seduction," supplied Gestefeld, with an embarrassed glance at Mother.

"Sí, yes! Seduction. The only difference is, when the seduction of the bull is over, you are not forced to marry. Ha! You will see. You will see."

Below, the bugler was at it again, this time calling forth the picador. The horse beneath him was old, and blindfolded. Across its chest was a leather apron, but that was an illusory protection at best. As soon as the picador stabbed his spear into the bull, the beast responded with fury and vented the whole of his rage upon the sightless horse. The picador leapt clear as the bull buffeted the screaming horse to the ground with his blunted horns and trampled it under his hooves.

The cheers were deafening. Men, women, and children were shouting as if the horse had done each of them a personal wrong. Even Gestefeld was clapping, if moderately.

Mother's hand was at her mouth while I shouted, "That was disgusting! He killed the horse!"

"But *sí!*" Bewildered by my outrage, my caballero patted my shoulder. "It is what the *caballo* is for. He is old, and would be put down in any case."

"So, after years of loyal service, the horse lives his final moments blindfolded and terrorized before being gored and given an agonizing, slow death! That's monstrous!"

He became grave. "I am certain your humane societies would prevent bullfights in the States. Your people would cry out against them. Yet do you not have prizefights, strong men trying to pummel one another to death? And do not your citizens clamor for admission to see executions, the lawful murder of men and women in health and youth?"

"In prizefights, all the participants are willing. And the executed are criminals."

He spread his hands. "The bull would be butchered for meat, and the horses put down for their age. Americans witness inhuman treatment to their fellow humans without concern, yet they affect holy horror at us for furnishing beef to the needy and taking out of *el mundo* a few old horses. Forgive me if I find the outrage misplaced."

To that logic, I had nothing at all to say.

The lanzadores were roping the still-kicking horse and dragging it from the arena as another picador came forward, again on a tired, ancient horse. This one could barely walk, and it died in the same fashion.

After that horrible display it was time, it seemed, for the main event. The crowd was shouting something like, *"Muerie! Muerie!"* which I assumed meant they were saying, "Kill him!" The judge signaled the bugler, who bleated out a few notes, and Juan Moreno stepped forward.

He first had to tease the bull with his cape, because by some bizarre law the matador was not allowed to kill the bull until it charged. I felt awful for the bull, who never seemed to see the man holding the fluttering cape he was chasing. He certainly did not see the thin sword that plunged into his neck, just between his mighty shoulders. Juan Moreno made a single stab that pierced the beast's thundering heart. In and out, it was skillful, scientific, and merciful.

Yet it seemed to take an eternity for the bull to concede the inevitable. He took two steps. His mouth opened and his tongue lapped the air. He stepped again toward the door to his cell, and almost made it to the fence, where spectators reached out to pluck his tail. He stumbled. Finally, he collapsed and lay still.

At once the crowd erupted, throwing gifts down to Juan Moreno: money, cigars, fruit, flowers, and feminine trinkets that belonged in a boudoir. Men tossed expensive sombreros, and the victorious matador, perhaps sensible of how costly a good hat could be, tossed them back to much applause.

Meanwhile, the lanzadores were back at work, lassoing the bull and dragging his carcass away, making room for another bull. And the whole thing started over again.

"How many bulls will be slaughtered today?"

"There are four bulls to a fight," said Gestefeld.

"Oh, good Lord!" I felt like gagging.

The next bull was much tamer, barely chasing the capeadores. He never charged, never pawed the earth. The crowd jeered this gentle soul, calling him a "weak woman," and the lanzadores had to come forward on horseback to rope him around his blunted horns and flip him on his side. Then, with admitted skill, they roped his feet, preventing his rising again.

At that moment, the clowns rushed forward to pluck the protruding banderillas from his shoulders and hindquarters. These colorful spears, now with the additional decoration of the cowardly bull's blood, were sold to the eager crowd.

At last the man with the wheelbarrow was explained. He was the butcher. He gave the beast a fast, brutal death by severing the piteous thing's spine.

"Elizabeth," said my mother, "my head aches. I think it was all the sun and exertion this morning."

Instantly, everyone leapt to their feet, me included. Grateful for Mother's intervention, I made our excuses and guided her toward the exit.

Gestefeld followed. I frowned in his direction, angry with him for exposing us to such brutality. "Don't you have to report all that?"

"I have another man here. He'll keep score for the paper. He's American, and more keen than the average Mexican. He's even taken part against the *toro embolado*." Seeing my unwillingness to ask, he said, "After the fight, another bull comes out with balls on his horns. Anyone who thinks they can best him with the cape is allowed to try."

"Amateur night," I observed.

"Exactly so." Gestefeld paused. "Forgive me for bringing you. But this is a key part to the Mexican character. You have to experience it at least once."

I pressed my lips together. "I suppose I'm grateful. And yes, I am glad I saw it. Quite the contrast to the beautiful ride."

"Beauty, bullfights, and opera. That is the heart of Mexico, Miss Bly."

"That may be so, Mr. Gestefeld. But you'll have to excuse us from the opera, tonight at least. I'm afraid I just don't have the heart for it."

TWENTY-THREE

LOST IN MEXICO

AFTER THAT EXHAUSTING SUNDAY I rose even later than normal. For once Mother did not object, having slept almost to eight o'clock herself. It was ten o'clock before I was dressed, and we decided to have a light day while I began to write of our adventures.

The writing took me several days, during which time we went out only in the afternoons, wandering Mexico City at a more leisurely pace. I did some follow-up interviews, took more notes, and tried my best to spell the Spanish words correctly. Sadly, as I was forced to pose my questions in English, I mostly became proficient in spelling *"No sé"*—"I don't know."

By the following Sunday I had three completed pieces, including a full-throated screed against bullfighting. With that horror behind us, we explored the various churches, as well as the museum. Even there we could not escape evidence of man's bloodlust. We saw the massive sacrificial stone that until recently had been part of the great basilica, but was currently displayed in the museum with the sensational claim that fifty thousand people had been sacrificed upon it. Covered in carvings of the sun and the moon, of men and strange hieroglyphs, it had a rude hole in the center. "For the blood," we were told.

Beholding portraits of armored Spanish conquerors and the feathered shields of natives, the juxtaposition made my heart ache. My sympathies were so firmly aligned that, when one day we saw the tree under which it is said Cortés wept after the events of La Noche Triste, I was singularly unmoved.

We attended the theatre, and experiencing the strange reverence the Mexicans had for the stories that unfolded upon the stage was just as exciting as if we understood the plays themselves. The opera was even better, as I doubted anyone understood the words. During intermissions,

Mother and I tried to piece together the narrative from the tenor of the tenor and the devotion of the diva.

It was during a play at the National Theatre that we had our first view of Mexico's president. Craning around from our place in the orchestra, I studied him. El Presidente Díaz appeared far more British than Mexican, with his swooping white moustaches and his close-cropped white hair.

"So that is what a dictator looks like," I remarked. Heads turned my way, and I felt both censure and fear from those heavy gazes.

Mother and I dined out often, at the invitation of our growing number of acquaintances: Señor Garcia, Mr. Gestefeld, and the ungracious Mrs. Carter. The young men began to swarm like locusts. My sheer disinterest offered them an unintended yet irresistible challenge, but romantic as it might have been to have a tempestuous Mexican love affair, I had no intention of "falling" for any of them.

One of my would-be beaus did give us cause for laughter. Thinking to impress me, he ordered a gift of linens and handkerchiefs embroidered with my initials. But as he was under the impression my name was actually Nellie Bly, I ended up with a suitcase full of beautiful linens with *N.B.* written in the finest embroidery!

The biggest temptation I experienced was smoking. Everyone smoked in Mexico. *Everyone.* I had thought myself quite used to cigar and cigarette smoke in Pittsburgh, where the air was filthy whether one smoked or not. But Mexico dropped the scales from my eyes. In America, a lady smoking drew more condemnation than admiration. Not so in Mexico, where a woman was hardly at ease until she had a twist of paper stuffed with tobacco fuming between her teeth.

No spot in Mexico was safe from tobacco, not theatres, nor railway cars—not even churches! It seemed to give everyone something to do, some idle occupation for their hands and their lips. Even little children could be seen puffing tiny clouds of tobacco.

Being entirely surrounded by it, I was tempted to try the filthy habit. It became especially enticing when Mrs. Carter informed me, with great gravity, that smoking reduced the appetite. As my stomach was still opposed to Mexican cuisine, the idea of being less hungry was appealing. But the presence of my mother and the calculations of the cost of even a mild habit quite made up my mind to keep my throat pristine.

The other scourge of Mexican society was the lottery. Promising a million pesos tomorrow for a single peso today, women and children sold these insidious tickets all over town. Imagining rich men growing richer with each ticket sold, I became enraged whenever I saw one.

We began to frequent certain haunts, usually more for their names than the food. One of the pleasures in Mexico City was found in the names of the establishments. Our landlady purchased her groceries at The Tail of the Devil. I had a pair of shoes custom-made for me at The Boot of Gold, and purchased a new blouse at The Way to Beauty is Through the Purse. If thirsty and abjuring Mijo's, we could visit Temptation, Reform, Dynamite, or Christmas Night, this last being found on the Street of the Back of the Holy Ghost, across the Bridge of Firewood. My favorite was The Coffee House of the Little Hell.

We were seated outdoors at Little Hell one evening, watching the parade of humanity, when I sighed deeply. "What am I doing here?"

Startled, Mother said, "You're reporting."

"Yes, the same tourist goop as anyone else." I flicked open my notebook and began riffling pages. "Does anyone care that Dr. Waterman will stay in Mexico a little longer, though his friend Mr. McGill of Freeport, Pennsylvania, is stopping at his silver mines in Durango before heading home? Or that Mr. Frederick Church of New York, the well-known landscape painter, has brought his family along for his second visit to Mexico? Or that no one has seen the writer Joaquin Miller, though he apparently arrived on the eighth and registered with no hotel, cutting everyone dead?"

"I think highly of a man who does not travel on his fame," said Mother.

Shaking my head, I closed my book. "That's hardly the point. Here I am, regurgitating nonsense about Americans in Mexico, just as I promised myself I would not do. I thought I could unearth a real story, *not* just tourist pabulum."

"Speaking of unearthing," said Mother with a wry sniff, "I doubt that anyone else would have mentioned the discovery of all those bones during the excavation of that new hotel."

I waved her humor aside. "Why did I come here? I mean, why not England, or France, or Italy? What, I hear Tom and Tony burbling about Mexico and suddenly I'm off on a mission, a crusade? Only this crusade is not to liberate anyone but myself from my doldrums. I haven't found a truly important story here. Now I'm wondering if I didn't run *to* Mexico, but actually ran *away* from home, because I'm no good at this work!"

Mother did not hug me, or quash me with kisses. On the contrary, she sounded harsh as she said, "Elizabeth. You have a unique talent. You do not plan, as most people do. You do not strive and toil, day after day, toward a single goal. No, you are walking inspiration. You capture lightning in a bottle. Lightning is gone before you can say it struck. But in the instant between the flash and darkness, you are able to grasp some truth, some fact—some *story*—that requires telling. But you cannot *summon* lighting. You can only wait for it to illuminate the sky. Inspiration has brought you this far. Trust that it will lead you on."

Turning away, I dashed at my eye, feeling surprisingly naked. It was one thing to be loved. It was quite another to be understood.

THE LIGHTNING STRIKE, WHEN IT CAME, was a literally explosive story with ties to people at home. The first I heard of it was at Mijo's, when Gestefeld said, "Miss Cochrane, you're from Pittsburgh. Are you going to the funeral tomorrow?"

"Funeral?" I asked, pulling out my notepad at once.

"For Jacob Heiney," he said, as if it explained all. Seeing my blank stare, he added, "There was an accident the other day on the Mexican National line. A native firefighter and an American engineer were killed. The engineer was from Pittsburgh."

"Oh! What happened?"

"A fire in the engine. Burst boiler. Happens more often than anyone reports. Hm, there's a story in that. . . Anyway, the Mexican government is releasing Heiney's body, and the funeral will be this afternoon. Thought you might want to attend."

"Thank you!" I said, earnestly. He told me the name of the church and I turned to leave for some research, then paused. "What happened to the native?"

"Hm? Oh, the usual. Buried in a communal pauper's grave."

At first I thought that comparison would be my story: a Mexican tossed into an unmarked grave with others just like him, while the white foreigner received a formal funeral. But that day I learned to not frame a story until I had all the details. Instead, I sowed the first seed in the dangerous crop I would harvest in Mexico.

I went to the funeral that afternoon. As we waited for the casket to arrive, I found other American railway workers to interview. Most were members of the Brotherhood of Locomotive Engineers, and attended knowing that there but for the grace of God went themselves. The late Mr. Heiney had been well-liked, and had been in Mexico to support his ailing father back in Allegheny County. One of his fellow engineers told me, "His goal was to put enough aside that, should anything ever happen to him, the old man would have enough to get by. Such a pity his father won't be able to see his son again. Or even his coffin."

As it happened, none of us saw the coffin that day. The afternoon drew on, the flowers wilted, and yet no remains arrived for the funeral. At last, someone sent to City Hall to ask where the body was. But the official in charge had gone riding, and no one was willing to release Mr. Heiney's remains without their chief's permission.

Naturally, there was some ill feeling, both about the wasted time and the disrespect for the dead man. Perhaps *he* was beyond caring, but the mourners were not. Action was called for.

What had been a simple human-interest story suddenly became something more. When an "indignation committee" was organized that evening, I attended, taking note of who was calm and who was outraged. The more heated voices belonged to women, which I found interesting. It was eventually determined that a select group would appeal to the head of the U.S. Legation in Mexico, Minister Henry Jackson.

The next morning I followed the deputation to Minister Jackson's office. He had just returned from Veracruz, where there had been an unfortunate accidental murder: a Negro cook on the train had been shot with his own firearm while instructing a young Mexican boy on how to hunt game. So the minister was already in rather low spirits as he listened to the tale of the aborted funeral. "We will look into this at once," he said, and called in the secretary of the legation, a Mr. Morgan, to expedite matters.

But the Mexican response was hardly expeditious. In fact, it was only when Mr. Morgan threatened a diplomatic incident that the body was finally released.

Being present when the casket arrived, I overheard a comment from one of the officials, delivered to the priest in charge of the service. *"Mantenga el ataúd cerrado."*

My Spanish had not improved, but I had retained one word from that first day of exploring. *Ataúd* was the word for *coffin.* And I recognized *cerrado* from the many times we had been turned away from establishments during the afternoon siesta. It meant closed. The official had told the priest, "Keep the coffin *closed.*" More, it had been said with special earnestness, and out of earshot of any of the Americans save me, who they'd discounted due to my youth and gender.

Intriguing.

The funeral took place somberly. Everyone paid their respects, and Minister Jackson even rose to say a few words. Veiled women shook their heads and sadly repeated, *"Ay-ay-ay,"* which I understood as a kind of lament. When it was done, I cornered Gestefeld, who hadn't been present the previous afternoon. The delay had turned this into a story worth at least half a column.

Pulling him aside, I said, "There's something wrong."

"What?"

"With the body. There's something wrong." I told him what I had heard.

"Of course they don't want the casket opened," he frowned in puzzlement. "He died in a fire."

"And the priest knows that. This was something else. There was a furtiveness in the official's warning. More than delicate American sensibilities."

Gestefeld recognized a fellow reporter's hunch. Taking me by the arm, he said, "Cry."

After a moment of surprise, I burst into tears, or a close imitation of it. Taking me to the front of the small church, he used a soft voice to ask the priest for a moment alone with the deceased. As he spoke in Spanish, I wasn't certain, but he seemed to be relaying that I was the engineer's mistress. Full of understanding, the priest excused himself.

"Well played," said Gestefeld. "You belong on the stage."

"Thank you, no." Recovering myself, I tried to lift the lid of the casket, only to find it had been nailed shut.

"Damn," said Gestefeld, heedless of blaspheming in a church. "This will make noise." He drew a pocket knife from his coat.

"Hurry," I said, looking about.

He went to work, wriggling the short knife back and forth beside each of the nails to raise the lid just enough that we might peek inside.

One peek was more than enough. I don't know what I expected to see, but I was surely not prepared for what I did behold. Gestefeld's breath hissed through his teeth.

The dead man was definitely in there, his face burnt beyond recognition. But that was not the horror. What we saw was like the detritus of an abattoir. Heiney's limbs had been hacked off, and his chest had been opened and turned inside-out. All of his parts were crammed into the casket at odd angles: a foot rested beside his head, and his fingers and hand sat where his shoulders sloped sideways.

I gagged as Gestefeld tapped the lid back into place. The priest reappeared, and I had no trouble feigning distress as Gestefeld offered our thanks and escorted me out.

When we reached the street I had enough control of my queasiness to say, "Why would they do that?"

Gestefeld looked rather pale himself. "Let's find out."

After a few discreet inquiries to his contacts in City Hall, the story came tumbling out. Apparently, the dead man had been removed from his casket on Friday for some reason, and then left out all day Saturday. When the officials tried to return Heiney to his casket on Sunday morning, they discovered he had swelled up too much to fit. When they suggested purchasing a larger coffin, their superior denied them funds. They were still fretting out a solution when Mr. Morgan made his threats, and so the Mexicans, in their desperation, sawed the body up, forced the bits into the original casket, and nailed it shut to avoid the inevitable outrage.

It was an outrageous story, and sensational. So I was shocked when I read that Friday's edition of the *Two Republics* and saw Mr. Heiney's name, and there was no mention of dismemberment of the corpse!

I hurried to Mijo's to confront the publisher. "You kept it quiet?!"

"Not the important parts," objected Gestefeld, clearly concerned by my tone because he waved his hand for me to calm down. "I wrote about the delay of the funeral, and the protests."

"But not the mutilation of Mr. Heiney's body!"

Gestefeld wore an expression I had not seen on him before. "I am forced to tread carefully, Miss Cochrane."

"What do you mean?"

"What I mean is this: I run an English-language newspaper in Mexico. Even if I do not accept a subsidy, as many do, I still require the goodwill of the government."

I stared at him. "And?"

"And this story makes the government look bad."

"It brings to light an injustice that the government should be glad to know about, so they can fire these men!"

"You think they did this without permission? They weren't willing to do anything while their boss was out riding, yet they would risk their reputations by doing what they did without being told?"

"Then their superior should be fired as well!"

"That's not how it works here." He drew out his cigarette case and lit one, drawing the smoke deeply into his lungs. "Two weeks ago, the editor for *La Crónica Tribunales*—the Court Chronicle—was denounced and imprisoned."

"For what crime?"

"Writing about a judge's ruling. He made no statement on the justice or injustice of the ruling. Merely writing about the ruling itself. He'll be released, in time. But he's fortunate."

"Fortunate how?"

His eyes on his cigarette, his answer was quiet. "I knew a liquor store owner named José Fausto. Originally Guiseppe Fausto, of Italy, his name meant *lucky* in his native tongue, but he was not lucky enough to be allowed to wag that tongue against the government with impunity. One night a man came in and ordered whiskey. As José turned to fetch it, he was shot in the back. Repeatedly."

"Was the murderer not arrested?"

"Who would have arrested one of the Serenos?"

I gasped. "He was a policeman?"

"Was, and is. He was arrested, then released for lack of evidence. They do not tolerate being made to look bad." Gestefeld shook his head. "I wish I had never told you about the funeral."

I dug my fists onto the tabletop between us. "Why? Because then none of this would come out?"

"I'm always glad when a truth comes to light. But let me ask, are you going to—no, of course you are. Better to ask, *how* are you going to write about it?"

"Just as it happened!"

Gestefeld pursed his lips. "Miss Cochrane, please take this advice. Be careful. Write the story, by all means. But write it with tact. And for all that's holy, avoid describing the insult done to the body."

Omit the most eye-grabbing part of the whole tragedy? I could already imagine Madden's headline: BODY HORRIBLY MUTILATED BEFORE BURIAL! But Gestefeld was in such earnest that I said I would take his advice to heart. He looked relieved.

I went home and wrote the story just the way I wanted to. The way Nellie Bly should.

The *Dispatch* ran it at the end of the month. It would be another month before the repercussions in my own life would ripple out, like waves in a pond after a rock had been thrown.

TWENTY-FOUR

UNCLEAN

I GRADUALLY BECAME ACQUAINTED WITH THE QUIRKS and rhythms of the city. Across from the Cathedral a band played in the evening on Sundays, Tuesdays, and Thursdays. On Mondays, all public entertainments were suspended, as were the operations of most restaurants, and one was expected to dine at home.

On the other hand, one was always expected to bathe out. Specifically, at the public swimming baths. The plumbing in Mexico City was absolutely unreliable, which did much to explain the choking sea of colognes and the obsessive smoking. Most people had clearly decided it was preferable to fill their noses with the smell of tobacco rather than the reek of their fellow humans.

However, at least once a week, men and women headed to the nearest public baths, just as they did in ancient Rome. It was a sight to behold: all the dainty señoritas trudging up the street, hair hanging askew, maids trotting behind them with towels and clothes.

Being without maids ourselves, Mother and I were often subject to scorn for bringing our own towels and soaps and such. A real lady never carried anything herself, not even her umbrella. One time, Mother fell a few paces behind me, and I wondered why, until I realized she was pretending to be my maid. For a moment I was tempted to allow her to pretend, but my better self came to the fore and I fell in step beside her. "We just have to lift our chins and brave it," I said.

The baths themselves were quite pleasant, though I had to wonder if all the neighborhood ladies would not much prefer to bathe in their own homes, as the rich did. It took me the better part of a week to realize there might be something more at work, but it finally dawned on me like the sun bursting through a cloud: *Oh! This is where women go to socialize away from the company of men!*

This was one of the major reasons I had no interest in a Mexican romance: the treatment of their women. Girls were considered ripe for marriage at age twelve, and boys at thirteen, which made women of thirty-five into grandmothers. Mother secretly suspected that men liked their wives young because of the luxuriant moustaches the women began to sport at thirty, often far more fine than those of their husbands.

Yet boys and girls were kept forever separate, even as babies. They were schooled separately, as had been the case in America fifty years earlier. Then, the moment they were of a "marriageable" age, they courted in the open street. The Juliet sat at her casement window, strumming her guitar. If her room was up high, her Romeo would pen notes to her that she would lift by a string. If it was on the ground floor, they might talk and even hold hands through the bars. This went on at all hours of the night and day. Sometimes two lads would arrive at the same time and duel, there and then, for her love.

If a suitor was in earnest, he would approach the girl's father. If refused, he had the right to swear out a writ that the father was a barrier to the girl's happiness, and then ask permission to elope. This often put the father in the legal position of being forced to allow his daughter to marry.

Either way, once the father gave his consent, the couple would first wed before a public official, and then, a day or a week or a month later, unite in a grand church wedding. Dressed in the finest brocaded white, the bride would be feted by one and all.

The moment she was married, however, the Mexican bride had nothing. Her clothes were all returned to her parents. Her dowry wouldn't be available to her until her parents died. Until then, she had to rely upon her husband for everything.

In return, she was expected to live a life of complete seclusion. As far as I could determine, a Mexican wife was allowed to eat, drink, sleep, and smoke, but was never allowed to be in the company of another man, and precious few women. Men often left their wives at home and attended the theatre or the bullfights with their friends. Or their sweethearts.

Having observed all of this, I felt astonishingly thick not to have realized why women made no fuss over not having plumbing in their own homes. Bathing provided them an excuse to join other women without scorn or suspicion, their sole chance for pure social interaction.

One morning, as Mother and I took our baths in twin tubs, I mentioned this. "How terrible to have husbands so suspicious that they cannot even entertain their friends!"

"Yes," said Mother.

"I mean, what is the point of living? How terrible is it to waste life waiting for permission to live?"

"I take your point, Elizabeth."

Missing the growing edge in her tone, I carried blithely on. "And what can be wrong with men that this is what they desire? To have no trust, no faith in the person with whom they share a life, to whom they have pledged their love and devotion!"

"Yes, Elizabeth."

"But the real fault is with the women. None of it could happen without their consent." I sat forward, sloshing water all around me. "That's the trouble! Women should band together and demand their rights!"

"Perhaps they will."

"I should write about it."

"Please don't."

That checked me. "What?"

"Don't write a call to arms for Mexican women."

"Whyever not?"

"They won't thank you."

"I don't aim to be thanked. I mean to spur them to action."

"It will do the opposite. They shall resent you for it."

I leaned my arms on the edge of my tub to stare at her. "Why?"

"Because, like you, they will feel they don't require protection." She paused, then added, "And for that matter, I don't require protection either, Elizabeth. Forgive me. *Nellie*." The way she said it, it cut.

I was utterly confused. "Mother?"

"You said you did not require my protection. Well, no more do I require yours."

"I have no notion what you're talking about."

"I'm talking about the fact that you keep bringing him up."

"Who?" She gazed at me, hard. Frowning, I cast about wildly. Then a dim notion flickered. "Ford?"

"Yes. Your stepfather."

"I don't keep bringing him up!"

"Oh, of course you do. Every comment about women who allow men to dominate them, control them, abuse them—they are all, every one, aimed at me."

I was genuinely shocked. "Mother, no! If anything, our time with Ford has made me see the plight of women more clearly. And you did what none of these other women were able to do. You freed yourself!"

That mollified her slightly. By the set of her jaw, though, she was still in a temper. Like Harry, she was slow to anger. Like me, she was slow to let it go.

But with the subject broached, it seemed time to pose a question that had been troubling me. "Mother—why do you never call him by name?"

Her nostrils flared. "I thought that would be obvious."

"Not him," I said quickly. "Daddy. You either call him 'your father' or 'the Judge.' Never Michael."

"Michael was my husband's name."

Her breath caught as soon as she'd said it, and I puzzled over why. *Of course Michael was her husband's name. He was my father. . .* It made no sense.

"Come." Rising from her tub, she reached for her robe. "We'd best dress and find someplace with decent food. I will even venture to try the tortilla soup Mr. Garcia recommended."

Emerging from my own tub, dripping wet, I suddenly recalled that she had been a widow when she'd married my father. "You mean Mr. Cummings! His first name was Michael as well!"

Her step faltered. "Yes," she said shortly, then retreated behind a screen to dry and dress herself.

Behind my own screen, I did the same with a furrowed brow. Mother *never* mentioned her first husband. I didn't recall even hearing his name until the divorce case, when Mother was interrogated as to her marital history.

My cheeks began to burn. As unromantic and practical as I was, it had simply never occurred to me that Mother had ever loved anyone beside my father. *A child's view of the world.* I felt a fool. Of course Mother had loved her first husband!

Which raised a new question.

As we emerged into the air, I suggested we take a walk before luncheon. Thus we were strolling through the park beneath the glorious midday sun when I asked, "Did you love my father?"

She started, and her face was momentarily suffused with offense. Then she softened. "Of course I did, Elizabeth."

"But not the way you loved Mr. Cummings."

She was silent for a time. "I loved Michael with the love of my youth. My love for your father was more mature. Which suited him, having already lived a whole life before I came into it. He was not interested in girlish fancies. He wanted someone to comfortably slip into the place of his lost wife. Whereas I did not want to be alone, and wanted no one to take the place of my departed Michael. Consequently, I carved out a new place in my heart for the Judge, which led to a very successful marriage."

"Harry's middle name is Cummings," I observed suddenly.

She nodded. "Just as Catharine is named for your father's first wife. At first I objected. But he wanted her to have a legacy, and I eventually decided to be flattered that he wanted to share that legacy with me. Of course, your half-brothers and sisters were furious. I think that was the moment Robert turned against us. I had not only replaced his mother in the Judge's bed, but even usurped her name. One of the many grudges they hold against me."

"Against all of us," I said.

She took my hand. "It was never aimed at you. I cannot think, had I been the one to die instead of your father, that they would have repudiated you so. They saw me as a schemer and conniver. You were caught in their cannon fire—that is all."

"They should have been mad at Father, not you."

"Oh, they were. But they deemed him too old and ensnared in the clutches of an evil grasping harlot."

"Mother!" I was shocked at her self-description.

She mistook my reproof. "Not all of them, of course. Just the elder ones. They could not forgive him for remarrying."

"Imagine being angry at Father!" I said, feeling quite exorcised by the conversation.

"Mm," said Mother between pressed lips.

Her expression gave me pause. "Mother—are *you* angry at Father?"

"Elizabeth, I'm furious at him!" All at once, like the boiler that had consumed Mr. Heiney, my mother positively exploded. "I sit up nights and rail against the Judge! *Judge*, indeed! So proud of that title, he was. The height of pretension. A mill worker who made a small fortune and was elected a local magistrate. Yet he died without a will. Without a will! What kind of judge does not leave a will? What kind of father dies without providing for his little ones?" Fifteen years of pent-up hostility suddenly burst its dam. "You know that Robert is calling himself 'squire' now? Just like his father, more eager to be *seen* as important and good, rather than *doing* good."

"Mother, he was a good man—"

"He was," she admitted, no less hotly. "He was more than that. He was beloved. And he took care of his children by Catharine. Your father married me to help raise them, even though Maryann was barely younger than I was. He thought that far ahead for the children of his first marriage. But not for us. Not even the smallest foresight. How could his children imagine me to be a schemer, when I didn't even force him to make his will! Quite the wicked stepmother, I was!" She threw up her hands. "Because of his thoughtlessness, after his death, I was less than dirt. Twice widowed, five children to look after. Money vanished, thrown out of my own home, having to live on my widow's dole alone."

"So you married again."

"Your father left me no other option," she said viciously. "The world was not going to look upon me as worth anything without a husband. I required a champion."

"And you got Ford." We had reached him at last. My stepfather, Jack Ford. "Do you blame Father for him?"

That checked her. I thought I knew her answer, and was surprised when she admitted it. "Sometimes. He certainly put me in a position where I had to marry again. But, no. Your father cannot be blamed for Ford. That mistake was mine. And you paid for it," she added, with a sorrowful look to me. Then, in her own defense, she added, "Not that there were many choices. Not eight years after the war, with all the good men dead or married already. And Ford had no pretensions. A plainspoken widower who was good with his hands. And he wanted me. You have no idea how appealing that was."

"You knew he drank." I tried not to make it an accusation.

Thankfully, she did not take it as one. "Michael drank. Mr. Cummings, I mean. So did your father, though not often. Nearly every man who fought in the war drank. I did not see it as an insurmountable vice." Her brow darkened. "What I did not realize was how deep his thirst went. Nor had any man ever offered me violence before. Before Ford, I had viewed women with blackened eyes as less clever in their choices, in their manner, in their life. How foolish that seems. . ." She reached over to flatten my bangs, then she stroked my hair. "I am sorry it made such an impression on you."

"Has it?" My natural defiance, though muted, was present. "Just because I haven't married Tom or Tony—"

"I'm speaking of the stories you write. I know you are proud of them, but I regret that I am responsible for your interest in women's issues."

"Responsible!"

"It was I who brought Ford into our lives."

"Mother!" I stopped on the grass and faced her, my fists digging into my hips. "Ford does not define me. No one has an easy life—at least, not anyone who has a life worth living. It doesn't take a man like Ford to make me interested in women's issues. I am a woman, and we live in an age that's about freedom and equality. Just because slavery has ended, does that mean we stop fighting other kinds of injustice?" I shook my head vehemently. "I'm only sorry that you had to endure Ford as long as you did. I'm sorry I couldn't protect you better."

"Pink. . ." She wasn't crying yet, but tears were forming in her eyes.

They were forming in mine, too. I was recalling one night where Ford had been beating her. She had tried to send us children to a neighbor's house, but Ford had demanded that we stay and watch. "They need to know what happens," he'd told her, removing his belt.

"I did what I could," I said plaintively, almost begging her forgiveness. "I'd distract him, or goad him into hitting me in place of you. I even hid his gun. After he pulled it on Albert the first time, I started hiding it, and he was always so drunk, he'd assume he'd misplaced it. Once I pawned it, and got Mr. Miller to tell Ford he'd done it himself." Sniffling, I laughed. "He must have thought he was going crazy."

From behind her hands, Mother said, "Mr. Miller? He knew?"

Halfway through wiping my eye, I stopped and looked at her for a long moment. "Mother, everyone knew. Even before that night, *everyone* knew. Do you think he kept getting jobs because he earned them? People hired Ford for odd jobs just to get him away from our house. Away from you."

Now she was weeping openly. Disregarding the stares of passersby, I put my arms around her. "We never blamed you, Momma. And he liked the boys. He never hit Harry, and Charlie could usually calm him down." I did not mention Albert, who had been surprisingly brave in those days. It was the last time we were allies.

After a time Mother lifted her eyes, her lashes glistening. "Elizabeth. Did Ford—did he ever lay hands on you?"

He had. She knew he had. He had struck me, shoved me, thrown me into a wall. Casually, never with all his strength. Mother had tended my bruises, made my excuses at school. I had been home "sick" many times in those years.

But that was not what Mother was asking. "No. No, he didn't."

"Thank God." It was said on a release of a breath she had been holding for a long time. "What about Catharine?"

"Not that I know of," I told her. "She was very little. And she didn't stand up to him. In fact, she was always his favorite. She made him laugh. Laughy Cathy, he called her. He only got mad at us when we stymied him, got in his way."

Mother was silent. While true of us children, that statement was certainly not true of her. By the end, everything she did was fodder for his fury. The meat was too dry. The bread was too flaky. There was dust on the rear bookshelf—as if he ever picked up a book. At home, anything might have made him rage. He would sit in his chair—the chair that had once been my father's, preserved with what little furniture we had been able to keep—he would sit there and sip his whiskey and fume, waiting for an opportunity to be outraged.

The worst parts were the days we were grateful for, the days when he was his other self: sober, funny, dapper even. He could charm us children when he chose. Tiny presents, bought with Mother's money, purchasing future forgiveness.

If it had been stable, perhaps we could have endured. But the violence had escalated, like the tension on a violin string just before it snaps. Mercifully, we had all escaped with our lives.

But only barely.

Our eyes red, our spirits sore, Mother and I dropped off our washing things, then lunched at the Little Hell. Yet, seated out of doors on a day too fine to be the end of February, our setting was far from hellish. The sun was bright and warm, and a cool breeze kept our skin from prickling.

If only the same could have been said of our tempers.

We spoke very little. I felt at once a little closer to Mother, and also resentful. I had not intentionally criticized Mexican wives in order to dig at her, and it had been unkind of her to think so.

Yet it was true that I had brought up Ford, indirectly, several times since the beginning of our trip. *Why did I do that?*

A cat came up to beg a scrap from our table. Distressingly, the fashion of bobbing horses' tails had become a mania for all domestic animals. This fat monster had neither ears nor tail, making him evilly sleek. As it clearly meant he was not homeless, I shooed him away. Though, thinking better of it a moment later, I wished I had given him some of my meal. A suitable punishment for begging for scraps.

"Pets might make an interesting piece," Mother observed. "The men have much bigger dogs here than at home. And the children keep sheep! It's delightful."

"Maria had a little lamb," I sang, and we both laughed. "Have you noticed that the needy people here keep birds?"

"Of course. A rooster and a few hens, and they return the investment. What cat can boast that much?"

"None, unless their owner is fond of mouse meat. Which this might be," I added, poking at my food.

"We tried to keep some hens, do you remember?"

I was surprised she mentioned them, as Ford had sold our hens to feed his bottomless thirst. The idea of Ford refused to leave our minds, just as the actual man had refused to leave our lives. Mother asked, "Do you ever talk about him? You and your brothers?"

"No."

"Never?"

I shrugged. "We all pretend he never existed."

Mother gazed off into nothing. "I wish he didn't have that power over you all."

"Over *us!*"

"I'm guilty of it, too. I don't want to even speak his name. That's a terrible power. But I avoid naming him because of what he did to you all."

"Mother, what he did to us was nothing compared—"

"Bruises fade, Elizabeth. It's far more bruising to my heart to think that Jack Ford was the father of my children."

"He wasn't ever a father to us!"

Mother shook her head. "In the way that matters, he was. He shaped you all. I look at my children and I see them face the world the way he taught them."

I felt cold, and my hands were numb. "What are you talking about?"

"Sweet little Harry, eager to please, afraid to ever do anything without approval. Poor Catharine, who played the pretty darling and made him laugh, married a man she has to do the same for. Charlie is so hunkered down inside himself, he's made himself impervious even to happiness. And Albert. . ."

I was fascinated to hear what she would say about Albert. Because what she had said of the others was absolutely true. So what had Albert learned from Ford? Casual brutality toward his family. To shirk hard work and let others labor for him. And to drink. Albert had often gotten drunk with Ford—first to distract him from Mother, later because he enjoyed it.

So when Mother opened her mouth, I was amazed when she said, "Well, Albert was the eldest, and least vulnerable to influence."

Inwardly, I sighed. No, she would never see Albert's perfidies. To her beloved firstborn, she was forever blind. But there was a question more pressing in my mind. "And me?"

"You? You have set yourself to be the antithesis of me: a woman independent of men. I cannot imagine that you would fight quite so fiercely against all the injustices you perceive against our sex had I not dragged Ford into our lives."

I might have responded with umbrage to the idea that Ford had shaped my life in any way. I could have acknowledged the truth of it, or railed at the idea of me being so weak-headed I could not find my own course in life.

I chose, instead, to laugh.

Lifting my cup, I said, "Then I would not be a reporter, and neither of us would now be in sunny Mexico, enjoying this terrible meal on this beautiful day. So here's to your choice of husbands, which brought us here!"

Her smile was a little strained as she joined me in the mock toast. "What about *your* taste in men?"

I felt my cheeks flush as one man in particular came to mind. I banished the Quiet Observer at once. "Whatever do you mean?"

"We began this conversation by saying you would not like to be a Mexican bride. I hope that does not mean you also eschew being an

American one?"

I set my cup firmly on its saucer. "Mother, there is no man I am considering for matrimony."

"Because you are not interested, or because you have not met one worth marrying?"

Neither was true. "There is no man in my life I could marry with an easy conscience."

"Ah. So you are waiting."

"I suppose I am."

"For whom?"

I smiled at her. "No sé. Though I do have some qualifications." I began ticking qualities on my fingers. "As women mature more swiftly than men, he would need to be somewhat older—at least ten years my senior. He would need to be smart without being pedantic. Ambitious, so he can have occupation. Wealthy, so he can have servants to do wifely chores whilst I lead the life I have chosen. Which leads to the most important quality."

"Yes?"

"He would need to give me my space to pursue my reporting."

"An ambitious, intelligent, rich man without an ego," summarized Mother, smiling.

I smiled down into my cup. "Yes, I'm afraid I shall never wed."

A week later, I met Joaquin Miller.

TWENTY-FIVE

THE PRINCESS AND THE BEAR

TUESDAY, MARCH 9 1886

TO CELEBRATE FAT TUESDAY, SEÑOR GARCIA escorted us to a soiree at the French Club. Amid the bright clothes and happy laughter, he spent the whole time lamenting, "Alas, Mexico is becoming far too civilized."

I sipped my lemonade. "How so?"

"Time was, the streets would be packed with men and women in masks, and huge battles were fought with eggshells and piñatas. But tonight? Who here wears a mask? Where is the secret assignation, the anonymous wooing, the thrill of mystery?"

"There are many fine costumes," I observed. Myself, I was done up as a native princess—if she were allowed to wear velvet with her feathers. Daringly, my dress barely reached my knees, and below it tall boots clung to my calves. Stunningly good-looking, they pinched like the dickens.

Satin seemed to be the fabric of the evening, either embroidered with silver and gold or else mixed with beautiful spring flowers. I noticed one gorgeous woman, her dusky skin draped in a cream gown adorned by red roses with actual butterflies pinned to them. Another couple—Señor Garcia informed me they were recently engaged—wore matching outfits covered in white fur pom-poms. It was evidently a family tradition, as the girl's parents were also dressed to match.

The band alternated between waltzes and Spanish danzas. Mother was happily dancing with some other ladies her age, this being a night where all was permitted. Indeed, this was a night where women could propose dances to men, as they could during a Leap Year. From his hints, Señor Garcia hoped I would ask him to the floor, and I was considering doing just that when Joaquin Miller came in.

His entrance shouldn't have been remarkable. He wore no costume. Though he was tall, his shoulders were not so very wide, nor was his English-tailored suit anything particularly fine.

Yet over those narrow shoulders he wore a bearskin, much cared for. And what mask could ever compete with that astonishing fat moustache, heavy slate beard, and those twinkling blue eyes?

Pausing in the doorway, he scanned the room. Then, with a laugh of reckless fatalism, he plunged in.

"Pardon me, Señor Garcia," I said, "but who is that just coming in?"

Señor Garcia loosed a wry chuckle. "That is Señor Joaquin Miller. A poet," he added, incongruously.

"Joaquin? Surely he isn't Mexican."

"Surely not," agreed Señor Garcia. "He is American, though with as much in common with you, señorita, as the night has with the sparkling day."

Obliged to acknowledge the compliment, I allowed him to take my hand and lead me in a dance. I noticed Mr. Miller's eyes tracing my movement across the floor.

When at such an affair, it was always a simple thing to brush the arm of someone in order to make faux-embarrassed introductions. After we finished dancing, I told Señor Garcia I was concerned for my mother, for she had not been well and all this dancing must have made her thirsty. Off he trotted to fetch us all drinks, and I was able, on the pretext of looking for my mother, to bump into the bearskinned back. "Oh! Forgive me!"

Turning round, Mr. Miller bared his teeth. "Never you fear, m'lady. This bear has had worse insults than that in its time."

"I'm looking for my mother," I said, unprompted. Then, lest he believe I was trying to escape, I paid homage to the bear. "He must have been very fierce."

"So he was! Though if he had known I'd drag his unhappy hide over half the known world, he might have been more forgiving. He's dined with royalty, has my old Orsino, and I've lost count of the times I've sat on his back on some stony floor to regale a crowd with my poor scribblings."

"You're a writer?" I asked, as if I had not already been told. We made proper introductions, and as I offered my name I added, "I'm a reporter, down here from Pittsburgh. I write under the name Nellie Bly."

I was disappointed that he hadn't heard of me. But he at least knew the song, and he sang a verse, as people were wont to do. I was equally eager to show off my erudition, so when he finished warbling I said, "Orsino. From *Twelfth Night*."

"Yes, indeedy!" Grinning, he turned to the musicians. "'If music be the food of love, play on!'"

"Qué, señor?" asked a guitarist, which made us both laugh.

Thankfully for everyone, Mother arrived just then, and I was busily making introductions as Señor Garcia returned with our drinks. After a few minutes of conversation in which only Miller or I got in a significant word, Señor Garcia decided that discretion was the better part of valor. Claiming to see someone he knew, he excused himself and moved off to look for a new dancing partner.

This allowed our little American trio to find a table along the wall and continue our conversation. "That is a very fine beard," I observed, restraining my hand from stroking it.

He confounded me by doing that precise thing. "It has been my constant companion for thirty-odd years, since back in my Mount Shasta days, ever since the damned Modocs put an arrow through my face. No, no exaggeration, I promise you! Came out the back of my neck. I'm told I was within a hair of death. Even now I don't recall anything from the year that followed. Probably the best year of my life," he added with a laugh.

Joaquin Miller had certainly filled his life with adventures. He spoke of his audience with Queen Victoria, the unexpectedly fierce handshake of the shah of Persia, and of the joys of wading in the California muck panning for gold.

Less than half his age and with none of his experience, my sole advantage was my two months in Mexico City. I told him about Coffin Street, which he said I must show him. I promised I would do so, and we began to make plans for the following day.

"Is your wife with you, Mr. Miller?" asked Mother. "If so, she must come along."

I frowned at Mother even as Miller's face clouded. "My wife, my wife. I suppose you could say, 'What wife?'"

"You have been married," she observed. I, too, had noticed the pale, indented band of flesh on his finger where until recently a ring had been. To me, this was an apt symbol of the effect of marriage, deforming the flesh and draining the skin of color.

"Uh-huh. Three times. None stuck. Guess I'm just too restless for a woman to endure. And I like my solitude."

"For a hermit, you seem to enjoy society."

His chest swelled as he laughed. "Well, Mrs. Cochrane, I like people well enough, so long as it's not the same people each day. I quite enjoy these soirees and salons, where people are polished like buttons and on their best behavior. It's the streetcars and sidewalks and markets and the everyday elbow-jostle that sets my teeth on edge." His brow grew troubled. "That was the trouble with Angie and me. She loved it, city life. Her concession was to move from New York to Washington D.C.—which you can hardly call the country life. So when I said we were moving out West, she decamped with our daughter back to New York, and that was that."

"I'm so sorry." I was simultaneously proud of Angie, furious with her, and grateful to her. That last was troubling.

"That must be hard," said Mother, "to be away from your child. What is her name?"

"Juanita." They spent several minutes discussing his little girl.

As much as I liked children, the topic was not excessively pleasing to me, so at the first opportunity I said, "Do you make your living as a writer?"

"How I wish! No, I made my mint during the Gold Rush in California. Now I scribble. Seems to go over well, though. What the devil!"

A fight had broken out nearby, with two men quarreling and a woman weeping. She had asked a handsome fellow to dance, and he had rebuffed her, citing her looks. Her brother was now avenging the slight. All three were quite drunk.

"So much for best behavior," I observed as we edged toward the exit.

"Isn't that the truth!" exclaimed Miller, instinctively putting his bulk between me and the violence.

Feeling responsible for us, Señor Garcia found us outside and offered to escort us home. Mother accepted before I could speak a word, so we took our farewell from Miller and rode in the late-night carriage back to our rooms, where Señor Garcia kissed my hand, but no more.

"I hope he was not offended," said Mother as we undressed before our mirrors.

"Why would he be?"

"Be he Mexican, American, Russian, or Chinese, no man ever enjoys being ignored for another."

"I didn't ignore him!"

"Not until you began conversing with Mr. Miller. Then you could hear no one else."

"That's not at all true," I said mulishly.

"It was like watching two opposing armies lobbing cannon fire at each other without cease." She said it with a knowing smile.

In fact, I did feel as if I had been in a battle. A skirmish of wits. I was reminded of Wilson. But Miller seemed to approve of me, which was refreshing.

And a little unsettling.

A S WE'D ARRANGED, WE MET Mr. Miller in the park just after two o'clock the following day, when the heat became more bearable. Together, we three traveled to Coffin Street. On the way he quizzed me. "So you're enjoying Mexico City?"

"Of course. Only. . ." I trailed off.

"Only?"

"The sights in the city have begun to assume a familiar look. I've seen all the ones that matter, and I've written about them as much as I think the *Dispatch*'s readers will care for. I am beginning to think of moving elsewhere."

He bobbed his chin sagely. "I know what you mean. However, there is something comforting in seeing the familiar, in things that haven't changed in several hundred years. This time around, I mean to visit all my old haunts. Remind myself of my youth."

Thus I discovered that this was not his first visit to Mexico City, only his most recent. I felt a fool, having described for him all the things which had to have been old hat to him. Yet when we reached Coffin Street, he marveled. "Little Nell, you are a second Columbus! You have discovered a street that has no like, and I have been over the world twice. It's quite fine, isn't it?" He gave a hearty laugh, then said, "One good turn deserves another. Follow me."

He led us up one street and down another until we reached the Street of the Jewel. "Here is a paseo inextricably linked to Love and its close companion, Despair."

"How so?" asked Mother.

He pointed to a door. "Here dwelt the vibrant Violante Armejo, with her husband Gaspar Villareal. Not a wealthy man, Gaspar, but he had enough to allow his wife to remain at home. Which suited her. She was averse to stepping outside, despite her incredible beauty."

"Or perhaps because of it," said Mother wryly.

Miller laughed heartily. "Perhaps so! Well, one day a young nobleman, Diego de Fajardo, was riding by. Thirsty, he called and asked a servant for a drink of water. As a gracious hostess, Violante instructed her servant to substitute wine for water. Feeling obligated to thank the lady of the house for the change in beverages, he dismounted and entered. Thus he found Violante in her hammock, garbed all in white, a vision of refinement, beauty, and perfection. The thanks had not passed his lips but he'd determined to win this angel from her husband."

I frowned. "Perhaps she had no wish to be won."

Miller wagged his huge finger in the air. "Perspicacious, Miss Bly! Day after day, Diego watched the house until he determined when he could find the lady alone. It was near nightfall when he spied Gaspar departing. Moments later he was inside the courtyard, falling at Violante's feet and professing his love. She spurned him, reproaching him with such vehemence that he saw his folly for what it was. He fled, and she began to head to her chamber to pray with her rosary. But she tripped on an object Diego had dropped. It was a gift for her: a bracelet he'd had made, with her name in diamonds, entwined with his own coat of arms.

"Just then, her husband returned, having forgotten his gloves. He'd observed Diego rush from his home, and seeing the gift, he drew his dagger. Without a word, he plunged it into her breast. As she died, he plucked up the bloody bracelet and journeyed to the home of Diego de Fajardo."

"And they dueled," I said, bemused.

"Not at all. Diego was awakened in the morning by his servants, who told him there was a strange sight in the street. Outside his door was Gaspar, dead by his own hand. Embedded in the door was the knife covered in both his wife's blood and his own. From the knife's handle hung the bracelet."

"How terrible," said Mother.

"Quite," I said, biting off my words. "It was too much trouble, I suppose, to speak to his wife before murdering her?"

Miller shook his head. "You're absolutely correct, of course. But there is something beautiful in it, is there not? Arthur and Lancelot, Tristan and Iseult, Romeo and Juliet. Love denied is poetic."

"Says the poet. This reporter thinks it's stupid."

Momentarily perplexed, Miller burst with sudden laughter. "Well, I can see this was a bust! Perhaps I can make up for it. I'm meant to join a party that's off to visit the Floating Gardens this weekend. Would you ladies care to join us? You said last night you were growing tired of the city. And it would make a glorious story for the folks back home."

It was no surprise to anyone that I immediately said yes. Anyone, except myself.

TWENTY-SIX

PERILOUS EYES

I HAD ALREADY PLANNED A VISIT to the famous Floating Gardens of La Viga, so as Joaquin and I set the date for an excursion to Lake Texcoco, I told myself this was purely a matter of happy happenstance, nothing more.

That morning, a Sunday, found me up early of my own volition for perhaps the first time in my life. I was surprised to find Mother still in bed.

"I have a terrible headache," she complained.

"Well, eat something before we have to leave."

"I am not going," she informed me from under her forearm.

"What?"

"I require a day to myself."

"What?"

"I would only hamper your enjoyment of the day. You can tell me all about it when you return."

My jaw hung open. Mother's aim was all too transparent. She wanted me to be alone with Miller. *What is she thinking?* Rather than remaining by my side, as a chaperone should, she was practically shoving me into the arms of a man we had only just met!

I said so, and she squinted at me from under her arm. "You could always cancel. Mr. Miller and his party will understand. And then you could stay and take care of me. " She placed a pillow over her eyes. "Though if you do remain, please stay quiet."

"Fine. Fine! I'm going." *It will serve her right if I do fall for Miller.*

Thus it was that I joined Miller and six of his American and British acquaintances—both male and female—in climbing aboard a train car labeled LA VIGA just as the sun was cresting the hilltops. They had purchased several luncheon baskets for the trip. Hearing that my mother was not to join us, they all made the appropriately solicitous statements, and then Miller said jovially, "More food for us, then."

Discussion on the first part of the journey was spent on safe territory, mostly touristy things, like translating signs that we passed or discussing oddities, such as a fortress that had been turned into a slaughterhouse. Then, some eight miles out of the city, the car stopped. Alighting, we were instantly set upon by eager boatmen, each clad in a similar suit of white linen shirt and pants.

"In Venice, the gondoliers wear black," observed Miller before bargaining our passage with the best-looking prospect. The one he chose had broad, powerful shoulders, which spoke well of his capability.

The eight of us followed him to his boat, a flat affair with a tin roof, some hanging linens to keep out the sun, and pink calico covering the seats. He said he would take us for six dollars, but Miller aggressively haggled him down to one. "It's the same all over. They don't respect you unless you drive a hard bargain."

Punting out onto the water, we experienced a unique version of market day. Boats on either side of us were packed full of produce, livestock, and marvelously colored flowers. I had never seen such roses! Daisies, honeysuckles, bachelor's buttons, and poppies that took my breath away. Miller offered to buy me a bouquet, but I preferred a wreath, which I could wear without interfering with my ability to take notes. He draped it around my neck, and we both smiled.

It was a day of smiles. From the shore, from other boats, smiles were directed at the two of us, seated together in the sun, while the others huddled in the shade of the canopy. "Everyone thinks we're lovers, on a clandestine excursion," I ventured softly.

It was a perfect opportunity to flatter me, but Miller did not take it. "More like a father taking his daughter out for the day. Granddaughter," he added wryly.

I laughed, but inside I felt a fool. *Have I misinterpreted what's happening? And why was that disappointing? Didn't I say I was uninterested in a Mexican romance?*

Our conversation turned to literature. It turned out that Miller personally knew all the great writers of the day, including Walt Whitman and Mark Twain. As I had finally devoured *The Adventures of Huckleberry Finn*, we discussed how it had utterly confounded expectations.

"Yes," agreed Miller, "old Sam's outdone himself."

"Sam?" I asked.

"Sam Clemens. Mark Twain to you."

"Oh." For some reason, I never imagined Mark Twain to be a pseudonym. How many readers believed my name really was Nellie Bly?

Miller was amused. "With a name like his, I'd change it too. Of course, I'm no one to cast stones."

I lit up. "Oh? And what name are you running away from?"

Looking sly, he lowered his voice so the others might not hear. "You promise not to spread it around? It would murder my reputation."

I lifted my hand, palm out. "I promise."

"Cincinnatus."

If he expected me to laugh, he was disappointed. "I think it a marvelous name! So where did Joaquin come from?"

He ducked his head. "I quite like the tales of Joaquín Murrieta. You know of him? The Robin Hood of El Dorado? He was everything a young man looks for in a hero: young, wronged, daring, and immortal."

"Immortal?"

"Nothing conveys immortality faster than dying young!"

I considered. "I can see taking his name while you were out in the wilds. Joaquin is more intimidating. But I will think of you as Cincinnatus. A citizen of the world." I could see he was pleased.

We passed through the customs gate, where I was outraged to discover how poor people on their way to sell at market were taxed above their ability to pay. The others and I discussed this at some length, with me stating firmly that government had no business crushing penniless people trying to make a living.

"Oh, I agree, Little Nell," exclaimed Miller. "The best thing government can do is to let people alone."

But that was a statement with which I could not agree. "No, the best thing government can do is see that everyone has a fair chance to live their life."

"Who's to say what's fair?" asked one of Miller's friends, a British man with spectacles.

"The law," I responded. "Without the law, it is the rich who will dominate. Impecunious people can't be allowed to make money, lest they themselves become rich and so pollute the exclusive power of the wealthy!"

Miller rubbed his neck. "Can't argue with that. But is it wise to pass laws that make everyone equal? Who then shines bright?"

"You only say that because you consider yourself anyone's equal. Whereas I, a woman, am not equal. By law, I am less than you. Is that right? Is that just? How would you care to have your life decided by something you have no control over, like your gender or the color of your skin?"

The two other women on the boat applauded. Miller stroked his beard, frowning. "Can't say I'd like it at all," he admitted.

"No, you wouldn't. Let me put it to you this way: you made your money in the Gold Rush. Did you have friends who went there, and didn't make a fortune?"

"Of course."

"Were they all lazy and foolish?"

"All? Certainly not. Some were, of course. But there were many who were simply unlucky."

"So luck determines all? Am I simply unlucky to be female?"

"I can't see you being unlucky at all." I could tell from his eyebrows that Miller's temper was rising. "Here you are with a good job any man would long to have, living in a foreign land, able to make your way with your wits. You got that by pluck and grit, by refusing to know your place. Little Nell, you are proof that if someone wants something badly enough, they can take it."

"Nothing of the sort! I'm proof of what you say—luck decides everything! I was lucky to be given a chance no other woman was afforded. Given that chance by the whim of a man! And look what I've been able to do with it! Now imagine if all women were afforded the chance, legally, to ply their God-given talents rather than cook and wash and clean and give birth."

"Then you would cease to be special. And I think you like being special, Little Nell. I think you like being unique."

That remark cut. For the first time, I saw what his wives might have found objectionable. At peace, Miller was an angel. Roused, he was a bear, ferocious and mean.

I turned from him, and he from me, and together we drifted in silence for a time while our companions filled the awkward space in over-awed exclamations of the local beauty. It was certainly gorgeous, but my thoughts were turned furiously inward as I crafted several cutting remarks for the next exchange.

It was impossible, however, to ignore the glory of the day and the beauty of the landscape. The shimmering water made a narrow lane between banks studded with trees that were more like pillars, tall and narrow and proud.

But I saw nothing at all that resembled what I had imagined to be a "floating garden." Looking past Miller, I said, "Boatman, where are the floating gardens?"

"There, señorita," he answered, pointing to an island in the center of the water.

"What, that solid, dry land?"

"No, señorita. With your permission we will take a canoe and go in among them."

"Con mucho gusto," I said with a smile.

Miller grunted in satisfaction. "There's the smile I was looking for."

I pulled a face at him as we clambered awkwardly into a little dugout barque, borrowed from the owners of a modest castle built of cane and roofed with straw. Our boatman dropped neatly into the water, which here was just a few feet deep. Gliding us along, he waded toward a stone bridge so low it threatened to behead us.

It was here that I discovered the truth: the Floating Gardens were, in fact, no such thing! I had pictured ranks of flowers and vegetation actually floating upon the water. At first glance, this seemed to be the case. But in reality the Floating Gardens were islands, each between fifteen and thirty feet wide, and solid enough to support cattle and horses, sheep and pigs. I know because I saw them! And there were homes, the quaintest little homes, each surrounded by hedges of roses.

The scents were intoxicating, and despite my disappointment at the gardens not actually floating, I joined the others of our party in plucking up the gorgeous water lilies to adorn our hair, our garments, and our baskets. Mischievously, I took a large one and planted it in Miller's fine beard. He laughed and placed another in my hair. Just like that, the group relaxed and everyone could again partake in the unadulterated pleasure in the day.

Yet I could not get over my disappointment. "Why are these called the Floating Gardens if they do not float?"

Miller shrugged. "I imagine they did float, in their youth. Starting as weedy children, they grew sinews of cane and put down roots. Slowly earth was drawn to them, and presto! Up sprang an island."

I wrinkled my nose. "So they are now in their dotage? Old age and rheumatism has stiffened their joints, leaving them forever stationary?"

"Speaking as your elder by several decades," said Miller with a grumpiness not wholly unfeigned, "allow me to object. Be kind to age, lest it be unkind to you."

"If I do live to grow old, I hope I have enough honesty in me to not lie about my nature."

He laughed. "Vanity makes an innocent lie look attractive. No, my Nell, the gardens do not float. But please do not spoil the pretty belief by telling the truth about them in your paper."

I cocked my head. "Are they any less beautiful for not floating? They are simply misrepresented, not maligned."

A smile twitched his moustaches as he hooded his eyes against the sunlight. "You mean to reveal all, don't you?"

"I may," I allowed. Certainly, I had imagined what a good story it would make.

"And will your revelations stem from a love of the truth?" he asked with interest that was both benevolent and malicious at once. "Or because you cannot bear to do what you are told?"

"It depends," I said, "on who is telling."

"I don't believe that for a moment," he answered.

We alighted on one of the islands, and as it was close to noon we broke open our baskets and picnicked. Miller's basket contained a dozen hard-boiled eggs, two loaves of bread, an ample supply of cold chicken, some ripe oranges and grapefruit, some sweets, and, to my utter surprise, a dozen bottles of beer.

To my raised brows Miller exclaimed, with absolute justice, "Well, we can't drink the water!"

Two members of our party were temperance advocates, and they declined our beer. This proved to be wise of them: unstoppering the first bottle, we discovered it had gone quite sour. "Damn and blast," said Miller with more resignation than vehemence. "It's so confounded hard to preserve beer down here. Maybe the next bottle will be better," he added, reaching for it.

"No, thank you!" I said. "I do not want to experiment with my stomach."

"I'll try it," said our neighbor, the male half of the temperance-advocating couple. "I don't drink, so I'm the perfect one to taste your beer. I can tell you if it's off without succumbing to its power." He glanced at his disapproving wife. "I promise, my love, I will not enjoy it."

So Mr. Temperance tested each and every bottle of beer. Strictly speaking, he drank more than was necessary to discover if the fermented brew had gone bad. I tried not to laugh as he began slurring his words, and Miller averted his gaze whenever a smile threatened to undo him. At last, Mr. Temperance attempted to stand and fell over, and we all laughed, save his wife.

Soon the other couples strolled off to explore, leaving Miller and me in the company of the dozing intemperate and his hot-tempered wife. There was not far to go on such a small island, and we could not help but see one young lady kiss her beau upon the lips.

"Ah, love!" sighed Miller. "'Love well who will, love wise who can.'"

I had just enough wit to realize he was quoting himself. "After three marriages, I'm surprised you believe in love."

"It's a poor poet who doesn't believe in love. 'Love is a smoke made with the fume of sighs.'"

"That's Shakespeare." I remembered part of the next line. "'A fire sparkling in lovers' eyes.'"

"'Being vexed, a sea nourished with loving tears. What is it else?'"

The next bit eluded me. "Something, something—'the source of bliss'?" I suggested. When he did not nod, I continued extemporaneously. "The cause of maddened anguish? The bulge in the lawyer's purse, made fat with breach of promise and divorce case fees?"

"Ha! I don't believe they had those in Romeo's day."

"If they had, Juliet might well have survived to lead a happy life. People often say what a great love story that is. But in a great love story, they'd live."

Miller wagged a weathered finger. "Ah, but that's hardly the fashion! A love cannot be great unless it is tragic, doomed. . ." He raised his brows and offered me an orange, "Or forbidden."

"Are you Adam, or the serpent?"

"'Neither, fair maid, if either thee dislike.' But as to love, it *must* be tragic, Nell! That way, you experience it fully. Marriage, of course, is the definition of tragedy. It is built into the very fabric of the wedding vow: 'till death us do part.' I may have my doubts about cohabitation, and even marriage itself. But my faith in love is unshaken. And there's no better place to be in love than Mexico," he said expansively, reclining upon his elbows to gaze up at the trees and sky beyond. "Perhaps that's why I came back. When I was last here, some six years ago, I—" He paused, shooting a glance to me.

Amused, I wafted him with my hand. "Go on."

"Well, I made an utter fool of myself over a dark-haired lass with smoldering eyes. I was only able to excise her from my brain by warning the world against her, and those like her." Stretching out upon his back, he recited:

> Some fragrant trees,
> Some flower-sown seas
> Where boats go up and down,
> And a sense of rest
> To the tired breast
>
> In this beauteous Aztec town.
> But the terrible thing in this Aztec town
> That will blow men's rest to the stormiest skies,
> Or whether they journey or they lie down—
> Those perilous Spanish eyes!
>
> Snow walls without,
> Drawn sharp about
> To prop the sapphire skies!
> Two huge gate posts,
> Snow-white like ghosts—
> Gate posts to paradise!
>
> But, oh! turn back from the high-walled town!
> There is trouble enough in this world I surmise,

Without men riding in regiments down—
Oh, perilous Spanish eyes!

If Miller's aim had been jealousy, he had shot true. *No one has ever written poetry for me! Well, not unless you count the neighbor boy when I was five.* And the day was stirring me, giving me a reckless itch. Taking Miller by the hand, I drew him to his feet. "You'll fall asleep if you stay there much longer. Come, show me the rest of the island."

It was an invitation, and he understood it. We strolled arm in arm until we were out of sight. Then he turned and, without a word, kissed me. I let him, and when he grew tentative I used my arms to draw him tighter. It occurred to me that my virgin status was more burdensome than precious, and I was half of a mind to be rid of it. *I could certainly never hope for a better setting.* And a man like Miller would not rush like a boy, but take his time. A poet, in a garden, in a foreign land—it was a poem itself.

And yet. . .

Miller had spoken the truth. Love was tragic. And while my flirtations with him were pleasurable, there was no tragedy here. No passion. No adventure. Only kindness, friendship, and reason. Later, I would look back at the girl I was then and think, *What a fool you were, to reject those. For those are the brick and mortar to a very comfortable kind of love.*

But something made me break away. Miller was a gentleman, proceeding no further than the lady allowed. I smiled at him to show my lack of remonstrance. He chuckled and said something amusing that I immediately forgot. *Not everything a poet says is worth remembering.*

Recomposing ourselves, we returned to the others and passed the rest of the day in a kind of quiet solitude, smiling wistfully. He bought me a hat, stark in black and white. Like the writing on the wall.

That evening, dancing to the blaring brass band we discovered in the square, I felt alone as I wrestled with myself. Joaquin was everything I was looking for in a lover: an ambitious, intelligent, rich man without an ego. Well, without *too much* ego. Still, on paper, he was the very man for me.

And yet. . .

That night, as my head hit my pillow back in my own bed, it was not Miller's face that swam into my imagination.

And *that* was a tragedy.

TWENTY-SEVEN

DENOUNCED

I HAD BEEN SO BUSY WRITING my stories that I had not put much thought into how they were being received at home. Madden cabled when a subject I had touched on tickled his fancy, or when one palled. He was characteristically brusque. "More pulque, Coffin Streets, less museums."

If Madden was terse, Wilson was verbose, penning long letters full of newsroom talk, though never anything personal. He also sent me my clippings, which I appreciated, for I could see the growing size of my byline. NELLIE IN MEXICO was the header, and I could imagine the pride readers felt in their adventurous girl abroad.

But a letter Gestefeld received had me raging. Spitting mad, I wrote a public letter to my editor, my pen flying as it hadn't since I'd challenged Wilson's inane ramblings about "a woman's sphere."

For the last year I have been engaged on the staff of your paper and have endeavored, in my humble way, to perform my duties faithfully, careful not to take advantage of my being a woman, and yet without the least desire to be mannish. During my short newspaper career, I have experienced nothing but kindness not only from acquaintances I have formed, but from your managing editor and the Quiet Observer, to whom I owe everything. I came to Mexico with the intention of doing as well as was in my power, in the way of news for the paper. So far I have received but favorable comments from those I left behind.

The newly found friends here have endeavored to extend every kindness and courtesy to me and I, feeling my inability to do justice to their beautiful country, have refused all requests to see my letters. Some very anxious ones have written to private parties in Pittsburg and obtained the DISPATCH containing my communications. The other day, a gentleman received a letter from which I make this extract: "Nellie Bly is quite a scribe, but envious people hereabouts do say that it is not she, but a brother who writes the articles signed by her name. However, I believe this report to be false."

With the desire not to appear in a false light to my friends here, I have written this, which I hope you will favor me by publishing. Although they know that I am here alone with my mother, I desire that they may also know that Nellie Bly has no brother, and never had, to whom she was indebted for one item or suggestion in her newspaper efforts.

I practically stabbed the paper as I finished, picturing Albert's face. *Albert!* Without a shred of evidence, I knew Albert was the culprit, that he had been telling everyone that *he* was the true author of his sister's works. I didn't know what made me angrier: Albert's perfidy or the stupidity of those who believed it.

"Now Elizabeth," Mother chided more than once, "you have no proof."

It wasn't true. I had a lifetime of proof. But also a lifetime of experience that told me Mother wouldn't hear a word against Albert. It did nothing to mend my mood.

Certainly Miller, arriving to take us to the theatre that night, was shocked by my unexpected ferocity. Yet he seemed to like me the better for it. I was too furious with men in general, however, to even acknowledge his renewed attentions, or to feel bad about having led him on about his chances in romancing me.

That rumor was the spur I needed to redouble my reporting efforts. Mother and I traveled outside the city, taking trips to Zócalo, Guadalupe, Veracruz, and Jalapa. When we shocked the locals by carrying our own bags, I made sure to mention it in my next article: "The Mexicans surveyed myself and my chaperone in amazement. But I defied their gaze and showed them that a free American girl can accommodate herself to any circumstances."

I did not mention that we carried our own baggage because we were attempting to conserve our funds. After almost three months in Mexico, we had spent less than sixty dollars, a fact that made me quite proud. I was even praised once by a bald French gentleman who watched me, with my terrible Spanish, haggle with a porter who had insisted on carrying my bag onto a streetcar. He'd demanded that I hand over a dollar, but I'd talked him down to a quarter. The Frenchman stroked his white side-whiskers and said, "Well done, mademoiselle. I have fluent Spanish, and yet I foolishly paid him without trying to bargain!"

It was upon our return from one of these overnight trips that the first rumble began to quake my calm Mexican life. An urgent note from

Gestefeld asked me to meet him at the park near our abode. "I shall be there each morning at eight, and again every afternoon at four. Until we meet, do not approach Mijo's."

"That is alarming," said Mother when I handed her the note.

"I hope I have not offended someone," I said, trying to figure out what might have happened to cause Gestefeld's concern.

"Well, my dear, you can be a little acidic in your remarks about your fellow Americans."

"That's because I am trying to *not* be acidic about the Mexicans." My plan to speak contrarian good about the country had, at last, run afoul of reality. I liked so many of the Mexicans I'd met, and there was much beauty to absorb and enjoy. But since my arrival I had been cataloging injustices perpetrated against both the natives and the common Mexican people by their government. Mindful of Gestefeld's warnings, especially the story of the liquor store owner, I never critiqued the government in print—at least, not directly. Instead, I heaped eager praise on a renegade mayor who wanted to help the natives, or wrote about how frequently President Díaz was to be seen at the theatre, away from the work of his office. I tried to draw contrasts, excessively praising the good to draw a natural comparison to the bad. I thought I was being subtle.

But subtlety was not my strong suit.

When we finally met, Gestefeld's warning was stark. "You are in danger of being denounced."

"For what offense?" I asked at once.

He opened his briefcase and removed a clipping. "On March twenty-second, the *Dispatch* printed a story in which you mention editors from non-subsidized papers being jailed."

"Yes. I was referring to *Ahuizote*." This was a satirical antigovernment paper, like those found on every third street corner in Pittsburgh being handed out for free. "I didn't make a fuss about it."

"No," he said fairly. "But you mentioned it. And it was picked up." He removed more clippings. "Several other papers back home found the story to be of interest and ran it. Every one of them cites you as a source."

"Really?" My cheeks felt hot. *My reporting is causing a stir?* I stifled the impulse to do a little dance, as Gestefeld's gaze informed me this was not the moment for pride. "I take it these stories have made their way down here."

"Yes," he agreed.

"And been noticed."

"Yes."

"By the government?"

"Yes. But it's not the government that will denounce you. It is the other papers."

"What?!" I was shocked.

Glancing furtively around the park, he motioned for me to lower my voice. "The twenty-five or so newspapers that accept a subsidy from the government. They will claim that by singling out the editors who are not subsidized as being unjustly imprisoned, you are implying that all those who *are* subsidized are in cahoots with the Díaz government."

"Well, they are!"

Gestefeld sighed. "Of course they are. But you can't say that."

"So what are they threatening?"

"To claim you've violated Article 33."

"That sounds ominous."

"It's a provision in the Mexican constitution that designates the consequences of 'undesirable foreigners' who speak or write too freely about Mexico and Mexicans."

The warm flush in my cheeks vanished. "Consequences like imprisonment?"

"Or deportation, with a literal army of soldiers escorting you to the border."

"I think I'd prefer the latter," I said.

"I'm not certain you'd be allowed your choice," he said, exactly matching my grimly amused tone. "What will happen is that the papers will denounce you for slandering the Mexican people and the Mexican press. That will allow the government to investigate, saying they are only responding to the voice of the people."

"Very tidy," I said.

"The only benefit here is that you are a woman. The outrage in America if you were jailed would be disastrous for Díaz. It does not hurt that you are both young and attractive."

My face pinched up. "I think I'm insulted."

"Well, if it's any consolation, they might decide to have you die in an accident. A tragic warning to nosy foreigners."

"There go my little jaunts into the countryside," I joked, trying to remain jocular in spite of a very real chill.

"The good news is that they have another target. You remember Daniel Cabrera?"

I did. "He was at *Ahuizote* before it was shut down."

"He started a new paper this week. *El Hijo del Ahuizote*—the Son of *Ahuizote*. The front page was a caricature entitled 'The Cemetery Of The Press,' with graves for each paper the government has shut down. 'Independent Press, Rest In Peace,' it says."

I whistled. "I wish I was that daring."

"Don't. Daniel's gone into hiding. They may want to make you pay in his place."

"That's mildly terrifying. What should I do?"

"Allow me to head this off before they go to press about you. Let me arrange a meeting to plead your case. You will be full of wide-eyed naïveté and innocent love of all things Mexican, the picture of an American abroad. Can you do that?"

My heart was pounding. I thought of prison. I thought of my mother. I thought of the sneer on Albert's face back home. And I thought of my pride, weighing it against my own fear.

Biting my lip, I nodded.

WHEN I TOLD MILLER THE STORY, he was outraged on my behalf, and instantly protective. "We must put you on a train home at once!"

"I can't leave at once," I said. "I have to report on the Easter celebrations. And besides, everyone tells me the food will improve when Lent is over. You insisted I try some dish of lamb and peppers."

"That's hardly a reason to remain," insisted Miller. "I will send the peppers and the recipe to Pittsburgh. Your mother can make it."

"I would not know where to begin, having never tasted it myself," replied Mother. "No, I think we must stay and try it here before attempting it at home."

Her remark filled me with warmth. Though clearly nervous, she was on my side. Eventually Miller gave up with bad grace, and I didn't see him for a week as he sulked, doubtlessly composing complaining sonnets about mutinous mule-headed maidens.

The promised meeting took place in mid-April, in the offices of Gestefeld's boss, the owner of the *Two Republics*, Major Clarke. He was a cigar-chomping Texan who said nothing but made it clear by his presence that to trifle with me was to trifle with his whole paper.

Gestefeld and I sat on one side of a wide library table, while three representatives of the government-funded papers sat on the other. Their leader, seated in the center, was a careless man whose eyes alighted everywhere but on me. The Major sat at the far end of the room, smoking and apparently reading a local story in his own edition.

Gestefeld's voice was utterly polite as he presented my side of the matter in flawless Spanish. He insisted that I had made a small mention of something I had thought would be of interest at home. When the leader asked a question, Gestefeld studiously avoided looking my way as he rattled off a clearly defensive answer.

"Have they read my other pieces?" I demanded, pulling out a stack of clippings to share with them. "They are full of praise for Mexico and the Mexican people. Indeed, I have worked to dispel the myth held in America that Mexicans are lazy or less than honest. Here, see for yourselves." I pushed the stack across the table.

The leader of the trio waved his cigarillo dismissively. "No, no. *Un botón es suficiente.*"

I turned to Gestefeld. "What does that mean?"

He ignored me even as he continued to plead my case. I was forced to sit in uncomprehending frustration while my fate was decided by men speaking a language I did not know.

At one point they did reference my articles, pointing to my name. "They want to know why you publish under a false name, if not to hide your intentions."

"No woman publishes under her own name."

Gestefeld translated, adding a long and flowery explanation about women in publishing that I was glad I could not understand. Suddenly they all laughed, and Gestefeld patted my shoulder in the most patronizing way imaginable. I had an impulse to bite his hand.

At last Gestefeld smiled and heaved a sigh. It had been decided that I had no ill will for Mexico in my heart. "They agree that you may continue to write."

As if they could stop me, I thought, my arms sulkily folded. "Good."

"They will not denounce you," said Gestefeld, pointedly.

"Thank them for me." I looked at the leader. "Gracias."

The man grunted. As the trio departed they laughed with the Major and clapped Gestefeld on the back. One even offered him a cigar. And me? They did not even look at me, much less deign to address me.

Naturally, I was fuming. After they were gone, a smoking Gestefeld explained in more detail what had been said, and my anger mounted. He had gone to great lengths to use my being a woman in my favor. He'd described with great care my revulsion of bullfighting, which the other men had found charmingly girlish. One had even remarked that his daughter felt much the same.

"Did he say how old his daughter is?"

"She is almost eight."

Repressing my desire to strike something, I asked, "And what was that they said? When I asked if they had read my other writing about Mexico, what did he say?"

"He said, 'One button is enough'. Meaning, he did not need to see the whole garment. He knew from a single button that you were an enemy of Mexico."

"I'm not!"

"And I managed to convince him of that." He blew a smoke ring, then gazed at it proudly. "I assured them you had no idea that what you wrote could be insulting. That you did not understand the implication of praising the non-subsidized papers over the rest. That since you have been here the only negative story you have written was the one about bullfighting, and one could hardly blame a young lady for not enjoying blood sport. As I told you, they accepted this."

"So, in essence, they will leave me be because I am a naïve girl in a job that is beyond me, and that any offense I've caused was done in feminine ignorance."

"In essence," agreed Gestefeld reluctantly. "They have asked that, in future, you will keep to writing about the theatre and the sights and people of Mexico, and keep politics out of your work."

That was the last straw. "The Devil with that! I'll write about this meeting! Let them send me to prison! Then they'll see what bad publicity truly is!"

Gestefeld knew me well enough to stop me there, before I made good on my threat. "They wouldn't imprison you. They would either deport you, or else threaten you with violence. You, and your mother."

That sobered me. I stopped pacing, something I had not even realized I'd been doing. A danger to Mother? *No, I have to stop at once. Just do as they say. . .*

Something in me reared up. The part of me that refused to be quiet, or be told what to do. *No, I will not stop writing what I want to write. No, I will not be quiet when I see an injustice. No, I will sit not down and make them comfortable just because I am afraid and they are powerful.* If they were threatening me, it was because they were the ones who were afraid.

Afraid of me.

A flash of fire caught my eye. The Major was lighting a fresh cigar, waving the long match through the air to extinguish it even as he puffed repeatedly to get the vulgar thing going.

"Miss Bly," he said. "Every day I stroll down the paseo with my two daughters. And every day the Mexicans say, 'There goes Clarke with his two republics.' Droll, very droll."

I frowned. "Pardon me, Major, but I don't—"

He pointed his cigar at me. "I do not have room for a third republic. You are not my daughter. I can't walk alongside you every day, too."

Bristling at his paternalism, I looked him in the eye. "Thank you for your support today. And you are correct. I am not your daughter. Nor am I a child. I can walk on my own." And I walked out of the room.

AFTER THAT DAY, IT WAS ONLY a matter of time. Throughout May, I wrote many stories: about Easter, about the Feast of the Gamblers and the Feast of the Flowers, and about riding on a streetcar. I wrote about visits to Guadalupe, Córdoba, and the disappointing pyramid of Cholula. I wrote about the tree in the village of Popotla called El Árbol de la Noche Triste, where Cortés sat and wept his failure. I wrote about the business opportunities awaiting Americans in Mexico, from rubber to silk. None of this was objectionable.

But I was also investigating stories I did not mean to publish—at least, not yet. I interviewed journalists, shop owners, and even some soldiers. My questions were always innocuous, and I made sure to listen rather than prodding my subjects in any particular direction.

Sometimes they were loyal to President Díaz, speaking of his humble origins, his bravery in war, and his genuine fidelity to his wife. Sometimes they said things that, if published, would have seen them imprisoned.

Most of their ire was aimed not directly at Díaz, but at his right hand: former president Manuel González. I was told of the draining of the Treasury, of private debts passed off to the Mexican taxpayers, of the two-dollar lottery ticket bought by González accompanied by the message to the managers of the lottery, "See that this draws the prize today."

One memorable story of corruption was of the ancient hacienda whose owners were asked to sell their family estate for a tenth of its value. Upon their refusal, they suffered all manner of misfortunes. Their horses were shot and stolen. Their cattle, water, and even family members were poisoned. When the land was at last sold to González, it went for a paltry five percent of its value.

I learned of González's abandoned wife, who was living in poverty, and the affair between González and the daughter of Díaz. And also how Díaz, upon resuming the presidency that González had been keeping warm for him, passed a law garnishing a percentage of all government employees' salaries to make up for the two-million-dollar shortfall caused by his friend.

If asked, the men who related these stories could claim with perfect honesty that they had said nothing directly against President Díaz. But their implications were clear. When they told me of the failed attempt to blow up the president the previous November—as in the historical plot involving Guy Fawkes and James Stuart, the conspirators had been discovered and punished—they were not speaking ill of the government. They were simply sharing plain facts.

Those facts came to fill my notebooks, however, and they spoke for themselves: Ten million souls in Mexico, but eight million of them were natives, forced into perpetual poverty, without voice or vote. Two political parties, but without distinction. One excellent constitution, which on paper excelled the freedoms of our own, but a government that allowed none of those freedoms in practice.

I don't know when I first noticed the presence of the Serenos. It was a vague sense at first, that imperceptible animal instinct of being watched. Back in Pittsburgh I had always been aware of the men who followed me, trying to gain my attention and favor. Perhaps it was those experiences which helped to ring the first warning bells in my mind. But it was a mark of how very naïve I still was that I did not perceive the jacketed policemen as a threat.

Not until they made the threat explicit.

Walking home alone at dusk from a completely innocent interview, I found my way blocked by three large men in coats with piping and buttons that shone. They smiled at me. I smiled back. They did not, as Mexicans always did, step aside to let a young lady pass. Nor did they attempt to pass me. They simply stood, blocking my path.

I stepped to one side to circumvent them, and one of them took a lazy sideways step to intercept me. Naturally, I stepped to the other side. This was a mistake, as the move put me next to the wall of the building to my left. At once, the policemen stepped closer, one on either side of me, one directly in front, penning me against the wall.

The other two turned outwards, scowling at passersby who might have questioned this crowding of a lady on the public street. Still, I could not believe anything truly awful might happen. The sun was still in the sky, and this was a bustling paseo, with people passing in both directions.

But no one on the street said anything. If the Mexicans all around saw me—and they surely did—they chose to continue walking.

The man facing me said nothing. Summoning my courage, I looked him in the eye. "Yes?"

A smile twitched the lips of the Sereno. Slowly, with deliberate care, his hand rose from his side. It was empty—there was no hint of a weapon.

He reached toward me, his hand moving with aching slowness, inch by inch. Had he moved swiftly, I might have screamed for help. Instead, I remained frozen. His fingers climbed toward the center of my chest. I barely breathed as his forefinger and thumb closed over a button on my dress just below my sternum. He pinched the button, and held it.

My gaze lifted from his fingers up to his face. His expression was menacing in its utter blankness, its lack of threat, its utter disconnection from my humanity.

Suddenly, he yanked my button free. I gasped, then looked at him with my mouth hanging stupidly open.

Holding the button between his pinched fingers, the Sereno raised it between us so I could see it. Then, with the same awful slowness, he placed the button in his pocket.

For a moment he remained still, looking at my flushed face, listening to my staccato breathing, studying my trembling shoulders. Then, with exaggerated politeness, he stepped back, bowed, and waved for me to go.

I plunged past him and his companions, my hand instinctively closing around the new gap in my clothing. Walking as fast as I might without running, I hastened to our rooms, where I shut the door and leaned against it, my heart thudding against my ribs like a panicked bird's wings against its cage.

"Elizabeth?" asked Mother, rising from her seat by the window. "What's the matter?"

Squaring my shoulders, I forced myself upright. "Mother—it's time to leave."

One button was enough.

THAT NIGHT I SENT NOTES to Miller, Gestefeld, and Señor Garcia, asking them to see us in the morning. I spent the night with the chair propped against the door, wakeful and jumping at every sound.

In the morning I was a bedraggled mess as all three men arrived. I tried not to show my gratitude. But there wasn't much left of pride at the moment. I was, in essence, about to run away with my tail between my legs.

My note to Miller must have conveyed my state of mind. He showed me a pistol under his coat. "Those scoundrels! What kind of men threaten a woman?"

"The kind that are afraid of one," I said, trying to keep my spirits up.

"This is wise," Gestefeld assured me. Indeed, he looked quite relieved. "But we must be certain you get away safely."

I frowned. "What do you mean?"

"It's a long ride to El Paso," he said. "And away from Mexico City, you do not have the protection of your friends."

Garcia said, "Perhaps I should purchase a ticket and ride with you to the border."

"I'll do it." Miller almost bounded off, but I caught his elbow.

"Don't," I said.

"But if they arrest you on the train—"

"They won't—if you do me one last service."

Miller was all attention. "Anything!"

"Send a cable to George Madden at the *Pittsburg Dispatch*. Tell him we are on our way back home, and to have a reporter waiting to meet us at the station. And tell them to run the announcement of our return in tomorrow's edition."

Gestefeld bobbed his head. "Good thinking, Miss Cochrane. And I'll post something in tomorrow's *Two Republics* bidding you a regretful farewell. If your return home is advertised, they cannot delay you without fear of drawing attention."

"I'd still rather go with you," growled Miller. "Let Gestefeld send your cable home. I'm due to leave soon at any rate. I've lost my taste for Mexico."

I took his hand and patted it. "Not on my account, I hope, Cincinnatus."

Miller squeezed my fingers. "I should do much on your account, my Nell."

The intensity of his gaze made me recall the Sereno and the button. I stifled a shudder and drew in a breath. "That is very kind, Mr. Miller. But I am not a poetic lady in need of a knight. I'm a reporter, rushing home to file a story." I stepped back and held out my hand. "Besides, I have my mother to protect me."

Miller took my rebuff of his gallantry graciously, though I imagined he would later hail curses down on my head. *Amazing, that a man of his years can be so easily quashed by a twenty-one-year-old woman.* But I was not interested in his grand gesture, or his pistol and his gruff presence intruding on my story. I wondered, when it came to romance, if men ever grew up.

Our last day in Mexico was a panicked rush to pack, and I twice burst into tears, declaring that I would not go, I would stay and fight. Both times, I allowed myself to be talked out of petulant self-destruction. Thus I positioned myself to be leaving Mexico against my will, even if it had been my idea in the first place. A sorry sop to my pride, which everyone recognized and no one spoke of.

I took it out on Miller most of all. As we arrived at the station before dawn the following day, I acted as if it was his fault I was leaving. I even refused to allow him to carry our bags aboard. "We'll carry them ourselves," I declared, hefting mine. "I want to confound the Mexicans to the last."

"Not all Mexicans, I hope," said Señor Garcia.

I relented at once. "Of course not. Only your horrendous government."

Gestefeld bit his lip, holding back the warning that was all too clear on his face. With polite acknowledgements and many promises of immediate correspondence and continued good-will, Mother and I boarded the train—only to wait an hour before it pulled out. A very uncomfortable wait, expecting every moment to be dragged off the train and thrown into some prison, such as the one we had seen at the border where they shot prisoners trying to "escape."

I was annoyed at the gratitude I felt when all three men remained to watch us off, lest the secret police spirit us away before the locomotive began to move. But there we remained, smiling and waving at each other, for seventy-one minutes. I knew exactly how long it was because I kept throwing glances at the watch in my hand, spending the time between glances worrying my finger against my lucky thumb ring over and over.

At last the whistle blew, the doors closed, and Garcia, Gestefeld, and Miller vanished in a cloud of steam. We were off.

As we left Mexico City behind us, I found myself feeling ashamed of my cowardice, and I wondered what would have happened if I'd shown a little more backbone. Other reporters were willing to risk their lives for a story—was my decision to flee the mark of a woman's wilting courage?

I am not running away, I assured myself over and over as I watched the landscape race by. *I am removing myself from enemy territory to take up my best weapon.*

A free press.

IV

THE GODS OF GOTHAM

THE BEAUTIFUL WRECK

UNABLE TO TELL HER NAME OR ANTECEDENTS

The mysterious and beautiful young woman who wandered into the Home for Women at No. 84 Second Avenue last Friday, and from there was sent to Bellevue Hospital, is still there in the insane pavilion, but will leave late this afternoon for Blackwell's Island. Dr. Braisted, who is in charge of the pavilion and who at first thought that she was suffering from hysterical mania, said to the Telegram man to-day that she was undoubtedly insane.

She is about eighteen years old, of medium height, with dark brown hair, hazel eyes, delicate features and has evidently the air and tone of a well brought up girl. Her clothing consists of a dress of light-gray fashionably made material trimmed with black lace; her shoes are of fine material and No. 2½ in size. There is not the slightest mark on her clothing by which she can be identified. Dr. Briasted thinks that she is a native of a southern country, probably Cuba.

"I have not been able to learn anything of her antecedents or past history," says Miss Scott, the experienced head nurse. "I speak to her sometimes in French, and at lucid intervals she seems to understand what I say, and evidently at first made a mental effort to answer intelligently. She has evidently been properly raised and well educated. She complains of the quality of the food and the size of the cups and saucers and wants to be waited on. The same is the case in grooming herself, and evidently expecting some one to perform that duty. At one of her lucid intervals she said that her parents are dead, and at another time she spoke of traveling on the ocean with her grandmother; but she could not remember her name, and, in fact, her mind as to the past is a complete blank."

No one has called to inquire for the girl, and Dr. Braisted said that she would be sent to the Blackwell's Island Insane Asylum late this afternoon.

—*Evening Telegram*
Monday, September 26, 1887

TWENTY-EIGHT

HOME AGAIN

PITTSBURGH, PA
TUESDAY, JUNE 22 1886

DESPITE OUR FEARS, WE CROSSED the Mexican border without any trouble, and a week later arrived in Pittsburgh, healthy and whole. It was the height of summer, which somehow managed to surprise me. For some absurd reason, I had imagined there would still be snow upon the ground.

To my even greater surprise, a *Dispatch* reporter was waiting for me—I had forgotten that I'd asked for one. Even *more* surprising, he was there to interview me! Rather than being the author of the story, Nellie Bly became its subject.

I answered his questions without sacrificing the best parts of the story. Those, I planned to tell myself.

I went to work right away. It was comforting to march back up those dreadfully narrow steps and find my old desk waiting for me. I received the greetings of Madden and the other newsmen like a triumphant conquistador. The roaches professed disappointment that I had neither brought them gifts nor married a Mexican. "We had a pool going," they informed me.

"Who won?"

"Wilson," they said with a groan. "He insisted you would not spoil your trip by marrying." It was pleasing to think the Quiet Observer knew me so well.

My first sight of Wilson himself was prosaic enough. I marched right up to his desk and said, "I'm back!"

"So I observe." He had his shoe off and was eyeing an actual cockroach skittering around the corner of his rolltop. He smacked it down, checked the sole, and grunted in disappointment. "The return of Nellie the Kid. I'm sure there are no stories left to tell about Mexico. You've seen it all."

"I may have seen all," I said, disappointed in his lack of heartiness, "but there's much more to tell."

Wilson's sigh threatened to shatter his huge frame. "Then please, for the love of all that's holy, take your time writing it. Madden tasked me with correcting your articles. I have them all here," he added, opening a drawer in his desk. Sure enough, there in a neatly stacked bundle was every article I had written in the past six months. The top sheet was covered in blue pencil, and I had to assume all the rest were as well.

I felt a flush of annoyance. "I'm sorry I was such a burden." And I stomped off to my desk to throw myself into work. *Work. Work is the answer.*

Free at last to write without fear of prison, or worse, I unloaded barrel after barrel of ink into the dictatorship of Porfirio Díaz as if I was emptying the chambers of a gun. I wrote every story I had previously suppressed. I told the truth about the Mexican press, the government, and the military—several members of which had bragged to me that they looked forward to beating America in a war. *That* caused quite a stir.

But I didn't confine myself to government matters. I continued to write about Mexican culture, though with a less accommodating eye. I tried to be kind to the many friends I had made there, and especially to the wretched natives who had no one in their own nation to speak for them. But the treatment of women and the poor in Mexico? That, I savaged.

I was surprised when my stories started to be picked up all across the country, and even more shocked when I received invitations to speak at events—though not, I noted, at another soiree with a Mexican delegation. No, most invitations came from local societies wanting to discuss what was to be done for the poor Mexican natives. Attending these events and accepting their praise, I was initially hopeful as I listened to conversations about ways to help the natives rise up and reclaim their country. But I soon saw these tea-sipping women with their lapdogs for what they were: useless and vacuous. All of their solutions revolved around sending me back to Mexico to live among the natives and teach them about America's Founding Fathers. When I suggested that the ladies go themselves, they demurred.

My fury lasted until September, by which time I was fully returned to life at home, and ready to return to life as a *Dispatch* reporter.

But first I had another homecoming to make. The lawsuit I had brought against the executor of my father's estate was finally going to be heard.

It was my season for justice.

ALBERT REFUSED TO COME, BUT the rest of the family all made the trip back to Apollo to testify for me against Colonel Jackson. They carped, they complained, and they were clearly nervous. But they came. I tried to be grateful, and not resentful, that they weren't as enthusiastic about the lawsuit as I was.

The last time we, as a family, had been in the Apollo courtroom, the same courtroom my father had once presided over, it had been to testify in Mother's divorce from Ford. Even years later, I could still recite my own testimony, having learned it by heart:

> *My age is fourteen years. I live with my mother. I was present when Mother was married to J.J. Ford. I saw them married about six years ago.*
>
> *Ford has been generally drunk since they were married. When drunk, he is very cross, and cross when sober. I've heard him scold Mother often and heard him use profane language towards her often and call her names. A whore, and a bitch. I've seen mother vexed on account of his swearing and bad names and I've seen her cry.*
>
> *Ford threatened to do mother harm. Mother was afraid of him. I've seen Ford throw the clothes after being washed and ironed on the floor and throw water on them and seen him upset the table.*
>
> *The first time I saw Ford take hold of Mother in an angry manner, he attempted to choke her. This was sometime after they were married. The next time was in the Odd Fellows Hall on New Year's Night, 1878.*

Other townsfolk had testified about that particular night, so I hadn't been required to tell that story. Which was just as well, as it was as close as I'd ever come to death. Mother, too.

Now here I am, dragging everyone back to rake over the expired coals of our lives in Apollo. Troublemaking me, trying to get a little justice in the world. During the day's travel to our old town, I had the leisure to fret over the fruitlessness of dredging up our history once again.

In a pleasant twist, though, it turned out not to be fruitless at all. While I had known in my gut there had been shenanigans involved with our family's money, I had no evidence until the court-appointed accountants revealed to the judge what they had found. The Colonel had mingled our inheritance with his own personal funds. He had paid a low interest of return, regardless of the interest he himself had received. He had marked that he'd paid for me to attend two semesters at the Indiana State Normal School, not just one.

Worst of all, he had bought our home—which was maddening in and of itself—and had owed Mother a sum every six months for her widow's percentage of that sale. But in his accounting, he had recorded those payments as money intended for our upkeep, drawn from our own inheritances. Meaning he had paid for our house with our own money!

Ford's name came up, as there were several payments to him that had never been authorized by Mother. Some were dated after the divorce. It was that, more than anything, which finally raised the ire of my siblings. Suddenly Charlie, Kate, and even Harry were as furious as I was.

Yet, as wronged as we were, it was quickly made clear that we had become outsiders. Our cousin Tom Cochran, who was now the local pharmacist and married to Colonel Jackson's sister, not only made a plea to the judge on the Colonel's behalf, he also cut us all dead. Us, his own blood kin.

Nearly all of our old friends in the town did the same. The judge, sitting in my father's old chair, intimated over and over that the town would protect its own. Sensing the financial and reputational disaster about to come down on the old Colonel's head, the judge declared that he was appointing his own accountant to look into things further. "If there is money owed to the Cochrane family," he said, pronouncing the extra *e* we had added, as if to show how foreign we were, "time is needed to assess how much."

I heard this statement with burning satisfaction, magnified when Colonel Jackson shuffled out of the courtroom without meeting my eyes. It was clear what he'd thought girls were good for. They were good for robbing.

We would never see that money. I felt sure of it. Nevertheless, it felt like a victory. Mother, Kate, Charlie, and Harry all gathered around to discuss the judge's ruling. Harry, being himself, imagined that in a week or two we would have a windfall that could support us in a better life. Charlie, more practical, said that he was simply pleased to have shamed the old fraud who had stolen our money. Kate was with Harry, focused on the money—perhaps she was hoping it would be enough to pay for her anticipated divorce.

Only Mother was downcast. She kept repeating, "I'm so sorry." It was up to me to cast the judge's decision as a huge vindication, and insist upon a celebratory luncheon before our train the next day.

I knew that my siblings had looked up several of our relations while we'd been in Apollo. I had refrained, in part because of my own anger at them, in part because I'd be snubbed. This lawsuit would not have been necessary if not for their greedy behavior upon my father's death, and I was certain that my half-brothers and sisters would feel that it reflected badly upon them. Because it did.

After lunch, Mother said she meant to visit my half-sister Mildred, whom she had helped to raise. Charlie and Harry went to look up boyhood friends. Since little Beatrice was back at home being looked after by Charlie's wife Sarah, Kate was free to socialize with former friends as well.

Myself, I decided to avoid people and take a walk through my old stomping grounds.

So few of the streets held happy memories. There was the place where we had lived with Ford, which I equated with Hell. It looked nicer than we had left it—whoever owned it had clearly worked to repair and renew it.

I wondered if they might not have been better off razing the place and salting the earth. Surely the unhappiness we'd endured lived on, absorbed by the walls and the floors and the roof, enclosing a shrine to misery.

A block away from our old home was the grocery and confectionery store that Mother had tried to set up for Ford and Albert. The idea had been that they would manage the grocery side of the business, and Mother would make the ice cream herself. For a brief moment ours had looked like an ideal life, with a mother who made ice cream every day. But Albert and Ford had quarreled from the start, and it ended as all things did with Ford: with him drunkenly drawing his pistol while hollering threats.

The building had been bought by John Blair to expand his general goods store. I spied Mr. Blair as I walked past, and he looked much the same as he had when we'd caught and sold frogs to him as children. Before the fascinated eyes of the town boys, and one Pink Cochran, he would brain the frogs, chop off their legs, and then ship the legs to Pittsburgh. The worst part was that he would then release the amputated amphibians into the alley behind his store to crawl off and attempt to survive.

Most of us children were appalled by this. Not Albert, of course. He found it the funniest thing in the world, and would slap his knee and howl as the miserable creatures slithered and flopped until they died. Whereas Harry wept the first time he saw it, and never went back to the alley, nor did he catch any frogs for Mr. Blair, no matter how many pennies he could earn.

The town had grown since my childhood. Nearly a thousand people lived in Apollo these days. I reached the new part of town, rebuilt after the fire ten years earlier. I recalled that night vividly, when a single broken kerosene lamp had started a conflagration that consumed three square blocks of Apollo, including all the buildings by the canal. I was surprised to see the new buildings already had chipped paint and signs of wear.

There was Mr. Mills's tin shop, where he canned goods for the winter. And over there was Mr. Conn's leather workshop, known as The

Muleskinner. And at the top of the street was the Methodist Episcopal church. I wondered if Reverend Lemon was still there, and if I could still shock him into cursing.

There was the schoolhouse, all two stories and forty-five by forty-eight feet. I knew the exact dimensions because as children we had been forced to measure it for a school project. For four months each year, we had been instructed in the downstairs primary school by a parade of young women who'd taught us until they could marry and escape us. Older students were allowed upstairs, where Mr. Davis taught algebra and Roman history and Shakespeare.

The only times Mr. Davis had ever spoken to me were to admonish me for being too loud and unruly. It was true that I hadn't been a good student. When I told people I just lacked patience, I was accused of being greedy for attention.

And how could I not be? When I thought about my childhood, it was always framed by my struggle to be heard. *I had so much to offer, and no one to share it with.*

Yet whenever I tried to express myself it all came out wrong.

Once, there was a little girl, Sadie, who refused to allow certain girls to play with the barrel hoops along the river. Even though I was one of the favored girls, I found this to be unfair and told her so. She continued to deny the excluded girls access to the hoops, so I bit her on the arm.

That's me, the troublemaker. Always finding a way to lose to moral high ground.

As I trundled along the tracks of this train of thought, I found myself turning up Terrace Avenue. That was the name of the street, but no one called it that. It was Mansion Row.

It was home.

A mere two blocks from our house with Ford, here stood the house I had been born into. The house now owned by the same man who had cheated us of our inheritance. The house where my father had grown ill, still, and died.

It hadn't changed. The long steps still cut a path between twin stone walls to the main porch. Twin pairs of massive Corinthian pillars still supported the portico roof two stories high. The small triangular gable behind those pillars was still supported by a miniature set of similar pillars. It was all just the same, even down to the red-stained glass in a window on the second floor.

My brothers and I had never understood that single pane of glass, and it had been a game for us to avoid the crimson beam of light it cast as it slowly moved across the upstairs landing every morning. There had been times the game was deadly serious, as if that red light would burn us through or brand us like cattle. Albert claimed to be impervious to it, always walking right through it. Whereas little six-year-old Pink climbed over the banister and lowered herself, rung by rung, down the stairs just to avoid it. Albert would always ask. "Why do you make it so much harder for yourself?" And I would have no answer, save to finish the dangerous journey I'd started.

Then Father would arrive to pluck me out of danger just as my hands began to slip. He would flip me over his shoulder and parade me through the house, laughing, "My naughty little Pinky!" And I would reach down to scratch his back, which he pretended to love. That probably only happened once, but I recalled it so clearly it might as well have been a daily occurrence. It was the very definition of my father, and home, and love...

"Pink? Pink, is that you?"

I turned around at the sound of the voice. It took me five seconds to recognize the person inside the grown woman. "Lillie?"

"I heard you were back in town!" Lillie Elliot was the daughter of the local doctor and one of my old schoolmates. We embraced, then she hooked my arm and began chattering away. "They tell me you're a writer!"

"A reporter," I said, but then I wished I had left her thinking I was a writer. It seemed somehow more glamorous. "I just came back from six months in Mexico."

"Mexico! You must tell me all about it!" With that, she took me to her parents' home, where we had played together as children.

Her mother, Mrs. Elliott, was chilly toward me—I was certain she knew my cause for being back in town, and possibly viewed me as an unsatisfactory influence on her daughter. But Lillie had always been one of those happy, devil-may-care spirits, the person most of us wish we could be, but never are. She had never bitten Sadie. But then, she had always been allowed to play with the barrel hoops.

Over tea and cookies, Lillie urged me to talk about being a newspaperwoman. I did, but we soon fell into nostalgia, as old acquaintances were apt to do.

"You look so fine," Lillie said to me. "But I always think of you in white!"

"My whites never stayed white for long," I said, laughing.

"True. You were always up some tree or under some hedge. But every morning you were back, starched and perfect. Oh, how I admired your white stockings."

"And I wanted your black ones. My fondest wish was to be like the other girls."

"No, it wasn't," Lily said with the casual disdain one only accepted from very old friends. "You may not have liked how you stood out, but you were going to stand out no matter what you wore. You played with the boys as much as with us girls. And you argued! Oh, how we all trembled when you planted your feet and got all red in the face."

"Really? I seem to remember running away more than standing to fight." Thoughts of Mexico were still in my head.

Lillie laughed. "You always were quick. The twins used to say it took the two of them to catch their little auntie."

I had twin nieces. Born to my half-brother three months before me, it had been their joke to call little me their Auntie Pink. We had been playmates together, before the family rift.

Lillie said, "Oh, that reminds me! You've heard about Cora?"

"Robert's daughter?" She was another niece, three years my elder.

"Yes," chirped Lillie. "She married Thomas Henry. Can you imagine it?"

"T.J. Henry?" I erupted with an involuntary laugh. He had been a studious boy in our own year. I shamefully remembered teasing him on a number of occasions because I, a girl, was more adventurous than he. "He's married to Cora?"

"Yes! And they're in Pittsburgh, too. He's becoming a doctor. And it's your fault!"

"Mine?"

"Don't you remember? You used to sneak that book of medicine from your father's library and shock us all with pictures of organs and... organs." She tittered. "I guess he was able to look past his embarrassment and actually take in some of the words."

"T.J. is going to be a doctor," I repeated, bemused. My initial flush of surprise turned into a sludge of resentment. *Thomas has become a member of my family, and I have to learn of it this way? I have family in Pittsburgh and they haven't looked us up? Well, I don't want to see them, either!*

Before I grew too vexed, I changed the subject. "And you? Aren't you married yet?"

Lillie flushed. "Well, no. . ."

I smiled. "But there's someone."

Flushing deeper, she pressed her lips to restrain a smile of pure happiness. "Well, I don't know. Perhaps. Do you remember Jacob? Jacob Myers?"

I did. A handsome boy some nine or ten years older than us, with a single lock of hair that fell across his left eye. We had all made fools of ourselves over him. My face must have conveyed my admiration for her achievement, for she blushed an even deeper crimson and averted her gaze.

"Well done, Lillie."

She laughed and quickly said, "Nothing is certain. He wants to be more established than he is at present. But in a few years, maybe. . ."

"A few years! Why wait? He can certainly establish himself better with you by his side. You could find work and help him."

Lillie clapped her hands. "There's that sharp tongue! What about you? What romances does a newspaperwoman have?"

"I saw a great deal of a poet while I was in Mexico," I said evasively. "And each week I receive a proposal of marriage sent to me at the paper. But I have no serious suitors."

"Do you ever correspond with any of the proposers?"

"Heavens, no! Could you imagine what would happen if I encouraged them?"

"You didn't use to mind encouraging them," she said slyly.

"Lillie, you brat, I was four years old!"

But Lillie was reveling in making me relive my youthful romance. "What was his name? Willy? Billy?"

Through gritted teeth and suppressed laughter I said, "William."

"And how old was he?" she demanded, blinking in innocence. "Twelve?"

"That's what he told me. But he was probably lying to impress me."

Lily laughed. "Trust Pink Cochran to fall for a man three times her age!"

I felt a twinge in my stomach, one that I had to fight to ignore. Not long after that remark I thanked Lillie and her mother for their hospitality and, promising to write, took my leave.

What's the saying? "There's no going home again." That was certainly true for Apollo and Cochran's Mills.

What I had not yet learned was that it was also true for Pittsburgh.

TWENTY-NINE

NAUGHTY KID

SUNDAY, MAY 15 1887

"TELL ME, HOW WAS THE PLAY, Mrs. Lincoln?"
Dropping my gloves on my desk, I shot an outraged glance at Wilson. "That's an awful greeting, Q.O."

He held up his hands. "I know, I know. A terrible joke."

"Yet you never tire of telling it."

"How was the play?"

"Well produced," I said, settling into my chair. "The backdrops and costumes were very fine."

"Ouch."

Hanging my coat over the back of my chair, it was my turn to shrug. "I don't want to be critical."

Wilson leaned back, smiling. "Except that's precisely your job description."

I grunted in response and buried myself in my papers. It was true. Over seven months, I had gradually become the thing I had most dreaded: a "culture reporter."

It had started with Madden asking me to compare Mexican theatregoers with their American counterparts. Then he asked me to review the show I had attended to write the earlier story. Then he asked me to interview the leading actress of that company, which led to her next project and my next review. It was insidious. I was soon ensnared.

The terrible part was that it was so easy, and the trappings were attractive. I could dress well, be seen, have a fuss made over me, be offered prime seats and all kinds of perquisites. Just as if I were someone who mattered. Worse, I was being paid fifteen dollars a week! It was far more than I had ever gotten paid for exposing ugly truths about life in Pittsburgh.

There was a story there. How entertainment was the curtain behind which we swept all the unsavory truths of life. Only I would never write that story, because no one would ever publish it.

I had managed a *few* stories that felt like me. I had visited the Western Penitentiary and interviewed both prisoners and guards. And I had tried to revive the old factory girl series, but there was little interest. It was so much easier to go along with Madden's assignments, and I floated through them, feeling unmoored.

The worst part was the theatre itself. It wasn't like I was being sent to experience the great works of Shakespeare—the plays were insipid. The previous evening I had watched a feeble imitation of Kate Castleton's infamous turn in Edward Rice's *Pop*, which was less a play than a series of suggestive songs and dialogue strung together for men to hoot at. The most famous ditty, the one that had cemented Castleton as a star, was "For Goodness' Sake, Don't Say I Told You":

> I'm going to whisper some words in your ear,
> But for goodness sake don't say I told you;
> Whatever I say, and whatever you hear,
> For goodness sake don't say I told you;
>
> I think you'll acknowledge before you depart
> That I've unreservedly opened my heart,
> Whatever I know, I to you will impart,
> But for goodness sake don't say I told you.

The last thing I wanted to do was to write a review of that show. True, the audience had laughed long and hard. But as theatre, it had no meaning.

Just as my life had no meaning.

Everything about Pittsburgh was stifling. Yes, "Nellie Bly" was a name known to all the right people. She was invited to parties and courted rather assiduously by young men who wanted to defy their parents by being seen with a female reporter. Scandalous.

> I'm a sweet little girl, so all the boys say,
> But for goodness sake don't say I told you;
> And though I am innocent, just a bit gay,
> But for goodness sake don't say I told you;
>
> And all of my mischief is done on the sly,
> With a pout of my lips and a glance of my eye,
> I'm terribly proper, but awfully fly,
> But for goodness sake don't say I told you.

Since the fall I had received two proposals of marriage. One was unserious, from an old family friend named Humphrey Miller who, I think, pitied me. It was amusing for about half a second to imagine Joaquin Miller's face if I were to explain that my surname was now Miller as well. But that was about as far as that proposal went.

The other was quite serious, from a fellow reporter named Joe Gregson, whom I hardly knew. I rejected him as sharply as I could, to dash not only his hopes but those of any other would-be newsroom suitors.

The unfortunate result was that going into the office was that much more daunting. I was used to the boys pinching me as I passed, or ruffling my skirts, or leaving lewd sketches mixed into my papers. All that I could deal with. But my rejected suitor's alternating puppy looks and abrasive insults began to grate on my nerves.

Through it all Wilson just smiled and patted me on the shoulder with a consoling, "There, there." We were good friends at this point, Wilson and I. We had a perfectly good arrangement. We'd resumed our Friday walks, and week after week we would banter over women's rights and social justice and high ideas of morality and law and religion and humanity. But never anything personal. We were peers. We were colleagues. We were friends.

Only friends.

That year's Christmas party had been unremarkable. Knowing what to expect, I was not surprised to be greeted by Mrs. Wilson's enveloping embrace. Sissy complimented my Mexican hat, which was not Mexican at all, and I threw myself into being her confidante and dogsbody throughout the evening. She laughed and pinched my cheeks and reveled in my stories of Mexico and life in general.

"I admire you so much," Sissy confided in me after refreshing her sherry. "You embrace life. You seize it. You are the woman I wish I could be. So brave."

You are the woman I wish I could be. That phrase festered as Wilson was occasionally absent from his desk at the *Dispatch*. My ears strained for mentions of Mrs. Wilson's "condition." Men spoke of her spirits, alternately called "high" or "low." They spoke of her being "high-strung," or even occasionally "hysterical"—a word that bothered me, as it was exclusively applied to women.

I'd heard as much at one of the women's meetings, and looked it up to be certain it was true. The word *hysteria* came from the Greek *hysterikós*, meaning "suffering in the womb." The new procedure called the hysterectomy was often prescribed for women who were "overcome with emotion." Meaning the doctors believed the root of every woman's problems was to be found in her uterus.

This was not new. The ancient doctor Galen had claimed the disease was rooted in abstinence among passionate women. The cure for this was intercourse and self-release. Modern medicine had invented the term *hysterical paroxysm*, where it was the doctor's chore to "massage" the patient to release her pent-up "hysteria."

There was certainly no lack of patients to whom physicians might prescribe this treatment. Dr. George Taylor had become famous thirty years earlier by claiming that a quarter of all women suffered from hysteria. Among his list of symptoms was "a tendency to cause trouble."

If I was to be counted a hysterical female, woe betide the doctor who prescribed a "hysterical paroxysm" to me.

Though I felt a deep solidarity with Mrs. Wilson's condition, whatever it truly was, I never asked Wilson about it. I never mentioned his wife at all, and only asked after her if he first introduced her into the conversation.

Working on my review, another line from the silly ditty came into my head:

> If you are married of course you'll agree,
> But for goodness sake don't say I told you,
> That you a bachelor would like to be,
> But for goodness sake don't say I told you;
>
> For 'tis the right of the ladies—ancient and young,
> And what is a woman if she can't use her tongue,
> For a woman would talk if she hadn't a lung,
> But for goodness sake don't say I told you.

I turned to Wilson. "Would you like to take a walk?"

Wilson frowned. "Is it Friday already?"

I shook my head. "I need to stretch my legs. Theatre seats."

He glanced at his watch. "It's barely ten."

"We can fetch cigarettes for the roaches. We'll be heroes."

Chuckling, he put away his pen, shuttered his desk, and lifted his coat from the back of his chair. "Then, by all means, let us be heroic."

We walked out to our favorite stomping ground, the park by the old Block House. The Schenley family at least cared for their public spaces, if not their tenants. "What's on your mind, Miss Bly?"

"Why do you still use Bly?" I demanded. "You've met my mother."

Wilson raised his brows. "It is your professional name, and therefore the professional way to address you. If you would prefer I call you Miss Cochrane, I will endeavor to re-lay my mental tracks. I cannot promise I will always be successful. To me, you are the indefatigable Nellie Bly."

His answer made me ashamed of my question. Of course I wanted him to treat me as a professional. That I had seemed to suggest otherwise was troubling. To deflect my embarrassment I said, "The naughty Nellie Bly, you mean."

"Hardly," he replied as we strolled by the river. "You simply make me realize I am old. Perhaps I was born old. But I cannot keep pace with the times. Whereas you, kid, wish to hurry them along."

"Can equality be patient? Can justice?"

"Is that what's on your mind? Suffrage? We could have argued that in front the roaches."

"And they would have enjoyed it. No," I admitted, "it's not that."

"Then what?"

I didn't quite know, so I answered with a tangent. "Did you see that notice in the *Saint Louis Post-Dispatch*? Mr. Pulitzer is proposing to send a reporter up in a hot-air balloon and have him travel west as far as he can."

"How very Jules Verne," said Wilson.

"I wrote and offered to be the reporter."

Wilson chuckled. "Of course you did. And what did they say?"

"That the job was already taken, and it was far too dangerous for a woman."

"Well, it's not every day you can be chased out of a foreign country. . ."

"I'm serious!" I insisted.

"So am I!" From the crackle in his eye, I saw that he was. "Every life has some tedium. So will every profession. As a woman, you might not believe it. But name the most exciting job you can imagine, and I will show you how tedious it can be."

I elbowed his arm. "Is that how you view the world? Long stretches of boredom?"

"If we're lucky. I was there during an exciting time, kid. The war was enough excitement for a lifetime. Made me appreciate the tedium. I had hoped Mexico would be enough excitement for you."

"Are you never tempted to chuck it and go someplace else? With the book, you must have offers." Wilson had graduated to full-fledged author while I'd been away. He'd collected his newspaper columns into a book entitled *Quiet Observations on the Way of the World*, and it had sold moderately well.

Wilson pulled a face. "A few. John Black at the *Bulletin* hounds me daily."

"Are you not tempted?"

"Kid, of course I am. But unless I have a reason to go, I might as well stay."

"That's inertia."

"It's stability. Doesn't that appeal to you?"

"That's the trouble—it does! Oh, Q.O., it would be so easy to make this my life! To walk in rarefied circles, judging art and spreading gossip. But that's not the life I want to lead. I want to matter. To make a difference. My happiest time was writing about the workshop girls. And uncovering corruption in Mexico. Those are the kinds of stories I want to tell. Except. . ."

"Except what, kid?"

I voiced my real fear. "Except they didn't change anything, did they? Those stories. They didn't make a lick of difference."

"Change is difficult," said Wilson. "It takes time. With the Factory Girls articles, you opened some eyes, mine included. And perhaps frightened some shop owners. The Mexican government was certainly frightened of you."

I snorted in a very unladylike way. "They're not frightened anymore. Now I'm the scourge of divas and mediocre playwrights. And the worst part is, even if I left the *Dispatch* and moved to another paper, within six months I would be stuck in the same rut, my wheels spinning up useless dirt on actresses. I need to go someplace where I would be allowed to chase important stories."

"So work it backwards, kid," advised Wilson. "Who is telling those stories? What newspapers dare to do that kind of work?"

Several leapt to mind. "The *Sun*. The *Herald*. The *Standard*. The *World*."

"Uh-huh. You notice what all of those papers have in common, kid?"

I did. They were all in New York.

To distract from that uncomfortable truth, I challenged him. "Why are you always calling me 'kid'? I'm not a child. Neither am I a lost little lamb."

"Goat," he said. "A lamb is a baby sheep. A kid is a baby goat."

"Oh, that's much better!"

"I'm afraid, ancient as I am, I still view you as young. Or, if you like, I think of you as always kidding me."

"That's me," I sulked. "Always the kidder."

He raised his brows and looked down at me, his gaze significant. "Like you're kidding yourself about your plans."

"Why am I staying in Pittsburgh, you mean? I don't know. What is there here for me?"

"Your family?" suggested Wilson.

I shook my head. "I live in a house with them, but none of them share my dreams. They have their own lives."

"Even your mother? She stayed by your side in Mexico."

"We're closer than we've ever been," I confessed. "But her life goals are not mine."

"What are your life goals, then?"

Under the shade of a fat oak tree I stopped to face him, hands on my hips. "Don't play your reporter's tricks on me, Q.O.—I know them too well!"

Facing me in return, he spread his hands wide. "How can it be a trick if you know it? I'm a columnist. I like lists. Give me three life goals."

I bit my lip. "To work for a New York newspaper."

He ticked off his finger. "That's one."

"To reform the world."

Another tick. "Two."

"To fall in love."

Tick, with a smile. "That's three."

"And to marry a millionaire."

A breeze moved the branches, and the sun dappled his face with light. "Four! Unless you combine three and four together, as I hope you someday will."

I stared at him. "Too late. Unless you're a millionaire and have been hiding it all this time."

Shock turned him to stone, the laughter on his face trapped in amber. I didn't wait, but stepped up on my toes and kissed him right on his frozen mouth.

After a moment he began to respond. For that single instant, I was every kind of alive. Wrong, and right. Exultant, and ashamed. It was not my first kiss, but it was my first kiss of love.

It would also be my last. Pulling back, Wilson stared at me, his face ashen, his eyes filled with a hundred thousand kinds of sadness. The look on his face was heartbreaking. It was such a betrayal, my saying it aloud.

I had made things worse. I'd dragged him over a line that could not be uncrossed. I quickly said, "I'm sorry," and fled, leaving him there under the shade of that oak, with only hints of sunlight filtering down to touch him.

Wilson and I were only friends.

I had just ruined a perfectly good lie.

HEART THUNDERING IN MY EARS and hammering at my breast, I pressed through the city, oblivious to my surroundings. All I could see was Wilson's face, his shock, and the hurt I had caused him. With revolting irony, verses of the previous night's ditty came unwanted to my mind:

> I'm awfully modest, and awfully shy,
> But for goodness sake don't say I told you;
> But in spite of it all, I like fun on the sly,
> But for goodness sake don't say I told you;

I'm sorry, so sorry for hearts that I break,
I know it ain't right, but I certainly take
In that line what is commonly known as the cake,
But for goodness sake don't say I told you.

I don't care a fig for this mere surface show,
But for goodness sake don't say I told you;
I never get fast, though I never go slow,
But for goodness sake don't say I told you;
I don't think that all of the goodness we see
So carefully labeled, is goodness for me,
It is only pretense, and I call it N. G.,
But for goodness sake don't say I told you.

That's what I was: no good. At least, not for Wilson. What right did I have, pressing my affections on him? What claim could I make that would repair the terrible wrong to his wife?

Joaquin Miller came to mind, and the story he'd told of the house on the Street of the Jewel and the unwanted suitor who ruined three lives in one moment of boldness.

I am Diego de Fajardo, the dishonorable suitor. Wilson is my Violante, the innocent spouse. If I stay here, I will ruin him.

Not that he would end up dead in his jealous wife's arms. This wasn't Mexico.

Nevertheless, I thought, *I must save him. From me.*

What was wrong with me, anyway? Didn't all the great writers say it was far more beautiful, more poetic, to pine from afar, rather than live the messiness and ugliness of life? Love was perfect, life was not. Better to keep one's love pure by never intruding life upon it. Better to live a life of chivalry.

The writer in me began to reframe the story. At this moment there was only a kiss. One perfect kiss in a lifetime of muck and hardship. *If I disappear now, that kiss will remain: untouched, unsullied, unspoiled. If I vanish now, I will be like one of those old chevaliers, like a knight of King Arthur's.* I would vow to do great deeds in the name of a love that would never be acted upon. A pure love, a dream of love, for whom one went on quests, like Galahad or Perceval, like Don Quixote.

Don Quixote was mad.

For some reason, that thought made me laugh. Didn't madmen laugh? Madwomen, too, it seemed. That was the other meaning of *hysterical*, after all.

My mind made up, I remained away from the office until I was sure Wilson had gone home. When I finally entered the newsroom, I skirted the remaining roaches and went directly to my desk.

The light was still on in Madden's office. I thought of telling him, but why bother? I simply packed up my few things into my bag, ran my fingers over my typewriter, and put on my coat and hat.

Before skipping down those steep steps for the last time, I stopped by Wilson's desk. Heart hammering, I unfurled his rolltop, filched his beautiful pen from its drawer, and pulled out a scrap of paper.

My first attempt was too daring. I tore it up and settled for something breezier:

> *Dear Q. O.—*
>
>   *I'm off for New York. Look out for your Naughty Kid.*
>
>   *Nellie Bly*

Nothing objectionable in that! Except perhaps the word *naughty*. But anyone reading it would see it as an insult, a flinging back of the thing he'd called me so many times.

There would be no fooling Wilson. He would understand what I was doing. And why.

I tucked the note into the corner of his blotter so it wouldn't be immediately obvious to anyone else. Then I walked out of the *Dispatch* for the last time.

An hour later I was on a train to New York City.

THIRTY

GOTHAMITE

NEW YORK, NY
SUMMER 1887

NEW YORK WAS A DISASTER from the first.

I emerged from my train wearing my best Mexican hat—the black one with the white band Miller had bought for me—bedecked with dried flowers from the Floating Gardens. After cabling Mother and telling her not to worry, I found a hotel. Appalled at the expense, I immediately looked to secure a more permanent lodging.

I ended up renting a room on West Ninety-Sixth Street, on the Upper West Side of Manhattan. My landlady was a Polish lady called Mrs. Pesetsky, and the furnished room cost almost six dollars a week.

This was of no concern, though, as I was confident I would land a job long before my savings were whittled away. After all my notoriety in Pittsburgh, I assumed I would only have to walk into a newspaper and say, "I'm Nellie Bly!" and they'd fall over themselves offering me work.

Oh, how naïve I was.

For all of June and July my routine was exactly the same. I would force myself to wake with the sun, dress smartly, gather my bag and portfolio, and then walk the unpaved dirt roads, past goats grazing in vacant lots, over to the Ninety-Third Street station to catch the Ninth Avenue Elevated train. Untrusting of my fellow lodgers, I took everything of value with me, tucked in my bag to prevent theft.

After disembarking a half hour later on Barclay Street, I would walk five blocks east to Park Row, where all the great newspapers had their offices. Then I would trudge from Barclay to Broadway, across Ann Street to Gold, up Gold to Spruce, and then back to Park Row. At noon I would pause in City Hall Park to take a meager bite of lunch, usually an apple or a slab of bread. Then back to Nassau Street, and the area known as Printing House Square.

At each place I would enter, carrying my clippings and letters of introduction, and ask to see the editor. The greater newspapers all had elevators. It was thrilling to reach my floor and step off quickly, as I often imagined the cable snapping in the instant I crossed from the car to the hallway, resulting in me being sheared in half.

I would then walk down the hall to knock on whatever door looked most imposing, introduce myself to some clerk, and wait to be rebuffed.

I was never disappointed.

It didn't matter the publication. Be it the *Sun*, the *Herald*, the *Tribune*, the *Mail and Express*, the *Times*, or my highest hope, the *World*—wherever I went, the door was closed in my face. Often literally.

It was humbling to learn how few newsmen had even heard of me. Of those that had, none were interested in hiring a female reporter. One editor at the *Tribune* had actually read my Mexico reports. Far from being impressed, he was indignant. "Who was the gent you stole the idea from? Don't you feel guilty that his family is now starving?"

So it was back to the elevator—its descent matching my hopes—and then out into the bustling street, where everyone had purpose but me.

Still, this ritual afforded me a good tour of New York, which boasted more of everything—more skypiercers, more horses, more streetlamps, more restaurants, more bustle, more people. It was said that one of every three hundred people in the world lived in New York City.

And it certainly had more wires: telephone wires, telegraph wires, electrical wires, ticker tape wires. The whole web of New York cables would have made all the world's spiders curl up their legs in envy.

Unfortunately, among its many impressive excesses, the Empire City was also notable for an abundance of filth and rudeness. One June day it rained, and all the horse droppings became a river of excrement that flooded the sidewalks and sent both men and women scurrying to higher ground. There was a joke I often heard repeated in those first weeks: "What is dirtier than some streets in New York? Other streets in New York."

They can grouse all they like, I thought. *Until their tongues are coated with the soot from a Pittsburgh steel mill, they don't know from dirt.*

But for rudeness, New Yorkers were unmatched. I soon became accustomed to it, and was pleased to cause several shocked looks by swearing like a native after being jostled on the train one morning.

Not that everyone understood me. The sea of languages was vast and deep in New York, as were the kinds of people. Coming from Pittsburgh, I was quite used to the sight of Negroes, but my long-standing home had almost no Chinese or Indian people. I had grown accustomed to Mexicans in Mexico, but it was a shock to see them on New York streets. The denseness of their poverty was palpable. Every day I wondered what they had endured to make it to the Land of Opportunity.

My first goal was to avoid ending up in their shoes. Trying my best not to spend money, I made it my habit to visit the library and check out a new book each week. I should have been taking home Ovid or Aristotle, yet I found myself borrowing novels by Wilkie Collins, Archibald Clavering Gunter, and Hugh Conway. *The Woman in White, Mr. Barnes of New York,* and *Miss Rivers's Revenge*—novels of romantic locations and mysterious women in distress. Trash, but thrilling trash.

I attended as many free lectures as I could find. At least once a week I would head down to Cooper Union, the great philanthropic institution just north of the Bowery dedicated to the pursuits of art and science. The reading room was always stocked with periodicals from across the country, and I devoured them looking for clues to employment. Sometimes I would visit the auditorium, if a particular topic caught my interest, which allowed me to socialize in a perfectly respectable way while enjoying a brief escape from the hurly-burly of New York's streets.

Sometimes, though, I would walk down by the ferries, look at all the destinations, and imagine taking a journey. I would walk by the port and watch all the posh people disembarking from massive ships, their poorer counterparts struggling along gangplanks from steerage, where they had stayed for weeks without sight of the sun. I both pitied and admired the steerage gangs—not only for their pluck, but for the adventure they had endured. I wondered if they would be as disappointed by New York as I was.

Each evening I would retreat to my single room to do my laundry and write new story pitches. I had several I thought were good, including a New York version of the Factory Girl series. I also noted the many immigrants, and wondered what their experience had been in coming to America. There was a story in that, if I could find the right door into it.

And get past the doors that kept me out.

I hoped that sheer doggedness would achieve what optimism and confidence had not. I had to wear down their resistance.

Yet to wear them down, I had to remain. To remain, I needed money. My savings were already dwindling. Mistrusting my fellow lodgers, I kept my money with me at all times, safe in the bottom of my handbag. Between the bag and my little portfolio case, all of my life—past, present, and future—was literally in my hands.

I began to regret my shabby treatment of Madden, whom I'd left without even a word. After all, he'd taken a chance on me out of the clear blue sky.

I hadn't quite realized how rare that was. Not only that, he'd taken me back after I'd quit.

If he'd done it once, he might do it again. Close to penury in mid-July, I swallowed my shame and wrote to him:

> *Dear Mr. Madden,*
>
> *Greetings from Empire City! I saw a show on Broadway last night. It was pretty swell, and I thought the folks back in Pittsburgh might be interested in hearing about it. I've enclosed a review, in case you'd like to have Nellie Bly working for you again. Give my love to the roaches!*
> *—N.B.*

Sorry I left you in a lurch, but can I write for you freelance until I find a real job?

It was true about the play. I'd used my old *Dispatch* press credentials to get into the Lyceum Theatre to see *The Highest Bidder*. The play had been running for two months, and the owners were happy to think a fresh review might draw out-of-towners.

I imagined Madden reading that letter and pacing his office, ranting about the little girl who he'd taken in and given work—even given a name!—only to have her stab him in the back. Twice!

It had felt good to just vanish. Naughty, wicked, joyful. I felt like I'd pulled off a heist, or swindled my way into someplace I wasn't allowed. In reality, I had just been childish. Nellie Bly, always burning bridges she might need to re-cross someday. Running away from what was hard to face.

Running away. Is that who I am? The troublemaking girl who runs away?

They say blood is blue until it touches the air. That's how it's always been with my feelings. They look one color when they're inside me. The moment other people see them, they change color and become something completely different.

At last, a letter came from the *Dispatch*. Enclosed was a blessed, blessed check, along with an admonishment:

> *Stick to culture writing and don't step on McCain's toes.*
> *—Madden*

Oh, thank you, thank you, thank you, Madden!

George McCain was the *Dispatch's* New York correspondent, who I'd met at Wilson's Christmas parties. He'd never been much interested in me, and would therefore be unimpressed by my arrival. Hopefully, he would not be threatened.

At least, not until I gave him cause.

Relieved that the Nellie Bly byline was still good for something, I began to write exactly the kind of stories I had come to New York to escape. I wrote about puffed sleeves, about faux-Greek hairstyles, and the new—and ridiculous—trend of women wearing their hats back to front. I wrote about such pressing questions of etiquette as "Should a man remove his hat to a woman on an elevator?" Dreadful stuff. Worse, it was precisely the kind of reporting that would keep me from being taken seriously by the crusty old men behind the editorial desks, the ones I needed to impress to get the kind of job I was after. But it kept me housed and fed, so I did it and tried to stay grateful.

I did enjoy a few of the many plays I reviewed that summer, though I found *Tartuffe* to be remarkably unfunny. It was so didactic about hypocrisy that it was quite impossible to laugh. And every week some theatre was giving up the ghost. Overwhelmed by constant losses, the National Opera Company in New Jersey filed for insolvency, just one week after I had gone there to review Gounod's *Roméo et Juliette*.

One play I was excited to see was an adaptation of a penny dreadful I had devoured entitled *Called Back*. It featured a heroine who haunted both the hero and the audience alike. Pauline was never given to shouts or frantic ranting. Instead, she was eerily listless. When asked to speak, she would offer the bare minimum of human response. Never rude, never desperate, she was the image of detachment, and all the more disturbing because of it. I was struck by the actress's performance—absence of life or reaction was more unsettling than overacting. She showed the power of stillness.

Being me, however, I longed for more meaty stories. Great potential stories abounded that summer, from the sappy to the sensational. There were charges of corruption among the umpires when the Detroit Wolverines won in ten innings at home against the New York Metropolitans. It was shockingly revealed that one Ann Dyer, who had died four years earlier, had made her fortune by dressing in rags and sitting three days a week at the corner near the Barclay Street ferry, begging. The rest of the week she took her alms and invested them in real estate. Over in Five Points, the Grand Duke Theatre was demolished to make room for a six-story tenement house.

The story that would most interest Pittsburghers that summer was the murder of the clerk-turned-athlete Joseph Quinn, fatally shot at the corner of Second Avenue and Thirty-Eighth Street. The accused murderer, Danny Lyons, was a Pittsburgher. Apparently the two men had quarreled over a woman at Billy McGlory's tavern, with Quinn knocking Lyons down and Lyons swearing to kill him the next time they met. Determined to make good on his word, Lyons allegedly went out, borrowed a gun, and lay in wait for Quinn on the evening of July 5. A single shot caused a wound that ended Quinn's life an agonizing hour later.

For seventeen days the manhunt ranged the country, with Detective Mullarky and Officer Duncan tracing Quinn from New York to Philadelphia, from there to Pittsburgh, on to Chicago, and then back to Pittsburgh. Mullarky and Duncan were utterly surprised to discover that the murderer they had been chasing through those two hot summer weeks was already in custody, held unknowingly by the Pittsburgh police for trying to pawn some stolen jewelry.

Now being brought back to New York for trial, Lyons was declaring Quinn's murder had been self-defense. All manner of stories circulated, with Captain Ryan of the New York constabulary giving statements hourly, it seemed.

I longed to report this story, and even asked if I could assist McCain. I was given a firm "No" from Madden. McCain was the *Dispatch*'s *real* correspondent in New York. I was there for culture and nothing more.

An idea occurred to me: *What if I can scoop McCain and get the details of Lyons's defense myself?* I wouldn't send them to Madden, I told myself. I would bring them directly to McCain. Perhaps we could share a byline. Or maybe gratitude would let him farm out a few smaller murder stories to Nellie Bly.

But how am I to discover the truth before McCain? The answer seemed obvious to me. I would bypass the police entirely and head straight for the district attorney who would be prosecuting the case.

It only took a few smiles at the courthouse to discover that Assistant District Attorney Nicoll was in charge. I took the stairs up to his office, propelled by the first stirrings of a real story I'd had all summer.

Unfortunately, what had seemed a stroke of genius to me was apparently commonplace to seasoned crime reporters. Nicoll was already giving a statement to other reporters outside his door. Worse luck, one of them was George McCain.

He spied me just as Nicoll was saying, "Mr. Lyons is pleading self-defense. He says there was never any woman. He maintains Mr. Quinn assaulted him on numerous occasions because Mr. Lyons refused to waylay and beat a Post Office inspector named Meehan, against whom Mr. Quinn allegedly had a grudge. Mr. Lyons maintains that on the evening of July fifth, Mr. Quinn assaulted him with a stick, and that only then did Mr. Lyons fire his revolver, striking Mr. Quinn fatally in the stomach. This is an obvious fabrication, as we have a dozen witnesses who heard Mr. Lyons threaten the life of Mr. Quinn at McGlory's, as well as the testimony of the woman he maintains does not exist. Nor was there any sign of a stick before the borrowed gun was fired. As to that, why borrow a gun if he did not intend to use it? We have the testimony of the gun's owner, who says—"

"Bly." McCain had edged away from the crowd of reporters to come my way. Clamping my elbow, he hauled me painfully down the hall. "What the blazes do you think you doing here?"

I probably looked as miserable as I felt. "I thought I could—"

"—steal a march on my story and show me up to Madden," snarled McCain. "You better believe I'll be writing to Madden about this. Now get out of here before I—"

"Who's this, George?" asked a man in a nice suit and polished shoes. He looked like a lawyer.

"Nobody, Henry," snapped McCain.

"I'm another reporter from the *Dispatch*," I said, yanking my elbow free. "I got my signals mixed. I didn't know George was already here."

The man leered as he held out a hand. "The more the merrier, Miss. . ."

"Bly," I said quickly, shaking his hand rather than allowing him to kiss mine. "Nellie Bly."

"Assistant District Attorney Henry Macdona, Miss Bly. A pleasure to meet you. Please, if you ever need any help with a story, my office door is open." He took me in, top to toe. "My home, too, if you're ever lonely. It's a big city. Never hurts to have friends in high places."

"Bly doesn't make friends," said McCain harshly. "She loses them before they know they were even close." He jerked his head toward where Nicoll was still talking. "You have anything more to add?"

"Me? I wish. No, I'm stuck on a boring piece of telegraph fraud. Empire and Bay State. Want to write about that? No, I didn't think so."

"I will," I offered at once.

Macdona laughed aloud. "But who would read it? No, I need a real case. This Quinn thing has been quite the headline-grabber for Nicoll. That's what I need. A scandal with weeks of coverage."

"Election's next year, isn't it?" observed McCain.

Macdona opened his hands. "Never too early to start thinking about it."

I opened my mouth, but McCain cut me off. "We have to be going, Henry. Don't fret. This is New York. Another scandal's always around the corner."

"One can only hope! Lovely to meet you, Miss Bly. George," he added familiarly as he strolled off to his office with an air of resigned smugness.

The whole way down to the street I was apologizing, explaining, and wishing I had concocted a better reason to be there. By the time we reached the street, McCain had cooled off. "Fine. I won't write Madden this time. But I swear, if I see so much as a boot heel mark at a crime scene—"

I held up my right hand. "I vow, you won't see me chasing a courthouse story again. I promise."

Nodding, he asked if I required a ride anywhere. Wanting only to escape, I declined, choosing to spend my own money on the train home.

Heigh-ho. Back to the women's pages for me. As summer dragged on I was certainly feeling down, desperate for a windfall of luck, or inspiration.

Then, in August, I received both, and seized them, determined to never let go.

THIRTY-ONE

INTERVIEWS

LIKE EVERY INSPIRATION IN MY LIFE, it started with a letter. Addressed to me and forwarded from the *Dispatch* offices, it was from a young woman asking what I thought a woman should do to get a job in a New York newspaper.

Devil if I know, I was tempted to reply. *You'd have to ask the newspaper gods of Gotham.*

And that's when I got the nifty notion to do just that.

The next day, looking bright as a penny, I approached the offices of the *New York Sun* on the corner of Spruce and Nassau. Not as an applicant, but as a reporter after a story. That story was: why did these papers not hire women?

Less impressive in stature than many of its neighbors, what the *Sun*'s offices lacked in height they made up for in history. Climbing the twisting spiral staircase, I looked about at what had once been the headquarters of Tammany Hall's Boss Tweed and imagined the stories this place had once been privy to. *If these walls could talk, what tales they could tell. . .*

Arriving at the newsroom, I barreled in. Apparently New York newspapermen wore their hats indoors—I later found out it was an old tradition, dating from a time when men feared removing their hats in the newsroom, lest they be stolen. Despite having made an appointment, I endured an insultingly lengthy wait. The *Sun*'s own reporters would certainly have chafed at having their time so wasted. I decided they were waiting for me to give up.

Clearly they did not know me. When the morning was worn to nothing and I had still not budged from my seat, I was grudgingly admitted to the great man's inner sanctum.

Mr. Charles Dana was exactly what I'd once expected Madden to be:

bald, with a majestic beard of white whiskers that reached his breastbone. This was a man who had assisted Horace Greeley at the *Tribune*, had been second assistant secretary of war and liaison between the War Department and Ulysses S. Grant, and had opposed more presidential administrations in print than I had lived through. The *Sun* was presently striving mightily to bring down President Cleveland.

Glaring at me over round gold-rimmed spectacles with the air of a man who had far more important matters demanding his attention, Mr. Dana invited me into his office. "I can grant you five minutes, Miss. Please, have a seat." He offered me an armless hard-backed chair before settling himself into his own leather-upholstered swivel chair behind his black walnut desk.

I glanced at the impressive number of bookshelves lining the walls, at the charming revolving bookshelf beside his chair, and at the rather off-putting stuffed owl perched atop it. The taxidermist had done an exceptional job—it looked more alive than Mr. Dana.

Feeling my heart race, I took out my notebook. "Mr. Dana, I'm writing a story about women journalists in New York. Do you think women are capable of being reporters?"

His grandfatherly brow wrinkling, he took his time before answering. "I think, if they have the ability, there is no reason why they should not do the work as well as a man."

I scribbled his words, feeling heartened. *A hopeful answer!*

But then he continued. "I do not think they can, however, as a class, do equally good work, for the very reason that women have never been educated up to it in the same manner as men. A few years since, there were no women journalists. Even now they are not regarded with editorial favor in New York. In the West, where good men are not plenty, clever women are employed. Here, there is a superabundance of first-class men."

"You mention education," I said. "What education is that?"

"Well, if I could have my way, every young man setting out to be a newspaper reporter should learn Greek and Latin, after the old fashion. Not only does a knowledge of Sophocles and Horace allow a man a keener insight into any story he might cover, be it a horse race or a political one, it also strengthens a man's grasp of language and grammar. I abhor nothing so much as a typographical error."

I thought of Wilson and his blue pencils. "I see. Are you opposed to women as journalists, Mr. Dana?"

"No," he said with deliberation. "If a woman can do assigned work as well as a man, there is no reason why there should be discrimination to her disfavor." He drew in a long breath. "And yet! While a woman might be ever so clever in obtaining news and putting it into words, we would not feel at liberty to call her out at one o'clock in the morning to report at a fire or a crime. In such a case we never hesitate with a man. That is why the latter is preferable."

I employed Wilson's trick of saying nothing, and found it worked, even on old newspaper hands. Mr. Dana could not allow the silence to go unfilled.

"Miss Blythe, foremost a newspaper must be a bringer of luminescence. For that, one requires facts. And the fact is that men report stories more accurately than women. Accuracy is the greatest gift in a journalist. It is difficult for most people, when told that two and two make four, not to write that they make five, or three, or anything except the exact truth. Women are generally worse than men in this regard. They find it impossible not to exaggerate."

I managed not to say, *You mean exaggerations like that one?*

Mr. Dana continued. "The best newspaperman I ever had could not write one line of correct English. But he was valuable because he always gave the facts. We could find plenty who could write, and this man always furnished them with the facts. An accurate man or woman is invaluable to newspaper work."

Hearing that, I pounced. "Have you many women applicants for positions on the *Sun*?"

"Not very many, no. We have a great number of male applicants, but not women."

Save, of course, myself. "But you do think women have a chance in the journalistic field?"

He spread his hands in a show of affability. "Anyone with ability has a *chance*. There is always a demand for people who have ability or talent, and I presume it would be appreciated in a woman as well as a man. But men are preferable because they are educated up to the business."

"So how does a woman secure a position in a New York newspaper?"

I saw his eyes twinkle with amusement. "I really cannot say." Revolving his chair to the side, he removed his glasses and began rubbing them with his vest tail. "Where have you worked, Miss Blythe?"

"At the *Pittsburg Dispatch*."

"Ah, yes. Well, it is a very clever, bright paper." He omitted the word *little* only for form's sake. "What kind of work did you do there?"

"I exposed the conditions of female laborers in workshops and spent six months as a foreign correspondent in Mexico until I was chased out for exposing the corruption of the Díaz government."

That made him squint for a moment. He chose to quiz me about Mexico, trying to catch me out, and I was able to parry his thrusts with actual *facts*. "And where did you go to college?"

"I did not." Recalling the age Madden had assigned me upon hiring me, I said, "I have been a newspaperwoman since seventeen."

"Ah." Mr. Dana looked away, smiling as if I had proved his point.

"But I can report the facts," I added.

"I'm certain you can, I'm certain you can." He stood. "But you must excuse my belief that, as men have been educated to the business, they are always preferable to women who have not. Now, if you will forgive me."

A moment later he was headed for lunch, and I was left to exit the newsroom through a haze of cigar smoke and offended fury.

So much for the *Sun*!

THE REVEREND DR. GEORGE HEPWORTH of the *New York Herald* was an avuncular figure, with a face like a Founding Father: thin-lipped and serious, yet expressive. His eyes were enormous, and enormously dark. A doctor of religion, he was a practicing clergyman as well as a publisher. Every Sunday, in place of a lead news story, he would publish a sermon, written, he said, "in the hope of smoothing the pathway of the troubled and furnishing them with stepping-stones to higher things." Typical titles for his sermons included "Why We Suffer," "All Men Are Self-Made," and "Little People Who Have Little Lives."

"Be seated, please," he said as I entered his office.

After the *Sun*, I'd decided to try a different tack. "Dr. Hepworth, I want a position at the *Herald*."

"Yes?" He adjusted his glasses to better peer at so demanding an interviewer. "What can you do?"

"Anything," I replied.

He looked startled. "Well, that's what the *Herald* is in search of. We want talent, and we are always glad to give everybody a trial. Sometimes we are compelled to search for the person we desire. Mr. Bennett has told me to allow every reporter to try writing editorials." This was a reference to the paper's owner, James Gordon Bennett, who had inherited it from his father, and was equally as famous as a champion of journalists as he was for urinating into a grand piano at his fiancée's dinner party. "I try first one and then another. And what if I am disappointed innumerable times? I am bound, some time, to find the talent we are in pursuit of, and when that occurs the reporter chosen has secured himself a permanent position. Just as soon as the man with that talent is found, I'll transfer him from the reporters' room to the editorial desk."

"Do you object to women entering newspaper life?"

"No, I do not object."

I heard the *but* coming long before it arrived.

"But still, there are many things about it not suitable for women. I could not think of sending one to the police of higher criminal courts, as I could a man. Even if I did, the officials there would give her as little information as they could, in order to get rid of her, and very likely, just as she was leaving, the most important news would take place. Now, a male reporter would stay there and hear and judge of the cases for himself. As all that the paper cares for is the news, it could not afford to be represented by someone continually liable to lose important information.

"But crime and criminals, though important, do not engross all our columns," he continued, "and there is much other work women can do, and do well. In this respect I might specify the gathering and writing of clerical, fashion, and society news. Until, however, the public demands a different kind of news, so long will women be unable to serve as all-around reporters. The very sources from which we obtain a larger portion of our news render it an impossible field for a woman. On account of the sensations and the scandals which are demanded by the present popular taste, a gentleman could not, in delicacy, ask a woman to have anything to do with that class of news. That is what bars her from reportorial success, absolutely."

Writing frantically, I longed to ask him if a man could have gotten the women of the workshops to open up to him, or gained the confidence of so many Mexican sources who underestimated the writing ability of a mere woman. Aloud, I simply said, "Do you favor employing women upon the work they *can* do?"

"Yes." He seemed relieved. "Because on such news matters they are preferable to men. But, do you know, they are a restraint in an office? The men do not feel at liberty to take off their coats or rest their feet on the desks. And then, I might as well add, they are too much of a guard morally. When they are within hearing, men cannot give vent to their feelings in the language all grades of angry men employ. Consequently, the result is apt often to be serious." He glanced at me, to see if I was shocked at his implication.

I avoided the salacious, if only to prove that a woman could, and drove in to the point. "If you are not opposed to women, why don't you employ more?"

Uneasy, he fidgeted behind his desk. "Because, the work which they can properly do being limited, there is no demand for their services. We have a woman, an old journalist, whom we are sending to Ireland. If a woman has the same ability and the same means of securing news as a man, she has the same chance upon the *Herald*. What we demand is the best, and we don't care what form it comes in. When we find what we want, we are willing to keep it at any price. We have men in our employ who have been here forty years. If they are sick for a month, or a year, their salary goes on just the same. If they die, they are assured a respectable burial." He smiled at me. "So you see, Miss Bly, we are as fair as the circumstances allow. And, as I said, it would be ungentlemanly of me to offer any other work to a lady."

My reply was very unladylike, giving the lie to his comment that only men used salty language. Yes, it was unprofessional, and surely reinforced what he thought of female reporters. But the stunned look on his face as I gathered up my notes was worth it.

Well done, Pinky! Burning bridges at the Herald, too. Nellie Bly, architectural arsonist, was in perfect form.

"WOMEN ARE UNSURPASSED AS REPORTERS in a few fields," enthused Robert G. Morris, editor of the *Telegram* as we strolled out of his offices on his way to another meeting. "They can go to a reception and obtain every little detail of the event which a man misses entirely. Why? Because a man must examine minutely a woman's costume in order to describe it, where a woman would take the whole thing in at a glance. And while a man is getting one dress, the woman has every costume in the room. She is familiar with everything that belongs to a wedding, reception, ball, or similar event, and has it all for use, while a man does not even know enough to ask sensible questions. Woman understands women, as a man never can. So why should she not be able to write of their ways and habits?"

He checked the time, and I saw that Mr. Morris kept to the new fashion of carrying a watch in the head of his walking stick. "Women are more ambitious than men and have more energy, if anything."

He paused, and I was sorely tempted to offer his *but* for him.

"But yet," he said sorrowfully, "their work has its limit on the papers. Not because they are not smart enough, but because they are women. If there was an emergency, just as we were ready for the last edition, I could not send a woman sliding down the banister and have her return up three flights of stairs four at a time. That's where the man gets the best of her as a New York reporter. Now, if you'll excuse me." He tipped his hat and hurried off to more important matters. Likely, lunch.

MR. MILLER OF THE *TIMES* did not insult me by using lunch to escape me. Rather, he insulted me by eating his lunch in front of me. He had a tray sent in from one of the local restaurants, another habit that was *en vogue*.

"I cannot say personally," said Mr. Miller as he leaned over his soup, "what the feelings of the profession are in regard to women journalists, because I have never talked the matter over with my acquaintances of the press."

An interesting statement, given that he proceeded to parrot the exact same excuses put up by Dana, Hepworth, and Morris. He began with the exception that proved the rule. "We have had a lady on this paper for years who reports on the cattle markets in a manner which far surpasses that of any man. She is an authority on all questions of that kind. But I cannot say what women are like on other kinds of work. I have heard city editors say that they are a bother, but I cannot of my own knowledge testify to that being correct." He smiled as he swallowed, as if his lack of position proved his good nature.

"You have no objections to employing women?"

He patted his mouth with an embroidered napkin. "I can see no reason why a woman should not be employed and receive the same compensation," he said, before launching again into the common cant. "*If* she has the same ability, and can work like a man. There is an old prejudice in New York against the employment of women in this field. We have so many experienced men who come to New York that we don't care to encourage women. I cannot say why the West is more liberal in this respect, unless, as the common belief is, they have not the able men required, and they do not want to pay the men's salaries. But I cannot be quoted as an authority, having had no experiences in the premise." He paused to consider. "You had better call to see the editor of the *Mail and Express*. I think they have been quicker than any other paper to give work to women. They have a gentlemanly force, which makes it a desirable place for women."

I did just that, hoping the *Mail and Express* was the exception to the rule. And, to start, it seemed this might be the case.

"Women are invaluable to a newspaper," asserted Mr. Foster Coates, editor in chief. "There are certain things they can do, and in a talking style peculiarly their own. Their manner of reporting certain events can never be equaled by a man. There is a peculiarity in expression entirely feminine which pleases and attracts readers."

Then he proved his exceptional nature. In place of the ubiquitous *but*, he supplied an *of course*.

"Of course, their work is limited, due entirely to the class of news which abounds in daily papers at present. For general, all-around, or emergency work, they are not available. Their dress, constitution, and habits of life keep them from the routine of a reporter's work."

I managed to keep my sigh of disappointment soundless. "What work do you think a woman can do, Mr. Coates?"

"Oh, society, fashion, and general gossip are entirely suitable for a woman, and she for them. Articles on travel, and special articles, such as fill our Saturday and Sunday editions. Dramatic and musical criticisms. Domestic, charitable, and religious news are all within her sphere. Are you well?"

I'd cringed at the word *sphere*. "Perfectly. Please, go on. What else is a girl reporter good for?"

"Oh, interviewing prominent people, book reviewing, and many other things can be done by her in a style that men can seldom reach. I consider, from an experience of fifteen years, that her services are invaluable to a bright, widely circulated paper. Women are always anxious to read what women write, and the knowledge that a woman has charge of some special department in a paper secures permanent readers, not only among her own sex, but among men as well. There is a prejudice in New York against women, and until they are tried it will never be removed. When once a newspaper has had the services of a bright and clever woman it finds, as I have stated, that her place is hard to fill, and that she is invaluable."

So, it's best not to hire a woman, lest they become too valuable to employ!

After a week of interviewing the most important men in American journalism, the gist was, "Of course a woman should have the job, so long as she has the experience and ability, but as she'll never get hired she'll never have the experience, and since we won't dare send her on dangerous or difficult assignments, she'll never be able to do the job. And men are such beasts, a woman shouldn't have to work with them, and if she tried, it would prove onerous to the men, unable to indulge their bestial selves."

In short, "We have more women now than we want, and women are no good anyway."

I had never been more determined to prove them wrong.

THIRTY-TWO

DESPERATION AND DISASTER

O F ALL THE PAPERS IN NEW YORK, the one I most wanted to work for was the *New York World*. Since its purchase by Joseph Pulitzer, the *World* had set the pace for all the newspapers of New York, and therefore the entire newspaper industry across the country.

Every edition was chock-full of smart reporting matched with unstinting sensationalism. Local politics and arts coverage were balanced against grisly crimes and crimson-faced gossip, replete with drawings. The names of its writers were known nationwide: Nym Crinkle, Henry Guy Carleton, Sol Pringle, and the sardonic humorist Bill Nye, an old friend of Wilson's.

In Pulitzer's hands, the *World* offered eye-popping headlines, contests, puzzles, events, and an incredibly strong editorial presence. In four years, the famous financier had turned around an ailing enterprise and reinvented how the news was delivered. As a result, circulation had risen from twenty thousand readers each Sunday to two hundred thousand.

At the *World's* helm was Colonel John Cockerill. Notorious for his irascibility and abrasiveness—as well as for killing a man—he had a fearsome reputation. A year earlier the *Journalist*, which regularly wrote about the newspaper industry, had called him "unquestionably the best news editor in the county."

Therefore, he was the one I most wanted to impress.

I walked into the *World's* offices at 31–32 Park Row and took the elevator up to the penultimate floor. Despite several electric lamps, it was surprisingly dark, with the bulk of the massive U.S. Post Office building next door casting a long shadow over the windows.

Passing rows of desks, I spied a curtained workshop where artists were busily re-creating gruesome or salacious images related to the news. The room positively hummed with energy, and I felt an urge to throw myself into a vacant chair, call for a copy boy, and simply hope no one noticed.

I paused by the desk of a tiny fellow in a bow tie. "I'm Nellie Bly. I have an appointment with Mr. Cockerill."

"Colonel," corrected the clerk.

"Colonel Cockerill," I corrected at once.

Mr. Bow Tie pointed to a long railway bench that covered nearly the whole wall. "You can sit there."

I did so, bracing myself for another long wait. But, unlike my visit to the *Sun*, it took only three minutes before I was ushered into the smoke-filled office of the editor in chief of the *New York World*.

Colonel Cockerill was handsome in an oversized way. His head was enormous. So, too, was his frame. Unlike Wilson, though, his size retained no boyishness. He was a man with a strong, straight nose above a rounded chin that stuck out enough to catch the light. His massive walrus moustache covered his mouth almost entirely. He kept his thinning dark hair quite short, parted on the right just above his rather prominent ears.

The only softness about him was to be found in his eyes, which were liquid and dark. But they were a trap belying his nature, like a silk glove over a steel fist. I knew he'd shot and killed a man in St. Louis while defending a piece he'd written against someone running for Congress. *Is that same gun sitting in his desk now?* I wondered.

I later found out he had never been a colonel in any army—unless one viewed the newspaper industry as a sort of militia. His father Joseph had been member of the U.S. Congress representing a district in Ohio before joining the Union army, rising to the rank of colonel, and being brevetted brigadier general on the field for gallantry. His brother Armistad had also reached the rank of colonel. But John Cockerill had been too young to fly so high. No, the title was honorary, and constantly galling to him.

Yet I saw the reason for the title. He was a man others wanted to follow.

He didn't stand to take my offered hand. Maybe because what he was reading was all-engrossing. Or maybe because it would have dislodged the dusting of cigar ash that blanketed his waistcoat like snow on the hills of Allegheny.

"Colonel Cockerill, my name is Nellie Bly and I'm here from the *Pittsburg Dispatch* on a story about women in newspapers."

Still he didn't look up from what he was reading. "Why would you do that?"

"Do what?"

"Work in newspapers. Why not get a bachelor and form a syndicate of your own?" He looked up long enough to offer me an unamused grin. I was wasting his time, and he wanted me to know it.

Without invitation, I took a chair and removed my notebook. "What do you think of women as journalists?"

Throwing down his papers in exasperation, he leaned back and worked his cigar. "I think they can do some things well enough. What they are fitted for, however, they don't want to do. There are society events which no man can report as well as a woman. Yet they always claim to hate that damned style of work, excuse my French. Fashion work and women's news they can also do, and do in a manner worthy of the highest goddamn praise, forgive me. We do not encourage women here, because we have a blasted deluge of good men unemployed. All the good journalists of the United States flock here to seek a livelihood, and in larger cussed numbers than we can ever provide for. Consequently, we don't encourage women. What they are fitted for is so blamed limited that a man is of far greater service. However, the *World* does employ two women," he added, in the typical sop, "so you see we do not object personally."

If he had thought to put me off by cussing, he had failed. I'd heard far worse growing up with Ford. "Do you think women will ever be able to do more than they do now on the papers?"

"Not unless public tastes demand different news. I don't think women journalists will ever be in great demand in New York. There is a feeling against them—not from experience, but from the want of it. We all want originality and brightness, dammit, and I don't think it would be refused if found in a woman. Yet no editor would like to send a cherry out in bad weather or to questionable damned places for news. We have as many as twelve dad-blamed applications daily from men, but very few from the ladies. When they do apply, we tell them to send in their blessed articles. If they are particularly clever, we accept them. If not, we refuse. They are generally," he added, puffing his cigar for emphasis, "of the latter class."

Finishing my notes, I said, "So, to summarize, women should not expect to take jobs that are better suited for men."

The Colonel looked pleased. "Exactly. I'm sure there are good women reporters. However, what they are fitted for is so limited that a man is of far greater service."

I stood. "Thank you, Colonel. Oh, I was meaning to ask, how did the balloon story go? I haven't seen any mention of it."

Colonel Cockerill grunted. "Drifted into nothingness."

"What a shame. Perhaps if you'd had a woman onboard, the public might have stayed interested."

Under his grotesque moustache, a corner of his mouth curled. "Perhaps."

Heading for the door, I turned at the last moment, unable to leave well enough alone. "Do you still keep a gun in your desk drawer?"

"Always." This time the Colonel's moustache definitely twitched. "But I'd never use it on a woman."

"At least you're consistent," I said as I passed through the door.

I WROTE MY ARTICLE FOR THE *DISPATCH*, offering up the editors' suspiciously similar quotes without commentary. My only personal touches came in the introduction, where I indulged a bit of self-pity:

> Last week I received a letter from a lady, ambitious and presumably young, who is desirous of becoming a journalist. She asserts that she longs for the empty glory and poor pay of the calling, and asks if it be advisable to come to New York to enter the desired career. Not wishing to bear the responsibility of her blasted hopes on my fragile shoulders I decided, before answering, to obtain the opinion of the newspaper gods of Gotham.

I was quite proud of that last turn of phrase. And while I truly meant what I said about empty glory, an unworthy part of me hoped to discourage other young ladies from coming and stealing my thunder. For part of me was secretly terrified that some intrepid young woman fresh from boarding school might see my story and take up journalism before I could establish myself in New York.

Which I was determined to do. Now more than ever.

The story ran two days later under the headline WOMEN JOURNALISTS and created a surprising sensation. The story was picked up all across the country, especially in the West, where they took offense to the many digs at their expense. Most heartening was the mention the article got in the *Journalist*, the very same publication that had previously praised the Colonel's hiring perspicacity.

But if I had hoped my public shaming of these great men would open a door for me, I was disappointed. I applied again at every institution, but I was again turned away. I was forced to console myself with the thought that a shut door could not be any more shut. *Though perhaps it can be latched on the inside. . .*

Back to writing pieces on hairstyles and fashion, I trudged through my daily routine: room to train, train to Park Row, office to office, Park Row to train, train to room. Over and over, I encountered daily defeat. It was hard not to take such rejection personally.

My only breaks were either shows to review or events at Cooper Union's lecture hall. One Thursday afternoon in September I attended a lecture on Dante, which I was surprised to find enthralling. The sheer variety of Hell was fascinating, and I particularly enjoyed learning that the poet had used his published works to settle personal scores, ruining his enemies for all eternity in his writing.

Afterwards, I noticed a gray-haired man in the uniform of a police captain. My reporting instincts lighting up, I walked over and introduced myself. "Good evening. I'm a reporter for the *Pittsburg Dispatch*."

The man tipped the brim of his hat. "Captain McCullagh, Miss. What can I do for you?"

"I was wondering if you're expecting any trouble at a Dante lecture. Any demons lurking about?"

Captain McCullagh chuckled dutifully. "No, Miss. Not that I've seen."

"Then why are you here?" I pressed.

He chewed his lower lip. "This is not always a safe neighborhood, Miss. I want to be certain young ladies like yourself are not inconvenienced."

"Five Points?" I asked, showing my knowledge of the local gangs.

"Just some hooligans. Now why don't you go on home, Miss."

"I told you," I said, my fingers itching. "I'm a reporter."

"That you did. But there's no story here, Miss. . ."

"Bly. Nellie Bly."

His face brightened. "Like the song!"

Now it was my turn to be vexed. "Yes, like the song."

"Now there's a coincidence," he said. "He died not far from here."

"Who?"

"That Foster fellow. Found him in his room, covered in—well, in a sorry state."

It occurred to me that I had no idea what had become of my namesake's composer. "What happened to him?"

"He was ill, fevered. Coming from his bath, he fell across some furniture and ended up with a gash in his neck. That's how we found him. Rushed him to Bellevue, but he died." He looked me up and down. "You could hardly have been born by then. But you said you're from Pittsburgh. Are you named for his song?"

"Yes," I said, heading home. "And no."

That story bothered me deeply. As I rode the train home, I kept coming back to it. Stephen Foster had come to New York, only to die naked, fevered, in a pool of his own blood.

And his creation? What had Nellie Bly come to New York to do?

Face against the glass, I stared at the city, softly singing one of the late Stephen Foster's songs:

> Let us pause in life's pleasures and count its many tears,
>> While we all sup sorrow with the poor;
> There's a song that will linger forever in our ears;
>> Oh! Hard times come again no more.

'Tis the song, the sigh of the weary,
Hard times, hard times, come again no more.
Many days you have lingered around my cabin door;
Oh! Hard times, come again no more.

As we arrived at the Ninety-Third Street station, I reached down to lift my portfolio and handbag. My fingers found the portfolio, but not the handbag. I leaned over, hand questing under my seat and all around my feet.

Nothing.

Heedless of feminine propriety, I dropped to my knees and stared at the impossibly empty floor. My handbag was gone. Stolen!

I was immediately overwhelmed by a sinking feeling, that combination of disbelief, despair, and self-reproach which hits you when you realize you've done something dreadfully foolish. Rising to my feet, I looked wildly around, staring at the hands of the men near me.

There was no sign of it.

Oh God. Oh God.

At first, I was frozen. Lifeless. Then, stumbling like a drunkard, I raced to the station agent and explained in a palpitating voice what had happened. He was sympathetic, but immobile. "I can spread word for the conductors to look for your bag. But whatever was in it is likely gone. I hope it wasn't too much money."

I'd had almost a hundred dollars in that bag. My life savings, plus everything I had earned from the *Dispatch* in the last two months.

Leaving the platform, my brain went to Dupin and Holmes, the detectives of Poe and Doyle, or police Inspector Bucket and Detective Cuff from Dickens and Collins. What would they do?

They would have noticed their bag being stolen, that's what.

Staggering home in a daze, I was just turning the corner when I jerked to a stop as if I'd impacted a brick wall.

The money is gone. There is nothing to be done. There is no remedy. So what are you going to do, Nellie? Are you going to go to your room to sulk and rail at your stupidity? Are you going to wither away like Foster, alone and helpless? Are you going to use this as an excuse to go home, defeated? Are you going to just throw yourself into the river?

Or are you going to do something to fix *your situation?*

Decision launched me back the way I had come, toward the train. I made it only a few steps before realizing I had no money to reboard the train. Reversing course again, I ran home and burst into the entryway. "Mrs. Pesetsky? I have a favor to ask."

I explained what had happened, making it sound like much less money than it had been—an inconvenience, not a disaster. I did not want her to start worrying about the rent. "Could I possibly borrow enough for a train ticket into the city?" Looking more confused than concerned, she gave me the dime that would carry me both downtown and back.

Back on the train, I viewed my fellow passengers with fresh suspicion, eyeing every man's hand to see if he carried my vanished handbag. Of course, there was nothing.

Alighting downtown, I braced myself. *This is the moment. Either admit I am licked, or change my fortune by taking charge of it.*

I headed for the *World*.

"I'M SORRY, MISSY," SAID THE LOBBY GUARD with a paternal smile. "It's after hours. No one is allowed upstairs."

"I'm a reporter," I said.

He nodded politely, even as his smile said it was the least likely thing he'd ever heard. "I see. Do you have any identification?"

My credentials were in my stolen bag. "I'm Nellie Bly with the *Pittsburg Dispatch*."

"I'm sure you are," he said, clearly disbelieving my whole story. "But I'm afraid it's after hours, and they're busy putting the paper to bed. You understand, I'm sure. It's like it must be with your children—better not to disturb them once they're down."

Willing my arms not to fly up and start pummeling him, I spoke in the calmest voice I could conjure. "I'm here to see the Colonel. I interviewed him last month, and he said if I ever had a story worth his time, I should bring it directly to him."

It was a bald-faced lie. But I was determined to enter the building by hook or by crook.

The guard looked at me dubiously, then squinted in slow recognition. "I do recall seeing you here."

In fact, he had seen me nearly every day for two months, coming in and out with my portfolio. I'd caught him looking at my booted ankles, as if hoping for a glimpse of stocking. If I'd had a more memorable figure, he might have remembered sooner.

"Yes," I said. "I've got a story for the Colonel. May I go up? Or is Colonel Cockerill going to have to explain to Mr. Pulitzer why the *World* missed out on a sensational story?"

Confounded, he let me into the elevator, and I pushed the button for the right floor just to prove I knew where to go. *First hurdle cleared!*

The next hurdle was the little twerp with the bow tie, sitting alone in the newsroom just outside the Colonel's door. I marched up to him. "I have an important story for Colonel Cockerill."

"Come back tomorrow."

"It's urgent."

"Too bad, Miss. Come back tomorrow."

I walked to a nearby desk, hauled a chair from behind it, and settled myself into it. "I'll wait."

He rolled his eyes ostentatiously. "Miss. Please. You can't."

At another time, his exasperation might have been amusing. Now it was only an obstacle. I folded my arms.

He tried ignoring me and going back to his work. I remained seated, staring at him. He wrote. I stared. He fidgeted. I stared. He started to get up, thinking to walk away and so leave me alone. I tensed, eyeing the door beyond him. He must have noticed, for he thought better of his errand and returned to his seat.

Finally, he tossed down his pencil and sighed. "Do I have to call the guard?"

"Not if you give me five minutes with the Colonel."

"They're not my minutes to give," he said, which I thought was a good answer.

"Then please, Mister. . ."

"Marsh."

"Mr. Marsh, tell the Colonel to brush the ashes from his waistcoat and give me five minutes."

Startled by my intimate knowledge, Marsh clung obstinately to his opposition. "I'm very sorry, Miss. The Colonel is far too busy preparing the paper for edition."

"And he'll want to decide if this story should go in it."

Marsh thought he spied a hope to get rid of me. "I could ask a reporter to speak to you."

I gazed back at him with a basilisk stare. "Are you a reporter?"

"Excuse me?" he repeated, blinking twice.

"Are you a reporter?"

"Of course I—"

"I've worked in newspaper offices both here and abroad, and I've never heard of a reporter giving up his story to another reporter. Maybe you do things differently at the *World*, but that's unheard of at any paper I've ever worked at. I talk to your editor only."

"Well, you can't."

"Fine. I'll take my story down to Charles Dana at the *Sun*," I said, building on my strategy with the guard downstairs. "He'll critique my grammar, but at least his gatekeeper is a stuffed owl, not a stuffed shirt." Marsh looked rightfully affronted. I pressed on. "Or maybe Doctor

Hepworth. He'll be writing his sermon for Sunday's edition, but he'll see me. Wherever I take the story, I'll make certain the Colonel knows he could have had it, but for an officious little clerk who was too frightened of the gun in his desk to bother him with a story. I'm certain the Colonel respects cowardice among his staff. Mr. Pulitzer, too."

I'd gone too far. Clearly too far. But I held my breath in hope as Marsh looked me up and down—not as a man might assess a woman, but as a reporter weighing up an untrustworthy source.

Finally, he shook his head. "I'll see the Colonel. But I'm not promising he'll see you," he added, clearly hoping to return armed with full authority to throw me out.

By the look on his face when he returned, he was disappointed. "Five minutes."

I bolted out of the chair and into the Colonel's office.

His waistcoat was a different color, providing a blue background for the ashes, making them now look like clouds. He glanced at me as he stubbed out his cigar. "Good evening, Miss. Marsh says you have a story. Pitch it."

I took up station before his desk, thinking fast. He was a direct man. He wouldn't care about stolen purses or life's savings. He wouldn't respond to a needy woman's pleas. He wanted blunt and to the point.

Which suited me to the ground. "Immigrants," I said. "The voyage to America is hard. I'll go to England, then return among the poverty-stricken men, women, and children coming to New York to make a better life."

"We have lots of immigrant interviews," he said, waving his hand.

"I won't just be talking to them. I'll *be* one of them. I'll ride back in steerage. Eat their food, sleep huddled with them, breathe their air. I'll tell the story from their point of view."

Cockerill's left eye narrowed just a fraction. I'd seen the same glazed excitement in Madden's face as he'd imagined layouts and headlines, but never so intense.

He snapped back to the present. "There are objections."

"Name them," I said.

"The obvious ones. A woman at risk."

"Other women endure it every day. Hundreds of them."

"If you got into trouble, we wouldn't be able to help you."

"Of course not. I wouldn't expect it. I am perfectly capable of helping myself. I survived alone in Mexico for six months, with the whole government against me."

His mouth curled beneath the moustache. "I don't want a riot onboard either."

"I'm no rabble-rouser. I'm a reporter."

He killed time by taking out a fresh cigar from a carved mahogany box and lighting it. Waving the long match in the air and puffing hard, he finally gave a bob of his overlarge head. "I'll consider it. Come back tomorrow."

I couldn't have hoped for more. Yet boldness had carried me this far, and I was in no mood for uncertainty. "No."

His eyebrows lifted. "No?"

"Accept it now, or I take it to the *Sun*."

Colonel Cockerill gazed at me coolly. "Oh, you will, will you?"

"Yes," I said simply.

He stared at me, ash dropping unheeded from his cigar. He drew in a deep breath through his nose, then began moving with sharp decision. Opening a large checkbook, he scribbled something, tore it off, then tossed it to the edge of his desk. "No, I don't think you will."

Trembling inside, I picked it up. It was a check for twenty-five dollars.

Plucking his cigar from his mouth, he aimed it at me. "That's a retainer. You've been paid, so you can't take it anywhere else. Your pitch now belongs to us. We'll use it, or we goddamned won't. Either way, no one else does." He stood, towering over me from across the desk. "Now, I'm taking this upstairs to Pulitzer. You can come back tomorrow and hear his answer." His eyes narrowed. "And if you ever again give me another goddamn ultimatum—"

I cut across him. "I'll wait."

"What was that?"

Raising my chin, I said, "I'll wait to hear what he says."

His jaw worked silently for several seconds. Then he loosed a cannon-shot laugh, gestured grandly to a comfortable chair across his office, and stalked out, shaking his head.

Shaking myself, but all over, I hastily unbuttoned the front of my dress and stuck the check into my camisole. Making myself respectable again, I toyed with my lucky ring, twisting it again and again around my thumb.

Slowly, I began to laugh, my eyes flooding with tears of relief. They say necessity is the mother of invention. If that's true, then desperation is the father of inspiration. I had done it! I had gotten past the gatekeepers, pitched a story, and not been told "no."

Not yet, at any rate.

It was almost twenty minutes before I heard his step outside, by which time I had composed myself. When Cockerill shut his office door, I was able to look him square in the eye.

"Mr. Pulitzer says no."

It was an almost physical blow. Before I could stop myself, I was protesting. "Why not? Did you—?"

Cockerill fiddled with the mahogany box on his desk, drawing forth a new cigar. "I pitched it hard. But he has a good reason. For a reporter new to the paper, we need a story that's more local."

My eyes were hot, my breathing short. But I couldn't allow myself to blubber. *Not here, not ever.* "I understand."

Wondering if I should leave, if I should give the check back, how on earth I would get to it with decency, I watched him finally get his cigar going. Huge head engulfed in a cloud of foul smoke, he looked at me.

"Mr. Pulitzer suggests a different story."

THIRTY-THREE

MAD WHISPERINGS

THURSDAY, SEPTEMBER 22 1887

"WE'VE BEEN HEARING RUMORS," the Colonel said, perching on the edge of his desk, "about the women's sanatorium on Blackwell's Island."

A thrill ran down my spine. Located on the East River, Blackwell's Island housed undesirable modern institutions: a prison, a charity hospital, a workhouse, an almshouse. In short, all the places unwelcome within the city itself.

Among them was the Woman's Lunatic Asylum. It was a name that conjured nightmares all on its own. But as Cockerill was watching me, I made sure not to quail.

"A while back, I received a tip from a friend at the *Sunday Argus* in Washington. He'd gotten a report from a woman whose friend died in there. Pneumonia, they said. It wasn't the first rumor we've heard. Now, such places always have rumors. But these are goddamn persistent. Problem is, we don't have a blasted shred of proof. They're all behind barred windows and locked doors, and we can't get anyone who works there to talk. As for the inmates themselves, even if we were able to interview them, they'd be dismissed out of hand for being, you know—"

"Crazy," I finished for him.

Cockerill nodded. "Mr. Pulitzer and I have been mulling ways to get information from inside. We discussed it just now, and it was our opinion that if you're willing to risk the dangers of steerage, you might be willing to do something perhaps even more dangerous, but also more goddamned important."

Perched at the very edge of my seat, I said, "You want me to pretend

I'm mad."

He blew a cloud of smoke toward the ceiling, then fixed me with his velvet gaze. "Exactly. We want you to feign insanity, get yourself committed to the madhouse on Blackwell's, and bring back the true story of the conditions inside." He puffed again, staring at me through the sulfurous cloud. "Can you do it?"

I smiled. "I can try."

After a moment of study, he added a caveat. "'Course, there may be nothing at all in it. One hears these things. Madhouses breed mad stories, most of them wild exaggerations or romantic drivel about love denied and gone mad."

"Like Empress Carlota," I murmured.

"What is that, a damned novel?" Before I could correct him he said, "I swear too goddamn much. It bother you?"

"If it's how you talk to your reporters, it doesn't bother me a goddamn bit."

The Colonel's moustache twitched. "Good. Okey, back to Ladies' Bedlam. As I was saying, there might be no fire, only smoke from the frenzied imaginations of madwomen."

"What do I write if that's the case?"

"You write about the women. That's the damned beauty, no matter which way it pans out, there's a story in it. If there's abuse, that's the story. No abuse, write about the kind of women who end up in there. Real goddamn sob stories. There but for the grace of God, like that." He frowned at me. "We're not asking you to go there to make up sensational revelations. Write things up as you find them, good or bad. Give praise or blame as you think best, and tell the goddamned truth all the time."

"You mean, be a reporter."

"Don't be sarcastic. I don't know you." The Colonel drummed his fingers upon the edge of his desk. He saw me staring and offered a sheepish grin. "Started as a drummer boy during the war. Always helps me find the center." He scoured me with a scorching gaze. "You think you've got the courage to go through with this? You'd need to play mad the whole time. Make them believe it. You can't ever let on who you are or what you're after."

"I understand." I'm sure my excitement showed.

"Even if things become intolerable, you must en-goddamn-dure. Maintain all aspects of insanity to such a degree that you can fool the goddamned doctors. Live for a week among the insane without being found out by the goddamned authorities. You think you can live that lie?"

I laughed. "Oh, Colonel! I have lived one kind of lie or another all my life."

Colonel Cockerill frowned. "Even now?"

"Even now."

He grunted. "This could work. No one will expect it. Hell, if you manage to pull it off, half the city still won't believe it. But you'll come out with a damned good story." His eyes narrowed as he studied my face, at the moment suffused with happiness and excitement. "I am concerned about that chronic smile of yours."

Unused to a man telling me *not* to smile, I quickly schooled my face. "When do I start?"

He continued to stare, as if worried my smile might burst uncontrollably forth again. "As soon as you're able. What name will you use?"

"I could use my real name. Elizabeth Cochrane."

"No. Too close to Cockerill, they might get suspicious. Besides, it should be close to your *nom de plume.*"

"Nellie. . . Brown," I suggested.

The Colonel tried it out. "Nellie Brown. Plain. American. I like it."

I laughed suddenly, thinking of the Mexican name confusion. "And I have handkerchiefs with the initials *N. B.* embroidered on them."

"Settled, then. Nellie goddamned Brown it is."

"How long will I have to be in there?"

"I'd say a week. Can you manage that?"

"Yes," I said, with such easy confidence that I almost believed it.

The Colonel waved at the door. "Off you go. We'll be watching. If you can't get in or if you're found out, come back to this office to let us know. Otherwise we'll see you in a week." He held out a hand. "Good luck."

As we shook, a distressing thought occurred to me. "Once I get in, how will you get me out?"

"No idea," answered Cockerill with a shrug. "But never fear. We'll get you out, even if we have to tell who you are and why you're there." He jabbed his cigar at me. "Only get in."

TEN MINUTES LATER I WAS on the street. All of New York seemed brighter, friendlier, and more vibrant. Forgetting the Colonel's injunction not to smile, I grinned all the way home. Three hours earlier, I had been at the end of the road. Now I had not only recovered a quarter of my lost fortune but I was being offered a story that was at the heart of everything I had worked on in my career. Downtrodden women and institutional corruption, mixed with adventure and a challenge to my wits. It was wonderful!

Toward the end of the ride home, I began to settle down and focus.

I have to start making plans now, tonight, this minute. Returning to my boardinghouse, I assured Mrs. Pesetsky that all was well. "I have a new assignment, and I was paid in advance," I said, to her great relief.

She looked slightly more dubious when I added, "But I have to make some noise tonight. I have to rehearse being a madwoman. It's, ah. . . for a play."

She patted my shoulder. "So long as you don't disturb the other lodgers, dear."

Up in my small room, I undressed, tucked my check away, and then began to imitate insanity. I began with the violence I'd seen portrayed in stories and on stage. I likely frightened Mrs. Pesetsky and the other ladies as I flung myself about my room, achieving little more than barked shins and a banged elbow.

Fortunately for us all, my rehearsal was short lived. After just ten minutes, I was panting like I had skated the whole evening at Rinkomania. Violent madness was not only dangerous, but *exhausting*.

Clearly this form of madness is not going to work.

But how else to be mad? I'd done my best to avoid insane people on the street, and had not the faintest notion of their actions, their movements, or their styles of speech. Worse, not only did I have to fool average people, but also doctors and alienists with years of training!

My only brushes with insanity had been in literature. I tried to conjure madmen from my memories of various novels, but they all seemed unsustainable in their frenzied ways. *Perhaps*, I thought, *the source of madness is an unending wellspring of energy.*

But then I recalled the novel *Called Back* by Hugh Conway, and the "madness" of Pauline. The actress in the stage version I'd seen had done such an amazing job of being disturbing in the role by *not* looking at people, and seeming utterly listless! Pulling a well-loved copy from my shelf, I thumbed through the pages, looking for a particular passage. I found it halfway through Chapter Five, where the hero related his frustration with his new wife's mental condition:

> How shall I describe her? Madness means something quite different from her state. Imbecility still less conveys my meaning. There is no word I can find which is fitting to use. There was simply something missing from her intellect—as much missing as a limb may be from a body. Memory, except for comparatively recent events, she seemed to have none. The power of reasoning, weighing, and drawing deductions seemed beyond her grasp. She appeared unable to recognize the importance or bearing of occurrences taking place around her. Sorrow and delight were emotions she was incapable of feeling. Nothing appeared to move her. Unless

her attention was called to them she noticed neither persons nor places. She lived as by instinct—rose, ate, drank, and lay down to rest as one not knowing why she did so. Such questions or remarks as came within the limited range of her capacity she replied to—those outside it passed unheeded, or else the shy troubled eyes sought for a moment the questioner's face, and left him as mystified as I had been when first I noticed that curious inquiring look.

I put down the book, aflame with excitement. It was perfect. Rather than manic energy, it required merely blank, bovine simplicity. Not heightened emotion, but an utter lack of it. I would build a wall around myself. Make myself impervious to questions or ideas or pleading or reason.

The Colonel had been concerned about my smile giving away the game. Because women were expected to smile. So I would be a woman without smiles.

That gave me the happy idea of stripping away, not adding to, my usual behaviors. I plunked myself before my mirror and gazed at myself in earnest, watching for habits to break.

Be still. Breathe. Stare. Ooo, stare and don't blink! Never blink!

I practiced long into the night, turning up the gaslight as the sounds of the other boarders faded to nothing. I conjured up memories of paintings with titles like "Ophelia" and "Portia," their far-off look of sadness, that very gothic despair. Gothic in Gotham.

As the world outside became unsettlingly quiet, so did I. At about one o'clock, it struck me that I should go to bed. Then I thought of the Macbeths. Lack of sleep had driven Macbeth mad, while each night Lady Macbeth sleepwalked through all her sins.

I determined not to rest until I was committed. *Nellie Bly shall sleep no more!*

Seizing upon this thought, I pulled down ghost stories from my shelves and read them in snatches and starts, hunting out the most unsettling or gruesome scenes. Around three o'clock I realized I was hungry, as I had entirely missed supper. *Should I sneak downstairs and wolf down a bit of bread and butter?*

No. Be hungry. Be tired. Become the desperate thing you want to be seen as. Who knows? Perhaps by simply being hungry and tired, you can be taken for mad.

To keep myself awake, I started pawing through my wardrobe. *How does a madwoman dress?* To keep to my theme, I decided she would dress simply. Hunting up a fashionable dress, coat, and hat, I laid them upon the bed to examine them. The dress was gray cheviot with brown trim, a little frayed at the hem but with sleeves cut in the latest style. The gloves were made of brown silk. The hat was a black straw sailor's hat trimmed in brown, with a veil of thin gray illusion that reached only as far as my nose. A perfectly respectable outfit for a woman who should have better.

I removed the labels from my chosen attire, and then began to fret about what items to bring with me. My *N.B.* handkerchiefs, of course. A little money. A good pencil. A reporter should have a notebook, but surely that would be suspicious.

Unless I fill it with nonsense! Giddily, I tore some pages from an old Mexican notebook and scribbled gibberish into it. I passed the rest of that dark September night in my shift—the lights in my room blazing, my eyes watering, and my stomach roiling—as I read snippets of haunting tales and scribbled mad notes to myself.

As the sun threatened the horizon, I found myself cloudgazing. The fluffy masses seemed to move with intractable slowness, forming too-perfect patterns in the air. Objects in the still room hummed with a life of their own. The air seemed thick, oppressive.

I was mad. Or close enough to be getting on. "Time to go."

Startled by my own voice, I realized that speaking, too, was a weapon. "Don't mutter. Speak plainly, but nonsensically. As if there's any sense in the world."

I started to make my toilet and then checked. "No, don't comb your hair. Let your bangs hang askew. Leave your toothbrush alone." I couldn't resist the soap, though, and I scrubbed my skin raw, wondering how long it would be until I had another opportunity to wash.

I dressed fastidiously from head to toe: no button out of place, no cinch not fastened. I gave my little room a last fond look. *Who knows when I'll see it again?*

Then, outwardly calm, I went out to my crazy business.

M Y FIRST ORDER OF BUSINESS was to find a new boarding-house, one that had never seen me, where I could be Nellie Brown with no trouble. From a directory I selected the cheapest one in the busiest neighborhood: the Temporary Home for Females, Number Eighty-Four, Second Avenue, in Little Germany, just north of the Bowery, where prostitution and gambling dens flourished.

Two blocks from the house where Stephen Foster had died.

That's unsettling. I wondered if it was an ill omen, starting my venture so close to the death place of the father of "Nelly Bly." But I shook myself and dismissed the premonition.

Still, as I rode the train into the city, I had a sudden thought of self-preservation. *Someone should know where I am. Just in case.*

I thought of telling McCain, or even writing to Madden. But I couldn't share the story with another paper.

I thought of Mother. *I'm checking myself into a madhouse. Come get me out if I'm gone too long. Love, Pinky.* I could only imagine giving her a heart attack with such a letter.

I thought next of Wilson, and that thought lingered. It was dramatic, and a trifle fanciful. But, no. I knew his nature. Wilson would hasten to New York to rescue me, spoiling my whole enterprise in order to play the knight. And I didn't want saving. I wanted insurance. Also, if somewhere deep down I wanted to know if he *would* come for me, if he *did* care for me, I was too stubborn a coward to test it.

So, no one close to me. No one who might worry for me. Who, then?

With an amused groan I realized exactly who it should be. I got off near City Hall, and soon was in the office of Assistant District Attorney Henry Macdona.

Just to dispel any improper thoughts he might have, I began speaking the moment the door was closed. "I remember you saying that you were looking for a scandal that would keep your name in the papers."

Up to now his eyes had been alight with lechery, but they suddenly kindled with a different kind of desire. He waved me to a seat. "Please, Miss Bly. I am all ears."

He reacted with understandable incredulity to my assignment, but I was so matter-of-fact about the whole thing that he began to think me quite a prodigy. "And you say you've done this kind of thing before?"

"Yes. I infiltrated the factories of Pittsburgh, posing as a workshop girl. And I spent six months in Mexico, investigating corruption in the Díaz government."

Those were both gross exaggerations. I had only worked in one factory, and I had certainly not gone to Mexico to uncover corruption. But Macdona was impressed. "What do you want from me?"

"Advice," I said. "And a promise that you will vouch for me should I require assistance in freeing myself from that awful place."

He nodded slowly. "And in return. . ."

"In return, you will have the first crack at any malpractices I uncover. After the *World*, of course. I will give you all the information prior to the *World* publishing my findings, and you will then be able to act on them the moment they are made public."

"Exclusive access?" he asked in a singsong quaver.

"Until the stories are published. Then the public will have them."

"And the moment the public starts demanding action, I'll have the subpoenas ready and signed. And the story will continue with the investigation and the findings, the hearings, perhaps even some action in the legislature. . ." Snapping back to himself, he said, "What if you find nothing at all?"

I shrugged. "Then there is no story and no scandal. But with so many rumors. . ."

He considered, then slapped his hands together. "It's certainly worth the attempt. Yes, you have my word. I will keep an eye out for you, and assist you in any way I can."

"Excellent," I said. "First, you can tell me this: how does one go about getting one's self committed?"

He leaned back in his chair, considering. "Hmm. There are really only two reliable ways. Either you can have someone commit you out of concern for your person, or you can create some kind of scene or disturbance and have yourself committed by the court."

I was already planning on the latter tack. If I were to be committed by a court of law, there wouldn't be any suspicion that I was faking. "What are the courts looking for?"

"They'll look to see if you're completely alone. If you have a friend or relative, they'll attempt to foist you off on them first."

"I have obliterated every trace of my identity. No card, no labels on my clothes. Nothing to let people know even where I am from."

"Good. Next, they're looking at someone who might be dangerous, or prone to danger. Someone incapable of keeping herself safe. That's the largest consideration, I believe. Will she harm others, or herself? That's what will weigh on the judge's mind. And is she pitiable enough? Too truculent and she might be sentenced to jail instead."

That aligned neatly with my chosen form of madness. "That's perfect."

Macdona looked at me dubiously. "I wonder if you possess the fortitude for such an ordeal. You're so small. . ."

"'Though I be little, yet am I fierce,'" I said, misquoting Shakespeare.

"It means not only fooling the alienists, but also some policemen and a judge."

"I'm sure I can do it." I stared at him with my new, unblinking, preternatural stillness. "Already I feel quite mad."

Macdona blinked several times, and I saw a shiver pass down his spine. "Yes," he said with an uneasy laugh, "I can see that."

THIRTY-FOUR

LUNATIC LODGER

FROM CITY HALL, I DECIDED to walk to Second Avenue. I couldn't have anyone tracing my taxicab, and I wanted to arrive as mysteriously as possible.

It was a strange sensation, going someplace with the deliberate intention that they would deem me mad. I worked to dispel my growing feeling of guiltiness. Also my temptation to giggle.

At last, I arrived at Matron Irene Stenard's Temporary Home for Females, a dismal tenement house with no aspirations beyond mere functionality. I drew in a deep breath, then pulled the bell.

The door was thrown back with a vengeance by a short blonde girl just entering womanhood. "Yes?"

Putting on my best dreamy voice, I asked, "Is the matron in?"

"Yes," barked the girl. "She's busy now. Go to the back parlor and wait." Stepping back, she flung the door wide.

Feeling less guilty after such an unkind greeting, I passed through the front parlor, aware of three women listlessly engaged in sewing or reading. A little boy stared at me from behind his mother's skirts.

The back parlor was a lightless room, colder than the September air outside, and furnished with uncomfortable armless chairs. I found one with an upholstered seat in desperate need of dusting. Removing neither hat nor gloves, I simply sat as if unaware of the cloud that rose to either side of me.

The wait was long enough to allow me to take in every aspect of that chilly room: a wardrobe, a desk, a half-empty bookcase, an organ, and a scatter of chairs. The windows butted up so close to the next building that hardly any daylight squeezed through. Two peeling panels in the striped wallpaper showed older paper beneath. The newer paper was discolored near the lone gas jet, currently unlit.

Eventually, a lean woman in a pinched dark dress erupted into the room and cannoned a single word at me. "Well?"

"Are you the matron?" I asked in a slow, unconcerned way. Eyes not quite focused, I might have been talking to a spirit hovering behind her. *Best to get started at once.*

"No," snapped the slender woman. "The matron is sick. I'm her assistant. What do you want?"

"I want to stay here for a few days, if you can accommodate me."

"I have no single rooms. But you can share with another girl. I'll do that much for you."

"I shall be glad to share," I said evenly, already thinking of how to convince a roommate of my madness. "How much do you charge?"

"Thirty cents a night." From her voice she half-hoped I would cry 'Alas!' and depart.

I opened my little purse and let her see the full contents, or lack thereof. I had brought just seventy cents with me. The sooner my funds were depleted, the sooner they would throw me out. A girl without funds was a girl without friends.

I handed her nearly half of my ready money, which vanished into a tight grip. "You'll have to wait here until I can arrange a room. It won't be soon. I have other things to do."

Half-risen, I made no reply, but simply sat again, releasing a second cloud of dust, and returned my vacant stare to the faded wallpaper. Expecting an argument, she was clearly bemused. "What's your name?"

I looked past her. "Brown. Nellie Brown."

"I'll put you down in the book." She stalked off, leaving me on my own once more.

That wait was dreadful. I longed to rise and pluck a book from the shelf, inspect the desk, press the keys of the organ to see if it even played. But I kept utterly still, listening to myself breathe. Each swell of my lungs became the most interesting sound in my mad little world.

Suddenly a bell downstairs clanged loud enough to rival the doorbell. At its signal, the women in the front parlor rose, and others came trudging downstairs from various parts of the house. All of them headed sheeplike to the basement, where dinner was obviously being served.

No one spoke to me. No one invited me to join. So I continued to sit, vacuously staring. Part of me wanted to chew my cud.

The temptation to laugh was growing upon me. Despite my determined attempt at blandness, a few chuckles started in my clenched belly and forced their way up through my throat and nose. "Stop that," I warned myself.

"Don't you want something to eat?"

I almost jumped. The assistant matron was staring at me. She had clearly heard my chortle, or else my admonition.

Looking up at her, I said simply, "Yes."

"Then come downstairs!" She almost shouted it, consternation propelling her past indifference to exasperation.

Rising unhurriedly, I followed her to the basement stairs. "What is your name?"

"Mrs. Stenard."

So she had been lying when she said she was not the matron. *Easier, I suppose, to pretend to be a functionary.*

I stopped on the uncarpeted stairs, produced my notebook, and wrote her name crossways in a margin. I could feel her disconcerted gaze on me—no woman likes being written about by a stranger. Then I put the notebook away and, without acknowledging her at all, continued down the stairs.

The basement was even more disheartening than the back parlor. The floor was bare, and the wooden tables were unvarnished, unpolished, and uncovered. Two gas jets sputtered and a lone oil lamp flickered, casting the meal into gloom from the start.

I was surprised by the number of chairs gathered at the bare basement tables: at least twenty, of which eight were presently filled. Room was made for me at a table with three other women. I smiled vaguely at them, not looking any in the eye, and they resumed their desultory talk, neatly excluding me.

The blonde girl appeared in an apron, clearly now playing waitress. Fixing me with a look of indiscriminate hatred, she planted her arms on her hips and rattled off, "Boiled mutton, boiled beef, beans, potatoes, coffee or tea?"

"Beef," I said slowly. "Potatoes. Coffee and bread."

"Bread comes with it," she said disdainfully, already off to the kitchen.

Sooner than I expected, she returned with my order on a battered metal tray that she clattered down in front of me. The food was unappetizing, and I only made a feint of eating it as I listened to the lifeless conversations around me. There was nothing of any interest, just simple scraps of human interaction to fill the void between this meal and the next.

I began feeling unaccountably angry with myself. I was here to play on the credulity of these women when I should be championing them. Men like Wilson believed this kind of life was good enough for any respectable woman, when in truth it was not fit for a mouse. Let any man exist here for even a few hours and he would rebel, cursing the government, the charities, and his God in a single breath. Yet these women endured this colorless life day in and day out!

But I had a job to do. Swallowing my pity, I watched as each woman crossed to a desk in the corner where they paid Mrs. Stenard for their meal. Taking my nibbled meal without comment, the little blonde gave me a worn red ticket. On it was marked 27 CENTS, which I dutifully paid. Within two hours I had run through nearly all my money.

The meal being over, there was nothing to do but return to my chair in the back parlor. There I sat in enforced idleness for the longest afternoon of my life.

The other women avoided the back parlor in favor of the front, where at least there was more light. I watched them through the connecting doorway. Most sat in equal stillness, waiting for night. Or death. A few filled the time with lacework or knitting. One woman kept nodding off, only to wake herself with her own snores. I hoped she would not be my promised roommate. Another sat reading and scratching her head, occasionally uttering an admonishing, "Georgie!" at her son without looking up from her book.

Georgie himself was a terrible brat. Once, he rushed headlong into the back parlor to deliberately butt my arm with his head. Discovering a target that did not fight back, he repeated his impression of a ram. And again.

This cannot stand.

As it was out of character for "Nellie Brown" to admonish anyone, I had to deal with it a different way. Removing my blank gaze from the far wall, I fixed it upon Georgie.

Georgie stared at me with a stupid grin fixed across his sticky mouth.

I stared at him.

He fidgeted.

I stared.

He squirmed.

I ran my tongue across my lips.

He ran, screaming in terror.

Score to the madwoman of Allegheny.

Throughout the whole day, the front bell would clang, and woman after woman would arrive to look for a room. Blondie would thunder to the door with unwelcoming scowls, having been distracted from her constant muted singing of hymns and popular songs. With the single exception of a lady in from the country for a day's shopping, every one of the prospective residents was a working woman, sometimes with a child in tow.

As the meager daylight dimmed, Mrs. Stenard came in to light the gas jet. Perched on her low stool she frowned at me. "What is wrong with you?"

I looked up blankly, saying nothing.

"Have you had some sorrow? Some trouble?"

"No," I replied vaguely, concealing my surprise. "Why?"

"Oh, because," she answered in the role of the all-knowing matron, "I can see it in your face."

I offered wide-eyed astonishment. "You can?"

"Yes," confirmed Mrs. Stenard, stepping down. "It tells a story of great tragedy."

"Well, everything is so sad," I said haphazardly.

She reached out to pat my shoulder. "You mustn't allow it to worry you. We all have our troubles, but we get over them in good time. What kind of work are you trying to get?"

"I don't know." I felt a stirring of unease. The last thing I wanted was to elicit sympathy. "It's all so sad."

Pulling a chair closer, she sat. "Would you like to wear a nice white cap and apron and be a nurse for children?"

Children like Georgie? Thank you, no! Drawing out one of my monogrammed handkerchiefs, I covered my face. "I've never worked. I wouldn't know how."

"But you must learn." With benign harshness, Mrs. Stenard waved a hand toward the front parlor. "All these women here work."

"Do they?" I said in a whisper of amazement.

"Of course they do, Miss Brown. They are all good ladies."

"Miss Brown?" I asked, blinking.

"That's your name, isn't it?"

Recalling the Spanish word for *brown*, I said, "Yo soy Nellie Moreno."

That confounded her. "But, Nellie, you said it was Brown." Clearly frustrated with me, she yet persisted in her helpfulness. "You must be tired. Rest will do you good. And socializing. Talk to these other women."

Suddenly, I spied a route to dispel her well-intentioned mothering: Albert's trick of calling me a liar when he himself was lying, of cheating when he was cheating. Might not a lunatic accuse others of lunacy?

Lowering my head so that my hat almost concealed my eyes, I confided, "They look horrible to me. Like crazy women. I am *so* afraid of them," I added, my unblinking eyes meeting hers.

A variety of emotions fluttered across Mrs. Stenard's face, but she remained dogged. "They don't look very nice, true. But they are all good, honest, working women. We do not keep crazy people here."

We'll see if you can say that come morning! That thought brought up my laugh again, and this time I let it out, dropping my handkerchief a fraction so she saw my smile. In a voice pitched just loud enough to be overheard in the front parlor, I went on. "They all look crazy. I promise, I am afraid of them. There are so many crazy people about, one can never tell what they will do. So many murders committed, and the police never catch the murderers. They *never* catch them!" From somewhere I found a noise—half laugh and half sob—that would have been given a rave by even the most jaded theatre critic.

It was amusing to see how swiftly Mrs. Stenard was out of her chair and across the room. Remembering her step stool, she darted back for it. "I have more lamps to light. I'll come back to talk with you after a while." She exchanged looks with the ladies of the front parlor as she passed.

She never did come back.

Eventually the supper bell jolted the house, and the midday parade repeated, this time with more people. There were fewer choices, as supper was merely the leftovers from dinner. In the basement a few women eyed me askance, but none outright avoided me. Yet.

Back upstairs after supper, I found both parlors full, with not enough chairs to go around. With the solitary gas jet in each room and a little oil lamp in the hall between, we were all cast in a sickly glow, shadows dancing upon half our features.

As all the chairs were taken, I was unable to sit and stare. I wondered if I might not achieve a swifter effect by engaging a couple of these women. I wanted to be on my way to the madhouse as soon as possible, if only to escape this dreary place. A few nights here and I might actually gain admittance to Blackwell's without any performance on my part!

Noting two particularly chatty women, I floated up to them. "Excuse me. My name is Nellie Moreno. I am lonely. May I join you?"

I must have been an odd picture, still in my hat and gloves, circles under my wide, unblinking eyes. But they were kind and gracious, and one of them moved to share a seat with her friend, making room for me. They introduced themselves as Mrs. King and Mrs. Caine. From their accents I knew their origins, at least in the vaguest sense. Mrs. King was a Southerner, while Mrs. Caine hailed unmistakably from Boston.

Their conversation itself was uninteresting, but they made a point of attempting to include me. I just stared back at them, making no reply beyond a shrug or a muttered, "I couldn't say."

They did not seem unduly concerned. Perhaps they thought I was shy, or simple. Having achieved such success with Mrs. Stenard earlier, I decided to again try out my accusation. "Everyone here looks crazy," I confided in them.

Mrs. King laughed in a genteel fashion. "Listen to you. Are you not from the South? Your accent says y'are."

I agreed that I was from the South. I decided to agree with everything, and if I was contradicted, to simply be confused.

"Where did you receive schooling?"

"In the convent," I answered, inventing.

Mrs. Caine explained she had come to New York for a job correcting proofs on a medical dictionary. "But I have been ill of late, and lost my place. I think tomorrow I must give in and go home to Boston. Do either of you know what time the Boston boat leaves?"

"Nine-seventeen." Too late, I caught myself. Nellie Bly knew the timetables of the ferries, but not Nellie Brown. *Except now she does.*

"Thank you, Miss Moreno. What about you? What work are you in search of?"

"I don't think I should like to work," I remarked blankly. "I think it is quite sad that there are so many people forced to work at all, like peóns at the hacienda."

That was the moment they looked at me as if I was truly crazy.

"Hacienda?" said a new voice. A brunette not much older than me came over to join us. "That's a Spanish word! It means *house.*"

"Do you speak Spanish?" asked Mrs. King.

"I take lessons." Smiling at me, the brunette employed a Spanish more fluent than my own. "*Buenas tardes. Me llamo* Dorothy. *Como te sientes?*"

Panicking, I answered, "*Buenas tardes*, Dorothy. *Cómo estás?*"

"*Estoy bien. De dónde eres?*"

Dónde—that meant where. She was asking where I was from. "*La hacienda.*"

"*Dónde está la hacienda?*"

I shook my head. "No sé." *I don't know.*

She kept pressing, and between evasions I invented wildly, stealing huge swaths from Huck Finn: the dead mother, the abusive father, the sailing up the Mississippi. I might have even mentioned the Widow Douglas. *How are they not catching on?*

I was running out of phrases to evade her. Dorothy was going to spoil my whole plan, and it was all my fault for trying to be clever by using Spanish words.

Feigning a sudden pain, I put a knuckle to my forehead and bit my lip until tears came to my eyes. Looking up, I stared into their eyes. "It's gone. It's all gone."

The trio was quite startled by my tears. They might have tried to comfort me, but the little blonde came up to us. "It's time for bed."

"I'm afraid." I leaned close. "All the women here look crazy."

"You—you have to go to bed," said the young teen.

"Must I? Could I not just sit on the stairs all night?"

"No," said the girl, recoiling.

Mrs. Stenard came over. "You cannot remain here. Or everyone in the house will think you are crazy."

"Me? But I'm not crazy." *The surest way to get people to believe you are a thing is to deny it.*

By this point, every woman in that parlor was looking at me with extreme unease. Lifting me by the elbow, Mrs. Stenard escorted me to the stairs. I did not resist, simply repeating, "But why can't I sit on the stairs? I'm not crazy. They're the ones who are crazy."

In an attempt to distract me as we climbed the stairs, Mrs. Stenard said, "Do you have any bags?"

"Yes," I said.

"Where are they?"

I looked around the landing as if searching. "I don't know. I don't see them. . ."

Rising from the crowd of women watching me, Mrs. Caine ascended. "Let me take her." Mrs. Stenard was only too happy to hand me off, allowing Mrs. Caine to escort me the rest of the way.

Leading me into the room I was to stay in, Mrs. Caine sat me down in a chair and talked soothingly while she unpinned my hat and took down my hair. She was incredibly kind, and I wish I could have been grateful. If the world were full of Mrs. Caines, there would be far less misery and loneliness.

But her kindness was not an aid to my deception. So when she suggested I remove my coat and dress, I said, "I don't want to undress. Not in a house full of crazies. I want my things. Where are my things?"

By now, other women had gathered at the door to watch. As soon as I refused to undress they started muttering.

"Why, she's crazy enough."

"Poor loon!"

"I'm afraid to stay with such a crazy in the house."

"She will murder us all before morning!"

"Fetch a key and lock her in the room!"

One woman proposed sending for a policeman, and I wanted to say, *Listen to her!*

Again, Mrs. Caine championed me. "What has she done? Who has she harmed? She is merely confused, and likely tired. A good night's sleep will see her restored."

The woman I was meant to share the room with shook her head. "I won't stay in the same room with her for all the Vanderbilts' money!"

Mrs. Caine stepped between them and me. "Then I will stay with her!" And shut the door in their faces. She turned to me. "I should have asked. Is it all right with you?"

"I should like it of all things," I replied blankly.

So the kind and good Mrs. Caine became my roommate. She was not so trusting, however, that she could ignore me and my strange behavior. Eventually, she decided to mimic me and remain in her clothes as she laid herself down on the lone bed. "Would you not like to lie down as well?"

"No." I was so tired that I feared I would fall directly asleep the moment my head touched the pillow. Instead I said, "What is your Christian name?"

She seemed comforted by so normal a question. "Ruth."

"Like from the Bible," I said.

"Like from the Bible," she agreed.

Known for her kindness and devotion. Racked with guilt, I sat next to her on the bed, but faced the wall.

What a terrible night I gave her. Just as she would start to nod off, she'd jerk awake to look at me in fright. In the between times, she would ask me questions: how long had I been in New York, how old was I, where else I had lived, how did I fill my days, and more along those lines. To every question, I would simply answer in my dishrag dampness, "I forget."

Before midnight, she was close to tears. "Your eyes are terribly bright," she said. "They shine so. I fear for you."

"Why?" I asked her. "I am perfectly well. Only I have this headache. . ." I started mentioning the pain in my head at intervals, knuckling my forehead to show the spot.

Suddenly, we heard a scream from elsewhere in the house. There was a commotion in the hallway as everyone tried to pack into our room. But Mrs. Caine assured everyone the scream had come from neither her nor me. The ladies all peered at me, sitting fully dressed on the bed, staring at the wall.

Another door opened, and in moments the screamer was confessing. She had been wakened by a terrible nightmare—of me! "I saw her, the mad one in there! She was rushing at me with a knife in her hand! She meant to murder me!"

"She has been in our room all night," snapped Mrs. Caine. "She's made no threats against anyone. She says her head hurts."

"Has she not slept, even a little?"

"No," confided Mrs. Caine softly. "She is very strangely behaved. I'm afraid for her."

"I'm not afraid *for* her," said the screamer, perfectly loud. "I'm afraid *of* her!"

Mrs. Caine closed the door on the hallway gaggle and slowly returned to sit upon the opposite side of the bed.

"What was that cry?" I asked, unmoving.

"One of the girls had a nightmare," she said simply.

"I'm not surprised," I answered. "In a house filled with those crazy women, they must all suffer nightmares. It is why I do not like to sleep. I wish I had a gun."

That remark was more frightening to poor Mrs. Caine than any I had previously made. "You don't have one?"

I shook my head. "No." Fixing her with my eyes, I allowed a little hope to creep into my dream state. "Do you?"

"No. Thank Heaven, I do not."

I sighed and resumed staring at the wall.

Reassured that I was unarmed, Mrs. Caine eventually fell into a sound sleep. Relaxing a little, I crept to a chair across the room. It was uncomfortable, which helped me stay awake as I looked for some way to fill the time.

I posed myself a question: what had brought me to this place, this pass, this moment in time? From my earliest deeds, could I ever have imagined I'd be sitting in a miserable boardinghouse feigning madness so I might gain admittance to an insane asylum?

That brought a smile to my lips. *No, I don't think in all my wild youth or angry teen years I could have conjured such an outcome.*

How did I get here, then?

That was an interesting line of thought. I began laying the rails of the track that had brought me to this place. Over the course of that long night, the pages of my life were turned up and I stood face to face with myself.

If that's not crazy-making, I don't know what is.

THIRTY-FIVE

BEFORE THE JUDGE

SATURDAY, SEPTEMBER 24 1887

ACCORDING TO CHARLIE, ONE of Father's favorite stories to tell us at bedtime was Robert the Bruce and the spider:

When the good king was in prison, he saw a spider spin its way from one of the ceiling beams of his cell to another, only to fall. Six times the spider spun, and six times the spider fell.

Six times have I fought against the English and failed, thought the Bruce to himself as he watched the spider closely. *Now if the spider fails again, I too shall give up and abandon the fight for Scotland.*

But the spider did not lose hope. Robert the Bruce forgot his own troubles as he watched, fascinated, as the little spider swung herself out upon her slender line. Would she fail a seventh time?

No! The thread was carried safely to the next beam and fastened there. The bridge was made, and could be built upon.

And Robert the Bruce threw off grief and despair and continued his war for independence until he achieved victory.

When dawn broke, I was watching a mouse in the corner of the room, trying to read in its frightened skittering portents of the future. The idea seemed quite reasonable.

I watched the mouse make its way up to the bed beside Mrs. Caine. Feeling pity for her, I moved to shoo it away. It fled, leaving me with only cockroaches to watch. They came together and seemed to converse. I wondered if I was the subject of their conversation. It seemed lengthy, and quite involved.

They all skittered off as Mrs. Caine woke. She let out a little noise of surprise to see me still up, still in my clothes, and still watching her. But, being irrepressibly sympathetic, she came over to take my hands. "Oh, poor dear. Still lively as a cricket?"

Thinking of the roaches, I said, "I'd rather be a cricket."

"Poor, poor thing. Oh, would you not rather go home?"

"I should," I agreed, "very much."

"Then tell me where home is and I will take you."

She was so kind, and I was so tired, my eyes welled with tears. "I do not know where my home is!"

In that moment, it was true.

She fetched a cloth and bathed my brow, all the while talking in soothing tones. She kept trying to coax me to recline in the bed and get some sleep. Failing at that, she wrapped me in a blanket and kissed my forehead. "Poor child. Poor child."

Knowing how little true kindness there is in the world, I felt rotten forcing this beautiful soul to waste so much upon me, who did not actually require it. She held me back that morning until all the other women had broken their fasts and gone off to work. Then she led me to the basement for coffee and a stale bun. I ate in silence, then returned to my room.

She followed, still asking questions. "Where are your friends?"

"I have no friends." I looked around. "I have trunks. Where are my trunks? I want my trunks."

"We shall find them," she assured me over and over. "We shall find them."

The clock was ringing nine when Mrs. Stenard appeared at the door. I immediately asked after my trunks.

In an indecently eager tone she suggested I go out and look for them. "Perhaps they're where you left them yesterday."

"No! I will not leave until my trunks arrive. And until this terrible headache goes away!" I pressed my knuckles to my forehead, hitting myself several times with them. "How I wish I had a pistol!"

"A pistol!" cried Mrs. Stenard.

"She doesn't have one," said Mrs. Caine quickly.

Mrs. Stenard did not seem reassured. "Why does she want a pistol?"

"For protection against the crazy girls," I said, still pressing my knuckles against my head.

"Fetch a policeman," said the young blonde harshly from the door.

Mrs. Stenard tried for another three minutes to convince me to go looking for my lost trunks. Then she gave up and, fetching her bonnet, announced she would be back soon. My heart started beating in hope. *Has the time come at last?*

Indeed it had. When Mrs. Stenard returned, she had two police officers in tow. They wore long blue coats and flat caps with short brims that barely shaded their eyes. Like most New York coppers, they sported thick moustaches. Also like most policemen, they were big—far bigger than me.

They burst into the room ready for anything. Clearly, Mrs. Stenard had played up my "insanity" to gain their help in ejecting me. When they saw a woman sitting and staring vaguely at the space between them, they were nonplussed. Softly, Mrs. Stenard said, "I want you to take her quietly."

One policeman cracked the knuckles of his right hand. "If she don't come along quietly, I'll drag her through the streets."

That sent a shiver up my spine. *But it would make a good story. . .*

Mrs. Caine intervened with a plan. "She says she's missing her trunks," she told them in a low tone. "If you say you are taking her to find them, she may go with you."

The policeman with the uncracked knuckles squatted in front of me. "Miss. Miss, can you hear me?" He snapped his fingers in front of my nose, and I shifted my head to gaze in the direction of his face. "I'm officer Bockert. I understand you've got some lost trunks?" I nodded enthusiastically. "Would you like to go find them?"

I recoiled slightly. "I'd be afraid to go alone."

"I'll go with you," said Mrs. Stenard, surprising everyone present. I'm not sure if Mrs. Caine's goodness had shamed her, or she simply wanted to make sure there was no chance of me returning. Whatever the cause, she arranged to walk me to the nearest precinct station, with the two policemen trailing behind to watch me from a respectful distance.

Mrs. Caine helped me with my hat and veil, and then led me to the basement where she kissed me and blessed me. "I hope you find what you have lost."

When she said that, I almost cried.

Mrs. Stenard and I exited the building by the rear door. I imagine she wanted no one to see the crazy lady. She led me to a neighboring street, and from there the few blocks to the station house. Officer Bockert and his brutish partner followed us, a fact I gathered from Mrs. Stenard's frequent reassuring glances back.

Reaching the 15th Precinct station, I experienced an unwelcome jolt. Standing beside the front desk was the sturdy police captain I had spoken to just two days earlier, the one who had informed me of the details of Foster's death. Captain McCullagh was in conversation when I arrived, but he noted me and watched as Mrs. Stenard brought me to the desk.

Coming in after us, Officer Bockert casually stepped behind the desk and addressed me. "Very well. Let's learn a few things. Are you Nellie Brown?"

With McCullagh so near, I sought desperately for a name that was not so close to Nellie Bly, and recalled my playful lie the previous evening. "Yo soy Nellie Moreno."

"She said that last night," interjected Mrs. Stenard.

He frowned. "Does she speak English?"

"Like a native. Nellie, you said your name was Brown, isn't that right?" Enjoying their confusion, I nodded. "Sí, Moreno."

"Nellie Marina, alias Nellie Brown," said Bockert, writing. "And where do you come from?"

"*No sé.*" Much further and I would have to revert back to English. *Or I could try out my dusty French*, I thought.

Fortunately, Mrs. Stenard burst into speech. "She's been like this since yesterday. She arrived with no luggage and asked for a room for the night. Then she sat by herself in the dark all day, not conversing with anyone, just staring at the wallpaper. When I tried to talk to her, she accused me of being crazy, and of all the other women in the house of being crazy too."

"Sí, loco," I said with a limp kind of nod. I didn't recall accusing her of being crazy, but it was all one.

Mrs. Stenard leaned close to the officer. "I think she is a good girl who's been driven mad by some inhuman treatment."

The officer looked for my response to this incredible statement. I simply gazed over his head at the chipped paint on the wall. "Come over here," he said to Mrs. Stenard, and the two stepped aside for a few minutes.

When he returned, he was all smiles. "Miss Marina. Come along with me. I will find your trunks for you. But first we must have you tell your story to the judge so he will understand."

"The judge?" I asked.

Though relieved by my use of English, he was fearful of my potential hysteria. "I mean the man at the express office. We call him judge. He'll know where your trunks are."

"Oh. I see." I swiveled my head toward Mrs. Stenard. "Are you coming?"

"Yes, dear." Now that I was clear of her house, the matron was enjoying her part in this drama.

Officer Bockert gestured toward the door. "Shall we go?"

"Con mucho gusto," I told him.

EMERGING BACK INTO THE STREETS of New York in the autumn sunlight, our strange trio drew stares as we strolled. The mention of a judge had made me giddy, and I played up my insanity along the way, pointing at strangers and saying, "I've never seen a man like that before. Who is he?" Or, "That woman is crazy. I can tell, just look at her."

"I think she is a foreigner," observed Bockert over my head to Mrs. Stenard. "You can hear traces of an accent."

Accent? What accent? Well, if they want one. . .

I began employing the cadence of speech I'd heard in Mexico, tossing in the odd word in Spanish. I just hoped I wasn't being too ham-fisted about it.

Apparently I wasn't. Other policemen became interested as we passed. So, too, the urchins in their ragged clothes, looking for a day's entertainment. One of these overheard Bockert telling a brother officer about my circumstance and instantly the boy cried out, "Here's a lady off her rocker!"

At once the children swarmed, pestering Bockert. "What's she up for? Murder? Did she murder someone?"

"Say, copper, where'd you get her?"

My favorite was the boy who cried out, "She's a daisy!" Meaning I was marvelous, the cream of the crop, the very best. By which I took it that I was the most entertaining thing going that morning.

Mrs. Stenard did not like the attention of the children. Myself, I wanted to laugh. Instead, I studied them as they studied me, using my unblinking stare to make them retreat in horrified fascination.

When we reached the Essex Market Courthouse, Bockert maintained his fiction. "Here we are, the express office. We shall soon find those trunks of yours!"

There was a crowd all around the courthouse, so the children couldn't follow us in. Instead, they waved farewell. "Goodbye, crazy lady! Have fun in Bellevue!"

I raised my hand a little, as if confused. "Do they think I'm crazy?"

"No, no," said Bockert quickly. "It's the way kids speak nowadays."

"Oh." I looked at the crowded courthouse door. "Have all these people lost their trunks?"

"Yes." He shared a look with Mrs. Stenard. "Nearly all of these people are looking for trunks."

"That's very careless of the shipping company. But then, most of these people seem to be foreigners."

"Yes," agreed Bockert, "they are all foreigners. Just landed. They've all lost their trunks, and it takes up most of our time finding them."

"That's very kind of you, Señor Sereno," I told him. "To be helping people with their trunks."

Officer Bockert smiled fleetingly, now convinced I was utterly insane. I could hardly blame him. He thought that I thought his name was Sereno. *This is fun!*

He led me into the courtroom packed with hard-bitten men and hard-used women. Abuse, poverty, and neglect were etched in the lines of every face. Scattered throughout, well-pressed, well-fed officers of the law watched with indifference. There was only so much misery the human heart could behold, day after day, until it became hardened.

Behind a high desk at the far end, I spied a kindly looking gentleman whose placard read JUDGE PATRICK G. DUFFY. He smiled and chuckled, acting as though he were dealing out the milk of human kindness wholesale.

But I did not want kindness. I wanted condemnation. *This will take finesse.*

Bockert went up to the desk before us and explained matters to the judge, who called Mrs. Stenard up for confirmation. Meanwhile, he sent another officer over to take my statement.

"What's your name?"

"Nellie Brown." During the walk I had remembered that if I did not use the name Nellie Brown, Colonel Cockerill would not know how to find me—which was a terrifying thought. "I have lost my trunks. Would you fetch them please?"

My request made no impact on him. "When did you come to New York?"

"I did not come to New York," I said, mentally adding, *I've been here for months.*

That brought him up short. "But you're in New York."

"No," I insisted in a pitying tone, "I did never come to New York."

A nearby man, waiting for his turn before the judge, said, "She's from out west. I grew up out there, that's a southern accent."

"No," replied another eavesdropper. "East coast. Boston, maybe."

I was startled. Since arriving in New York, I had attempted to polish away any trace of accent. After Wilson's remark that when angry I sounded much as Shakespeare would have, I had been acutely aware of my cadence. But apparently it wasn't just anger that tilted my tongue. Without realizing it, in sleeplessness and faux madness I had fallen back on my native Apollo lilt—which these people found confusing and confounding!

The officer taking my statement turned to the judge. "Your honor, here's an odd case. This young woman doesn't know who she is or where she's from. You might want to move her up the line."

The judge waved me over, speaking with surprising harshness. "Come here, little girl. Lift your veil!"

Remaining where I was, I answered in a freezing voice. "To whom do you think you are speaking?"

Startled, the judge ameliorated his tone. "Come over here, my dear lady, and lift your veil. Please. If you were the queen of England, you'd have to lift your veil in my courthouse."

Queen of England? Ha! Thank you, Apollo accent.

"That is better," I said, my accent crossing the globe as I crossed the room. "I am not the queen of England. But I will lift my veil." And I did.

One look at me and the judge was suddenly paternal. "My dear child, tell me, what is wrong?"

"Nothing is wrong," I said, adding a haughtiness to my vacuity, "save that I have lost my trunks, and this man," I pointed to Bockert, "promised to bring me to where they may be found."

The judge rounded on Mrs. Stenard accusingly. "What do you know about this child?"

"Nothing!" protested Mrs. Stenard, no longer enjoying herself. "She gave her name as Nellie Brown, and came to the home yesterday asking to remain overnight."

"The home? What do you mean by 'the home'?"

"I run a temporary lodging for working women." She gave the address.

"What is your position there?"

"I am the matron."

"Well," said the judge, less suspicious now, "tell us all you know of this pitiable creature's case."

Mrs. Stenard told the story with fair accuracy, while I gazed around in blank admiration of the paint. When she had finished, the judge asked, "Had she any money?"

I decided it was time to get a word in. "I paid her for everything, and the eating was the worst I ever tried."

There were snickers all around us. Mrs. Stenard reddened.

Judge Duffy leaned back in his chair and steepled his fingers. "Poor child, poor child. Well dressed, and a lady. Her English is perfect, and I would stake everything on her being a good girl. I am positive she is somebody's darling."

The laughter that remark elicited was much louder, and it was the judge's turn to redden. I was able to hide my face behind my handkerchief before I burst into laughter myself. It would have been awful to be so close and give away the game.

Full of consternation, the judge hastily explained. "I mean, she is some woman's darling! A mother's joy! I am certain someone is searching for her. I would be, I promise you." Surprisingly, I saw tears in the judge's eyes. "She reminds me of my daughter, Sarah. She even looks like her. Poor Sarah!"

This quite cooled the laughter. No one waiting for a judgment would want to be seen mocking the judge's dead child. Then Judge Duffy said something that chilled me to the bone. "I wish the reporters were here. They could ferret out something about her, I'm sure."

They might indeed! The last thing I wanted was to be recognized by a fellow reporter. Thinking fast, I waved at the crowd. "These men are impudent. I do not want to be stared at. Take them away. Or else I shall go." And I took the opportunity to pull down my veil once more.

"That is a very fine hat," said the judge. "Do you recall where you bought it? Or who gave it to you?"

"This is not my hat," I told him. "I don't see what my hat has to do with my trunks."

"We'll find your trunks. Did you come here by boat?"

"No. I came here like everyone else."

"By train, then?"

"Yes, by railroad. That's the way I always travel."

"From where?"

"From home."

"Where is home?"

"No sé."

"No say? Why are you refusing to say?"

"I'm not."

"Then where is home?"

I shrugged. "No sé."

The judge was fit to be tied until it was explained to him that *no sé* meant *I don't know.* "Oh, poor thing!"

Our impromptu comedy routine went on like this for some minutes, until at last the judge leaned down to consult with his clerk. "I have no idea what to do with her. Someone must take care of her."

"Send her to the Island." The officer who had interviewed me was eyeing me suspiciously.

That sent Mrs. Stenard into a genuine panic. "Oh, don't! Don't! She's a lady. It would just kill her to be put on the Island!"

I wanted to throttle her. The last thing I needed was sympathy and kindness. Looking blankly at her, I said, "I would love being on an island. Are my trunks there?"

Judge Duffy's brows were creased. "I fear some foul work here. I believe this child has been drugged and brought to the city."

Why does he keep calling me a child? I scowled at him for a moment, and I think it helped him to a decision.

"Make out the papers so we may send her to Bellevue for examination. Probably in a few days the effect of the drug will pass off and she'll be able to tell us a story that will curl our toes."

"What name should I use?" asked the clerk. "Brown, or Moreno?"

"Moreno sounds more her natural name." The judge glanced toward the door. "I wish the reporters would arrive. They're always here begging for a story, and now that we have one worth their ink, they're nowhere to be found."

I knew it was too early in the day for most reporters, but I dreaded their appearance. "I would not like to stay here. Everyone is looking at me with such crazy stares. And my name is Nellie Brown."

Judge Duffy nodded patronizingly. "Officer, take Miss Brown to the back office. I'll be there in a moment."

Gathering up some papers, the judge followed Officer Bockert, Mrs. Stenard, and me to his little office in the rear of the courtroom. There he seated himself and smiled at me. "My dear, may I pose a question?"

"Of course," I said, remembering not to smile.

"Are you from Cuba? Is that where you come from?"

For the first time, I broke character by snorting out a little laugh. *Whatever put that idea into his head?* But as I had determined to be agreeable to anything said to me, I answered gamely, "Yes! However did you know?"

Judge Duffy bobbed his head in self-satisfaction. "Oh, I knew it, my dear. I knew it. The name Moreno—that is a Cuban name. Now, tell me where in Cuba? What part?"

Specifics were dangerous. "In the hacienda."

"A farm! I thought so. Do you remember Havana?"

"Si, señor, it is near my home. How did you know?" I asked in wide-eyed amazement.

"I knew it from the first," he assured me. "Now, won't you tell me the name of your home?"

"*No puedo*," I said, and held my palm to my forehead. "I have a terrible headache. It's here all the time, and I can't remember things. I don't really mind. The memories, they trouble me so. I don't want them troubling me. Everybody is asking me questions, and it makes my head hurt."

"Well, no one will trouble you anymore." Judge Duffy looked to Mrs. Stenard. "Could you not keep her a few days, until this passes?"

Thank Heaven, the matron shook her head. "I dare not. The other ladies are all afraid of her. If I bring her back, they'll leave."

Judge Duffy puzzled, then suggested, "What if the court made up the difference?"

Drat his kindness, and drat her unlooked-for pity! Together they might conspire to keep me out of the madhouse. Before the matron could reply I declared, "I won't go back. The cooking is terrible, the cockroaches have meetings, and all the women there are crazy. I won't go back unless I have a pistol."

That put a stop to their kindness! Standing, Judge Duffy patted my shoulder. "Very well, very well. No need for pistols. Just sit here and rest.

I'll be back soon." Out he went, leaving me alone with Mrs. Stenard.

The matron looked distressed as she took my gloved hand. "I'm so sorry, Miss Brown. I wish I could. . . I had no idea they would—I mean, I hoped they could help you find your people, not send you to the Island. . ."

"Cuba is an island," I said, embracing my ridiculous new history. "And perhaps my trunks are there."

The door opened and the other officer put his head in. "Reporter's here."

I drew a breath. "The judge said I was not to be troubled!" It came out almost hysterical.

Mrs. Stenard hurled an accusatory look to the officer, whose shoulders were raised defensively. "Fine, fine. No insanity in that, at least. Sorry, bud. You heard the lady."

As the door closed behind them, I feared I had behaved suspiciously. It was the most assertive I'd been the whole day. Mrs. Stenard's hand patting had ceased, and she was frowning at me.

I leapt up. "Everyone is looking at me. You are, he is, they are. *Todos!* It is bad enough to be kept in a house with crazy women who stare and stare and won't let me sleep. But to have everybody looking at me, when they should be looking for my trunks! I do not understand," I moaned as I paced the judge's office. "I won't stay here. I want my trunks. Why do they bother me with so many people?"

Starting to panic, Mrs. Stenard was grateful when the door opened to admit Judge Duffy and another man. For a second I feared he had brought the reporter back, and I said, "No more people! *No más, no más!*"

"There, there, my dear." The judge shut the door behind him. "There is no one else coming in save me and my friend here." *Sotto voce*, he spoke to his companion. "I think this poor girl has been drugged, doctor. Anyone can see she's a good girl. I'm interested in her case, so be kind to her."

Doctor! Now we're getting somewhere. From the corner of my eye, I saw that he wore the uniform of an ambulance surgeon. He stepped forward. "Miss? Please remove your veil. I must examine you."

He seemed quite down-to-earth and practical. Doubt flooded over me. *How can I fool a doctor?* But there was nothing for it. I lifted my veil and allowed him to guide me to a chair.

"She looks like my sister," said Judge Duffy with such sadness that the reporter in me longed to ask him for his life story.

"Put out your tongue," said the doctor.

I did nothing. He pressed his lips together. I did the same.

"Put out your tongue when I tell you."

"I don't want to."

"You must," he explained brusquely, wagging a finger. "You are sick, and

I am a doctor."

I wondered if it would be too much to bite his finger. *Probably.* "I am not sick. I only want my trunks."

"You won't get them if you don't stick out your tongue."

Expelling a sigh, I pushed my tongue slowly out of my mouth. He stared at it, then, without asking permission, took my pulse at my wrist and listened to my heart with his stethoscope. I held my breath, hoping to raise my heart rate.

Next he lit a match and held it next to my face, staring into my eyes as he moved it around. I stared unblinkingly ahead. Extinguishing the match, he said with an almost savage harshness, "What drugs have you been taking?"

"Drugs?" I asked, genuinely surprised. So far, ignorance had worked best. "I do not know what drugs are."

Mrs. Stenard swooped in to say, "Her eyes have been like that ever since she came to stay. They have not changed once." I wondered how she knew. Then I wondered if there truly was something wrong with my eyes.

Standing, the doctor turned to the judge. "I believe she has been using belladonna."

"I am a little nearsighted," I said, again with complete honesty. "I am not sick. No one can make me stay where I do not want to be. I want to find my trunks and go home."

The physician took out a slender leather-cased notebook and scribbled several notes. "That's all right. I'm going to take you home."

I nodded imperiously. Mrs. Stenard started to cry. Judge Duffy said, "Be kind to her. Tell them to be kind to her, and do all they can. She looks like my sister, you see?"

At the doctor's order I rose and collected myself. I was shocked when Mrs. Stenard embraced me. Judge Duffy patted me repeatedly on the shoulder. Then, guarded once more by the stalwart Officer Bockert, I was marched through the chattering courtroom to a side door leading to an alleyway, where an ambulance was waiting.

We paused by an office filled with men and books. One of them called over. "We should question her for the record."

"No point," retorted the doctor. "It's useless. She can't answer you."

No more questions? What a relief!

A crowd had gathered. It seemed the children from the walk over were quite efficient little gossips. Dozens of eyes were on me as the doctor urged me into the alley. A burly man stepped forward, suggesting he put me in the ambulance. I knew the kind. His hands would be everywhere in the guise of "helping." Fortunately, Officer Bockert refused and led me to the ambulance door himself.

A painted NO. 5 was the legend behind the single horse. The rear wheels were larger than the front, and the driver had a cozy little wooden canopy to cover him from inclement weather. Inside, I could see a kind of low bed for patients, with a bench along one side for the doctor to sit.

"This is a curious carriage," I remarked. "I've never seen one like it."

"It's quite comfortable," said the doctor tersely.

I held back. "I don't think I should like to ride in it." It took them two more minutes of convincing before I allowed them to help me inside. I was told to lie down atop the hard bed with a tattered yellow blanket. "I've never reclined in a carriage," I observed.

"Oh, it's for your comfort," said the doctor, whose name I still did not know. He sat at the back and closed the curtains when the crowd pressed close to gape at me. He punched the roof three times. "Let's go, Stanley!"

The ambulance jerked forward, causing the crowd's noise to swell. All the children ran alongside us, calling out, "Bye-bye, Wide-Eye! Toodle-oo, Screw Loose! Watch out for scurvy, Nervey!"

Happily, I was prevented from laughing by the need to hold on for dear life. The ambulance driver evidently feared someone would catch us up and set me free.

Whereas I was exactly where I wanted to be.

THIRTY-SIX

BELLEVUE

AT THE END OF OUR WILD RIDE, the ambulance passed through a brick archway and came to an abrupt halt. A voice shouted, "How many!"

"Only one, for the Pavilion!" the driver answered.

The carriage door was thrown wide, and before I knew what was happening, a rough-handed man with whiskey breath was hauling me into the air as if I were a bear being baited.

"Easy, Clyde!" snapped the ambulance doctor. Cradling my arm gently, he said, "I'll take her myself."

Turning my nose up imperiously at the brutish Clyde, I walked with royal poise on the doctor's arm. As we went, I noticed another crowd just beyond the archway, back the way we'd come. They could hardly have heard about me, and so they must have been simply in search of cheap entertainment.

What a sad existence!

Though no sadder than the place I soon found myself.

My first impression of Bellevue Hospital was of unrelenting hardness. A far cry from the original Belle Vue mansion, this was a wide quadrangle enclosed by brick buildings three stories high. They were covered with a latticework of iron balconies and fire escape stairs, with patients of one kind or another lounging and smoking on them. Only one of the enclosing buildings lacked this adornment, and I wondered if it housed the famous morgue, and so did not require a fire escape.

Heading left, we climbed curved steps to a magnificent portico, one taken from the old Federal Hall where George Washington had been sworn in as the first president. Passing under this august transplant, we entered a dusty office filled with bored men toiling over books. One of these opened his ledger to a new page and rattled off the same questions I'd been asked all morning.

This time I simply refused to answer, allowing the ambulance doctor to reply for me, adding in a confiding murmur, "She's too insane to tell you anything that matters."

I watched as the papers were filled, signed, and filed. Marveling, I thought to myself, It can't be this easy, can it? *Surely there has to be some kind of proof, some test, some measure of certainty!*

Apparently there wasn't.

It was then that I made up my mind. *From this moment forward, I will drop all pretense of madness.* I'd keep my answers vague, but henceforth I would do nothing to seem crazy. I would simply be myself and see how expert these doctors actually were. *Let them catch me if they can.*

"Very well," said the clerk. "Take her to the Pavilion."

The rough Clyde was determined to manhandle me. As he grasped me a second time, I shook him off with a fierceness that surprised him. "How dare you touch me! The judge ordered this doctor to escort me. I will go with him, and no one else."

Clyde did not like my protest, and was about to grab me again when the ambulance doctor said, "I'll take her." Scowling, Clyde shook his head. But he did leave us.

My friend the ambulance doctor led me through the quad and across a well-manicured lawn to the insane ward. The two rows of trees along the path were all evenly spaced, as if the order of the setting might aid disordered minds.

The building called the Pavilion was visually far more appealing than any in the quad, its brick being trimmed with white. Yet I noted there were bars on the windows of the second floor. The third story was set back for a wide balcony with a white-pillared railing. The recessed façade of that uppermost floor held a series of mournful doubled windows that looked like sad eyes on a white, mouthless face.

No, not at all disturbing.

The door to the Pavilion was on the left-hand side as we approached. We were met there by a white-capped nurse who nodded and smiled at me in a perfunctory way. "And who is this?"

"Nellie Marina" said the ambulance doctor. "She is to wait here for the boat."

A shriek from inside the Pavilion made me jump. A horrific sound, it caused my blood to curdle like week-old milk.

In honest fright I grasped the doctor's arm. He patted my hand. "My, what a noise the carpenters make."

Carpenters, my eye! Genuine fear ran through me. Somehow all my anxiety had been directed at getting in, getting the story, and getting out. I had spared no thought to the women who would be my peers for the next week: the madwomen of New York.

It suddenly struck me like a hammer. *There are crazy people in here!*

The doctor started detaching me from his arm. "You must now go with her," he said pointedly, then glanced to the nurse, who reached for me.

I clutched my companion's arm tight. "You're not leaving me!"

Prying himself gently away, the doctor said he must. "I have an amputation to assist. You wouldn't want to be there for that."

"Indeed not." With a show of reluctance I let him go. "But I don't want to stay here without you."

"I'll be back, I promise. Soon!" It was a lie, and we both knew it.

"Come inside, please," said the nurse. "There's a chill in the air."

And so I entered an insane asylum.

It was not, I hoped, my last stop. That would be Blackwell's Island. But even if I was found out here at Bellevue, I had at least part of my story.

I looked around, trying to memorize everything. A long uncarpeted hallway stretched away to my right. It had the look of having been scrubbed so hard it had gone past cleanliness all the way to worn out.

Passing through a heavy door, I entered a wide hall furnished only with benches and frayed willow chairs. At the rear stood massive iron doors fastened by a padlock, while doors on either side led to bedrooms.

Just inside the door was a room for the nurses. On the opposite side was a room with clear signs that it was where food would be served. It occurred to me that I had not eaten since the previous supper, and then hardly at all. "I'm hungry."

Ignoring me, the nurse called out, "Mary?"

From the right-hand room appeared a stout Irishwoman in a black dress. Her cap and apron were starched a perfect white. A parcel of keys hung at her waist. "Aye?"

"This one's for you," the first nurse said, handing over my paperwork.

"Very good. Hello, dearie," said Mary to me with a smile as wide and kindly as one could hope. "What would your name be?"

"I'm Nellie," I replied with a little caution.

Mary's smile widened. "What a darlin' name. I'd be Miss Ball. Come and have yourself a seat. It'll be time for luncheon soon enough. Until then, take your ease. We're all friends here."

I advanced tentatively into the wide room. It held only three women. All were huddled into themselves, for it was absurdly cold with the windows open. The September air was piercing. I wondered if cold was a cure for madness. Certainly, it prevented excessive activity.

Time to start reporting. I began by approaching the youngest of the three ladies, seated in one of the willow chairs and gazing sadly out the window.

"Good morning," I said.

She looked up and smiled carefully. "Good morning." Her voice had an Irish lilt.

"My name is Nellie. Nellie Brown."

"Anne Neville." We shook hands. Hers were like ice, even through my glove.

"Do you mind if I sit with you?" I asked.

"Not at all," she said pleasantly, waving a hand without vigor. She had the appearance of being exhausted. But, despite the deep circles under them, there was no hint of madness in her eyes.

Not knowing how else to approach the matter, I said baldly, "What brings you here?"

"Too much work," she answered. "God help me, I'm just so tired."

"Tired?" I asked.

"Yes. I've been a chambermaid, but I became ill. I was always cold and tired. I went to the sisters' home for a rest, but my nephew couldn't afford to keep me there. He's a waiter, and lost his position. He'll get one soon," she added, quick to excuse lest I think ill of him. "He's applying at Delmonico's. But until he is in funds again, he sent me here."

I couldn't tell if the "sisters' home" was her actual sister's home, or a home run by nuns. It hardly mattered. "Besides being run down, is there anything wrong with you mentally?"

"No." She said it simply. "The doctors ask curious questions. Sometimes I suspect they're trying to confuse me. But there's nothing at all wrong with my brain."

She seemed so normal, I ventured a dangerous comment. "You do know that only insane people are sent here."

Miss Neville sighed. "Yes, I know. But I can't do anything about it. The doctors refuse to listen, and it's useless to plead with the nurses." She studied me. "You don't seem crazy, either."

"They think I am," I said. "But I'm sure that when I see a doctor it will all get sorted out."

She looked at me pityingly.

Excusing myself, I tried the other two patients. Miss Weeder was full of giggles and absurd statements, but she seemed in no way dangerous. I'd met women at dinner parties who were just like her.

Whereas Mrs. Fox was quiet and sullen. After introductions, she said to me, "My case is hopeless." After that, she turned to face the wall and would not speak to me again. It seemed more like self-pity than insanity.

Taking a moment, I withdrew my little notebook and added their names and stories, inserting in some nonsense so it might draw no attention.

I felt my first stirrings of a story. None of these ladies would have been out of place on the street, or at the boardinghouse the previous evening. Why were they here?

During my conversations, I had missed a shift change. Nurse Ball had been replaced by a fair-skinned blonde with sharp features. She marched up to me and snapped, "Take off your hat."

"I shall not," I said. "I will want it on the boat."

"You're not going on any boat. You might as well know it now as later. You are in an asylum for the insane."

Acting as though this was news to me, I said, "I am not insane. I wish to leave."

"It will be a long time before you get out if you don't do as you're told," she hissed with unaccountable venom. "Take off your hat or I shall use force. All I have to do is ring the bell and help will come running. It won't be gentle. Will you take it off?"

"No, I will not." Apparently Nellie Brown disliked being bullied quite as much as Nellie Bly did. "I am cold, and I want my hat on. If you take my hat off, I shall take off your cap!"

She was about to retort when there was a call from the door. "Miss Scott!" With a nasty look for me, she hurried off.

Once she was out of sight, I removed my hat and gloves. It was no part of my plan to be evicted for being troublesome. When Miss Scott returned, she sniffed once in satisfaction, then informed us it was time for lunch.

Returning from her break, Miss Ball instructed us four ladies to gather at a bare table with a bench before it. A moment later she produced a tin platter with ice-cold beef that had once been so boiled that it was falling apart in strands. The lone potato that accompanied each hunk of meat might never have been cooked at all.

I took the tin plate with no joy. "This is a server fit for a dog, not a woman."

"Well, you're not wrong about that," laughed Mary Ball, and to my surprise she fetched a proper china plate. When she was close, she said, "Have ye any pennies about ye, dearie?"

I blinked in surprise. "What?"

"Pennies. They'll take 'em all anyway, dearie, so you might as well hand them to me."

My heart sank. So much for Miss Ball's smiles and kindness. Shaking my head, I told her my purse had vanished. I did have a dime and some pennies in a pocket, but decided to keep them for future need.

As Miss Ball sighed her disappointment in me, I tried the food. Even with my stomach in painful knots, I couldn't force down that hunk of unsalted blandness. Taking back the tray, Miss Ball fetched me a glass of milk and a soda cracker, for which I was very grateful.

With at least something in my belly, I had only to endure the cold. After an hour I crossed over to the little room where Miss Ball and Miss Scott were seated. "The cold in here is unbearable."

Surprisingly, it was Miss Ball who scolded me, even if her tone was kind. "Now, dearie, you're here on charity. You canna expect feather beds and a warm chimney."

I noted they were dressed quite warmly. "Then may I go to bed, where at least there's a blanket?"

"No," said Miss Scott.

"But it's so cold in here!"

Rising with an ejaculation of disgust, she opened a drawer and withdrew a tattered gray shawl. She shook the moths from it and handed it to me. "Here."

Pinching it with two fingers, I examined it. "It's rather ratty."

"Some people would get along better if they were not so proud," she snapped. "People on charity should not expect anything at all. People on charity should not complain."

As there was no arguing with these statements, I wrapped myself in the shawl. I found myself enveloped less in warmth than in a musty smell. Fortunately, my nose was running from the cold, making the odor less offensive than it might have been.

I went to a chair far from any window, where I pulled the shawl over my head and huddled into a ball. After two days with no sleep, fatigue claimed me, and I dozed off into an uncomfortable, if welcome, slumber.

I AWAKENED AS THE SHAWL WAS JERKED off my face. I jolted upright, forgetting for an instant where I was, and ready to shout at Albert for his latest mean trick.

The sight of Miss Scott recalled me to my surroundings. But it was not she who had removed my shelter. It was a doctor, who was now frowning at me. "I've seen that face before."

My heart stopped. I was found out.

Keeping to my role, I leaned forward with an eagerness I did not feel. "Then you know me?"

"I think I do," said the doctor, dragging over a chair and perching on its edge. "Where did you come from?"

"From home."

"Where is home?"

"Don't you know?" I asked.

"They say you're from Cuba."

"That is what they say, yes."

He took my pulse and examined my tongue. "Tell Miss Scott all about yourself."

"No. I will not talk to women."

From the little smile he showed, he enjoyed that. "What do you do in New York?"

"Nothing." It was mostly true.

"Can you work?"

"No, señor."

"I see. Tell me, are you a woman of the town?"

I felt my cheeks flood crimson. "I do not understand."

He took my reaction as guilt. "I mean, have you allowed men to provide for you in exchange for your favors?"

The only decent response was to slap him. But he might deem me violent and so lock me away from the other women. Swallowing my outrage, I shook my head. "I don't know what you mean. I have always lived at home."

"At home, with a man?"

"At home, with my mother."

"Mother, is it? Is she like you? Do you call her mother because she has lots of girls?"

I was utterly beside myself. Next to this doctor's calm insinuations, Albert was the height of chivalry. "I call her Mother because she is my mother."

"Where is she, then?"

"At home. I wish I were there." In that moment, I meant it with all my heart.

After several more questions that were more prurient than probing, the doctor rose and said to Miss Scott, "Positively demented. I consider her a hopeless case. She needs to be put where someone will take care of her."

Thus I passed my second medical examination. Because I would not confess to whoring, I was clearly mad.

Thirty-Seven

Not a Humbug

TWO MORE WOMEN ARRIVED at the Pavilion that day. One came while we were attempting to consume a broth of gruel. She was accompanied by a boy Harry's age, and looked to be his mother. The boy placed her on a bench, chatted with Miss Scott, and then just nodded goodbye and left. When she joined us, I tried to chat her up as I had the others, but she spoke only German. I did get her to write her name in my notebook: Mrs. Louise Schanz. She seemed utterly bewildered by her surroundings, but when Miss Ball brought over some sewing, Mrs. Schanz set to it with dexterous competency.

At five we were given bread and tea, neither of which were edible. Miss Ball allowed me to repeat my lunch of a cracker and milk. I was eating these and watching Miss Scott light the gas jets—which blessedly meant the windows had to be shut—when the last miserable soul entered.

By the flickering light, I spied a girl of my own years. Her hair was short, almost hacked off, and I knew it for the look of someone who has had a severe fever.

I offered her my bread and tea, and she took it like a mouse, skittish but eager. I asked her to sit. "I'm Nellie."

The young lady sipped the tea and nibbled the edge of the bread. It took her a long time to answer. "Tillie," she said at last. "Tillie Mayard."

"Nice to meet you, Tillie. What brings you here?"

"I've been ill," she said, half-reaching up to her hair before catching the movement. "I must look a fright. I had a fever. Bad. I'm better," she added swiftly, lest I recoil in terror. "But my nerves are a mess. My friends have sent me here to be treated."

Heaven preserve me from such "friends," I thought. Looking at her too-thin face and shaking hands, I found I didn't have it in me to tell her where she truly was. She would find out soon enough.

The clock had barely chimed a quarter past six when Miss Ball informed us it was time for bed.

"But it's early," I said.

Miss Ball's good cheer was imperturbable. "I'd like to be headin' home, dearie, so you'll all have to be in your beds now. You weren't planning on holdin' a dance, were ye?" Laughing, she assigned us each a room and told us to undress. We were each given a cotton-flannel gown to wear while our clothes were tied into neat bundles with our names on them.

I was not tall by any measure, but the nightgown they gave me must have been a child's, as it barely reached my knees. Shivering, I asked for something to keep me warm.

With that same smile, Miss Ball slipped me an extra blanket. "That there's a rare privilege, so be sure to appreciate it."

I pushed down on the bed, testing it. Hard. Feeling under the sheet, I found an oilcloth that was near frozen. I touched the pillow. Being stuffed with straw, it crunched.

Nothing for it. Dizzy with sleeplessness, I settled down and wrapped my two blankets around me, tucking them under my feet and pulling my knees up to my chest. Early as it was, I was ready for sleep. *What was it Macbeth called it? "Balm to hurt minds. Chief nourisher in life's feast. Sleep, that knits up the raveled sleeve of care. . ."*

My sleeve stayed unraveled. The cold kept me awake for a long while. I tried my best to warm that oilcloth, knowing that once warmed it would retain that warmth. But it had been chilled all day, and was retaining the cold instead. *I am an iceberg atop some arctic sea.*

At last, my whirring mind slipped into unconsciousness. *Blessed, blessed sleep. . .*

I was awakened by the nurses being relieved by the next shift. They all chatted loudly, the night nurses asking about all six of us "loonies." The remarks they passed were perfectly insulting. I heard myself described as stuck-up and prideful, but someone who would bend under pressure.

My eyelids were drooping again when I heard a male voice saying my name. "I'd like to see Miss Nellie Brown, or Nellie Marina."

"How did you get in here?" demanded a nurse. "You know reporters can't come in!"

"Come on, Alice. It's just for this story. My editor wants the scoop on this Nellie Marina who Judge Duffy was so sweet on. What's she like?"

"I have no idea, I just got here. And no, I'm not waking her up just for you!"

"Let me at least see her belongings, then. Give me that, at least."

I was revolted to hear the nurse give in, imagining this man pawing through my clothes. I was grateful I had nothing to mark me as a reporter, or as Elizabeth Cochrane.

I heard him exclaim, "So it *is* Nellie Brown!" I was confused, until I realized he must have found my monogrammed handkerchief.

He was disappointed with this discovery, however, for he began pestering Alice again. "Come on. Give the *Sun's* readers something!"

The Sun! My mind filled with images of Mr. Dana and his stuffed owl. So proper, so condescending. Meanwhile, his reporters were out pestering nurses for muck on a poor mad girl.

Alice was frustrated, though by his persistence or her own inability to dish the dirt, I couldn't tell. "I don't know anything except that she's hopelessly insane."

Satisfied at last, the reporter from the *Sun* departed, and I rolled over to try again to sleep.

Not fifteen minutes later, the door to my room banged open. I jolted and threw the blanket over my head. From the door the nurse called Alice said, "Nellie Brown? A doctor is here to speak with you." From under my blanket, her voice was difficult to read. *Is that disgust, or concern?*

A handsome young doctor walked in, smooth as any gentleman at the club. I heard the nurse call him Dr. Fitch. Strolling past the nurse, Dr. Fitch waved her off and seated himself beside me on the bed. "Cold in here," he said, perfectly normally. "Aren't you cold, Nellie?"

"Yes," I said.

"Well, let's do something about that." Dr. Fitch put his arm around my shoulders and indicated I should lean into him. Despite a flurry of misgivings, I did so, husbanding his warmth.

Only then did I notice the second man. He had closed the door behind him. He was of middle years, with wide sideburns and a peculiarly intense stare.

Fixed on me.

The doctor spoke in a cheerful voice one might use with a child. "Well, how do you feel tonight, Nellie?"

"Oh," I said slowly, "I feel all right."

He made a tut-tutting noise. "But you are sick, you know."

"Am I?"

"You know you are. Now, they tell me you're from Cuba. When did you leave?"

"You know Cuba?"

"Yes, very well. So does my friend here. We've been there many times. Don't you remember him? He remembers you."

How could he, when I'd never been to Cuba in my life! The hairs on the back of my neck were standing on end. "No. No, I don't remember him."

"No? But he remembers the man who brought you here. It was a man, wasn't it? Who brought you to New York? I read the notes of your interview, Nellie. You were a good girl, and you lived with your mother and a lot of other good girls. I bet you were warmer there. Would you like to be warmer here? My friend has a very warm heart, and tender. He'd like to help warm you."

All this time the man by the door said nothing. He simply stared at me, breathing hard.

I slid from the doctor's grip and moved as far as I could from them, pressing my back into the cold wall. The room was redolent with danger. Looking the silent man right in the eye, I said, "No. I do not remember him. But I will now. I will remember both of you."

Dr. Fitch's smooth manner fell away as he shot a glance toward his companion, whose eyes never left mine. At last, the quiet fellow gave a single shake to his head. The doctor rose at once, opened the door for the other man to pass, and then offered me an angry glare before slamming it shut on me again.

It was several minutes before I could breathe normally.

My shivers now had nothing to do with the cold.

AFTER THAT I COULD NOT SLEEP, so I listened. The shouts from the male ward upstairs did little to soothe my nerves. Between those cries and the irregular banging of the ambulance gong as new patients arrived at Bellevue, there was more noise than any human could slumber through. Far from being knit up, my sleeve of care was more frayed than before.

The night nurses liked to read to each other from shilling shockers and penny dreadfuls. Every half hour they galumphed down the hall in their hard heels, sounding like a regiment on parade as they opened each door to check on us. I could hear from the groans and sobs in my neighboring cells that I was not the only one wakeful.

The night dragged on, and I focused on keeping warm. Slowly it got better, my chills went away, and I didn't jolt awake at every sound. . .

"Come, come. Time to get out of bed!"

Miss Ball yanked my blankets off me, and I was surprised to discover I had indeed slept a little. Miss Scott was throwing open my window, letting in a burst of cold air. Thrusting my disordered bundle of clothes into my arms, she instructed me to dress.

The cold breeze was motivation enough, and within moments I was fastening the last button. "Why is it kept so cold in here?"

Miss Scott deigned to answer. "They refuse to turn on the heat until October. You'll have to endure it."

"Five days?" I asked, horrified.

She smirked. "You won't be here that long."

I had almost forgotten about Blackwell's Island. *Surely it can't be worse than this place!*

Miss Scott led me to a washstand, where my fellow patients were busily washing their faces. When our ablutions were done, we were trooped back to the wide central room with the barred windows and spare furnishings. Breakfast awaited us. We were told it was chicken broth, but it might as well have been old laundry water. I choked it down.

Then we underwent a strange sort of shearing. While Miss Ball tidied up the breakfast bowls, Alice and the other night nurses armed themselves with scissors and began paring our nails. Mine were cut right down to the quick. I felt like a declawed cat. Which was exactly the idea.

About nine o'clock a new physician appeared, Dr. Field. He was older, and walked with a knobby cane, which I found a little threatening. I eyed him suspiciously, especially after Dr. Fitch's visit the previous night.

But Dr. Field only checked his pocket watch as I was ushered toward his perch in the nurse's sitting room. Without looking up from my papers he said, "Name?"

"Nellie Moreno."

That got his attention. "Then why did you give the name of Brown?"

"*Moreno* means *brown*."

He tossed a frown at me. "What's wrong with you?"

"Nothing," I said plainly. "I did not want to come here, but they brought me. I want to go away. Will you let me out?"

He sighed. "If I were to take you outside, would you stay with me? You wouldn't run away the moment you were on the street?"

"I can't promise that I wouldn't," I answered.

"Exactly. You're staying." Settling in, he rattled off a list of questions. "Do you ever see faces on the wall?"

"Yes." *In pictures.*

"Do you ever hear voices?"

"Yes." *When people are speaking.*

"Do you ever hear voices at night?"

"Yes," I said, remembering the night nurses' ceaseless prattle. "There is so much talking I cannot sleep."

"I thought so. What do these voices say?"

"I try not to listen to them. But for instance, last night they were talking about Nellie Brown, and then of some silly romance stuff. And sometimes they say they know me when they don't. Not at all."

"That will do. Miss Scott?"

As Miss Scott started to usher me out, I said, "Can I go away?"

"Yes," replied the doctor with a small chuckle, "we'll soon send you away."

"It's just so very cold here."

"That's true," he said with a shiver. "Miss Scott, the cold is almost unbearable. You'll have some cases of pneumonia if you're not careful. Now, bring in the next one."

Taking up a station just outside the door, I listened to this interview, and the next. They were exactly the same as mine, with the same questions. Only, the other women did not say they saw faces or heard voices. Denial seemed to make no difference. *If they are not to be believed, why bother asking the questions?*

The sole benefit to the doctor's morning visit was that we were all provided with shawls, and the windows were closed. But the rest of the day was a repeat of the day before, down to the food.

The monotony was only broken up by reporters coming to the windows and calling for the girl from Cuba. I covered my head and told them to go away.

"Are you famous?" asked Tillie in a whisper. Poor thing, she had not yet cottoned on to where she was. Or she was remaining willfully ignorant.

"No," I told her through my shawl. "People are just interested in a mystery."

"What mystery?"

"Who I am," I said, regretting it already.

"And who are you?"

"I'm just a girl with no one to speak for her."

She patted my hand. "I'll talk to my friends when they come for me. They'll look after you as well."

I almost wept on the spot, and had to hug her to prevent her from noticing. That required removing the shawl from over my head, and the reporters at the window—there were at least a dozen—were finally afforded a view of my face.

To my fury, some were allowed in to talk to me, though the answers I had for them now were pat. I would mention my trunks, and Cuba, and crazy people. It became a game to answer as truthfully as possible without breaking my story:

Who is your father? "I have no father." *What happened to him?* "He died." *Where did you come from?* "Home." *Where were you going?* "New York." *Where did you learn Spanish?* "I never learned Spanish." *How did you travel?* "I always go by railroad." *Why did you come to New York?* "To get a job." *What kind of job?* "The kind where I don't have to answer impertinent questions!"

Growing bored, I tried out my French, which prompted one of them to mention New Orleans. I agreed that I had come from New Orleans, and they leapt upon this fresh clue.

One reporter was from the *World*, but he seemed as eager as the rest, and I doubted he was in on the secret. Both Mr. Pulitzer and Colonel Cockerill were likely to play their cards close to their vests.

Dr. Field returned that afternoon to question me again. He pretended to examine my coordination, making me stand and stretch out my arms and wiggle my fingers, then touch my nose. No longer playing simple, I obeyed his commands without the least hesitation.

But he wasn't at all interested in my dexterity. He wanted to pose questions, none of which had to do with my sanity. He kept on asking about my supposed lovers. I had the sense that there was a good deal of money at stake for him. Doubtless the *Sun* reporter was still trying to find answers to the mysterious insane girl. It was almost tempting to mention Miller and his bearskin coat just to shock them, but that would only prove his evil thoughts correct.

After a while he piqued my temper, so when he asked, "Have you ever been married?" I told him, "You are too old for me," which made the nurses laugh.

Leaving in an annoyed huff, Dr. Field was waylaid by Tillie Mayard. "Doctor! One of these women just told me this place is a home for the insane!"

Leaning on his cane, he gazed back at her with little pity and great condescension. "Have you just discovered that?"

"Please, why was I sent here? I'm not mad! I've been ill, is all. My friends said they were sending me to a convalescent ward! I do not belong here. Please, let me gather my things and I'll go."

Dr. Field actually laughed in her face. "There's no rush, Miss. You won't be leaving in any hurry."

"If you were any kind of doctor, you'd know at once that I'm perfectly sane."

"A sane woman would not be here in the first place."

Tears streaming down her face, Tillie grasped his hand in both of hers to plead with him. "Why not give me some test, some examination?"

The doctor pulled his hand free. "We already know everything we need to. Now calm down. You won't improve your case by getting agitated. Certainly the nurses on Blackwell's won't like you any better for it. Be calm, and get better." He limped his way through the door.

Tillie burst into wracking sobs, and I spent a good part of the afternoon soothing her.

An hour or so later, the warden of Bellevue, Mr. O'Rourke, came for a visit. Ignoring Tillie, he chatted me up. Like everyone else, he was very interested in "Nellie Brown." I took the trouble of making Miss Mayard's case, but he breezed past that to quiz me. "What are you playing at?"

A chill ran through me. "Playing?"

He folded his arms. "You, my dear girl, are a humbug. You may have fooled these others, but if you're not here to pull some trick, I'll eat my hat."

"I don't know what you mean."

"Of course you don't. Well, I can't contradict the doctors and simply throw you out. But the joke's on you, Miss Brown, or Marina, or whatever you call yourself. If you think you're getting a free trip to a sinecure, you are in for a rough surprise. Blackwell's is no holiday, and you're not a treasured guest. So speak up now, in your right wits, and I'll have you examined again and released."

"I don't want to be examined again," I said tartly. "But you can see my tongue if you like." I stuck it out at him.

The warden almost smiled. "Suit yourself. But don't say you weren't warned."

He returned late in the day to show me off to a collection of men and women in fancy dress clothes who had read about my case and were eager to lay eyes on me. I found it to be so odd, stopping by an insane asylum before heading to the opera or a concert. But entertainment came in all shapes and sizes. The warden was more than happy to oblige, hoping I might somehow give myself away.

I declined to give them a show, yet they left quite satisfied, loudly discussing the possible causes of my madness. The warden simply shook his head at the folly of rich people and mad girls alike.

That night was just like the former, though I was able to sleep a little. Before going to bed, I told the nurses I did not want to see Doctor Fitch again, and they said he would not be in that night. There was a look of understanding among them, and I felt a sudden burst of fury. *They suspect what's going on, and do nothing? Fellow women?*

But the night nurses all seemed focused on the prurient. Each time they saw I was awake they would insinuate things. "Missing your lover? Dreaming of your great romance? Look how low you've fallen! Hope it was fun while it lasted!"

Somehow a narrative had been constructed of my life: I was a rich girl who had left Cuba and run away to New Orleans with her lover, only to come to New York to be prostituted, which had eventually deprived me of my wits.

It was amusing—until I thought of all the girls and women who passed through that place, and the stories made up about them to keep them there.

Then it was not amusing at all.

V

INTO THE MADHOUSE

NELLY MARINA OR BROWN

SHE TELLS A LITTLE ABOUT HERSELF,
BUT IT IS A MYSTERY YET

Nelly Marina, who also calls herself Nelly Brown, the pretty crazy girl who was sent from Bellevue to Blackwell's Island a week ago yesterday, and about whom there is believed to be a romance, has not been claimed. Her case is diagnosed as melancholia, and Dr. Ingram considers it a very hopeful one.

"Am I sane or insane?" is a question she frequently asked Dr. Ingram. She speaks French, Spanish, and English perfectly. She is traveled and is very familiar with Southern customs. She says her parents are dead. Her mother was a Cuban and her father an Englishman. She once lived in New Orleans, she says, but she is careful not to reveal anything that might lead to her identification. She promises that she will soon tell all about herself.

Emille Voltier, of Toulouse and Bourbon Streets, New Orleans, wrote to The Sun to ask the girl if she was Lottie Peters. Lottie Peters, Voltier wrote, was a friend of his who had disappeared from New Orleans, and about whom he was greatly troubled. Nelly said yesterday that she was not Lottie Peters, and that she knew no girl of that name or no man named Voltier.

Morena is Spanish for Brown. The hospital authorities could easily have written Marina for Morena, so that the girl's giving two names may be merely additional corroboration of her story instead of a suspicious circumstance.

—*New York Sun*
Wednesday, October 5, 1887

THIRTY-EIGHT

HALL SIX

MONDAY, SEPTEMBER 26 1887

AFTER BREAKFAST THE NEXT MORNING, we were informed that we ladies could expect to leave for the island at one-thirty in the afternoon, and should prepare.

A little better rested, if still hungry and bedraggled, I felt a frisson of excitement. *Blackwell's Island is my goal, and by tonight I will be there!*

Assuming I survived the morning.

The reporters were swarming again. I hoped they had no access to Blackwell's. This business would be much easier without all these nosy parkers trying to expose me.

Warden O'Rourke appeared just before lunch. "Last chance."

"I do not want to talk to you." An idea occurred to me. "Not after Dr. Fitch."

The warden frowned. "What about Dr. Fitch?"

"The night before last, he brought a man into my room and said we knew each other, and that he would like to help me stay warm. I told them to go away. But the nurses let them in. A man with wide sideburns and a mean stare."

The warden's brow darkened with every word I uttered. At the man's description, he rocked back a little on his heels. "Is this true?"

"It is," I said. "But then, who would believe a madwoman?" I moved off, hoping I had done some good.

I was given back my hat and gloves, and Miss Ball allowed me to keep the tatty shawl. In return, I gave her the last of my pennies.

"God bless you," she said, kissing the coins. "I'll pray for you. Cheer up, dearie! You are young, you'll get over this."

I allowed myself a slight smile. "I hope so. Adios, Señorita Scott!" She shook her head at my cheerfulness, but waved nonetheless.

My giddiness was dangerous, but nothing could pierce the aura of excitement that surrounded me, not even the handsy handling of Clyde, who brought me roughly to the ambulance. A pack of medical students watched as my fellow inmates and I were loaded into the wagon. Clyde got in with us, the doors were locked from the outside, and we were off.

I felt as though I was part of a triumphal parade. After all the false starts and frights, the worries of exposure, and the fear of maintaining my disguise, I had succeeded! I had gotten myself committed to Blackwell's Island! Victory for Nellie Bly!

My mood was certainly a contrast with that of my fellow loonies. Anne Neville, Tillie Mayard, Mrs. Fox, and Mrs. Schanz were all sad-faced and sullen. Their sole distraction was averting their faces and holding their breath against the foul reek of Clyde's exhalations. *Did he eat onions for breakfast?*

Reaching a wharf, we were led out in reverse order, meaning I was last. The police had been called to keep the mob away, and I had a panicked moment, fearing yet another possible moment of exposure.

I threw the shawl over my head as Clyde dragged me down the plank onto a boat. A gust of sea air brought his breath into my nose and I staggered, which he took for resistance. "Now, you! I knew you'd be trouble!" I gasped as he wrenched my arm nearly out of its socket, propelling me into a dirty cabin that reeked even worse than his breath. All the windows were closed, and I clutched the musty shawl to my nose to hold out the terrible stench of feces and urine.

More women were brought in, and we all sat in discomfort on long benches. The only open space was an empty bunk at the far end, befouled by some past patient. I was horrified when they placed a sick girl onto that cot. If she had not been ill before, she surely would be soon!

Two massive nurses brought aboard one more woman unknown to us. Not a patient, she bore a basket of scraps of old meat and chunks of bread. As meagerly fed as I'd been, I did not proposition her for a sample.

But I was less fearful of her food than I was of the nurses. One had a dress made of brown and white striped bedticking. The other had attempted style, and missed the mark, with her feathers and brocade and clashing blouse and jacket. She would have been comical, save for the fearsome scowl she wore.

The door was locked, and as the boat began to move I discovered a truth about myself: I did not enjoy being on the water. The smell was definitely a contributing factor, but my whole world narrowed to resisting the urge to vomit at each swell and drop of the boat. Recalling my proposed trip to England and back in steerage, I felt a wave of thankfulness that Mr. Pulitzer had chosen this assignment instead.

The nurses conversed in low tones, discussing troublesome patients, handsome doctors, and mutual dislikes. They made lewd remarks to the men outside the door, and scowled at us if we dared to look their way. Both chewed tobacco, expectorating with a precision that was, if horrifying, genuinely impressive.

My entire body was a clenched fist as I breathed through my mouth and fought to keep down my gorge. At one point I felt a change might help my stomach and my nose, and rose to look out the window.

At once the grosser of the pair lowered her terrifying brow. "Sit. Down."

Her words were redolent with violence, and I did not even think to challenge her, but sat down at once. This was a fight I would lose, and badly.

The boat paused once to let off the sick girl and the old woman with the basket. At the next landing, it was our turn. "Everybody off."

My companions shuffled out, and once again I was last. As I emerged a man gripped my left arm so hard I could feel the bruises forming. The fearsome nurse took my other arm in an even rougher grip, and together they marched me up a plank, onto the shore, and toward another ambulance.

"What is this place?" I asked the man hurting my arm.

"Blackwell's Island," he said matter-of-factly. "An insane place you'll never get out of."

I proved my insanity in that moment by showing him a triumphant smile.

They shoved me into the waiting ambulance with the others. As we passed him, I noticed that the driver wore a prisoner's uniform, while a uniformed officer watched us all. The frightful nurses did not accompany us into the ambulance, and I confess I was relieved to see the backs of them.

In their place we were met by a tall, thin, kindly-faced woman in a brown and white striped dress, with a white apron and cap. She climbed up top of the ambulance. At the last moment, a letter carrier jumped on behind her. Then we were all off.

I've done it! I'm on Blackwell's Island! I couldn't resist a small laugh of triumph. "Ha!"

That drew looks from my fellow travelers. "I can't see what's cheered you so," said Tillie Mayard with lamenting accusation. "Ever since we left Bellevue you've looked positively happy."

I opened my hands. "Positive is the word. No matter where I am, I try to laugh and be happy."

"You do know where we are, don't you?" she insisted, on the verge of tears once more. "This is Blackwell's Island Lunatic Asylum!"

"But you're not crazy," I reminded her. "So why worry?"

"Because what if the doctors here are like Dr. Field, and don't listen?"

"Then we'll make them listen," I said, full of confidence.

"She's right, though," observed Anne Neville. "I never saw anyone change so suddenly. You were so quiet these last two days, Nellie. Now you look actually delighted."

"Maybe I'm where I belong," I chirped.

They all looked at me as if I were truly mad. Seeing them so depressed and disheartened, and rightly so, I felt ashamed and made an effort to modulate my feelings.

I needn't have bothered. In a few hours, I would be as miserable as anyone who ever lived.

"THANK GOD THEY CAME ALONG quietly," said the happy-faced nurse as she descended. She spoke with a trace of a Germanic accent.

The officer grunted in response and opened our door as if expecting us to rush him. But we clambered docilely out and gazed around at our new home.

My stomach had just been settling when our carriage had lurched past one particular low building. The stench from it had been so horrible that I'd been compelled to hold my breath—and pray it wasn't the kitchen. But away from those noxious smells, I could breathe once more, and off the waters I finally regained my equilibrium. So I was able to note the surroundings along with my companions.

The Asylum grounds consisted of a series of long buildings set amidst exquisitely manicured lawns. The entrance facility was a massive octagon, five stories tall, made of bluish-gray stone quarried right on the island. The only things imported to Blackwell's were the elements of society that society was uncomfortable to see.

The Octagon was perversely beautiful. But I noted at once that its design caused the building to be much taller on the left side than the right. *A sinister building*, I thought.

Inside, under a high dome, a fantastic twisting staircase curled counterclockwise up to the heights. As I gaped upward with the others, I fancied that even the direction of the stairs was indicative of the unnatural bent of the place.

We ascended the stairs to the first level, where we were led left through a narrow vestibule. The nurse used the keys hanging from a green cord at her waist to lock the door behind us.

The sound of that clicking lock punctured my inflated euphoria. *I now have to survive a week among the truly mad. Day and night, minute and hour, in the company of gibbering, possibly violent lunatics. Eat with them. Sleep with them. Be one of them.*

Then I imagined what it was like for Tillie and Anne and the others. To hear that click and know that this was their home until reason or death offered release. The possibility of this being home for the rest of their lives had them all quaking. My own knees were unsteady, and I would be there only a week!

We were escorted down a long, uncarpeted corridor, where we came to a wide room labeled HALL SIX. It was filled with women. And such women! Their clothes were a uniform combination of an underskirt and a cheap white calico dress. Their hair was matted, disheveled, and loose. They sat doing nearly nothing at all, in a dreadful silence that seemed worse to me than howls of madness.

The nurses told us to sit, and we obeyed. Several patients made room for us, staring curiously.

One patient marched up to me, bold as the brass of the nurse's buttons. "Who sent you here?"

"The doctors," I said.

Her gaze overflowed with a suspicious hostility that made me uneasy. "What for?"

"They say I'm insane."

She squinnied at me. "I can't see it in your face."

I was relieved when the German nurse barked out, "New girls, step forward! Time to see the doctor." My inquisitor slunk off and I followed the nurse to some rooms at the end of the hall.

Hoping someone with so gentle a visage might have a soul to match, I tried my first overture to the German nurse. "May I ask your name?"

I could tell it was a mistake the moment it left my teeth. "Be quiet," she snapped. "No talking."

Despite her harsh reply, I did learn her name a moment later as she knocked and entered the doctor's office. "Dr. Kinier?"

"Ah, Miss Grupe. Did you meet our new arrivals?"

She answered with an odd coquettish giggle. "I like to go down in the wagon. It helps to break up the day."

"And the open air brings out the roses in your cheeks," replied the doctor.

A smile was on her face as she emerged, but it was not for us. Producing a list, she said, "Matilda Mayard, come here."

Tillie obeyed, and I listened while they measured her height and weight, and then asked her a series of perfunctory questions. She answered them with complete lucidity, and politely but insistently pleaded her case throughout. At no point did she lose her composure as she described her recent illness and insisted that she was suffering nothing more than "nervous debility" from her time in sickbed. Her reasonable requests for more tests, for belief, for justice, all fell on deaf ears.

Up until then, I had still had a shred of faith in the system, and in the doctors in whom we reposed our trust. It evaporated when Tillie was returned to us without a single word of sympathy or hope.

Mrs. Schanz was examined next. She went dutifully in, but as she could not understand a word that was said to her, she was unhelpful, replying only in German. The doctor kept repeating his questions louder than before, as if sheer volume could penetrate the language barrier. At last Dr. Kinier turned to Miss Grupe. "You're German. Speak to her for me."

"Doctor," stammered Miss Grupe, suddenly on the wrong foot, "I have not spoken German in years. I can barely understand more than three words."

The doctor was having none of it. "Go ahead. Ask her what her husband does."

After a few more protests, Miss Grupe posed some halting questions in German. Mrs. Schanz replied eagerly, hoping she had at last found an ally.

"I think she says her husband is a carriage driver," answered Miss Grupe.

"There now," laughed Dr. Kinier. "Your German is perfectly good! What was the use of lying to me?"

"I cannot speak any more," insisted Miss Grupe, and indeed she refused to translate any further questions from the doctor, or any statements from Mrs. Schanz, despite her tearful pleadings.

The interview with Mrs. Fox went just the same. The doctor seemed far more interested in teasing and flirting with Miss Grupe than in eliciting information from his patients.

When her turn came, Miss Neville answered the questions quite calmly. At one point she said, "God save me," to which the doctor said, "Are you very religious?"

"I hope so."

"I take it you pray?"

"Of course."

"When you do, does anyone answer?"

"All prayers are answered. We just don't always understand the form it takes."

"Interesting, interesting." I wondered what madness he took from that perfectly reasonable answer.

When at last it was my turn, I went in and took the indicated seat opposite the doctor's desk. He didn't look up from a large book full of notes. "Name."

"Nellie Brown."

"Where is your home?"

"Cuba."

The doctor's head came up with a start. "Oh-ho! A celebrity! Miss Grupe, this is the girl from the papers! Did you see the stories?"

"Yes." Miss Grupe eyed me with sudden hostility. "I saw a long piece in the *Sun* yesterday."

"I'll be right back," he said, racing out of the office.

Alone with me, Miss Grupe glowered over folded arms. "Take off your hat and shawl," she snapped.

Her spite, not her authority, led me to obey, and I sat with eyes downcast at the worn red carpet under my feet until the doctor returned. "Couldn't find the paper," he said. "There must be one around here somewhere. Anyway, as I recall she threatened other women in her boarding home, fooled the judge into thinking she was drunk or drugged, and then claimed not to remember anything at all about who she is."

"I didn't threaten anyone!" I said indignantly.

He entirely ignored me. "What color are her eyes?"

Leaning close, Miss Grupe used the opportunity to pinch my face and pry my eyes wide. "Gray."

Unless rage caused them to change that day, my eyes had always been hazel. The doctor, who might have seen for himself if he'd only looked, wrote down her reply. "What's your age, Miss Brown?"

"Nineteen last May." Ever since joining the *Dispatch*, it had become natural to lie about my age.

Scratching that down, he glanced at Miss Grupe. "When's your next pass?"

Again, she gave that girlish laugh that seemed so unsuited to her years. "Saturday."

"You'll go to town?"

"Why, doctor!" They both laughed, then she added, "Yes, I'll go to town."

"I know you'll paint it red. Measure her."

I was led across the room to stand upright while a measure was lowered to touch the top of my head.

"What does it say?" asked the doctor.

"You know I can't read it," replied Miss Grupe. It was not said with shame, like her denial of speaking German. This was flirtatious. *Is she really pleading ignorance to gain his admiration? Are there really men who enjoy stupid women?*

Apparently so. The laughing doctor wagged a finger. "Yes, you can. You did it just a minute ago for the last girl. How tall is she?"

"There are some figures here, but I can't tell."

This went on until Dr. Kinier got up from his desk and came close. "Five feet, five inches. See?" And he took her hand in his and led it to the right number on the measure. She didn't even look to where he was pointing, but gazed instead at him. I wondered if they'd notice me leaving.

Next, I was put on a scale, and again Miss Grupe pretended to be unable to read the numbers. "You'll have to see for yourself, doctor!"

"One hundred twelve pounds," I reported in a clear voice.

Miss Grupe scowled at me as the doctor wrote it down, addressing her as he did so. "What time are you going to supper?"

The rest of the interview went just like that. I was incidental, an object to be noted and processed while they carried on their odd and disturbing flirtations.

Only at the end did I make a statement. "Doctor Kinier, I am not sick. I do not belong here. I do not wish to stay here. You have no right to shut me away without a proper examination."

"This was a proper examination." Writing two words in his book, he nodded to Miss Grupe. "That will do."

Our exit brought me near his desk. Though upside down, I could plainly read the diagnosis:

"Hopelessly insane."

THIRTY-NINE

RUB, RUB, RUB

WE WERE LED BACK TO THE sitting room of Hall Six, and I finally had the time to take it in. Longer than it was wide, it was desperately crowded. I started counting. There were forty women in that room. With us, forty-six. In a place designed to hold half that number.

As at Bellevue, the windows were all open, and women huddled together for warmth. The bare yellow benches, made to hold five, overflowed. They had straight backs and looked very uncomfortable. The most desirable seats were beside the two stoves that heated the room. But as that was where the nurses liked to congregate, most patients opted for a seat along the wall, where at least they were safe from the wind.

Sunlight from outside was crisscrossed by shadows from the iron bars on the windows. The white walls of the room were made interesting only by three lithographs: two of Negro musicians and a third, bizarrely, that was a portrait of actor Fritz Emmet, his head bursting through a wooden panel, and his tousled blond hair covered by a brown cap. The smile on his face was as disturbing as anything around me.

I was pleased, at least, to see how clean the place was. After the foul stink of the boat, I had feared a place of squalor and filth. But Hall Six was immaculate. My respect for Miss Grupe and the other nurses increased.

Looking for an open seat, I spied a chair placed before an ancient square piano. I went to sit down, but was intercepted by a different nurse. Like Miss Grupe, she was in her twenties, but tall, with her hair pulled severely back. This was Miss McCarten. "Do you play the piano?"

"I do."

That surprised her. "Prove it."

Desperate for entertainment, my fellow inmates began encouraging me to play, so I sat down and lifted the cover. Striking a few keys, I winced.

"How horrible! I've never touched a piano so out of tune."

"What a pity." The nurse's voice oozed with sarcasm. "We'll have to get one made to order, just for you."

Closing my ears against the awful untuned strings, I began picking out "Home, Sweet Home." My fingers were cold, so I mis-hit a few keys, and with the tuneless thuds of several strings it was hardly a creditable performance.

Yet the ladies of the Hall Six did not seem to mind. Most were silent, with just a few muttering or humming along with the lyrics:

'Mid pleasures and palaces though we may roam,
Be it ever so humble, there's no place like home!
A charm from the skies seems to hallow us there,
Which, seek thro' the world, is ne'er met with elsewhere.

Home! Home! Sweet, sweet home!
There's no place like home,
There's no place like home.

I saw Tillie weeping silently and I slowly trailed off. Several women asked for me to play more, but I shook my head.

Miss McCarten wrenched me up from the seat. "You won't play? Then get away from here." She banged the lid of the piano down and hauled me bodily up to a table near the door.

Behind the table sat a woman with ugly red blotches on her cheeks and forehead. She asked me, "What have you on?"

"My clothes," I replied.

"Don't be smart," snapped Miss McCarten. She then lifted my dress and skirts, reciting a litany of what she found as the other woman dutifully took notes.

Just as she was finishing, someone shouted, "Go out into the hall!" The nurses scuttled out at once, while the inmates in white calico rose and began heading for the door. One took pity on my obvious confusion. "That means supper."

There is a camaraderie in shared misery. We new arrivals kept together as we followed the other women out. I mimed a spoon to Mrs. Schanz, to which she nodded grimly.

Every window along the corridor was open, and the chill wind whistled past us, around us, and, it seemed, through us. We were kept standing there for at least a quarter of an hour before being marched through a door to a narrow landing, where we again halted before a gaping window.

We newcomers were slightly better off than the others, since we still retained our street clothes. Anne Neville leaned close to me. "How can the nurses leave these wretched women in the cold?"

"It's brutal," I agreed.

But as much as I pitied these women, I was marking them for my story as well. About a half dozen were busily chatting with the air. As many more were laughing or crying, having broken some emotional tether. The rest stood dully gazing and shivering, though one scraggy-haired crone kept nudging me with her elbow and winking at me. Her three lonely teeth were prominent as she confided, "Don't mind them, love. They're all mad."

Emerging from the dining hall, Miss Grupe called out to our assembly, "Stop at the heater and get in line, two by two. Mary Hughes, get a companion. Alice, do I have to say it again? Get. In. Line!" My breath was taken away when she struck some woman on the ear, causing the poor wretch's head to bang into the woman beside her. Both reeled for a moment. Yet they said nothing, showed no defiance at all. They just stood meekly and shivered.

When order was brutally established, we were allowed to enter the narrow dining room—where all semblance of order vanished in an instant. Women rushed at the tables where food was set out: a bowl of weak pinkish tea, a black hunk of buttered bread, and a small saucer of five prunes for each patient. It was meager fare, yet the women of Hall Six clambered over backless benches to claim their share, heedless of decorum.

At once, I saw why. Theft was paramount in those early moments of dinner. One portly woman ran from table to table stealing small saucers of prunes and dumping them into her own saucer, which overflowed. Then she tossed back her saucer, downing all the stolen prunes before they could be stolen back.

The sight of her made me laugh, which cost me my own bread, as the woman opposite me filched it with no compunction at all.

Yet even in Hell, kindness can be found. Another patient, seeing me bereft of bread, offered me hers. "I couldn't, no," I replied with real thanks. Then I turned to Miss Grupe. "I don't seem to have any bread."

Though it was obvious what had happened, she leered at me. "Ate it already? You're a greedy one. Forgotten your home, but not how to eat."

"I have not eaten since before we arrived. May I have a piece of bread, please?"

Expecting to be denied, I was surprised to have a hunk of bread hurled down in front of me. I tried a bite, only to discover her generosity had a dark amusement behind it—the butter was rancid, utterly inedible. Miss Grupe lingered long enough to laugh at my gagging.

When she had gone, a young woman with the bluest eyes I'd ever seen said, "No one can eat the butter. You are allowed to ask for it plain."

Thanking her, I decided not to press my luck and instead turned my attention to the prunes. Only two looked healthy. An eager neighbor down the row was watching me like a hawk, and when I put the rest aside she asked for them. I slid her the saucer and lifted my tea.

At that point I knew to expect little, but even so, I could not manage more than a single sip. I hadn't expected sugar, so the bitterness was no shock. What curled my tongue was the heavy metallic taste, as if it had been brewed in copper. I pushed it away, and another patient slurped it up at once.

Seated beside me, Anne Neville looked worried. "You must force the food down, Nellie."

"I can't," I said simply.

"What if you get sick? In here, that might make you truly crazy. A good brain requires a good stomach."

She was right, of course. But the very thought of ingesting any of that meal made my stomach roil. Never had I expected to long for Mexican food! How good a tortilla heated on a stone sounded just then.

With so little food being offered, the meal was over in a trice, and we were led back to the sitting room of Hall Six: our home from then on.

As we entered, several women begged me to play on the piano again. The nurses encouraged me as well, though with less kindness and more intimidation. But that was not the fault of the patients. "Very well. I'll play."

"And I shall sing," offered Tillie Mayard, surprising me. Smiling at each other, we crossed to the piano and discussed possible tunes. "What about 'Rock-a-bye Baby'?" she asked. I played, and after a halting start, she began to sing in such a pure voice, she might never have been ill at all.

It was amazing what music could do for the heart. As I listened to Tillie's voice transport those weak, unbalanced, and unhappy women to a place beyond suffering, a plane beyond cares, I thought of Saint Augustine, who once said, "He who sings, prays twice." I was no great believer in the God of the Bible, but never had I been closer to the divine than in that moment, in that hellish place.

We moved on to "Oh! Susanna," which led me to cheekily suggest another Stephen Foster song, "Nelly Bly." But Tillie did not know the words, so I played "Skip To My Lou," which was so bright and jaunty that several women got up to dance.

That was too far for Miss Grupe. Or perhaps it was the lyric "Rats in the bread box, what'll I do?" that moved her to slam the cover down, almost pinching my fingers. "That's enough. New girls, follow me. The rest of you, sit down and behave!"

The air was suddenly charged. Some residents lowered their eyes. Others gazed upon us pityingly. Still more leered eagerly. Whatever was coming, it would be unpleasant.

I had no idea.

Miss Grupe led us along with no sign of gentleness or compassion. It was a hard enough thing, being in so uncertain and precarious a position, to look for any small kindness or hope of relief, and find none. It was even worse to pray for indifference, and find only cruelty.

She pointed to a door, and I was the first through. It was a bathroom, dank and chilly, but clean—the three sinks along the wall positively gleamed. The single cast-iron tub in the center of the room was new enough to have faucets, with taps for both hot and cold.

A woman was waiting for us. She was dressed in the clothes of an inmate, her copper hair shot through with iron and tied in an untidy tail at the back of her head. She stood beside the filled tub, chattering happily to herself. At least, I presumed it was happy chatter. She often chuckled at her own remarks, repeating the words, "Rub, rub, rub." In her hands she held a large, discolored rag.

Rolling up her sleeves, Miss Grupe said to me, "Nellie Brown, take off your clothes."

I looked at the women who had followed me in—the other nurse, Tillie, Anne, Mrs. Fox, and Mrs. Schanz. "Not here, surely."

"Here, and now," insisted Miss Grupe.

I clutched the buttons of my dress. "No."

Stopping her preparations, Miss Grupe raised her brows at me. "No?"

"It is not decent. You cannot expect a young woman to disrobe in front of strangers, to bathe in a place so public."

"It's a public institution, so all your baths will be public from now on." Miss Grupe enjoyed her little joke so much that she repeated it. The woman near the tub laughed along with her.

Then Miss Grupe's face hardened. "Undress, or you'll be sorry."

I clutched my clothes tighter. "Do you have no decency? To be naked, here?" I waved my hand at the watching women. "It's crazy!"

Miss Grupe grinned without amusement. "Then it shouldn't be a problem."

I shook my head. "I won't."

Miss Grupe signaled to Miss McCarten and together they began to remove my clothing by force. Being concerned for the clothes, I begged them not to tear the fabric. But they had no such concern.

At last, everything was gone save my final undergarment, the same piece I'd set out from home in four days earlier. Combining drawers with a chemise that buttoned down the front, it was now glued to my body by my locked legs and arms.

They took hold of me, undoing the buttons, and hauling the straps down over my shoulders. This exposed my breasts, and I couldn't even raise my hands to cover them, as they were pinned to my sides. Laughing, the two nurses tugged the one-piece down to my belly.

Rather than continue in this grotesque burlesque, I released my legs, hopped out of the garment, and leapt gracelessly into the tub.

Pins and needles of ice struck my every sense, and I loosed a strangled scream. The water was freezing! Despite the presence of the hot water tap, no one had turned it on! Shaking, I reached for the tap.

Miss Grupe laughed. "Go ahead. It doesn't work. Now be still."

I waved a hand at the onlookers—not just my companions, but the other women of Hall Six who had come to gawk at the spectacle I was making. "At l-least make them g-g-go away!"

"Shut up, will you?" Taking me by the scruff of the neck, Miss McCarten dunked my face into the water. I swallowed a mouthful, and it was a long moment before she drew me up again, choking.

"Come on, Maggie. Time to work."

"Rub, rub, rub," said Maggie as she lifted a bar of soap from a tin pan and proceeded to rub it all over me, scouring my back, arms, and legs. Miss Grupe and Miss McCarten hauled my arms wide so that Maggie could access my chest, stomach, and nethers. Then she went at my neck, up across my chin to my face.

"Not my hair!" I shouted as she ran the bar of soap over my head.

Crazy Maggie paid no heed. "Rub, rub, rub!"

That's when I began to sob. I was frozen, not from the cold, but as one who had been struck by lightning. *Who would do this? Why?* I huddled in a ball, my knees drawn up and my fingers clutched crossways over my chest. My hands were already blue, and my chattering teeth were the only part of me that moved.

They wrenched another gasp from me as a fresh bucket of ice water was thrown over me. I sat up straight, arching my back. Clearly an experienced hand at this torture, Miss Grupe took advantage of my involuntary movement to unload a second bucketful in my face. With water already up my nose and down my throat, the third bucket made me honestly believe I was drowning.

They dragged me gasping and shivering from the tub. To think that just moments before I had been concerned with modesty! My once-pretty hair hung in limp, viny tangles across my face and shoulders. My cheeks were blue and dripping. My hazel eyes were shot through with red. I must have looked like a drowned cat.

Looking into the faces of my companions, their expressions were so comical, so astonished, so horrified, I had no choice but to burst into a peal of laughter. Which likely made me appear all the more demented.

With no thought of drying me, the nurses fitted me into a short Canton flannel slip. Letters on the back branded me LUNATIC ASYLUM, B.I.–H.6.

Meanwhile, it was already Tillie's turn. Oh, how it broke my heart! As terrible as the experience had been, I would have gladly subjected myself to a second bath to preserve her. She wept, weakly protesting her feeble health and recent illness. "My head is still sore from the fever."

"Shut up," answered Miss Grupe. "It'll be over soon."

"Can she at least rub more gently?" pleaded Tillie.

Miss Grupe snorted. "There's not much fear of hurting you. Shut up, or you'll get it worse."

Tillie did shut up, though her torrent of tears was the only fresh water added to the tub, which they hadn't bothered to drain after my ordeal. I hoped I had at least warmed the water for her.

I was not allowed to stay to see her out of the tub. Miss McCarten bustled me into a room with six beds. *If not privacy*, I thought, *at least I'll have company.*

Shivering in bed, I was wrapping a blanket around me when Miss Grupe appeared, soaked to the elbow. Marching over, she wrenched me by the arm. "This one has to be put in a room alone tonight. I imagine she's noisy."

"I won't be n-noisy," I stammered, but she paid me no mind as she frog-marched me down the hall. Stopping before Cell 28, she said, "In here." With a shove, she deposited me into the bare stone room.

The only furniture was a bed, bolted to the floor. Freezing wet, scrubbed raw, feet naked, my modesty in tatters and my sanity hardly better, I shivered in my threadbare flannel slip.

Before she shut the door I asked Miss Grupe, "May I not have at least a nightgown?"

The nurse stared at me stonily. "We don't have such things here."

I gestured to the slip clinging to my body. "I cannot sleep like this."

"I don't care," replied Miss Grupe. "This is a public institution. Those who take charity should be thankful for what they get."

"The city pays to keep this place up," I protested, and then added, "and pays people to be kind to the unfortunate souls brought here."

She didn't laugh. Nor did she pity me. In plain, simple terms, she spoke her truth. "Don't expect any kindness here. You won't get it." With that, she closed the door. I heard it lock.

Dazed, I crossed to what passed for a bed. Tentatively, I stretched myself upon it. For some reason known only to God, it had been made high in the center, so I was in danger of rolling off onto the floor.

Clinging to the bed, I put my head down, flooding my thin pillow with water. My soaked slip transferred some of its dampness to the sheet. I pulled up the blanket, a too-short affair made of black wool that scratched the parts of me it deigned to cover.

Curling into a ball, I bit my lip, hard. *This was what you wanted*, I told myself. *This is what you asked for.*

THE ONE BLESSING OF MISERABLE EXHAUSTION was that it made it easier to succumb to sleep. As the door had been locked, I expected to be left alone all night.

Once again, I was wrong.

Heavy footsteps in the hall startled me awake, and I heard the unlocking and locking of cells. I waited with heavy-lidded impatience for the turning of mine.

The door opened, revealing new nurses in brown and white striped dresses, with copper buttons and white aprons. One carried a lantern which she flashed before my groggy eyes. "This is Nellie Brown, from Cuba."

"Oh!" exclaimed the other. "The one from the papers."

"Who are you?" I asked blearily.

The one without the lantern smiled. "I'm Miss Burns, the night nurse, dear. Now you get to sleep, and sleep well."

Already suspicious of kindness here, I sought for an ulterior motive, even as she locked the door once more.

Of course, being awake, I could not again fall to sleep. I wondered if I should ever sleep soundly through the night again. Hearing the locks turn on Cells 29 and 30, I had an unsettling thought. *What if a fire should break out?* With bars on the windows and heavy locks on all the doors, how would a patient escape burning to death? Would the nurses risk themselves to free us? It was not even a possibility. We would all roast alive.

Well, said a sardonic voice in the back of my head, *at least we'd be warm and dry.*

I pulled the blanket up to my chin, thus exposing my feet. Curling up once more, I moved my head to the driest part of the pillow and prayed for sleep.

It felt like hours before I finally drifted off, dreaming of La Viga, and Joaquin Miller, and a poem he'd written just for me, called "The Crazy Señorita de Blackwell." He recited it as he wove water lilies into my hair while I drowned in my own tears.

It was only my first night in the asylum.

FORTY

MOST PECULIAR CASE

TUESDAY, SEPTEMBER 27 1887

I WOKE UP SPEAKING SPANISH, A happy accident that I assumed would only help my story. *Unless it means I'm truly going mad. . .*

But no, my last dream before waking had been, if not real, at least based in reality. I was in Mexico, at a bullfight. Only I was the picador, and the bull grinned like Albert. Mrs. Wilson was in the stands, cheering the bull on, her cheeks flushed in excitement. Bessie Bramble applauded softly with her gloved hands as a lapdog drank tea from a saucer on her knee.

Then all at once I was on the train tracks, running after a train while cowboys chased me on horseback. Only they couldn't be cowboys! They didn't wave! They didn't wear red sashes! Their fine moustaches curled like those of a pantomime villain, and they wore the black coats of Mexican policemen.

Serenos! They're coming for my buttons! Oh, my buttons! I ran harder after the train. Mother was sitting there in the last car, looking back at me as she knitted, shaking her head with a "tut-tut."

I called after her, reaching my arms for her as Wilson came and sat beside her. He added his voice to the "tut-tut." They started alternating, first him saying "tut," then her. They smiled at each other.

"Tut," said Mother.

"Tut," said Wilson, who sounded just like my father.

There was a tap on my shoulder, and I turned around to see Ford pointing his gun in my face. "*Por favor, no,*" I said, holding up my hands. "*No más.*"

My shoulder shook again. "Get up. Get up, Nellie Brown, this minute!"

I shrugged the hand away. "*Por favor. . .*"

The next thing I knew, the window was being thrown open, sending a harsh blast of frigid air that propelled me from the bed like a leaf in a gale.

Prying my eyes open, I stared around in confusion. The first shoots of light were sprouting. It could not have been half-past five.

I am in the asylum, I told myself, panting. *On Blackwell's.*

It was a strange thing to awaken in such a place and feel relief. *There is nothing so fearsome as what we have in our own heads.*

A new nurse stood before me. Her wide toad's face featured a mouth that turned down at the corners, merging with the deepest frown lines I had ever seen. The blonde hair under her starched cap was limp and lifeless. The cap itself was more ornate than those worn by the other nurses, and I sensed that this was the head nurse I had heard spoken of: Miss Grady.

She demanded, "Who were you asking for?"

"*Mi madre.* My mother."

"So you remember your mother?"

"No." Too late, I remembered I was supposed to have no memory. "I mean, I remember her face. But not her name. She has so many names."

That drew a grunt. "What about your father? What are his names?"

"El juez."

Her eyes flickered and her hostility grew. "A Jew?"

"No," I said quickly. "No. A judge."

Slightly mollified, she said, "There's only one judge here, and He says you're damned. Now, take that off and put this on."

I gazed at the thin folds of white calico, the same as worn by the other women of Hall Six. "May I not wear my own clothes?"

Miss Grady folded her arms. "You'll take what you're given and remain quiet."

With no hope for modesty, I did what I could. Turning my back, I removed my flannel slip. I saw bruises all over my skin. My wrists and elbows and knees all ached as if I suffered from rheumatism. Still wet, my hair clung to my neck in a chilly embrace.

Naked, I took up the offered garments. There were only two: an underskirt made of coarse dark cotton, and the dress. I quickly tied the strings of the underskirt and then lifted the dress, a tight waist top sewed onto a straight skirt. As I buttoned the waist, I started to laugh—the underskirt was a full six inches longer than the dress.

"I don't suppose you have a mirror?" I asked, chortling at the absurdity of it all.

Taken aback, she became angry. "What are you laughing about?"

I waved to indicate the picture I presented. I was hardly tall, and could have easily understood a dress that was too large for me. But to have found one so ludicrously short?

"It's what there is. Unless you'd prefer to be naked."

"No, thank you." Past Miss Grady's scowl, I saw several inmates hurrying down the hall. Recalling the rush to dinner, I hurried to follow.

Apparently it was the time for ablutions, though they were thankfully less violent than the night before. The bathroom held only two towels, to be shared between forty-six women. Looking at my mentally wrecked sisters, several of whom had the most furious eruptions on their faces, the idea of wiping my face after they had left their burst pustules on the cloth was horrifying. I forewent the towels and used my underskirt to dry my face after washing at a tap.

I heard a scraping sound behind me as patients dragged a long, backless bench in from the dining room. Miss Grupe and Miss McCarten followed with combs in their hands. We were instructed to sit in turns, six women at a time. I was in the first group.

I braced myself, but was utterly unprepared for the torture to come. I'd heard the phrase, "I'll give you a combing," but it had never made sense before that moment. With my hair still matted and clumped from the night before, combing would have been an arduous task under the best of circumstances. As it was, I yelped and winced as my head was jerked and yanked with no trace of mercy. My eyes watered, but I set my teeth.

When it was over, I asked for hairpins. Instead, they had a patient—a perfectly nice woman called Mrs. McCartney—plait my hair into a single long braid at the back of my head. The bottom of the braid was tied off with a red cotton rag that had once scrubbed dishes.

Passing by, Miss Grupe surveyed my results. "Can't you do something about those bangs?"

Mrs. McCartney shook her head. "I'm sorry, Miss Grupe. They're too short to stay back in the braid." Miss Grupe clucked her tongue, but I was allowed to keep just that much individuality.

I was relieved, having feared she'd simply cut them off, or perhaps tear them out by the roots. By this time, nothing was past belief.

Our hair combed, Miss Grady escorted us to the central room. Perching on a bench at the far end, I watched for my companions from the day before. Being a trifle nearsighted, it was difficult, especially since we were all identically coiffed and dressed.

I spied Tillie, clearly recognizable by her short hair, and waved her over. "I had my own comb," she said at once with feeling, "but Miss Grady took it from me. I wanted to comb my own hair. It's not as if it's any chore at the moment," she added, running her fingers through her short locks.

"Be grateful. At least you were spared that one ordeal. How did you sleep?"

"I nearly froze to death." Indeed, she was pale around her mouth and eyes. "And the noise kept me up all night. Oh, Nellie, it's dreadful! My nerves were already unstrung before I came here. I don't know how I can endure."

"You'll endure because there's no alternative. Help will come, I promise. Stick it out a week, maybe two, and things will improve."

I stopped myself from saying more. I desperately wanted to comfort her, but there were other women about, and Miss Grady was at the door. Having only just penetrated this hellscape, I had no intention of giving myself away yet.

However, there was one thing I could do. Telling Tillie I'd return, I marched up to Miss Grady. "Several of us are cold. May we have more clothes? Our shawls from yesterday at least?"

Miss Grady's toad mouth widened. "Shut up. We don't have shawls for everyone, so there'll be no special favors. You have all you're going to have."

I could see where Miss Grupe learned her manners. The fish rots from the head. "We'll share," I offered.

"Then share what you have, if you like. Makes no difference to me. You'll get nothing more." She left to collect the next group.

Turning to rejoin Tillie, I spied a newspaper on a chair by the nurse's station. Glancing furtively about, I plucked it up and carried it back to the bench.

"What have you got there?" asked Tillie.

"Sunday's copy of the *Sun*," I replied as I perused it. It did not take me long to find the article Dr. Kinier had mentioned.

WHO IS THIS INSANE GIRL?

SHE IS PRETTY, WELL DRESSED AND SPEAKS SPANISH

SHE WANDERED INTO MATRON STENARD'S HOME FOR WOMEN AND ASKED FOR A PISTOL TO PROTECT HERSELF — IS HER NAME MARINA?

A modest, comely, well-dressed girl of 19, who gave her name as Nellie Brown, was committed by Justice Duffy at Essex Market yesterday for examination as to her sanity. The circumstances surrounding her were such as to indicate that possibly she might be the heroine of an interesting story. She was taken to the court by Matron Irene Stenard of the Temporary Home for Females at 84 Second Avenue. The matron said that Nellie came to the Home alone about noon on Friday, and said she was looking for her trunks. She was dressed in a gray flannel dress trimmed with brown, brown silk gloves, a black straw sailor's hat trimmed with brown, and wore a thin gray illusion veil. The closest questioning failed to elicit any satisfactory account of her. During the night she frightened the minister by insisting that she should have a pistol to protect herself. She said that she had some money in a pocketbook, but somebody took it away from her. Her voice was low and mild, and her manner refined. Her dress was neat fitting. The sleeves were the latest style.

In court Nellie was not even terrified into giving any account of herself when informed that she was charged with insanity. She was perfectly quiet and went willingly with the matron. The burden of her talk in reply to many questions put to her by the matron and Justice Duffy was this:

"I have no father. He is dead. I don't know where I came from. I am going to New York. The hat is not mine. I have forgotten how to speak Spanish. Oh, how many questions they ask me, why should they ask me so many questions? I want these men to go away. That man is a reporter. I don't want anything to do with reporters. I came on a railroad. That is the way I always go. I don't see why my private affairs should be made public. I came to try and get work. But I do not know how."

The girl had in her pocket thirty-three cents wrapped in white tissue paper, and a black memorandum book in where there were some rambling and incoherent writings. One sentence was: "Jay Gould sends people to Siberia." Justice Duffy took a good deal of interest in the girl, and telegraphed for an ambulance. A physician from Bellevue Hospital, who came with the ambulance,

talked with the girl, and could get no definite information from her. He expressed the opinion that she was demented. She was taken to the hospital, under commitment for five days, for examination as to her sanity. If pronounced insane she will be committed permanently to the insane asylum. All officials who have seen her are of the opinion that she has come from comfortable surroundings.

Justice Duffy expressed the opinion that the girl was under the influence of some drug, and that she had been ill-treated.

Matron Irene Stenard said last night that when she was in Brooklyn last Thursday she saw the girl wandering aimlessly about. She noticed her from the fact that she had on no wrap, and it was quite cool, and then she wore two veils. The next she saw of her was on Friday, about noon when the girl came to the Home. She said her name was Nellie Brown, and that she had come to stay. At dinner she was perfectly rational, but about 5 o'clock in the afternoon she began to cry, and complained of pains in her head. Matron Stenard asked her if she was in trouble, and she grew hysterical. When asked her name a second time, she gave it as Nellie Marina. That matron said, "But, Nellie, you gave it as Brown a few minutes ago."

She remembered being educated in a convent near New Orleans, and spoke of the rigid rules. When asked where she used to live, she replied "on the hacienda," but could not tell where that was. The servants, she said, were peons. An inmate of the home who had been taking Spanish lessons spoke a few words in that language, and the unfortunate girl began to converse in Spanish. Suddenly she put her hand to her head and exclaimed, "It is all gone." After that she could not recollect a word of Spanish. She also said that she spoke French and Spanish.

According to the story she told an inmate of the Home, her mother died at her birth. Her father, whose name she gave as Juan Marina, she seemed to remember perfectly, and her grandmother, who kept house for them. After the death of her father she was under the care of one called Ignatius or Ignatia. She spoke vaguely about sailing on the Mississippi, and another of the inmates of the Home intending to go to Boston asked what time the Fall River boat left. The demented girl immediately told her, and also said that the boat did not run on Sundays. There was not a mark of any kind on her clothing. Her shoes, the matron said, were evidently not American made.

At Bellevue Hospital it was said last night that the girl was probably suffering from hysterical mania. Thorough physical examination established that she was not suffering from the effects of any drugs whatever. Physically, she was perfectly healthy, and evidently had been well taken care of. A further examination will be made as to her sanity. The doctors say that it is the most peculiar case that ever came into the hospital.

I burst out laughing. *I am "the most peculiar case" they've ever seen?* And what was this nonsense Mrs. Stenard was spouting about seeing me wandering the streets with no wrap and two veils? She had never seen me before in her life!

Tickled by the nonsensical story concocted for me by my fellow housemates, I tried to recall what I had actually said in my broken Spanish. *Where had Ignatius come from?* It took me a moment to realize it had been transmuted from Huck Finn's guardian, Douglas. Was my diction that poor?

Amused as I was, the story was cause for mild concern. I had never intended to make such a spectacle of myself in coming to Blackwell's. I could only hope it would not give away the game too soon.

Still, recalling my annoyance with the *Sun*'s reporter my first night in Bellevue, I felt a certain satisfaction. The more the *Sun* kept making a fuss over me, the more foolish they would look when the truth appeared in the *World*. Colonel Cockerill and Mr. Pulitzer would surely appreciate blackening the eye of their fiercest rival! That would show the stodgy Mr. Dana. *Men report facts better than women? I think not!*

Engrossed in the *Sun*, I did not notice until Tillie tugged my arm that we were being called to break our fast. I was positively starving, and I braced my stomach for disappointment.

We were again lined up like Noah's animals, two by two, and left standing in the cold before being released to a frenzy of food fighting. The latest offering was a bowl of cold tea—possibly the same tea from the night before— along with a slice of buttered bread and a saucer of oatmeal. We could have a globule of molasses for our oatmeal, if we liked.

I was ravenous, but I recalled the advice from the previous night and asked for my bread unbuttered. When it came, it was little better than dried dough. Inspecting it, I found a spider embedded like a fossil in the side.

Setting it aside, I tried the oatmeal with molasses, but it resided in my mouth like an unwelcome wad of phlegm and simply would not descend my throat. In my desperation, I did at least manage the tea.

After breakfast we returned to the sitting room, but did not sit. Miss Grady divided us into groups, and I received another revelation. I'd been impressed at the cleanliness of the place, mentally complimenting the nurses on their fastidiousness. Now I learned what should have long been obvious—the nurses had nothing to do with it. We patients were expected to clean every room, including the nurses' own.

I was set to doing laundry, washing out linens in the company of a dozen others. I'd once tried my hand at being a housemaid, and failed miserably. But I certainly had enough experience with our own household chores to make a good job of my share. I waited in vain for praise from Miss Grady or Miss Grupe, however.

There were very few shirkers, with everyone fearful of being singled out. But I managed to make a few new friends during that wash. One was named Josephine, a broad-shouldered, broad-chested, broad-hipped figure of French womanhood. Another was the sweet Mrs. McCartney who had shared her wisdom with me the night before about unbuttered bread, and had braided my hair that morning. Then there was Mary Hughes, who appeared perfectly sane to me. We helped each other, recognizing through small acts of kindness a kind of kinship.

Before I could quiz them as to their circumstances, however, I was called away to see the doctor yet again. Having just settled in to get some reporting done, I was annoyed. "Why?"

"Don't ask questions!" Miss Grady glanced me up and down, her lip curling at the ridiculous difference between the lengths of my dress and my underskirt. "You can't wear that to see the doctor, stupid girl. Annie!" Miss Grupe scurried over. "She can't see the doctor like this. Get her changed, and quickly." Thus I procured a dress of decent length, if no better in quality.

As we passed the cells, I noted that the beds all now had white counterpanes, making them look far more appealing. I supposed it was for the same reason as my dress: the sake of appearance.

While examining me, Dr. Kinier took no note of my dress, nor of my sanity. He was simply interested in listening to my heart and lungs, checking my pulse, and raising my eyelids to examine my pupils. It was far more effort, with far less flirtation, than he had shown the day before.

The reason for this sat in a chair on the far side of the room: Assistant Medical Superintendent of Blackwell's Island Asylum, Frank H. Ingram. My first impression of him was of youth. He could hardly have been much older than I was myself. Indeed, Dr. Kinier seemed to be his contemporary, save that he had attempted the addition of a heavy moustache.

Dr. Ingram was clean-shaven, with a shock of unruly fair hair that fell across his bright brown eyes. His almost lipless mouth was set in a perpetual smile. With his light side-whiskers, he seemed like an amiable puppy.

Yet this puppy had an acute mind. He posed only three questions to me.

"Do you often find that your thoughts race faster than your ability to express them?"

"Yes," I answered with complete truth.

"Do you often have trouble finishing a project or chore?"

"Sometimes," I admitted.

"Do you find that your inability to complete tasks is usually someone else's fault?"

I took a moment to consider that one. "No. It is my responsibility."

Dr. Ingram's eyes narrowed at that. Then he took my hand. "It has been a pleasure, Miss Brown. Lovely to meet you. And it's odd—I hear no trace of the accent everyone has been talking about. How long did you say you've been in America?"

"As long as I can remember," I told him with a smile.

RETURNING TO THE SITTING ROOM, I spied Miss Grady with a book and pencil and started. *Those are mine!* She was reading through my notes, randomly underlining her favorite of my "insane ramblings."

I marched right up to her. "Those are mine. May I have them back, please?"

Miss Grady's toad-like mouth widened and she croaked, "No."

Anne Neville approached to take up my cause. "It is hers. She had it when we arrived."

"You're imagining things, both of you," said Miss Grady.

I was anxious to make notes on my stay so far. "That book helps me remember things."

Miss Grady radiated contempt. "You can't have it, so shut up and get back to cleaning." She laughed at my shocked expression as if she were a villain from a play. Then she opened a drawer and placed my book into it, on top of an assortment of playing cards, dominoes, and a half dozen other entertainments denied these women who would be so desperately grateful for them.

I was about to argue, but Anne took my arm and dragged me away. "It's not worth another bath."

My shoulders drooped. "God's truth."

I had never imagined that a woman such as Miss Grady existed in the real world. There were cruel men, of course. But the notion of cruelty for the sake of cruelty was as unfeminine as. . .

As a female reporter.

FORTY-ONE

LUNATIC

THE CLEANING COMPLETE, WE MADWOMEN were reassembled in the sitting room. "It's a clear day," said Miss Grady to us. "Get your shawls and hats. We're going for a walk."

All the experienced residents raced about with the excitement of children going on holiday. There was some fighting over a selection of white straw hats, the kind bathers wore at Coney Island. None were fit to grace a lady's head, so drooping and worn they were. Pulling on my own, one of the last to be claimed, I peered through the shredded brim that dropped across my eyes. I again wished for a mirror, for sheer amusement.

I'd lost Anne Neville, and under hats and shawls, we were nearly indistinguishable. "Anne? Anne, where are you?"

A figure further down the hall mimicked me, and Anne emerged from anonymity. "Nellie!"

"Quiet!" snapped Miss Grupe.

But we had found each other and so were partners in our two by two procession, just behind Mrs. McCartney and the French Josephine. As we marched along, Anne and I snickered at our appearances. "I look ridiculous? You should see yourself!" Such was the nature of human hope—there was always room for laughter.

Traversing a route I had not yet seen, through several impressive locking doors, we at last came out the back of the building and onto the grounds.

Blackwell's Island was lovely. It was long and narrow, and one could see the shores of Manhattan on one side, and Queens on the other. It was queer to imagine this pocket of madness floating between them.

Madness had not been the start of Blackwell's. The prison had come first, and then the prison hospital. Only after that had a wider variety of undesirables been shipped here. The criminal, the sick, the insane, the insolvent—all the dregs of society, nestled into its very heart.

Perhaps we were a cautionary tale. Anyone strolling the edges of the river could point and utter a quick, "There but for the Grace of God." Certainly, our column of comical marchers offered a pitiable spectacle as we paraded in pairs in our shawls, hats, and uniform dresses, kept in line by sergeants disguised as nurses, drilling us for our battle for sanity.

I had to wonder—if the goal was a pleasant walk, why were we not allowed onto the grass? Why were we kept to the hard paved walks, forbidden to commune with soothing nature? I remembered thinking when I arrived what a comfort all the pretty greenery must be to the unfortunate souls trapped here. *What a jest! It's more taunt than comfort.* Walking beside paradise and never allowed to partake. Some girls tried to surreptitiously lift a red-gold leaf or a fallen nut from the ground, a small allotment of nature to cling to. But the eagle-eyed nurses always made them throw their little bit of God's comfort away.

We were accidentally allowed one pleasure that morning. It was the day of the long-anticipated yacht race between the Scottish Thistle and the new-built American boat, Volunteer, for the America's Cup race. We cheered Volunteer, and for the span of time they were in view, racing ahead of the Thistle, life seemed remarkably normal.

Returning to our perambulations, we passed a group of women from another ward. They had different dresses, though their hats were the same. So, too, were their hangdog looks and vacant eyes. Some talked to themselves, and these were let to babble. Whereas if I ventured a remark to Anne, I was scolded and threatened.

Passing the gaggle of women, I had to cover my face with my shawl. How they reeked! I felt momentarily grateful for my bath the previous night, and then thought how horrible it was that I should be made grateful for such abuse.

I was often singled out during that awful walk. Nurses from other halls, having read of the crazy Cuban girl, called to Miss Grady to discover which was she. The head nurse took great delight in bringing me out of line to be ogled.

"Oh, she's a wild one," Miss Grady told them. "You've never had a girl as mad as her!"

As we had only met that morning, and I had done absolutely nothing but what I'd been told, I wondered how she could dare to make such a mendacious statement. But it was clearly a badge of honor to have the maddest girl on the island, and her exaggerations only burnished her reputation.

As we continued our walk, I saw other buildings—a scrub brush factory, a match factory, a laundry—all manned by patients who went unpaid for their labors. Slavery may have been forbidden at law, but it was clearly still in practice!

We turned a corner and Anne Neville suddenly exclaimed with excitement, "A merry-go-round!"

Spying the carousel, I smiled at once. It was wondrously incompatible with the experience so far. If I had seen a bullring I would not have been more amazed.

"That's for Fridays only," whispered Mrs. McCartney. "And only if the nurses care to start it moving." Once more our hopes were dashed, which seemed to give the nurses a gross kind of satisfaction.

A sudden commotion ahead drew my attention. Somewhere just out of sight, women were shouting curses, or singing, or praying, or preaching, or all of them together at once. We came to a halt to let them pass, and the sight of them was more than I could endure. Each was fitted with a wide leather belt. A cable rope as wide as my hand was looped through each belt, binding them together. At the end of the rope was a cart bearing two women, both patients, being towed along by their resentful fellows. Nearly all of them were making some noise or other, absorbed by their individual freaks of mind.

One of the women in the cart was screaming at a nurse. "You beat me! You beat me, and I won't forget it! You want to kill me! Kill me!" And she dissolved into tears of utter despair.

Leaning close to Mrs. McCartney, I said, "Who are they?"

"They are from the Lodge," she whispered back.

"The Lodge?"

She indicated a building with high steps on the far side of the walk. "For truly violent cases. They have men in there, too, but only two halls, whereas they have four for the women."

It was shocking to think that there might be twice as many violent women as there were men. I counted the rope gang as they passed. Fifty-two. If that was one hall, then there were over two hundred women in the Lodge alone. Which set me to wondering how many women were held on the island.

"God help them," murmured Anne, turning from the rope line. "It's so dreadful, I—I cannot look."

I did look, but soon wished I had not. An ancient grandmother with hair the color of clouds spoke to the sky as if appealing to join it. Another large woman was bound into a straightjacket and dragged along by two nurses. Crippled, blind, old, young, homely, pretty, they all marched along, a senseless mass of humanity. There could be no worse fate.

I made eye contact with one, a blonde waif with the deepest blue eyes I had ever beheld. Instantly, she began talking to me, though I could not hear her words over the din. I was grateful, for her smile was so malignant, so terrible and unnatural, that I was shaking with a very real fear. She kept looking at me as she passed, craning her neck to lock my gaze until she disappeared beyond a bend.

Miss Grady saw my shakes. "Don't like them, do you? You wouldn't want to be on the rope, would you?"

"I should say not," I replied in a gasp.

"Then be sure to do as you're told."

We passed another pavilion known as the Retreat. According to Mrs. McCartney, this was second only to the Lodge. Printed across its door was the legend WHILE I LIVE, I HOPE.

I thought Dante's warning was more appropriate.

WHEN WE RETURNED TO OUR HALL, it was time for luncheon. By this point, the wait was as familiar as the detestable food: soup, a cold potato, and a hunk of spoiled beef. Not granted even the dignity of cutlery, my fellow patients slurped, gnawed, and tore at the food as best they were able.

Swallowing what little I could—horribly, I found I was growing accustomed to it—I decided to settle into my role of reporter and started to subtly interview the residents of Hall Six.

A handful were truly ill, and these could be recognized right off. But as far as I could see, the majority who lived there were no less sane than I was. Indeed, several were far moreso. Unlike me, they had not been locked up of their own volition.

Luncheon ended and we returned to the sitting room, where we were instructed to sit still upon those hard benches for the entire afternoon. Mrs. Schanz took up some knitting, as did others. Inmates were expected to make clothes, especially the shawls. I tried my hand at it, but I had never been skilled with such crafts. *Why in Heaven's name are there no books?*

Still, I had a task I could perform while knitting. For the next few days I had to prize the histories of these various women. For them, it proved a pleasant way to while away the time, gossiping. For me, it was a radical education.

I began with Mrs. McCartney, who had been such a comfort. She would not say why she was there, but with tears in her eyes she did mention that she had hopes that someday her husband would liberate her.

From her I moved on to the large Frenchwoman, Josephine Despereaux, who seemed perfectly lucid as she explained her situation. "*Toute ma famille est en France. Mes amis aussi. Je ne sais même pas comment les contacter, faites-leur savoir que je suis en vie. Ils n'ont aucun moyen de me trouver, et je n'ai aucun moyen de me libérer de cet endroit infernal.*"

Though my French was weak and long-dormant, I understood the gist. Staying in some boardinghouse, one morning she had become ill at breakfast. They had called for two officers, and she had been unable to make herself understood. She had first been relieved to be taken by an ambulance, but then she had been taken from Bellevue to Blackwell's and made to understand she was not in there for illness, but for insanity. "*Quand je suis arrivé, j'ai crié que j'étais là sans espoir de libération, et pour avoir pleuré,* Mademoiselle Grady *et ses assistants m'ont étouffé jusqu'à ce qu'ils me blessent, car ça a été malade depuis.*" Indicating Miss Grady, she covertly mimed choking with both hands. When I gasped, she laid a quick hand across my arm to silence me, obviously fearful of more such treatment.

A thin German girl named Louise—*Are most German women named Louise?* I wondered—had also received beatings from Miss Grady. "Because I am unable to eat the horrible food they give us. Nor ought I be compelled to freeze for want of proper clothing. Oh! How I suffer from *mutterseelenallein*! I pray nightly that I may be taken to my papa and mamma!"

"Mutter. . . Is that a disease?"

She shook her head sadly. "It is the feeling of being so alone, not even your mother loves you."

"Oh!" I thought it a marvelous word, describing a feeling I had felt so very often. "Do you know where they are? Your parents?"

"They are here," she said, waving her hand around us. "They died, and they stay near me until I can join them."

That cooled my heels a bit. But other than the delusion that her dead parents were with her all the time, she seemed rational—though her eyes looked a little bright, and when I held her hand she seemed to be quite warm. I worried she was coming down with an illness.

Perhaps it was her growing fever that loosened her tongue. She told me a tale that seemed eerily similar to my own experience in Bellevue. Only in her case, the evil doctor who visited her in the middle of the night was Dr. Field. She remembered him because of his cane.

"One night, at Bellevue, Dr. Field arrived and said he wanted to examine me. I was in bed, very tired of the examinations. Especially his questions, which were very *unhöflich*." I looked confused, and she sought the correct word. "Rude? Yes, rude."

I nodded, having undergone the same thing from Dr. Field. I imagined the night nurses hovering by the open door, listening to his salacious questions. "Go on."

"I answered his questions a long time. When I said 'I am tired of this. I will talk no more,' he grew very angry, very red in the face. 'Won't you? I'll see if I can't make you.' I thought he would strike me. But his crutch he set down and onto the bed he climbed, over me. He pulled my blanket and put his hands on my—" She indicated her breasts. "Pinching them so hard I cried out!"

I gasped. "What did you do?"

"Straight in bed I sat up and shouted at him, asked him what he thought to do! He told me he wanted to teach me to obey when he spoke to me. And he smiled. Smiled! *Ach du liebe Zeit!* If I could only die and go to papa!"

I patted her hand, picturing Dr. Field limping around on his knobby cane, taking money from reporters, pinching girls who didn't answer him. And Dr. Fitch, with his midnight visits and pandering act.

I had previously been afraid of a fire in this place. Now I wanted to burn it all down.

ARRIVING AT BLACKWELL'S, I HAD assumed that the nurses were charged with tending to the patients. That afternoon, however, I came to understand that the nurses viewed the patients as nothing more than sources of amusement. Being both new and notorious, I was a favorite target. Miss Grupe and Miss Grady attempted several times to draw me out. At first, they mocked my supposed forgetfulness:

"Nellie, you've forgotten yourself! Your dress is back to front!"

"Oh, that Nellie Brown, she would forget her head if it wasn't attached."

When that failed to get a rise from me, they focused upon my supposed love affair:

"Was he handsome, Nellie? Of course he was. He was handsome, and rich, and took you dancing, and you fell for him, did you not, Nell?"

"Certainly, she did! Nell fell right to Hell!"

Again failing to draw more than disdain from me, they at last settled on their favorite taunt—the report that I was afraid for my life:

"They're coming to get you, Nell," said Miss Grupe.

"That's right," agreed Miss Grady. "With poison. You'd best not drink your tea tonight. Or you'll sleep better than sound, you'll sleep like the dead."

When even this proved not to move me, they moved on to easier prey. One of their longtime favorites was old Matilda, a tiny woman who whispered to steam heaters, complaining of her lost fortune. Miss Grady and Miss Grupe tried to get the poor old biddy to offer insults to Miss McCarten, with whom they were quarreling that day. But Matilda did not fall for the trick, so Miss Grady called her close. "I have a secret for you." When Matilda leaned down to hear, the nurse spit in her ear.

I started to my feet in outrage, but Anne pulled me down. "Don't, Nellie! Speaking out only makes it worse."

The fact that she was right did nothing to cool my anger.

LATE THAT SECOND AFTERNOON, THE SUPERINTENDENT of Blackwell's Island arrived in Hall Six. His name was Dent, and the nurses greeted him with special obsequiousness. Walking through the hall, he addressed the occasional woman who looked sane enough to converse. In a slow Southern drawl he would ask, "How are you today?"

Every one of them replied that they were perfectly well, thank you. This, when they were blue with the cold and shivering, or stiff and sore from sitting all afternoon.

"Why don't they complain?" I asked Mrs. McCartney.

"Because if they do," she answered gravely, "the nurses will beat them."

"Surely not!" I exclaimed.

A woman called Mrs. Cotter glanced my way. On my other side, Mrs. McGuiness grunted. But no one said anything more.

Superintendent Dent brought in a doctor called Flint to examine me. Unsure why I merited such attention, I used the time he was taking my pulse to tell them how cold it was. "I require no medical aid. But Miss Mayard does. You should transfer your attentions to her."

They did not answer me, but Tillie, having heard her name, came forward. "Please doctors, I am ill. I just recovered from a fever, and I feel it creeping in upon me again. Please, may I be allowed to rest and recover?"

The doctors utterly ignored her, prompting me to say, "Why don't you listen to her?"

Miss Grupe took Tillie hard by the arm and dragged her back to the benches. "After awhile, when you see the doctors will not notice you, you will quit running up to them. If they pay attention to you, else everyone will be doing it."

Meanwhile, Dr. Flint was frowning. "Interesting. Her pulse and eyes are not those of an insane girl."

Superintendent Dent shook his head. "In such cases, tests are useless. She is hopelessly mad. Look at her face. Her cheeks are bright. And that fiery look in her eyes? The mark of a lunatic."

If anger marked me as crazy, I was indeed a lunatic.

THERE WAS NO BATH AFTER DINNER, thank God. Again, I was shut away from the others, and I curled up on the terrible convex mattress, hoping for sleep. But I was kept awake for at least an hour by an elderly woman in the next cell begging for death. "God, take me home! Leave me to die!"

The next morning I looked out for her. She was easily seventy years of age, and blind. The nurses laughed at her as she tottered into benches and tables. When she tried to remove her uncomfortable shoes, they made two patients force the shoes back on her feet.

"You complain about the cold," sneered Miss Grupe. "But you try to strip naked every time we turn."

"They hurt my feet," protested the old woman. "Please, may I have a shawl?"

"Knit one, and you can have it." Miss Grupe laughingly speculated what such a shawl might look like. "A crooked spider's web!"

Giving up the fight over her shoes, the old lady tried to simply lay down on a bench, but Miss Grupe jerked her up by the arm. "What do you think this is, you old whore, a boudoir? You can't lie down here!"

"Please, give me a pillow and pull up the covers," gasped the old woman, nearly delirious. "I am so cold." She shivered in the same meager clothing as the rest of us, while the nurses wore coats and loved to discuss their warm undergarments in loud, taunting voices.

Miss Grupe sat on the bench beside her. "Here, sweetie. This will warm you." And taking her cold hands she pressed them savagely inside the old woman's dress. Gasping, the blind woman protested, which prompted Miss McCarten and Miss Grady to join in, warming their hands on the shrieking woman's face and neck.

I watched this, no longer needing my book. The actions of Miss Grupe, Miss Grady, and Miss McCarten were branded across my brain, forever etched into my psyche. I felt my hand twitch as though I was already writing of them for the whole world to see.

It was now Wednesday, and I complained yet again of the cold. It was becoming a ritual. I'd complain, and one of the nurses would say, "Shut up." Once I said it along with Miss Grady, who was none too pleased.

Eventually, Miss Grady said, "Fine. We have some flannel underthings you can have, if only you'll shut up." She took me to one of the cells and offered me the smallclothes, which turned out not to be small at all, but ludicrously huge. They fell off my shoulders and down my body, even when tied. "I can't wear these," I said, laughing.

"That's what we get!" complained Miss Grady, appealing to the ceiling. "You complain, we help, and you complain some more! Some thanks we get. Take them or shut up about being cold!" So I took them, and when no one was looking, I gave them to Tillie.

I was growing seriously concerned for her. Barely recovered from her fever, she was feeling the cold as much as anyone, and she could not have consumed more than a few nibbles of food since we'd arrived. Anne and I rallied around her, trying to keep her upright during that day's walk and all that wearying sitting.

I had never in my life been as tired as I became sitting on those benches. Patients would shift, prop one foot beneath them, or sit sideways—or even on their knees—if only to make a change. The nurses were relentless in scolding this behavior, forcing us to "Sit properly!" If we protested, we were given the now well-known refrain: "Shut up."

After just two days, my own behind was desperately sore, and several other women had long since shed delicacy, openly discussing their piles, weeping sores, and bleeding from all the relentless sitting.

Even setting aside the physical discomfort, I wondered what it was supposed to be doing for their sanity. *What are these genius doctors thinking, having these women sit from six in the morning to eight at night?* Fourteen hours interrupted only by one walk, then back to the "sitting room." Never had there been a more apt description. Sitting, with nothing more. No books, no drawing, no games, no sport, no real discussion even. It was a game of endurance, and a rigged one at that.

Endurance was the thing Tillie lacked. That afternoon I tried to chide her into singing if I played a little music—something the nurses could tolerate, for they were as bored as we were.

But Miss Grupe ordered us to stop. Having discarded the blind woman, she had devised a fresh distraction and did not like to have it disturbed.

Her distraction's name was Sarah Fishbaum, a little Hebrew girl with dark features, not much older than me. I only learned her story through the taunts of Miss Grupe, who drew Sarah close to the stove. "Now Sarah, tell me true. You'd like to have a nice young man, wouldn't you?"

Sarah had very little English, but tried to be amiable. "A young man is nice, yes."

Miss Grady snorted while Miss McCarten smiled absently. Miss Grupe positively glowed. "What about one of the doctors, Sarah? Wouldn't you like to have one of the doctors?"

"I like the doctors, yes," said Sarah agreeably.

"Should we talk to the doctors for you? Would you like that?"

Sarah's eyes lit up with hope. "Please, yes! Talk to doctors for me!"

"But which doctor, Sarah?" pressed Miss Grupe while the other two laughed behind their hands. "Who is the best young doctor? Dr. Kiniear? Dr. Ingram? Not Dr. Dent, surely. You don't like the older ones, do you, Sarah? No, you like young men. That's what your husband says. He says you like all the young men, so he put you here, where there are only women. But the doctors are men, Sarah. So there's your hope. Now, Dr. Ingram will come by this afternoon. What will you say to him, Sarah?"

"I know what she should say," offered Miss Grady. "Sarah, tell him you don't like moustaches. Too itchy. Tell him he has a nice smooth face."

Miss Grupe bobbed her head. "He'll appreciate that, Sarah. Truly he will. Men like to be complimented by pretty girls. And you're a pretty girl, aren't you, Sarah? That's what all your husband's friends say. . ."

When Dr. Ingram came in, Sarah did as she had been bidden and said she did not like moustaches. Thankfully, Dr. Ingram was too kind to find fault in her, and spoiled the nurses' fun by agreeing. "That's what I say. Too itchy. It's why I shave each and every morning." He patted the top of her head and passed along.

I was careful not to let the disappointed Miss Grupe see me smiling.

T HAT AFTERNOON TWO NEW ARRIVALS broke our monotony. One was called Carrie Glass. As she shuffled into Hall Six, she was clearly confused by her new surroundings. "This one was born an idiot," Miss Grupe said, mimicking her dragging foot and slow speech. Not understanding that she was being mocked, Carrie laughed, possibly believing she had made a friend. My heart shattered for her.

The other was a German immigrant named Margaret Bentz who had been hired into a home as a cook. She seemed perfectly well, though as we welcomed her she had furious tears in her eyes.

"What brought you here?" I asked.

"My temper," she said, bitterly pouring out her story. She had just finished cleaning the kitchen of her employer's home when two chambermaids came down and deliberately soiled it. Now, Miss Bentz was one of those women who could not abide untidy things—usually considered a fine feminine trait. "So I quarreled with them. Called them some unkind names, perhaps, but in German, which neither of them speak. Still they called an officer, and I was taken away. Me! Now they say I am insane! Because I allowed my temper to run away with me?"

"Don't speak German to Miss Grupe," I advised. "She's embarrassed to be foreign."

"Which one is she?" When I pointed, she said, "Oh, yes. She struck me already when I tried it."

"What did you do in reply?"

"Nothing. I intend to remain quiet and prove I am able to keep my temper."

This was the clearest anecdote I had gleaned for my article all day. Most inmates were reluctant to share their stories within hearing of the nurses, who were always eavesdropping. Only during meals, walks, or those intervals where the nurses were distracted could I prize personal information from my fellow madwomen.

There were a handful of Negroes among the predominately white inmates of Blackwell's, and only one in Hall Six. Octavia Ballard must have been nearing fifty years, and proved utterly indifferent to my questions—until I mentioned children. "Children? *They* put me here. Of the four of them, there were none who would take me home. Their brothers would have, but they're dead. Four alive, four dead and waiting."

I did not ask for what, or whom, the dead were waiting. "Where's home?"

A wrinkle appeared between her brows. "Preston."

"Where's that?"

"Nova Scotia."

"Canada?"

She shook her head, not in disagreement but in apathy, and would answer no more questions.

Mrs. Ballard's silence was juxtaposed to Mrs. O'Keefe's endless chattering. She talked to no purpose and could not seem to stop, but her prattle was soft, like the sound of water by the shore.

Rebecca Farron had the palest skin I'd ever seen. Even a hint of sun and she burned. She was docile and demure, and offered the nurses no amusement—she was far too sane. In the midst of a long conversation about music, I leaned close. "Rebecca, why are you here?"

"I was sick," said Rebecca simply.

I hesitated. "Mentally?"

"Heavens, no. What gave you such an idea? No, I was simply overworking myself in a factory and I broke down. I ran out of money, and I applied to the poorhouse until I was able to work again."

Again I hesitated, but could not help myself. "Don't you know that they don't send needy people here unless they are insane?"

She shrugged. "I realized it after I arrived. But they said this was the place they sent all the needy women who cannot work." She pointed to two others. "They come here each Fall, when the weather turns cold. By spring they are miraculously cured, only to relapse come autumn."

I made a mental note to interview these two habitual inmates. "And how have you been treated?"

"I've escaped a beating so far," whispered Rebecca, making a sign to ward off evil. "Though I've certainly been sickened by the sight of them. You had to take a bath when you came, yes? It was the same for me. But I had been so ill that the doctors had told me not to bathe. Miss Grupe dunked me anyway. It took me weeks to regain my strength. Frankly, I'm amazed I recovered at all."

Which made me all the more concerned for Tillie, who was weakening hourly. Anne and I tried to keep her company and shield her from the nurses, of whom we were growing more and more afraid with each new casual cruelty.

That afternoon a woman I had not yet met, a Mrs. Turney, was removed from the sitting room to "assist" Miss Grupe in preparing dinner. When she returned, she was holding her wrist. Her eyes were wet, and her hands trembled. Asked what ailed her, she shook her head. "It's nothing. Only a burn."

"How did you get it?" I asked, when no one else would.

"I was slow making the tea," she answered.

At dinner that night I was gnawing fruitlessly at a blackened hunk of unbuttered bread when I heard a noise that chilled me more than any I'd heard there. It was faint, as if it came from some distant cellar. I had heard women crying, and even the occasional man—their voices carried across the island from their pavilions. But this wail, so desperate and high, brought tears to every eye.

It was the wail of a baby.

Crazy Maggie began to cry. Mrs. O'Keefe's constant prattle became a lullabye:

> Lullaby, and good night,
> You're your mother's delight,
> Shining angels beside
> My darling abide.
> Soft and warm is your bed,
> Close your eyes and rest your head.
> Soft and warm is your bed,
> Close your eyes and rest your head.

Though several more of us began to cry, none spoke. Some common consent, some deep bond, kept us all in silence. To acknowledge that terrible, helpless wail would burst a dam that could not be mended.

FORTY-TWO

CRUEL INTENTIONS

THURSDAY, SEPTEMBER 29 1887

I T SEEMED THAT DESPITE MY NOTORIETY I'd proved myself untroublesome, for I was moved to a room with six beds. I'd hoped to be placed with Tillie and Anne, and I received half my wish. Anne's bed was just across from mine. Afraid to talk, we smiled at each other throughout that third night. An enormous comfort.

The next morning, the world outside was gray and foggy, and the chill reached right into the tiled floor. I heard the nurses discussing a sick girl, and at once I feared for Tillie, but a quick search of the benches at the wrenching coiffurie revealed my friend shivering beside one of the steam radiators.

The missing girl was the German girl Louise, who had been assaulted by Dr. Field back at Bellevue. She hadn't eaten in all the time I'd been there, but allowed Crazy Maggie to filch all her food. Eavesdropping on the nurses, I learned that Louise was in bed with a high fever. Miss Grady told Miss McCarten, "Go check her temperature, Alicia. See if she's faking."

Miss McCarten returned several minutes later. "She's not faking. Her temperature is one hundred fifty degrees."

Hearing that absurd number, I snorted with amusement. Miss Grupe whirled on me. "How high has your temperature ever gotten?"

"Not that high," I offered.

Suspicious, she glared at me. Was I simple, or was I mocking them?

Miss Grady stood. "I'll go try." When she returned, she declared that Louise had a fever of ninety-nine degrees. That, at least, seemed possible. And in this place, a fever was nothing to laugh about.

"Well," said Miss Grady, "starve a cold, feed a fever. She has to be made to eat." They ordered Josephine to take more rancid food up to the sick girl. "And tell her if she doesn't eat, I'll force it down her throat."

After three days on the island, I had the routine of the place down pat: morning combing, breakfast, cleaning, a walk, sitting, lunch, sitting, supper, sitting, bed. My own routine also solidified. Each morning I would ask the nurses for more clothes for all the women, a request that was always denied. I would talk to every doctor I saw and say simply, "Am I sane or am I not?" I would care for Tillie as best I could, and work with Anne to keep her spirits up. I would play upon the piano for half an hour. And I would move among the women to learn their stories.

The more I heard, the more important this story became. For example, during Thursday morning's walk across the eerily foggy grounds, Mrs. Cotter spoke of her own horrible treatment with a resignation that made her all the more tragic:

"One day I thought I saw my husband coming up the walk over there. A trick of the light. It wasn't him, just a doctor. But because I broke the line, I was sent to the Retreat. The nurses there beat me with a broom handle." She winced, touching her side. "I think they did something to my ribs. It's still hard to breathe. Then they bound me hand and foot, twisted a sheet about my throat, and threw me into a bathtub of ice water. They held me under until I thought I was going to die. When I awoke, they started cursing me for frightening them. 'Not like the other girl!' they said, and beat my head against the wall and floor. They tore out my hair by the roots. See? I fear it will never grow back."

I was speechless. Even seeing the clumps of missing hair, I wondered if she could have imagined these events, if only because I needed to believe such things didn't happen. "Other girl?"

Shooting a frightened look at the nurses, Mrs. Cotter pressed her lips together. "Talk to Bridget."

Bridget McGuiness was a medium-sized woman of perhaps thirty, though already her red hair had tendrils of silver woven through it. I had not yet tried to talk to her, for she seemed preternaturally quiet. According to Mrs. Cotter, there was a reason. Though I was uncertain how much more horror my heart could hold, I knew that every reporter accepts a good tip.

I had no chance to talk to Bridget that afternoon outside the nurses' hearing, so I took the trouble to chat her up about subjects that would be of no interest to Miss Grupe or Miss Grady: the weather, her favorite flowers, music. Music seemed to be the key to conversation. I had not realized how much the inmates of that place appreciated my brief stints on the piano each day.

That afternoon when Dr. Dent came through for his inspection, Mrs.

Turney unexpectedly rose from her bench to approach him. Showing him her burned wrist, she said boldly, "Miss Grupe did this to me."

All of us were transfixed. The middle-aged woman herself was shaking with fear as Dr. Dent called Miss Grupe over. "Well? What about this?"

Miss Grupe employed her softest tone. "She's absolutely right, poor thing. It's my fault. I asked her to help me make the tea for supper last night. She was burned by the pot. I should never have demanded so much of her."

The doctor nodded sympathetically. "I'm sure it's no one's fault. Did you soak it in cold water?"

"No, doctor," said Miss Grupe, looking at Mrs. Turney. "But I certainly shall."

Dr. Dent patted Mrs. Turney on the shoulder. "You'll be better soon."

Mrs. Turney cowered away. She had dared. She had failed. She would be punished.

"I did that too," said Bridget softly.

Lowering my gaze to my knitting, I said, "What's that?"

"Complained. I argued all the time when I first got here. Told them I was perfectly sane, demanded release. After a week they decided I was 'troublesome.' Sent me to Retreat Four."

"You were on the rope gang?"

Bridget nodded, her mouth barely moving as she spoke. "The beatings there were something dreadful. I've been beaten before, but never so viciously. Pulled by the hair, held underwater, choked, kicked."

"No one saw?"

"Nurses always keep a quiet patient near the window to warn if any doctors approach."

"And the doctors don't care?"

"They don't believe it's happening. Say we're imagining it."

"How can a woman imagine a bruise?"

"You saw Mrs. Turney. We must be hurting ourselves. If we try to tell the doctors, the nurses hurt us worse. She's in for it," she added, looking at Mrs. Turney.

"Did you tell?"

"No. I was held underwater until I promised I wouldn't. When that's happening to you, you'll promise anything."

"So you never fought back?"

Bridget raised her eyes to mine. "Once. Once, I did. I picked up a chair and swung it at the nurses. Broke a window, threatened to use the glass to cut them if they didn't leave me be."

Her daring had me breathless. "What happened?"

"I was transferred to the Lodge."

It was such a dire pronouncement, so full of meaning and so final, that we sat in silence for a long time. "I've seen the Lodge. It looks fearful."

"Worst place on the Island. Dirty. Stench is awful. Flies swarm over everything. Food is even worse than here, and we eat off of tin plates. Bars are on the inside, not the outside. That makes a difference."

"Is everyone there violent?"

Bridget snorted. "There are women who've been there for years. Not violent at all. Perfectly quiet and docile."

"Then why—?"

"To do the work. Who else would do it, the nurses? They're too busy beating the patients to clean and wash."

"Is that how they are made docile? Beatings?"

Glancing across the room, Bridget considered. "Starvation works more than the drugs. The drugs make you crazy. Morphine calms you for a day, then you hunger for it. And chloral makes you wicked thirsty. I've seen women wild for water from it, and the nurses refuse to give them a drop. I remember crying for water until my mouth was so parched I couldn't speak. But I guess I made enough noise, because I earned another beating. Broke two of my ribs that time, jumping on me."

"Oh, dear Lord," I gasped. "Did the doctors do nothing?"

"Like I told you, the doctors know nothing about it. And if we talk, we're beaten worse than ever before. They use a broom handle, and hurt us, you know. Inside."

Disgusted, I sat for a while in silence. I could tell that Bridget was done, but I was not. Weighing how long we'd already been talking, I ventured one more leading remark. "Mrs. Cotter mentioned a girl. . ."

Bridget's head came up with slow suspicion. "Who are you?"

"Me? I'm just. . . I'm Nellie Brown. I'm new here."

"Why are you asking all these questions?"

"I just want to know more about this place."

Bridget glared at me. "I don't know what she's talking about." And that was all she would say to me.

I felt my heart racing in my chest. If I hadn't already had enough horrific reporting to do, I now had a mystery girl whose fate I had to discover.

THAT AFTERNOON THERE WAS ANOTHER new arrival, which had me wondering if Hall Six was some kind of holding area for new patients until they could be sorted more permanently. It made sense, being located so near that twisting entrance. I wondered what happened to the women when they were moved out of this hall.

This new patient was named Urena Little-Page, and to Miss Grady's delight, she was easily provoked. Still in her street clothes, Miss Grupe took her to see Dr. Kinier, just as had been done to me. When they returned, the nurse wore a sinister smile upon her face.

"Now Urena, I have one more question for you. How old did you say you are?"

"I'm eighteen," said Urena.

Now, I had lied about my age many times in my life. It is a woman's prerogative. But if she was eighteen, then I was no more than six. It was an absurd assertion, one that much amused the other nurses.

Catching on, Miss Grady lifted a document. "The doctors say you are thirty-three."

"I'm eighteen," insisted Miss Little-Page as tears formed in her eyes.

"Truly?" Miss Grady's toad-like face glistened with contentment. "Were you born in a leap year? Or do you only count every other birthday?"

"I'm eighteen years old!" cried Miss Little-Page, ripping the document out of Miss Grady's hand. Then she balled it up and hurled it at the head nurse. "I'm eighteen! I'm only eighteen! You can't treat me this way!"

Miss Grady only laughed, continuing to taunt her. "Let me think! If you are thirty-three, you were born in '54, were you not? If you lived through the war, you must recall it."

Miss Grupe and Miss McCarten joined in, demanding she reveal her birth date. The pitiful woman could not, simply insisting over and over that she was eighteen. She began to plead, "I want to go home! Let me go home!"

Their amusement fading, they told her to shut up and sit with the other women. But they had riled her too far, and when she wouldn't obey, they slapped her face to stop her crying.

They misjudged, however, for it only made her cry all the more. With the speed of a serpent, Miss Grupe grasped the weeping woman by the throat. "Be quiet, or I'll make you quiet!" Choking and gasping, Miss Little-Page flailed her arms. The other nurses restrained her.

"Take her to the closet!" snapped Miss Grady. Together, they dragged the deluded creature out into the hall.

They were gone for several minutes, and returned straightening their uniforms and scowling. The rest of us hunkered our shoulders as if bracing for a storm. I started to whisper to Mrs. Cotter, but she gave an emphatic little shake of her head.

The only patient in Hall Six now making any noise was Mrs. O'Keefe, pursuing her constant low chatter with nobody. Miss Grady's desire to punish had been awakened, and she stormed over to the old, slate-haired woman and hauled her out of her seat. "I've told you to stop with your babble!"

Mrs. O'Keefe was not so far gone that she didn't recognize her danger. She appealed to all of us, crying, "For God's sake, ladies, don't let her beat me!"

"Shut up, you hussy!" Taking hold of the old woman's hair, the head nurse hauled her out of the room and down the hall. I could hear her cries growing fainter and fainter. Finally, they ceased altogether.

A minute later, Miss Grady returned and nodded to Miss Grupe. "That settled the old fool for a while."

I found myself unable to knit, my hands were shaking so. But not in fear. In rage. *I have to get out of here and tell this story.* The only thing keeping me calm was the thought of how famous these terrible women were about to be.

No, not famous. Infamous.

A T OUR URGING, AND KNOWING she had to keep up her strength, Tillie tried to eat that night. But after one bite she was overcome with nausea. Leaping up, she fled from the dining room, and we heard her vomiting in the toilets.

Already in a foul temper, Miss Grady said, "Wonderful. All it takes is one whiff of sick to make them all start churning their guts. Alicia, go and tell her she better steel her stomach or she'll be sorry."

Obeying, Miss McCarten left the dining room. Miss Grady was near the door, leaving only Miss Grupe to walk among us.

There was a sudden rush and clatter behind me, and I turned in time to see Mrs. Turney hurl the steaming contents of her soup bowl at Miss Grupe's face.

There was a frozen moment as Miss Grupe stood mouth open, eyes wide, arms akimbo. Then with a breath like a volcano erupting she shrieked, "You little hussy!"

Miss Grady took charge. "Annie, go clean yourself up. You are relieved for the evening. And you!" She grabbed Mrs. Turney by the back of her neck, braid and all. "I hope you enjoyed your last meal in Hall Six. Tomorrow you're going to the Lodge."

There were gasps all around me. Mrs. Turney protested vehemently as she was dragged from the dining room, and just like that we inmates were left alone. At once we all started talking, asking questions, retelling Mrs. Turney's act of bravery with the tea.

Returning, Miss McCarten shouted, "Shut up, all of you! Unless you care to join her. Be quiet and eat!"

I started to stand. Miss McCarten turned her glacial stare on me, and I sank back down again, ducking my head.

"That's right," she said in triumph. "You sit there and be quiet, Nellie Brown."

Bent over my food, I did not eat. I did not even realize when dinner was over until we were chivied back to the sitting room.

I don't know how it began. All I knew was that tears were flowing down my face. Try as I might, I could not control them. At last, I broke into huge, ugly sobs, my nose dripping and my mouth dragging in huge desperate breaths.

"What's the matter, Nellie?" asked Anne.

I shook my head. On my other side, Tillie began stroking my arm. "It will be fine, Nellie. It will be just fine. Shhh. Shhhh."

"She should be quiet," advised Mrs. Despereaux in an undertone, her accent adding a sibilant hiss. "The nurses."

I could not help myself, even when I heard Miss Grupe saying, "I knew she was noisy." I wondered why she had even come back. Yet her voice only propelled me further into helpless paroxysms of torrential weeping.

"Put her back in her cell tonight," said Miss Grady.

Never had I felt so helpless. Shuddering, I thought with fear of how completely we were in the power of our keepers. We could all weep, and wail, and plead—for release, for bread, for kindness, even—all to no avail.

Eventually fatigue set in, and the tears began to slow as we marched off to bed. I wanted to ask if I might stay with the others, but an invisible hand clamped over my mouth to prevent me. So I docilely followed to Cell 28, took off my dress, and sat on the bed.

And thought.

Why did I lose my composure so thoroughly? I had never cried with such abandon in my life. Not when Ford beat me and Mother and Albert. Not when I discovered I could not return to school. Not even over Wilson. I had not cried like that since. . .

Since Father died.

My father, who had called me Pink. My father, who had failed us so badly. Not only by dying, but by not providing afterwards. My father, who had adored me and abandoned me. Making me the lonely orphan girl named Pink. A frightened girl who pushed her way to the front so no one would see she was afraid. Afraid she wasn't brave enough, or smart enough, or lovable enough. All she was, at heart, was angry. *Only girls aren't supposed to be angry, are they?* Sugar and spice and everything nice. And that had never been Pink.

It isn't Nellie Bly, either. But Nellie Bly was different. Nellie Bly was bold and daring, never afraid. *Look at the things she did: newspapers, factories, Mexico. Look what she's doing right now!*

I wanted to be Nellie Bly. Nellie Bly was brave. I was not. I might pretend to be brave, but that night I'd faced a moment that required bravery. And I had frozen.

Is that who you are? Who you have become? You ran away from Mexico when faced with danger. Even with Wilson, rather than be brave and dare the world to judge you, you ran away. Are you a coward? Are you really that timid? That fearful? That. . . womanish?

I was surprised by the heavy turn of a key in the door's lock. The night nurse, Miss Burns, opened my door and saw me sitting there. "It's ten o'clock. You should sleep, Miss Brown."

"I know." My voice sounded small.

She hesitated, then said, "It is easier to sleep if you lay down."

"I know."

Her advice sounded well-intentioned. So far she had been kind, at least in comparison to the other nurses. I could almost hear her shake her head before she closed the door.

I hoped she had just gone for coffee, or to read. No such luck. There were returning footsteps, my door opened, and Miss Grady stormed in.

"You are determined to be trouble." The head nurse was wearing her nightclothes.

"I am not bothering anyone," I said softly.

"Liar. You are bothering me. I am bothered. If I were not bothered, I would be in my bed right now. This is bothersome. You are bothersome. Go. To. Sleep."

"I am quiet, I am still. Why may I not sit and think?"

"Because this is the time for sleeping. And the less thinking you do, the better off you will be here. Believe me. Ah, here it is." Miss Burns arrived with a glass that she handed to Miss Grady. Though the light from Miss Burns's candle showed the liquid was clear, I knew it was not water.

"This will make you sleep," said Miss Grady

"Help you sleep," amended Miss Burns.

Coming close, Miss Grady held it under my nose. "Drink it."

From the powerful scent, it was probably chloral hydrate. I recalled with fear the stories of women who had become addicted to that wretched stuff. More than simply resistance now, this was becoming a battle for my wits. "No, thank you."

"Drink it down this instant."

"I will not," I answered.

"You are determined to be troublesome, aren't you?"

"No," I said with growing mulishness. "I simply do not want to sleep just this moment."

Miss Grady waited a long moment before storming from my cell. Miss Burns said, "Please try to sleep." And she shut the door.

A victory. *See, I am not a coward.*

My inner voice did not reply. Perhaps it suspected trouble.

Ten minutes later I was considering putting my head on my pillow when again I heard the clack of the heels on the floor outside. The door opened and Dr. Kinier stepped into my cell, the offensive glass in his hand.

"Nellie Brown," he said with drowsy boredom, "drink this and go to sleep."

"I do not want to sleep just now. And I do not want to lose my wits."

"Too late for that," he said with dark humor. "Just be a good girl and drink this and we may all go to our beds."

Biting my lip, I shook my head.

That brought an immediate change to the air. Dr. Kinier set aside gentleness, and even politeness. "Fine. Fine. If that's the way you want to be, I won't waste any more time with you. Miss Grady, fetch me a syringe."

Panic flooded through me. If they injected the foul stuff into my body, there was no hope of resisting. But if I swallowed it. . .

"I will drink."

Smug with satisfaction, Dr. Kinier held out the glass. Then he withdrew it for a moment. I was confused. Reaching into his bag, he withdrew a phial and before my eyes he doubled the portion in the cup. Only then did he put the glass in my hand.

I wondered what would happen if I smashed it. *You will probably end up in the Lodge.*

Miss Grady's toady face was expansive with anticipation. "Drink it."

I opened my mouth and drank it down at a single gulp. The doctor made me open my mouth to prove I had swallowed, then patted me on the head. "Good night, Nellie Brown." He left.

"Put your head on that pillow and give yourself over," instructed Miss Grady. I curled up on the bed, and put my head on the pillow. Nodding once, she departed.

"Sleep well," said Miss Burns with sad kindness, and shut the door.

No sooner had I heard the heavy lock turn over than I leaned over the side of my bed and pressed two fingers into my mouth and down my throat. I was already dazed, my eyelids drooping, but I forced myself to press on.

It took several tries, and I worried at the retching noises I was making. But after two minutes there was a little pool on the floor, and the chloral was allowed to try its effect there.

Returning my head to the pillow, I stared at the darkness, feeling woozy and weightless. Scenes started drifting before my eyes, in strange hues of brown and orange. I could hear music, a chorus of "Auld Lang Syne."

And I was fourteen again, and singing by a piano, trying to spite Ford by enjoying New Year's Night.

I am there, and it's all so real. . .

HOLIDAYS ARE A DREADFUL TIME. Because Ford loves them. I think he likes the excuse to drink without guilt. Every Christmas, New Year's, Easter, Fourth of July, he insists on big celebrations and becomes enraged if things are not just right. He always catches Mother out for small imperfections: the bunting is hung wrong, the food isn't ripe enough, the candles aren't bright enough. Nothing Mother does is ever good enough.

Christmas and New Year's Eve are both awful, vibrating with violence and nastiness. A snickering Ford tries to teach little Harry to call Mother a "black-eyed devil."

To relieve our hearts, Mother has taken us to the New Year's Night celebration thrown by our church at the Odd Fellows Hall on Main Street. Little children run about, but I am expected to sit with Mother and the other ladies, chatting.

I hear the commotion from the floor below us, smell the reek of whiskey as Ford barges up the stairs, cringe as he storms toward us with his pistol. "You inconsiderate bitch! I'll kill you, even if you were the last woman on earth!"

He points the gun at my mother's head.

For the first time in my life I'm glad to see Albert, who jumps on Ford with two other men. I reach out and clutch Mother's hand, dragging her down the back stairs and into the street. Breathless from running, we come at last to the Kings' home, where Mother hides behind the chimney while Mr. King stamps up and down the room swearing and calling for Ford's head.

I feel the sickening lurch when, next morning, Mother takes us back home.

Back to him.

"I love him," she tells us. "It will be better now."

I won't be better. It can't go on. *Why is everything spinning?*

Ford is here, a cocked hammer, vowing never to drink again. It's my job to make the gun go away. So I needle him as only a fourteen-year-old girl can. Night after night, I never let up. If there's a politician he detests, I heap praise. If there's a neighbor he despises, I sing paeans. If there's an opinion he holds, I deride it.

Time hurtles by. In March he swats my head.

In July he strikes my face.

In August he throws me into a wall.

In September our house of cards comes crashing down.

"I think Mr. Stitt's new horse and wagon is nowhere near so fine as the one Mother used to own," I say, slurring my words. "You know, the ones she sold to pay your debts."

His hand goes up and I clench my jaw. But Mother steps between us. "No. No more."

That ignites him. Swearing at us all, he is terrifying as he pummels the furniture to splinters, punches holes in the walls, shreds baskets of flowers, kicks a hole in the rocking chair's wicker seat. The next day he's still in a state, taking all our freshly ironed clothes and dragging them through the backyard, pouring bucket after bucket across them. At dinner that night he smashes his coffee cup on the floor even as he waves the carving knife in the air. He flings a bone at Mother, and when she flings it back, he finally draws his pistol.

I know that pistol so well. A Remington New Model Army with a long octagonal barrel and a walnut handle, scored and chipped. Having stolen it many times and secretly unloaded it even more, I've considered firing it. One shot and I can save my family.

But I don't have the gun. He does. And he's pointing it at Mother's head.

Suddenly I'm between them, looking down the maw of that pistol, wondering if this is the moment.

Albert puts his body between me and the gun and yells, "Mother! Run!" Albert and I keep getting between Ford and Mother as he tries to aim. Finally she's out the door, and Kate and Henry and Charlie too.

That's when Albert turns and runs.

Leaving me alone with Ford.

Who fires the gun.

It's an impotent shot, through the empty front door. But the bullet passes within a foot of me. I feel its passage through the air, smell the cordite even as my ears take in the snap.

I want to turn and run. But I'm the last outlet for his rage. If I show fear, he will put a slug between my tiny shoulders. So I stand here, staring, waiting.

"Your mother's a whore, and a bitch, Pinky. And you're just like her."

"I hope so," I tell him.

He doesn't hear me. "You are. No sense in your head. Want to be a boy, don't you, Pinky? Want what you haven't got."

"I don't want anything you've got." With that, I turn and march toward the front door.

My ears strain for the snap of the hammer falling, the pop of the powder igniting, the punch of the bullet.

It doesn't come. I jump as the door slams behind me. It locks.

Just like the lock on the cell door here on Blackwell's.

G ASPING, I ROLLED OVER AND VOMITED again. I was desperately thirsty, but kept spitting, attempting to get the last of the foul chloral out of my body. Struggling to stay on my feet, I staggered to the corner, wedging myself against it and pressing into the wall for strength and support.

Ford! It had been so *real*! It was as if I could still feel his presence in the cell. I slammed the back of my head twice against the stone wall, using the pain to ground myself in the real world.

That memory—I had tried not to think about that night for the last nine years. *Nine years?* I thought of the date. September 29.

It will be exactly nine years tomorrow.

I marveled at the thought. Was it the anniversary that had dredged all this up? Was that the cause of my tears this night, a burst dam of memory? Or was it the look McCarten had given me, making me feel as small as I'd been during those five years with Ford.

I could not be ashamed of my younger self. I looked back at her with awe. She had been fearless.

No, not fearless. She had been afraid. But she had also been determined. Her determination had proven greater than her fear.

Hunched in the corner, slowly reclaiming my thoughts, I recalled how after that day we'd never seen Ford again. He'd stayed in the house tearing up the floorboards and nailing the windows and door shut. No one knew what he was doing, save when he snuck out a second-floor window for liquor.

After a week, Albert and Charlie had ventured back and found the house wrecked. Ford had disappeared after smashing all the furniture in a final act of spite.

That's who Grupe and Grady and McCarten were. They were spiteful creatures, unhappy souls who took out their unhappiness on others.

As my head cleared, I pushed upwards, sliding my back against the wall until I was standing. Lifting my face to the window, I looked up into the night sky, recalling that moment, alone with Ford. The gun pointing at me. Certain I was going to die.

I tried to feel now what I had felt then. It wasn't bravery. The only time women were told to be brave was when they had to endure a hardship. All

the people in Apollo had told Mother to be brave when my father died.
They said it when our money vanished. They said it whenever Ford went
wild.

Bravery for women was enduring men.

No, I hadn't felt brave.

I had felt defiant.

I had felt determined.

I had felt strong.

I had felt *beautiful*.

Returning to the bed at last, I placed my head upon the pillow and, for
the first time since I came to Blackwell's, I slept well.

Forty-Three

Sane Decisions

Friday, September 30 1887

I WOKE TO THE SOUND OF RAIN. The weather mirrored how I felt. Gray at the edges, but cleansed. And determined.

Word of my nighttime ordeal had spread, and I found myself hugged several times as we washed faces. The comb that ran through my hair was gentler than any morning before. I was an object of pity among madwomen.

I tried to be grateful, but mostly I felt resentment. I was fine. Or rather, I would be when I was able to tell my story.

My spirits were high because of my certainty that I would soon be leaving this infernal place. I found cause to be grateful to the *Sun*'s reporters for creating such a fuss over "Nellie Brown." The Colonel could not have missed the story.

He had said I would be here for a week. This was my fifth day on Blackwell's, and I'd been in Bellevue for two days before that. Which meant that the time of my release was either today, if he counted my time in Bellevue, or on the coming Monday if he did not.

This gave me extra determination to find out all I could before I was sprung. Perhaps it was overcompensation for my timidity the night before, but though I felt a little unsteady on my feet, my heart and mind felt ready to grapple with anything.

My renewed self-assurance was tested almost at once. We were all suffering in the sitting room when Miss Grady cried out, "Listen to this!" Holding my book, she began to read aloud from a passage. "'I fear the Quiet Observer will never adore me as I do him. It is enough to love, is it not? It is enough. It is enough.'" She looked about with triumph. "The

Quiet Observer! Ooh-la-la!"

As the other nurses laughed, I flushed. I did not recall writing those sentences, but no one else could have. Had I really been so tired those first few days that such a sentiment could have bubbled up unnoticed from the recesses of my heart? Or were the things I thought so deeply buried actually near the surface?

Miss Grupe drew closer to me. "So. The 'Quiet Observer.' That's what you call him, is it? Your young man who has driven you mad? Does he like to watch you? What is he observing, your lover?"

"He's not—"

"He's not what?" asked Miss Grupe eagerly.

Any comment I made would only fuel their mocking fire. I looked up at her. "It's very cold in here. May we have our shawls?"

Snorting in frustration, Miss Grupe walked away. If I wasn't going to entertain her, she had better things to do.

Shortly thereafter, Dr. Flint entered, his hands in his pockets. When I waved him over, he said, "How are you, Nellie Brown? I trust you had a sound sleep."

"I'm perfectly well. Only it is very cold in here."

"The cold is in your mind," he told me.

I indicated the nurses. "They are wearing coats. Are their minds unsound? Your hands are in your pockets. Is yours?"

Frowning, he turned to Anne. "Anne Neville, why aren't you sewing?"

"Because my eyes are weak," she answered. "Sewing hurts them."

"That doesn't make any difference." He spoke without a trace of kindness. "Others here have weak eyes and they have to sew. The sewing must be done." He turned to me. "Nellie Brown, why don't you sew?"

"Because I do not want to," I answered.

"That doesn't make any difference either. The sewing must be done. Will you not sew?"

"Sewing is just in your mind, doctor."

His face reddened as he took in the suppressed smiles from the ladies around me.

Before he could devise a punishment, Mrs. Cotter tugged his sleeve. "Doctor, it is Friday. You said that I would be going home this week. I hope that is still true, that I am."

"No, you are not," said Dr. Flint roughly. "You might as well know it now."

Mrs. Cotter wavered for a moment, and then burst into tears. Dr. Flint shook his head, muttering, "Have to find another position. So many weeping women."

"There might not be so many weeping women," I said, full-voiced, "if you took our feelings and thoughts into account."

"Nellie Brown," he began.

"Miss Brown, if you please," I snapped.

He gritted his teeth. "Nellie Brown, I understand you were dosed with chloral last night. I presume your current agitation is the after-echo of your distress last night."

"I was in no distress last night until they came into my room and threatened me!"

"You're becoming hysterical. I hope we don't have to dose you again."

Keeping my voice as calm as possible, I said, "Yes, threaten to dose me rather than engage in a debate you know you'll lose. You do not listen to the women here. Miss Mayard over there is deathly ill, and you refuse to even examine her."

Tillie was pale and shivering, her teeth chattered, her skin was pale, and the rings beneath her eyes were fearful. Yet still he declined to see the obvious. "Am I the doctor here, or are you?"

I put my arms around Mrs. Cotter, who bawled into my shoulder. "I am uncertain if I am. But I know you are not."

His jaw unhinged as he chewed air for several seconds. Then he raised a hand. Whether it was to point at me or strike me, I do not know, for he was stymied by the arrival of Dr. Ingram.

This lone good doctor spied the weeping Mrs. Cotter and came hurrying over. "What's the matter?"

Returning his hands to his pockets, Dr. Flint walked away as Mrs. Cotter explained what he had told her. Patting her hand repeatedly, Dr. Ingram said, "Look, Mrs. Cotter. I will do everything in my power to get you released. Now smile once before I leave you. I cannot leave you in tears."

He had to repeat himself several times before she could accept what he said. But when her head came up, she wore a broad smile on her tear-stained face. "There's a good girl."

Before he could move off, I caught him and told him of Tillie's growing illness. Then I added, "You recall the book I asked for? The book I brought here with me, that Miss Grady claimed was hers? She was reading aloud from it this morning, and it is undoubtedly mine—the nurses asked me about it. I would like both that and my pencil returned to me."

"I'll see what I can do," assured Dr. Ingram.

Soon it was time for our walk. This was the promised day of the carousel, but the weather prevented any thought of it, and we were made to march around the sitting room just as if it were the outdoors. We even wore our hats.

I went to partner with Tillie Mayard, thinking to be her crutch. Oddly, she shied away from me at first. Only when I persisted did she relent. "It hurts to walk," she told me. "I have a toenail growing downwards." Indeed, she limped the whole walk, leaning heavily on my arm. Between that pain and her fever, she hardly said a word, and those few she did say made little sense.

After lunch we heard the most terrible caterwauling. "Hurrah! Three cheers! I have killed the devil! Lucifer! Lucifer! Lucifer!"

A redheaded Irish pixie appeared, staggering like a drunk. Her soaked street clothes marked her as a new arrival, but they were only half on, and she was immodestly slipping her shoulder out of her unbuttoned blouse. "Lucifer! Lucifer! I gave it to ye, devil!" She pronounced it "divil."

She lurched into the room to face the women on the nearest bench, which included Louise Schanz and Margaret Bentz, who had found a bond in their shared German ancestry. Leaning into their faces, the new girl said, "They always said God made hell, but He di'int!"

"No," I murmured to Anne beside me. "The state of New York did."

LATE IN THE AFTERNOON, FLINT and Ingram returned. By then the much-amused nurses had gotten the new girl, Pauline Moser, to cease undressing and sit beside them. As Dr. Flint entered, Miss Grupe pointed to him and whispered to the Irish lass, "Here's the devil, coming for you. Go for him! Show us how you give it to him!" Thankfully, the girl was too invested in singing hideously obscene songs to bother with the doctor.

While Dr. Ingram sought out Mrs. Cotter to discuss her release, I marched up to Dr. Flint. "Miss Tillie Mayard is very ill. She has been for several days. And she has an ingrowing nail in her foot that is troubling her—"

"Have you one?"

"Me?" I blinked, surprised. "No."

"Then keep quiet and allow others to speak for themselves."

"Are you going to examine her?"

"I am not answerable to you, Nellie Brown."

You will be. Aloud, I said, "What are you doctors here for?"

"To take care of the patients and test their sanity," he replied in a biting tone.

I put my hands on my hips. "Very well. Try every test on me, and tell me: am I sane or insane?"

"There is no need. You are here already."

I wished I had studied Latin more, for there was a phrase that I could not remember that would have been particularly cutting in that moment.

Lacking the words, I had to try a different tack. "That explains the laziness of the doctors here."

"Laziness!"

"There are sixteen doctors on this island, and excepting Dr. Ingram, I have never seen you pay any attention to the patients. How can a doctor judge a woman's sanity by merely bidding her good morning and refusing to hear her complaints? Even the sick ones know it's useless to say anything, because the answer will be that it is their imagination."

"Well, it is!" He was growing quite hot. "That's the nature of insanity!"

Unlike him, I had preserved my temper this time. "Doctors take an oath, do they not? Does your oath mean nothing?"

"I—I never—this is an outrage—!"

"Excuse me, Miss Brown." Dr. Ingram interposed himself between me and the blustering Flint. "May I have a word with you?"

He meant it kindly. But I was in no mood to retreat, so I pointed toward Flint. "This is the most impudent man I have ever met! He is paid for work he does not perform, and lords himself over us as if we should worship the ground upon which he deigns to trod."

"Well, that is the nature of doctors," said Dr. Ingram agreeably. "Pardon us, Dr. Flint. I must speak with Miss Brown." Taking me gently by the arm, he led me out into the hallway and down to his office, where he offered me a chair.

"Thank you," I said as I sat. "Now. Did you ask about my book?"

"I did. But first I have a question to ask you. Is your real name Lottie?"

I blinked. "What?"

"Lottie. Is that your name?"

I started to laugh. "No!"

"The name Lottie Peters means nothing to you?"

"Nothing at all," I said, with complete honesty. "Why? Who is she?"

"We thought she might be you."

"Whyever would you think that?"

"There is a woman missing from New Orleans of that name. One of her friends, hearing of your case, thought you might be she."

"Oh, for Heaven's sake!" I cried. "Perhaps if you all were practicing medicine rather than amateur detection there would not be so many sick women here!"

Dr. Ingram raised his hands. "I know, I know. None of us do as much as we should. But I promise you we do all we can."

"*You* do," I allowed. "I cannot say anything kind about the other doctors here."

"So, to be clear, you are not Lottie Peters? You've never heard of her?"

"I am not Lottie Peters," I assured him, "nor have I heard her name before this minute."

He wrinkled the corner of his mouth. "It is strange. You seem so very clear on that point, yet so vague on your own history. It is as though there is a block, a partition, walling off the truth of your past."

Of course, he was perfectly correct. A wall of my own making. "Perhaps the return of my book will aid my memory."

He held up his hand. "I have asked that it be returned to you. Though Nurse Grady says you only brought the book. That the pencil is hers."

"Of course it isn't! What good is a book without a pencil?"

He leaned forward. "Nellie, please. Try hard. Fight your imagination. Why would Miss Grady say it was hers if it wasn't?" I shook my head. "What is it, Miss Brown?"

Taking a breath, I spoke to him as I would to a friend who was wasting his life. "You seem like a kind and decent man. But you have no notion what's happening here, do you? The beatings. The monstrous threats. The cruelty."

He looked concerned, and for the span of a moment I thought he believed me. "You were given chloral last night. You might still be a little confused."

Disappointed, I closed my eyes. "I'm not confused, doctor. I know what's real. Better than you do, it seems. The nurses are tyrants. They beat the patients. Not me, thank Heaven. Not yet, at least. But the cruelty they display is obvious to anyone with eyes."

"The nurses are a handful of women charged with caring for hundreds. I'm sure accidents happen."

"Accidents! It's astounding how many 'accidents' happen to the patients who fall afoul of Miss Grady and Miss Grupe. And what if there was a real accident? Tell me, what would happen if there was a fire? All the cells are locked at night. What would happen to the women inside?"

"The nurses are expected to open the doors," he said simply.

"You know positively that they would not wait to do that. These poor women would burn to death. You *know* that."

Unable to contradict me, Dr. Ingram sat silent. That silence was utterly damning.

"Why don't you do something to remedy all this?" I insisted.

"What can I do?" he replied with real anguish. "I offer suggestions until my brain is tired, and what good does it do? What would you do?"

"Are you asking the insane girl? Well, I'd start by putting in locks joined by a single crank. I've seen them, they work. Turn the one crank and you can unlock every door on that side. Then there would be some chance of escape. Now there is absolutely none."

Dr. Ingram turned in his swivel chair, a new expression on his kind face.

"What institution have you been an inmate of before you came here?"

I blinked. "None. I never was confined in any institution, except boarding school, in my life."

"Then where did you see the locks you describe?"

Too late, I recognized my mistake. I had seen them reporting on the new Western Penitentiary in Pittsburgh. But I could hardly say so. No, having given him a supposed clue about myself, he could freely ignore the good sense to my argument. "Oh, I saw them in a place I was in—as a visitor."

"There is only one place I know of where they have those locks," he said, "and that is at Sing Sing."

To him the inference was clearly conclusive. I couldn't help myself. I burst into laughter. "No, Dr. Ingram, I assure you! I have never been in prison in my life."

Then I sobered a little. "Until now."

W HEN THEY RETURNED ME TO the sitting room, I was immediately confronted by Miss Grady, who slapped my book into my hand. "You need to learn to stop talking to the doctors. They're not the ones who are with you night and day. Watch yourself."

I had a mad impulse to brain her with the book. I raised it as if to look at it, but before I could make up my mind, the new girl, Miss Moser, began shouting. "You devil! I'll give it to you!"

Beside the newcomer, Miss Grupe was pointing to the photograph of the Negro minstrel. "You mean this devil?"

"I'll give it to you!" With her fists doubled, the pixie hurled herself at the picture, smashing it.

Miss Grady pushed past me to join Miss Grupe in wrestling the redheaded waif to the floor.

I had the impulse to leap in and join the fray on the side of the pixie. After all, I needed a complete picture of this place. That meant seeing the Lodge up close. Or at least the Retreat. *If I am to explore the whole depravity of this wicked place, do I not have an obligation to experience it all?*

Giving in to my impulse, I was starting forward when someone caught my arm. It was Bridget McGuiness, who guided me to a bench far from the fracas and sat me firmly down. "Whatever you're planning, don't."

"I don't know what you mean," I said, but unconvincingly.

"I know that look," said Bridget. "I saw it last night on Mrs. Turney. Why do you want to pick a fight with the nurses?"

"Pick a reason. They made fun of my book. They're cruel. They deserve a good kicking."

"All you'll get is a ticket to the Lodge."

I raised my chin. "If that's what happens, so be it."

Bridget's eyes narrowed. Then, all of a sudden, the story she had withheld days before came tumbling out. Not as gossip. As a warning. "While I was there, a pretty young girl was brought in. She fought. Called it a filthy place, said she didn't want to be there. Nurses didn't like her complaining. They took her, beat her, held her naked in the bath, threw her on her bed." After a moment, Bridget shrugged. "Morning came, girl was dead. Doctors said she died of convulsions. That was all."

I stared into her eyes, weighing a hundred factors. "That's murder."

"Yes," said Bridget evenly. "Yes, it is. So stay out of the Lodge." Her warning delivered, she stood and moved away from me as if I had a contagious disease.

The nurses were now dragging away Miss Moser, who was tearing her own hair. Doubtless, she was being taken to the closet for a beating.

I was not afraid of a beating. Lord knew, Ford had taught me that injuries heal.

But death doesn't.

I recalled my interview with Colonel Sirwell two years earlier. "Pick your battles wisely," he'd said. "When you take ground, you must hold it. Plant your flag and stand."

I had planted my flag here on Blackwell's. It was enough to hold it. It was not bravery to court death, nor was it cowardice to pick my battles.

One button was enough.

Forty-Four

Transfer

Saturday, October 1 1887

I WAS A LITTLE DISAPPOINTED NOT to be freed on Friday afternoon. In fairness, I had only been there for five days, and had yet to experience a weekend on Blackwell's. Nevertheless, I felt certain that come Monday I would be away from this vile place. *Then let these nurses come into my sight!*

By Saturday morning, I was glad I had stayed. Tillie was in a dreadful state. Touching her forehead as we sat on the benches in Hall Six, I discovered that she was burning up.

Enough was enough. I was marching up to the nurses huddled beside the steam heater, when there was a sudden gasp behind me, followed by cries. Turning around, I saw Tillie had fainted dead away. Anne had caught her and was trying to revive her.

"Let her fall on the floor!" Miss Grupe told Anne. "Teach her a lesson."

I was opening my mouth to berate their inhumanity when a nurse I did not recognize entered. "Dr. Dent wants Nellie Brown."

"This is she." Rising to cover the commotion at the far end of the room, Miss Grady dragged me forward by the arm. "Take her and good riddance."

Is this it? Is this my deliverance? I felt a swell of relief, and immediately regretted it. *What about Tillie?*

I followed the new nurse out of Hall Six, through that curious entryway and up the twisting stairs and to the office of Superintendent Dent. "Here is Nellie Brown, Superintendent."

Upon entering the office, I received a double shock. The first was the sight of Dent and Dr. Ingram chatting with seven men who were obviously reporters, based on their pencils and notepads.

My second shock came when I recognized one of the men: none other than George McCain, my fellow reporter from the *Dispatch*!

Seeing me, his eyes widened, and I prayed he would not spoil the game. To forestall any outburst from him, I turned to the superintendent. "Dr. Dent, Miss Tillie Mayard has just fallen into a fit in Hall Six. She is feverish, and the nurses are doing nothing for her."

The superintendent frowned, then quickly smiled for the reporters. "I'm sure it's nothing. But I will go at once. Please excuse me. Dr. Ingram, remain with Miss Brown."

I was offered a seat, and all seven reporters gazed eagerly at me, pencils quivering. McCain was seated furthest away, and was entirely quiet as Dr. Ingram fielded the first question. "What's the matter with her, doctor?"

"Her case is diagnosed as melancholia," said Dr. Ingram.

"Is there any hope?" asked the man from the *Sun*.

"Oh, I am very hopeful." Dr. Ingram laughed. "Every day she asks the same question. 'Am I sane, or insane?' A hopeless case does not question her sanity. The fact that she has doubts is an excellent sign."

The questions turned to me. One man tried to catch me out by speaking in Spanish, another in French. I answered them in English, but made clear I understood them. I continued the fiction about my parentage, and vehemently denied being the missing girl Lottie Peters.

"I feel better every day." I looked directly at McCain. "I promise you, soon I will tell all about myself."

Either he didn't understand my hint, or he ignored it. "Excuse me, Miss Brown—Nellie—I wondered if you knew me."

I raised my brows politely. "How should I know you?"

"I feel we've met before. I'm just having a hard time remembering where."

"If I knew you, why would I not say so?"

"Perhaps you don't wish to know anyone. Or be known."

I laughed. "I am known! But I don't want to know you. Any of you. I can't imagine why in the *world* I would want to know reporters. You look for all the *world* to be strangers. What in the *world* possessed you to talk to me?"

If he doesn't understand that heavy-handed hint, he's denser than I thought. Still, I thought to add another clue. "What is your name?"

"McCain," he said.

Shaking my head, I said, "Ay-ay-ay," using a Spanish lament I had heard often in Mexico. "I know no McCain. I knew a Mrs. Macdona once, in Cuba. I talked to her all about my life. She would take me out of here."

Feeling ignored, the reporter from the Sun said, "Do you want to be here?"

Still looking at McCain, I chose my words carefully. "I keep telling them that I do not. This place is like a strange story, one I would not have ever believed. I tell them I am sane, but they do not believe it. I feel like a quiet observer, watching my own life here. It would make quite a tale."

"Oh, our readers are very interested," said the *Sun*'s reporter as McCain slowly folded his notebook closed.

Dr. Ingram looked at his watch. "Gentlemen, that's as much time as we can allow. I'm afraid Miss Brown must look to her recovery."

They thanked the doctor and said farewell to me as they exited, trying to elicit one last statement. I simply stared at them. When it came to McCain, I gave him the slightest of nods.

He winked, and I released a small sigh of relief.

Dr. Ingram saw that relief as he closed the door. "Sorry about that. They've been hounding the superintendent all week. We thought the best way to dismiss them was to give them what they want."

"I see." I paused. "Dr. Ingram. May I ask you a personal question?"

"You may ask," he said with a wary smile. "I'll not promise to answer."

"It is very impertinent," I said. "You may re-evaluate my sanity."

"I think you'd better ask it at once, then, don't you?"

I looked at him gravely. "What does the *H* stand for?"

He blinked. "Excuse me?"

"Dr. Frank H. Ingram. What does the *H* stand for? Several of the girls are wondering, and they've taken to making wagers. Hamish is the favorite contender, but also Harrison, Horatio, Horace, and Homer."

"That's quite a fanciful list!" said Dr. Ingram, laughing. "I'm afraid it's nothing so bold. In fact, I now hesitate to tell you, as it will seem far too prosaic."

"Then I think you'd better tell me at once, don't you?"

He laughed, a real laugh, as one caught off guard. "Harold. Frank Harold Ingram."

"Did you always want to be a doctor?"

He puzzled for a bit. "I'm not sure I thought about it in those terms. My father was a banker, and expected me to follow in his footsteps. But when he died, the doctors were all helpless. I suppose I wanted to understand what they could not."

"So you came to New York to study medicine. When was that?"

"About ten years ago." Meaning he was about twenty-six or twenty-seven.

"What led you to mental disorders?"

"Is this your revenge? Is it my turn to be interrogated by a reporter?" Still, he answered. "It is a field open to interpretation, and of sudden interest. If we are to understand people's actions, we must understand their motives. Motive matters, Miss Brown. Motive is the key to understanding, and understanding is the key to empathy. We have so little understanding for our fellow man. So many cannot comprehend a problem unless they have themselves lived it. And people alienated from themselves are the most lost, and most in need of understanding."

"Do you know the poet Joaquin Miller?" I asked.

"I don't believe I do."

"There is a line from one of his poems." And I quoted:

> In men whom men condemn as ill
> I find so much of goodness still.
> In men whom men pronounce divine
> I find so much of sin and blot
> I do not dare to draw a line
> Between the two, where God has not.

The doctor had begun rearranging the chairs, returning them to their places. "I wish I knew more of poetry. So much truth in so few words." He paused, a wistful smile on his face. "I had a professor at Bellevue who said what seemed to me to be the wisest proverb I shall ever hear. 'It doesn't matter what you choose to learn, so long as you learn to learn deeply.' That, to me, is key. Once you have learned how to explore a subject, wring from it every ounce of meaning, and you can then attack any subject with the same ferocity. It strikes me now that the same applies to empathy. Once you have learned to have compassion for one group of people, it is hard not to have equal sympathy for another group. Compassion is a bucket above a bottomless well. We can always find more, if we so choose. It only goes dry if we choose not to lower the bucket."

"So you believe lack of compassion is a choice?"

"Not necessarily," he said, lowering himself into a chair, properly distant from mine. "Not always. At first it is ignorance. An inability to look beyond one's self. But from the moment that bucket is first dipped, from that time on, it is a choice. Once a soul has learned to have compassion for one downtrodden soul, it must be an active decision not to have compassion for another. Learning cannot be unlearned. It can only be ignored."

"What allows people to ignore their compassion?"

"When they fear compassion will prove costly. Which it never is. Compassion is the best of humanity. It is the backbone of all good religion, and all good medicine. People turn their back on compassion when they feel they are losing control. So they label others not worthy of their compassion. Negroes. Immigrants. Women. The bankrupt. The diseased. People who are—"

"Inconvenient," I supplied.

"Inconvenient?"

"I will tell you a secret, Doctor Ingram. Most of the women here are no less sane than you or I. Very few are a danger to themselves or to others. But here they are, because there is no other place for them. They are not mad. They are inconvenient."

"Surely not!"

"You think not? I have been told often enough in my life that I am crazy. Crazy for not wanting to marry. For not wanting children. For wanting to work. For not wanting what I was supposed to want, and for wanting things denied to me. I was called crazy for being troublesome, loud, inquisitive—inconvenient." I waved a hand to the walls around us. "That's what all these women have in common. They are inconvenient. To their husbands, their children, their relations, their community. To society. They are inconvenient, and too poor to pay for that inconvenience. I doubt you have any rich ladies here on the Island."

"No," he agreed. "I doubt we do."

"Madness in the rich is eccentricity. They can afford to be inconvenient. Think of that word, *convenient*. I find it insidious."

"Why, what does it mean to you?"

"What does it mean to *you*?"

He rallied gamely. "I suppose it means *easy*. Comfortable. At hand. Something that requires no effort. A thing to make life easier."

"That's what the world wants women to be. A convenience. A balm to their hurts, a comfort to their nights, a grease to the tracks of their lives. Any woman who is not one of those things is damned as being mad. Crazed. Hysterical. *Insane*."

I fell silent, and Dr. Ingram stared as if trying to peer inside my head. "I confess, Nellie Brown, your case confounds me. You seem so very lucid, I wonder you are in here at all. I have no doubt that you have a hopeful future before you once you are released."

"I fear that will never come so long as I am on Hall Six. The nurses there are wickedly cruel." I recounted the worst offenses I had seen Miss Grady and Miss Grupe perform.

After two minutes Dr. Ingram held up a hand. "I know sometimes women have a difficult time getting along. It's just something in your nature."

"There it is!" I cried, rolling my eyes. "You refuse to believe what I say, because it would be inconvenient. It would disorder your world. Whereas if a man was beaten, choked, doused with ice water, he would be believed. You say a lack of empathy is a choice? What are you choosing right now, doctor?"

That brought him up short. For a moment he worried his lower lip.

Then he said, "What if I were to transfer you to a quieter ward?"

"And Miss Neville and Miss Mayard, if you please. All three of us."

"I'll do what I can. Miss Mayard may be too ill. You said she had a fit this morning? She might be better off where she is."

"I promise you, she is not."

BACK IN HALL SIX, I FOUND Tillie sitting upright, her head in her hands. I went to Anne. "What happened?"

"Dr. Dent came, took hold of her forehead, and pinched it until her face was crimson. She came to herself, so I suppose it worked. But she has a terrible headache now."

I went directly to Tillie and wrapped her in my arms. "Oh, my dear! I wish I hadn't sent him. I only hoped he could help—"

"Why did you go?" asked Tillie harshly.

"I had to go to the office. They had reporters there."

"I thought so." She looked at me, and there was venom in her fevered eyes. "What name did you give them?"

"What?"

"What name did you give them? Nellie Moreno? Nellie Brown? Lottie Peters?" Her face hardened. "Or was it Tillie Mayard?"

"Tillie, what—?"

"You admit it! You said you were me! You're passing yourself off as me to be released." Her head swayed as she poured forth with a passion I had not seen in her. "There's no reason for me to be here! I'm not crazy! But you are! You are! You're happy to be here, you keep asking everyone questions so you can learn all about us and then, when one of us is ill, you can pretend to be her and get released!"

Shocked, I kept my voice soothing. "You're not well, Tillie."

"Of course I'm not! That's why you can prey upon me this way. You're a devil. A devil!"

Across the hall, the pixie picked up the cry. "A divil! A divil!"

Tillie paid her no mind. "It won't work. You'll see! You'll see, my friends will know you're not me and you'll be right back in here and I'll be free. . ."

I tried to reason with her, but she had only wicked things to say. She worked herself into such a lather that I had to retreat, much to the amusement of the nurses. For the rest of the morning I kept my distance from her, for her sake as well as mine.

An hour later Miss Grady called, "Nellie Brown. Come out into the hallway." Thinking of the promised transfer, I obediently joined her.

Once out of sight of the other patients, the head nurse raised a finger and jabbed at my face. "You ratbag hussy. You damn wagtail. You forget all about yourself, but your memory works fine when you talk about us to the doctors. Little guttersnipe. It's a lucky thing for your hide that you're being transferred, or I'd pay you for remembering me so well to Dr. Ingram." She leaned back into the doorway. "Anne Neville! You come along too. You're being transferred."

Startled, Anne quickly stood, causing Tillie to leap up as well. "See! See! She's getting out by pretending to be me!"

Miss Grady grinned nastily. "Don't have many friends, do you?"

"Please look after her," I said. "She's not well, surely you can see that."

"I certainly don't see as much as you do, you preening tart. Now come along. And don't forget your damned book."

With no other belongings to speak of, we followed Miss Grady out of Hall Six and up the stairs to Hall Seven. There she transferred us to the care of a nurse called Miss Hart. "Good riddance."

Miss Hart studied us with distaste. "Oh, so you're troublesome, are you?"

Anne and I exchanged a look. "We don't mean to be."

First we were taken to see a new doctor, one Dr. Caldwell. He chucked me under the chin as if we were old shipmates, then began the litany of questions. As I was tired of refusing to tell where my home was, I spoke to him only in Spanish. He grew frustrated, especially when I laughed at the crinkle in his tiny nose. After that he left me alone. As I was led from his office to my new abode, I heard him say to a nurse, "Extra restrictions for that one." I wondered what that meant.

Hall Seven looked rather nicer than Hall Six. It, too, was hung with cheap pictures and had a piano. But, being on a higher floor, it was brighter. Better, it did not vibrate with the fearful crouchings of its patients.

The real difference was the music. The piano in Hall Seven was in tune, kept so by a remarkable patient called Mattie Morgan. She had worked in a music store before her commitment, and now devoted herself to teaching all the lucid inmates of Hall Seven how to sing.

The moment I entered, she rushed up to me. "Do you sing? What is your range? Alto, or soprano?"

"Soprano," I said.

"Yes, you have the neck for it. And you?" she demanded of Anne.

"Soprano as well."

"That's a pity. We have too many sopranos at present. Ah, well. Perhaps we can extend your range."

"I also play piano," I offered.

"Oh, do you?" She seemed less than impressed. "Excellent. Let's hear."

Feeling I had entered an audition rather than a lunatic ward, I dutifully crossed to the piano and began to play. Unimpeded by the painful clunks of ill-tuned keys, my playing grew bolder, more confident.

"That's very well," said Mattie when I finished. "Though I should watch my tempo on the bridge, were I you."

I might have been offended, but a little later I heard her play. A true virtuoso, Mattie could have played in any concert hall in Pittsburgh without fear.

She was also a skilled teacher. All the women in her little choir sang on pitch, with good breath support. The artiste of the hall was a Polish girl called Wanda. She was an even more gifted pianist than Mattie, able to read the most difficult music at a glance, and her touch and expression were perfect.

That first day I found life on Hall Seven almost pleasant. Women were allowed to chat, not sit in rigid fearfulness. Not that the nurses were particularly kind. There were four: Mrs. Kroener, Miss Fitzpatrick, Miss Finney, and Miss Hart. I did not see such cruel treatment as downstairs, but I heard all of them make ugly remarks and threats, and Miss Hart made a habit of twisting fingers and slapping faces if anyone was unruly.

Nevertheless, they were not immune to the pleasures of Miss Morgan's music, and none owned that positive delight in cruelty that Miss Grupe and Miss Grady possessed.

No, that was reserved for the night nurse.

Miss Conway met us after our dinner—which was still awful—and told us in the plainest manner that she was cross. "I'm in a foul mood tonight, so no lip!"

As I changed for bed, I discovered Hall Seven was quite different in one respect. Already in scarce supply below, modesty here was nonexistent. Each patient was made to undress in the hallway, in plain view, and then fold our day clothes and leave them outside our doors until morning. Only then could we enter our rooms and put on our nightdresses.

Watching the others, Anne and I glanced at each other. "Miss Conway? Could we not change in our rooms?"

Miss Conway marched right up to me. Inches from my nose, she hissed, "If I ever catch you even trying such a trick, I'll make you regret it."

With weary reluctance, I stripped naked, feeling Miss Conway's eyes on me the whole time. When I squatted to lay my clothes on the floor, she remarked, "Why so dainty, Brown? Hardly anything to be modest about."

Flushing with shame, I padded into my assigned room and hurriedly donned an unclaimed nightgown.

While washing before bed, I found there were no basins in the bathroom, only old metal buckets suspended over the taps. I wondered if the buckets were ever cleaned. I was certain that if I asked, I would be the next one to clean them.

I shared my new room with five other women. Three went at once to their beds and curled up. Not wishing to make an enemy by displacing anyone, I waited for the other two to lay claim to their cots before choosing mine.

But they made no move toward any bed. One began to pace the room. The other knelt beside the window, gazing out at the night.

Tentatively taking an unclaimed bed, I closed my eyes.

It seemed that Hall Seven had no rules about patients having to sleep at night. Miss Conway never came in to scold the two insomniacs. One sat by the window while the other ranged the room, often passing my bed, her gown brushing my mattress. Her name was Doris, a fact I learned because she talked about herself in the third person. "Doris will have her revenge. Oh yes, on Din and Gillespie and Coley and Adams—oh yes, on Adams." As she prowled, she raved in shocking terms, and I soon discerned she was searching for someone she wanted to kill. I was desperately glad it was not me. There was something to be said for the harshness of Hall Six after all.

The sleepless patient by the window was a middle-aged woman with the most wonderful illness. Her name was Vanessa, and she had a scrap of newspaper that she would hold up to the sky. By the moon's light she "read" aloud the most imaginative, beautiful, romantic stories. I lay listening for hours, entranced. History and fantasy combined into marvelous epics. I wish I had written them down, for I could never have invented such magnificent tales.

Daybreak erased her conjuring powers, and she remained mute through the weary process of day, only to come alive again with the dimming of the lights.

Vanessa was the only madwoman for whom I felt envy.

ON SUNDAY THE QUIET AND OBEDIENT patients were allowed to go to church services. I'd seen the small Catholic chapel on the island, and I was told there were also Protestant services. Apparently, I was considered neither quiet nor obedient, because I was not afforded the chance to go.

Hall Seven had a visitor that morning. She had come to see her cousin, bringing with her a small babe in arms. Spying the baby, one patient rushed close. "Oh, please—I have been away from my five little ones so long. May I please hold her?" Reluctantly, the mother handed over her baby to the maternal madwoman, who was suffused with joy.

She spent the next three-quarters of an hour singing and talking to the child, while the infant's mother relaxed. "What a good nanny you would make," the mother remarked, at which the patient glowed.

Things altered when the mother wanted to leave. The madwoman claimed the child was hers, that the mother was attempting to steal it. With the help of the nurses, the mother recovered her child and fled, and the miserable madwoman's howls for the child agitated everyone on the ward.

I was able to note all this in my book, for I had been given a pencil. It felt like a blast of freedom, that little bit of wood and graphite. Though not as fine as my own, I was hardly about to complain. It was astonishing how, when we have been deprived of them, the smallest things could become the biggest blessings.

The day went on, with music and chatter as I got to know these women as I'd done the ones below. There was a Mexican woman who delighted in speaking Spanish to me, no matter how little I could reply in her native tongue.

I worked extra hard to record details, not just from Hall Seven, but from my whole time on Blackwell's. I had to cram in as much reporting as I could manage, for the next day would be my last on the island.

Casual cruelty was still present. At bedtime that night, two patients complained of dry throats and begged for a drink of water, but Miss Hart and Miss Conway refused to unlock the bathroom, when it would have cost them nothing.

Despite being thirsty myself, I made sure not to complain. Nor did I sleep that night for excitement. I thought of all the things I would do when I was out of this terrible place. Take a proper bath. Have a proper meal. A beefsteak and a sweet potato. Some fluffy, crusty bread. A ripe piece of fruit. An apple, or maybe a pear.

Then I would write up my story, telling it first to the *World*, then to the world. It was certain to be a sensation, and I needed to remember every bit of my experience, both here and in Bellevue. There was a word for what I had been through, but I was so tired I could not recall it just then.

As Vanessa told her stories and the girl called Doris prowled around muttering threats, I stayed up all through Sunday night making notes on the events of the past week. At times, I found myself philosophizing in writing:

> *What a mysterious thing madness is. I've watched patients whose lips are sealed in a perpetual silence. They live, breathe, eat. The human form is there, but that something, which the body can live without but which cannot exist without the body, was missing. I wonder if behind those sealed lips there are dreams we ken not of, or if all is blank?*

Just as sad are those cases where the patients converse with invisible parties. I've seen them wholly unconscious of their surroundings, engrossed with an invisible being. Yet they obeyed any command, in about the same manner as a dog obeys his master.

One of the most pitiful delusions of any of the patients is that of a blue-eyed Irish girl here on Hall Seven, who believes she is forever damned because of one act in her life. Her horrible cry, morning and night, "I am damned for all eternity!" strikes horror to my soul. Her agony seems like a glimpse of the inferno.

Yet, as I told Dr. Ingram, the majority of these women are not mad. They are merely inconvenient to society. And so they are placed here, in this human rat-trap. It is easy to get in, but impossible to get out.

Oh, my prophetic soul.

FORTY-FIVE

No Exit

MONDAY, OCTOBER 3 1887

I SPENT MONDAY LIKE A BIRD on a clothesline. The slightest vibration had me up and moving to the windows, or else toward the door. Every step in the hall, every voice heard below, every turn of the hours, I was certain was the herald of my emancipation.

There were visitors being given a tour. They paused to listen to Miss Morgan play on the piano, clustering close to her until one whispered, "You know she's a patient." Then they all retreated as if she had leprosy, leaving her equal parts amused and indignant.

A lady called Gwendolyn received a letter, the first I had seen delivered to any patient. Apparently, it was such a rare occurrence that it was considered a treat, and all the women of Hall Seven begged Gwendolyn to read it out, crowding around her to drink in news from the outside world.

I was not among them. Instead, I was staring out the window.

"Where have you gone?" asked Anne.

"Gone?" I said, startled.

"You must not become of those." She nodded across the room to a woman staring vacantly at nothing. "The ghost women. Not even here, just haunting this place. I would not be surprised to see them walk through a wall."

"This place probably does have ghosts," I said, and I swear I felt a chill pass through me.

Luncheon passed, and there was still no sign of a caller for me. That afternoon, Anne and I were told we would be working in the scrub brush factory on the island. *A factory girl once more.*

I protested, saying, "I am expecting a visitor."

"No visitors," Miss Hart told me. "You're on restriction. Dr. Caldwell's orders."

So that's what he meant! I trudged off to the factory, wishing I had not been so petulant with him. What if the doctor's order kept the Colonel's agents away from me?

Oh, God—what if he can't get me out?

That was a thought that festered rapidly. What if they had petitioned the court and been rejected? Or, horribly, what if he had decided I was too *inconvenient* to rescue? I'd embarrassed him in the *Journalist* with my story about hiring women. Was he a man who would sacrifice a woman for the sake of his pride?

Is there a man alive who wouldn't?

But no, the Colonel was not a villain. He had murdered a man once, true, but in self-defense. He would not murder me this way.

Though he might not think it murder. He might think, from my mad rush to pitch him an insane story about hiding in steerage among the flotsam of Europe, that I was actually deranged.

Oh, dear Lord. Does he think I belong here?

At that moment my hand was full of badger hair, which I was busily knotting together to turn into the bristles of a man's shaving brush. The work was monotonous and brain-achingly simple, and only lasted three hours. Then we were back in Hall Seven, and Miss Morgan was playing, and women were dancing. Some of the doctors even stepped in to take a waltz around the room with their favorite patients.

I looked for Dr. Ingram, but he was not there, so I strode up to Dr. Caldwell. He mistook my purpose and grasped me in his arms for a polka.

"Doctor," I said, trying not to step on his toes as we hopped along, "I should like to have the restrictions removed."

"Oh, now you speak English, do you?" he asked knowingly.

"Perfectly. And I am hoping for a visitor."

"Why? No one has visited you yet. Save for those pesky reporters. Never you fear. I've given the word that they should be turned away. They shall not bother you again."

Turned away! "I would not be bothered!" My voice was strained, and not from the dancing.

Spinning me around, his knowing smile broadened. "I thought so. You like attention, don't you? All this fuss about the mystery girl. I doubt half of your story is true."

As the other patients cheered and clapped, I decided to take my fate in my own hands. "You're correct. My story was false. I'm not Nellie Brown. My name is Nellie Bly, and I'm a reporter for the *New York World.*"

He laughed. "Anything for attention! I've seen it often in women here.

Don't worry. After a time, the need becomes less intense, and these fanciful delusions will fade." Releasing me, he took the arms of another girl, leaving me wide-eyed and aghast. As he moved off, he began humming the tune that shared my name.

I had revealed the truth, and it had not mattered. I was not going to be believed. I was in a madhouse, which proved I was insane.

DURING OUR AFTERNOON WALK, MY AGITATION finally got the better of me. I wanted to walk with Anne Neville, but the nurses said I could not because her dress would not match mine in color. They liked their color coding in Hall Seven. I persisted. "I have walked with Anne since we first arrived, and I will walk with her today." Miss Fitzpatrick looked me over. "You walk where you're told."

A week earlier, I would have given in. Instead, I caught hold of Miss Fitzpatrick's elbow and held on. The nurse tried to pry my hand free, and was surprised that she could not. When Miss Fitzpatrick raised her hand to me, I said in a cool voice, "Don't try your beatings on me. I am perfectly sane, and will not go easy."

Miss Fitzpatrick's lips curled into a taunting smile. "What are you going to do? You have no help, and all I have to do is call out and a dozen nurses would help me to make you obey."

My laugh might have sounded a little hysterical. "Do you know what? If I wanted to leave here this instant, I could merely go down to the river, jump in, and swim across. Once in New York you would never have Nellie Brown again as a patient."

"Try it," said Miss Fitzpatrick. "We'd all like the show."

It was tempting. It was so tempting. But out of the corner of my eye I saw Anne mouth the words *The Lodge*. Instantly, I subsided. Mad as it sounded, if I was to be free, I could not try to get free.

Dutifully, I took my place among the dresses of my color. I hated the look of triumph on Miss Fitzpatrick's face.

The walk held no joy for me that day. Nor for the trees, which had finally begun to lose their leaves.

THAT NIGHT I WAS LIKE Shakespeare's Juliet just before she drinks the Friar's potion, imagining all the scenarios that might bring about her doom. Perhaps the Colonel had fallen ill. Perhaps he'd had a stroke, and was at that moment prone and insensible in some hospital, with the secret of my mission trapped in his brain. *Why, oh why did I not send*

a letter to Mother telling her about my assignment? Why did I not take more precautions, extra insurance, some additional means of extricating myself from this hell I blithely entered of my own free will?

I calmed myself with thought of Macdona and McCain. Both men knew I was in the asylum, and if Macdona knew why, McCain could certainly guess. They would see me freed.

Except. . .

I had spurned Macdona's ham-handed flirtations. And I had tried to poach one of McCain's stories. Those were reasons enough for them to wash their hands of me, a silly girl who didn't know what was good for her. In over her head. What an example to make. "This is what happens to a girl who doesn't know her proper sphere."

Sphere. Wilson. What would he say to all this? I could almost hear him: "Well, you naughty girl, you've done it now. I tried to warn you. But you're so stubborn, you can't be taught. You have to experience everything. Laborious factories, dangerous Mexicans, it's not enough for you to observe, you have to thrust yourself in there and be part of the story. Well done. Only now you're trapped as a subject in a story they'll never let you report."

No, Wilson would never be so cruel. If McCain carried my news to him, the Quiet Observer would move heaven and earth to get me free. He would do anything for me. I was sure of it.

Anything, save love me.

Doris had fallen asleep on the floor, which meant my only companion in wakefulness was Vanessa. She was back at the window, her hair unbraided and free, reading a fantastical tale from her newspaper. Naturally, it was a romance.

"Joyous, joyous Tuesday," said Vanessa. "Once upon a Tuesday, there was a darling young lady named Bianca Rose who wore her hair quite long, in two impossible braids. Just before midnight, she was sitting before a crackling fire in her home writing an urgent telegram to her love, who was taking ship that night for Ceylon. She knew what she should write. She should say her sister, her Pearl, was deathly ill, and their cousin Joseph had gone out West to find a fortune and never returned. The town practitioner of medicine told the lovely Bianca Rose that she must send to all her kin, for Pearl might not recover from this blinding fever that left her either raving or simple. What Bianca had told no one as yet was that she was feeling the creeping fingers of fever upon her own face, inside her own eyes. Without help, without aid, without care, she and her brother would never survive.

"So Bianca Rose looked at that spare telegram form, thinking of the only man she had truly loved in all her life. Knowing her sister needed her, and would never stop needing her, Bianca Rose had spurned him—at the same time, fracturing her own heart into a thousand pieces. Rejected, her love had gone far away, heartsick and bereft, promising never to return to trouble her.

"Now she wrote to him the words she should have spoken: 'I write you a note of celebration, of love, of poetry. It takes so little to make me smile because of thought of you. Let us celebrate every hour on the hour the celebrations of the hour just past. I love you.' And she signed the form, 'Your White Rose.'

"She sent it off, that expensive message that carried no news. It was worth it, because it carried the truth. She loved him. She could not let him think that she did not. And she could not worry him with her illness. If he returned, let it be for love, not for fear. Let it be for love.

"Pacing the floor of the master bedroom, she heard Pearl groaning across the hall. The striking of the clock echoed through the hallway. One o'clock. Two o'clock. Three. Quietly, she slipped downstairs to sip a bit of tea. As she reached the bottom, she noticed the doctor, asleep on a divan in the parlor. Poor man. Bianca Rose roused him and sent him home to his wife, a friend through the ladies' mission, who often came along to hold Bianca's hand. They would chat amiably, each knowing the danger underneath the idle talk.

"When the doctor was gone, Bianca Rose remained outside, sitting on the swing under the tree and losing herself in memory. When the clock struck five, she returned to her room, resigned to a little sleep before another grueling day.

"Bianca Rose was just nodding off when she was startled by a knock on the door. The doctor shouldn't be back. She rushed to the foyer, opened the latches, and flung open the door, hoping—not daring—to believe.

"There he stood, framed against the rising sun, not even a scrap of luggage, and unshaven face. 'I love you,' he told her. 'I could not stay away.'

"Being loved was a new experience. People had told her they loved her before. But she had never believed it until this moment.

"And they lived happily ever after," said Vanessa, holding up her creased newspaper for proof.

The tears on my cheeks were proof of her power as a storyteller. To love, and be loved. So simple, yet what we all longed for.

I might never have another chance, I thought. And so I picked up my pencil and wrote the words I had never dared to even frame as thought:

> Dearest Q. O.,
> *The fact that you'll never read this means I am, for once, free to be honest. It goes against the grain, honesty. For a reporter, it's all facts, no feelings. And the facts of us demolish my feelings.*

Fact—you are a married man, a devoted husband.

Fact—you are nearly twice my age.

Fact—you have never shown more interest in me than as a polite friend and mentor.

Fact—I love you.

Yes, here I am, you think, a silly girl with a crush. But believe me when I say the love I have for you is as much fact as feeling. My heart is full of you, you infuriating man. To think I should love a cheerful curmudgeon, an old-fashioned man with last century's ideas. A man who approves of me as a friend, yet disapproves of me as a person, a woman, a fellow being. I long in equal measure to strike you as to kiss you.

Fact—I like your wife, and pity her, and admire you for your dedication to her. It is a mark of love, endurance. How can I watch you endure the pains of your marriage and then fail to endure my own infatuation with you? That would make me unworthy of you. The only way to be worthy of your love is to deny myself that very love. How perfectly trite. How very gothic. I am a "type."

What's genuinely amusing is that the tale spun about me by the doctors and nurse and reporters is not far from the truth. They say I was made mad through a love spurned and jilted. Why else would I be here, but that it's true? When I came to New York, and Blackwell's, I was not just running toward my career. I was also running away from you.

You think me adventurous. In a certain light, I suppose I am. But at heart I am a coward. Because the one adventure I did not dare was you.

Don't think I did not consider an affair. But even if you would have considered such a thing (I know you would not), affairs, by their nature, end. They are temporary, impermanent, finite. Were I to give in to temptation, I could not endure the inevitable ending. "Better to have loved and lost than never to have loved at all?" Perhaps, if your love has died. But to enter a love knowing it is doomed? Wonderful for novels, dreadful in reality.

No, it's better to love from afar and feel pride in not imposing that love, adding my burden to your already overweighted shoulders. I know they are as broad as mine are narrow. But I can bear the weight of my love for you. It is a delightful anguish.

You started me on this path. I shall continue to walk it, no matter the result. Because I hope to make you proud of me.

I hope I have shown what girls are good for.

I closed my book and clutched it tightly to my chest, closing my eyes as well. Tomorrow was unknown, and unknowable. There were only three things in life of which I could now be certain. My vocation. My mother's love. And the love I carried like a secret torch within me.

Inconvenient. But beautiful.

"**N**ELLIE BROWN?" SAID MISS HART. "You have visitors." Stunned, I remained seated on my bench in Hall Seven. "What?"

"Visitors. In Dr. Ingram's office. Quick now!"

As I set down my knitting and rose, Anne said, "Who is coming to see you?"

"I have no idea," I replied, hardly daring to hope. *Has the Colonel come himself? Or Macdona? Or. . .*

My fanciful thought was the McCain had cabled Wilson, and the Q.O. himself had come to pull me free of this morass. If this had been a novel, that's what would have happened.

Instead, I found Dr. Ingram sitting with two men. The first I had never seen before in all my life. He was in his thirties, with flaxen hair and a face marked by childhood pits. The second man was familiar, but I could not immediately place where I had seen him. He was also on the youngish side, with thin brownish hair and pince-nez glasses perched across his wide nose.

"Nellie," said Dr. Ingram, "these men have come to see you."

"Oh?" I asked warily.

The pitted-faced fellow removed his hat. "Miss Brown, my name is Peter Hendricks. And you know Mr. McDougall."

"Do I?" I looked to the other man, trying desperately to place him in my memory.

"Nellie, it's me, Walter!" cried this Mr. McDougall. "I'm so relieved to see you. Frannie and I read all about you in the papers, but we never dreamed that the mysterious waif was you!"

Frannie? Unsure how to play along, I said, "As you can see, it is me. How is Frannie?"

"Worried sick about you," said McDougall with a wag of his finger. "She even wrote her father, the colonel, about it. And the colonel hired Mr. Hendricks here."

Cheeks flushing, I was careful not to betray my delight. "I feared the colonel had forgotten all about me."

"Hardly," said Mr. Hendricks. "His language has been quite colorful. Well, you know the colonel."

"Indeed," I said, with the hint of a smile.

Dr. Ingram was delighted. "Excellent! Certainly you seem to have jogged her memory." He waved us all to chairs. "Nellie, Mr. Hendricks here is a lawyer. He says that Mr. McDougall and his wife are willing to take charge of you. That is, if you would rather be with them than here in the asylum?"

I made a show of thinking before saying, "Yes. I should prefer that. When would I leave?"

"Soon, we hope," said Hendricks. "We must get a judge to sign the form." He turned to Dr. Ingram. "I trust there will be no problem getting Miss Moreno released."

"None at all. She has been very well behaved, and a thorough delight to speak with. I regret, Miss Moreno, that I shall no longer have the pleasure of your company. But I trust you will be happier with your friends."

"I trust so as well. Walter, please thank Frannie for me. And the colonel. I cannot wait to tell him all about my adventures."

"He's eager to hear all about it."

"You have to go back to Hall Seven for now, I'm afraid," said Dr. Ingram as he rose to escort me to the door. "And if you can, refrain from telling the others. You know how excited they can get."

Before leaving, I turned to Mr. Hendricks. "Oh, I do have one request."

"Yes, Miss Moreno?"

"Whenever you arrange my release, could you have a proper meal waiting for me?"

M Y RELEASE CAME SOONER THAN I had dared imagine. I was in a double line for our morning walk across the grounds. We had paused because one of the other lines had some commotion ahead of us. Being nearsighted, I had trouble seeing at that distance. "What's happening?"

Mattie was craning her neck. "One of their ladies has fainted dead away."

Squinting hard, I saw this was the truth. Beside me, Anne gasped. "Nellie—it's Tillie!"

"No!" I broke the line, but many hands hauled me back into place before the nurses saw me. As I strained against them, I saw Miss Grupe and Miss Grady forcing Tillie to stand and trying to compel her to walk. "They mustn't! They should take her to the hospital."

"Nellie Brown!"

It was a male voice, which made all heads turn, including that of little Tillie.

Hendricks and McDougall were walking alongside Superintendent Dent, who held in his hand my papers of release.

I turned to Anne. "I'm leaving." She burst into tears, and we hugged each other. In her ear I whispered, "I'll come back for you."

From her own line, Pauline Moser called to me. "What's to do, Nellie?"

"I am going home!"

"You never say!"

Word spread like wildfire, and women from both halls broke their lines to rush up to my liberators and plead with them. "I'm a friend of Nellie's, she can't live without me, take me with you!"

"I know her best! She slept in the cell next to mine!"

"I'll cook for her! I'm an excellent cook."

Never shy, Pauline Moser didn't bother with words but simply attempted to kiss McDougall on the lips.

By the time the nurses had swatted them all back, the suits of both men were rumpled and in disarray. Dr. Dent waved at me. "Hurry, Miss Brown. Don't dawdle!"

Anne released me and I hurried over as if my chance at escape might expire. Dent told me I should collect my things and dress in my own clothes, which a nurse would collect.

As both lines of women trudged in opposite directions, I waved to my friends, kissing my fingers to them. "Adios!"

At the last moment, a small figure broke her line and raced back toward our little cluster. Staggering with delirium, Tillie threw herself into McDougall's arms. "Please, sir! You must know me. You inquired after me. She's an imposter! I'm the real one! I am Nellie Brown!"

I was so shocked I wanted to cry. McDougall attempted to extricate himself from Tillie's manic grip as the superintendent angrily waved a nurse over.

"The poor thing!" Miss Grupe took Tillie by the arm, putting on that simpering voice she used in front of the doctors. But the grip on Tillie's arm produced a gasp of pain. "She's not her best self today, as you can see. Come along, Tillie dear. And calm down. The best thing we can do is go on with our daily routine."

With her arm held in a viselike grip, Tillie was too weak to resist. But she threw me such venomous glare that I took a frightened step backwards.

"Wow! What a bug!" laughed McDougall softly. "Lucky for us that nurse was here."

I turned a look like Tillie's on him. "She was as sane as anyone when we arrived. It's this place that has driven her out of her wits."

The superintendent started to protest, but I didn't bother to hash it out at that moment. In a few hours, I would be able to do far more for these women than just raise my voice.

A nurse took me inside and helped me collect my things, and I changed into my modest attire. The shawl I had brought from Bellevue was among my clothes, and had passed to them its musty smell. But I did not mind. It was my souvenir from this place: a tattered wrap of insanity that perfectly symbolized everything I had experienced.

In my own clothes once more, I was taken into a proper bathroom, and for the first time in ten days I saw myself reflected. My lips were chapped. Huge circles hung below my eyes. Tangled into a rough braid, my hair looked waxen and unkempt. And there was a fire in my eyes that I could not recall ever being there before.

That's when it came to me. The word I had been looking for. *Crucible.* And I had passed through mine.

Ten minutes later we were on the boat, leaving Blackwell's Island.

FORTY-SIX

THE STORY

"**Y**OU MADE QUITE A GODDAMN SPECTACLE of yourself." I was once again in Cockerill's office. "Is that a problem, Colonel?"

"Problem? You want to know if it's a problem that the whole blasted city is talking about this crazy little girl from Cuba?" He glowered for a moment. Then his face broke into the widest of grins. "It's a goddamn masterstroke! The *Telegraph* and the *Herald* bit hard on the story, and Christ, have you seen the fuss the *Sun* kicked up over you?"

"I saw one story," I replied.

"One! They ran a story every other constarned day! They played up the 'poor lost crazy girl' for all it's worth! They're going to look mighty goddamned foolish come Sunday—oh, it'll be delicious! Am I boring you?"

Having finally consumed a proper meal, the effect was unexpected—I felt sleepy, my eyes drooping of their own accord. But I shook it off. Digestion could wait. "No, Colonel."

"Good. Now, I understand there's a real story here. A story beyond *you*, I mean."

"Colonel, you have no notion. They beat the women, strip them naked, douse them with ice water, starve them. One woman even died in their care."

His eyes looked like a child's at Christmas. "The doctors do this?"

"The doctors choose not to know. It's the nurses who are so wicked."

"The goddamn nurses?!"

"And Colonel—most of these women are as sane as you or I."

He slammed his hands together. "That's terrific! I mean, it's a damned shame," he amended at once. "But I'm glad we chose to investigate."

"Do you want me to tell you about it?"

"No, I want you to write about it, now, this minute. I've got the gist. It's terrible, that's why we sent you. Now, you write it. We'll set you up at a desk. And get everything to McDougall so he can start drawing it. I'm glad he got a look-see."

"I've already described some scenes for him." On the trip back, I'd learned why McDougall seemed familiar: I'd seen him beyond the newsroom curtain, where the artists dwelled, adding sensation to every story. It was clever to have sent him, giving him an in-person view of the place.

Having spent most of my meal—my delicious, delectable, delightful meal—describing my experiences to McDougall and Hendricks, they had lost their appetites while I discovered what a wealth of material I had. I warned the Colonel, "It's going to run long."

"The longer the better!" cried the Colonel. "We can break it up across two Sunday editions. How she got in the first Sunday, and be sure to buy the *World* next Sunday to see what happened to her. It will be a smash!"

I was clearly no longer needed, and my fingers were itching to start. On my way to the door, I paused. "Did the *World* run any pieces on the lost girl?"

"Of course. Would have been damned suspicious not to."

"I'd like a copy."

"I can do you better. We've kept clippings from all the coverage of Nellie Brown, Nellie Marina, Nellie Moreno, the lost waif, or whatever goddamn thing they were calling you that day. I'll have them sent 'round to your desk. Now get writing!"

Within ten minutes I was assigned my very own desk in that busy newsroom. Other reporters shot me covert glances under the brims of their hats. I was the only woman in the whole place.

But I had no time to engage with them, or even acknowledge their stares. I was too busy earning my place among them.

THE STORY RAN THE SUNDAY after my liberation, October 9, and I was giddy with thrills and fears. Already, rumors were spreading that "Nellie Brown" was an imposter, and everyone was trying to find me. I'd stayed in seclusion, only going back to my boardinghouse once, staying instead at a nearby hotel so I could work on the story right up until it went to press.

At one point during the five days before the story broke, as we worked over one of the many drafts, I said to the Colonel, "You don't mind this bit here?"

"What, this bit where you keep yourself awake by thinking about your life? Why would I mind that?"

"I've been told," I said primly, "that I should refrain from placing myself at the center of my stories."

"Whoever said that is a dad-blasted moron. You *are* the center of this story. You are the reader's eyes and ears. They have to feel they know you, that they can trust you. You are the face of the new journalism!"

I couldn't help flushing. "You think so? Truly?"

"If you aren't, you soon will be." He winked at me. "I'll make sure of it."

Late Saturday night I was granted permission to watch the giant rolling pins lurch into action, and was gifted with the very first edition, the ink barely dry.

The headlines alone were heart-stopping:

BEHIND ASYLUM BARS

THE MYSTERY OF THE UNKNOWN INSANE GIRL

REMARKABLE STORY OF THE SUCCESSFUL IMPERSONATION OF INSANITY

HOW NELLIE BROWN DECEIVED JUDGES, REPORTERS AND MEDICAL EXPERTS

SHE TELLS HER STORY OF HOW SHE PASSED AT BELLEVUE HOSPITAL

STUDYING THE ROLE OF INSANITY BEFORE HER MIRROR AND PRACTICING IT AT THE TEMPORARY HOME FOR WOMEN — ARRESTED AND BROUGHT BEFORE JUDGE DUFFY — HE DECLARES SHE IS SOME MOTHER'S DARLING AND RESEMBLES HIS SISTER — COMMITTED TO THE CARE OF THE PHYSICIANS FOR THE INSANE AT BELLEVUE — EXPERTS DECLARE HER DEMENTED — HARSH TREATMENT OF THE INSANE AT BELLEVUE — "CHARITY PATIENTS SHOULD NOT COMPLAIN" — VIVID PICTURES OF HOSPITAL LIFE — HOW OUR ESTEEMED CONTEMPORARIES HAVE FOLLOWED A FALSE TRAIL — SOME NEEDED LIGHT AFFORDED THEM — CHAPTERS OF ABSORBING INTEREST IN THE EXPERIENCE OF A FEMININE "AMATEUR CASUAL"

All this before a single sentence of my own text. McDougall's art set off each section, with rather unflattering sketches of me through every stage of the affair. I had to wonder if my chin was that pointy, or if I sometimes lacked a mouth entirely.

However, I was in no position to complain of my treatment. The Colonel had dedicated two whole pages of the Sunday feature section to my narrative. Never before had I been given so much room to tell a story.

Moreover, he let me sign my name. There were veteran reporters at the *World* who did not have a byline, but Nellie Bly did.

That night I collected every excerpt about "Nellie Brown," carefully clipping each out with my nail scissors and pasting them in order in a book. Strung together, it was like the narrative from one of my shilling shockers. Reading it through, I felt I really had overplayed the part. I did not recall saying half of what was ascribed to me. *Did my hands truly tremble?*

But it was certainly sensational! Worthy of the most dreadful penny dreadful. And Monday would bring the biggest shock of them all. More nervous about the reaction to the story than I had been on my last night on the island, I couldn't sleep for my anxiety and excitement. It was an interesting mental struggle, as I chided myself over and over.

Do you care about the story, or about Nellie Bly becoming famous?

"Both. If I'm successful, I can tell more stories like this. I can effect real change."

And be loved for it.

"And hated, I'm sure."

Why care what other people think of you?

"Who doesn't care what people think of them? Anyone who says they don't is lying. Or a lunatic."

When I realized I was actually speaking my responses out loud, I laughed uncomfortably, reminded of Crazy Maggie. *Rub, rub, rub.* Or Vanessa, with her beautiful nocturnal flights of imagination.

Curled up in my own bed at Mrs. Pesetsky's, I fell asleep imagining what people would be talking about in the morning.

T HE STORY OF MY TEN NIGHTS in the madhouse was a smash, a sensation. It sold out within hours, and when I came in to the *World*'s offices I found dozens of telegrams and messages from horrified and admiring readers.

On Monday, the story was carried across the country, first by Mr. Pulitzer's other papers, then by everyone else. It seemed this was far more than a local story. What most distressed editors and readers everywhere was that doctors and supposed "experts" had been so easily fooled by a slip of a girl with no formal training in anything.

Yet the appeal went beyond that. The story had grabbed the imagination of Americans everywhere.

"It's you," the Colonel said, brushing ash from his waistcoat as he stood to pat me once again on the shoulder. "They only have girls like you in books. Here's one in life." He puffed his cigar, then jabbed it at me. "Don't get cocky, and finish writing the rest of the damned story."

While my story made national headlines on Monday, the other local papers were mum. The "esteemed contemporaries" line must have rankled them. Worse, we had caught them entirely flat-footed. All they could do was reprint parts of Sunday's *World*, which was galling in the extreme.

Some did just that, though not the *Times*, who dropped the story of the mystery girl entirely.

The *Sun* seemed to ignore it as well, doubtlessly aggrieved over having been taken in so thoroughly.

On Friday, they had their revenge.

I WAS AT MY DESK AT THE *WORLD*, refining the details of my ordeal in the bath, when I heard shouting from the Colonel's office. Heads turned when something crashed, and for a second I thought the editor had taken up target practice with his pistol. "Bastards!"

Bursting from his office door, he stalked over to me and slammed a newspaper down on my desk. "The bastards! The goddamn bastards!"

Relieved I was not the source of his rage, I found myself looking down at the front page of the *Sun*'s evening edition. In the two right-hand columns ran a lengthy story:

PLAYING MAD WOMAN

NELLIE BLY TOO SHARP FOR THE ISLAND DOCTORS

NINE DAYS' LIFE IN CALICO

THE SUN FINISHES UP ITS STORY OF THE "PRETTY CRAZY GIRL"

QUESTIONED, PRESCRIBED FOR, LOCKED IN A BARE CELL EVERY NIGHT, UNIFORMED IN FURNITURE GOODS, BATHED BY ALIEN HANDS, WASHED REGULARLY WITHOUT HER OWN HELP AFTER EVERY MEAL OF COARSE FOOD—SILLY AND UNCOUTH COMPANIONS, IN WHOSE CHILDISH PLEASURES SHE DID NOT JOIN—HER DECEPTION SUCCESSFUL—INCIDENT OF HER ADVENTURE AND OFFICIAL ACCOUNT OF IT.

With the Colonel angrily huffing above me, I tried not to smile. To have my name placed so prominently in another paper's headline was a real coup. And they began with four paragraphs recounting the entire tale as they had reported it, before revealing what we had told the *World*'s audience two days earlier:

Soon after she was discharged from the asylum a rumor was heard that the girl was a pretender, that she never was affected mentally, and that she had taken the course she did to secure a commitment to the island for the purpose of writing about her experience in the asylum. This rumor soon settled upon our young woman known as Nellie Bly as the heroine of the adventure. She has been doing newspaper work in New York for several months, and is the metropolitan correspondent of a Pittsburgh newspaper. Her mother is the widow of a Pittsburgh lawyer. She is intelligent, capable, and self reliant, and, except for the matter of changing her name to Nelly Bly, has gone about the business of maintaining her self in journalism in a practical, businesslike way.

How flattering! I was impressed they had already learned so much about me, though I was annoyed by how much they got wrong. *Father, a Pittsburgh lawyer? And what was that sly comment about changing my name?* No woman wrote under her real name, and only a handful of men did. Nevertheless, they were helping to make Nellie Bly a name known in every household in New York.

Reading further, my delight in my budding notoriety turned to icy fury. My own account on Sunday had ended with my arrival at Blackwell's Island. The *Sun* had picked up my story there:

The asylum is a gloomy, dark gray stone building, L-shaped in plan. In its courtyard the ambulance stopped, and Dr. D.F. Kinier, the officer of the day, and the attendants of the reception ward made ready to receive the patients that Miss Grupe had brought to them.

Nellie was conducted up the stone steps, through the narrow door, and along a naked-walled and bare-floored entry to the right a few steps. Then across the threshold of an open door she stepped into Hall 6, the reception ward. She was still silent. Partly from the purpose of simulating insanity, and partly from the effect of a nameless dread and chill, she moodily and silently tramped down the bare corridor with its rows of open doors and bare, cell-like bedrooms.

Growing more outraged by the second, my eyes skipped down from point to point:

Under these conditions and circumstances, it is easy to believe that Dr. Kinier found the patient very much depressed. She helped him out, and in answer to his persistent and diligent questioning she furnished further and corroborative symptoms to support the diagnosis of dementia and melancholia. Her answers were monosyllabic... When asked if she heard voices, she answered yes... she also kept her hand applied to her head all the time... as a final and finishing stroke, she relapsed into the silence that had marked her advent... Nellie took her place in the sitting room of the ward, another of the charges assigned to the care of attendants Miss Annie Grupe, Miss Alicia McCarten, and Miss M. Grady...

I turned the page, horrified to find four more columns—the *Sun* had dedicated as much space to my story as the *World* had! Worse, they were making me out to be both a clever actress and a terrible, self-indulging snob!

When Nellie saw the clean white-pine table, without sign of table cloth or napkin, already set with what was evidently all that was to be expected either in the way of food or pottery or plate, she could not keep from her face an expression of dissatisfaction... and the nature of the service also seemed to fail to come up to her ideas. When seated, she complained of the fare. She displayed a sufficiently good appetite... the attendants, who are instructed to report upon the failure of any patient to eat, found no occasion for such a report about Nellie... The interval between tea time and bed time is given up wholly to amusements in the sitting rooms. While on this Monday evening the other patients were as usual passing this time in playing various games, in playing upon or listening to the piano, or in dancing to its tones, Nellie received the attention of the attendants... their efforts to come to an understanding with her had not met with any degree of success.

Referring to the mattress upon which I had tried to sleep, they said: "It was a bed that would be considered comfortable enough by anyone who had never been used to any better, but it was one upon which the frame accustomed to the luxuries of curled hair and elastic springs would vainly try to repose." *When have I slept in a luxury bed in my life?*

An unhappy night ending in chloral... with some fitful dozing that was scarcely less restless than her wide-awake moments, she passed the first three hours of the night in a most miserable fashion. At the end of that time she received a sleeping dose of chloral from the night doctor and seemed glad to get it...

"God damn them!" The paper crumpled in my hands. There were four columns I hadn't read, but I could no longer see straight. "'Seemed glad to get it'? 'Diligent questioning'? 'Good appetite'! I'll—I can't—what do they think—those *bastards*!"

Seeing that my fury dwarfed his, the Colonel's rage gave way to amusement, and he laughed as he slapped me grimly on the back. "Come on." He gestured toward his office.

"I didn't tell them any of this!" Shaking the offending *Sun* as I scurried after him, I was suddenly fearful for my job. "I swear, Colonel, they didn't get any of this from me!"

"Girl, I know that," he assured me, standing behind his desk and lighting a fresh cigar. "You may be a good actress, but your anger is all too real. And you're not stupid. You wouldn't undermine your own story, even if

you'd had the time. No, it's my fault. I should have seen this coming."
He chuckled without amusement. "Those rotten bastards! Scooping us
on our own story. It's why they were quiet all week, you see. The *Sun*'s
been burnt, and the best way to burn us back is to scoop us on our
own goddamned story. We should have run the second half yesterday. By
waiting a week, we gave the *Sun* an opportunity, and the crafty bastards
took it. I'm impressed."

"They got all this from the doctors and nurses," I said, thinking aloud.
"Why would they talk?"

"Because they know damned well what you're able to do to them, so
they're desperate to get their version out first. The *Sun* is about to be the
asylum's best friend. Both have been made to look the fool by you, and
for their own reasons both are going to work mighty damned hard to
discredit you. You noticed how they were all praise at first? Insult through
dad-blasted compliment. They'll keep calling you 'clever' and 'resourceful,'
all they while implying 'devious' and 'deceitful.'"

Numbly I said, "They're going to use being female against me."

"What else can they do? They've had to admit they were taken in by a
little girl. That's never going to go away. So they're going to make *you* go
away instead."

From Monday's lofty high, I was on the verge of despair. "What can we
do?"

"Do?" The Colonel pointed his glowing cigar at me like a cannon. "We
goddamn *destroy* them, that's what we do. We crush these bastards the way
only Pulitzer can. We'll make them the fools and buffoons they're terrified
they are."

At last I understood why everyone called him Colonel. I was ready to
take up arms and march down Newspaper Row to shoot at the *Sun*. "How
do we start?"

"First, did they get anything wrong in their piece?"

"It's more of a wonder they got anything right!"

"How much of the story they ran is true?"

"None of it is true!"

"You said you were given chloral."

"Not that first night!"

"You didn't refuse clothes?"

"What? No." I hadn't gotten that far into the story. "I complained when
the clothes didn't fit!"

Puffing furiously, the Colonel started nodding. "Good. That's good. Are
there enough false statements in there to make a story?"

"Oh, yes!" Barely halfway through, there were a dozen things I could
refute. "Definitely."

"Then write it, right goddamn now. We'll run your second half on Sunday as planned, but we need to hit back immediately after. You pen a piece refuting every lie they put into print, and we'll run it Monday. Hit them hard in their facts. They had to have rushed it, running out to Blackwell's and interviewing everyone they could lay hands on. They're desperate, and that makes them vulnerable. Rub Dana's nose in it." He chortled. "Pulitzer will be thrilled. Nothing sells better than two papers duking it out. They can have a few nights to think they've got one over on us. Let them sleep happy. It'll be the last good rest they have. Come Monday they'll see what it means to take on the *World*'s star reporter Nellie Bly."

It was everything I could do not to burst into tears and hug him. Instead I went to my desk to pour my vitriol into print. The worst part was that it meant I had to read the rest of the article. The staff on Blackwell's lied about event after event, and the paper went out of its way to believe them, even offering flattering praise. "Miss Grupe is tall, graceful, and fair. Her face is of rare prettiness, and she seems to be particularly pleasant and good-natured." I imagined her using that terrible ingratiating simper with the *Sun*'s reporter. It made my blood boil.

So did this statement: "Nellie, with her companions of Hall Six, took a ride on the carousel in the first afternoon, but made no manifestations of pleasure or interest while doing so." *I never got to ride the carousel!*

The article ended with statements from four doctors and four nurses. The doctors' statements were all to be expected, and at least as accurate as their bias allowed. What drove me to the brink of madness were the statements from the four nurses:

Miss M. Grady states as follows:

She made no particular disturbance in the hall except to talk to other patients and to endeavor to incite them to ask for other clothing and apparently to make trouble by interfering with the patients as above mentioned. She asked me for extra under clothing for herself and refused to take it when offered. She was disrespectful to the attendants, making faces and endeavoring to make trouble through other patients. She played a little on the piano. She had a good appetite and slept well. She had a good memory and impressed me as putting it all on.

Miss Alicia McCarten states as follows:

She talked with the other patients, telling them they should not do what the attendants told them, acting in an insolent manner; said the attendants here were not ladies and the doctors not gentlemen. She asked me for a cigarette one day. She impressed me as being of a very disagreeable disposition. She conversed but little except with patients.

Miss Annie Grupe reports as follows:

She never spoke to me in a polite manner, was insolent in her conversation, answered very shortly, conversed with some about Cuba, and said she formerly lived there, and thought she was there now. She conversed with the other patients, and tried to incite them to ask for all manner of things, apparently to make trouble and was disrespectful in her manner. She complained of being cold, and when more clothing was given her she refused to put it on.

Miss C. Kroener says:

Nellie Brown was received in Hall 7 Oct. 1, and was asked to change her clothes by the attendants, which she did, but refused to wear the dress given her as it did not suit her complexion. She refused to walk with any patient except Annie Neville, who had always been her companion since she was admitted to Bellevue Hospital. I asked her if she could play the piano. She said yes, but she would not play here. I asked her if she would sew or do some work. She said no, not while here. She was very rude and saucy sometimes, and inclined to make other patients the same. In fact, she did make one patient very noisy and excited for some three or four hours. Otherwise her general behavior was good.

Those rotten women! I honestly did not think I could hate anyone the way I hated Ford and Albert, but my time at the *World* had proved me horribly wrong. My one consolation was that there was no mention of Dr. Ingram. Either they hadn't interviewed him, or they had and he'd refused to say anything evil about me.

The truly wicked part of the article came at the very end. The *Sun* and Blackwell's attempted to discredit me through the most despicable means they had available: the wretched women I had befriended during my stay. In my Sunday article I'd written that I had found neither Anne nor Tillie to be mad. In answer, the *Sun* published the asylum's notes on both of them:

Anne Neville; 33; Ireland; single; Bellevue; never been visited; no history from friends; formerly in Utica Asylum; there for several months; has delusions concerning religion; says she sees visions; hallucinations of sight; apparitions of visitors from heaven.

Matilda Mayard; 25; United States; admitted Sept. 26, 1887; Bellevue; delusions of persecution; thinks people have conspired against her; conversation irrelevant and rambling; at times she won't talk at all; refuses to answer questions; still in reception ward under observation. Oct. 11— Fluctuations of the case make it impossible to determine to what ward she should be assigned.

They haven't sent her to a hospital? She's still in Hall Six? This is monstrous!

I started writing my rebuttal with relish, refuting lie after lie. The list was huge, as I corrected the record on what I wore, my interview with Dr. Kinier, my riling up the other patients to make a better story, my supposed threats of suicide—large and small, I addressed it all. There were mistakes in the sequence of events, and loads of lies told by nurses to make themselves look better, lies that were easily done away with. Brick by brick, I tore down their monument of mistruths.

By the time my rebuttal was ready for print, it was four columns long, and the headline read UNTRUTHS IN EVERY LINE. The opening sentence had Cockerill strutting about swearing with joy:

> On my first arrival in New York the editor of THE SUN said to me in an interview, "There is nothing so valuable as a reporter who gives facts; who, when told that two and two make four, puts it four instead of three or five." I have always been particular in stating only facts in all my work, but never did I confine myself so closely to this rule as in my story of "Behind Asylum Bars." As THE SUN undertook to prove that I really passed ten days as an insane girl on Blackwell's Island, I would like to correct the many mistakes and misstatements which I counted throughout the six columns recently published about me in that journal.

"Take that, you pompous old fossil!" crowed Cockerill after reading it aloud for the fifth time to the whole newsroom. "How he'll kick himself for giving you that interview. And this: 'I was not in the least fatigued, and my nerves are and were always remarkable for their strength. I have faced what seemed positive death, yet I never felt my nerves even twinge.' What death have you faced?"

I thought of Ford, but said, "I was run out of Mexico by their government for exposing corruption."

"That's my adventurous girl!" Chortling, the Colonel turned again to the newsroom. "This one has more goddamned backbone than the lot of you!"

That statement cemented my role for the rest of my life as a reporter. To keep the Colonel praising me, to keep the World's attention, I would have to court danger in every story I chased. It wasn't enough to expose the ills of the world. Nellie Bly had to expose herself to them as well.

THE CIRCULATION OF THAT SUNDAY'S *World* was the highest that year, and that afternoon I found an envelope on my desk with a check in it for a hundred dollars. It had Mr. Pulitzer's signature on it, and came with a hastily-scribbled note with just two words: "Good job."

I was thinking of what I could do with that money—rent an apartment, buy some new clothes, send some money to Mother—when the Colonel stopped by my desk. "Congratulations. I've already had a phone call from the mayor. He's in a lather. It's a god-blessed thing to behold."

Putting the check away, I said, "What happens now?"

"Now? Now everyone scrambles for cover while we milk this story like a dad-gummed cow."

"No."

He checked. "No?"

"Colonel, I've been through this before. I write a story exposing some horrible thing, and then move on to the next one. We cannot let this just become another story. Things have to change. Those women need our help. They need justice."

The Colonel grinned. "You want justice. I want to sell papers. Which is great news for you, because in the end it's the same damned thing. There is nothing better, little girl, than a righteous goddamned cause. Let the story drop? Are you actually insane? The *World* is about to become the loudest blasted voice for these poor souls in the history of, well, the world. With Nellie Bly leading the way."

FORTY-SEVEN

NELLIE BLY

THE WORLD THEIR SAVIOR
HOW NELLIE BLY'S WORLD WILL HELP THE CITY'S INSANE

HEADLINES LIKE THOSE CONTINUED FOR the next two months, as the *New York World* became the foremost champion of women's rights and Nellie Bly was transformed into the brave heroine of a story too fanciful to be fiction.

Letters poured in from across the country praising my pluck and gumption, and stories ran everywhere about me personally. I was suddenly more than a reporter—I was a celebrity! I received offers to lecture, and even one from a Broadway producer to act out my great story on the stage. "You are obviously a performer of no small talent, to have achieved such a feat as feigning madness!"

Kind as that was, I had no desire at all to leave the *World*. And I had still yet to meet Mr. Pulitzer. Hilariously, he was cornered by one of the roaches while he stopped off at Union Station in Pittsburgh on his way back from St. Louis. When he was asked about me by the *Dispatch* reporter, Pulitzer called me "bright" and "plucky." "She is well-educated and thoroughly understands the profession which she has chosen. She has a great future before her." Nice words to hear from a boss I had yet to even see!

Nearly everyone in Pittsburgh laid claim to me. There was even an incredibly sweet tribute from Bessie Bramble, who wrote that great editors of New York:

. . .had scarcely got done saying that women could not cross the "great gulf" that separated them from reporters of the first order of enterprise, or words to that effect, when behold! Nelly Bly steps in and performs a feat of journalism that very few of the men of the profession have more than equaled. She has shown that cool courage, consummate craft and investigating ability are not monopolized by the brethren of the profession. By her clever woman's wit she has shown how easily men can be humbugged and imposed upon—and men hitherto deemed smart and experts at their business at that.

It was adorable how she managed to tweak me from afar by misspelling my pen name. I wondered if Madden had caught it and let it stand. Probably.

I got in a little nose tweaking of my own as I wrote to Mother, asking her to come out to visit now that I could treat her with style. I sent love to Charlie, Henry, Kate, Beatrice, and little Grant. "And I hope Albert is telling everyone he knows that his little sister has become a real success." She wrote back at once, promising to come soon, but with no mention of Albert.

The one person in Pittsburgh I most longed to hear from remained silent.

I N NEW YORK, THINGS WERE MOVING swiftly. A grand jury was impaneled, and I was called to appear. I had hoped to help Mr. Macdona with his career, but when I arrived he grinned and shrugged. "Story is too big. My boss wanted it for himself. But thanks for trying, little girl!"

I took an oath to tell the truth, the whole truth, and nothing but the truth—and then immediately lied about my age. I told them I was twenty, when I was now twenty-four. It had become such a habit, I'd done it before I could even catch myself. Thankfully, Albert wasn't there to contradict me.

The grand jury was made up of twenty-three men, and I had to wonder if these men would even care for the conditions of impoverished women. I told my whole story from the beginning, and was pleased to see them listen with evident fascination. And when Assistant District Attorney Vernon M. Davis suggested the whole grand jury visit the island to see the place for themselves, one man on the panel said, "Can Miss Bly come with us, to show us around?"

"If she's willing," said Mr. Davis.

"I should be glad to," I said.

In truth, I was anything but glad. I had hoped to never see that place again, and I was honestly afraid of going back and being trapped there— I'd had nightmares for weeks about just that. But I also longed to know what had happened to Anne and Tillie and all the rest. And I wanted to stand before Miss Grupe and Miss Grady, face to face, their equal in status and freedom, and repudiate them in the terms they so richly deserved.

We went the next day, starting at Bellevue, with the idea that it would be a surprise visit, no warning given. But somebody in the government clearly wanted to protect the institution from a further drubbing at my hands, because it wasn't long before we were joined by one of the charity commissioners and Dr. MacDonald of Ward's Island, another of New York's floating pens of undesirables. The doctor made a point of walking up to me and shaking me by the hand. "Boy, are our faces red," he said loudly for all the grand jury members to head. "You certainly pulled the wool over our eyes. But that's newspapers for you! Anything for a good yarn!"

The implication, of course, was that I had made up most of the events in my reporting. Withdrawing my hand, I said, "I wish the yarn had been duller, and there had been no story to write in the first place." After that he did not try to speak to me, only around me.

The boat ride to Blackwell's was a vastly different experience than my previous trip to the island. As we churned along, one of the jurors said, "Is this the boat you rode on your first journey over?"

I had to laugh, gesturing around the boat that practically sparkled with cleanliness. It had to be next to new. "No."

Mr. Davis asked the commissioner why we were not riding on the usual boat. "Oh, it's laid up for repairs."

I began to worry. The asylum had had two weeks to clean up their messes, to make things sparkle with newness and comfort. With a sickening twist of my stomach I realized that the nurses would have forced the inmates into a devilish state in order to make things presentable. *How much were those women made to suffer to make them presentable for official New York?*

Our arrival seemed to confirm my fears. The first signal of cosmetic change was the absence of certain key characters in my story. If I had been looking forward to facing my tormentors, they had all vanished. Miss Grupe, Miss McCarten, and Miss Grady were all absent from the island. No one would say more than that.

Our guide for the "impromptu" tour was Superintendent Dent. He had last seen me dressed in a calico sack and a frayed sun hat, with my hair askew and huge circles beneath my eyes. My comely appearance clearly startled him, as did my freezing manner.

As the jury interviewed several of the nurses who were present that day, Dr. Dent came close to me. "I am glad you did this. Had I known your purpose, I would have aided you."

"Oh, really," I said dryly.

"Honestly, we have no means of learning the way things are going except to do as you did. Since your story was published, I found a nurse at the Retreat who had watches set for our approach, just as you had stated. She's been dismissed."

"And Miss Grupe? Miss Grady?"

"We are investigating them. I expect them to be dismissed as well."

"They should be charged with assault at the least."

"You may be right. But it would be hard to bring charges." His meaning was plain. What jury would convict on the testimony of a madwoman?

I began to notice how rehearsed the stories of the nurses seemed. So did Mr. Davis, who splendidly caught them out in several contradictions. He pounced on one particular statement. "Wait. You say you were told where you should stay when we visited. So this grand jury visit was discussed?"

"Y—yes," admitted the nurse, a woman I did not know.

"Who discussed it with you?"

Her eyes shot guiltily to Dr. Dent, who looked pale. "Yes, well, we suspected we would receive an inspection of some kind or another. It was only natural that we should prepare."

Mr. Davis turned to the superintendent. "I suppose I should direct my questions to you, since all these nurses are only repeating what you've told them to say. Talk to us, Dr. Dent, about the baths. Do you know if they bathe the women in warm water or cold?"

"Warm, I'm sure."

"Oh, you're sure, are you? So are the nurses. But if we were to ask the patients?"

"Well, I confess, I'm never present during their baths, for obvious reasons," he added with a self-deprecating chuckle. No one laughed.

"So you have no firsthand knowledge of whether the water is warm or cold. What about women forced to wash in old water left by other patients?"

"Again, I'm never present for these things, so there's no real way for me to be absolutely certain—"

"Does that extend to cruelty toward the patients? If a nurse decided to mistreat one of the inmates here, you'd have no way of knowing, because you're not present when they do it? Is that going to be your excuse for everything? If not you, what about the other doctors here? Surely they must have eyes, even if you don't."

Dr. Dent drew himself up haughtily. "I'm sorry to say, not all the doctors here are competent. The fact that Miss Bly was able to deceive them is proof enough. But that is the fault of our budget. If we had more funding, we could pay the doctors more, and hence hire physicians of higher quality."

I lifted my hand. "Mr. Davis, may I ask a question of Dr. Dent?" The assistant district attorney gestured for me to proceed. "Doctor, may we please speak to Anne Neville?"

"Who?"

"Anne Neville. She arrived the same day I did. When I left here, she was assigned to Hall Seven."

"I'm not certain I recall her. We do have so many women coming and going, I can't hold them all in my head."

"Really? Because you gave her official diagnosis to the *New York Sun* on October eleventh. Both hers and Tillie Mayard's, making their medical conditions public. I should like to see them both. As of that date, Miss Mayard was still in Hall Six. Will you send for them, please?"

"I shall try to find them." Frowning, Dent spoke in hushed tones to another nurse.

"What about Mrs. McCartney? Or Mary Hughes?" I asked.

"Ah! Mary I remember. Some relatives called and took her away."

"Where?"

"How should I know? I only remember she was as happy enough to leave as you were yourself."

We were given a tour. The beds were improved all around, with finer mattresses than any I had slept on. They all had springs rather than straw. Likewise, the kitchens were unbelievably transformed, sparkling with fresh cleanliness. Two barrels of salt stood conspicuously open right beside the door. The bread brought out to us was white and flaky. In the bathroom up in Hall Seven, the buckets were gone, replaced by proper basins.

The whole time, Dr. Dent and I played a dire game of cat and mouse. I would ask after a woman I had known, and the doctor would send a nurse to find out about them. Each time, the result was negative.

Mrs. Cotter? "Discharged."

Bridget McGuiness and Rebecca Farron? "Transferred to other quarters."

The belligerent German girl, Margaret Bentz? "We can't find her."

They denied all knowledge of the Mexican woman in Hall Seven. "There has never been such a patient."

Louise Schanz? "She was transferred out of Hall Six, but we have no record of where."

"Your record-keeping seems terribly lax," I remarked tartly after a half dozen more such answers. "Is that due to budget as well? What about Josephine Despereaux, the Frenchwoman?"

Dr. Dent clucked his tongue. "Alas, you can't see her. A sad case. She's dying of paralysis."

"What? She was the healthiest woman here!"

"Apparently not. Ah, I'm told we have located one of your friends. Why don't you go to Hall Six and wait there while I fetch her."

Hall Six was empty when we arrived, and the nurse escorting us said, "All the patients were having such fun on the merry-go-round, they asked if they could stay outside a while longer."

I was flabbergasted, fearing the jurors would buy this pack of lies.

Then they brought in Anne.

It had only been two weeks, but she had altered in appearance. She was all bones, like someone after a dreadful illness. She did indeed appear mad, and she stared at us with distended eyes.

Then I saw her hands trembling with fear, and I instantly knew what had happened. The nurses had informed her she was to be examined by a group of men. That was enough to terrify any woman in that place.

As Dr. Dent brought her forward, I turned to Mr. Davis. "Let me speak with her first. She knows me."

He hesitated, perhaps fearing I would interfere with his witness. But looking at her erased any notion of undue influence. This place had already done that. "Go ahead. Gentlemen of the grand jury, let's give Miss Bly a chance to reacquaint herself with her friend."

Dr. Dent did not like that. He was forced to choose between staying with the grand jury and controlling what I said to Anne. He chose the former, shooting the nurse a dark look.

As the men stayed at the far side of the open sitting room, I approached my friend. "Anne? Anne, it's me. It's Nellie. I said I'd be back for you. Here I am. Do you remember?"

"Nellie?" she asked dully.

The moment I heard her voice, I knew she'd been drugged. As I drew close to her, I could smell the chloral on her breath, which brought back my own night with that wicked stuff. "Anne, did they give you some medicine to calm your nerves?"

She nodded. That explained the delay in bringing her to us.

"Anne, these men are all friends of mine. I want you to tell them the story about us coming to the island, just like it happened."

"Why?"

"Because they don't believe me," I said. "They think I'm crazy."

Her voice grew soft. "Will they put you back in here?"

"I hope not," I answered.

I had to blink back a welter of tears as she took my hand and said, "I'll protect you, Nellie."

The men of the grand jury approached and sat on those hard benches that now had pillows across them. I put Anne in a chair and stood beside her, holding her hand and saying as little as possible so I could not be accused of prompting. After he tried twice to direct her answers, Dr. Dent was told to remain silent as well.

To my blazing triumph, Anne told the story exactly as it had happened. She kept calling me Miss Brown, proving she knew me by no other name. She spoke of our meeting, our journey here, and our daily life, answering the jurors' respectfully whispered questions.

Mr. Davis said, "Have things changed since Miss Brown went away?"

"Oh, yes," answered Anne. "When Miss Brown and I were brought here, the nurses were cruel and the food was too bad to eat. We did not have enough clothing. Miss Brown asked for more all the time. I thought she was very kind, for when a doctor promised her some clothing, she said she would give it to me. But ever since Miss Brown was taken away, everything has been different. The nurses are very kind and we are given plenty to wear. The doctors come to see us often and the food is greatly improved."

If Dr. Dent looked stricken at that, it was nothing compared to my features the next moment. The residents of Hall Six were returning at last from their walk, and I saw Tillie. She was like the ghost of a person, emaciated and staggering. Her hair had grown out a little, and now flew away in wild strands too short to braid. She looked the maddest of the lot, and I could not bring myself to point her out to the jurors for fear of frightening her. She didn't recognize me.

I kissed Anne as we departed. She clutched me, looking right into my face. "Did I help? Did they believe me?"

"They did," I assured her. "They did."

"Good. Good. God bless you, Nellie. God bless you and keep you safe."

I have no idea what the jurors thought of me, weeping all the boat ride back. Nor did I care.

NELLIE BLY LED THE WAY

THE GRAND JURY REPORTS ON ABUSES
AT BLACKWELL'S ISLAND ASYLUM

ITS EYES OPENED BY "THE WORLD'S" ACCOUNT OF THE HORRORS OF THE PLACE—CONDEMNING THE JUNIOR PHYSICIANS AND THE NURSES AS INCOMPETENT—RECOMMENDING THE EMPLOYMENT OF FEMALE DOCTORS

The October Grand Jury finished its investigations of the condition of the Female Insane Asylum on Blackwell's Island yesterday and at noon filed into the Court of General Sessions and made its presentment to Judge Gildersleeve. The investigation was the immediate result of THE WORLD's disclosures concerning the management of the institution. Miss Nellie

Bly, who spent ten days in the asylum under the direction of THE WORLD was the chief aid of the Grand Jury in its inquiry, and on her testimony most of the recommended changes are based. The Grand Jury, accompanied by Miss Nellie Bly, visited the Female Insane Asylum on Oct. 18, inquired into the method of conducting the institution, and examined a number of witnesses, including the physicians and nurses in charge of the asylum.

THEY HAD BELIEVED ANNE. EVERY WORD.
    Even as the district attorney's office was handing down indictments against the nurses, doctors, and administrators over at City Hall, Mayor Hewitt recommended allocating over a million dollar increase to the Department of Public Charities and Correction, citing my story in the *World* as his reason.

I was present during nearly all the various court proceedings, either as a witness or a reporter. I ran into McCain there, and thanked him profusely for not exposing me on the island.

"I was afraid you'd run right out and wire to Madden that I had gone insane. And then he and Wilson would come riding out on white horses to rescue me."

"Can't imagine Madden on a horse," he laughed. "And Wilson's gone."

"Gone!" I felt a sudden panic.

"Took a job at the *Bulletin*. His farewell article was a laugh riot. You should have Madden send you a copy. If he's still speaking to you."

Breathing again, I felt my face bunch up in wonder. "Won't he be?"

McCain laughed. "How many times have you quit on him now? Still, I suppose he can't argue with success. How does it feel to be the most famous woman in New York?"

"I'm hardly—"

"And the luckiest! You know about Golding, right?"

Louis Golding had been at the *Dispatch* during my first year. "What about him?"

"He's the syndicate reporter at police headquarters. He just happened to get left behind on the day you were brought it. If he'd seen you, believe me, he would have said so. I suppose it's better to be lucky than be good. Did I hear something about a book deal?"

"Yes," I admitted, biting my lip against that last remark. Clearly McCain was envious. *Well, let him be!* "I've been taking offers all week to turn the story into a book. Of course I accepted the one with ties to Mr. Pulitzer."

"Of course. Now I'm sorry I didn't let you take that murder story this summer. It's not everyone who can say they were scooped by Nellie Bly! Well, ta, girl wonder!" He walked away with another laugh, leaving me with very mixed feelings.

I wrote to the *Dispatch* at once, and received a letter back from Madden, with a copy of Wilson's farewell article. It was hilarious, and very sad.

A FEW DAYS LATER, AS I RACED down the courthouse steps to file my story, a man's voice called out to me. "Hello! Miss Brown! Miss Brown—Miss Bly, I mean."

Turning, I almost gasped. "Hello, Dr. Ingram."

"It's good to see you out in the world." He gestured toward the courthouse. "Quite a mess, isn't it?"

"Yes, it is. Wait, they're not coming after you, are they?" Of all those on Blackwell's, I had singled out Dr. Ingram alone for praise.

"No, no. But I'm not in Dent's good graces, let me tell you."

I balled up my fist. "He's saving his own skin by sacrificing everybody else."

"I couldn't say. It doesn't matter, anyway. I've resigned. My last day is in two weeks."

"Oh! That will be such a loss for the unhappy women there. What will you do?"

"Start my own practice. I have quite a recommendation, it seems, from a famous reporter." He shook his head. "You made fools of us, one and all. And rightly so."

I placed a hand on his arm. "You were the only one who showed any human decency at all."

"And isn't that damning with faint praise! But I'm glad you think well of me." Dr. Ingram placed his hand over mine. "It means a lot, actually."

The moment was suddenly charged with something new. Acutely embarrassed, my heart racing, I withdrew my hand. "That's—very kind of you to say. Especially to a fraud like me."

"Fraud? You are, forgive me saying this, you are the most authentic person I have ever met."

"Thank you." He might have said more, but I looked at the lowering sun. "I'm so sorry. I have to make a deadline."

He stepped back at once. "No, of course. Do your work, Nellie Bly. I'm sure I'll see you again, even if only here." He smiled at me.

I flashed him a smile in return as I trotted down the steps. Thanks to those years at the *Dispatch* and those awful, steep stairs, I was never in danger of tripping again. Even when I was running away like a frightened deer.

Dr. Ingram!

I'D JUST MOVED INTO MY NEW APARTMENT on West Seventy-Fourth Street. It was more space than I had ever had to myself, and I was trying to furnish it carefully rather than in a rush. I had bought a bed, a dresser, and a wonderful new rolltop desk, with a fine banker's chair to sit at. I didn't even have art for the walls yet, or more than a few dishes. But I had my writing desk!

Still distracted by thoughts of Dr. Ingram, I pushed open my door, gathered my mail from the floor, and sank into my lone chair, tossing the letters across my desk. I was bent over, unlacing my boots, when I spied a familiar scrawl across the front of one envelope.

Forgetting the second boot, I tore open the long-awaited letter and read the words in Wilson's fine hand:

Dear Kid,

I don't know what to do first, congratulate you or castigate you. As you doubtless expect the latter, I'll confound you by saying how very proud I am at the incredible job you've done. It was a smashing piece of journalism, and reading the story, I could hear your voice in every line.

You were insane to try it, of course, which I suppose explains how you were able to do it. You must never, never, ever take such a risk again. My heart cannot take the strain. It truly cannot. I write this knowing that you're already planning some insane new danger into which you are going to thrust yourself, to the awe and approbation of all.

I'm sure you've heard of my departure from the dismal Dispatch. I just could not endure the place any longer. Without your insouciant presence, the place grew stale and lifeless for me. Like yourself, I was in desperate need of a change, if only of scenery. Naturally, my solution was not as drastic as yours. You have more courage, my kid, than I could ever lay claim to. I admire you immensely.

Otherwise, all is the same. My wife is well, and I am as happy as I can ever be. It gives me great joy to know that you have risen to your proper height, and that readers far and wide feel for you what I do.

I do not blame you for not writing, as I am certain you have entirely dismissed me from your mind. I just want to assure you that my friendship for you is as warm as ever it was. And to bind you to a promise that, should you ever be in such dire straits again, you will not hesitate to demand my help.

In a perverse way, you have proved me right. I maintain my

original thesis: a woman's sphere is encompassed by a single word:
"home." And your home, my naughty kid, is the World. Indeed,
the World is lucky to have Nellie Bly in it.

You've indeed shown me what this one girl, at least, is good for.
This is Nellie Bly's world now. We mortals merely live in it.

Your friend,
Erasmus Wilson
The Quiet Observer

I sat staring at that paper for at least an hour, wringing a thousand meanings from it before eventually deciding to take it in the only allowable way—at face value.

He had offered friendship. That was all I could in good conscience offer him in return.

I thought of the letter I had penned that last night on Blackwell's. I'd torn it from the notebook before allowing the Colonel to see my notes. Now I took it from my desk's top little drawer and unfolded it. The clarity of that night, the rawness of it, the beauty of it—all of that remained.

But I could no more send it to him now than I could have that night, trapped in Hall Seven. It wouldn't be right. It wouldn't be fair.

Still, hadn't he hinted at some of the things I felt? Wasn't his reference to his strained heart, his warm friendship, him missing my presence—weren't they all veiled appeals? Or was that only in my mind?

Taking out a fresh sheet of paper, I wrote my reply:

My dear Q.O.,

I was so glad to get the letter which you have been owing me a long while. Mr. McCain gave me word that you had quit the Dispatch. I was surprised.

When I read your farewell to the roaches, I sat down and had a long "think" about you. Dear Q., I could see you after all was done for the last time, take up a few papers, quietly slip them in the outside pocket of your overcoat, and quietly and lonely go down those steep, dirty, dark old stairs. I felt in reading that you thought there was none you cared so much for, or none cared so much for you, as the speechless roaches. Was that it? And so to them and them alone you bade farewell.

Where shall I see you when I go to Pgh? For I am going just as soon as I can. Mrs. Mellon of the East End is going to give a reception for me and she has asked for your address because she wants you to be there. Won't you go, Q.? I should be so glad. There will only be a small number of congenial people present.

McCain and I have buried the hatchet, as much as it will ever be, between us.

I have no desire to do other work than what I am at. I will not lecture or go on the stage, so long as this pays. They are very good to me in the World office, and no one but Colonel Cockerill dares say a word to me. Somehow they treat me as if I was a pretty big girl. I don't object, so long as it pays.

I wish you could come to New York. I'd show you the town— that is, with your permission. Write to me often, Q. I am afraid you don't like me half so well as you used to. Write often and let me know what you are going to do next.

Give my regards to Mr. Muller and Mr. Black, and accept much love for yourself.

Longing to see you, I am, as ever,
Your Naughty "Kid,"
Nellie Bly

There. I had put myself out there. I had told him as much as was decent. He could ignore me, but only if he truly wanted to. If there was an ounce of him that felt as I did, he would come.

He will come.

IN THE END, THE INCREASE in the city's charity funding wasn't quite as much as the mayor asked for. Still, it was the largest hike in spending in the city's history, jumping from under $1.5 million in 1887 to more than $2.34 million in 1888. Some of this money was specifically allocated to Blackwell's for new bathrooms, a double oven for the kitchen, and funds to remodel the Lodge—suddenly deemed "unfit for habitation"—and turn it into an amusement hall.

My sense of triumph was tempered by the certainty that it was not enough. It would never be enough. But for once—just for once—Nellie Bly had made a difference.

That was just the start. Already, I was working on three other stories. One was a version of the old factory girl bit, only at the places where a girl was expected to work for nothing for the first several weeks. Another was about sham employment agencies. Both had promise, but the story I was most eager to tackle was the buying and selling of unwanted babies. One of Nellie Bly's readers had written in with the tip that these illicit traders placed ads in newspapers with suggestive medical terms. Some of these ads even ran in the pages of the *World*.

Coming home one day, I bumped into my neighbors. A lovely couple, they were dressed for the theatre. We exchanged pleasantries and I was about to shuffle by them when the man said, "Oh, did he find you?"

"Did who find me?"

"The man who was looking for you," said my neighbor. "He said he had come all the way from Pittsburgh to see you."

"He's quite handsome," his wife said, and then giggled when he chided her.

I felt the blood drain from my face, and then rush in again. "What did you tell him?"

"I said you kept all kinds of hours, but most days you're home after seven. I hope that's all right."

"It's wonderful!" I cried, and dashed rudely up the stairs, only thinking to call out, "Have a wonderful time! Thank you!" after the door had closed.

I made certain everything in my apartment was neat and put away— *thank Heaven there isn't much to clean!*—and then quickly changed into a new blue dress with a small bustle that collected all the fabric of the skirts. I fixed my hair, considered putting on some makeup, decided not to be so forward, and then sat on the edge of my bed, smoothing my skirts with the flat of my hands over and over until I was afraid I would wear clear through the fabric.

At last, there was a knock on my door. I leapt up and raced to open it.

"There you are," said a hated, drawling voice. "Finally!" Albert pushed past me into my apartment. He looked around and snorted. "I thought you were doing well. Can't you afford more than one chair?"

Behind him was Mother. Seeing the expression on my face, her smile faded. "You said to come. I thought we would surprise you."

"You have." Laughing and shaking my head, I filled the awkwardness with a hug. "You have!"

"I came by earlier," complained Albert. "Glad I didn't bring Mother. The train ride was long enough without her having to wait around for you to come back. Your neighbors look like snobs, by the way."

"Takes one to know one," I said over my shoulder.

"Pink," chided Mother. Apologizing, I led her inside.

We went out to dinner—my treat, of course—and I showed them around the city that was now my own. Albert worked hard to belittle everything, but I could tell he knew how envious he sounded, and eventually he spied a saloon and said he would meet us at home. "Unless I find someplace with a bed for me to sleep on."

After he had gone, I took Mother to Newspaper Row. I pointed to the World Building. "This is where I work now. This is my life."

I felt my mother's hand under my chin. "Elizabeth. Why are you crying?"

Looking at her through damp lashes, I managed a smile. "I don't know! I have found what I am good for. That's enough, isn't it? I mean, that's more than most. Isn't that enough?"

Taking hold of my arms, Mother fixed me with her gaze. "No, Elizabeth. It may never be enough. Not for you, my little troublemaker."

Slowly she smiled. "But it's a start."

                                                                FIN

AFTER WORD

Late one April evening in 2016, sitting at my desk not writing, an article in the *Atlantic* caught my eye. The premise was that there were more female action stars a hundred years ago than there are today. Most were in the mold of *The Perils of Pauline*, with an intrepid young woman leaping off horseback or clinging to the side of a train.

Intrigued, I started looking up these films referenced in the article only to discover that most of the daring fictional females they portrayed were newspaper reporters. Of them, the majority were based on Nellie Bly.

The name rang a very specific bell. In the second season of the television show *The West Wing*, the president's amorous intentions are thwarted one evening when he belittles the achievements of Nellie Bly, whose statue First Lady Abigail Bartlet had just unveiled. No longer in the mood, Abbey gives him a short biography of Nellie, which Jed again puts down. Needless to say, the night does not work out the way he planned.

That being my sole knowledge of this intrepid reporter, I typed "Nellie Bly" into The Googles and stayed up deep into the night reading, knowing I had struck gold.

Female characters drive historical fiction. My trouble has always been that the historical women who fascinate me—Cleopatra, Anne Boleyn, Boudicca, Isabella of Spain, Eleanor of Aquitaine—have all been done, and done well (I have the same problem with King Arthur stories—sure, I'd like to write one, but it's been done). Moreover, I have a deep resistance to writing about queens or princesses. In looking for a heroine, I wanted an exceptional woman who rose from nothing to make her mark.

As a writer, I was waiting for the right woman to come along.

In Nellie Bly, I found her.

Here I had the chance to explore early Feminism, a piece of history largely ignored in the fabric of American history. If Nellie is mentioned, it's for pioneering undercover journalism. Totally true, but hardly the whole story. It wasn't just how she got the stories. It was the stories she chose to tell. Fought to tell. Nearly died to tell.

What snagged *my* attention was how she became a reporter in the first place. Maybe because I love origin stories, maybe because it struck me as both brave and pointed. I was utterly thrilled by the story of the outraged letter that directly led to twenty-year-old Elizabeth Cochrane becoming the investigative reporter Nellie Bly. To me, that story sums her up. She was utterly incapable of remaining silent when facing injustice. Nearly one hundred and fifty years later, her outrage is still palpable. Her energy, her drive, her vanity, her vitality, her vulnerability—it's all right there, laid bare in the pages of her stories.

After falling down a midnight internet rabbit hole, I couldn't resist. The next day, setting aside all plans of *Star-Cross'd* sequels or the long-awaited Othello novel, I dove into the research and started to write.

You hold the result.

For sources, I've been blessed by two recent nonfiction examinations of Nellie Bly's life. The first is *Nellie Bly: Daredevil, Reporter, Feminist* by Brooke Kroeger. This is an exhaustive and amazingly researched work, examining every aspect of Ms. Bly's life, making all kinds of connections between the professional and the personal. I simply could not have written this novel without Ms. Kroeger's work.

The other recent work to which I owe a debt is Matthew Goodman's *Eighty Days*, an examination of Nellie's trip around the world. While those events are not depicted in this novel, his buildup to her journey is a magnificent look at her life, incredibly well-written. And his framing of the story, matching Bly with Elizabeth Bisland's counter-trip, is utterly brilliant. If you want to know what comes next for Bly, you cannot do better than *Eighty Days*.

Both Ms. Kroeger and Mr. Goodman were of direct help to me as well, graciously sending newspaper clippings that were missing from various library collections, and being generally encouraging about the novel itself.

Among other sources were *Bylines: A Photobiography of Nellie Bly* by Sue Macy; Sensationalism: *Murder, Mayhem, Mudslinging, Scandals, and Disasters in 19th-Century Reporting*, edited by David B. Sachsman and David W. Bulla; *Nellie Bly: First Woman Reporter* by Iris Noble; *The Amazing Nellie Bly* by Mignon Rittenhouse; and *Mexico City: A Cultural and Literary Companion* by Nick Caistor.

Of course, the best resources available to me were Nellie Bly's own writings. For the historical novelist, having the words of one's subject is a tremendous advantage. This was my first time having such access, and I found it equal parts wonderful and daunting. Wonderful, because I had her story right there, in her voice. Daunting, because she had already covered most of the events in this novel herself, in great detail. I wanted to incorporate those articles into the fabric of her life's story, and quite often I have used a phrase or sentence from her own writings.

But that way danger lies. Again and again, I had to weigh her writing against the story I was telling. Just as I could not simply copy her work and present it here, I had qualms about substituting my own words when hers exist. This was a unique problem, and a marvelous one to have. I've tried to ameliorate it by using her experiences as the starting point for my research. Extra details about Pittsburgh, Mexico, and New York are filtered into her own firsthand accounts. Yet I'd be insane to abandon her own experiences—if she chose to write about them, they're important to her story! Especially in Mexico, I've used her own observations as the canvas to paint the story about her life. The great thing for me in that stretch was the presence of her mother, whom she omitted entirely from her articles. I hope that the Mexico and Madhouse sections of the book have more to them than simple regurgitation of her own books, both of which are well worth reading.

I've also tried, in my feeble way, to mirror her style—her preferred words, her tics, her modes of expression. I searched her writing for favored phrases and words. Still, times change—styles, too—so I have made her a bit less passive in her writing voice. I've also corrected several grammatical infelicities, especially in her Spanish (and, for the record, I adore Mexican food. In this novel, I merely reflect Ms. Bly's own feelings on the matter).

One of the most interesting elements of this story is that Nellie is such a terrific reporter—except when it comes to herself. Her version of herself in her stories is fascinating, not only for the flattering elements she presents, but also the unflattering elements she omits. Just as she got caught up in the lie of illness or lack of funds when she left school, there are times when she is caught out in some exaggeration or other. She lied about her age nearly her whole life, even under oath. When it comes to Nellie Bly talking about herself, she is an unreliable narrator. This offered a marvelous challenge in crafting a whole person out of everything we know about both Elizabeth Cochrane and Nellie Bly.

It is not my job to discern her minor exaggerations from the facts. It's my job to tell a good story. So when faced with two differing accounts of events, I try to side with the more interesting for the narrative, as well as the one that makes the most sense.

All of this culminated in the "Madhouse." Nellie has already given us her account, in her own words. In fact, she gave us three versions of it—the one printed in the *World*, the expanded book version, *Ten Days in a Mad-House*, and an 1889 piece for *Godey's Lady's Book* that she entitled "Among the Mad."

Now, I'm not saying I don't believe her account—quite the contrary, I have taken her version of events as gospel. But, like the gospels themselves, there are elements omitted from the known story. I've worked them in, creating (I hope) a richer tapestry for the narrative, as one can do in fiction. I trust that what she says happened. I don't always trust her part in it.

There are certainly enough characters in Nellie Bly's own account of Blackwell's to populate this novel and many more (Miss Grupe was apparently the inspiration for Nurse Ratched in Ken Kesey's *One Flew Over the Cuckoo's Nest*, and Miss Grady makes an appearance in one of Bly's later works of fiction as a child-killing nurse). To their number I have added just one in passing, a real woman culled from the census records of the inmates of the Willard Asylum for the Chronic Insane near Seneca Lake. Octavia Ballard was one of just fifteen African American women incarcerated there between 1870 and 1900, out of a total of 1,107 women. Nellie does not mention seeing black women, but she would have, and so in my novel, she does.

Also, the way Nellie presents her stay on Blackwell's Island becomes more episodic than chronological, as if she wrote out her strongest memories rather than a day-by-day account. I aimed for the latter, building in stray facts she left out and elements from her own life that she would never have shared with the public.

Note—what was the 15th Precinct in 1887 is the 9th Precinct today, as there was a citywide renumbering of precincts in 1929.

Something happened after the initial publication of this novel. While researching the sequel, I stumbled across an actual historical discovery. After her famous race around the globe in 1890, Bly quit reporting for three years and took a lucrative job writing serial novels for a weekly newspaper published by Norman Munro, her book publisher. No complete copies of the *New York Family Story Paper* exist today. We only knew the titles of two thanks to her letters and one stray issue that lives at Villanova University. So Bly's novels have been lost for 125 years.

Until December, 2019, when I found them. All *eleven* of them.

I spent the next fifteen months having them transcribed and edited, some by me, some by friends. They are an amazing window into Bly's mind, a collection of breathless gothic romances inspired in part or in whole by her reporting. These are now available, known collectively as *The Lost Novels Of Nellie Bly*. Check them out! You won't be disappointed.

While I was adding the back matter to those volumes, I ended up transcribing a slew of her articles as well. So while I was releasing Bly's own writing, I decided to do the one thing no one ever had—publish her complete reporting. That series begins with *Nellie Bly's World*, a four-volume collection of all her work for the *New York World*. Though by doing this, I have rather given away the game for the next novel. . .

I owe thanks to several people. Beyond Kroeger and Goodman, I would like to thank Kathleen Hale, supervisor for public services at the State Library of Pennsylvania, for hunting up several articles for me. Likewise, allow me to thank Shayna Marie, along with Erika Lorraine and Tamara Cyleste, for doing legwork at the Carnegie Library of Pittsburgh for me, and to Klenton Willis for putting us together. Also huge thanks to Tara Sullivan and Karin Borgeson for being among my early readers, with tons of feedback. And my friend and audio producer Judith West.

A huge thanks to Gianni La Corte and Giovanna Burzio for their enthusiasm and being the first to shepherd the novel to publication—and for giving it a title!

An enormous, unending, awestruck "Thank you!" to Robert Kauzlaric for his truly incredible work editing this beast. I've been lost in the wilderness for many, many years. To find an editor in one of your best friends, with whom you have shared stages, pages, and living spaces for nearly two decades now, is just magic.

The soundtrack for this novel has been a nonstop loop of Suzanne Vega, Tori Amos, the Cranberries, and the Sundays, with a dollop of Adele on top. The sole exception is Dirty Bourbon River Show's version of Stephen Foster's *Nelly Bly*, which is utterly terrific and very un-Foster-y.

For movies, I had the terrific *Spotlight* running at least once a month, often far more, along with *All the President's Men*, *The Hunger Games* series, *His Girl Friday*, *My Man Godfrey*, and all the best Maisie Williams episodes of both *Game of Thrones* and *Doctor Who*.

Finally, I have not succumbed to the writerly instinct to add romance where none existed. Bly's relationship with Wilson lasted her whole life, and his. We have her letters to him, which means he kept them. Whereas she burned all her correspondence, presumably to keep any letters she received away from prying eyes.

I did make just one alteration to her letter to him at the end of the book, making it McCain who told her the Q.O. had left the *Dispatch*, instead of a random character we had never met.

Her relationship with Wilson is too rife with conflict and desire to ignore. He was both father figure and love interest, and their story is almost perfectly Gothic: they are thrown together, they have feelings, but he has an invalid wife, so they remain apart, writing to each other through the decades to come. It's one of those stories too heartbreaking to be anything but real.

But Nellie Bly has many years of adventure ahead of her. Wilson is a part of those years, but so are so many other rich characters, not least of them Cockerill and Pulitzer, who now have a celebrity to exploit. As well as Albert and Mary Jane, who see in the person of Nellie Bly a means to regain the wealth and social status they lost when the Judge died.

Most fantastic of them all is Nellie herself, who has barely begun rocking boats and making a name for herself. The next few years are the richest of her career as a reporter.

I plan a few novelettes covering stories Bly wrote between the fall of 1887 and the summer of 1888. The first is entitled *Charity Girl*, in which she goes undercover to find out what happens to unwanted babies in New York—a story that would heavily influence the end of her career. In another novelette, *Clever Girl*, Bly travels to Albany to expose a corrupt lobbyist.

The next full-length novel is entitled *Stunt Girl*.

Cheers,
DB

PREVIEW OF

CHARITY GIRL

NEW YORK, NY
SATURDAY, OCTOBER 29, 1887

"I'M GOING TO BE A PUBLISHED AUTHOR!"
I said this aloud to my empty apartment, so there was no one to hear my exciting news. I had just signed the lease, and had barely a stick of furniture. That didn't trouble me—eager as I was to outfit my new home in New York City, I didn't want to buy anything that was less than perfect. Having pinched pennies since the age of six, I knew better than to play the drunk when flush. *You never know when disaster will strike.*

In fact, disaster had struck almost exactly a month earlier. On the twenty-second of September my bag had been stolen, and it contained nearly one hundred dollars: all the money I had in the world. I couldn't even afford to pay the rent on my shabby little furnished room uptown.

However, the experience made me realize something about myself: crisis brought out the best in me. When pushed to the brink, I could be devilishly resourceful. That night I borrowed enough money to take me downtown to Newspaper Row and marched into the offices of Joseph Pulitzer's *New York World* and pitched them a story.

They didn't buy it.

Yet Pulitzer's prize editor, Colonel Cockerill, was impressed by my pluck and gumption, and he suggested a different story: getting myself incarcerated in the Woman's Lunatic Asylum on Blackwell's Island to expose the goings-on there. At the time, I had no idea it was a repeat of a stunt performed a decade earlier by a man. All I knew was that it was a chance to prove myself—while also peeling back the curtain on misdeeds against women. So I played shatterpated and got myself committed.

I'd emerged three weeks ago—*Was it only three weeks?*—with a story that had made my moniker a household name. Well, not my *actual* moniker. No one knew who Elizabeth Cochrane was. But everyone knew the name Nellie Bly.

Which was how I ended up with the letter in my hand. It was from the publisher Norman L. Munro, offering me more money than I could have hitherto imagined for the rights to publish my story from the madhouse: a whopping five hundred dollars! Considering that I had started off at five dollars a week, and had made only twenty-five dollars for the madhouse exposé, it was a small fortune.

Hence my new, if empty, apartment on West Seventy-Fourth Street. Compared to the furnished room I'd occupied all summer, it was a palace: six large rooms with a private hall, a bathroom with a tub, and a kitchen with a range. There was a common freight elevator in the building for groceries, and a janitor's service was included. The rooms were outfitted with gas chandeliers, steam heat, and fairly decent woodwork. I even liked the wallpaper. All for twenty-two dollars a month—a steal.

And I wouldn't be alone for long. Even before the book deal, I had sent to Pittsburgh and asked—well, told—my mother to sell her house and come live with me. I did it partly out of duty, partly as repayment for all the trouble I'd caused her over the years, and partly because we had been good companions during my months reporting in Mexico.

There was another, less worthy reason as well: I wanted to show up my brothers.

Of my four siblings, the oldest two were both married and employed. But Charlie had remained at Mother's house even after his wife had produced a bundle of joy. And Albert, the eldest of us all—and Mother's favorite—now lived in a fine house of his own in Pittsburgh, yet he hadn't invited our twice-widowed, once-divorced mother to live with him. No, *I* had done that. In New York, no less. Me, the troublemaker. Me, the heck-raiser. Me, the one Albert considered undignified and incapable.

It was petty of me, but it felt so good to throw my money and success in their faces.

However, if I really wanted to show up my brothers and impress my detractors—of whom I had many—I needed to continue making my name. Knowing enough to strike while the iron was hot, I had been on the lookout for another story just as good as Blackwell's Island. I had to keep producing unique pieces for the *World*. Every Sunday that Nellie Bly had her name in print was a victory.

My male colleagues resented my sudden success, which seemed to have struck from out of the clear sky. Few of them rated a byline, and they all thought I got mine simply because putting a woman's name above a story gave it the level of sensationalism that Colonel Cockerill prized.

While I understood their resentment, I dismissed it. They had enjoyed their exclusive "no girls allowed" clubhouse for long enough. They could open the doors to admit just one lone girl. *If they don't like it, well, they can lump it. Nellie Bly isn't going anywhere but up.*

To do that, however, I had to find another story.

I'd gotten some initial inspiration from a passing comment by the *World's* lawyer. His tip led me to stint of impersonating a woman in search of work to expose the underhanded practices of New York's employment agencies. These swindlers fleeced women by demanding money in exchange for empty promises to find them placement. It wasn't as exciting as my stay in the asylum, but it made for a good story, and it fit all of Cockerill's criteria: it was titillatingly sensational, it had a strong moral component, and—most important—it was exclusive. The piece would run in the World tomorrow.

But today, I thought, I need to figure out what to write about next. And it needs to be big.

Fortunately, I got help from the World's readers.

I hadn't known what kind of letters to expect after the Blackwell's Island exposé. Praise, I'd hoped. And, yes, there had been laudatory notes from all quarters: doctors, housewives, bricklayers, even a circuit court judge! My favorite was the one that extolled me for giving those madhouse quacks "such a magnificent black eye with such a tiny fist."

On the other hand, there had been many letters condemning me for thinking I knew better than the doctors and nurses, and even some claiming I actually *was* mad and deserved to be locked up for the rest of my life. Though I'd tried to laugh those off, they lingered in my mind far longer than the praise.

However, by a fair distance the majority of the response had consisted of letters telling me where I should investigate next. Within days I'd collected a catalog of outrages that would make a normal girl take to her bed in a faint. Whereas I found them to be full of exciting possibilities. *What does that say about me?* I wondered as I flipped through my stack of recent correspondence.

Amid all the swindles and scandals, one story leapt out to sock me right in the chin. Instantly, I knew what outrage I would be swinging at next.

Babies. Specifically, unwanted babies.

The typewritten letter read:

> *Dear Miss Bly,*
>
> *I have followed your work since the days of your journeys to Mexico, and read with heartfelt sorrow of the plight of the natives of that magnificent but misgoverned country. It was with mingled delight*

and dismay that I learned of your arrival in New York through your articles on the misdeeds on Blackwell's Island. Delight, that such a smart, insightful girl reporter was present in this metropolis; dismay, that you had to undergo such an ordeal. It is my fervent hope that you never again place yourself in such a dangerous predicament. Please count me among your admirers.

I am writing because I would like to know what becomes of unwanted infants in this city. Without giving details which such a talented reporter as yourself could easily use to identify me, allow me to say that I am a well-off man who, through my church, recently became aware of an unmarried girl who was with child. It was my intention, with the aid of our pastor, to assist the fallen female in a Christian way. We discussed with her the various institutions available to assist her and her expected child. But just as she approached her joyful day she disappeared from our church. Not much later I saw her on the street. As she was clearly no longer bearing, I, meaning nothing but well, congratulated her on her deliverance. First she pretended not to know me. Then she pretended she had never been pregnant at all. At last she said she gave her son away and, cursing me, departed from my sight.

I do not want to invade her privacy, so I will not presume to offer up her name, which is likely an alias. Yet since that chance encounter I have been unable to sleep, worrying about that newborn child. Is he still alive? Where could she have taken him? And how many more children like him are given up each day in this massive city? What becomes of them? Where is it best to donate money? I have asked at my church, and they advise me to give to them. But I am moved to give funds where they are put to the best use. After all, as they say, I cannot take it with me.

I also worry of extralegal means. My wife called on a Mrs. Gray who advertises manicures and vapor baths. She was horrified to discover the house full of new mothers and their babes, and she had the worst feeling that the infants were not there to be cared for.

She was too frightened by her experience there to ask any more questions. We discussed it and decided I should write to you. If there is any fearless ferreter of truth in our Gotham, it is Nellie Bly.

Would you consider looking into the plight of unwanted infants in New York? I can think of no one better suited to the task.

Pitying Philanthropist

My initial reaction to the letter was outrage, naturally. My second was suspicion. *Does he have an ulterior motive?* Yet the writer seemed sincere. He wasn't after this particular woman or seeking her child, which had been my first concern. In fact, I was surprised a man had written this letter—which I recognized as a troubling statement on my opinion of the average male.

Whoever it was that had written, they traveled in wealthy circles. Only the best homes and businesses had typewriters. There had been only two at the *Pittsburg Dispatch*, and even at the *World* there weren't more than a dozen. Mr. Pulitzer claimed he wasn't yet convinced of their longevity, but Cockerill had privately confided the real reason to me: Pulitzer was subject to terrible headaches. It was bad enough when the presses were running, but the clacking keys and ringing returns drove him from his office in an agonized state. So Mr. Pulitzer preferred that his reporters use their Blackwing pencils.

Returning to the letter, I considered the subject matter. I had certainly heard of girls who became pregnant and disappeared, only to return without their child. I wondered how much happier my own sister might be if she were not a mother. Things were not looking well for her marriage. What if their relationship had soured before the birth of Beatrice? Where would Kate have gone?

To Mother, of course. And the family would have seen her through, as we would do if someday she left her louse of a spouse. But what about the girls who couldn't go to their mothers? What about the girls who hadn't married first, but had "fallen" for a man? I certainly knew enough of those. I thought of Ada, probably still toiling away in the smelly cigar factory, letting her hair down at the end of the day to pick up men on the streetcar in order to gain a dinner.

I felt a pang of guilt. I had built the foundations of my career thanks to Ada, and how long had it been since I'd thought about her? Too long. *I am not a good person.*

Whereas the writer of this letter certainly *was* a good person. He seemed genuinely interested in helping—though it did not escape me that it wasn't the women he wanted to help, but rather the children. Because women who gave up their children were abominable, of course. Inhuman. Unnatural. Not worth caring for.

Still, it was a good cause. Better still, it was a good story. And it had a sharp "hook." I had landed a honey with the madhouse, and while I was under no illusion that they would all be such smash sensations, this one felt like it had the potential to build on the legend of Nellie Bly, Crusader for Social Justice. If I did it right, it might just keep my name in the papers and prevent the Colonel and Mr. Pulitzer from thinking my success to be a flash in the pan.

So where do I begin?

READ **CHARITY GIRL**
ON SALE NOW FROM SORDELET INK

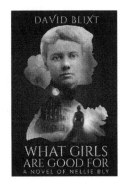

WHAT GIRLS ARE GOOD FOR
A NOVEL OF NELLIE BLY

Nellie Bly has the story of a lifetime. But will she survive to tell it?

Based on the real-life events of the tiny Pennsylvania spitfire who refused to let the world change her, and changed the world instead.

CHARITY GIRL
A NELLIE BLY NOVELETTE

Fresh from her escape from Blackwell's Island, Nellie Bly investigates the doctors who buy and sell babies in Victorian New York. Based on real events and her own reporting, Nellie Bly asks the devastating question - what becomes of babies?

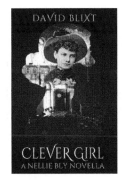

CLEVER GIRL
A NELLIE BLY NOVELLA

A blizzard has frozen all of New York, and Nellie Bly is going stir-crazy when she and Colonel Cockerill plot out her most daring undercover assignment yet: she's going to trap the most crooked man in politics, Edward R. Phelps, the self-styled "King" of the Albany lobby.

COMING SOON:

STUNT GIRL

A NOVEL OF NELLIE BLY

BY DAVID BLIXT

THE MYSTERY OF CENTRAL PARK

A rejected marriage proposal and the corpse of a dead beauty confound Dick Treadwell's hopes for happiness, until his beloved Penelope sets him a task: she will marry him if he solves— *the Mystery of Central Park!*

EVA, THE ADVENTURESS

Nellie Bly's ripped-from-the-headlines novel of a poor girl determined to revenge herself upon the world, only to find that, in the battle between love and revenge, only one can triumph.

NEW YORK BY NIGHT

Setting out to solve the bold diamond robbery, millionaire detective Lionel Dangerfield finds himself in competition with Ruby Sharpe, daring young reporter for the *New York Planet*. Will "The Danger" solve the case before Ruby can steal the story—and his heart?

ALTA LYNN, M.D.

A prank goes awry and Alta Lynn finds herself wed against her will. Leaving love behind, she throws herself into the study of medicine, only to find that love has other plans for her!

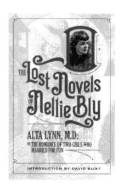

WAYNE'S FAITHFUL SWEETHEART

Beautiful Dorette Lover is rescued from poverty when she finds work as an artist's model. That same day she witnesses a seeming murder. To protect the man accused, she agrees to become his bride—only to fall desperately in love with him!

LITTLE LUCKIE

Luckie Thurlow longs to be accepted by society and gain the man she loves. But she harbors a dark secret—she is the daughter of the murderous Gypsy Queen, who plans to use Luckie to gain her own revenge!

IN LOVE WITH A STRANGER

Kit Clarendon is in love! Trouble is, she doesn't know her love's name. But she is determined to track him down and force him to love her! A wild pursuit filled with disguises, desperate deeds, and declarations of love as Kit determines to go through fire and water to win him!

THE LOVE OF THREE GIRLS

An heiress in disguise, a factory girl with dreams of wealth, and a sweet child of charity are forced into rivalry when they all fall in love with the same man! Murder, fever, fallen women, and a desperate villain conspire against—
the love of three girls!

INTO THE MADHOUSE

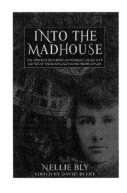

Never before collected! "Who is this insane girl?" asked other papers, completely taken in by Nellie Bly's plan to infiltrate Blackwell's Island. The complete reporting surrounding her daring expose, including details not included in her initial accounts and her scathing rebuttal of the doctors' excuses!

NELLIE BLY'S WORLD - Vol. 1
1887-1888

Bly's complete reporting, collected for the very first time! Starting with the stunt that made hers a household name, Nellie Bly spends her first year at the New York World going undercover to expose frauds, sharpsters and boodlers, interviewing Belva Lockwood and Hangman Joe, and tackling Phelps the Lobbyist!

NELLIE BLY'S WORLD - Vol. 2
1889-1890

Bly's complete reporting, collected for the very first time! Nellie buys a baby, has herself followed by a detective and arrested, interviews Helen Keller, champion boxer John Sullivan, and convicted would-be killer Eva Hamilton, all before setting out on her greatest stunt of all, a race around the world!

COMING SOON:

NELLIE BLY'S WORLD, Vol. 3 & 4
NELLIE BLY'S DISPATCHES, Vol. 1 & 2
NELLIE BLY's JOURNALS, Vol. 1 & 2

ALL FROM SORDLET INK

ABOUT NELLIE BLY

Nellie Bly was born Elizabeth "Pink" Cochran. Her father, a man of considerable wealth, served for many years as judge of Armstrong County, Pennsylvania. He lived on a large estate called Cochran's Mills, which took its name from him.

Being in reduced circumstances after her father's death, her mother remarried, only to divorce Jack Ford a few years later. The family then moved to Pittsburg, where a twenty-year-old Pink read a column in the *Pittsburg Dispatch* entitled "What Girls Are Good For." Enraged at the sexist and classist tone, she wrote a furious letter to the editor. Impressed, the editor engaged her to do special work for the newspaper as a reporter, writing under the name "Nellie Bly." Her first series of stories, "Our Workshop Girls," brought life and sympathy to working women in Pittsburgh.

A year later she went as a correspondent to Mexico, where she remained six months, sending back weekly articles. After her return she longed for broader fields, and so moved to New York. The story of her attempt to make a place for herself, or to find an opening, was a long one of disappointment, until at last she gained the attention of the *New York World*.

Her first achievement for them was the exposure of the Blackwell's Island Insane Asylum, in which she spent ten days, and two days in the Bellevue Insane Asylum. The story created a great sensation, making "Nellie Bly" a household name.

After three years of doing work as a "stunt girl" at the *World*, Bly conceived the idea of making a trip around the world in less time than had been done by Phileas Fogg, the fictitious hero of Jules Verne's famous novel. In fact, she made it in 72 days. On her return in January 1890 she was greeted by ovations all the way from San Francisco to New York.

She then paused her reporting career to write novels, but returned to the *World* three years later. In 1895 she married millionaire industrialist Robert Seaman, and a couple years later retired from journalism to take an interest in his factories.

She returned to journalism almost twenty years later, reporting on World War I from behind the Austrian lines. Upon returning to New York, she spent the last years of her life doing both reporting and charity work, finding homes for orphans. She died of pneumonia in 1922.

Books by Nellie Bly

JOURNALISM

Ten Days in a Mad-House

Six Months In Mexico

Nellie Bly's Book: Around the World in 72 Days

NOVELS

The Mystery of Central Park

Eva the Adventuress

New York By Night

Alta Lynn, M.D.

Wayne's Faithful Sweetheart

Little Luckie

Dolly the Coquette

In Love With a Stranger

The Love of Three Girls

Little Penny, Child of the Streets

Pretty Merribelle

Twins and Rivals

ABOUT DAVID BLIXT

David Blixt is an author and actor living in Chicago. An Artistic Associate of the Michigan Shakespeare Festival, where he serves as the resident Fight Director, he is also co-founder of A Crew Of Patches Theatre Company, a Shakespearean repertory based in Chicago. He has acted and done fight work for the Goodman Theatre, Chicago Shakespeare Theatre, Steppenwolf, the Shakespeare Theatre of Washington DC, and First Folio Shakespeare, among many others.

As a writer, his STAR-CROSS'D series of novels place the characters of Shakespeare's Italian plays in their historical setting, drawing in figures such as Dante, Giotto, and Petrarch to create an epic of warfare, ingrigue, and romance. In HER MAJESTY'S WILL, Shakespeare himself becomes a character as Blixt explores Shakespeare's "Lost Years," teaming the young Will with the dark and devious Kit Marlowe to hilarious effect. In the COLOSSUS series, Blixt brings first century Rome and Judea to life as he relates the fall of Jerusalem, the building of the Colosseum, and the coming of Christianity to Rome. And in his bestselling NELLIE BLY series, he explores the amazing life and adventures of America's premier undercover reporter.

David continues to write, act, and travel. He has ridden camels around the pyramids at Giza, been thrown out of the Vatican Museum and been blessed by John-Paul II, scaled the Roman ramp at Masada, crashed a hot-air balloon, leapt from cliffs on small Greek islands, dined with Counts and criminals, climbed to the top of Mount Sinai, and sat in the Prince's chair in Verona's palace. But David is happiest at his desk, weaving tales of brilliant people in dire and dramatic straits. Living with his wife and two children, David describes himself as "actor, author, father, husband - in reverse order."

WWW.DAVIDBLIXT.COM

PLAYSCRIPTS

ACTION MOVIE - THE PLAY BY JOE FOUST AND RICHARD RAGSDALE
ALL CHILDISH THINGS BY JOSEPH ZETTELMAIER
CAMPFIRE BY JOSEPH ZETTELMAIER
CAPTAIN BLOOD ADAPTED BY DAVID RICE
CHURCHILL BY RONALD KEATON
THE COUNT OF MONTE CRISTO ADAPTED BY CHRISTOPHER M WALSH
DEAD MAN'S SHOES BY JOSEPH ZETTELMAIER
THE DECADE DANCE BY JOSEPH ZETTELMAIER
DR. SEWARD'S DRACULA ADAPTED BY JOSEPH ZETTELMAIER
EBENEZER: A CHRISTMAS PLAY BY JOSEPH ZETTELMAIER
EVE OF IDES BY DAVID BLIXT
FRANKENSTEIN ADAPTED BY ROBERT KAUZLARIC
THE GRAVEDIGGER: A FRANKENSTEIN PLAY BY JOSEPH ZETTELMAIER
HATFIELD & McCOY BY SHAWN PFAUTSCH
HER MAJESTY'S WILL ADAPTED BY ROBERT KAUZLARIC
IT CAME FROM MARS BY JOSEPH ZETTELMAIER
THE LEAGUE OF AWESOME BY CORRBETTE PASKO AND SARA SEVIGNY
THE MAN-BEAST BY JOSEPH ZETTELMAIER
THE MAN WHO WAS THURSDAY ADAPTED BY BILAL DARDAI
THE MOONSTONE ADAPTED BY ROBERT KAUZLARIC
MY ITALY STORY AND LONG GONE DADDY BY JOSEPH GALLO
NORTHERN AGGRESSION BY JOSEPH ZETTELMAIER
ONCE A PONZI TIME BY JOE FOUST
THE RENAISSANCE MAN BY JOSEPH ZETTELMAIER
THE SCULLERY MAID BY JOSEPH ZETTELMAIER
ANTON CHEKHOV'S THE SEAGULL ADAPTED BY JANICE L BLIXT
SEASON ON THE LINE BY SHAWN PFAUTSCH
STAGE FRIGHT: A HORROR ANTHOLOGY BY JOSEPH ZETTELMAIER
A TALE OF TWO CITIES ADAPTED BY CHRISTOPHER M WALSH
WILLIAMSTON ANTHOLOGY: VOLUME 1
WILLIAMSTON ANTHOLOGY: VOLUME 2

NON-FICTION

ORIGIN OF THE FEUD BY DAVID BLIXT
TOMORROW & TOMORROW BY DAVID BLIXT AND JANICE L BLIXT
FIGHTING WORDS: A COMBAT GLOSSARY EDITED BY DAVID BLIXT

WWW.SORDELETINK.COM

Nellie Bly

Manufactured by Amazon.ca
Bolton, ON

29860268R00258